James H. Graff

Lady Wedderburn's Wish

A Tale of the Crimean War

James H. Graff

Lady Wedderburn's Wish
A Tale of the Crimean War

ISBN/EAN: 9783337248079

Printed in Europe, USA, Canada, Australia, Japan

Cover: Foto ©Andreas Hilbeck / pixelio.de

More available books at **www.hansebooks.com**

LADY WEDDERBURN'S WISH.

A Tale of the Crimean War.

By JAMES GRANT,

AUTHOR OF "THE ROMANCE OF WAR," "FIRST LOVE AND LAST LOVE,"
"THE GIRL HE MARRIED," ETC.

A NEW EDITION.

LONDON:
GEORGE ROUTLEDGE AND SONS,
THE BROADWAY. LUDGATE.
NEW YORK: 416, BROOME STREET.
1871.

CONTENTS.

LADY WEDDERBURN'S WISH.

CHAPTER I.

THE DESPATCH BOX.

"THE Colonel has written to the effect, that the regiment has received 'letters of readiness' for foreign service, and that the *route* for the East may come at any moment."

"My dear boy, Cyril, and you will be leaving us."

"For old Gib or Malta in the first place, and the Crimea after," continued Cyril, glancing again at the letter he had just opened ; "but the Colonel adds, that until I am telegraphed for, my leave of absence may remain intact—it is a little anomalous ; but he is a thorough good fellow, the Colonel !"

"And what of Horace ?"

"There is no word of Horace, dear mother ; but he will probably be detailed for the depôt."

"My darling Cyril !" exclaimed the anxious mother, as her eyes filled with tears, and her upper lip quivered.

The "darling" referred to was a handsome young fellow of five feet ten or so, with a thick curly brown head of hair, shorn short to the regimental pattern, and most unexceptionable whiskers ; one who rather considered himself as the model officer of the Royal Fusileers, in which distinguished corps he —Cyril Wedderburn, then on leave of absence—held the rank of Captain ; and now having laid the Colonel's letter beside his plate—for the family were at breakfast—he forthwith, and with appetite unimpaired by the prospect of a speedy and too surely perilous change of scene, attacked the drumstick of a devilled turkey.

Gervase Asloane, the family butler—a portly individual, in an ample white waistcoat and suit of black—had but a few minutes before placed the Russia leather despatch box, with its brass plate, bearing the family arms, &c., beside Sir John Wedderburn, who had unlocked it, and distributed the contents among the party at table, which consisted only of Lady Wedderburn,

Miss Flora M'Caw, her companion, a Highland maiden of doubtful age but undoubted pedigree ; her two sons, Cyril and Robert ; her nephew, Horace Ramornie, son of a deceased sister, and who was junior lieutenant in Cyril's regiment ; and a visitor, Chesters of Chesterhaugh, a gentleman of whom the reader may hear, perhaps, too much in future.

There were no missives for Miss M'Caw ; there never were any, so she had long since ceased even to affect that one might come.

"One letter for Horace," said Cyril, while decapitating an egg.   "Well, old fellow, what says your despatch—' to amount of account rendered,' eh ?"

"It is only some mess-room gossip from Probyn of ours."

"A kind fellow is Probyn."

"No word of the war as yet, Cyril, so our leaves are safe," added Horace Ramornie.

"And our lives too, for a time, eh, mamma of mine ?   A pink cocked hat for Bob, or invitation, or a love letter, of course ? But what is up with you, Chesters ? you look disturbed, as they say on the stage."

"Perhaps I do," whispered Chesters.   "I have again backed the wrong horse, and lost a pot of money, at the last Liverpool Spring Meeting.   The rain fell in torrents."

"And the course was soft ?"

"Soft as butter," replied Chesters, filling his mouth with toast to check a rising malediction.

"How *can* you talk so gaily and so lightly, Cyril ?" urged his mother, reproachfully, with her fine eyes more full of tears than ever.

"Why, mother, dearest, any way, both Horace and I must have had to leave you soon ; the spring drills, the bore of coaching up for the half-yearly inspection, will soon begin, and then quit we should inevitably."

"In May ?"

"Yes."

"And this is March ; it is hard—very hard !   I had formed such pleasant plans for you."

"Why don't you forward them to the Horse Guards—they might soften the hearts of the Commander-in-Chief and Adjutant-General ?" said Cyril, laughing.   "Another cup of coffee, Miss M'Caw, at your leisure," he added to that demure personage, who daily officiated at the magnificent silver urn and Wedgwood breakfast equipage.

"My dear Sir John," exclaimed Lady Wedderburn, suddenly, as her eyes now fell on her husband, who had remained perfectly silent, "what *is* the matter ?   You look quite pale, and—and—the letter you have read is wafered with black !"

" And edged with black, too," added Robert Wedderburn, a thoughtless, but rather pretty looking lad, about eighteen, with curly yellow hair and dark grey eyes. "What's up, papa— ' whose mare is dead ?' "

But the Baronet did not answer immediately ; he permitted the hand retaining the letter to drop upon his knee, and his chin sank upon his breast as his head drooped forward, and he seemed to become lost in thought. Then all eyes, including those of old Gervase, the butler, were turned inquiringly towards him.

"Sir John Wedderburn, Bart., of Nova Scotia, and Willow- dean in the Merse—creation, 1628," as the heralds have it, was a remarkably good-looking man, and fully six feet in height, though he *did* stoop a little now, being past his sixtieth year. His features were cleanly cut, and very noble in contour, and benign in expression, his eyes a clear grey, and his white hair started in spouts from his forehead to fall back wavily like a lion's mane. His hands, though brown—for he never wore gloves—the whip, the gun, the rod, or the weeder seldom being out of them—were well shapen and aristocratic in form, while his costume—a suit of coarse grey tweed and long brown leather leggings, as he sat at table, with a silver whistle at his button-hole, and a dogwhip in his pocket—only required his old wide-awake hat, with its row of flies and fish-hooks, to complete it ; but the aforesaid hat hung in the hall without.

"My letter contains most mournful and sudden news, Katherine," said he, as a tear started to each of his eyes—an emotion all the more painful, as he was a man quite unused to the melting mood.

" You will perhaps permit me, dear Wedderburn," said she ; on which Cyril took the letter from his father's passive fingers and handed it to his mother, who lifted her gold eye-glass, and, after a pause, read as follows ; but not without great difficulty, as the handwriting was tremulous, and in some places degenerated to an almost illegible scrawl :—

" The Choultry, Madras.

"MY DEAR BROTHER JOHN,—My physician and old friend, of the Palmacottah Light Infantry, worthy Doctor Chutnay, who has just left me (and who will forward *this* to you), has told me that my hours are numbered now. Before this heavy fever fell upon me, I had fondly hoped to be with you once again, to inhale the pure, cool breeze that sweeps over the purple Lammermuir and all down bonnie Lauderdale ; but God has willed it otherwise. I cannot live more than two or three days at the utmost, and have only strength to write, that I bequeath to you my most valuable possession on earth—my only child Gwendolcyne—whom I know that you and dearest Katherine will love and cherish, even as your own boys, for the sake of her mother, who, to the hour of her death, loved you all so well.

"The impulsive blood of her mother's old Welsh race is in my girl's veins, and she is a warm and enthusiastic creature ; so I pray you, as one so soon to face his God as I, alone can pray, that you will be her guide and protector. She will be rich ; see that she marries worthily ; guide and watch over her lonely steps, dear John, and love—love to—but my head swims. I cannot pen another line. Be a father to my little Gwenny, and believe me your affectionate brother,

"WILLIAM WEDDERBURN."

While all listened to this in respectful silence, and the letter was passed between the brothers for re-perusal, Sir John had thrust aside his breakfast, and with his chin resting on one hand, sat gazing into the far vista of the sunny lawn, lost in sad thoughts; but Lady Wedderburn very deliberately examined the letter in which it was enclosed, and a document which came with it.

The letter was from the physician, Doctor Chutnay, and was dated from the cantonments of the 3rd Madras N. I. It stated that "the deceased expired on the second day after the letter was written, and that his daughter, Miss Gwendoleyne Wedderburn, would leave Madras for Europe by the next P. and O. liner that came into the Roads, and that herewith he begged to enclose a copy of her poor father's will.

William Wedderburn, the younger brother of Sir John—younger by six or seven years at least—had spent half his life in the Indian Civil Service, and had realised a handsome fortune by his lucky speculations in the staple produce of India, such as cotton, indigo, rice, and coffee ; and by his will it would appear that, save a few thousands bequeathed to Sir John, he left the bulk of his property, more than three hundred thousand pounds, to his orphan daughter, including a "garden-house" like an Oriental palace on the Choultry Plain, shares in the Agra Bank, Indian Stock, and—Heaven only knew all what more !

The contents of this letter affected all at the table in various degrees.

Lady Wedderburn had scarcely—and her sons had never—seen, though they had heard so much of this rich Indian uncle, who yearly sent home such magnificent and graceful (because suitable) presents to the family. He had been a kind of myth to all, save Sir John ; so personally his death stirred no deep or tender chord in their hearts.

Her first idea was that the thousands now so suddenly bequeathed would be a seasonable aid in pushing on Robert at college and bringing him out for the bar ; also in purchasing a majority for Cyril in some regiment that was *not* going to the East ; and then, if the orphan cousin was handsome, who could say what might happen? the Madras heiress would make an excellent wife for one of them.

Her next thoughts ran on the fashion and expense of mourning, for the whole household, even to the lodge gatekeepers, would require to be put in black. Was a black hammer-cloth necessary for the carriage? Gaiety, they could have none of it for a time—a confounded bore, Robert thought, "when a fellow had so many invitations on hand and in prospect." Then as the little heiress would be here anon ; which rooms was she to have? The best of course, after her own. All these ideas swept in quick succession through her busy brain.

Chesters of Chesterhaugh thought of the heiress's thousands and his own ugly betting-book. He played with his knife and fork ; wondered what she was like, and ventured to enquire her age.

" She will be eighteen in May. Poor girl ! and quite an orphan ; but so rich, Captain Chesters ! "

The poor companion sighed, for she too had been long friendless ; but no lacs of rupees ever fell to the great Celtic line of the M'Caw.

Horace Ramornie remembered that eight years before this he too had come an orphan to Willowdean, but " so poor ; " and now he had no thought or interest in the matter, save surprise to see tears falling silently over the bronzed cheek of bluff and jolly Sir John Wedderburn. But the memory of the latter was wandering away into the past, and he could recall the lithe, supple, and handsome figure of that dead brother, a blue-eyed and golden-haired lad, as he went forth to seek his fortune in the sunny East, with mingled hope and sorrow in his heart, and their mother's tears and kisses lingering on his cheek ; and he could recall many a happy, happy hour they had spent together under yonder old trees, under the roof of Willowdean—days of nutting and bird-nesting in the summer woods, of trouting in the Leader and Whitadder ; or wandering, truant-like, by many a harvest-field and lone burn-brae ; of tricks they had played upon their tutor ; of depredations committed in the vineries and hot-houses ; and their awful fear of discovery, which was more than half the charm of the whole adventure ; of all their rides and rambles, their boyish hopes and mutual aspirations ; and now—*now* he was dead and buried, far, far away in an Indian grave, an old, shattered, fever-stricken man.

It seemed so difficult to think when he looked across the room to where hung a portrait of the little Willie of the vanished years, a laughing and golden-haired boy ; and Sir John muttered, with something between a sigh and a sob in his throat—

"Yes, Willie, I shall be a kind father to your orphan girl, whate'er betide !"

"Gwendoleyne is a pretty name," said Cyril, approvingly.

"I am so glad you like it," observed his mother, following her own ambitious thoughts.

"Rather romantic though. There is *one* I like that is more simple."

"Her mother was a Welsh lady—one of the Ap-Rhys of Llanchillwydd," added Lady Wedderburn, in an explanatory tone. "But she died, poor thing, at Madras, when Gwenny was about three years old, and I wonder that uncle William did not send her home to Europe long ago ; but then she was his only child, and he would have missed her so much !"

As the conversation was now taking a domestic turn, and Sir John Wedderburn was evidently disturbed by the tidings—for, instead of his brother's death, his final return had been anticipated,—Chesters, who hated the dark or gloomy side of anything, thought he had better go, as he had only ridden over to see a horse of Cyril's ; yet he lingered for a time, smoking a cigar with him and Robert on the terrace before the mansion, while Lady Wedderburn was engaged in family council with her husband.

CHAPTER II.

THE WILLOWDEAN.

THE manor house of Willowdean is situated in the Merse, which, with Lauderdale and Lammermuir, forms one of the three great subdivisions of Berwickshire, each of which possesses distinct natural features ; but the former has been long celebrated in Scottish annals for its rich scenery, its industrious population, and plentiful harvests, while the sterner Lauderdale is bold and rugged, and Lammermuir is lone, bleak, and dreary, all purple morass or pastoral hill, being, in fact, a vast sheepwalk.

Built on the site of an old Bastile-house, that had many a time been burned or stormed, restored and stormed again, by English armies and Warden raiders in the times of old ; lastly, when the Bandes Françaises under D'Esse d'Epainvilliers were in full retreat from Haddington during the wars of Mary of Lorraine, Willowdean we may describe as a handsome modern house, of aristocratic appearance, with a peristyle of eight Ionic pillars, in the pediment above which were the Wedderburn arms —a chevron between three mullets ; while their motto—*Fortiter et recle*—was carved in large Roman letters on the frieze. The rooms were lofty, the double drawing-room, when its folding doors were slid into the wall, forming a stately salon for dancing, when all its rich furniture was removed, and the Karl Harrgs, Fosters, and Gilberts, that adorned its walls, were alone left behind.

There was, of course, a noble billiard-room, where many a game was played by Cyril and Chesters, not always to the advantage of the former ; and a great conservatory filled with the rarest exotics, where more than one graceful acacia drooped over statues and fountains, was lit at night with roses of gas made at the home farm.

The park had been under grass for centuries, if it was ever ploughed at all. Tradition said that Leslie's six thousand cavalry had grassed there a night or two before the battle of Philiphaugh ; and there, as its vista stretched far away to where the purple Lammermuir bounded the distance, far beyond the invisible fence that marked its actual limits, the brown fallow deer might be seen in summer browsing or lying under the ancient oaks and beeches, half hidden among the green fern and pink foxglove ; and that nothing might be wanting in effect, some stately peacocks spread their spotted plumage over the white balustrades of the terrace before the façade of the mansion, to which the gravelled carriage drive approached by a semicircular sweep on each side, through the smooth and velvet grass.

Every comfort were there, and every luxury—ice-pit, vineries and forcing-houses, stables and kennel—yet the means of the worthy Baronet were far from adequate to his expenses in this aspiring age, and in Willowdean, as in many a less pretentious dwelling, there was too often a struggle to "keep up appearances."

Perhaps no part of the house was furnished more luxuriously and elegantly than Lady Wedderburn's boudoir, the hangings and furniture of which were blue satin and silver ; but few objects there were more treasured than certain Burmese idols, three-headed gods, triple-trunked elephants, and other hideous little monsters, in bronze and ivory, which her beloved Cyril had picked up amid the "loot" at Moulmein, and brought home for "dear mamma," when he was a boy ensign, in his first red coat.

And now for a little account of some of our *dramatis personæ*.

Captain Wedderburn, though a frank, honest, and good-hearted young fellow, was and ever had been a spoiled child of fortune. Pronounced by aunts and nurses "a love of an infant" when crowing and nestling in his silk berceaunette, he had gone to Rugby a bold and beautiful schoolboy, and left college to join his regiment a dangerously handsome man. He had been pretty successful in all the little undertakings of the gay life he led—the career of a soldier in the flirting times of peace. The horse he backed was pretty sure to win ; he could keep his wicket against the prime bowler of the garrison, and march off the field with his bat on his shoulder : he won the prize at every pigeon match, rode straight to hounds, pulled a capital stroke oar, and was deemed one of the best round-dancers in the Royal Fusileers. There was one thing he had *never* been able to do, viz., to beat his acquaintance Chesters at cards or billiards, "and thereby hangs a tale." Few men among those distinguished Fusileers had been more petted, spoiled, fallen-in-love-with, or so lucky among the ladies as handsome Cyril Wedderburn, who became rather fastidious in consequence.

A prime hand he was in arranging picnics, or a social "spread" on the roof of a drag at race or review, and he affected to dabble in music too, for he had a fine voice, and many a mysterious air he had bribed the band-master to "fudge out of another," and dedicate to some pretty girl about whom he dangled till the *route* came ; and it was his great—yet most ungrateful—boast, in mess-room parlance, that "no bit of white muslin had ever hooked him yet."

There was one sweet, pale face, however—but of *that* anon.

His cousin and brother-officer, Horace Ramornie, though nearly as much petted and admired, was much less a man of pleasure than Cyril. He was by no means so showy an officer or so fashionable a man, yet he was a lad of very striking and interesting appearance, now in his twenty-second year ; slender, graceful, and gentle-mannered, with nearly regular features, and a skin of an olive tint ; yet with bat and foil he had held his own against the best at Sandhurst. He had wonderful dark hazel eyes, eyes that, as Cyril said, "were bright enough and soft enough for a girl, and were quite thrown away upon a fellow like Horace."

The lad had been a hard student, for he knew—and had perhaps been taught to know from his boyhood—that he was dependent on the Wedderburn family for his commission, in the first place, and for his little yearly allowance in the second ; therefore, he was chiefly vain of having won a step in the regiment, that he was a lieutenant, and that three letters, *p.s.c.*, after his name in the Army List, showed that he had already passed his final examination at the Staff College, and was fit for any appointment the Commander-in-Chief might bestow upon him.

Though amid the expense which their household and Cyril's allowance—especially when on home service—entailed, together with Robert's prospects, Lady Wedderburn did sometimes

deem Horace somewhat of "a drag," she could not forget that
he was her dead sister's only son ; and as she doted on the
tomes of Douglas, Burke, and Debrett, she was vain of his
direct descent from an old, old Scottish line, that stretched far
beyond the Wedderburns of the Merse into remote antiquity ;
for the lad was descended from fierce Sir John Ramornie, the
audacious and implacable, the companion and false friend of
the helpless Duke of Rothesay, whom, as history tells us, he
seized near Strathtyrum, and starved to death in the Castle of
St. Andrew's in 1402, and from Alexander de Ramorgny, who
had a free gift of Pitglassie in Fife from Robert Duke of
Albany, and so forth ; so Horace, though only a subaltern in
Her Majesty's service, enjoyed an historical name, one among
the best of many of Scotland's "unlanded gentry," though
Pitglassie and all had gone in recent bank failures, very little
store he set thereon, as he walked to and fro on the terrace on
that breezy March morning, enjoying a pipe of Cavendish and
listening to Chesters, who was descanting most fluently on the
merits of certain horses and dogs, and on certain races that
were on the *tapis*, but descanting in vain, for Horace was not
a betting man.

Ralph Rooke Chesters, of Chesterhaugh, a neighbouring
proprietor, whose lands were deeply dipped in debt, enjoyed the
local rank of Captain, having once been a cornet in a cavalry
corps, which he had left "somehow under a cloud," as the
phrase went. He was not without a certain amount of good
looks, and had undoubtedly a gentlemanly exterior. Yet he
was a *blasé* man, of some forty or five-and-forty years, who had
seen and known a vast deal of the world ere half that time
was past. His nose was very red, his cheeks were blotchy,
and his sandy-coloured hair was already thickly seamed with
grey. There was a perpetual sinister and watchful expression
in his pale grey eyes, and usually a compression about his thin
cruel lips, the secret workings of which his sandy moustache,
luckily for himself, concealed.

On this morning he wore a rough suit of heather-coloured
tweed, with leather gaiters and baggy knickerbockers, a round
jacket, scarlet shirt, and Glengarry bonnet, the vile composite
costume of the fast Scotchman "of the period" whose limbs
will not pass muster in the kilt ; and on the left side of the
said Glengarry he wore a huge and pretentious silver badge,
the crest of the Chesters (a tower), to whose line he certainly
was no ornament ; and Cyril Wedderburn, who was very
fastidious in his own toilette, disliked this style of dress
intensely, and even when shooting or fishing never adopted it.

His new horse—a fine bay hunter, with dark legs—had fully
met Chesters' approval. The stables, the dog-kennel, and the

2

loose box had been duly visited ; they had tried a stroke or two
in the billiard-room, with a glass of Madeira and a biscuit, ere
the Captain again announced his intention of going.

"I daresay, Wedderburn," said he, "you must feel it a
thundering bore, this death of an old uncle you scarcely ever
saw ? It will spoil all your fun, having to play propriety here
till your leave is up."

Cyril, like Robert, was perhaps thinking so, but had not the
coarseness to put his thoughts in words.

"Uncle William was my father's favourite brother," said he,
evasively.

"Order my horse, Asloane," said Chesters, as the butler was
leaving the billiard-room with the salver and decanters.

"Are you going already?" asked Cyril, in a tone of equal
indifference and politeness.

"Yes, if you will allow me. I am rather *de trop* here—
family grief, house of mourning, and all that sort of thing," said
Chesters, smiling as much as he ever smiled ; "but perhaps you
will look me up at Chesterhaugh to-morrow, and pot with me
at six, and then we'll have a little mild play ; not extravagant,
remember ; only guinea points."

"All right, I'll be there ; thanks," replied Cyril, but in a tone
of more indifference than cordiality.

Cyril Wedderburn courteously accompanied Chesters to the
nearest gate-lodge on the verge of the park, and then he
galloped off.

"That is not the way to Chesterhaugh," said Cyril to the
lodgekeeper.

"No, Maister Cyril," replied that official, with a leer ; "but
the Captain gangs as often by the road that leads to Lonewoodlee."

This man did not speak unthinkingly, for his tone and manner
made the brow of Cyril contract, and he felt his cheek flush
with anger, for the inference to be drawn from those simple
words was far from being a pleasant one to him.

"Chesters at Lonewoodlee ! By Heaven, I must look to
this !" he muttered, as he turned and walked slowly back to
the house.

<hr />

CHAPTER III.

LADY WEDDERBURN'S HOPE.

DINNER at Willowdean, even when only the family were
present, was rather a stately and cumbersome meal ; yet Cyril
and Horace, accustomed latterly to the splendour and glitter of

the regimental mess, perhaps liked that it should be so. A service of plate covered the great walnut-wood sideboard. The damask cloths, the elaborately cut crystal, the blue and gold china with the Wedderburn arms—crest, an eagle in full flight, with the motto, *Fortiter et recte*—which figured on everything from the ice-pails to the salt-spoons, all betokened taste, luxury, and moderate wealth ; while candelabra lit with gas shed a flood of brilliant light over all. Save a few feet of polished wainscot round the room, the floor was entirely covered by a rich deep Turkey carpet. Long and narrow, the apartment had four lofty windows at the end ; these opened towards the Lammermuir Hills, but were now, at six P.M. in the month of March, shrouded by heavy maroon-coloured hangings with broad gold binding.

The three servants in attendance were each a perfect "Jeames" of the most approved order, so far as calves, whiskers, and livery went ; for the traditional good old-fashioned servants who lived and died in their master's household, and were as hereditary as the family pictures and plate, like many other Scottish things of the best kind, exist only in romance, and are gone with the past.

The party which assembled at table when Asloane rang the house-bell at six, was of course somewhat reserved and taciturn for a time. They conversed but little, or in low tones, till the cloth was removed, and that little ran chiefly on the weather, or consisted of the courtesies of the table, till Mr. Asloane had placed the elaborately cut decanters in a row before his master, bowed, and withdrawn.

Sir John, though grave and even sad in expression, had already been able to think calmly over his "poor brother's" death, in conjunction with certain long projected improvements on the property—more particularly the erection of a new wing to the stable-court, and a central clock tower ; and yet ever and anon he would come forth with some fond or kind reminiscence of Willie, for he seemed at times to live in the past, and could scarcely realize the idea that he had died an elderly man at last.

Cyril's thoughts rose chiefly upon what the gatekeeper had said so casually ; thus he was taciturn, almost morose, and fidgeted with his cuffs and studs or whiskers, viciously cracking walnuts as if in the shell of each he crushed an enemy.

His brother Robert was probably thinking that if their uncle William had left *him* something out of his lacs of rupees, he might have cut the Bar, for which he had no great fancy, and betaken himself to the profession of a man of pleasure ; while young Horace Ramornie had no thoughts of the matter, for he was the least considered in that small family circle, and so made, perhaps, a more subst..ntial dinner than any of them.

Lady Wedderburn, (*née* Katharine Douglas, daughter of a poor but aneient family in one of the Wards in Lanarkshire) was no longer young ; she was past the prime even of middle age, but still had great remains of beauty. Her cast of features and the brilliance of her dark grey eyes were unchanged, though wrinkles had taken the place of dimples, and her once blaek hair was streaked with silvery white.

Her small and lady-like hands showed the minute wrinkles and blue veins of time ; yet they were well-shaped and beautiful hands still ; and though she had several rings on them, fully a half of these were black euamel and pearls—the rings in memory of friends and relations she had survived.

The great remains which she possessed of a high class of beauty rendered her still pleasing, and Cyril, a very fastidious connoisseur in fine faces, always admired his mother's more than that of any other woman. She was his model, yet men rarely fall in love with their imaginary models. Her dresses were always rich, the colours well ehosen, and in fashion adapted to her years, for she had the art which so few possess— that of growing gracefully old. A fall of rich white lace pinned prettily over her stately head fell with lappets at each side, finishing a coquettish demi-toilette that somehow became her matronly character.

"Pass the wine, Cyril ; you are very silent," said Sir John ; "and let us drink kindly to the memory of your poor uncle Willie."

"My dear Sir John," said Lady Wedderburn, still pursuing her own secret thoughts, after this little ceremony was over, "on again looking over our dear William's will, I observed that his property is conveyed away to eertain trustees, of whom *you* are the chief, for the bchoof of that darling child Gwenny, whom I already begin to love—quite as a daughter, indeed."

A grave kind of smile spread over Sir John's face, and Cyril, after a swift but furtive glanee at his mother, proceeded to crack more nuts ; but no one replied.

"I do so long to sce her," resumed Lady Wedderburn, toying the while with some grapes, her head pensively on one side, and her eyes cast down. "If like her mother, she will be a very beautiful girl, Cyril."

"Indeed—I never saw her mother," replied Cyril, with provoking indifference, as he played with his long whiskers.

"I don't think there were many girls who in the bloom of their twentieth year surpassed Gwendoleyne Ap-Rhys !" observed his mother, emphatically.

"Pass the port, Horace," said Cyril ; "that Madeira is like

our mess tap, rather heady, but makes a capital 'whitewasher,' however."

"Makes a what?" asked Lady Wedderburn, with a tone of pique. "But a girl with three hundred thousand pounds will prove a serious responsibility to us."

"Get her married offhand," said Robert, bluntly.

"That is the very kind of marriage to be guarded against," replied his mother. "Thus we must be careful whom we introduce to her. She will prove a great comfort to us, however, Wedderburn, when the dear boys are back to their regiment and Robert is at College."

"I quite concur with you, Katharine, about the introductions," said Sir John. "One thing is clear, that after Cyril goes I shall not have that person Chesters coming about Willowdean."

"He is no particular friend of mine," retorted Cyril, almost haughtily, while he coloured with annoyance. "I only met him at the Lothian Racing Club : he knew Probyn and other fellows of ours, and so we came to talk of horses, and turn a card or two, that is all."

"A card or two to your loss, as I am aware ; but he is a bad style of man, and not the kind of companion I wish you or Horace to make."

"My dear papa," replied Cyril, who, when in his father's presence, never forgot the influences of boyhood, "after a fellow has been eight years in the line, been round the Sand Heads at the mouth of the Hooghly, and marched all through Central India, if he can't take care of himself, he never will."

"I know that Chesters got into a scrape in his regiment, and then into the hands of the 'Chosen People,'" said Horace, laughing.

"An easy matter to do so," added Sir John. "Chesterhaugh, with its rents, won't stand a stud of horses, a pack of harriers, a yacht on the Clyde——"

"Besides a French *danseuse*," interrupted Cyril, under his breath and with a swift glance at his cousin.

"He rooked that young French officer who was travelling here," said Sir John—"what was his name?"

"The Captain De la Fosse," said Miss M'Caw, softly, for the flatteries of the Frenchman were still deep and soft in her memory, when he spent a week at Willowdean.

"Thank you—yes, De la Fosse. He rooked him so completely that, but for my assistance, he would have had serious difficulty in getting home to France."

"Ah, well : don't let him marry cousin Gwenny," said Cyril, once more applying himself to the port. "But here is a chance for you young fellows, Bob and Horace. Why don't you toss up for who is to enter stakes for the heiress ?"

"Fie, Cyril! How can you talk thus—how make a jest so unseemly at such a time—of your own cousin too?" exclaimed Lady Wedderburn, with heightened colour and unusual asperity of tone.

" Why, mother dearest——" began Cyril, with surprise.

" You might give yourself the preference."

" The right of the first-born," added Robert, sententiously.

" Nay, nay, I am not a marrying man. What the deuce should I do with a wife, when the regiment has got its ' Letters of Readiness,' too ?" asked Cyril, again having recourse to the nuts, with a gloom in his dark blue eyes.

" Or Horace either, if it comes to that," said Lady Wedderburn, a little pointedly. " But under all the circumstances, I do not see why you should now go to the East at all, Cyril."

" Why *now* more than yesterday?" asked Cyril, who seemed to be in a cynical mood of mind. "I daresay you think me far too fine and handsome a fellow to be shot or bayoneted by some filthy Russian linesman, and then flung into a hole or a trench by the wayside, as better men have been."

" Oh, Cyril, what a horrible idea !" exclaimed his mother, while tears started to her eyes ; " but there is our neighbour, Lady Juliana Ernescleugh, on the first rumour of war she had her son, the Master, transferred to the Scots Fusileer Guards, and I don't see why I should be worse treated than she is."

Cyril and Horace laughed on hearing this, and the former said, contemptuously—

" I do not think Lady Juliana made much by that move, as the Brigade of Guards are also under orders for European Turkey."

" At all events, when Gwenny comes home—for this house is of course her home, Sir John being her nearest kinsman and chief trustee—I trust that you two boys will do all in your power to soothe and console her after the terrible loss and affliction she has undergone."

Horace Ramornie coloured, for he felt himself omitted in this charge ; but then she was no relation of his.

" Of course," replied Cyril, who, after a pause, began now for the first time to perceive how the current of these remarks tended ; " but our time for all that sort of thing—at least, mine and Horace's—will be short, and a telegram from the Colonel may whisk us off by the first train at any moment. Gwenny—Gwendoleyne—the name is pretty enough, smacks of Mudie's, and the novel in three volumes octavo—we must leave the care and the reversion of her to you, Bob."

"She won't have any tinge of colour about her, I hope?" said that personage, simply.

"What a griff you are! Come out for the Scotch Bar; you would certainly shine there, Bob, if nowhere else," said Cyril.

"Well, a Welsh girl," persisted Bob, who was at the age when most young men are flippant; "she'll have black eyes, of course, with the proverbial cheek bones of the Celt and the Cymri—a high-crowned hat, and a scarlet handkerchief."

"A nice costume to wear at the Choultry, when the thermometer is at 108° in the shade. Bob, you are the veriest griff I have met since I left Chowringee."

"I am getting utterly provoked by this tone and the tenor of these remarks. Really the young men of the present day are becoming quite insufferable!" said Lady Wedderburn, actually darting an angry glance at poor Horace, who had scarcely spoken. "Cyril, and you especially Robert, seem to forget that her mother was a lady of one of the best families in Wales, and that her father was your uncle."

"Yes," added Sir John, stiffly; "Ap-Rhys of Llanchillwydd, is a name second to none in the annals of the old Principality."

"Then, papa," continued Bob, "when Gwenny comes home, we'll all have to go in for Burke, Debrett, and pedigree?"

"Reared in India, and away from all home influences, the girl will too probably place such things at their true value," said Cyril, still more unwittingly shocking his aristocratic mother; "though of course she may, if she please, go far beyond the Wedderburns up to the first Prince of Wales, or Howel Dha, at least."

"Come, come; no quizzing," said Sir John, a little severely. "Remember that she is an orphan."

"And so rich," added Lady Wedderburn, plaintively. "Miss M'Caw," she continued, with a bow understood by that lady, who, when no other was present, always sat on Sir John's right hand; and then the four gentlemen rose as ceremoniously as if they were all strangers, while she retired to the drawing-room with her companion.

The latter, who had been pretty when young, was now well past her fortieth year, and having a pedigree—as what Highlander has not?—she had sighed with secret impatience and envy, perhaps bitterness, while listening to much that we have recorded; for she too, as well as the heiress, had come of an old Celtic line that had furnished its patriotic victims for the field and scaffold; and among her private *lares* she treasured an old locket of red gold, containing a lock of "the Prince's" golden hair, given by his own hand, on the retreat from Derby, to her great grandsire, the great M'Caw of the '45, who died like a hero in the human shambles at Carlisle.

She had resided some ten years of an aimless and hopeless life at Willowdean, and had not been without secret thoughts on one or two occasions of entangling Cyril in a matrimonial affair ; but he had seen too much of the world even as a boy, and was daily seeing too many fresh young faces to be caught so easily—so all such hopes were past and vanished now.

She was a calm, quiet person, who, under a tolerably ladylike exterior, concealed much of that discontented pride, fawning, and subservience, which are too often the leading characteristics of the modern Celt.

"I do beg that you will not consider Ralph Chesters as in any way a friend of mine," said Cyril, resuming a thread of the past conversation, after his brother and Horace had betaken them to the billiard-room ; "for I fully agree with you that he is not the style of man to meet ladies."

"Especially one who is such a monetary prize as your cousin," said Sir John, pointedly.

"But he talks of going to the army of the East."

"In what capacity ?"

"An officer of the Bashi Bozooks, or some such distinguished force," said Cyril, with a hearty fit of laughter.

"And a good riddance his absence will prove to the Merse," added Sir John, as he rose to join Lady Wedderburn, leaving Cyril to smoke on the terrace, where he walked to and fro in the clear cold starlight, with his eyes fixed on a dark spot that was barely distinguishable on the hill side, two or three miles off. It was a dense grove of trees, which seemed to have a peculiar attraction for him, and its outline became more distinct when the moon arose.

"Have you been talking to Cyril?" asked the lady, as her husband entered her boudoir, and, not without some doubt and hesitation, deposited his burly person in his rough tweed suit on one of her blue and silver *fauteuils*.

"Yes," said he, rubbing his forehead with an air of perplexity.

"Seriously, I hope ?"

"About Chesters—oh, yes."

"Tush ! I mean about Gwendoleyne."

"No ; but it seems to me that you are already—even on the first day our melancholy news has come—disposed to press your views and wishes too plainly upon Cyril."

"How so ?" asked Lady Wedderburn, curtly.

"In the choice of a wife, most men like to please themselves, not other persons."

"But surely, Wedderburn, you would wish to see this alliance brought about ?" said she earnestly.

"Undoubtedly ; but Cyril is just the style of young fellow

to run rusty—to kick over the traces—if worried about the matter. I know that I should have done so."

"He can have no previous attachment, for never a letter comes here, save from some of his regimental friends, and Horace and Robert see them all."

"But, my dear Katharine," urged Sir John, gently, as he stirred his cup of coffee, "we must consider also the girl's inclinations, her tastes, her sympathies."

"What right has she to have any at her years ? I am sure I had none !"

"Complimentary, Kate, for you were just about her age when you married *me*."

"Ah, but that was a very different thing. I did not possess three hundred thousand pounds."

"You possessed much that had far more value in the eyes of John Wedderburn," said the old gentleman, as he stooped, kissed her upturned forehead gallantly, and to end this matter, went forth to have a look at his horses, and think over the proposed additions to the already magnificent stable-court.

CHAPTER IV.

LONEWOODLEE.

WITHIN a few miles of this splendid and luxurious modern mansion a very different scene was passing in another dwelling.

In a bleaker part of the Merse, more immediately adjoining the Lammermuir range of hills, was situated the house of Lonewoodlee, a fine example of what a Scottish fortalice required to be in the troublesome times of the sixteenth century. "It grotesquely associated with its rude strength the fantastic ornaments of a more powerful and civilized people—a type of what the French alliance must often have produced among the gentlemen of the age—the rugged nature of the Scot, with the style and manners of the mercurial Frank."

It was a small square tower, with round corbelled turrets at the angles ; but as it has changed hands since then, and been strangely modernized within the last three years, the reader may look for it in vain as we shall describe it.

Numerous loopholes, designed for arrows or arquebuses, were in the angles of these four turrets, in the sills of the windows, and round the floridly carved entrance-door, over which were the arms of the family, with the legend in quaint letters, in bold relief—

"*Y̔is tovr finished be Oliver Levenox, 15th Aprile, 1560, is ovr inheritance.*"

It was grey, gaunt, lichen spotted, and solitary, and was surrounded by a grove of ancient trees on the pastoral slope, from
whence it took its most characteristic name of the Lonewoodlee.
It was more immediately girt by a massive wall, which had once
been for defence, but was ruinous now, for the long-tufted grass
and fragrant wall-flower flourished along its cope, and the iron
gate had long since fallen from its hinges, while the proud court
was almost covered by the grass that sprung up between the
stones.

Even prior to the period of which we write, some fifteen years
ago, an attempt had been made to modernize the tower a little,
by removing the rusted iron gratings from the windows and
enlarging them ; but still the dwelling was gloomy, in consequence of the enormous thickness of the walls and the vaultings
of the lower basement.

Among the wood around it were many trees that had sprung
from seedlings of the ancient ash, which, by the law of an early
Scottish king, every man who built even a cottage was bound to
plant near his dwelling for shafts, when the "spear, six Scottish
ells in length," was required to bear back alike the Norman
knights and Saxon infantry of England.

Many a gloomy old Border legend was connected with the
Tower of Lonewoodlee, and like some other ancient families,
the proprietors had their warning when fate was nigh—an
unpleasant, however romantic, adjunct ; for it was said that
when a Lennox was to die, as the moon rose above a certain quarter of the Lammermuir hills, the shadow of a large
human hand—the hand of destiny—was cast on the eastern
wall, with the forefinger pointed at length ; and the local
papers actually asserted that such a shadow was visible before
Major Lennox was killed at the battle of Waterloo.

Within all was gloomy, dilapidated, and darkened by time ;
the furniture was full forty years old, and some of it was still
older.

In the dining-room, or hall, the sofas were square-elbowed,
of horsehair, and furnished with back-squabs ; the chairs were
of dark blue leather, and in the corners were circular stands for
curious china, large shells, and so forth. With cotton furniture,
or coloured calico, a meagre attempt had been made by a neat
female hand to render gay the apartment that passed as a
drawing-room, where the chiffonnières of wood, painted white
and gilded, the white marble girandoles (minus half their crystal
pendants), and everything else, were old-fashioned, shabby,
and worn, for they had been the new furnishing of the mansion
when George III. was King, and the mother of the present
proprietor had come home a blooming bride.

Here and there, in oval frames, or bordered only by black oak mouldings, were portraits of a far older period than any of the Georges, as the black wigs and breastplates of the subjects evinced. Every way it was an old and worn-out establishment, where everything looked mouldy and fading away.

On the same March evening when the maroon-coloured curtains were drawn at Willowdean, and the pompous old butler was placing the row of glittering decanters before Sir John Wedderburn, an old man was seated in a high-backed leather chair, which was studded with rows of brass-headed nails, seeking to warm his limbs at the fire, which blazed cheerily enough in the great stone chimney of the dining-hall at Lonewoodlee. The grate was old-fashioned, like everything else there ; it was a mere iron basket, adorned with four brass knobs, and placed upon two square stones, quite unsuited to the form of the fireplace. Thus the heat of the roaring pile of coals, turf, and bog-oak roots, went all up the great tunnel-like vent, with a column of sparks.

Oliver Lennox of Lonewoodlee looked much older than his years warranted, for his wasted figure, clad in a well-worn Indian dressing-gown, or *robe-de-chambre* of the shawl pattern, tied by a cord and tattered tassel, was bent severely, and his face was furrowed by disease and the emotions of the mind, rather than time, for he was not more, perhaps, than fifty-five years of age.

His right elbow rested on the arm of his chair ; his chin was placed in the hollow of his hand, and his keen, restless, yet clear blue eyes were fixed dreamily on the ruddy flame that lighted up his sharp aquiline features, and turned to threads of glittering silver his thin white hair that had once been a rich dark brown.

Seated on a tabouret or little stool by his side, was his daughter Mary, a girl not quite of twenty years ; perhaps the only true friend whom many reverses of fortune left him ; his sole attendant, save a couple of female domestics ; others seldom remained long at the Tower, as a querulous master and a gloomy house, which had moreover the steady reputation of being haunted, rendered service unattractive at Lonewoodlee.

Mary knew he was dying of some internal and mysterious disease with which the doctors had totally failed to grapple--that, in spite of her affection and their skill, of her prayers and their potions, he was slowly and surely passing away from her ; and she left nothing unsaid or undone to soothe, by sweet devotedness, what she knew to be too probably the few months of his last year on earth.

He had survived the winter, but might never live to see the

summer ripen into autumn, and the golden corn waving on the upland slopes that were his own no more.

To God and herself alone were known the terrible thoughts of Mary Lennox in the long, sleepless hours of the weary nights she passed ; yet unswerving in her filial duty, tenderly nursing and ministering as only a woman—only a daughter or wife— can nurse or minister to the wants of a querulous patient ; springing from her pillow with cheerful and affectionate alacrity, to anticipate his every wish, and smiling to hide the sorrow that preyed upon her own heart.

Pale and sad usually, her face was beautiful ; yet sadness had not been its normal expression, but rather the result of local influence. Her features were not quite regular, but there was a divine delicacy about them : her finely lidded eyes were of that blue-grey which is aptly termed violet colour, and her mouth and chin were beautifully formed, so were her tiny ears and hands. Her whole figure, which was *petite* rather, and the contour of her head, with its masses of rich brown hair, were eminently lady-like and indicative of high breeding and tender culture ; and a charming picture she would have formed, as she sat then, with her father's passive left hand locked caressingly in hers, and her soft little face upturned to his, every feature teeming with affectionate solicitude.

Her dress was plain, inexpensive, and simple, for their means could not afford her many luxuries ; but her starched cuffs and collar—made and dressed by her own hands—and the tiny velvet riband around her slender white neck, made it quite a pretty toilette, while, save an old ring or two that had been her mother's, she was destitute of ornament ; and there the father and daughter sat long in silence, while the blustering March wind soughed in the old wood without, and the flood of red and wavering light from the capacious fireplace fell upon their faces, and fitfully too upon the portraits of those ancestors, who, if their exchequer had been as low as that of Oliver Lennox, would have chosen just such a moonless night for a quiet ride among the beeves on the southern side of the Border.

Oliver Lennox had once been a man of considerable influence in the Merse, and had even contrived to shine, for a short sea- son, in London society. But deep play, some unlucky bets at Newmarket, one or two vexed law pleas with Sir John Wedder- burn, in which he had been nonsuited with great loss, domestic cares of many kinds, particularly the deaths of his wife and several children, all combined to break him down in health and spirit.

Much of his land had gone, piecemeal, to satisfy the creditors his London career had raised around him, and now the little that remained of Lonewoodlee was mortgaged to the utmost ;

and having but a bare annuity, he knew too surely that when he died there would be neither home nor shelter for his Mary.

He was a proud, fiery, and irritable man, who would brook neither the pity of his friends nor the scorn of his enemies; and the knowledge that his only child—his gentle and delicate daughter—would be left to the mercy of the world, or to support herself by the accomplishments she possessed, maddened him, so that there were times when his mind wandered, and *then* it was that the soul of Mary Lennox seemed to die within her with sorrow and terror!

"Shall I play to you, dear papa?" said she softly.

There was a wonderful chord in Mary's voice that made it very seductive, but she had to repeat the offer three times before the sense of it fell upon his drowsy ear.

CHAPTER V.

MARY LENNOX.

'SHALL I play to you, dear papa?" she repeated for the third time.

"No, Mary, no." said he, peevishly. " Your piano, child, is in that shabby chintz-covered den you call a drawing-room."

"Oh, papa! what served poor mamma may very well do for me."

"And I fear we can't afford a fire there as well as *here*."

"But if I keep the doors open you could hear me. The cold is not great to-night," she urged.

"No—no, child, thank you; but I wish to think."

"To-morrow, papa, I shall have my poor old piano brought here, and then I shall play to you some of the airs you love so well."

"Pet Mary—but music makes me sad."

"But it soothes you too, papa."

"Your voice, my darling, would soothe anything, even the rage of a lion," said he, as he drew her head upon his knee and held it caressing there between his tremulous hands; "but it sounds so much like your mother's, that—that—even while I love to listen my heart grows sad and sick within me! Music possesses such vast power, especially over a shattered nervous system, and more than anything else can conjure back the past, the lost, and the dead! But," he added, suddenly, with a louder tone and a strange gleam in his eye, " where is your brother Harry; why is he not here to-night?"

Then a kind of wail escaped the lips of poor Mary, and the

tears started to her eyes, for she knew that his mind was wandering again.

"Oh, papa!" she moaned, and looked at him imploringly.

"Where is he?" demanded Mr. Lennox, impetuously, and his
eyes flashed in the red light of the fire; then he struck his hand
upon his brow as a gleam of memory came to his aid, and he
said, in a choking voice, "I forgot myself! God help me—God
help me! True, Mary—true; my boy is lying in his Indian
grave, far, far away, where the bones of the Briton and Sikh lie
thick on the battle-field. But you must remember the night I
saw him here—here, in this very room!"

"I was but a child of eight years when poor Harry died."

"Yes; and when I saw him."

"Oh, papa, that is a wild idea; as absurd as—as ——"

"What, girl?"

"The shadowy hand."

"It is not so, and it was not so! It is not impossible, Mary,
when death, more especially a violent one, strikes at a distance
one who is dear to us—dear as your brother Harry was to me—
that some intuition, some mysterious presentiment announces
the event. How often have I told you that as I sat here in the
twilight of evening in this chair, and on this very spot, reading
the Gazette of the killed and wounded on that disastrous Indian
field, some secret impulse made me glance towards the end of
the room, and there I saw the figure, the form, the face of your
brother, regarding me mournfully and tenderly for a moment,
and then all faded away. I was terror-struck, but deemed it
fancy! Again I turned to the fatal Gazette, and the *next name*
that caught my eye among the killed—the killed in action—was
that of my own boy, Harry Lennox!"

"Hush, papa, oh hush!" said Mary, looking round anxiously;
for it was this story to which her father was fond of referring
from time to time, that had won the Tower, among the vulgar,
the reputation of being haunted, so that domestics were terrified
to remain, though the place was within a mile or two of the rail
to Berwick.

After a long pause he drew a deep breath and spoke again.

"Did I not hear, or was it a dream—for I have strange dreams
sometimes—that Wedderburn's son buried him—buried my
boy?" said he, in a tremulous voice.

"Yes, papa," said Mary, eagerly; "Cyril Wedderburn buried
poor Harry, and stood by his grave in that distant land. He
did more, papa: he cut off a lock of his hair for—for you."

"I could bless him for that, but for his father's sake. I hate
that elder Wedderburn. I hate his flaunting wife," he continued,
raising his voice and his clenched hand. "I hate the whole
brood of them, and shall never cease to curse——"

"Oh, dearest papa, do not—do not speak thus!" cried Mary, imploringly, as she placed a hand upon his mouth, and saw with growing terror the fire, as if of incipient insanity, flashing in his eyes.

The paroxysm of rage into which he lashed himself when he thought of his lost lawsuits, especially one in which Sir John Wedderburn asserted and made good his right of pasturage upon a certain part of the Lee, which the Lennox family had claimed as theirs alone for several generations, weakened him so much that Mary was glad to give him a soothing draught, and get him to his bedroom for the night.

After this he became more seriously ill, and there were more frequent aberrations of intellect. Sometimes he imagined himself in the hunting-field, and then he would shout in a quavering and childish treble—

"Tally ho! tally ho! Hallo, my Lord Wemyss, what's up at the high fence yonder? By Jove, John Wedderburn's brown mare is at fault—her off forefoot is caught in the wires—and over they go, nag and rider! I hope the young scoundrel's neck is broke at least!"

And Mary wept as she heard the fierce wish, which referred to some sporting adventure years ago, when her father and Sir John were much younger men, but seemingly no better friends.

Next night she had her piano moved close to the drawing-room door, so that she might play to him as he lay abed in his own room. She had a magnificent voice, and it had been highly cultivated. She exerted herself to the utmost to please, and played and sang him to sleep, as one might do a fretful child. Then when she was assured that his slumber was sound, she kissed him softly, assumed her hat and veil, her cloak and muff, and hastened from the Tower and its desolate court, to where some one she well knew was awaiting her, at an angle of the wood—but in this we are somewhat anticipating our story.

Two or three dreary days and nights followed his last outburst of mental fury, and a certain revulsion of spirit and corresponding bodily weakness followed it. Then he became more calm and coherent, after some opiates had been administered by his medical attendant, the young parish doctor, whom the charm of Mary's presence rather than her father's necessity, rendered a pretty regular visitor at Lonewoodlee; but in the hours of her tearful watching, the querulous old man unwittingly stuck many a barb in his daughter's heart.

"I feel weaker every day, Mary dear. I won't be long a burden or a trouble to you," he would say; "for something whispers to me that I cannot last long now. Old and weak—old and weak—half blind and well-nigh toothless!"

"Papa," said she, imploringly, "do not talk thus! You are not yet sixty years of age."

"I know, darling; but the poor human machine is worn out for all that. Look at Wedderburn! How hale and strong he is, for fortune has ever favoured him and his family, child; while with me—with me—oh, how is it with me? Ah, truly says Ossian, that 'age is dark and unlovely, and that the race of men are like the leaves of woody Morven; they pass away in the rustling blast, and other leaves lift their green heads on high.' So—so shall I soon pass away, Mary; but dearest you are weary?"

"I am not, papa," sighed the girl.

"Your eyes are red and dim. To bed, Mary—to bed. Place the sleeping draught at hand, then kiss me and leave me. Good night."

Then she would slip away to her room, the door of which was always left ajar, so that no sound might elude her ear in the night; and she would pray and sigh herself to sleep.

A day came anon when her father was too weak to leave his bed, and from thenceforward he became more than ever a confirmed invalid.

The sturdy but shambling old shooting pony, on whose broad back he had been latterly able to take a little exercise by a trot to Polwarth or Prestonhaugh, enjoyed a complete holiday; and time, as marked by the old-fashioned repeater at Mr. Lennox's bed-head, passed slowly indeed!

And as he lay there, day after day, and too often night after night, wakeful, and filled with keen and anxious thoughts, he strove to picture—to fashion out—the future of that lonely daughter whose life was, he hoped, to extend far beyond his own. He had plenty of time for this profitless employment, for, save Captain Chesters or perhaps the parish clergyman, no one ever dropped in to talk with or enliven him now, for his ailments and complaints against friends and fortune, his whims and fancies, rendered his society unpalatable to all save poor Mary.

There was no rousing him to take an interest in anything; and news of the coming war fell dull upon his ear. In vain did Mary read to him of our preparations for the Crimean war; that already the Russians and Turks had come to blows, and the former been defeated at Oltenitza, with the loss of three thousand seven hundred killed and wounded; that a Turkish squadron had been destroyed by the Russians, and the town cruelly bombarded; and that the British fleet, under Sir Charles Napier, had sailed for the Baltic from Spithead; that the destruction of Cronstadt was confidently expected, and so forth.

Oliver Lennox deemed the worthy minister an utter bore, and viewed his attempts to soothe or console him as simply impertinence, which his proud and fiery spirit resented. Of Chesters he felt doubtful, and knew enough of the world to fear such a visitor and such a friend for his unprotected daughter. He knew his own debts and difficulties, his own poverty, and that the annuity he possessed would die with himself, and then what would be left for her—work—starvation —death!

It was horrible to lie there—helpless, fettered hand and foot as it were, weak, powerless, and inert, weaving such dark, bitter, and distracting fancies! He writhed and wept on his pillow, and muttering, "Mary—Mary! my daughter—my daughter!" would press his thin wan hands on his burning breast, as if to stifle thoughts that would not be stifled.

"I have been rash, wasteful, and unfortunate," he would often say, "but what have you done, my poor Mary, that you should be stripped of your inheritance? for this Tower, built by Oliver Lennox, and all the land around it, even to the Whitadder, form your inheritance; but it must pass away to others —others—oh, my God! while such people as those Wedderburns live on, surrounded by every earthly blessing!"

"Calm yourself, papa," said the hopeless girl, in a choking voice; "all may yet be well. Your health will revive with the warmth of spring."

"The spring grass will be sprouting on the sod that wraps me, Mary; and there I would lie in peace could I but see your future, child—if God would only in His kindness lift the veil that hides it from me! But, from the land of shadows, perhaps I may so see it—I may see it, and be a guide and a watch over you."

Though Mary heard much of this querulous grief, she never became accustomed to it; but seemed always to suffer the agony of his death by anticipation when he spoke thus.

"Fear not, papa, fear not for me," she was wont to reply, while caressing his head on her bosom. "If I lose you, I must trust then to God only."

"To God and yourself, darling; but there are times when I think with fear that—that——"

"What, papa?"

"That Ralph Chesters seems to love you."

Mary trembled and grew pale as she said—

"Do not speak of this again, I implore you, dearest papa."

"I am glad you don't like him; but what brings him here so often!"

"To see you, of course, papa," said Mary, as her pale cheek reddened.

3

"An old man sick and ailing!   I don't believe it; but when was he here last?"

"Three days ago."

"Did you see him?"

"No; when alone with him, his presence becomes intolerable to me."

"Why—how?" asked Lennox, eagerly, and half-raising himself in his bed.

"There is an expression in his eye I do not like; moreover, I never leave your room save when you are asleep."

"Thanks, my darling; that is kind and good; but beware of Chesters, for he is a dog that bites but does not bark."

"Have no fear for me so far as *he* is concerned," said Mary, emphatically.

"It is well.   Kiss me, child, and then I shall try to sleep."

The girl kissed him tenderly, restraining her tears as she did. Then with tremulous gentleness, her pretty, small hands adjusted the pillow and coverlet, ere she glided noiselessly away.

Often had Mary pictured—for she was a sensitive creature and full of imagination—how utter her helplessness and loneliness would be when her father was gone; and notwithstanding all the love which *another* had succeeded in kindling in her heart, she longed and prayed that in the hour her father was taken, she might be taken too!

CHAPTER VI.

TWO LOVERS.

"BEEN fishing to-day, Cyril?" asked Robert Wedderburn, with a quizzical expression in his face, as his brother assumed his hat, gloves, and whip in the hall prior to riding out.

"No," replied Cyril, curtly, and colouring with some reason, as he had gone forth for four consecutive days with his rod, and returned with his basket empty : the fishing was merely a pretext to be alone, for he would have been clever indeed to have found trout or perch on the upland slopes of the Lammermuir, where Horace and Robert had seen him, while shooting hares and rabbits near Lonewoodlee.   "I dine with Chesters to-day," he added.

"You go betimes?" said Robert, suspiciously.

"I want to give my new bay nag a breather—to have a few miles' gallop ere I go to Chesterhaugh," replied Cyril, as he rode off.

It was one of those dull March evenings when the sun sets

at six o'clock, as Captain Wedderburn dashed on at a rapid
pace towards Lonewoodlee. The more fertile part of the
Merse was soon left behind, and after a ride of three or four
miles among heathy and grassy slopes, striped here and there
with bright green where the track of the Lammas floods had
run towards the Leader or the Whitadder rivers, he saw the
old grey Tower, whose four round turrets, cope-house, and
chimneys stood clearly defined against the evening sky, over-
topping even the ancient timber that grew around it.

Thatched cottages with whitewashed walls, and the ruddy
firelight glowing through their small square windows ; hedgerows that were in process of being lopped and trimmed ;
gardens where the fragrant earth had been newly turned up,
and where tufts of the white snowdrop and rows of the yellow
crocus or purple violets were appearing, had all gradually
vanished, and Cyril found himself amid a voiceless and pastoral
solitude, dotted only by black-faced sheep, or huge round
boulder-stones, and where here and there a sable gled or raven
hung aloft in mid air—a black speck amid the amber glory of
the twilight sky—as if on the outlook for the dead wedder or
other carrion that might be lying in some moss-hole or mountain
burn.

"By Jove, this place is well named the Lonewoodlee, for it
could not well be lonelier !" thought Cyril, as he rode into the
thicket of trees. There was no obstruction, for the enclosure
or boundary, once a dry stone dyke, had fallen down, and all the
place was bare and open. He threw the bridle of his horse
over a branch, and, as the twilight deepened, he turned very
deliberately towards the mansion on foot, and as he did so, the
rabbits and hares flitted before him from among the deep rank
grass.

In spite of the coldness—almost amounting to hostility—
between their families, Cyril Wedderburn and Mary Lennox
loved each other dearly. He had met her from time to time at
races and country balls, occasionally in the houses of mutual
friends. These meetings had not always been pleasant, for
latterly they were at times the result of contrivance, as Mr.
Lennox, from the peculiarities of his temper, would not have
heard of this intimacy with patience.

On the other hand, Cyril was dependent on his father for his
allowance—no man can live on his pay in any regiment now, so
least of all was it possible in the Royal Fusileers ;—and while
her father lived, Mary, under any circumstances, could not think
of marriage, and so some three years of a secret and undecided
engagement between these young people had slipped away at
the period when this story opens.

Cyril did not enter the desolate looking courtyard, lest he

might be seen by either of the two female domestics who now composed the sorely reduced household of Oliver Lennox. All was silent in the empty stables and ruined coach-house, and the entire place looked gloomy in the extreme to the eyes of the young officer, accustomed to his father's more spacious and magnificent mansion, with its great oriels of plate-glass, and he sighed when he thought of Mary.

Suddenly, through an open window on the second story, there came the swelling notes of a beautiful and tender soprano voice —a girl's—as she sang the grand old Christmas hymn, accompanying herself upon a piano, which, though a fine one, was nevertheless somewhat old-fashioned and not exactly a grand trichord.

"Poor thing! God bless her kind heart! she is singing to the old man," said Cyril, while he listened intently, with his head reclined against the wall, as if to absorb every sound. "So my little fairy sings in Latin!"

> "Adeste fideles,
> Læti triumphantes ;
> Venite, venite in Bethlehem :
> Natum videte
> Regem angelorum :
> Venite adoremus,
> Venite adoremus,
> Venite adoremus Dominum."

It was a strange song for a young girl ; but, in fancy, Cyril could see the old man listening, and perhaps beating time with his fingers on the coverlet or pillow of his bed, as he was soothed away to sleep. The notes pealed out on the calm evening air with a startling effect, each one stirring a chord in the loving heart of the listener without ; for as his own soul—yea, and dearer than his own soul—did he love the singer, who, after a pause, dashed into a plaintive little Scottish song, and then, quite as suddenly, into the beautiful solo, *Cujus animam*, from the "Stabat Mater" of Rossini.

At last she ceased. He heard, or thought he heard, the piano closed softly ; and in a minute more, with her eyes beaming, her damask cheek glowing with pleasure, as she threw up the veil of her smart little hat, Mary Lennox glided round the corner of the Tower, with her cloak on and her little hands in her muff.

"At last, my darling—at last we meet!" said Cyril, as he drew one of her hands through his arm, and believing that no human eye saw or ear heard them, led her into a denser and darker portion of the grove that grew about her old paternal home.

"I have been singing to poor papa."

"So I thought, Mary ; and he is now asleep?"

"Yes," replied Mary Lennox, with a bright smile ; for her meetings with Cyril, though stolen and hasty, were the only bright spots in the usually dreary tenor of her life, and she looked up at her lover admiringly and tenderly. His rough suit of tweed, his grey round felt hat, and scarlet shirt, very open at the neck, became his style of manly beauty well, and showed that he belonged to the class of society which can affect and afford so simple and careless a mode of costume.

" There is no word of your leave being cancelled ?"

" None, dearest."

" Thank God for that !" exclaimed the girl, as she clasped her hands.

" Four whole days have passed, my Mary, and yet I have not seen you !" said Cyril, half reproachfully, while he drew her close to him, gathering her fondly and gracefully to his breast.

" My poor papa has been so ill," she urged, as her eyes filled with tears, and her head sank wearily, yet confidently, on his shoulder.

" I regret to hear it. Poor old man ! I wonder if he will ever receive me ?"

" It would madden him, the very thought of doing so, Cyril."

" This sentiment is very foolish."

" He has neither forgotten nor forgiven that last unhappy dispute about your claim of pasturage on the lower part of the Lee."

" Bother the Lee ! The basket of grapes and peaches I sent from the hothouse ——"

" They came ; thanks, darling Cyril ; but papa suspected some friend's kindness—pity he called it—and the fruit was thrown to the dog in the yard."

" Folly again."

" It is restless pride, Cyril ; the pride that fights with poverty," pleaded Mary, with a sigh.

Cyril regarded her anxiously. He could perceive that much of her girlish simplicity was passing away ; that there was a sadness in her eyes, and about her whole demeanour a more womanly grace perhaps ; but she was growing paler and thinner in her battle with life—a life that would have been utterly cold, hard, and cheerless, but for the ray of light his love was shedding on it.

" Our households imagine us to be but cold and distant acquaintances, if even so much as that. Could they but peep in here and see us now," said he, as he covered her little face with kisses ; for Cyril was merely supposed to lift his hat in the simplest courtesy to Mary, if he passed her on the highway or at church, where she could go but seldom now, in consequence of her father's ill-health, and as for their carriage and horses, they had long become things of the past.

"Oh, it is a great horror to me, Cyril, to be separated as we are," she began.

"As we are supposed to be, you mean, Mary dear."

"And to meet as we do by stealth, practising such dissimulation."

"It is intensely absurd that I, a Captain in the Line, a fellow who has been eight years in the service, should stoop to it."

"Unless for *my* sake, love?"

"True, Mary, true. What would I *not* do for your sake, my sweet pet?"

"But it is degrading to us both, and where will it end?" she said, plaintively.

"It shall end when we are married, darling. Oh, Mary! nightly my dreams are of you, and daily my thoughts. You seem thus to be ever near me, with me, and by me!"

"Oh, Cyril, it is very good of you to love me so."

"Who could help loving you?" was the enthusiastic response.

"Your mamma does not," said she, smiling; "and neither does Sir John; so how much would they hate me did they really know all."

A gesture of impatience escaped Cyril.

"I must and shall end all this by declaring our engagement; and should my allowance be cut off, which I can scarcely anticipate, I can exchange into an Indian regiment, and maintain my wife as other men do."

"But my poor papa?"

"True; and then, I am under orders now for the East!"

"We are very unfortunate," said Mary, while her tears fell fast.

"How unlucky that Mr. Lennox and Sir John have been at cross-purposes so often, in courts of law, at public meetings, elections, and county matters, actually about the very mode of hunting with the county pack. Never were two men more antagonistic; yet is it not strange that—that——"

"We should love each other so tenderly. Is that what you were about to say, Cyril?"

"Yes, Mary darling."

"But what would they say if they knew of our meeting thus?"

"Why torment yourself by thinking of it? Your father would storm finely, I doubt not; mine be loftily indignant; and as for my lady mother, it would be a case of hysterics and sal-volatile. But I do not see why their silly views should ruin our peace, Mary."

"Ah, did Sir John but know how weak and feeble my poor papa is now, that his ebbing life is only a matter of time, he would surely come over and forgive him all."

Cyril scarcely thought so, all the more when he remembered

the rich young cousin who was to arrive so shortly at Willowdean ; but he looked silently into Mary's eyes of violet-blue,
they were brimming with tears, and her face wore a sad and
wistful expression. Perhaps she was marvelling how it would
be with her when all was over—when Cyril was before the
enemy, and that parent, so beloved, had passed away.

"Our engagement seems wrong without the consent of our
parents," she murmured, in a low voice ; "and times there are,
Cyril, when—when I seek to school myself to the task of
releasing you."

A dark and startled expression shot over the fine face of
Captain Wedderburn for a moment, for somehow he connected
this innocent speech with the idea of Chesters ; but shrinking
from putting his thoughts in words, he merely said—

"Your father might well forgive *me* for loving you, Mary, if
he would remember how I carried off your brother's body in the
face of the enemy, after making a rally and charge with the
bayonet at the head of my own company, or rather the survivors
of it, at a terrible risk and under a fire of grape from the brass
guns of the Sikhs. He might remember, too, how I laid the
poor lad in his last home, a lonely grave under a palm tree,
near the banks of the Sutledge."

"Alas ! he remembers nothing coherently ; and there are
periods when he actually thinks that Harry yet lives, and in
moaning terms he entreats him to approach the bed and take
his hand."

"And you have neither seen nor met any of my family during
my last absence with the regiment, Mary ?"

"No ; and it is better that I have not done so."

"Oh ! why, Mary ?"

"Fearing your return, I suppose, or that your brother Robert
might fall in love with me——"

"Why, Mary, Robert is a mere boy !"

"He is about nineteen ; and boys of nineteen fall in love
sometimes," said Mary, smiling.

"Well, darling, well ?"

"Fearing the result of these contingencies, your mother has
slighted and put many an affront on me. Pardon me for saying
so, dearest Cyril, but I cannot forget that my father, though
poor, is Lennox of Lonewoodlee."

Cyril Wedderburn struck his heel upon the ground angrily.

"My own Mary," said he, "this style of thing is utterly
absurd ; it is like the romance of a family feud, Romeo and
Juliet—Montague and Capulet, reproduced by an irritable old
gentleman and a match-making woman who thinks no woman
good enough for her eldest son."

"You don't know my papa," said Mary, plaintively, and yet resentfully.

"I do. I know him to be rash, extravagant, fiery, and passionate ; but pardon me, dearest, I must not forget how dearly I love his daughter."

"Cyril," said the girl, earnestly, "reared as you have happily been amid the ease and affluence of your own family, you know not the curse of being a poor gentleman."

"Don't I, by Jove ! when bits of blue paper come back, protested or unaccepted, and the Colonel and Paymaster look grave !"

"As I said before, I know not how all this will end. I only know, that irritated by losses, by poverty, and quarrels, how unforgiving my poor papa has become ; how implacable ; and that without some reconciliation with Sir John, I never could dare to speak of—of——"

"Of me ?"

"Of that which is the only happiness of my life—our engagement ; and my heart bleeds and upbraids me for deceiving him, when lying thus on what may prove his deathbed !"

Cyril did not reply, for his lips were pressed to those of Mary, and her tears were mingled with their kisses.

"Situated as we are, Cyril, our engagement may be a long one ; that I don't mind, as I could never leave papa in his present state ; but then it may be a hopeless one for me—that is, papa and I are so poor, so very poor ! You do not know the struggle we have with the world, for all his land is gone, save the patch the old Tower stands on."

"It *is* a cruel and bitter world," said Cyril (though he, a favourite of fortune, had not found it so), "and you, my tender Mary, are a deuced deal too good for it."

"All are not bad or bitter though ; there, even Chesters of Chesterhaugh——"

"What of him ?" asked Cyril, sharply.

"Finding me weeping one day about a bill of papa's that had become due when we had not a shilling to meet it, he—he——"

"Took it up, I suppose ?"

"Yes, Cyril ; he lifted a load off my heart by doing so ; but I dislike being under an obligation to any one—to him least of all."

"And this bill, what was the amount ?" asked Cyril, gloomily.

"A two hundred pounds bill, Cyril."

"Why did you not write to me ?"

"I did not like to do so," she replied, blushing.

"Had you not faith in me ?" he asked, impetuously.

"Yes, love ; but not in myself. What sound is that ?" she added, starting from his arms.

"Only the hoofs of a horse on the highway," said he, and as they listened the sound died rapidly away on the evening air.

They had been quite unaware, so absorbed were they in each other, that in the twilight gloom and under the shadow of a great larch-tree, a *third* person had been lurking and listening ; one who, when he saw their lips meet, had involuntarily raised his hand and loaded hunting-whip, and with an unuttered malediction—all the deeper for being voiceless, on his cruel white lips—had stolen away, mounted his horse, which, like Cyril's, was concealed in the thicket, and galloped off.

This lurker was no other than Ralph Rooke Chesters, who, intending to visit Mary in passing homeward from the county town, had been compelled to depart, with his heart full of jealousy and his head scheming vengeance.

And now, after a few more tendernesses, Cyril bethought him of his dinner engagement.

"I shall get that bill out of Chesters' hands, if I can," said he ; "one never can tell the use to which he may put such a document, and now good-bye, my darling. At noon to-morrow look for me here ; and at twelve to-night look at your ring and think of me, for at the same moment of time I shall turn to mine and think of you."

They separated, and Mary lingered by the Tower-gate till the last sound of the bay hunter's hoofs died away in the distance, and then she stole on tiptoe back to the bedside of her sleeping father. She had been with Cyril barely an hour, and as if it had been five minutes only, had that delightful hour sped away.

*　　*　　*　　*　　*

Punctually at twelve that night the girl looked at her ring and murmured the name of her lover, while a beautiful smile spread over her soft pale face, for she was full of romance and enthusiasm.

"The dear fellow ; he is now thinking of me !" she whispered to herself, as she laid her tiny watch on the table in the dressing closet, one of the four little turrets, and proceeded to let down the masses of her rich brown hair prior to arranging it for the night ; but ere the minute hand had gone many seconds beyond the hour of twelve a distant sound came to her ear—a sound that rapidly grew louder.

It was the clanking of hoofs, as a horse in mad career swept along the hard beaten pathway near the Tower. The heart of Mary beat faster, she scarcely knew why ; she threw open the little window of the turret and looked out upon the starry but moonless night, and as she did so the cry of a man in distress or terror came plainly upward to her listening ear, and when dying away on the wind it sounded strangely like the voice of Cyril Wedderburn.

But after a time she put aside that idea as too absurd! Would he, a finished horseman, ride like a madcap at that break-neck pace, and utter a shout like a tipsy brawler on passing Lone-woodlee?

And yet, she knew not why, she felt unhappy about the circumstance; and this anxiety increased when the following day passed, and the subsequent evening; and yet she saw or heard nothing of Cyril Wedderburn.

CHAPTER VII.

SUSPENSE AND DREAD.

At noon on the morrow, the time he had promised to come, she looked for Cyril from the turret window of her room, which commanded an extensive view of the road that wound through the grassy and pastoral district. From that turret window and along the same road had more than one ancestress of Mary looked for her husband returning from the Scottish wars, in the times of Cromwell, Montrose, and Dundee, and looked in vain.

Through her lorgnette Mary studied every figure that approached on foot or horseback; there were not many, perhaps three or four only, during the entire day; but there was no appearance of Cyril Wedderburn, either mounted on his favourite bay hunter or afoot with rod and gun.

So for that day the thicket was unvisited; no fond whispers were uttered under the old larch-tree, and when midnight came she looked at her ring as on the preceding night in the vague hope that he might be doing the same, and thinking of her, wherever he might be.

Three days—to Mary, long, anxious, and dreary days—passed away. Knowing that his leave of absence from the Fusileers was so short, she grudged every hour he spent with others, when he passed so few with her, and now a new source of terror occurred. Had the war broken out suddenly, and Cyril's leave been cancelled? But surely he would have written, and however sudden his departure, should have made an effort to see and to bid her farewell.

Was he ill? That was not improbable, as for three days now the parochial Sangrado, Doctor Squills, had not been near Lonewoodlee; but then she knew that such rich folks as those at Willowdean would depend more on the greater medical talent, for which they could telegraph at any moment to the metropolis.

She was in an agony of suspense; their residence was not a cheerful place, so visitors were few and far between, and she could learn no tidings of the only other being whom, beside her father, she loved on earth.

On the fourth day, one of her domestics, Alison Home, an elderly woman, who had noticed her feverish anxiety without suspecting its cause, announced that a person on horseback was approaching the house—coming indeed at a gallop over the Lee. Then Mary rushed to her window, only to be disappointed, as she recognised at once, not Cyril Wedderburn on his long-stepping hunter, but the rather awkward figure of Doctor Squills, on his barrel-shaped Galloway cob.

The Doctor was a suave, well-meaning, fair, florid, and passably good-looking man, about thirty-five or forty years of age, anxious to please all, and to spread the practice in a district where the people were so healthy, that, save for his parochial salary, and one or two retired Bengalees with large livers and purses, he must have starved, his patrons being as few as his patients. Mr. Lennox was certainly a permanent, but far from a lucrative one; yet the Doctor was kind and attentive, all the more so that he had naturally a secret desire to stand well in Mary's estimation, and whenever he visited Lonewoodlee, he almost unconsciously made a more careful toilette than usual.

She received him with a genuine smile of welcome in the gloomy little dining-room, with its deeply embayed windows, its dingy old family portraits, the two great horsehair sofas and veteran chairs and tables, of the shabbiness of which, by long use and wont, she had ceased to be ashamed, though the pretentious coat-armorial of the Lennoxes was carved in stone above the fireplace, at the richly moulded jambs of which there still hung on each side those steel chains by which the fireirons were secured in the good old Scottish times, when guests would quarrel over their cups, and if their swords were left in the hall, were wont to enforce their arguments with the poker and shovel, if not thus secured to the wall.

"By that bright smile I augur well of my patient, Miss Lennox?" said Doctor Squills, taking Mary's hand between his own, patting it the while, and seeming very much disposed to retain it as he seated himself, for it was a lovely little hand indeed.

"Thanks, Doctor Squills—papa has been singularly easy and free from pain for three days past," replied Mary, making an effort to retain her impatience for some news of the outer world.

"That is good—very good. The composing draught taken as usual, I suppose?"

"All according to your orders. I am a good little nurse, I hope," said Mary, with a smile and a sigh.

There was a pause, and then the Doctor said,

"You have heard the great news, of course, Miss Lennox? but we'll talk of it after I have seen your papa. Is he awake just now?"

"Yes," said Mary in a breathless voice, for the idea of "news" terrified her, and she seemed as one frozen, while the Doctor, after leisurely depositing his hat and gloves on the table, where with trembling hands she was placing a decanter of wine, and cake of her own making, from an antique buffet—with his bland smile of professional sympathy and jaunty step, took the way which he knew so well, to the bedchamber of Mr. Lennox.

What "news" had the Doctor? was it of war and peril, of hasty departure, of sickness or sorrow, of joy and triumph, or what? The Doctor knew nothing of her interest in Cyril; so, could he be referred to?

Poor girl! she was not left long in suspense, for the Doctor soon came sliding in with the same jaunty air, saying—

"Pulse regular, head cool, breathing good. Complaining of appetite too; capital! Give him any reasonable thing he may wish. Strength must be kept up at his years, you know, Miss Lennox—at his years especially."

"And you think papa better to-day?"

"Indubitably so—beyond my expectations."

"Thank God for that!" said Mary, fervently.

It was only a brief rally before the great catastrophe; but the good-hearted Doctor had not yet the courage to tell her so.

"You spoke of news, Doctor?" said she.

"Ah—sad—sad—very sad, indeed! Those poor folks are greatly to be pitied."

"Who—where?"

"The family at Willowdean."

"Pitied for what?" exclaimed Mary, starting as she grasped with a white and trembling hand the arm of the sofa on which she sat.

"The awful loss which they have too evidently sustained," said the Doctor, pouring out a glass of poor Mary's indifferent sherry, as he remembered that he had a ten miles' ride over the hills before him.

"What loss? what has happened? Oh, tell me, tell me, Doctor, for the love of Heaven!"

"Is it possible that you have not heard what, now, all in the county know?"

"No—no—no; I have heard nothing," said Mary, wringing

her hands piteously, while her dilated eyes, her blanched visage, and quivering lip betrayed a depth of emotion for which the Doctor, who knew of the coolness between the families, totally failed to account. " What *do* you mean ?" she added.

" The disappearance—the death, no doubt—of young Captain Wedderburn, Sir John's heir apparent, the heir to so fine a property, and a title among the oldest of our Nova Scotian baronets—and with a rich wife in prospect too—one we hear worth half a million of money. It is a great and unparalleled calamity, and his family are plunged, as you may well suppose, in the profoundest affliction—the affliction of the wealthy and noble is always *profound*, it would seem, to judge from editorial sympathy—and to be in depth far beyond anything that the middle class or poor folks can have any idea of," added the Doctor, with a sigh, which was perhaps induced more by cynical repining than pure sympathy, as he drank his sherry, and then turned to Mary, and saw, with some amazement and alarm, her crushed and wobegone aspect.

" Disappearance—death ?" she thought. "Oh, what does this mean ? Do I hear aright ? Am I mad, asleep, or dreaming ?"

" I see, my dear Miss Lennox, that your tender susceptibilities are greatly shocked ; but I can only tell you what I heard, and what the local papers of this morning contain ; but first, take a glass of wine, and then listen to me. Take it pray, nay, you must," and the kind Doctor forced her to swallow that which nearly choked her, and then resumed in his chirruping, gossipy manner, "'the terrible catastrophe' happened thus—on Wednesday last—let me see, was it Wednesday or Thursday ?"

" Wednesday, I suppose. Go on, in the name of mercy !" said Mary, in a voice all unlike her own ; the rich chord was gone, and a cracked unearthly sound now remained.

" Yes, my dear Miss Lennox, it *was* on Wednesday, for the *Berwick Warder* has it so—Captain Wedderburn dined with that gay man of the world (rather too gay he is), Captain Chesters, at the Haugh, but did not return home. His non-appearance at breakfast next morning—though Mr. Asloane rang the great house-bell thrice—created no alarm among the family, as it was supposed he had remained overnight with his new sporting friend and would probably turn up about luncheon time ; though as Chesters was only a recent acquaintance, it excited a little surprise at Willowdean that Captain Wedderburn would tax his hospitality. *That* I learned from Mr. Asloane himself, as I had to ride over to see one of the laundry-maids who had a whitlow, which I treated successfully by ——"

" Oh, go on—go on, I implore you !"

" It was on her right thumb—well, you are impatient, I see. After a time a whisper came of his having left Chesterhaugh before midnight on Wednesday. This was alarming. If so, where had he been for these twelve hours past? The butler came to Lady Wedderburn at the usual hour about orders for the carriage, or horses for riding; they were both postponed, and the luncheon was delayed. Master Robert, his cousin, Lieutenant Ramornie, old Asloane, all the gamekeepers, gardeners, and grooms; even Sir John, and the Master of Ernescleugh, with all his people, proceeded to beat the woods, shrubberies, the park, and all the roads, but did so in vain. No traces of the Captain were discovered until yesterday, when a hat—a grey felt wide-awake, known to be his—was found at Buncle-edge, and his silver-mounted whip at Falaknowe, about a mile further eastward. There were no traces of blood, however. Pardon me, for I seem to shock you: but last night the darkest tidings of all came from Lady Juliana Ernescleugh. A horse known to be his, a fine bay hunter with black fetlocks, which he had purchased from her son the Master, was found by some of the Dunbar fishermen sorely bruised, battered, and drowned, with saddle-girths reversed, beside the rocky cleugh or beach, somewhere near Fast Castle. So what has happened, how he has perished or by what means, and as to where his body may be lying, whether on the land or in the sea, we are as yet helplessly and hopelessly in the dark. It is a terrible and melancholy catastrophe, and affects you deeply, I see, my dear young lady. I know not whether you ever saw Captain Wedderburn, but he was one of the finest young men in the Merse."

As the Doctor concluded this harrowing story, calmly and quietly, but unwittingly dealing death-stabs in her heart, poor Mary Lennox sank quietly back with eyes closed into a recess of the sofa; she was icy cold, and but for his presence and the means he took to recover her, by forcing her to take more wine, she must have fainted.

A stupor or torpor seemed to come over her. She became stunned, blind, and almost deprived of the power of volition. She knew not what to think or believe, or what to do. Aware of the stern necessity for keeping up appearances and for preventing the secrets of her heart from becoming patent to a stranger, she made a vehement essay to start up and question the Doctor again, only to find that he had been gone for nearly an hour and she had known it not. Neither she knew nor cared what instructions regarding herself he had left with her two startled and dismayed domestics.

She only knew and could only realize that her lover, her affianced husband, the secret husband of her heart, had perished by some miserable death, whether the result of foul play or some terrible accident she might never know; and now she recalled with grief and terror how she had heard a horse galloping madly past, when she looked at her watch on that fatal Wednesday at midnight ; and the wild cry, the prompting, as it seemed, of fear or of despair, that came upward to her ear; and how she had associated that cry with the voice of Cyril Wedderburn !

And his horse had been found at Erneseleugh, near Fast Castle (the Wolf's Craig of Scott's romance), and she knew how frightfully steep the rocks are there !

Her kind, her handsome, and her loving Cyril ! Never again would his strong arm caress her slender waist, or his love-lit eyes gaze tenderly into hers ; and now all his soft and loving ways came vividly before her, mingled with a dreadful sense of calamity and loss, till the very tears— tears which she longed to mingle with those of his haughty mother—almost choked her as she lay on her bed, prostrate on her face.

On Wednesday she had seen him last, and this was Sunday forenoon : she could hear the bells for service ringing in the village church about a mile distant to remind her of the fact, and that four days—four days in this age of steam and telegraphy had elapsed without trace or tidings of her lost one !

Then she became suddenly aware that her father was ringing his hand-bell furiously, and was querulously, even peevishly, demanding her presence for something.

Her tears, and the cause of them, she was alike compelled to conceal ; so after bathing her eyes hurriedly, she tottered away to attend him as usual.

CHAPTER VIII.

MARY'S MISTAKE.

She regretted that she had permitted her emotions to overpower her so much in the presence of the Doctor, and that hence he had been allowed to depart without further questioning when she had so many inquiries to make. From Alison Home and her other domestic she could gather nothing, save that on the same Wednesday, at midnight, they had both heard the swiftly-ridden horse pass along the roadway, and also the strange cry of the rider.

Could it be possible, she was ever asking of herself, that they would meet no more ? Never more in the thicket, never more at the stile in the lane at the end of the Lee ? that she should never again be gathered to his breast so kindly and so tenderly ?

Cyril's love had made her very happy ; so much so that it often inspired her with gratitude to God for blessing her so, and no shadow had ever rested upon it, save the secrecy they were compelled to practise, as they hoped, for a time only, and being both proudly spirited, they had felt that necessity a degradation and source of irritation. Now all that and the love itself had passed away, and a cloud of thought and gloom black as midnight, seemed to envelop the pale girl as she sat alone in the little chamber, gazing listlessly at the sunlit scenery, and with no sound in her ears save the beating of her heart.

Oh, had her brother Harry been spared to her, thought she, Cyril's friend and comrade in India, how differently might she have been situated ! How she longed to rush to Willowdean and prosecute inquiries there, but dared not even give expression to the thought !

Only lately she had been anticipating in dread the withdrawal or expiry of his short leave of absence, and his departure to Turkey with the proposed Allied Army. Now she felt that to see him going forth even to face the perils and chances of the threatened Russian war would be a welcome exchange for the present doubt and horror she endured.

All that day no food passed her lips, and as evening drew on the dread of enduring another night without some further intelligence proved too much for her grief and impatience ; so the craving to go forth and inquire personally—she could not trust to the discretion of her servants, and shrunk instinctively from their morbid surmises—became so strong, that on finding her father sleeping calmly and peacefully after the slight repast he deemed a dinner, she dressed herself in haste to go out—but for where and to whom were her next thoughts ?

The nearest house was Chesterhaugh ; it was little more than four miles distant, and though she shrunk from the idea of seeing or being seen by Captain Chesters, she resolved, come what might. to question his gatekeeper, as if casually, about the last he had seen of Cyril Wedderburn ; for as the coldness between the two families was pretty well known in that secluded district, she felt assured that the man would imagine her to be prompted by the merest curiosity.

As she set forth on foot, she sighed when passing the empty coachhouse and the stables where the hoofs of horses and the rattle of their stall collars were heard no more. She was young, active, and would walk the distance in an hour ; yet not to repine a little when she thought of all that should and might have been, was perhaps impossible.

She did not anticipate that the gatekeeper could add much to the alarming details already furnished by the Doctor, yet she longed to see him as one who, however humble, had been the last who looked on Cyril's winning face and heard his cheerful voice ; moreover, the utter solitude of her home had proved on this day intolerable. She dared not speak of the occurrence to her father, for he would be the last perhaps to express genuine sympathy ; so the desire to move abroad, to speak to some one, to be doing anything but sitting still and brooding, became an irresistible impulse.

Full of her own thoughts as she walked on, she did not perceive how stormy clouds had enveloped the afternoon sun ; that the dull grey mist was rolling swiftly along the grassy glens and upward to the slopes of the Lammermuirs, and with how melancholy a sound the wind shook in gusts the leafless trees of the old wood near the Tower, while on the hill sides the shepherds were driving fast their flocks to the thatched *bughts*, or sheepfold in sheltered places. Neither was she aware that her chief domestic, old Alison Home, was looking after her with mingled admiration and compassion, as if reading something of her secret, when she passed out upon the highway ; for Mary Lennox, though charming at times, was looking unusually handsome, graceful, and compact in her smart velvet hat and plume—the wing of a golden pheasant shot for her by Cyril— her cuffs and muff of grey Iceland duck, her jacket of sealskin (imitation, we are sorry to say), her veil drawn tightly over her pretty face and ears, and her skirts looped up, less to show the scarlet petticoat, taper ancles, and balmorals, than for activity, as she set forth.

Which of all those hoof-marks she could trace upon the road were those of Cyril's fatal horse? How often had she walked along that road to church and to the nearest market town since they had lost their carriage, but never with a heart so heavy, and with such a sensation of being benumbed and stupefied with grief.

"Sorrow, misery, and horror!" she muttered from time to time. "Oh what a life is before me now ! Cyril, Cyril !" and at the sound of his name, even on her own lips, the tears rolled forth beneath the closely drawn veil, and the little hands were wrung convulsively within her muff.

Every moment she thought that she *must* see him coming to meet her ; it seemed impossible that he could be thus blotted out of existence ! All appeared chaos and confusion to Mary as she walked on ; the order of events and the course of time seemed to be alike inverted.

It appeared as if years had elapsed since she had last seen Cyril—last stood in his close embrace in yonder thicket, and heard his loving voice, while the events of years ago seemed to have happened yesterday ; even his arrival from India, when she was much younger, with her dead brother's sword and

4

watch, his rings and lock of hair, and the happy subsequent
time when his and her secret intimacy began. How much had
passed since then ; they were lovers, and engaged, so solemnly
too—and now—the mass of unuttered thoughts seemed to rend
her heart !

Circumstances had given her few friends, and now she sorely
felt the want of one.

School companions, girls from town and elsewhere, with gay
and happy home circles, had occasionally broken the monotony
of her life by becoming her guests ; but she grew painfully conscious that owing to the dreary seclusion of the old Tower,
where few sounds met the ear save the bleating of sheep or the
whistle of the curlew, and also from her father's querulous
eccentricity, they curtailed their visits, and seldom or never
came again. Then, as he ailed so frequently and aged so fast,
she could not accept invitations in return, even those given by
neighbours so near as Lady Ernescleugh and others, who were
disposed to be kind to the lonely little Chatelaine of Lonewoodlee.

Ere long she reached the handsome iron gate and grotesque
little lodge of Chesterhaugh, beyond which she could see the
sweep of the gravelled approach that led to the house. The
park was perfectly bare and open now, as the thriftless Captain
had long since converted into cash every tree on the estate ;
and the park itself, once his father's pride, was now let to a
grazier of cattle.

Mary was flushed and breathless as she approached the gate.
She had walked very quick that she might the sooner return,
and she had not been insensible to the fast increasing coldness
of the temperature, the howling of the March wind, and the
gathering of dark masses of cloud in the east, hastening, or
anticipating by nearly an hour the shades of evening.

She was in the act of questioning old Tony Heron, the lodgekeeper, who approached her respectfully with a hand at his hat,
" if the tidings were true that Captain Wedderburn "—how her
voice faltered as her quivering lips pronounced the name—
" had really suffered by some accident after leaving Chesterhaugh," when the sound of hoofs struck her ear, and before the
man could fully reply, Captain Chesters—in nearly the same
costume in which he had breakfasted at Willowdean—dashed
up, accompanied by his favourite and only groom, Billy Trayner,
to whom he at once threw the reins of his horse on dismounting.

" Good morning, Miss Lennox," said he, lifting his hat with
profound courtesy.

" It is evening, rather," said Mary, covered with confusion
and annoyance by this unexpected *rencontre*, " and I must not
delay lest poor papa——"

"Ah ! to be sure ; but the old gentleman was all right, fast asleep, Alison told me, as I stopped for a moment at the Tower to inquire for you in passing. But to what good fairy is the humble house of Chesterhaugh indebted for the honour of a visit from you, Miss Lennox, and alone too?" he added, as he led her very deliberately inside the gate, which the keeper shut; "and you have no demon of a duenna or chaperon. It beats cock-fighting, 'bangs Banagher,' as O'Grady of ours used to say."

" You make me feel more and more the extreme awkwardness of my situation by this banter, Captain Chesters," said Mary ; "but——but——"

"Out with it. You came to ask about young Wedderburn !" exclaimed Chesters, bluntly.

" Yes, sir," said the lodgekeeper officiously ; "she was just asking me when you rode up, and I was about to tell her——"

"That according to our old Scottish proverb, 'a fu' man and a fasting horse go quickly home'—but, by Jove! Cyril Wedderburn went rather further than he quite reckoned on."

" I ask pardon, sir, but I think you are wrong," said the man, touching his hat; "the Captain was not the worse of wine, though his horse seemed mad."

"How the devil should you know anything about it? Silence, Tony !"

" I let him out, and shut the gate."

" Then shut your mouth now, or speak only when you are spoken to," said the Captain, furiously, on which the man slunk into his lodge, abashed.

" Poor Cyril Wedderburn !" said Mary, biting her nether lip to control her emotion.

" He left Chesterhaugh quietly enough, but his horse was disposed to be restive, straining hard on the curb, and so forth, and would seem to have run away with him. It is a very mysterious and melancholy affair," added Chesters, drawing off one of his riding gloves ; "but if you will permit me to lead you into the house I shall then tell you all about it, at least, all that I can pretend to know."

" Thanks, no, excuse me," replied Mary, hurriedly, as she was nearly swept away by a sudden gust of wind, while hail and snow came on suddenly with great force and density. " Good Heavens !" she exclaimed, " it is quite a storm. I must take shelter here a few minutes, if you will permit me."

" In my gate-lodge? Impossible ! Absurd ! Come with me into the house, and if the blast does not lull in a few minutes, I shall have the pleasure of driving you over to Lonewoodlee."

Mary looked rather despairingly through the bars of the handsome iron gate, and saw the bleak wide moorland waste she had traversed whitening fast, and that the road was becoming more and more obscure, as the snow covered and the darkness overshadowed it; and while her tears and her repugnance to accept the invitation increased, she said—

"Thank you, Captain Chesters; you are very kind. I was most rash to come; but I could scarcely walk back now, and alone too."

"To walk alone; the thing is not to be thought of. And do not talk of thanks, you owe me none. Do permit me." And taking her hand with all the suavity he could assume—for Chesters was harassed in aspect, having been questioned and cross-questioned by the Procurator Fiscal and the constabulary till he was sickened by the name of Cyril Wedderburn—he conducted Mary into the house of Chesterhaugh, where she had not been for several years, since she was a little girl and led by her father's hand.

Through the marble-floored and oak-panelled entrance-hall, which was hung with spoils of the field and chase—trophies of arms brought by Chesters from India, tiger skins, skulls and horns, with a multitude of whips and spurs, cloaks and riding-boots; thence through a long corridor, that in his father's time had been furnished by magnificent cabinets of buhl and marqueterie, and hung with fine old paintings, all of which had gone, like the trees of the park—he led her into a handsome and well-appointed dining-room.

Though the assurance given by Chesters that he had left her father asleep but a short time before was not strictly true, it tended to soothe Mary's mind a little till the shower of hail that crashed on the windows of the room disturbed her, all the more that the closely-drawn curtains, and the twelve waxlights in the chandelier of Florentine bronze suggested ideas of night-fall, though the hour was barely six o'clock.

Chesters courteously drew a chair for her near the fire, and led her to it.

"Permit me to relieve you of your muff and hat. Won't you even lift your veil?" he entreated, as he leant, half caressingly, over her chair; but Mary was determined to remain in all her walking gear, to be ready for departure, and said—

"Captain Chesters, do kindly order Trayner to drive me home without delay."

"Why such haste?"

"I perceive that you are just going to dine."

"And will you not share my poor bachelor fare, and by your presence shed a light over my lonely board for an hour or so, and then I shall drive you home in person?"

But Mary was resolute. No food had passed her lips; but she had dined, she said, long ago, by her papa's bedside. Go she must, and at once, she added, and was only pleased that her tears and her blushes of irritation were hidden by her tightly drawn veil, as with a very peculiar expression in his face, Captain Chesters languidly rang the bell for Trayner.

Unlike her gloomy paternal residence, and unlike the more elegant and modern mansion of Willowdean, the house of Chesterhaugh had been built in the reign of George II., when art was at its lowest ebb in Scotland, and taste was studied less than solid comfort. It was a great square block, three stories in height, with all its chimneys clustered in the centre ; the roof sloped down from them in the pavilion form, and the outside walls were roughcast with gravel and lime ; and poor Mary thought sadly of her own older-fashioned and more sordid home, and of the few comforts that surrounded the declining days of her father, as she surveyed and contrasted with a rapid glance all the details of the spacious and lofty dining-room of Chesterhaugh—the walnut-wood furniture so elaborately carved, the chairs of green morocco, the crimson damask window-curtains with their gilded cornices, the many pictures in which horses seemed to predominate in place of men ; the brilliant plate console mirrors, in which all these objects were reproduced in two endless perspectives ; the elegant ironstone dinner-service of pink and gold, laid for Chesters ; the massive plate ; the claret airing near the fire—and she marvelled how all this luxury was supported, when remembering that the Captain had the reputation of being a spendthrift, a bankrupt, and worse.

She little knew that Cyril Wedderburn, when last he had been in that room, had sat in the very chair she now occupied ; but Chesters remembered the circumstance, and a disdainful smile crossed his face as he did so.

Again and again he pressed her to take wine ; but Mary steadily declined ; and at last, after being rung for thrice, Mr. Bill Trayner appeared—a very good specimen of a smart but unscrupulous groom, small in stature, with a long body and short bandy legs, a mean and narrow forehead, sleek black hair, shorn short, with a circular lock or curl plastered on each prominent cheek-bone, and with sharp, cunning eyes.

Bill was a Scotchman of Newmarket growth, and to all the worst points of the national character, added the roguery that may be so easily gained in the atmosphere of the betting-house, the stable-yard, and training-ground. He kept a betting-book as well as his master, whom he was always ready to second in mischief, and to betray, if it suited his private interests to do so.

A perfect oracle on all matters pertaining to the turf, he knew by heart or rote all the entries and engagements made at the various race meetings throughout the country ; and knew shrewdly which horses were the best to back and which were likely to be scratched.

"How about the waggonette, Trayner?" said Chesters. "You know I have no other carriage, Miss Lennox," he added, parenthetically, to Mary.

"The waggonette, sir," repeated Trayner, trying to fathom the meaning of a peculiar glance his master gave him.

"Yes, the waggonette with the patent springs," resumed Chesters, with a remarkably knowing wink.

"The springs is broke, sir," replied Trayner, with a similar mode of telegraph, when he glanced at Miss Lennox, and took in the whole situation.

"Broken—the devil they are!"

"All to smash, sir.'

"Then the waggonette won't be in working order for——"

"Not for ever so long, sir."

"Then I must walk, and at once!" said Mary, rising from her chair. "I have not a moment to lose."

"Walk? Listen to the rising blast and the crash of the hailstones," urged Chesters.

"Ah, there's more there than hailstones, Miss," said Trayner. "It is a regular feeding storm. The snow is some inches deep already."

"Oh, my poor papa!" exclaimed Mary. "If he is awake and calling for me! Surely the lodgekeeper will accompany me?"

"The two old women at Lonewoodlee will surely suffice as attendants for a couple of hours."

"Hours? Impossible, Captain Chesters!"

"That will do, Trayner. You may go," said Chesters, and his *fidus Achates* vanished with a leer, which he conveyed to the servants in the hall below, together with the information that "the master had been and gone and done it again. Here's a lark! He's got that girl of old Lennox's, and means to keep her in Chesterhaugh all night if he can—only she seems spirited, and likely to kick over the traces."

Mary had seen something of the man's expression of face as he retired, and she felt that in her anxiety and grief for Cyril Wedderburn she had made a mistake it was too late to remedy now; but it was destined to have a fatal effect upon her interests and happiness at a future time.

CHAPTER IX.

A SNARE.

SHE rushed to the window and drew back the heavy damask curtains. Snow—snow and hail on the bitter blustering wind of March had whitened all the moorland waste, and was deepening fast there.

She permitted the curtain to drop from her tremulous hand, and returned in a kind of despair to her seat ; for although the distance between her and home was short, the night was too wild for her to venture forth alone.

"It will serve no purpose your taking this little delay so much to heart," said Chesters. "You must have patience. Pray compose yourself, and do lay aside your wraps."

"Excuse me, I cannot," replied Mary, in a choking voice.

"And so you came to ask about young Wedderburn !"

"Yes," faltered Mary ; "but only of the gatekeeper as I was passing."

"That young muff, the Master of Ernescleugh, is making himself excessively busy in the affair."

"But they are—alas ! must we say *were*—neighbours—friends," urged Mary, with surprise at his tone.

"That is no reason why he should have come to me thrice with the people of the Procurator Fiscal in the prosecution of inquiries. He should join his regiment in London, or his papa, my Lord Ernescleugh, at his government in the Ionian Isles, and leave Cyril Wedderburn and his fate to the family and the local authorities ; but he'll linger on here no doubt, and enter stakes for the heiress."

"What heiress ?"

"Haven't you heard about her ?" asked Chesters, with a languid but malevolent smile.

"No."

"Sir John Wedderburn's brother William has died lately at Madras, and left his whole fortune, some three hundred thousand pounds at least, with a palace in the Choultry, to his only daughter—a girl, who is coming to Willowdean as her new home. She is a great beauty, they say ; and Mamma Wedderburn," he added, a little spitefully, "had an eye on her as a wife for Cyril."

"I know nothing of it," sighed Mary.

"Ah, but I do. I was at breakfast with the family on the morning the news came, and I read the whole intention in Lady Wedderburn's face and manner ; but now, as Cyril has gone, that legal prig Bob will very likely have a chance of making her a prize."

Mary only answered these surmises so slangily expressed by her silent tears ; but while he spoke she remembered, as one in a dream—for she had not slept since she heard them—the words of the Doctor about a rich bride in prospect for her lost Cyril.

But the rumour excited neither jealousy nor fear. Oh, what did it matter now !

She looked so exquisitely lady-like as she sat with her little hands folded in her tiny muff which rested on her knees, and her veiled face upturned to Chesters, that he—no bad judge of breeding in women or horses—thought what a creditable-looking wife she would make for him or any man; but she was poor, and he was up to the ears in debt; thus neither her poverty nor her beauty excited his pity, though they gave quick suggestion to his worst passions. He loved Mary in a fashion of his own; but he knew that the wife for him must have money, and poor Mary had none.

Full of grief as he saw she was for the terrible and mysterious disappearance of Cyril Wedderburn, Captain Rooke Chesters was far too judicious, or far too cunning, to press any suit of his own just then. He could wait his opportunity; but he thought that if by luring or detaining her under any pretence in his own house for a few hours, he could compromise, or place her in a false position, it would achieve all he wanted at the time.

All that day, we have said, she had not taken food, yet he pressed her in vain to join him at dinner. She felt weak, ill, and giddy. The room seemed to become larger and larger still; its further end appeared to recede as if to a vast distance; all around her became like a species of phantasmagoria, and only by a violent effort of her own will did she resist the faintness that was stealing over her.

She was in an agony of mind as the hours of the stormy night wore on.

She pictured to herself her ailing and querulous father asking for her, in an alarm that might prove detrimental to his shaken system—missing the poor wan girl, who, in her faded dressing-gown, was at all hours of the weary night ever at hand to give him the medicines or soothing draughts prescribed for him by Doctor Squills; ever ready to arrange the pillows; to caress him and bathe his hot and tremulous hands or aching head with cold water, with Rimmel or other aromatic vinegar; and she was here—*here* at Chesterhaugh, imprisoned by the darkness, the hail, and the snow!

Chesters had his own dark purpose to achieve, and as he forsook champagne for claret, and idled over his walnuts, he viewed her impatience and her mental agony with perfect composure, though treating her with well-bred sympathy the while.

But, as the night wore on, Mary felt more and more the awkwardness, the ultimate doubt and danger of her position, in being thus alone, without a lady friend or chaperon, in the house of a bachelor; and more than all, one who bore such a local reputation as Ralph Rooke Chesters! She was conscious that the very servant—he of the inevitable calves and plush—

who removed the dinner and brought in maraschino and coffee, inspired by some of Mr. Bill Trayner's knowing remarks and cruel inferences in the servants' hall below, regarded her with curious eyes.

It has been said that "even bad men have some good traits in them, and that selfish men are capable of *feeling*."

Perhaps it may be so ; but Chesters was incapable of sensibility or caring for any one but himself, and was destitute of a single good trait or generous emotion ; so even while watching Mary's restlessness, agitation, and her evident dread of the detention she was undergoing, he muttered, inwardly—

"Pshaw ! women can't help loving those who love them ; so I'll make a bold attempt to cozen, if I cannot crush or win her !"

It was perhaps a little dangerous for Mary that, though she often expressed and displayed a great aversion of Chesters, there were *times* when she did not altogether feel it ; for few women can *hate* a man who professes to love and consequently admire them : yet, seeing the full sense of her false position, she began to hate and fear him now.

Should the story get abroad that she had spent some hours in his house, under any circumstances, it was a *contretemps* that might cost her dear ; for how would the censorious world interpret her conduct or acknowledge her reason ? That she had come to inquire about the fate of Cyril Wedderburn, and been storm-stayed, few would believe, for what vital interest was *she* supposed to have in the lost heir of Willowdean ?

Alas, alas ! for secret loves.

Secluded though her life had been at Lonewoodlee, she knew quite enough of the world to be aware that a young lady could not, with propriety, visit a gay young bachelor as she appeared to have done—one to whom she was neither related nor engaged —and it was this consciousness, together with the craving desire to be again by her father's side, that made her so steadily resist taking any refreshment, even coffee, or doffing any part of her costume, and which made her writhe under the well-bred commonplaces uttered by Chesters, such as that he "hoped she wouldn't fret. What the deuce was the good of it ! The storm must soon abate ; indeed, it was abating now. It is very unfortunate, no doubt," and all that sort of thing ; adding, "but it is very stupid work this, and we should do something to amuse each other."

Yet he could neither soothe nor amuse her ; he could not leave her for the smoking-room ; neither could he smoke in her presence, and so betook him to champagne dashed with brandy, a perilous mixture, through the influence of which some very daring ideas began to form in his cunning brain.

Bad, bold, and daring as he was, Rooke Chesters would

scarcely have ventured to trepan a girl of Mary Lennox's
undoubted rank in the county into a false position, but for his
perfect knowledge of her father's helplessness, his poverty, and
the bill he possessed.   Moreover, the only man who would
have protected her—the lover whose arms he had seen around
her in the thicket—was gone, no one knew where or how.

"There is a climax in this life," says a writer, with stern
truth, "a climax in mental and bodily pain, after which we can
feel no more, and after it all other sources of emotion appear
tame by comparison."   And this climax had poor Mary passed
already.

Cyril was gone ; her father she knew was dying ; and when
he went, who would she have to care for, to study, or to love?
Hence for a time, perhaps, she cared less what happened to
herself, till the massive black marble clock on the mantelpiece
struck the alarming hour of eleven.

"Eleven !   I have been here five whole hours !   Oh, I shall
go afoot, if I die on the moor !   I cannot and must not stay
here another moment !" she exclaimed, starting from her chair
and moving towards the door.   "Oh, papa—my own papa—
how much you may have missed me !"

"Be not in such a hurry, pray.   I had a pleasant surprise for
you," said he, laughing.

"How, Captain Chesters ?"

"Trayner must have patched up the springs of the waggonette by this time.   He is a clever fellow, Trayner, and if
the horses are put to, I shall take you over in a few minutes."

"Oh, thanks—a thousand times thanks !"

"No thanks are necessary."

Again he rang the bell, and said, with perfect calmness, to
the servant who answered the summons—

"Tell Trayner to get out the waggonette, if it is ready ; trace
the horses, and bring it round to the front door."

Without perceiving in the least the intelligent glance that
passed between Chesters and his domestic, Mary could know
that she had been deluded and drawn into a species of snare,
the object of which she did not then quite clearly comprehend.

In a few minutes more the tramp of horses' hoofs and the
muffled sound of wheels amid the snow without were heard,
and Mary rose, her face almost beaming with delight through
her veil, as she took his proffered arm to be led forth on her
way home at last.

The waggonette, a very handsome "bang-up affair," as
Chesters deemed it, was drawn up close to the flight of steps
which led to the entrance door ; and the long lines of radiance
from its two silver lamps shone far amid the white waste of
snow in the now treeless park.   The storm had ceased, the wind

had passed away, and the clouds were divided in Heaven over-head ; the stars shone out with frosty brilliance, and the night was calm and clear, The steam from the quivering nostrils of the impatient horses curled up in white wreaths above their heads.

Chesters lifted Mary—somewhat lingeringly, even caressingly perhaps, as he did so—upon the front seat, and carefully folded a warm railway-rug over her shoulders ; then buttoning the leather apron across her knees as he took his seat beside her. Mr. Bill Trayner vaulted up behind, and away they went, yet it was close on the hour of twelve (midnight) ere they were clear of the lodge-gates, the drowsy keeper of which observed with surprise the lady who was *still* his master's companion—Miss Lennox of Lonewoodlee !

As Chesters bent his face close to hers, he thought the time had come when he might venture to say something tender, and the champagne he had imbibed caused him to do it bluntly.

" Women, like men, may love many times in life ; but none, Miss Lennox, as I now love you—believe me, I speak from my heart."

" At this time I entreat you not to torment me in that way," said Mary ; " in Heaven's name, I implore you !" she continued.

" Ah, you think only of Cyril Wedderburn !" was the spiteful rejoinder.

" I do," said Mary, a dash of anger mingling with her grief, as her tears fell fast again.

" I am a lover as well as he was."

" Of mine do you mean ?"

" Yes."

" No, sir—no," replied Mary, firmly. " I cannot permit· you to talk thus, and take advantage of my situation."

" What the deuce do you mean ?" he asked, bluntly.

" That you are no lover, though a love-maker."

" Are they not the same ?" asked Chesters, with unaffected surprise.

" Nay, Captain Chesters, the difference between them is great."

" As you please," said he, biting his nether lip, while he lightly touched the horses with the lash about the ears.

The lodge-gate had scarcely closed behind them when a mounted gentleman, wearing an Inverness cape of rough material (which, like his half-bullet hat, was coated with snow), and long black overalls, came up at a hard trot, accompanied by a diminutive groom. On passing the waggonette, he curbed his horse abruptly back upon his haunches, and half looking round, cried cheerily—

"Hallo, Chesters, old fellow, where are you going? A bitter night for March!"

"Very. Good night," replied Chesters, without stopping; for the speaker was young Everard Home, the Master of Ernescleugh, who was very much surprised to see a young lady leaving the gate of Chesterhaugh at that time of night, and alone with Rooke Chesters! But in a few minutes he was perfectly enlightened on the subject by his groom, who rang the lodge-bell on pretence of wanting a light for his cigar.

A terror seized Mary lest she might have been recognized by these men. She said nothing of it to Chesters, for the deduction was humiliating; but her tears fell again, and she whispered in her heart—

"Oh, what matter is it? I have no Cyril now!"

She was soon deposited, with great politeness on the part of Chesters, at her own door, and in her anxiety and irritation she darted in and closed it, forgetting even to thank him for his escort.

Her father had slept soundly for hours; but now he was awake, and calling alternately for her and his dead son Harry, upbraiding them both for neglect, and threatening that he would break his own neck when next he rode to the hounds, "even as he once hoped that fellow Wedderburn had done;" and Mary's heart died within her, when she found his intellect thus wandering. But the brave girl cast aside her wrappings, took his old head carefully in her tender arms, and strove to forget, what might be nervous fancy only, that her two drowsy domestics who had seen her arrive in Chesters' equipage, looked somewhat oddly on her, and at each other.

CHAPTER X.

CHESTERHAUGH.

LET us now recur to a few nights ago, for the unravelling of much of this mystery.

With the soft memory of a minute and delicate little face that had been for nearly an hour so close to his own in the dark thicket, and all unaware that he had been observed or watched, Cyril Wedderburn rode at a hard gallop from Lonewoodlee, and ere long had reined up at Chesterhaugh, tossed his bridle to the obsequious Bill Trayner, who tugged his forelock as he led admiringly away the bay hunter, and then Cyril was ushered into the same dining-room in which Mary Lennox was afterwards to spend the weary and anxious hours we have described.

"Glad to see you, Wedderburn," said the host, taking his proffered hand ; "punctual to a minute nearly."

"Nay, scarcely. I'm a quarter of an hour late," replied Cyril, who was flushed by the rasping pace at which he had ridden the few miles that lay between Chesterhaugh and Willowdean.

"The salmon won't be spoiled, I daresay," said Chesters, with an imperceptible smile ; "but it takes one some time to get round that thicket at Lonewoodlee, if one's horse don't clear the stile. After your ride, have a B and S."

"Thanks ; no. I suppose you mean brandy and soda ?" said Cyril, who disliked slang, and who coloured a little at the reference to the thicket at Lonewoodlee.

"A glass of Madeira then, or a nip of Kimmel ?"

"Neither. I have an excellent appetite, and don't wish it spoiled."

"Cautious !" muttered Chesters, under his moustache, as he eyed with covert malevolence and suspicion the open and handsome countenance of his guest, who sat in a lounging yet elegant attitude in one of the soft elbow-chairs.

"Covers for two only, I perceive ; so we dine alone ?"

"Yes. I wanted Home of Ernescleugh to join us ; but he is engaged. By-the-bye, I should have asked your cousin Ramornie and your brother Bob, but——"

"Robert is not a player, neither is Horace, and we meant to turn a card to-night," said Cyril, coldly, and evidently disliking the assumption of familiarity in the other, who was but a recent acquaintance.

"I knew that—hence my omission."

The real reason was, that when Chesters played he disliked to have spectators.

"And now let us to dinner," he added, as they seated themselves at table.

The viands were all that could be desired, and the wines also were unexceptionable. Cyril was not a toper, so the suggestions of Chesters to try various heady vintages fell flatly on his ear, as he contented himself with pale dry sherry, an occasional glass of Sauterne, and after dinner adhered rigidly to claret, greatly to the disgust, apparently, of his entertainer.

Their conversation ran for a time on the topics of the day ; the increasing prospects of a war in the East ; the departure of our fleet for the Baltic, with hopes that "old Charlie Napier would knock Cronstadt to pieces ;" and the chances of the "sick man at Stamboul being," as Chesters phrased it, "snuffed out by the Russians," unless France, Britain, and Sardinia were prompt in succouring him.

Then came local matters, the pack of harriers, the master of the foxhounds, and his new mode of hunting the country ; race meetings and sporting news of various kinds, till after the claret jug had travelled pretty often between the two, Chesters, with his own secret purposes and his own ends in view, began to talk on matters more nearly concerning themselves ; but not until the cloth had been removed and the servants had withdrawn.

"When does your Indian cousin arrive ?"

"Don't exactly know," replied Cyril, curtly.

"Ah ! when you are in Turkey, Lady Wedderburn will have to play the duenna closely with the heiress—three hundred thousand pounds, by Jove !"

"Her fortune is said to exceed that."

"Fellows will swarm round her like flies round a honey-pot." Cyril made no reply, but toyed with the embossed grape scissors.

"Will your family winter in Edinburgh or London ?" asked Chesters.

"In London, of course ; if they don't remain at Willowdean."

"Edinburgh is a seedy place, after all, with its legal prigs and tradesmen's daughters—'merchants,' as Dr. Johnson laughingly said they called themselves. What would she do amid its 'upper ten dozen ?' No suitable match would be there, and small amusement among its dreary gaieties."

"You talk bitterly of the Athens of the North," said Cyril, smiling.

The truth was, that Chesters had been black-balled at one or two of the clubs there ; his proposal, that character was estimated at a low figure indeed. After a pause, he said, abruptly—

"Why don't you cut the service now——"

"On the eve of a war !" exclaimed Cyril.

"Yes ; and cut in for the heiress. I should if I were you, and I think Lady Wedderburn would like it."

"I trust, Captain Chesters, and I doubt it not, that Lady Wedderburn will leave me to choose for myself," said Cyril with considerable hauteur at what he justly deemed presumption in the other.

"Don't take it up that way, my dear fellow. *Pardonnez moi*, and let us say no more about it. Will you try a glass of my port ? I have some that has been thirty years in the cellar ; it belonged to my father when he was master of the foxhounds, and he was as good a judge of wine as of horses."

"Thanks ; no. I'll adhere to the claret. It is one of the curses which attend the heir to a fortune or a title—even a baronetcy," resumed Cyril, with reference to Chesters' advice, and feeling considerably ruffled, "to have his matrimonial views or intentions made the subject of debate and speculation among aunts, match-making mothers, and meddling friends. This or that girl will be suggested to him, and perpetually thrown in the way till he shudders at her name ; while the one he might prefer—the one whom perhaps he loves in secret—is deemed unsuitable, and is sedulously kept from him."

"Ah, yes—very true," said Chesters ; and as the voice of Cyril grew gradually tremulous, the memory of the former recurred to the recent scene in the thicket, and a pang of jealousy shot through his heart.

Chesters and Cyril alike loved the pure and simple-minded Mary, and it was perhaps strange they should *both* do so, as they were so different in their habits, tastes, and nature. The former was a man without soul or heart—selfish and sensual. The latter was innately refined, so his love was as full of delicacy, tenderness, compassion, and spirituality, as that of Chesters was mere earthly passion, amid which he could calmly see with satisfaction that ere long death, debt, difficulties, and utter friendlessness, with the loss of Cyril by separation, would cast the hapless girl completely at his mercy !

The same image filled the minds of both these men at the same time, but each viewed it from a very different point.

"You know Oliver Lennox of Lonewoodlee, I presume, being so near a neighbour ?" said Cyril.

"Of course ; all in the Merse know him for a crotchety old pump."

"That is not what I mean ; do you know him personally ?" asked Cyril, with marked annoyance.

"A little."

"You visit there, probably ?"

"Well—no—I cannot be said to do so," drawled Chesters, while he watched Cyril with half-closed eyes. "Who the deuce would go there, unless——"

"Unless what ?"

"One went after the girl."

"Do you mean his daughter ?" asked Cyril, swelling with secret anger.

"Certainly. I don't mean either of his two old female domestics. Pass the claret jug, please."

"I was a fool to accept this fellow's invitation," thought Cyril ; "I shall have a row with him yet, and I must forbid his visiting Lonewoodlee at all hazards, even if I declare myself to the old gentleman. I must take care of Mary, and watch over her if he cannot do so. That bill, too—Chesters would never be so liberal as to take it up without some ulterior purpose."

After a minute's silence, during which each had been covertly eyeing the other.

"You took up a bill of old Mr. Lennox's, I have heard," said Cyril, as if casually; "that was most kind and generous of you."

"Not at all—not at all; but who told you of it?"

"I forget—heard it incidentally somehow. Have you destroyed it?"

"No," replied Chesters, as he stuck his glass in his right eye and looked Cyril full in the face. "I have it here," he added, drawing from his breast pocket a handsome Russian leather case (girt with an elastic band), wherein he kept various odds and ends, I O U's, memoranda of races and coursing matches, with veterinary recipes, &c. ; and taking the fatal slip of blue paper, showed it to Cyril, and replaced it in the pocket-book.

"It has been noted and protested!" exclaimed Cyril as a flush crossed his face. "Why did you not destroy it—what piece of cunning is this?"

"Come, come, Wedderburn, that is rather a harsh term. I had it noted and protested, because, although I took it, I cannot afford ultimately to lose the money. Have some more wine?"

Cyril Wedderburn shook his head.

"Come—one glass of Madeira, as a 'whitewasher,' and then I ring for coffee."

But Cyril rose from the table and would drink no more. His mind had become imbued by mistrust and suspicion; yet he felt a desire to obtain that bill if possible, and he might do so amid the play he had promised to have with Chesters; so after the bay hunter's good points had been fully discussed, after the stables, the gun-room, the billiard and smoking-rooms, had all been lounged through, in a snug little parlour, with a box of cigars, and some brandy-and-water beside them, they sat down to cards—an act of folly on the part of Cyril Wedderburn.

The monetary difficulties of Rooke Chesters were nearly as great as those of the so-called "proprietor" of Lonewoodlee; but he possessed the skill and the means of supplying his exchequer which the other had not. His carefully studied betting-book, his intimacy with most of the horsey men on the turf, his means of getting secret information, his sharp practice and dexterous hand with cards, billiards and dice, seldom failed to keep him in tolerable funds, though most of his land was mortgaged, and he had more than once sought the sanctuary of Holyrood when his difficulties had been greatest; and it was with this clever schemer that Cyril Wedderburn sat down to be regularly "plucked."

CHAPTER XI.
CHESTERS' "MILD PLAY."

LIKE many other apartments—even the bedrooms at Chester-haugh, the little parlour was hung with pictures of lean, bony, gaunt horses, with little particoloured jockies perched on them; and Cyril, as he cast a glance at them, thought by contrast of the soft tender works by Greuze, the sombre Titians, the Raphaels, the Canalettis, and Correggios, which adorned the walls of Willowdean, interspersed with stately and creditable looking portraits of his forefathers, who had been all good men and true in the times of old.

Several packs of new cards, a dice-box, &c., were produced, and while carefully selecting a cigar each, cutting the ends thereof, and so forth, Cyril reverted to the subject of his favourite new horse.

" And so you like my bay hunter?"

" Amazingly ! he has all the fine points of thoroughbred—an ample chest, compact body, broad loins, a small head and thin neck, the legs all bone and muscle; if with these he has the requisites of courage and temper——"

" I am sure he has both, though I have never tried him yet; but what the deuce shall I do with him if we go on foreign service?"

" You should have thought of that before buying him ; but as the night is so cold, I would give him a warm mash with some nitre in it."

" A warm mash—why?"

" You came here at a rasping pace, and the animal may cool too much. I would have his eyes and nose spunged too, after your return."

" Do you think such necessary?" asked Cyril, with great simplicity. " I know you are a judge."

" Rather."

" I am somewhat ignorant of horses."

" Shall I ring for Trayner?"

" If you please."

Chester lit his cigar and rang the bell, but on hearing steps approaching, he rose, and said—

" I'll speak to Trayner myself about it : excuse me for a moment," and quitting the room he gave some instructions to the groom in an undertone. Cyril afterwards remembered hearing an expression of surprise escape the man, but little suspecting the vile trickery to which his horse and himself were about to be subjected ; he began to think, that could he reconcile or explain away the affair of the bill, Chesters was perhaps " not

5

such a bad style of fellow, after all ;" and no doubt the brandy-and-water he was imbibing went far to strengthen this conclusion.

"I've made it all right about your nag," said Chesters, reseating himself at the table and fixing his glass in his right eye ; "and now for a little mild play—what is it to be, écarté or casino, or five-card cribbage ?"

"What say you to écarté ?"

"Well, Wedderburn, écarté be it — the regular gambler's game."

Chesters arranged the pack into thirty-two cards, withdrawing the twos, threes, fours, fives, and sixes.

"How many points shall we have ?" asked Chesters.

"Five. Cut for the deal."

They did so, and it fell to Chesters.

"Take another jorum of the brandy-and-water. Do you like those cigars ? I could spare you a hundred or so. Oh, no thanks at all : they are quite at your service. Three cards to you, and three to me."

While Chesters chatted thus, to throw the victim off his guard, the latter played in a careless manner that was usual with him, talking and smoking all the time, and quite unaware how the whole faculties of Chesters were absorbed in the game, which is one of a nature wherein foresight and nice calculation are of a necessity so requisite, and thus he was no match for his host, who, after permitting him to win two or three games at guinea points, proposed to increase the stakes to five guineas.

Now flushed with play, Cyril rashly assented, and the game went on.

"I mark the king !" said he. "By the way, that ring of yours, Chesters, is a splendid one."

"An onyx."

"So I see. Are those arms yours ?"

"No ; it belonged to that Frenchman, Louis De la Fosse, whom your father befriended. We played for it, and I won it."

"Did you actually take the poor fellow's ring ? A family relic, perhaps !"

"Well, I might have lost mine but for my superior play. Bravo ! that card plays out the four tricks."

"The world is apt to shake its head at such gaming as yours and his was."

"Pass the decanter. Deuce take the world and its head too ; though it shake till palsied, what is it to me !" cried Chesters, laughing bitterly.

"But the world is censorious."

"So are all one's goodnatured friends—'d—d goodnatured

friends,' as Scott, I think, calls them. The Frenchman, De la Fosse, lost some thousands to me by backing no less than three losing horses at the Derby."

Cyril found that he had rapidly lost nearly two hundred pounds, and declined to play more.

"Not even to have your revenge?" asked Chesters, with feigned surprise, in which something of disdain was mingled.

"No," was the curt reply.

"Why, man alive, what do you mean?" asked Chesters, in a slightly bullying tone, with his glass shining in his eye.

"Simply that somehow, Captain Chesters, I do not like your mode of playing."

"Then we'll drop this and try casino : it is a good game for two."

"Agreed—five guinea stakes, as before."

They cut for the deal, which fell to Cyril ; but though he won several games, which only served still further to flush and excite him, in the end he found he had no better luck than before ; and ere long, instead of getting up Mr. Lennox's bill, he rose from the table minus two hundred and fifty pounds and had given his I O U for three hundred more. The time was close on midnight then, and he insisted on having his horse brought from the stables ; so once more the acute Mr. William Trayner was summoned.

Already repenting deeply the extreme folly into which he had been lured by a man for whom he felt at heart only contempt, and resolving never more to pass the threshold of Chesterhaugh, Cyril—already pondering whether he would get the money lost from Robert or his doting mother—put on his riding gloves, took his whip, and descended the steps to where his bay horse stood in the starlight, champing on the bit and pawing the gravel with impatience.

Had he looked round at that moment, he might have detected a strange and unfathomable smile on the face of Chesters.

The horse seemed very restive, swaying away when he put his foot in the stirrup, so that he mounted with difficulty, and gathered up and shortened the reins.

"Allow me, for a moment," said Chesters ; "there is something wrong about the curb chain, I think."

"The bridle's all right, sir," urged Trayner, who still held it in his hand, while Chesters very deliberately lengthened the straps a hole or two. "You'll do now, Wedderburn. Touch him with the spur. Good night."

"Good night ; thanks," cried Cyril, and away his horse went like the wind ; and he was barely clear of the lodge gate when he found the animal was totally unmanageable, and moreover had got the bit firmly between its teeth !

CHAPTER XII.

THE LAST OF THE BAY HUNTER.

" He is rightly named Rooke Chesters," muttered Cyril, as his horse began to caracole sideways along the high road, " for he has *rooked* me to some purpose. By Jove ! I can never confess my folly to my father, after all his warnings too. Halloa, old nag, what is the matter with you ?"

He now became sensible that his horse was becoming extremely restive ; something was wrong with the bridle he knew, but the conduct of the animal rapidly became so outrageous that he feared to dismount lest it should kick him or run away, in which case he felt that he would cut a ridiculous figure before his own household, by arriving on foot and whip in hand without his nag. His father and brother he knew would quiz him unmercifully. Dismount ! Pshaw ! the idea was not to be thought of. So being a good horseman he kept his saddle, and endeavoured by every means, first to soothe, and then by the whip to control, the growing fury of the bay hunter, but strove in vain.

It was swelling, trembling, and panting with rage ; its quivering ears lay backward flat, its head was outstretched, and its bloodshot eyes turned back, till at times he could see the white of them in the darkness.

After plunging and rearing, and endeavouring by every means to throw the rider, and after twice attempting to crush him against the park wall of Chesterhaugh, he suddenly flung out his forefeet, and with a fierce snort of rage, galloped at a terrible pace along the high road. The beautiful bay of which Cyril was so proud, as showing all the best points of a fine English hunter, seemed now changed into a tearing devil !

The curb chain was loose, the bit was clenched between its teeth, the reins were powerless, and Cyril Wedderburn could no more control its actions than he could rule a whirlwind.

Ploughed fields and gates, stackyards and farmsteadings, houses and cottages, all sunk in darkness, even as their inmates in sleep, were all passed with frightful speed, and seeking only to keep his seat till the animal became exhausted, Cyril trusted to his skill as a rider, and let the hunter take its way.

The open waste of Lonewoodlee, the dark thicket, and the quaint old Tower with its corner tourelles, were quickly at hand. As he swept past, Cyril saw the light in Mary's window: nay more, he saw her figure for an instant, and then it was that the irrepressible cry which Mary heard escaped him ; for he had begun to fear that there was more than the warm mash fermenting in the interior of his maddened nag ; that the animal had been drugged, as there were few "horsey" tricks of which Ralph Rooke Chesters, and his man Bill Trayner, were ignorant.

As this exasperating conviction forced itself upon him, he conceived the idea of stunning the horse by a blow between the ears.

His riding whip had a ponderous silver handle, and with the thong twisted round his right hand, he dealt upon the hunter's head a downward stroke that might have felled an ox ; but instead of finding it sink beneath him as he confidently expected, so that he might leap from the saddle, a fresh gust of rage seemed to inspire the horse, which actually bounded from the earth, and snorting, panting, and quivering afresh, it went blindly and madly thundering onward in its fierce career.

This was at Falaknowe, where the whip which had dropped from his hand was afterwards found.

For a time he had thought that the horse might know its way home, and stop at the park-gate of Willowdean ; but gate and lodge had long been left behind, the woods and house of Renton too ; the rising ground beyond was soon devoured by the rapid hoofs, and Cyril might have said, with Mazeppa, as alarm gathered in his heart—

> "All behind was dark and drear,
> And all before was night and fear.
> How many hours of night or day
> In those suspended pangs I lay
> I could not tell ; I scarcely knew
> If this were human breath I drew—"

for before him were the impending bluffs of a rocky shore, and the dashing billows of the German Sea !

By stern use of his spurs, burying the sharp rowels in blood, he had forced the animal to clear by a flying leap more than one closed toll-gate ; but the idea pressed upon him, that if he lost his seat or was dashed on the hard road, to be found a bleeding mass of broken bones, of what the emotions of the mother who doted on him, of his tender Mary, of his ambitious father, and of all his friends would be, if he were brought home to Willowdean an unsightly corpse ; and now, as death seemed close and nigh, innumerable episodes of his past life— good, bad, and foolish—came thronging fast upon him, as he rode this terrible race. With these came a longing for vengeance upon Chesters, and a loathing of the infuriated brute that bore him. How he longed for a loaded pistol, that he might put a bullet through its head.

Cyril was an excellent horseman, and had always been a little vain of his riding ; but now he was becoming worn out.

After a twenty miles run, the horse had now left the high-

way, and was traversing one of those large fields (of some forty
Scottish acres or so) that are peculiar to the Merse and West
Lothian.   It had been recently ploughed, and as the hunter's
small hoofs and slender fetlocks sank deep amid the soft and
loamy soil, while its panting and breathing grew harder, Cyril
hoped that it was weary and would soon stop ; but the hope
was vain.

Cyril's fingers were powerless with grasping the twisted reins
of the useless bridle, and his arms ached and tingled to the
shoulders with the long strain upon them ; his whole body
trembled, and he felt that little now would dismount him, so
fast and furious had been the career of his runaway steed, so
many the leaps he had made over gates and walls of turf and
stone, over high hedges and deep water-courses ; a regular
steeplechase over everything that came in his way.   The
roughest hurdle race was as nothing compared with it ; and
now, we have said, before him lay the sea.

He knew the ground well, and the whole locality ; he had
too often rambled there bird-nesting when a happy, heedless
boy, and while hunting or shooting in manhood ; and he knew
also every foot of that terrible shore from Eymouth to the
Bridge of Dunglass ; and he was aware that at the end of the
field he traversed there was no enclosure, no wall or hedge, no
boundary but the giddy verge which overhung the sea that
foamed some forty feet below.   So now the time had come
when he must cast himself from his saddle or perish.

He released his right foot from the stirrup-iron, but somehow
omitted to clear the left so readily.   In a moment he was on
his back among the soft loamy furrows, and dragged furiously
along ; the next, he felt himself shot fearfully through the air,
which seemed to whiz upward past him.

"God—oh, God save me !" escaped him, while his mother's
face, and Mary's too, flashed on his memory, with Mary's gentle
voice and tender eyes, as he fell through space ; and ere he
could again respire he found himself headlong in the midnight
sea, with the black water closed above his head.

Panting he rose to the surface, but to sink again and again,
for he was weak, powerless, and breathless ; yet being a good
swimmer, when he rose the third time he kept himself afloat
and looked around.

He was free from the fatal bay hunter now.

High over him towered a ridge of those black, beetling rocks
which bound the shore and culminate in the cliffs of Fast
Castle and those of St. Abb, covered with sea fowl, and with
the foam of the German Ocean rolling against them.   The
moon, which had been hitherto veiled by a mass of clouds, now
emerged from them, and as she was waning from amid the

ragged edges of the floating vapour, her light, cold, pale, and ghastly, shone along the tossing sea.

Even if he could have protracted his existence by swimming, in the end he must perish ; for all along that shore no footing place or sandy beach was nigh, and the waves, he feared too surely, would dash him on the bluffs a battered corpse.

Already his horse, with true instinct, had turned to the shore and swam through the billows, which dashed it again and again upon the wall of rock the slippery face of which it beat and pawed with its hoofs in vain to find a footing.

A mass of weedy and isolated rock some yards from that perilous shore caught the eye of Cyril in the moonlight. The waves boiled and seethed around but not *over* it. There he would find footing he hoped for a time, till daylight broke and his situation might be seen from the land or the sea ; and with a prayer of thankfulness to Heaven in his heart and on his lips, he swam boldly and reached its slippery apex by grasping the seaweed that covered it.

Cold and drenched he sat there with the white waves seething round him ; and he could remember that many a time when he was a boy he had striven, by tossing stones from the cliff above, to hit this identical rock which now afforded him a temporary place of safety.

Ere long he felt sensible that the water was rising, that the tide was flowing inshore, and might in time, perhaps, cover the rock, in which case he was certain to be washed off and drowned.

The moon soon disappeared behind that stupendous rock which is crowned by the ruins of Fast Castle, and is inaccessible on all sides, save by a narrow neck of land, and then a double gloom seemed to fall upon the sea. About a mile off he could see a solitary light in the window of a house upon the shore, the light too probably of some watcher by a sick bed ; and wistfully and yearningly he regarded it, as he sat, or crouched rather, on that isolated rock, perishing miserably within a few miles of his splendid home.

There he knew that by this time all would be a-bed, after his father, his brother, and Horace Ramornie had had a few amicable strokes at billiards, and after his mother had grown weary of weaving out the future of the coming heiress ; and he knew that Gervase Asloane, the old butler, would be sleepily awaiting his return from Chesterhaugh.

One other light was visible for a time ; it was on board a large steamer about eight miles distant in the offing, where gradually it passed out of sight as she sped on her way to England or Holland.

To shout, Cyril knew was worse than useless ; few craft ever ventured near that iron shore, and there his voice would be heard by sea birds only.

Poor Cyril Wedderburn!　He had not been much given to
prayer since he became a man of the world, or since he had last
lisped his childish orisons at his mother's knee; but now, in his
hour of desperate need, he invoked God earnestly for deliver-
ance from a death so early and so terrible as that which menaced
him : and by a strange idiosyncrasy of the human mind, amid
these pious thoughts, and amid the bewildering horrors of his
situation, there occurred to his ear and his memory scraps of
mess-room songs, of frivolous banter, and operatic airs, as if in
grotesque mockery, till he feared he was going mad !

Suddenly a terrible cry—a cry that seemed to belong neither
to Heaven nor earth—a cry altogether dissimilar to any other
sound he had ever heard before, pierced his ears. Its singularity
of tone made the pulses of his heart stand still.　Were the tales
he had heard of the water kelpy, and his shrieks of triumph
over the drowning, true after all?

No other sound followed but the monotonous dashing of the
waves, the hiss of the surf upon the rocks, and the voices of the
now startled sea birds as they were roused from their nests by
that unearthly yell.

It was the death scream of his drowning horse ; for a horse,
when in extremity of terror, can utter a dreadful cry at times ;
and now its body floated passively in the eddy round a wave-
beaten promontory, the sport of the billows, and Cyril, with
little regret certainly, saw it tossed to and fro in the starlight,
till it disappeared, and that was the last he saw of his fatal bay
hunter !

And now another deep invocation of God escaped him, for
he became assured that slowly, but steadily and terribly, the
rising tide was closing round him !

CHAPTER XIII.

GRIEF.

IN his exciting conversation with Mary, worthy Squills, the
village doctor, had not over-rated the grief and consternation
which the great catastrophe excited among the bereaved family
at Willowdean.　"There are days in some lives which are so
full of pain that no term of after years, no joy or peace of after-
granting, can enable us to think of them without a shudder,
even to the last hour of existence."　So was it with Lady Wedderburn then, on that black fatal day, and for many a day
after, when memory went back to the terrible shock her nervous
system had received.

Accustomed from her infancy to all the perfect repose and

care that wealth, position, and prosperity so frequently inspire, this calamity seemed beyond all her power of realization as a fact!

The absence of Cyril from the formal morning prayer read by Sir John (the Wedderburns were rather High Church), and from breakfast, excited no great surprise ; and when it was reported from the stable-yard that neither he nor his horse the famous bay had come home last night, the natural conclusion of the family circle was that he had been pressed to remain at Chesterhaugh, and would doubtless ride home in time for the family luncheon ; but Sir John, who disliked some of Rooke Chesters' proclivities, particularly his proneness to gamble, was surprised that his son (usually so careful and fastidious in his acquaintanceships) should so far tax that person's hospitality.

When Lady Wedderburn, in her gay little dressing-room, was in deep consultation with Miss Flora M'Caw about her style of mourning for her Uncle William, of Madras, and the proper sets of jewellery, jet, silver, or gold, to be worn therewith, and also when the season for second mourning arrived, the startling tidings came, in the form of a vague rumour at first, that her son Cyril had left Chesterhaugh about midnight, and had now been absent, unaccounted for, none knew where or how, for twelve hours !

For one so extremely regular in all his habits and so temperate in conduct, this seemed incomprehensible, and every hopeful, vague, and wild surmise was indulged in only to culminate at last in the fear of some terrible accident or outrage, and yet the people of the district were peaceful and orderly.

Then, as the Doctor had related to Mary, Horace Ramornie, and all the household, assisted by friends and neighbours, set forth to search the country. His hat was found at Buncle-edge, and his whip at Falaknowe, five miles nearer the sea ; but Lady Juliana Ernescleugh sent her son, the Master, with the darkest tidings of all, that Cyril's well-known bay hunter had been discovered drowned, and fearfully bruised and battered, among the rocks eastward of Fast Castle, and then the conviction that a dreadful calamity, the details of which were incomprehensible, had taken place.

The Coastguard were set to work, the shore was searched, and, save where the rocks were impassable or inaccessible, every creek and cranny were examined between Broxmouth and the Redheugh shore ; a fleet of fisherboats dragged all the water in the vicinity, but all their seeking was vain.

No further trace was found of Cyril.

The telegraphs were at work, with descriptions of his person and clothing, and rewards were offered for information, with no better success, and thus four days of agonizing suspense and horror were passed by the family at Willowdean.

All the servants sorrowed for Cyril, the feminine portion especially ; he was so handsome, and always so smiling and suave ; and old Gervase Asloane, on whose back he had ridden many a time when a boy, wept for him, and Miss Flora M'Caw wept too. Solitary, and of a necessity selfish though her life had been, she felt genuine grief for the loss of so fine a young man, and recalled the secret hopes and tender passion in which she had once ventured to indulge when the heir of Willowdean was in his mere boyhood, in the time that seemed so long past now.

Messages and cards of condolence poured in from friends and neighbours; and among others came a black-edged note, per Mr. Bill Trayner, from Rooke Chesters, expressing profound sorrow for the untoward event, and enclosing Cyril's I O U for three hundred pounds, which "he hoped Sir John Wedderburn would find it convenient to liquidate, as he was just about to travel."

"Oh, detestable taste !" exclaimed Horace Ramornie, with a flush of anger and contempt on his handsome face ; but Sir John, though his brown, manly hand trembled the while, signed a cheque for the amount, and enclosed it to Chesters without a word of comment.

He then looked sadly at the I O U, the last words, no doubt, his son's hand had traced, and with a sigh threw it into the fire.

When the second and third day passed, Lady Wedderburn was too ill to leave her bed, and it required all the skill of Doctor Squills, and all the solace of Miss M'Caw, with the aid of camphor, sal-volatile, and Rimmel's vinegar, to save her from a succession of fainting fits.

Cyril was gone—gone for ever !

These words seemed ever in her heart and on her lips, and to be written, as it were, in letters of fire upon the wall, and this feeling seemed to fill the air around her. The stunning sense of her bereavement was most keen in the wakeful hours of the night and of the early morning. Then it seemed to rush like a flood upon her. Never more would her slender fingers run caressingly through his rich dark hair ; never more would his soft and beautiful, yet manly eyes, turn affectionately to hers ; never again would his voice, always so sweetly modulated when addressing her, fall upon her listening ear.

A lonely girl at Lonewoodlee was full of exactly similar thoughts, sorrows, and memories ; yet those of the bereaved mother were perhaps the deepest — the most keen and the hardest to bear. Cyril was her first-born—the apple of her eye.

To her he was beautiful as Absalom was to David, and as she thought of that, she repeated in her heart—

"Oh Absalom, my son, my Absalom,
Would to God my life would ransom thine !"

Had Lady Wedderburn seen Mary Lennox then, and known the common cause of their grief, she might have forgiven and even loved her ; but she had never yet connected the idea of Mary with her son.

When Cyril was absent with his regiment—the Fusileers—the sight of his empty chair, his vacant place at table, always inspired her with sadness ; but she knew that he was no longer a boy, and could not be kept for ever by her side. Now his place would ever more be vacant, or filled by a terrible shadow —an unseen presence only. Even his grave she would never look upon ; and every relic of Cyril—the portrait painted of him, as a cherry-cheeked boy ensign, in his first red coat and epaulettes, with pipe-clayed belt and black bearskin ; the lock of his hair which had never left her bosom since he joined his regiment, then warring on the banks of the Sutledge ; his unused books, his bed, the soft cambric pillow-case his cheek had touched, his favourite meerschaum pipe, lying where he had last left it—all became as something sacred in her eyes, and inspired her with bursts of the most passionate grief.

The schemes she had been so fondly forming for his aggrandizement, by marriage with his rich cousin who was coming home, were all forgotten now ; and in the bewilderment of her grief she almost forgot to pray. Poor Lady Wedderburn was stupefied ; and the snow of that sudden storm which imprisoned Mary Lennox at Chesterhaugh added, while it lasted on hill and moor, double desolation to her heart, for the gloom of the weather adds keenly to the grief of the imaginative and impressionable.

Where was now the future she had pictured, with Cyril's children crowing and nestling upon her knee? Robert, her younger son—the future Baronet—yet was left to her ; but at present all her sorrows, tears, and regrets were for the lost one.

CHAPTER XIV.

AN UNWELCOME VISITOR.

"THE fifth day, and no news of him yet—no trace, save the dead horse ! By Jove ! what can have happened ? I meant only to break a few of his bones, or spoil his pretty face, perhaps, for Mary, and nothing more. Where the devil can he have

drifted to—the coast of Holland perhaps? Handsome of the
old boy to cash up the I O U. Wish it had been for six
hundred, though?"

Thus thought Ralph Rooke Chesters, when on the afternoon
of the fifth day—on Monday—after the disappearance of Cyril
he dismounted at Lonewoodlee, under the door which bore the
quaint legend, and presenting his card, asked for Miss Lennox.

"Miss Lennox was at home," Alison said, and ere long she
received him in the gloomy apartment which passed for her
drawing-room, with its chintz-covered furniture, its chiffonnières
of painted wood, its old-fashioned girandoles, and the meagre
finery of her mother's bridal days, to which her own eyes had
become accustomed. Her piano stood open, for though her
heart was full of grief, she had been compelled to sing and
play to amuse her father.

"To what do I owe the—the pleasure of this visit?" said
Mary, politely yet coldly, for the memory of yesterday's snare
haunted her unpleasantly, and secretly she resented it.

"My anxiety lest you should have suffered from the snow
(now nearly gone, by-the-bye) and the cold drive in an open
waggonette," replied Chesters, with as soft a smile as his face
could assume.

"Thanks ; I am well," said Mary, still more coldly, for there
was something in the manner of Chesters which inspired doubt
and dislike. Yet he placed his hat on the table, brushed a
speck off his tweed knickerbockers with his handkerchief, and
quietly seated himself with the air of a man who meant to
remain.

"And the old gentleman. How is he?"

"As usual," sighed Mary ; "very weak and ailing. I know
not with what ; and I don't think that Doctor Squills knows
either."

"Get some other skill than this cub of a parish doctor possesses. Send to town—to London or Edinburgh."

But Mary shook her head and sighed again as she thought of
their slender means ; and there was a pause, during which she
hoped that he would soon go, as she had to be at the railway
station at a certain hour to receive certain medicines which the
Doctor had ordered from Edinburgh for her father's use.

She was conscious that Chesters was regarding her earnestly ;
indeed he had been unable to get out of his evil mind the effect
of her pretty and ladylike little figure while she sat so many
hours in his dining-room last night; so he had come in the
prosecution of his nefarious suit ; but old as he was in the ways
of the world he lived in, he felt an awkwardness in his mode of
advancing it ; for Mary looked so provokingly calm and composed, and so exquisitely ladylike ; her beautifully dressed hair

so gorgeous in colour and quantity, with her plain but perfect toilet, and her only ornament, a simple brooch, nestling at her pretty neck.

To Mary's eye he looked older to-day and less careful in his costume ; his nose was certainly redder, and the blotches on his cheeks were deeper in colour ; his watchful and sinister grey eyes were more restless in expression, and it soon became evident that he had been imbibing freely, though the day was yet young. Wine, or something worse, alone could have made him depart from his policy of yesterday and blunder on as he did while the young girl's grief was so fresh and keen.

He rose, and coming close to the chair in which she was seated, laid his hand on the back of it, touching her rounded shoulder as he did so ; and lowering his voice, he said—

" Miss Lennox ; or may I call you Mary ?"

" Yes, if you choose. You have known me since I was a mere child."

" I have served in India since then," said he, with an ill-concealed grimace ; for he winced at the remark, or what it inferred ; and oblivious of the tender scene he had witnessed in the thicket, and the grief which filled her heart, he said—

" I am come to ask you if you will allow me to love you, Mary Lennox ?"

" I can neither prevent people from loving or hating me," she replied, evasively ; for she remembered the bill which he possessed ; the power it gave him over her father, and she trembled in her heart.

" Ah, Mary, who could hate you ?" he whispered, bending still nearer her face.

" But I beg that you will not speak of love to me."

" Why ?"

" For a reason I care not to give. Pray let that suffice," urged Mary, as she bit her lip and kept her pale face averted to hide the tears with which her eyes were filled.

" Then you love another ?" said Chesters, bluntly.

" That is my affair, sir."

" But you do ; or shall I say, *did.*"

" As you please," replied the girl, wearily, shrugging her shoulders, and her words seemed to come from her heart.

" At least, I have a kind of admission from your own lips," he resumed, with a half-muttered imprecation under his sandy grey moustache, and with a dangerous gloom in his false and sinister eyes. " But do you know your own mind ?"

" I trust that I do," was the gentle reply.

" You are right to speak doubtfully."

Mary changed her seat to the other side of the fireplace ; for, as his face came nearer hers, a kind of shiver passed over her.

"I do not understand you, Captain Chesters," said she, haughtily, as she erected her pretty head, and looked at him intently and steadily.

"I say you are right to speak doubtfully, for at your years a girl scarcely knows her own mind," he resumed more tenderly, again drawing near her and attempting to take her hand. "It is quite possible to love one person at one time, and another much more at a future time ; and thus you might love me. Who is the writer that says, ' we may love with but a part of our nature—for the heart must love something—until we chance upon a being our every nature sympathizes with ; one that will awaken new faculties to love with ; one that we can love with all the love we gave the first, with still more added—a being made for us, and us alone.' "

Chesters poured out this quotation at a breath, for he was sensible that his utterance was becoming thicker, and a smile of disdain passed over Mary's face.

"I don't know who the writer is," said she, with growing irritation, as she rang the bell, "but it all sounds very French—like some of the maxims of Jean Jacques Rousseau. One thing I am sure of, Captain Chesters ; my nature would never sympathise with yours, and I could never—pardon me for saying so—marry a man old enough to be my father."

Chesters ground his teeth at this reply, and a little hollow and bitter laugh escaped him ; for with all his open and secret admiration of Mary, which was genuine enough—as the charms of her person and manner were undeniable—a marriage with her formed no part of his plans. He was about to renew the subject, when old Alison appeared, in answer to the summons of her young mistress, who said—

"Ask, please, if my papa feels well enough to see Captain Chesters."

"He has just been inquiring for him, Miss."

"Good. Come with me, Captain Chesters, if you are so disposed. Papa sees so few, that your visit will be quite an event."

Now Chesters, with all his suavity and plausibility, when he had an object in view, could rarely give much sympathy to any one or anything, and above all, he hated the boredom of illness or sickness in himself or others, felt just then only anger at the quick mode in which Mary cut short his intrusive love-making ; but he bowed, and followed her into the room where poor Oliver Lennox lay in the bed from which, it was too probable, he would never rise. The oppressive odour of the sick room in such a chill season, and in such a house, where the walls were of such enormous thickness, was unpleasantly perceptible to Chesters, and had the result of making his recent potations more seriously affect his brain.

However, being withal a well-bred man, he shook the thin wan hand of Mr. Lennox with apparent cordiality, made the usual polite but conventional inquiries about his health, and received the same unmeaning and querulous replies, which he had heard a score of times in the same place.

Weak and worn though he was, could Oliver Lennox but have seen into Chester's heart, and read the plans he cherished there, he would have smote him by his bedside!

Propped on pillows which his daughter's tender hand had arranged, Mr. Lennox, looking twenty years older than his time of life warranted, had been lying the whole forenoon with his clear blue restless eyes bent on the muirland scene that stretched for miles away before his window—the acres upon acres that were no longer his own ; acres won and held by his forefathers in the old stirring times of Scottish raids and wars.

The snow of the unexpected storm had already disappeared ; the day really looked like one in spring ; the sky a deep blue ; the air soft and ambient. The bulb roots were expanding amid the prepared mould in Mary's little garden on the southern side of the Tower ; the primroses and wild violets were cropping up beneath the sprouting hedgerows ; the grass looked greener on the lonely hill sides and in the meadows, over which the shadows of the clouds were passing quickly ; and even the bleak Lammermuir looked less bleak than was its wont ; for the day was of a kind to make one feel content for the present, hopeful for the future, and prayerful to God.

Oliver Lennox felt its genial influence in his own fatuous way ; but not so his daughter, for her heart was rent by anguish for the loss of Cyril, and mortification for the annoyance which the suit of Chesters occasioned her.

" How kind of you to come and see an old broken-down fellow such as I am," said the invalid, turning his sharp aquiline face to his visitor, and presenting his hand for a second time.

" Not at all, my good friend. Glad to see you looking so well. Egad ! I shouldn't wonder to see you in the saddle again, scouring across the country—the leading man in the field."

But Mr. Lennox only shook his head and sighed despondingly, while Mary felt disgust for the untrue sympathy of Chesters, who stood sucking the ivory handle of his whip, while she rearranged with her quick hands the pillows under her father's head.

" It was just on such a breezy March day as this I hunted last, Chesters," said the invalid, with a sad smile. " We all came at a slapping pace through Oxendean, and round Buncleedge, till, oddly enough, a bed of sweet violets and primroses— only think of it !—in Renton Wood quite threw the hounds off the scent, and the fox escaped ! Since that day Oliver Lennox

has never been in the hunting field, or backed but an old Galloway cob."

"Take courage.   There is a good time coming, as the song
has it."

"My Mary is the veritable 'Brownie' of Lonewoodlee, who
cooks and watches in the night, and all that, so I should not
repine," said Mr. Lennox, with a fond smile, as he played with
her snowy and statuesque fingers ; "but her unwearying love,
and all her tender kindness cannot avert fate, or hide the out-
stretching of the Shadowy Hand."

"Oh, papa, do not—do not pierce my heart!" implored the
girl.

"How much more of life is there in this old grumbler yet?"
thought Chesters, as he actually gnawed the whip-handle with
his teeth, while watching admiringly the contour of Mary's
bust, the taper form of her white arms, and the high arch of
her instep, as she hung about her father's bed.

"You will be kind to her, Chesters, when I am gone," said
Lennox, in his usual querulous way ; and the request was so
much in unison with Chesters' own thoughts, that the blotches
deepened to scarlet in his face.

"Kind to her, Mr. Lennox?" he faltered.

"Yes. I leave so few friends behind me now, that Mary's
future fills my heart with intense anxiety."

"Papa dearest, fear not for me," said Mary, becoming deeply
agitated.

"Had your brother Harry but been spared—"

"Don't talk of poor Harry, papa," urged Mary, as her father's
mind was apt to wander then, and to confound the past and
the present together ; "do not talk thus, papa, when strangers
are present. You may live I hope and trust for many years to
come. 'God alone decides who shall live to suffer, or who shall
suffer and die.' I, perhaps, may be one of the latter."

A scarcely perceptible gesture of impatience escaped Chesters ;
but slight though it was, the quick eye of the invalid detected it.

"Well, I daresay I weary you. Take Chesters into the dining-
room, Mary, and give him a glass of Madeira, or brandy-and-
water, after the ride. I always took a horn after a gallop in
my day—the day that will never come again. Lonewoodlee
had ever a name for hospitality, and it shall not lose it while I
am above the turf, lassie."

"Thanks : then we shall adjourn to the dining-room," said
Chesters, and glad to escape from the sick chamber, he shook
the hand of Oliver Lennox, and ere long found himself in the
sombre little dining-hall, seated on one of the square-elbowed
haircloth sofas, and looked down upon by a few faded and
gloomy portraits of the Lennoxes of past times, in wigs, wide

cuffs, and pasteboard skirts, or breastplates of steel, just as Lely, Ramsay, or Medina had depicted them ; and somehow he thought that in all the faces of these dead men he could read something of scorn and scrutiny, so his eye avoided them, and he applied himself to mixing a stiff glass of brandy-and-water, while Mary hovered irresolutely near. She was all anxiety that he should depart, for in an hour now the train would be in, and she wished to receive in person the medicines that were coming for her father. She dreaded also to mention her errand or purpose, lest he might offer to accompany her, and give the affliction of yet more of his society.

But Chesters found himself perfectly comfortable. His din-ner-time was three hours distant yet ; the brandy-and-water proved quite to his taste—so, too, was Mary—thus he at once resumed the thread of their conversation, but in a more jocular, or as Mary justly deemed it, more insolent tone ; for helpless-ness and friendlessness encouraged this *vaurien*, while her rare beauty inspired his worst passion.

"Ah, Mary, we might be so jolly if you would only learn to love me a little." Then becoming maudlinly sentimental, he proceeded to quote Shelley—

"'See the mountains kiss high Heaven,
And the waves clasp one another ;
No sister flower will be forgiven,
If it disdain its brother.
And the sunbeams kiss the earth :
And the moonbeams the sea.
What are all those kissings worth,
If thou kiss not *me* ?''

"The order of that line should be reversed ; but, by Jove, my voice is getting quite feathery !"

He was becoming inarticulate, and almost tipsy.

"Captain Chesters," said Mary, gravely, "do not go on thus, I implore you ! You would pity me if you knew all—the hor-ror of living alone, or nearly alone, in this dreary house ; my sole occupation the sad, sad one——"

"Of what ?" said he, as tears choked her utterance.

"Soothing and amusing a dying father."

"Oh bosh ! my dear girl," was the coarse response ; "the old fellow may live long enough yet ; and I am sure that he would rather have me for a son-in-law—I who know so thoroughly the points of a horse and the secrets of the turf—a thoroughbred sportsman, who could take the county pack in hand, and, had I the means, would hunt the Merse and Lauder-dale as they never were hunted before—than yonder mooning fellow from whom you parted in the thicket on the night he disappeared. Ah, you sly puss, you little knew that I saw you there !"

6

Mary felt herself grow deadly pale, and then she flushed to the temples with anger, as these rude and almost fiercely spoken remarks, so wounding to her delicacy, fell on her sensitive ear. Again her hand went to the bell for the purpose of having Chesters shown to the door at all hazards of the future, but ere she could ring Alison Home's hard and wrinkled visage appeared, and she announced that "Captain Chesters' servant, Trayner, wished to speak with him immediately."

"Send him up then," said Chesters sulkily. "Most singular, this! What the deuce can the fellow want with me? I left him in the stables."

"He says, sir, that he has something for your private ear," replied the greyhaired domestic.

Now Chesters had so many strange involvements, and so many secrets to keep, that he very palpably changed colour on hearing this, and felt compelled to go to his servant, who had dismounted at the door, and was now dressed in livery, with an orthodox cockade and brown leather belt.

Mary only heard Chesters utter a fierce exclamation of astonishment in reply to a communication made by Trayner, who was coolly smoking one of his master's cigars, concerning "Willowdean and a telegram;" and then, without the courtesy of returning to bid her adieu, or making any explanation whatever, her unwelcome visitor rode off towards Chesterhaugh, accompanied by his servant; and Mary could see from her window that as they galloped along the road they were side by side and in close and rapid conversation.

About what?

CHAPTER XV.

THE SPRING EVENING.

ERE the night fell and the moonlight paled out on the Lammermuirs and on the sea, Mary was fated to hear what this secret communication was!

"What had happened at Willowdean—what was the nature of the telegram?" she asked of her own heart and of Alison in vain; the discovery of Cyril's body in the sea, or cast upon the shore perhaps, and even she who loved him so, yea as her own soul, dared not ask permission to look upon his pallid face again!

This conviction was a great, a bitter, and a mortifying grief! Well, well, if the world were going to pieces, she knew that she must attend to the health and wants of her father, and on looking at her watch, she found that she had not a moment to lose if she would be at the station when the train from the

North came in. She tied on her smart hat and veil, took her tiny muff, and set forth.

She might have sent Alison Home, but she had a craving to be a little abroad in the open air, for the atmosphere of the house seemed to stifle her, and there were times when the clamorous fluttering of her heart amounted to agony, and when she felt as one in a dream—one enduring sorrows not her own, but those of another.

She passed the thicket and the stile where she had been wont to meet *him* in the evening, and she glanced at both wistfully. No need was there now to wait with anxious heart to watch the clock, or wonder whether papa would be asleep, awake, or fretful when the time for trysting came. All was ended now! and yet as she looked at the rude steps of the stone stile, grey and spotted with lichens, it seemed to her as if she could, in her mind's eye, trace the outline of her handsome and winning lover's figure, waiting for her as of old—as he had waited only five days ago—her lost Cyril.

Never more! Oh, how much of sadness, of bitterness, and hopelessness, do these two words contain!

Save in a few hollow places on the hill sides, the snow of the preceding night had totally disappeared. The sunset deepened into a warm and russet glow on the summits of the pastoral hills, the air was balmy, and the chirping of the birds came clearly upon it, with the voices of children from a distance. The green buds were swelling in the hedgerows, and near a cottage which had once been a lodge of Lonewoodlee (now let to a cotter) she saw a group of rosy, barelegged "bairns" peeping with wonder into the first bird's nest of the season, which some unwary sparrow had built in the cleft of an open bush. The rooks were cawing aloft, the brown hares were gliding among the glistening furrows of the freshly ploughed fields, or "mains" as they are named in the Merse; there was a fragrance and odour of verdure in the air, and though the month is usually a rude and boisterous one, Mary, as she walked rapidly on, could not be insensible of the genial influence of spring.

Pausing at times, she looked fondly and sadly back to the gloomy old Tower, the tourelles, bartizan, and stone roof of which stood out so darkly against the bright blue evening sky. There, in the stirring times of old, by the Border Laws, or *Leges Marchiarum*, her forefathers had been compelled to keep a watch with alarm-bell and fire-pan, to give warning to the North, to Soltra and Dunpender, when the English crossed the Tweed or entered the Merse, and now their descendants trembled at the approach of an angry creditor! How long would her dwelling be there, and where would be her home when—but she thrust *that* thought aside as too painful, and hastened on.

She passed ere long the handsome modern gate and Grecian lodge of Willowdean, the pillared peristyle and white façade of which she could see at a distance between the trees of the park (or chase, it might be called in England), and an irrepressible sob escaped her for one who would never more be under its roof; and thus, with the tears welling but unseen beneath her closely tied veil, she entered the market town of Willowdean, which owed its existence and prosperity to the Wedderburns.

It is a quaint old Scottish Burgh or Barony, and was so long before the union of the kingdoms, remaining very much unchanged for more than a century after, and singularly so, as in Scotland nothing stands, for there whatever fails to "go ahead" must decline and pass away, like many of the burghs of Fife. It has stood almost unchanged, even by the railway, save for the erection of a few gayer shops and taverns—unchanged in its general aspect since Queen Mary made her famous ride to Hermitage, and from its aspect, its cross—a slender shaft of stone surmounted by a moulded unicorn—its kirk, and crow-stepped gables abutting on the street, its quaint outshots and turnpike stairs, one might expect to see the mailed knights of Mary, or buff-coated troopers of Leslie, fresh from Marston Moor, drinking at the market well, or "chaffing" the girls at the grated windows of the houses, some of which still show the iron crosses of St. John of Jerusalem.

The town once boasted of a castle, but after being burned by some Northumberland raiders in the time of Charles II., it has dwindled down to a few vaults and a green mound, the favourite resort of the children for games and play. Willowdean still boasts of a parochial barn, called a kirk, where God is worshipped according to the cold and stern form ordained in 1559 by the Lords of the Congregation, when Mary of Guise was Regent of the realm, enlightened Scottish lords who could barely make their mark like an Irish navvy, and who (could such an investment have been made) would have sold their fathers' skins to Queen Elizabeth.

This church had, however, attached to it the Gothic fragment of an older fane, still called the Lennox Aisle, and there lay most of the forefathers of her who now entered the street afoot, and sick and sad at heart.

To many of the "burgh merchants" in that little town was her father in debt, yet everywhere did Mary meet with respect; all touched their hats to her, for the memory of her father's open-handed youth was a popular one : and in a place so sequestered and out of the route of the tourist, even in fast-changing and radical Scotland, some more respect is paid at

times to the representative of an old family than might be
accorded to a wealthy *parvenu*, and all the more readily when
the said representative is a lovely young girl like Mary Lennox.
In the middle of the street—the town has but one, with a few
thatched closes or alleys diverging therefrom—she encountered
a group of little children dancing hand-in-hand and singing in
chorus one of those local rhymes which are so peculiar to the
Lowlands, as they came merrily along, enumerating, to an air of
their own, several localities, thus—

> " Braw Bughtrig and braw Belchester,
>   Leetholm and the Peel ;
> The lad wha gets a wife frae there
>   Will ever do weel ;
> But better far in Willowdean,
>   And bonnier will be see,
> If he'll ride further up the muir,
>   Unto the Lonewoodlee."

Then, as they suddenly perceived and recognised Miss Lennox,
the little creatures blushed and curtseyed ; and, but for the
chronic sadness of her heart, Mary could have smiled at the old
rhyming compliment to the alleged beauty of the ladies of her
family.

At last she reached the railway station, of which no description is necessary, as such edifices bear a strong family resemblance
all over Europe. There were the same liveried porters loitering
about that one sees everywhere ; passengers with labelled
luggage awaiting the up-train or the down-train ; the book-stall,
with its inevitable rows of yellow, green, or red novels, *Punch*,
and the *Illustrated News*.

Mary had not long to wait. With a shrill and vicious whistle,
the train for England swept out of the tunnel, a long pennant
of smoke streaming behind, and its crimson lamps flaming like
the eyeballs of a demon in front, for the twilight had deepened
to the gloaming now. Clang went the bell, the engine "slowed,"
and, amid the bustle, the opening and slamming of doors, the
production and notching of tickets, the choice of seats and
stowal of luggage, the darting of the thirsty into the refreshment-
room, and so forth—for all had to be adjusted and the train off
in five minutes, if it would avoid the express for Berwick—Mary
looked in vain for the familiar face of the friendly guard who
frequently did her little services, and who was to bring her the
important packet from town.

The man on duty this evening was a total stranger to her.

" A packet for you, Miss?" said he, in reply to her inquiries.
" What is the name ?"

" For Mr. Lennox, of Lonewoodlee."

" It was given to a gentleman in the train ; he offered to take
charge of it."

" By whom ?"

" The other guard, to whom he seemed well known, and to
whom he offered in person to deliver it."

" Singular ; a gentleman !" exclaimed Mary, in vague alarm
that the long-expected packet might be lost or stolen.

" Yes, Miss ; a regular gentleman, for he gave me a crown
when smoking in the van."

" But where is he ?"

" Yonder, on the platform, Miss. Seats, gentlemen, seats !"
and cutting short the conversation, the bustling official hurried
away, touching the brass-lined peak of his cap.

Clang went the doors and the bell ; the engine panted and
screamed, the train glided away, and Mary went towards the
gentleman indicated by the guard. He was speaking in an
animated manner to a few of the loiterers on the platform, who
had formed a group about him, and Mary fancied that he *had*
a small sealed packet in his hand.

Irresolute about addressing him, she lingered for a moment,
till something in his air and manner stirred a secret chord in
her heart, which vibrated painfully, and a low cry escaped her
lips, when the handsome face, with the well-known moustache
and tender loving eyes of the lost one, was turned towards her !

" Cyril !" she exclaimed, and would have fallen, but that his
arm was instantly thrown around her.

" Mary—Mary Lennox !"

It was he, but looking paler and thinner, and strangely attired ;
and they met thus abruptly amid a group of people on the open
and most prosaic of places—a railway platform !

Great though his excitement, Cyril Wedderburn had that
horror of a "scene" natural to every well-bred Briton, and
rapidly recovering his consciousness of the necessity for appearing calm and unmoved, he lifted his hat, and said—

" Take my arm, Miss Lennox : allow me to see you out of this
place. I have here the packet addressed to your father. I hope
to hear that he is better. Good evening, gentlemen and friends ;
thanks for all your kind wishes and congratulations."

He drew Mary's arm through his, waved his hat to the
people who had recognized and crowded about him on the
platform, welcoming his return—resuscitation, what you will—
with a genuine cheer that died away in a buzz of speculation
and wonder, for the Wedderburns were deservedly popular in
the district ; and then he led away Mary, who was in a state of
intense bewilderment, for much of utter terror was mingled with
her joy, so that her steps tottered as they left the station and
proceeded through the street of Willowdean, where the windows

of the little shops were beginning to be lit with feeble gas, or still more feeble candles, and from thence out upon the familiar highway that stretched beyond.

CHAPTER XVI.

A HAPPY WALK HOME.

"CYRIL," exclaimed Mary, in a low but piercing voice, while she clung to her lover's arm ; "in the name of mercy and for the love of blessed Heaven, explain all this terrible mystery !"

"Oh, my darling, my darling, how pale and wan you look !" he exclaimed, as he lifted her veil and kissed her tenderly.

"And you too, Cyril. But speak of yourself, not me," she added, dropping her head wearily on his breast, and giving way to a passionate fit of weeping. "What has happened to you, where have you been, and how have you returned in so sudden and unexpected a manner, from the grave—from the very grave, as it seems to me ? I have wept and mourned for you as one who was numbered with the dead ! Oh, the horror, the black, indescribable horror of those days and nights now past !"

"My tender, loving Mary !"

"Oh, Cyril, hold me up. I feel as if I could die just now—the shock of joy is so, so great to see you again ; to hear your voice, for the sound of which I have longed in a species of silent, gasping yearning, that no words can describe, and which God alone knows !"

"So have I longed for you, Mary," said he, in a broken accent, for her words and the tone of her voice moved him deeply, as it had in it that wonderful *tremolo* which added so much to its power.

Oh, was it real, and not a dream ?—each asked of their hearts —this clinging and gasping embrace in which they both indulged for a time, in a happy, happy silence, too deep for words.

After a pause, Cyril said—

"I telegraphed to my brother Robert that I should arrive by this train, and asked him or Horace Ramornie to meet me with the trap or carriage, and drive me home ; but there must have been some mistake, for neither are here, which is lucky, as I shall have the unexpected joy of a walk home with you, my darling Mary, my wee wife, who, strange to say, has been the *first* to greet me !"

So this must have been the telegram referred to by Trayner in his rapid communication to Chesters, who, in the true spirit of jealousy, fear, or malevolence, had ridden off, without mentioning it to her.

"Surely you would not have left *me* another night in grief and suspense?" said Mary, plaintively.

"Not another hour! I telegraphed to the family at Willow-dean, first, of my safety; and again that I was to be home by the evening train. I meant to have gone to Lonewoodlee by the way, my excuse for doing so being this packet, which I should have left for you, with a sufficient message, if we had failed to meet."

"But the mystery, Cyril—the mystery of your story; tell me all!" she implored, with a heart full of love and natural curiosity.

In a few words he rapidly sketched all the adventures of the night on which he disappeared—adventures he would yet have to detail to many a listener, but to few that would listen so lovingly and breathlessly as poor Mary Lennox—horrors that were to come back in many a dream! He told of his dining at Chesterhaugh; of the night spent in rash gambling there; of his desire, but failure, to get possession of her father's bill; and then how his horse had proved first restive and afterwards mad, and completely ungovernable; of the fierce race by Buncle-edge and Falaknowe—a ride like that of the Wild Huntsman of German renown—till he was borne right into the sea; of the narrow escape he had from being dashed to pieces; but how, by the aid of kind Providence, he had reached the fragment of isolated rock, and sat there in cold and misery, with the moon waning, the night deepening, and the tide rising round him, while all hope of reaching the land by swimming was futile, as the cliffs rose sheer like a wall from the sea, which was rolling with a mighty force against them; and Mary heard all this, with hands clasped upon his arm, with exclamations of compassion and dismay, with her eyes full of tears, and her parted lips revealing her closely set little teeth.

He described, that around him there wheeled flights of the snow-white solan goose, the black guillemot, the grey gull, and other sea birds; and that once there came a seal—a seadog, as the Scottish fishermen name it—which swam in circles round the rock, with its bullet-shaped head, black glittering eyes, and two fore-paws alone visible, as it paddled about; and often the memory of that incident came back in dreams, for he had envied the animal its amphibious nature, while the rising tide flowed over his feet and legs; and often, in the same visions of night, came back the sounds he had heard when there—the gurgling, the hissing, and the surging of the sea, as the ridgy waves succeeded each other in unvarying rage, round the rock on which he sat and against the cliffs that beetled over him.

Mary shuddered and shed many a tear while she listened, though Cyril appeared to speak somewhat lightly of the affair, as "a devil of a spill—an awful mess—a narrow escape," and so forth.

The strange weird scream of his dying horse was ultimately the means of saving him. It had been heard to seaward on board of a small fishing smack, the skipper of which lay to, and sent his little boat in shore to discover whence that unearthly cry proceeded; and two men who rowed it, and whose superstitious fears inspired them with the utmost unwillingness for the duty, fortunately descried Cyril by the starlight, and were just in time to save him. He swam off towards them, and was taken on board the smack, speechless with cold and exhaustion.

The kind fishermen took every means in their limited power to restore him; they placed him in one of the only two berths they possessed, for the entire crew consisted but of five men, and of these three were always on duty; they drew off his wet clothes, covered him cosily up, and gave him the only medicine they knew of—a totfull of hot stiff grog—and then he fell into a deep slumber.

When morning came, the smack was out at sea, on her homeward voyage to the coast of Angus. Cyril awoke feverish and ill. The atmosphere of the little den in which he lay was redolent of tar, stale herrings, and coarse tobacco, and every way was not conducive to a speedy recovery. His head ached fearfully; his whole frame felt as if bruised and battered; his senses wandered, and it was not until the evening of the second day that his preservers learned who he was; whence came the singular cry they had heard; how he chanced to be on that isolated rock, and that they would be well rewarded for having saved him.

The smack was light; they had sold their cargo of herrings to the French at Dunbar, and were anxious now to haul up for their own homes, somewhere about Montrose; but a head wind drove them into the North Sea, and four days elapsed before they succeeded in landing him at Lunan Bay, where he lost no time in telegraphing home, and starting by the first train for the Merse; and this was the solution of all that recent sorrow and mystery.

"Had my left foot not been freed from the stirrup in my fall, or had my horse not uttered that remarkable cry which attracted the attention of the fishermen, I had been lying now a drowned corpse in yonder sea, Mary," said Cyril, in conclusion.

Mary still sobbed, as she was terribly excited by the whole narrative; but joy made her face seem radiantly beautiful; and in a burst of confidence that was perhaps not overwise, she told him of Chesters' love-declaration to herself, and of his having been *en perdue* in the thicket on the night they had last met. Cyril's eyes sparkled with indignation ; he knit his brows, gave his moustache a fierce twirl, and said—

"I see it all, Mary. His jealousy made me the victim of some foul revengeful trickery, which I shall yet have unravelled and punished !"

Mary omitted to speak of her detention at Chesterhaugh ; for now the annoyance to which Chesters had subjected her more than ever by his address, her repugnance of him, the mortification she had occasionally felt as a high-spirited girl for the secresy of her love affair with Cyril himself, and the plans and precautions they were compelled to observe, were all forgotten in the joyous conviction of his safety—the charm of his manner and presence.

What delight to lean again upon his arm ; to feel her hand pressed caressingly to his side ; to look into his face and hear his voice ; and, ah ! how different were his tone and bearing from those of Chesters, when with genuine interest he asked about the health of her father. Was this evening walk not all a dream, a sudden madness ?

"Oh, Cyril, you do not know my papa !" she exclaimed, in answer to some remark.

"Save by sight, as mere neighbours, and not very friendly ones now ; but I wish I did know him."

"He is altering fast, and looking so fearfully wizened and pale, even I, who see him hourly, can perceive that."

"Poor old man !"

At last they were close to Lonewoodlee, where the old Tower and its dense thicket stood sharply defined in purple shadow against the last flush of light that lingered in the amber tinted west.

Mary still clung to Cyril, loth to part from one so recently and so suddenly restored to her, till he whispered softly in her ear—

"You forget, Mary dearest, that I have a fond mother at Willowdean, longing to see me too."

"True. I am most selfish in detaining you so long from all at home, and I have to read or sing papa asleep ; for he cannot read now, and his nights are so dull and lonely. Oh, Cyril, how I shall sing to-night !"

"Would that I were there to hear you. Good-night, my sweet Mary, until the usual hour to-morrow. Good-night."

Another moment and he was gone, and Mary lingered at the gate until his rapid footsteps died away.

"Where was all this to end ?" thought Cyril, as he walked hastily homeward. He felt, as a gentleman and man of honour, that this *secret* love for Mary Lennox was unjust to her, and might peril her good name ; it was trifling with her undoubted position and with his own, and he resolved that, come what might, he must ere long declare it to his family, despite the mohurs, rupees, and thousands of cousin Gwendolyne, and the ambitious views of his father and mother, the latter especially.

Mary had as yet but one thought, as she rushed with a happy heart into her room and threw off her hat and sealskin jacket ; that the first kiss after his return had been on *her* cheek, even before that of his mother.

Was this a little bit of the superstition or the selfishness which exists with all love? Perhaps so ; but then she had barely a bowing acquaintance with Lady Wedderburn, and situated as she was with her son, the humiliation of that circumstance was somewhat galling to Mary's pride.

But how wild was the joy of the impulsive girl ! How she sang and played that night for hours, lost in happy, happy dreams ! He had been restored to her again, her lover, the hope of her future life ; he who to her was " gallant and gay as the young Lochinvar ;" and yet, who in reality, was only a very good specimen of a gentlemanly officer of the Line. She forgot all about the tenor and brevity of his leave of absence, and that he might be summoned away at a moment's notice ; she forgot all but that he had been restored to the world and to her, and that he loved her, oh, so truly ! Of all fears she was oblivious for a time, till other thoughts than joyous ones stole gradually into her mind ; and then her white fingers strayed mechanically over the ivory keys of the piano, and her tremulous voice, like the last faint notes, died away.

Alas ! there can be no human happiness without some alloy !

She now recalled some of Rooke Chesters' malevolent hints and speeches about the wealth and beauty of the expected cousin, and of Lady Wedderburn's evident views concerning her and Cyril ; though from what precise source he drew those deductions was quite unknown, unless the ready invention of a mind inflamed by jealousy.

When this Indian heiress came, rich and lovely—for Chesters had assured Mary that she *was* lovely—would there be any change in their destiny? Oh, she must not think of that ; Cyril could never change, never forget all they had been to each other.

" Alas !" thought she, " this man—this Rooke Chesters, for whom I care nothing—can come openly to see me, to talk, and even, if I permitted him, to walk with me ; while Cyril—Cyril Wedderburn, who is to be my husband, whom I love so ; love as Heaven alone knows—I see only by stealth ! It is hard ; very hard ! but this is not a night on which I should repine," and she lifted up her hands and her soft eyes, while her heart was full of prayerful thoughts and gratitude, to Heaven.

"Forsaking may be human, but betraying is the vice of devils;" and Chesters only sought to betray, to lure, and destroy. Yet Mary knew not of that, though aware of his terrible character, for he had actually, but somewhat jocularly, spoken of marriage ; and Mary shivered at the thought.

In her small turret-chamber that night—the same from the window of which she had heard the wild cry and seen the galloping horse—she shed happy tears, as she prayed beside her little couch ; for the gloom that once enveloped her soul had departed, and all the bitter past seemed now a vanished dream !

CHAPTER XVII.

COUSIN GWENNY.

GREAT contentment and supreme happiness reigned at Willowdean, where long consultations were held by the gentlemen concerning Chesters, who had suddenly taken his departure to London. They had doubts of what to do, for suspicion was not proof, and Cyril had to conceal the espionage practised on himself at Lonewoodlee, and that jealousy had aught to do with the supposed treacherous trick played to his horse. Hence the whole affair seemed inexplicable to his father, his brother, and cousin, till in Cyril's mind there stole a kind of cloudy doubt even of Chesters' guilt.

"Could it be possible," he asked of himself, "that he could conceive and carry out a scheme so singularly infamous against an unsuspecting guest ?"

For the next day or two, Cyril found some difficulty in keeping his appointments with Mary, for his doting mother could scarcely trust her tall, curly-pated and heavily-moustached captain of Fusilers out of her sight, she had so much to ask and to learn : and nobly were the poor skipper of Angus and the four fishermen of his smack rewarded. Cyril, however, wrote little notes to Mary, making his excuses, and expressing his love for her ; and such notes were a great solace to her in her loneliness at home.

How trivial now seemed the adoption of mourning for Uncle William ; the suits of black for the family and servants, the note-paper and cards with sable edges and crests, when compared with the gloom of such preparations for the loss of the heir of Willowdean !

Cyril knew that of course he was his father's heir ; and that if God and the Russian bullets spared him in the expected war, he might in time become the Baronet of Willowdean ; but with all his interest, personal and sentimental, in the old family estate, he felt bored when his father talked to him, as country gentlemen *will* talk, of the probable appearance of the crops and the face of the country, of the farm and pasture land, of top dressing, subsoil, and tile drainage, especially for the lower meadows and three great fields of the home-farm ; the weight of pigs. "By Jove," Cyril would mentally exclaim, "the weight of pigs !"

He could feel an interest when the county pack was on the *tapis*, or when he heard that the covers would require looking to ; the patent powder to feed the pheasants ; the rooting out of weasels and foumarts ; of the new stables, and so forth ; but never in agriculture, which, in all its branches, he viewed and voted as an unqualified bore. Hunting after a night poacher, who occasionally visited the home-farm in "the glimpses of the moon," was more in Cyril's way than the alternation of green or white crops, and so forth ; but his thoughts, if not with the regiment, were ever at Lonewoodlec.

Horace Ramornie felt some interest in Sir John's topics, for though he had not an acre of land, he repined occasionally at the loss of the old patrimonial estates of his family, and felt somewhat too keenly his dependence on his uncle.

Lady Wedderburn was now intent apparently on the arrangements necessary for the reception of the expected ward ; but the chief thought of her mind was obvious to all, and she could not avoid recurring to it whenever she and Sir John were alone.

" I know that Cyril cannot quit his regiment with honour just now, when it has got letters of readiness," said she, on one occasion ; "but, dear Sir John, I should so like him to sell out, and reside quietly at home. He is not obliged to pursue his career as a soldier, like Horace, who is penniless."

" Quit !" repeated Wedderburn, testily, " I should think not. Quit on the eve of a war ! I would rather see the lad in his coffin than taunted with showing the white feather."

" In three days Gwenny will be here, and if she is so handsome as Doctor Chutnay of Madras assures us she is, she must be charming ! And if Cyril must go soon, I should wish —wish that he were married, or at least, solemnly contracted to her. You understand me, Wedderburn ?"

" Why such hasty hopes and plans, Kate ?"

" Because, as I have already hinted, some one else may marry her, and it would be an act of injustice to Cyril and ourselves to permit all her wealth to pass out of the family. Besides, our neighbour Chesters, every way a bad style of man, may see and admire her, with views of his own."

"If he ever should meet her, which after recent events I think barely probable," said Sir John, somewhat angrily.

"Then there is the Master of Ernescleugh."

"I don't envy your task as *chaperon*," said Sir John, laughing; "you will be in dread of every young fellow in the county! But suppose that the girl may have been foolish enough to fall in love with some enterprising subaltern on the overland route home—we hear of such results every day—some fellow in whose pleasant society she has been cast by sea and land for a month or more? She may come here engaged ; married, perhaps !"

The bare suggestion of such a catastrophe filled Lady Wedderburn with unutterable dismay ; all the more easily, perhaps, that the same fear had occurred to herself.

The three days glided away. By the evening train Miss Gwendoleyne Wedderburn was expected to arrive from London; and Cyril, who had not seen Mary Lennox for four consecutive days, resolved to take advantage of the incidental bustle at home to ride over to Lonewoodlee for an hour after dinner; but just as Gervase Asloane was removing the cloth, and placing the decanters before Sir John, Lady Wedderburn said—

"You are aware, Cyril, that your cousin will be at the railway station in two hours from this time ?"

"Yes. Does she travel alone ?" asked Cyril, with provoking indifference of manner.

"Alone. No. Could you imagine that she would do so ?"

"How then—with whom ? Has old Chutnay come all the way from Madras with her ?"

"She travels with her maid. You will, of course, go over with the carriage to meet her, as your father has complained of a twinge or two of gout."

"Can't Horace or Robert go ?" asked the Captain, bluntly, as he filled his glass with golden-coloured Château d'Yquem from a white crystal bottle.

"If Sir John cannot go, *you* should and must, as his representative."

"Why must the whole house be under arms because a little Indo-Briton is coming home ?"

"Cyril !" she exclaimed, lifting up her plump white hands.

"Besides, mamma, dear," said he, with something of his coaxing manner when a boy, "the fact is I have a particular engagement."

"With whom ?"

The Captain coloured slightly, gave his moustache a twirl, and said—

"Oh, what does it signify? To look at a horse I wish to take back with me to the regiment."

"Not a bay hunter, I hope," said his brother Robert.

"I have had enough of bay hunters," replied Cyril, with a short laugh ; and then he added, "Horace, my man, as your superior officer, I order you to go upon this tour of duty."

"With pleasure," replied Horace ; but Lady Wedderburn struck in—

"If Cyril is not courteous enough to go for his cousin, let Robert appear alone. Why trouble poor Horace?"

"Why not, mamma? What trouble can it be to look after a pretty girl? Let Horace go, by all means."

"But he is not her cousin!"

"What does that matter, Kate? Let him go also," said Sir John, while a droll but furtive smile was exchanged by Cyril and Horace Ramornie ; the carriage will surely hold three. I've known it come from a ball with six. Her maid may sit in the rumble with the servant— an arrangement which perhaps may be agreeable to them both. Asloane, order the carriage to be here punctually at seven."

Determined to have his own way, and no longer grieve Mary by his protracted absence, Cyril left the dinner table early, while Lady Wedderburn had serious misgivings about him ; and punctually at the hour ordered, the handsome family carriage, with its two bright coloured bays, with plated harness ; its two resplendent lamps, and a pair of spotted Dalmatian dogs in attendance, departed with Robert and Horace Ramornie for the railway station, from whence, in less than an hour, it returned with the heiress and her half-caste Indian maid, a tawny woman, whose dress, as yet, was a strange but ample scarlet garment, enveloping her whole person ; and the tall footmen were immediately in requisition to carry in her bullock trunks, portmanteau, and a huge "overland," covered with black canvas and bound with iron.

More than ever provoked and piqued by the unaccountable absence of Cyril at this interesting juncture, Lady Wedderburn —though after her late terror she felt she must forgive him everything—started forward with all eagerness as the drawing-room door was thrown open by Asloane, and a wonderfully handsome, and evidently highly-bred young girl, attired in a fashionably accurate suit of deep mourning, and all in the most exquisite taste, was led in by Horace and Robert, who saw—as the latter afterwards said—his mother's "company smile" brighten into one of genuine affection and sympathy, as she embraced and kissed on both cheeks the young heiress, of whom she was now to be the custodian and chaperon.

"Welcome to Willowdean, my dear, dear girl," said Sir John,

taking both her hands in his, and saluting her with great tenderness. "I am your old uncle Wedderburn ; yet not perhaps so *very* old, after all," he added, with a smile, while she looked wistfully and earnestly in his face, as if seeking to trace there a likeness to her dead father ; but though striving hard to do so, she failed, yet thought in her heart—

"I shall always love him, because he is my papa's only brother. And, dear Aunt Wedderburn, these are my cousins ?"

"One is your cousin Robert. Cyril you shall see ere long, Gwenny."

" Doctor Chutnay, of Madras, who was so kind to poor papa and me, has seen my cousin Cyril at Chatham Barracks, and says he is *so* handsome !"

"He is, indeed, Gwenny !" said Lady Wedderburn, greatly delighted by this remark ; " but now, dearest girl, you must be weary with your long journey, though you would stop at York and Berwick, of course. Permit me to see you to your room, or Miss M'Caw will do so, and take off some of your things, if your maid is too weary."

And with a bow of acquiescence, and a bright pleasant smile, the young lady, who had evidently made a most favourable impression on all, retired to her own apartments ; while Lady Wedderburn turned to Sir John, and said—

"A delightful girl—so charming and winning ! How provoked I am by Cyril's protracted absence—about a horse, too. Who goes to buy horses at night ?"

CHAPTER XVIII.

FIRST IMPRESSIONS.

FORTUNATELY for his mother's peace of mind, Cyril arrived even before his cousin descended from her rooms, where her own maid, Zillah, and Lady Wedderburn's abigail, had begun to unpack the huge overland and portmanteaus, which were filled with Indian marvels in the form of Delhi needlework and Champac jewellery of miraculous fabric ; Dacca muslins, ivory fans and puzzle-balls ; inlaid boxes of ivory and silver from Bombay, for essences and perfumes ; and now, with memory of the sad and tender kiss of Mary Lennox lingering on his cheek—a kiss all the sadder and perhaps foreboding, as she *had* heard of the arrival of this terrible Indian heiress—he had to welcome and salute his cousin, to whom he tendered many "apologies for an absence that was so perfectly unavoidable ;" and then came coffee, with a little repast for the fair traveller, who, though conscious that she was an object of undisguised interest, and as such, undergoing inspection, never betrayed the slightest confusion ; for the mode of life in India, and the nearly total want of privacy peculiar to it, together with the number of persons, faces, places, and scenes she had met on the long route overland, rendered her perfectly self-possessed, without, however, the least over-confidence.

Gwendoleyne Wedderburn was more than a pretty girl. Though colourless—even pale—she was in fact remarkably beautiful, with a vast quantity of fine dark hair, and very dark hazel eyes, with long black lashes, which she inherited from her Welsh mother, "Gwendoleyne Ap-Rhys of Llanchillwydd," as Lady Wedderburn frequently reminded her. Her hands and feet were beautifully formed ; she carried her head perhaps a little too haughtily ; but she was conscious of her own appearance, and had been petted and treated with extreme deference in the sunny land she had come from. Her mouth was very perfectly curved, and when in repose and not smiling—which was seldom—the upper lip resembled a little Cupid's bow, while the under was like a tiny cherry.

She formed, Cyril thought (and he was no bad judge), a perfect picture, as she sat a little apart from all at a small tripod table, with a little hastily-prepared dinner before her, served on Dresden china. Her figure, slight and graceful, clad in a crape dress, the blackness of which contrasted so powerfully with the dazzling whiteness of her shoulders as they gleamed in the light of the gaselier which fell in a flood about her. Her dress was cut low about the neck and bust—Lady Wedderburn thought a little *too* low, especially when her black lace shawl fell off. A necklet of jet beads encircled her delicate and slender throat, and save it and one magnificent ring of pearls and diamonds, other ornament she had none but her beautiful hair, which was dressed to perfection.

" Heavens ! if that should be an engagement ring !" thought Lady Wedderburn, as she glanced nervously at the girl's hand.

Her face was expressive of innocence and sweetness, just suggestive a little of pride ; and every moment she became more and more radiant as she became more familiar with those about her, and jested and chatted with her " three newly-found cousins," as she called them. Her manner and voice were sweet, and the girl was full of pretty ways ; thus every action of her head or hands was graceful.

" Suppose all these three young fellows fall in love with her, my Lady Wedderburn will be in a nice dilemma then ! And what is more likely to happen in a country house, where people have so little to do, and are so much thrown together?" thought Sir John Wedderburn, who was regarding her with a fond and

7

fatherly smile, and seeking to trace out some memory of his
brother, the Willie of other days—the days of rambling, riding,
and bird-nesting in Renton Woods and Willowdean—but save
a phrase or two which escaped her, he found none for a time.

Lady Wedderburn claimed nearly all the good points of
Gwendoleyne, as inherited from the Wedderburns ; but Sir
John saw that the girl was more like what her beautiful Welsh
mother had been when first she came to Willowdean on her
happy bridal tour, ere she went to India, the land of splendid
exile ; and Cyril, while he hung over her chair, while he conversed with her and looked into the bright depths of her dark
and liquid eyes, was thinking how different was the lot of this
wealthy and beautiful cousin as contrasted with that of the
lonely girl he had lately quitted, and who at that moment was
probably hanging about her father's sick bed ; and he felt that
his genuine and growing admiration of Gwendoleyne's beauty
was a species of treason to Mary Lennox.

Will he always think so ? We shall see.

Though the death of her father was a recent event comparatively, Gwenny was neither sad nor sorrowful now, save when
she spoke of him, and then would her voice become tremulous
and her eyes suffuse with tears, for she was soft and, by nature,
impressionable.

Since leaving Madras, she had been nearly six weeks on the
route home, in a splendid Peninsular and Oriental liner,
crowded with gay cabin passengers, officers of the Queen's and
East Indian armies, Civil Service men, &c.—happy fellows, all
coming home on leave or to retire altogether, as the case might be.

She had seen many marvels that were even glories to her
Indian eyes, since she had watched with tears, from the lofty
poop of the *Rajah*, the low, flat, sandy shore of Madras, so long
her home, with the Castle of St. George and all the white
minarets and gilded pagodas sinking into the blue sea, as the
vessel steamed out of the roads. She had seen Aden, with its
splintered rocks and arid shore of sand and ashes, where,
according to Mohammedan fable, once the rose-garden of Irem
bloomed ; and she had seen the sun's rays shining like the
Scriptural column of fire through the Gate of Tears, as she
sailed past Perim into the Red Sea. Then she spoke of Suez,
with its mosques and bazaars, and the exciting journey through
the desert ; and she clasped her pretty hands at the memory of
some of the scenes she had witnessed there : its occasional
horrors—camels, even men, lying dead, partly decayed or wholly
skeletons, and half buried in the shifting sand, with the black
vultures hovering over or perching on them, and for a background to the whole, the Pyramids rising in the distance, like
purple cones against a sky of fire and amber. And then there

was the awful thirst endured there—a thirst that rendered bitter beer, potass, and sherry, veritable nectar, however homely they may be deemed elsewhere.

Then came the Mediterranean, where she had encountered one of those sudden storms peculiar to that sea, when its waves changed from dark blue to pale green, and from thence to purple and silver, while the rain descended as if the windows of Heaven had been opened again. But old Gibraltar, its rock and town, its terraces and batteries, had filled her with delight, and so did everything else.

By that time, most of her *compagnons du voyage* were married ladies, old officers, or invalids—a statement which soothed some of Lady Wedderburn's fears—and so, chatting merrily, she told of all she had seen ; and, in the energy of her manner, and full of her narrative, which, somehow, she addressed chiefly to Horace Ramornie—but then he too had recently come home by the P. and O. route—when she laid, quite involuntarily, her soft ungloved hand, with its white modelled fingers, on his arm, the young man felt a thrill run through him, though he was not "a cousin"—a circumstance on which their mutual Aunt Wedderburn placed so much weight.

Did this new friend, this lovely girl, possess some magnetic power, or what was it? for Horace felt himself grow giddy with delight whenever she touched him.

She heard Cyril's thrilling story of his late terrible adventure, which was so keenly fresh in his mind and in the minds of all the household, but while she listened, it seemed to Lady Wedderburn, who was nervously observant, that her eyes, " whose lids seemed to be fringed with feathers from a bird's wing rather than with ordinary lashes, so thick and soft lay their shadows on her cheek," from time to time sought, not those of Cyril, but of Horace Ramornie.

Gwenny was soon found to be generous to a fault, and, by the suitable presents she lavished on all sides, she made friends with all. Her poor papa's magnificent hookah, with its snaky coil of silk and gold, and its pure amber mouthpiece, she had brought carefully home, with many other mementos, for her uncle Wedderburn. To Lady Wedderburn she gave a beautiful diamond ring, and made poor little Miss Flora M'Caw radiantly happy by a set of gold Champac ornaments, necklace, rings, and bracelets, that the Begum Sumroo, or even the terrible Queen of Delhi, might have worn with credit.

Three days saw her perfectly domesticated and at home in her new abode ; but many things there excited her surprise.

"How few servants you have, dear Auntie !" said she one day, "only the Kitmutgar Asloane—such a droll name he has ! —a few bheesties, syces, and ayahs, a butler, coachman, two

valets, and a few women.   How on earth do you contrive to do
with so few ?   We had nearly fifty at our house in the Choultry, besides six punkawallahs."

"Fifty ! where did you find beds for them all, Gwenny ?"

"Oh, they slept on mats, everywhere or anywhere—on the
stairs, in the corridors, on the roof, or in the verandahs, when
the rainy season was over."

"Such arrangements would scarcely suit Willowdean," said
her aunt, laughing.

The fireplaces, the carpeted floors, the total absence of a great
dark punkah swaying noiselessly overhead, all filled her with
a wonder that was almost childish.   Horace and Cyril could
both speak with her of India, having served there ; the former
two years, and the latter five.   Poor Bob knew nothing about
it, so, as he was rather ignored, he fumed a little in secret, and
thought to himself, "when those fellows' leave of absence is up,
I shall have it all my own way—patience till then."

All the ideas of the young heiress were odd for a time, being
of course those of an Indo-Briton.   The Indian summer had
just ended when she left Madras, and the Scottish spring had
just begun when she arrived at Willowdean, hence the verdure
was not so great as she might have found it in Devonshire.   The
fruit and flowers in the conservatory seemed all strange, puerile,
and meagre to her eyes.   Luxury and splendour there appeared
but little.   There was no state kept, she thought, at Willowdean ; no horde of half-nude native servants, obsequious to
slavery ; no camels, with gorgeous housings ; no elephants,
bearing gilded howdahs with silken curtains ; no dhoolie or
palaquin bearers, singing gaily as they trotted along.   She woke
at unearthly hours in the morning, to the astonishment and
annoyance of the butler and housemaids, and wished to have a
drive, as if she were still at the Choultry of Madras ; and then,
the perpetual clouds, and more than all the occasional mist
from the German Sea—white, dense, and palpable—filled her
with wonder, accustomed as she had been to the pure and deep
blue sky of Hindostan.

She smiled, and even laughed with provoking playfulness,
when Lady Wedderburn, who was fond of "talking peerage,"
expatiated on the historical and somewhat shady traditionary
glories of the Welsh race of Ap-Rhys of Llanchillwydd ; on the
famous Dafydd-ap-Gwilym-ap-Rhys, who inherited all the
virtues of Howel Dha, whose daughter had been his great-great-
grandmother, and gave him the blood of the Pendragons.   All
this sounded odd to Gwenny—very odd—for her papa had been
a man of the world, a thorough man of business, who stuck to
his ledgers and counting-house, always looking forward, setting
little store upon the past, and nothing at all upon a dead

Gervase Asloane, the old housekeeper, and other domestics, she somewhat shocked by using the piano on Sunday, and by yawning, more than a young lady should, in church—the parochial barn—oh, good heavens! how unlike it was to the lofty, airy, and white chunam-coated cathedral of the Bishop of Madras! Then there was no organ, and to her ears, the psalm-singing sounded but as a torrent of dissonant strains.

Her conversation for a time naturally enough ran on memories of the brilliant land she had left—the Choultry of Madras, with all its stately palaces, the black and the white towns, and the catamarans tossing amid the white and foaming surge, which there boils for ever on the shore; of chowries and mosquito curtains; of punkawallahs and tattywetters; of bheesties and peons, and other persons and things incomprehensible to Lady Wedderburn, who, however, was greatly delighted that Cyril could talk with her on such mysterious matters, and understood what she meant. But then, unluckily, Horace Ramornie knew all about them too, and had been in garrison at Vellore; still Bob sulked, and when Sir John laughed, voted it all "a dreadful bore."

She was astonished to find that people slept in their beds, and not merely *on* them; that blankets and broadcloth were used even in summer; that the butter was neither poured out like cream nor thickened with dead flies. The state of the thermometer was a source of perpetual wonder to her, and she said to Horace—

⸱ "Is it as cool always at Willowdean as on the Blue Mountains of Madras in the wet season?"

But greater surprises were in store for her, when winter came with its frost and snow, its skaters and curlers on loch and river.

With all her kindness and goodness of heart, Lady Wedderburn, in pursuit of her secret wish, was singularly injudicious.

Gwenny had come among her relations, an orphan. Horace Ramornie, though now a soldier, a young lieutenant of the Line, could remember the time when he, too, came to Willowdean in the days of his early orphanage, and the lonely hours when he lay in his little bed at night, seeing, in fancy, his parents' faces amid the darkness, and longing, with all a childish longing and yearning, "for a touch of the vanished hand, and the sound of a voice that was still;" and these recollections made him very tender in his manner to Gwenny, though Horace had ever a gentle and a winning way with all women, old as well as young.

"Cousin Horace," said she, on one occasion, "and you have been an orphan like myself; how strange!"

"Horace is *not* your cousin, but Cyril is," said Lady Wedderburn, in a pointed manner, as she passed through the drawing-room into the conservatory.

Her words conveyed a volume, for Gwenny blushed scarlet, and the young man grew pale.

"I am not your cousin, Miss Wedderburn—would that I were," said he, with a low sigh.

"Why, what difference would it make?"

"For then I might—might claim something more than mere friendship."

"Not my cousin?" queried Gwenny, her dark eyes dilating as she spoke. "Oh, I know that you are not, though Lady Wedderburn is aunt to us both ; but why call me *Miss*—say Gwenny, as Cyril and Robert do."

"Gwenny then," said Horace, tremulously and softly, for the girl's wonderful beauty bewildered, while her frank and candid manner charmed and entranced him ; but he felt a secret consciousness that, before Lady Wedderburn, to call Gwenny by her abbreviated name would be rather injudicious.

While shrinking from the idea of rivalling his cousin Cyril, and earning thereby the anger of such benefactors as his uncle and aunt, Horace Ramornie was in love with all the deep strength of a young man's first and genuine passion. The girl, as we have said, was undoubtedly beautiful, and if love will *glorify* all it looks on, to his eyes the face and presence of Gwendoleyne became as something divine, and Horace was intoxicated by her !

Night after night he lay awake for hours, feeding his soul with the idea of Gwendoleyne ; longing for and yet nervously dreading his recall to the regiment, amid this strange and fresh emotion that had grown in his heart, and which was alike his torment and delight.

He would sigh deeply and bitterly, clasping his hands in the dark, as he thought of his cousin Cyril's greater chances of success, his superior position, his attainments, and many genuine good qualities ; and also of his aunt's too perceptible opposition ; and then he would wring them like a love-sick girl, for Horace was by nature shy, impressionable, and enthusiastic.

Another was wringing her hands at times in Lonewoodlee, and weeping the silent tears of sad and bitter misgiving !

CHAPTER XIX.

SCHEMES.

LADY ERNESCLEUGH, a large, showy, and fashionable-looking woman, had driven to Willowdean with her son Everard, the Master of Ernescleugh, who was a lieutenant in the Household Brigade, on hearing of the new arrival ; and though the future lord was so wealthy that money was no particular object to him, the beauty of Gwenny, and the piquancy that was in all she did and said, impressed him favourably ; and now a series of dinners, picnics, drives to various places of interest, and even a pleasure excursion in his yacht, were schemed out ; but, to some of the former, and more especially the latter, Lady Wedderburn was decidedly opposed ; and the too recent death of Sir John's only brother afforded her a good pretext for doing so, and keeping Gwenny at home, while Cyril's leave of absence lasted, at least.

Lady Ernescleugh urged her to take Gwenny to London, and have her presented at the very first drawing room next season ; adding, that if Lady Wedderburn cared not about going to town, she would herself be only too happy to act as *chaperon* to a girl so beautiful and so certain to make a sensation ; but the watchful mother had no desire that the wealthy heiress should be lost to her Cyril in the splendid whirlpool of London society, while he, perhaps, was fighting the Russians. Heaven alone knew where, for as yet the scene of the expected war was vague indeed.

Her whole aim was to " bring the young people together," and in this instance it was overdone. Cyril saw through her scheme, though Gwenny did not ; and he was both amused and bored by it, for the master-thought evinced itself in many trifling ways.

" Gwenny, my darling," said she, one evening, in the drawing-room, " I am sure your cousin longs to hear you sing and play. Don't you, Cyril ?"

" Of course," replied Cyril, who had been furtively looking at the French clock on the white marble mantelpiece, and thinking it was almost time he was drawing near the stile at Lonewoodlee. " Of course, if she will so far favour us," he added, hastening to open the piano, set up the music-frame, and adjust the stool ; devoutly hoping the while that the performance would be as short as possible.

" I play little, and sing less now," said Gwenny.

" Gwendoleyne !" exclaimed Lady Wedderburn, as she shook her lace lappets and diamond pendants.

" Besides, dearest Aunt, Horace Ramornie is a critic, and I dislike to play before critics."

" You played and sang to *him* yesterday," said Robert Wedderburn, before Horace, who was about to deprecate being deemed a critic, could speak.

" True ; but he pressed me so," said Gwenny, with the faintest blush.

" Come, Horace, and press her again," urged Cyril, with a nonchalant laugh.

" Will you, then, favour me—us, I mean," whispered Horace, leading her to the piano, while his cheek reddened.

She seated herself at the instrument, spreading all her crape flounces over the stool, and began at once the prelude to some little air she had picked up abroad. Her voice was sweet and tender ; but neither the words of the song nor her execution were brilliant ; and Cyril, while he listened, admiring the while her ivory neck and pretty hands, was thinking of another whose fine voice, a glorious soprano, could thrill his heart to the core.

Lady Wedderburn often found her eldest son and his cousin in the conservatory—in the library, and even in the billiard-room ; and always left them discreetly, little thinking that Gwenny was in the first instance merely expatiating on the superior flora of Madras and the Carnatic ; in the second, perhaps selecting a book or so by Cyril's suggestion ; and in the third, that he, so far from talking of love when looking into the soft dark eyes of Gwendoleyne, was discussing most learnedly, cue in hand, on the screw and side-twist ; of losing and winning hazards ; of what a famous stroke Probyn of ours was ; of winning no end of scores off the red ball running ; of pool and pyramid ; all of which were as Sanscrit and Oordoo to the fair listener.

Busy with his steward or ground bailie, riding about one day or rambling the next, with weeder in hand, his sturdy legs cased in brown leather gaiters, and his wide-awake garnished with hooks and flies, Sir John spent most of his time out of doors, looking after his estate, seeing where trees were to be cut down or others planted, water-courses to be changed, or little bridges to be built ; and only once did he speak to Cyril of Gwenny, and even then at Lady Wedderburn's suggestion.

" If you mean to propose for your cousin, Cyril, you have my free consent. Do so, and do it at once. You know our maxim in hunting——"

" Never crane if you mean to take a leap ?"

" Exactly. And now I am off to see how the tile-draining gets on."

" Is she not handsome, Cyril ?" said Lady Wedderburn on one occasion, passing her arm through that of her son, as he stood, abstractedly, looking from the library window on the gravelled terrace, where Gwenny and Horace were feeding the peacocks with crumbs of biscuits.

" Of course she is handsome," replied Cyril, twirling his moustache ; " but——" and he paused.

" But what ?"

" One sees so many handsome girls in every garrison town. At such places as Canterbury they are thick as blackberries,"

"But few garrison hacks have three hundred thousand pounds."

"Few indeed," replied her gay captain, laughing. "And as for loving them, fellows only go in for that, mother dear, till the *route* comes. It is a very limited liability after all ; and then we leave them little pink notes—perhaps a lock of hair ; or simply send our servants with our august bits of pasteboard, scribbled P. P. C., for Dublin or Delhi, Brighton or Beloochistan, as the case may be ; the mess-plate is packed, the colours are cased, and away we go with the band playing, ' Good-bye, sweetheart, good-bye.' "

"Cyril, you will drive Gwenny to Coldingham to-morrow, and show her the ruins of the Priory."

"I don't think that a girl who has seen the vast rock-hewn temples of the Buddhists and the Pyramids of Egypt will care much about our old Priory. Besides she is to be driven there by Horace. *He* knows all about these old places more than I do ; and can tell her the whole story of how Edgar, King of Scotland, built it in the eleventh century, and gave it to the monks of Durham, and all that sort of thing."

"Horace ! It is always Horace," said his mother, with undisguised annoyance.

"Besides, 1 am engaged."

"How—where, and with whom ?" she asked, while the gloom deepened on her fair and open brow.

"Three questions, mother dear. You worry me ! How am I engaged ? By a previous arrangement. Where ? At Ernescleugh to dinner. With whom ? The Master. And now you have it all," said he, kissing her, as he used to do in boyhood.

Still she was dissatisfied, and taking his hand in hers, led him into her beautiful little boudoir—that toy chamber, with the blue satin and silver hangings, where she kept all Cyril's Indian presents to herself.

"Come," said she, as she closed the door, "I must speak with you seriously on the subject that is nearest my heart."

CHAPTER XX.

MY LADY EXPOSTULATES.

CYRIL's love for Mary Lennox was great ; all the greater that his heart was an honest one, and that so much of compassion was blended with his love. He knew that when he left her for the East she would be alone—most terribly alone—if her father died ; for with his life her means would pass away. So Cyril had been thinking seriously of a secret marriage, and thus

making for her such a provision or position as would compel
his family to support her honourably, if he fell in action, or
died of those diseases which follow an army into the field.

But he felt, on consideration, that proposing or effecting such
a measure would perhaps be an act of injustice both to Mary
and his family, placing her, perhaps, in a false position with
them in particular and the world in general.

Too well he knew that to announce openly his engagement,
or a resolution, to marry the poor and penniless Mary Lennox,
the daughter of a bankrupt and spendthrift, would excite the
greatest opposition—perhaps a quarrel with his father and
mother, whom he justly loved and respected.

On the strength of his opposition, Sir John might take very
high ground and cut off his allowance; without it could he
rejoin the regiment? and if he failed to do so, on the eve of a
war, where would his honour be as a soldier and a man? He
felt sure that even his brother Robert would open his eyes very
wide with wonder at such a matrimonial scheme; for he had
studied law long enough to have imbibed something of the
caution peculiar to the legal tribe.

Cyril's monetary difficulties were not trivial. He had come
on leave from an expensive regiment to retrench a little, and
within a few days he had lost the bay hunter, just after paying
Ernescleugh for him; and with what he had lost at cards with
Chesters, this made over a thousand pounds. Then he had some
gambling and other debts at headquarters; but no I O U's
were permitted to circulate in the Royal Fusileers, by a mess
regulation of that corps, where the word of a brother officer was
always deemed sufficient.

He felt worried on every hand, and once or twice his evil
angel whispered that, were Mary Lennox less winning, less
sweet, and more than all, less helpless, he might listen to his
mother's suggestions; but no sooner was the evil idea insinuated,
than the honest fellow crushed it in his heart. He could never
be false to his tender, true, and secret love!

With his mind thus agitated by conflicting thoughts, it may
be imagined with what patience he listened to his mother, who
still retained his hand confidingly and caressingly in hers, as
she seated herself by his side on a blue satin *fauteuil*, and
begun thus sententiously—

"The whole of this beautiful estate of Willowdean, when it
comes to you, as in the course of events it will, burdened as it
is by sundry old debts, and the allowances to your brother and
Horace Ramornie, will not yield——"

"And to you, mother dear."

"Don't talk of me; I have no wish to survive my dear
husband. Will not yield, I was about to say, enough for one

of your expensive tastes and habits ; therefore, a wealthy marriage is necessary."

"You flatter me ; but I love to be independent."

"And like many independent men, may end by making a fool of yourself," she added, with more bluntness of manner than was usual with her. "Pardon me, Cyril, but perhaps you have done so already.

"How ?"

"By forming some unsuitable, if not unworthy, attachment."

Cyril's handsome face flushed and grew pale under her scrutiny.

"Mother dear," said he, gently, "you never spoke to me in this strange tone before. Oh, why adopt it now ? I know what you mean and wish ; but do not ask me now, at least."

"Then if you will not be so attentive to your cousin as I wish, promise me one thing, Cyril."

"Twenty, if you choose, mother."

"That you form no hasty attachment elsewhere, and enter into no engagement without consulting me ?"

Again he coloured perceptibly, for he felt that the keen eyes of his mother were watching him, while the earnest grasp of her soft white hand tightened upon his ; but he replied, evasively, and with a laugh—

"I shall engage the Russians only. There, will that suffice you ? I beg your pardon, dearest mother," he urged, "but do let us cease this most unpleasant subject : and now I'll have a quiet weed in the conservatory."

But Lady Wedderburn was not yet done with him, and said, with growing excitement—

"Am I to conclude that you are a bad, or unnatural son, Cyril, who would repay my love and anxiety with banter ?"

"Because I won't propose to a woman—a girl I don't care for, and who does not care for me ? By Jove ! it is too absurd."

"Your interjections are not choice. If Gwendoleyne is beautiful in her eighteenth year, what will she be some time hence, in the full development of womanhood ?"

"Adorably lovely, I know ; yet I am in no mood to marry."

"No mood to marry her, perhaps," said Lady Wedderburn, with a sudden flash in her eyes. "Think of her wealth."

"I am ashamed to say that I have thought of it," said Cyril, with a sigh ; "all the more that I am pretty close run for money, both here and at headquarters ; but for Heaven's sake, don't let us have a row about Gwenny."

"A 'row !' How can you talk in this slangy mode to me ? How dare you, Cyril ?" she added, rising. "I thought that you rather boasted of your good taste over such men as Chesters of Chesterhaugh."

"'Pon my soul, you go beyond old Colonel Bahawder, of the depôt battalion!   But, my lady mother," said he, kissing her hand with playful respect, and caressing the braids of her black hair, which was now becoming seamed with white, "like some of the well-fed perch in yonder pond, I am content to coquette with the sweets and crumbs that come my way, even as Gwenny is now throwing them in ; but as for matrimony, that I leave to a sober-sided fellow like Robert, or a melancholy-eyed Romeo like Horace : and now that I think of it, she changes colour so visibly when Horace speaks to her, that I begin to suspect——"

"That he is in love with her?"

"No."

"What then ?"

"By Jove! that she is in love with *him*," replied Cyril, quietly selecting a cigar from a handsome case (embroidered for him by some confiding garrison beauty), and preparing it for smoking by carefully biting off the end, and heedless that his mother's eyes were sparkling with resentment.

"Are you aware that what I urge is also your father's wish?" she asked.

"Likely enough," replied Cyril, with growing annoyance. "There are Baronets as well as Knights of the Golden Calf, and both are more numerous than the Knights of the Golden Fleece."

"Go on, sir, go on ; though I never before heard you sneer at your good papa."

"How you pervert my words!   I do not sneer ; but in all this matter has poor Gwenny no right to be consulted ?"

"Not much ; she is so young, she is our ward, whom we are to see properly bestowed in marriage ; and where could she be given more properly than to one whom we have known from his boyhood ?"

"And a little earlier," said Cyril, laughing outright.

"You may—nay, you *must* win her, if you will only try, Cyril."

"But I don't want her.   By Jove! think of a fellow going in for matrimony and the corps having got its letters of readiness. I might be telegraphed away from the very altar—have to make a halt of it, a half-married man.   There would be a little melodrama for you !   The whole thing is absurd, mother."

"Well, when you return ?"

"Who can count on returning?   There are such things as shot and shell, shipwreck, camp-fever, frost and starvation, and so forth," was the gloomy response.   "I may be taken prisoner by the Russians, and never heard of again."

"Do not talk so, Cyril, I implore you.   Marry Gwenny and get on the staff.   If you will still soldier, let it be at home."

"If I do may I be—cashiered, that is all!"

Usually, Lady Wedderburn's manner had all the perfect serenity and unruffled calmness peculiar to good and gentle breeding, but now her brow, wont to be so smooth, became clouded over ; wrinkles actually appeared where none had been visible before ; her fine mouth became compressed, and an expression, almost of baleful spite, stole into her clear, dark grey eyes, as she drew herself up to her full height, and said, with half-averted face—

"I know to whom I am indebted for this steady opposition to my wishes."

"To whom, mother ?"

"That artful girl at Lonewoodlee. Ah ! servants will talk, and local gossips too !" and with a scornful sweep of her skirts, she glided from the boudoir, even as she did so repenting that she should leave in wrath the Absalom she had so nearly lost by a terrible fate !

"So, so, it's out at last ! Local gossips have been busy with Mary's name—curse them !" muttered Cyril. "Mamma has opened the trenches with a vengeance ! Well, I am not a boy, though she seems disposed to treat me as such. What is to be done now ? See my poor Mary about it, at all hazards."

As he glanced round his mother's luxurious boudoir, with its blue satin and silver hangings, its Aubusson carpet of pale green, studded with beautiful bouquets, its marble busts and alabaster vases, and tiny tables glittering with a crowd of handsome and elegant trifles, and thought of Mary's gloomy home, his heart felt sick and sore ; he sighed deeply, and entering the lofty and stately conservatory, lit his cigar, and threw himself on a sofa, to think over his plans for the future.

CHAPTER XXI.

THE TRYST.

AT the close of a recent chapter, it is mentioned that Mary Lennox had been shedding silent tears, and had not been without secret misgivings or forebodings of coming sorrow.

Situated as she was with regard to Cyril, it was scarcely possible that she should feel otherwise than restless when the absence of her lover, and the circumstance of his having unavoidably broken some appointments with her, were coupled with the hints of Chesters, and the stories told her by her two gossiping old domestics, of the wealth and undoubted beauty of the new resident at Willowdean.

Without absolutely cutting her—for that was a solecism in good breeding of which she would be loth to be guilty—Lady Wedderburn had too plainly held aloof from Mary Lennox in the few public places where they met ; and Mary had tolerated much of that "tabooing," but with a bursting heart, for she could not forget that the haughty offender was the mother of Cyril ; though how little could that scheming matron then know what Cyril was to Mary—what they were to each other !

Though Mary mourned in her loneliness when he was absent with his regiment, and moving then, as she knew, in a gay and fashionable circle, his letters were a constant solace to her ; and now that he was at home, though she trusted him—or strove to do so—to see him riding, driving, talking, and laughing with his cousin and other ladies, while he could only accord her a furtive smile or a polite bow, fretted, galled, and humiliated her ; for she could not forget much of her father's teaching, or that she was a lady whose forefathers had a name among the Scottish Border Barons long before the Wedderburns had an acre of land in the Merse.

She began to recall, perhaps too much, the artful insinuations of Chesters, and to brood over them till they sank deep into her heart. She began also to repine and fear a little when she heard of all those things—of such gaieties at Willowdean as the season of conventional mourning permitted ; and when she knew that he was constantly thrown in the society of this perilous beauty—when he was away for days with her and other ladies at race meetings and other places ; and now, through Doctor Squills and the Minister's wife, almost her only other visitors, came a rumour that he and she were to have quite a little cruise in the Master of Ernescleugh's yacht, to the Isle of May, to Coquetmouth, to Lindisfarne Abbey, and other places. So when she thought of all the advantages of propinquity, and remembered all she had heard and read of the pleasant intercourse that cousinship permitted, and how much more a recently known cousin might be likely to impress him than one long known from infancy like a sister, her poor little heart trembled within her !

One day, however, she was made happy by Lady Wedderburn bowing to her pleasantly, and even stopping the carriage to ask for Mr. Lennox, but that was in the fulness of her heart after the restoration of her son.

"So your mamma is coming round to me by degrees, at least, Cyril," said Mary, with a hopeful smile.

But Cyril knew too well what his mother's secret aspirations were, and answered only with a sigh.

Three days after this, gossips had been at work, and when Lady Wedderburn saw her in the little street of Willowdean she looked straight at the ears of her horses as the handsome carriage bowled away on the Ernescleugh road, without according a glance of recognition to Mary, who felt crushed and hurt

keenly, all the more so that she saw the dark eyes of Gwendoleyne remarking her with an expression of interest; and Mary
could judge for herself how great was the girl's beauty.

Mary knew that it was tradition in her family that two ladies
of it, both sisters, had died as nuns among the Cistertians at
Lennel, and somehow, now she often thought of those two
women, their reasons for becoming recluses, and wondered if
they had found within their cells the peace she feared she
would not find in the world. Then she smiled a bitter smile,
as she thought that nothing lasted for ever; that all things
passed away; that even Lennel was a shattered ruin, and its
cemetery, where the sisters lay, had been swept away by the
Tweed into the sea.

All unaware of the gloomy misgivings of her he loved, in
the evening after the long and unpleasant conversation with
his mother, Cyril, after riding from one of the gates of Willowdean as if going towards Greenlaw, the county town, turned
off abruptly by a narrow byeway, and took that for Lonewoodlee, for he was to meet Mary at the stile, which quite as often
as the coppice formed their place of tryst,

He was full of perplexing thoughts, and permitting the
reins to drop on his horse's neck, let the animal proceed at a
slow walk along the path which led only towards the residence
of Mr. Lennox.

He felt that some explanation, some more open and more
decided arrangement, were imperatively due to a girl of Mary's
position and character; but, as already stated, he dreaded the
opposition of his whole family; he dreaded the debts he had
contracted in his folly, and to marry on his pay—if his father in
his indignation reduced him to that—a pittance which barely
paid for his messing, glazed boots and cigars—would be the act
of a madman, even if Mary would consent to it; but then he
knew that Mary, even were she as rich as his cousin Gwendoleyne, would not do so at present, as she was chained by filial
love and duty to her father's sick-bed.

Well, that necessity freed him from one item of responsibility
in the awkward position of their affairs.

Cyril drew from his portemonnaie a ring; it was a plain
hoop, and so like a wedding one that it might have passed as
such, but for a single diamond of great value that was set
therein, and this altered its character. It was a tiny ring too,
and he trusted it would fit the dear finger for which he intended
it. With a fond smile he replaced it in his purse, and dismounting at the stile, threw the bridle of his horse over his
arm, and looked around him.

The stile was old and well worn by the footsteps of many a
wayfarer. It was simply formed by three great stones project-

ing from an ancient wall, and stood in a sequestered place, secret and lonesome, where the pink and white hawthorn usually bloomed and scented the air ere the end of May ; where the pendant cups of the bright foxglove and the blue-bell mingled with the brown autumn fern, among which the hare and rabbit lurked, and where hardy little thistles grew in every cleft, while over all towered the triple arms of a gigantic thorn of vast age, whereon many a Scottish outlaw and English moss-trooper had been hung "in his boots," as the phrase went, in the foraying times of old ; for the whole Borderland is full of such dark memories.

Around the pastoral hills stood up grim and silent against the red sunset sky. As Cyril looked on all these objects, so long familiar to his eyes, he pondered on what other scenery they might be resting ere long, and where that day month might find him ; too probably far away at sea, on board a transport crowded with troops, longing to be ashore and in front of the enemy.

And Mary too had often surveyed their meeting-place with wistful eyes and boding heart, thinking how lonely it would be when he should come no more, and how terribly desolate it seemed when he was supposed to be lost to her and all the world ; and how often had she shuddered at the story of the midnight race, the plunge, and the narrow escape—the rescue of her Cyril from a terrible death !

His mother's taunt was yet tingling in his ears ; and now, lest watchful eyes might be upon them, he almost dreaded to meet Mary at the accustomed stile or in the coppice ; for had not Chesters basely condescended to spy upon their meeting there ?

"Ah !" thought Cyril, "had I but known of such a circumstance on that terrible night, instead of sharing his sham hospitality, my hunting-whip and Rooke Chesters' shoulders had made an intimate and not to be forgotten acquaintance."

Cyril had but a minute or two to wait, when the slight figure of Mary, so lithe, graceful, and so compact, from her little round hat and feather to her brass-heeled Balmorals, came tripping down the pathway between two fields, and ascended the stile, from whence his ready hand now helped her down.

"Cyril, dearest Cyril, I have kept you waiting," said she, looking upward with a strange and earnest expression in her violet-blue eyes. Secure as she had been of his love, and familiar with it, there had always been a charming shyness in Mary's manner when with Cyril ; now it was sad and gloomy, though visibly she sought to conceal it, affecting to smile, and with her tightly-gloved hand to twirl, nervously, her parasol upon her shoulder.

"And what of your papa to-day ?" he asked.

" Kind Cyril, you always ask for him, my only and unfailing friend ; papa is sleeping : he always takes an after-dinner nap ; but when I watch him thus there always comes over me a horrible, an awful thought, Cyril !"

" What—which ?"

" If he were dead—DEAD—my dear papa, instead of only sleeping, what should I do then ?"

" Rely on me, darling," he whispered, and drew her close to him, and now he observed that Mary had her veil tied tightly over her face, to conceal her tears, perhaps.

" I can't kiss you through *that* thing, dearest," he urged, while endeavouring to remove it.

" Better not kiss me at all. Oh, would that you had never done so, Cyril !"

His fine dark blue eyes possessed usually a wonderful, a magnetic power of fascination in them ; but on this occasion they failed to reassure Mary, who, despite all her efforts at self-control, began to weep, and Cyril, with his natural abhorrence of a scene, felt more of worry than wonder.

" What *is* the matter ? Speak, darling Mary," he urged, tenderly ; for he could see that she looked wan, and a dark tinge that lay under each of her eyes, was visible through the purity of her skin.

" Oh, forgive me, Cyril, forgive me !"

" For what !" he asked, with growing wonder.

" For having doubted your affection ; but doubts did begin to steal into my head. I began to fear there was a change somewhere, and I have been praying humbly to God that you might not love me less now than before."

" Love you less ! I do not comprehend !"

" Yes, yes," sobbed Mary, nestling her sad little face on the breast of his black velvet shooting coat ; "for Chesters hinted to me——"

" What dared he to hint ?" exclaimed Cyril, striking his spurred heel into the gravel.

" Oh, pardon me, Cyril. I know not what I am saying. I have slept so little for two or three nights past. I never do sleep when I have not seen you, and Cyril, you seem always so gay and happy with her—I mean—those people with whom I see you at times."

" Gay, Mary ? Yes. I have to smile, like the Spartan boy, who had the fox under his mantle—the fox whose teeth devoured his vitals," replied Cyril, making rather a far-fetched simile. " One is not always happy when smiling. I think ever of you, when absent, of our coming separation, and the difficulties of our mutual position."

There was a pause, during which he looked tenderly and

8

lovingly into the violet eyes of Mary, and thought how dove-like, sad, and sweet, they were in expression.

Then he began to perceive her ruling thought by her leading question.

"Your new cousin seems to be a most attractive girl. Is she not so?"

"Very. Her eyes are gloriously beautiful, Mary."

"Oh, indeed," said Mary, while her nether lip quivered, her eyes drooped, and a pallor almost ghastly stole over her soft face.

"Yes, just like yours, except that the lids are not so finely formed, nor the lashes, though thick, so long."

"Am I to compare with her?" she asked, a little assured.

"Yes," said Cyril, smiling back at the wistful smile.

"Indeed!"

"Yes; but you would gain immensely by the comparison. But come, my dearest, there must be no pouting. no doubt of me, no jealousy of poor Gwenny. You know how dearly I love, and have ever loved you—ay, almost since you were a mere girl, when I came home from India, and brought your dead brother's sword and rings to Lonewoodlee; but listen to me now, I have much to say, and may not have so good an oppor-tunity again."

His left arm was round her waist: their right hands were clasped together, and as Mary's head drooped on his shoulder, her words became sighs or only half-articulated tenderness. She looked helpless and beautiful, soft and ladylike; and once more, in the tumult of his heart, Cyril, with broken accents, urged a private marriage, for her further security, in case the worst should happen to him; but Mary was firm, and with tears and paleness—not blushes—spoke of her father's health, and how she would not and could not, with honour to herself, marry even Cyril (whom she loved as her own soul) in a fashion such as he proposed, as it would insure the contempt of his family and the doubt of society; and this she reiterated again, firmly, sadly, earnestly, and with her eyes full of tears, till Cyril became convinced that the idea was impolitic, unwise, and not calculated to conduce to their future happiness.

He drew the glove from her left hand, and while placing the diamond ring upon her wedding finger—a slender little finger it was—he drew her still closer to his breast.

"Mary," he whispered, "my darling Mary, you are the secret wife of my heart. Never let this betrothal ring—the ring that binds you to me—leave your finger until I replace it by one that shall be consecrated!" and he kissed her on the eyes, and then the hand that bore the symbol which was indi-cative of affection long before the days of Juvenal.

"As your wife, Cyril, I shall ever deem myself; as your widow, should we never meet again!" said Mary, in a soft, low, agitated voice.

And with something of a prayer in his heart, Cyril lifted his hat, as he kissed her once more. After this they became more composed, even more happy, perhaps, for their hearts became filled with a divine trust in themselves and in the future.

"Yet what shall I do when you are far away from me, Cyril?" asked Mary. "Men love so differently from women. They have their avocations, occupations—their friends and amusements. The lonely woman can but brood and weep in silence: her heart thrust back upon herself as it were, for lack of the thousand little tendernesses and kindnesses that the man she loves can alone bestow."

"True, Mary; but do not repine thus, darling."

The twilight had deepened into the gloaming now, and even that was darkening fast; so leading his horse by the bridle, Cyril walked along the lonely hill-side path with Mary towards her home, and at last, with happy hearts, they parted at the end of the ancient thicket.

"Shall I see you to-morrow, Cyril?" she asked, as he mounted.

"It is impossible, Mary. I am engaged to dine at Ernescleugh, and that place lies in quite an opposite direction from this. Adieu, till next evening. Adieu, with a thousand kisses to you."

And he galloped away.

Mary's heart misgave her; he was to dine at Ernescleugh, with Everard Home. She had, with a reticence that was unwise and unlike her, shrank nervously from speaking to Cyril of her enforced detention at Chesterhaugh; but now she trembled lest the young Master of Ernescleugh had recognised her in the waggonette, and might speak of the strange circumstance of her being there with Chesters, and at such an hour.

The demon of doubt had been removed from her heart; but fear now took his place, and a time came when Mary repented bitterly of the reticence in question.

She was alternately happy and fearful—longing intently for her next meeting with Cyril, and resolved to tell him openly of the only secret that haunted her; and she was never weary of kissing and looking at the ring, the solemn link which bound her fate to that of Cyril Wedderburn.

And now, when she thought of the place where it had been placed upon her finger—the old triple thorn tree—there came back to memory a quaint legend connected with her family. It was a little ominous, so far as regarded the ring, and yet Mary laughed.

For local tradition avers that, in the days when Mary of

Lorraine was Regent of Scotland, Malcolm Lennox, younger brother of Oliver, who built the present Tower of Lonewoodlee, was a famous Border warrior, who caused an infinite deal of trouble and anxiety to the Governor of Berwick, the Captain of Norham, and other Wardens along the English Border.   Like his compatriot, Sir William of Deloraine—

> " A stark moss-trooping Scot was he
> As ere couched Border lance by knee.
> Blindfold he knew the paths to cross,
> By Solway sands and Tarra Moss.
> By wily turns and desperate bounds,
> He baffled Percy's best bloodhounds."

But one night he had got more wine than usual, when supping with the Laird of Thirlstane, and lost his way in Dogden Moss, where he must have perished, had not a beautiful young woman, who suddenly appeared, become his guide to firm land, and before daybreak he had betrothed himself to her, and placed on a finger of her left hand a golden ring.

Some nights after this, he was assailed by a multitude of wild cats, who seemed to have been holding a species of "sabbatt," or Walpurgis festival, at the triple thorn tree, and had to defend himself with a sword.   In the course of this strange *mêlée* he hewed the foreleg from one which had made itself particularly obnoxious in the assault ; and on the yelling grimalkins taking to flight, he found that his trenchant whinger had amputated, not the limb of a cat, but the fair and handsome arm of a young woman ; and on a finger of the hand he found his own ring, and knew thereby that he had betrothed himself to a witch !

He never recovered his horror of this adventure ; he became more reckless of life than ever, and perished some years after in the famous Raid of the Redswire, on the green ridge of the Carterfells, pierced by three English arrows.   This was the last conflict of any importance fought on the Borders prior to the union of the Crowns, and was chiefly remarkable from the circumstance that the Scots won the day by being well supplied with firearms, while the English had only the long-bow, with bill and spear.

CHAPTER XXII.

WHAT THE MORROW BROUGHT FORTH.

CYRIL found that a note had come from Lady Ernescleugh, inviting all at Willowdean to dine with her, *en famille*, to talk over their plans for the future season in London, when it came. "As for Edinburgh," she added, "with its eight assemblies, and a few club balls, all so mixed, it is not to be thought of in these railway times. What suited our grandmothers won't suit us, who have young folks to introduce in society."

So Cyril found that the carriage and pony-phaeton had been ordered, as all were going to the Cleugh, save poor little Miss M'Caw, whom Lady Ernescleugh had omitted, notwithstanding her long pedigree ; but then it was only a Highland one, as her ladyship thought, "and those people all boast of such, whether they are Peers of the realm or street-porters."

Ere long we shall have more startling events to describe than dinners, drives, or luncheons, and so shall only say that the "festive board" at Ernescleugh, a fine mansion facing the sea, and perched on a lofty eminence, was like any other in a wealthy and noble family.

Before the windows, stretched away in distance the vast extent of the dark blue German Sea, with here and there a white sail, or the long wreathed smoke of a steamer visible ; and just as the company sat down to dinner, they might have seen, had not the curtains been closely drawn, the light on the Isle of May, about five-and-twenty miles distant, at the mouth of the Firth of Forth, twinkling redly out upon the waste of waters.

Save the wines, everything on the table was Scotch : the fish were from the adjacent sea or the Leader ; the beef and mutton bred and fed on the Lammermuir hills ; the vegetables and flowers were reared by the gardener at Ernescleugh ; but all these figured in the bill of fare under French names, as *potages*, *poissons*, *relevés*, and *entrées*—a source of sore bewilderment to plain folks like the Rev. Gideon M'Guffog, parish minister ; Dr. Squills, the Lawyer, and the Baron Bailie of Willowdean, when once or so in the year they were invited to a state dinner at Ernescleugh.

Everard Home, the Master, a fashionable looking young man of a very good style, in absence of the Lord, his father, who was on diplomatic service in the Ionian Isles, placed Lady Wedderburn on his right. Sir John handed the hostess to her place, and Cyril, to his mother's satisfaction, led in Gwenny ; but then no other lady was present.

When Cyril looked at the unexceptionable wife his mother urged upon him, with her delicate neck and arms, so snow-white when contrasted with her black dress and jet ornaments, her rich Indian shawl of alternate black, gold, and scarlet stripes, diamonds flashing out here and there, as bright as her own eyes, his mind wandered away involuntarily to little lonely Mary, in her plain stuff attire, her sole ornaments a brooch and collar.

Lady Ernescleugh, a more showy, dowager-looking, and

though fair-haired, an older and haughtier style of woman than
Lady Wedderburn, with very good taste, wore a black dress of
the richest velvet, trimmed only with silver grey *grebe*, as all
her guests were in mourning, and both families had been
intimate for years.

As three of the gentlemen present belonged to the service, a
little shop would creep into their conversation, which ran
chiefly on the approaching war, and the mustering of arma-
ments by sea and land ; for by the London papers of the
previous day it was fast becoming apparent, as the Master said,
"that matters were looking less and less rosy in the East;"
and Lady Ernescleugh, who had recently got him transferred
from the line to the Scots Fusileer Guards, in the hope that he
might soldier only in London, and never encounter harder
service than might be seen at Windsor, in the Wellington
Barracks, at the Bank, or the Tower, was both alarmed and dis-
gusted to find that several battalions of the Household Brigade
were detailed to form a portion of the army of the East—the
force destined to protect Turkey from the Russians ; "those
barbarous Russians," she added, " whom she and Ernescleugh,
when he was Ambassador at St. Petersburg, found to be little
better than their forefathers are described to have been under
Catharine."

" The Semiramis of the North," said Robert Wedderburn.

" And we all know how wicked *her* times were," said Lady
Ernescleugh.

How little could Cyril foresee to what this conversation was
to lead ; when the young host said, laughing—

" By Jove, mother, there is more wickedness now in the
world than ever existed then. Yes, even among ourselves," he
added, wiping the champagne froth from his fair moustache,
" only we don't always see it."

" How, Everard ? I do not understand."

" It is more subtle, more refined, more cunning, and much
better bred."

" The latter is certainly some advantage," said Cyril.

" Besides, Wedderburn, we don't call our little peccadilloes
by such deuced hard names as our rough ancestors did—that is
all."

" I do not quite understand you, Everard," said Lady Ernescleugh, smiling, but with a little air of pique ; " you seem to
be aiming at something or some one."

Cyril, who had been talking to Gwenny, now became aware
that the Master was bending over his wine glass, and saying
something to Horace Ramornie, in a low tone, but laughing
and confidentially. He detected the name of " Mary Lennox,"
and after a time those alarming words, " By Jove, Ramornie, it

could not be termed a summer flirtation, as he was driving her home through the *snow*, at midnight, too. Queer, is it not? for we all know the fellow's character : but then the poor girl is so left to herself, in that old house by her ailing father, that"—here his voice sank lower—" but it is a pity, for she is *so* pretty !"

What had happened? To whom was he referring? Cyril felt his ears tingling, his heart grow still, and his face turn pale ; all the more so that the clear keen eyes of his mother were on him, and he remembered the conversation in her boudoir.

He burned with impatience until the three ladies withdrew to the drawing-room ; and the moment they had been bowed out, and he and the other gentlemen resumed their seats, ere closing up towards their young host, he very plainly asked, " what they had been talking about ?"

" The strangest thing in the world," replied Horace, with a serious expression in his quiet dark eyes ; " a scandalous story concerning the daughter of old Oliver Lennox, of Lonewoodlee. Of course, you know the girl ; by sight, at least."

" Scandalous !" repeated Cyril, making a violent effort to control himself, though there came a flash from his eye, lurid as that from a cannon's mouth, and there came a terrible frown from his brow, which he concealed by resting it on his hand. " And this story ?"

" Is, that she spent a night in the house of Chesterhaugh."

" Take care, take care," said Sir John ; " she represents one of the oldest families in the Merse."

" A fact !" persisted the Master of Ernescleugh, in a low tone ; " she spent there a night, or nearly so, about the time you were so mysteriously missing, Wedderburn. I was riding home from Greenlaw, accompanied by a groom ; there had been a severe fall of snow, and just as we drew near the gate of Chesterhaugh, it was opened by old Tony Heron, the keeper, and out came Rooke Chesters, in that bang-up waggonette of his, with Miss Lennox seated by his side. I could swear to her, though she was well muffled up in a railway-rug. The time was past twelve, and he was evidently driving her home ! Now we all know that ladies, old or young, don't visit Rooke Chesters. It is an ugly story, and I would rather not have known it."

Cyril's voice sounded strange, even to himself ; but he asked, calmly—

" Did you see her face, Horne ?"

" No. She was closely veiled ; but I know her little hat with the golden pheasant's plume.'

Cyril remembered that he had shot that pheasant.

"Did you speak with her?"

"No. We passed each other at a hard trot."

"Then what proof have you, beyond mere suspicion, that the lady was Miss Lennox at all?"

There was something categorical in Cyril's tone which made Everard Home tug his moustache ; but he replied—·

"My groom got a match for his cigar from the gatekeeper, Tony Heron, whose information put the matter beyond a doubt, and Chesters'groom, Trayner, confirmed the story next day, with many a joke Miss Lennox would not like to have heard. But pass the wine, the decanters stand with you, my Royal Fusileer."

What horrible mystery, worse even than that of his own disappearance, lay concealed under all this ? Was Rooke Chesters ordained by fate to be the evil genius of them both ? Heron, the gatekeeper, the groom of Chesters, and Ernescleugh were cognizant of the story, and Mary's name and honour were a joke and a source of vulgar and malevolent speculation in every servants'-hall and household in the Merse ! A *stunned* sensation came over him. Even were the story utterly false it was a terrible one, and the most degrading deductions would be drawn from it ; and even as he sat and thought over it, mechanically passing the decanter, and filling and emptying his glass, an age seemed to have elapsed since yester-evening by the stile—a mighty gulf to have opened between him and Mary Lennox.

"I usually make it a legal rule," said Robert Wedderburn, "only to believe the half of what I see, and nothing that I simply hear. These groom fellows may have been mistaken, after all ; but it is passing strange !"

Cyril could have embraced his brother for these words ; but still *the* story had gone abroad.

Cyril now remembered of Mary admitting that Chesters had addressed her in the language of love ; and yet she had ventured to spend some hours—gossips said a night—in the house, the house of a man with a reputation so tainted.

He also remembered her strange emotion when they last met. Was it compunction for her own perfidy, or affected doubt of his love, or neither, or what was it ? Alas ! he knew not what or whom to believe in now.

Her doubts must have been of herself and of her own faith ; not of him or his faith ! His Mary, so pure and gentle in eye and manner, to be subjected even to the glances of a man like Rooke Chesters was exasperating. What then was he to think of the companionship of hours ? He knew that Chesters visited occasionally her bedridden father, hence an interview could be nothing novel to either ; but fast in his passionate and impulsive heart, the emotions of jealousy, doubt, and mortification became predominant.

He almost loathed the master of Ernesclengh for his unwitting communication ; but he concealed all he felt, for the bitter conviction forced itself upon him, that if Mary Lennox were unworthy of his love, there would then be more reason than ever to hide that love from all. So those who saw him, as he sat at table chatting of politics, the coming war, the points of this horse or that terrier or pointer, could little have dreamed of the volcano that was in his heart, through which a hundred varying emotions were sweeping.

There were utter perplexity and keen distress ; shame and doubt, jealousy and wounded self-esteem. Could it really be the case that she had encouraged the advances of two—of Chesters and himself—as lovers, and on hearing of the loss of one who had gone, actually gone to the house of the other ? He had known of such things. There was his old flame at Canterbury, who had beaded the cigar-case ; but, pshaw ! she was a garrison-hack of ten years standing, and was known to every corps from Chatham to China.

What did it all mean, or what *would* it all mean ? To be the rival of Chesters would be humiliation enough. He was grieved and maddened by the whole affair ; for his secret love, the light and joy of his soul, was about to be quenched now.

His family—his mother, at least—had heard of it ; and knowing, as they and she did, the reputation of Chesters, could he speak now of making her his wife ; and yet he loved her so ! Surely she would be able to explain it all ; but still the ugly *cause* for explanation existed.

Why had she concealed the whole circumstances from him ? Why such reticence ? There was something in this fact that filled him with dire and dark suspicion, and but yesterday he had placed a ring on her wedding finger, a token of their solemn betrothal before God, and amid the silence of the starlight and the dewy evening he had tenderly taken her to his breast and called her his wife—" *the wife of his heart ;*" and yet she had acted thus in the time of his absence—of his supposed death—and made her name and honour the sport of gossips, of grooms and gatekeepers !

If so artful, why decline on any terms or pretence the proposal of marriage he had made her ? Chesters had insinuated something to her of himself (Cyril) and Gwenny, something to excite her jealousy and to pique her by her own admission ; thus they must have been talking confidentially, and to what purpose ?

So did he torment himself, viewing the circumstances in all its worst points. Glass after glass of strong, deep-coloured, and

heady old Madeira did Cyril imbibe ; and then others of Grande
Chartreuse and Curaçoa, by way of *chasse-café*, ere the gentlemen took their coffee and joined the ladies ; indeed Cyril,
though invariably most temperate, on this night seemed not to
care how much he drank, provided he drowned, or even
deadened, care for the time.

On entering the drawing-room he was painfully conscious, by
a peculiar expression, almost a radiant one, in his mother's face,
that Lady Ernesclough had told her the whole of this obnoxious
story, this horrible *esclandre*, about the girl he had hoped or
meant to marry ; to whom he was solemnly but secretly
plighted, and whom he loved with inexpressible tenderness.

There was a steady glitter in his mother's eye that provoked
him, and he turned to Gwenny, who was idling over the keys of
the piano, as if waiting for some one to speak with her.

He said something, he knew not what, and she replied
without his seeming to hear or understand her ; but she immediately began to play with more animation. How nimbly
and gracefully her white fingers wandered over the ivory keys,
making even them seem almost dull in colour by comparison ;
and he looked on, and turned the leaves of the music, as one in
a terrible dream, ignorant or heedless whether Gwenny was
playing a Highland Reel or the " Soldier's March" in *Faust*,
for the soul of him he could not have told, as he heard only the
voices of his mother and Lady Ernescleugh, as they lay back in
a crimson satin *fauteuil*, with their heads stooped towards each
other, and talking over their glittering fans.

" They are no doubt a strange set," said his mother, " that
small family of Lonewoodlee" (small, indeed ! thought Cyril).
" The father, a quarrelsome old person, has had, as you know,
endless law disputes with Sir John ; but luckily for us, has
always lost them. A spendthrift, he is now a bankrupt ; and
his girl, though so quiet and modest in aspect and manner,
must be a designing minx."

" But, my dear Lady Wedderburn, quiet ones are always the
deepest. 'Smooth waters,' you are aware," said Lady Ernescleugh, with a little laugh.

" And who knows what she may be, if all were known ?"

" The *esclandre* about visiting a bachelor of Captain Chesters'
proclivities does not surprise me a bit ; no doubt it is the
result of her bringing-up, or rather the want of bringing-up."

" She has been motherless for years," urged Lady Wedderburn, gently.

" Hence the result," replied Lady Ernescleugh, a cold and
haughty dame, who had never perhaps committed a solecism in
her life, and never pardoned one in others. " I am so glad we

have never had her here, though the girl is handsome and presentable enough."

"And now that Gwenny has come to Willowdean, my countenancing her, even by a casual bow, is impossible. I have already passed her at church and elsewhere before the story came out ; and one cannot be too careful whom one knows, for you are aware, my dear Lady Ernescleugh, that——" and here his mother's voice sank to a whisper, but Cyril was nearly driven mad by what he had heard.

"Dear Aunt," said Gwenny, "I do not know the unfortunate young person of whom you are talking——"

"And must never do so."

"But I am reminded of a maxim of my poor papa's."

"Ah ! and this maxim ?"

"Was always, 'Sift news first, and swallow it afterwards.' Proverbs are bad taste, I believe ; but he often said this when he heard wild stories of Thugs and Dacoits, of stranglings and poisonings, of men being carried off by tigers, and all the odd things that happen in Indian life."

"But, Gwenny," said Cyril, patting her white shoulder, and looking very much as if he would like to kiss her, "this is not India, but prosaic, self-righteous, and censorious Scotland."

"True, Cyril," added Horace Ramornic, who had also drawn near Gwenny : "the world here finds no fault with imprudence, or even wickedness ; but great fault with either being found out. So with this girl's rash visit to Chesterhaugh, in which there may have been no harm ; but I am sorry for her old father's sake, though I have rarely seen him, and sorry for her own."

"But the fact of spending four or five hours alone with an enterprising fellow like Chesters has an ugly sound about it," said Robert.

"You speak with the natural suspicion of a lawyer ; Horace with the generosity of a soldier," retorted Cyril, on whom all these remarks fell like molten lead.

Thus, one of the very ends which Chesters had in view when he took advantage of the snow-storm, and by a special false-hood, framed between him and Trayner, contrived to detain the restless Mary in his house, seemed on the point of being achieved ; for there are many men in the world like him—men who seek to blacken the reputation of the very girls they mean to betray, to forward their own purpose by dislocating them from the sympathy, protection, and even compassion of men.

As for the pity of their own sex, that is easily lost !

To Cyril the rest of the evening passed away like a night-mare ; and at last, to his infinite relief, the carriage and phaeton came to the door, and Ernescleugh, the frowning rocks, the sea,

and the distant light that twinkled on the Isle of May, were all
left behind as they drove homeward inland.

Sir John wished to smoke ; so he, Robert, and Horace were
in the open phaeton, while Cyril sat in the carriage with his
mother and Gwenny. Of what they had been arranging for
the London season he knew nothing, and cared less. When
that time came, he should be, he hoped, face to face with the
Cossacks.

He was sternly moody and silent, and both failed to extract
a word from him. His mother knew his secret ; with her he
was past acting, and endurance could endure no more.

She stole her soft hand into his—the hand that in infancy
and youth had never tired of caressing him—and whispered in
his ear—

"My beloved Cyril, a noble heart like yours was not meant
to be wasted on a worthless girl like Mary Lennox of Lonewoodlee."

Cruel words, though she said them ever so softly and tenderly ; but they put a finishing stroke to his misery, and he
started as if stung by a wasp.

On arriving at home, he hastened to his own room, and
desired Gervase Asloane, the butler, to bring him a bumper of
champagne ; and with the wine Asloane brought him a letter.
He tore it open. It was from Chesters, the first he had ever
received from him, and he rapidly perused it, with surprise and
rage mingling in his heart. It ran thus :—

> "Army and Navy Club,
>   London.

"My dear Wedderburn,—Glad to hear of your turning
up again in this sublunary sphere ; but sorry that I could not
stay at home to congratulate you in person. I suppose we
shall see all about it in the papers—*Bell's Life*, most likely?
I had to leave in haste, as Bill Trayner put me up to a good
thing or two, about to come off on the Turf. Sir John cashed
up your I O U like a brick ; but I mean to let Chesterhaugh—
put it out to dry-nurse—and go abroad, or take service in one
of the proposed foreign battalions. Have you made up your
book? The City and Suburban is the next good handicap set
for decision. Eugenie is said to be really a good thing. Those
who back her won't regret it. 10 to 30 are taken for Varna ;
and 1000 to 10 against Baltic." ["What the devil is all this to
me !" muttered Cyril. "Bah."]

"Awful scrape yours was. What the deuce did you do to
the bay hunter to render it unmanageable? How excited that
little girl at Lonewoodlee was about the affair. I had no end
of trouble, one night, before I got her consoled ; but *consoled*

she was in the end. And now, with best wishes, old fellow, believe me ever yours faithfully,

"R. R. CHESTERS."

"Insolent scoundrel!" exclaimed Cyril, before whom came in memory the mocking laugh, the sinister smile, and the green-grey, phosphorescent-like eyes of the writer, as he crushed up the jibing letter, and tossed it in the fire ; but not before he observed that it was sealed with the onyx ring which bore the arms of Louis de la Fosse, the young French traveller whom Chesters had so unmercifully pillaged at play.

There was a tone of banter in Chesters' letter, and of insolent reference to Mary, that filled the heart of Cyril with fury. What meant this sudden horror ? Cyril asked in his heart : an intrigue with Chesters at the very time when he himself was supposed to have perished by a violent and mysterious death. How could he question her about it without degradation to them both ? and yet as their mutual relations stood, confidence between them was necessary, most necessary. If he should speak of it, what would her answer be, yea or nay ? If the former, how was she to explain it away ? If the latter, must he believe her ? Oh, it was maddening ! An intrigue with Chesters—of all men in the world, Chesters !

Perhaps it was about her father's protested bill she had visited him. If so, what terms might not Chesters have made with her for it ? So, as jealousy makes the food it feeds on, he wove endless pictures of treachery and duplicity, and vowed to call out Chesters, and shoot him down like a dog, on the first available opportunity, forgetting that even then, in the year we were to storm the heights of Alma, duels had become out of fashion and forbidden.

He thanked Heaven for the prospect of a speedy war, and a hot one, too. Anything was better than enduring what he suffered. Would he resign his leave and rejoin the Fusileers at once, or remain till the last hour, and make fierce love to his cousin Gwenny ?

Perhaps it was all some horrible mistake, which might be easily explained. But why had Mary so studiously avoided all reference to the circumstance ? Desperately he clung to hope, and resolved himself to see about it. And now he, the heedless young officer, the man of pleasure and amusement, wealth and position, felt for the first time in his life that sickening and gnawing emotion of clamorous anxiety in his heart which Mary had endured during the suspense consequent to his disappearance, since Chesters had engendered in her heart a jealousy of Gwendoleyne Wedderburn, and never perhaps so keenly as on the evening she walked to Chesterhaugh.

Cyril knew that he should have no further opportunity of questioning the Master of Ernescleugh, as the leave of the latter was on the point of expiry, and he was to start by train on the morrow to rejoin his battalion of the Guards in the Wellington Barracks, London.

CHAPTER XXIII.

THE DAWN OF LOVE.

PRIOR to all this the intimacy between Horace Ramornie and Gwendoleyne Wedderburn had been ripening with a rapidity that her aunt, had she known of it, would have deemed "frightful" as well as fatal to all her hopes ; but still love had never been spoken of between them.

Busy about his estate and the farms thereon ; busy too about country matters, and the affairs of the little Burgh of Barony which owned him as patron and superior, Sir John Wedderburn spent much of his time out of doors, and a deal of it in his saddle. Cyril had been entirely occupied by his own secret passion, while Robert was sulky, and affected to be deep in his legal studies, reading up for a forthcoming examination, and frequently went alone fishing. As the household was in mourning there were few invitations given, and few visitors at Willowdean ; hence, in spite of all Lady Wedderburn's plans, Horace—not Cyril—and Gwenny were generally thrown together ; and what could be more natural than that the young people should learn to love each other !

Yet he dared not speak of the passion that was growing in his heart.

Lady Wedderburn had not been without a dread that the Master of Ernescleugh, young Everard Home, who was every way an agreeable and remarkably good-looking man, might "cut out" both her sons. Gwenny knew that he was the heir to a peerage, and rank would have much weight in the mind of an Indian-bred girl ; so she was thankful when his leave of absence expired, and he was recalled to London. She did not speak again to Cyril of Mary Lennox, either tauntingly or otherwise ; but once she said to her husband—

"Cyril has been looking pale and unhappy of late, and I know it must be caused by that artful girl at Louewoodlee. What does the foolish fellow go on about? Absurd ! It is only a girl's pretty face, after all."

"Have you forgotten the days of your own youth, and what your face was then to me as Kate Douglas? Ay, and is so still," said the good-natured Baronet, pinching her chin.

"True; but I didn't gad about the country alone on snowy nights with men like Rooke Chesters. Cyril is conscious of her unworthiness; so it is only the memory of a face that disturbs him."

"Don't worry poor Cyril; once with his regiment, he may forget all about her. Yet what does a poet say?—

> "'Only the face of a woman;
> Only a face—nothing more !
> But the memory of that sweet vision
> Comes back to my heart o'er and o'er.
> Only a woman's soft eyes;
> Only a look, that was all ;
> A glance that I chanced to encounter
> Still binds my soul in thrall.'

It was at a ball of the Caledonian Hunt, we first met, Kate. And never forget you were once young."

Gwendoleyne Wedderburn thought there was some analogy in the destiny of herself and Horace from the fact of being so young, and having come, like herself, to Willowdean in his boyhood, without father or mother. Horace was a smart subaltern in the Line now, and had quite considered himself a man in all respects for a few years past; but Gwenny loved to think of him as the lonely boy he had been ; for his manner was grave and gentle, and his voice and smile were ever sweet and pleasant to her.

Cyril, we have said, was pre-occupied, and Robert had enough of the student in him to be somewhat brusque, so Horace she preferred undisguisedly, to the infinite chagrin of Lady Wedderburn; and, if truth must be told, somewhat to the amusement of Sir John, who, though he would have been pleased enough to see his son with a bride so suitable and wealthy, was an enemy to all match-making.

The large and stately house of Willowdean, with its shady library, its galleried conservatory, its long corridors hung with valuable pictures, and its spacious garden, was a pleasant place for such sweet companionship; and whatever young Ramornie did, when not with Gwenny, was always done as if in a kind of dream to occupy the *blank* of time when he could not be with her.

How would time be occupied when they should be parted, perhaps to meet no more !

The garden was older than the house, having belonged to his predecessor, the ancient mansion, "the peel and fortalice of Willowdean;" thus its yew hedges and boxwood borders were thick and dense beyond any to be seen in gardens of more modern date ; and in the centre stood the ancient sun-dial, by the gnomon of which Sir John's forefathers had set or regulated their round silver watches that were like turnips in shape, and had perhaps wooden wheels that were worked by "thorl and string."

As yet the garden was only in bud, and there for the first time Gwenny heard with wonder the voice of the cuckoo when she and Horace were planting some rare Indian seeds which she had brought from the Choultry ; and she sighed when reflecting that he must be so far away when these seeds became flowers in all their tropical glory ; and when (then so bleak and bare), with its famous ribbon-borders of every imaginable colour, the hedges of azaleas and drooping fuchsias under the shelter of the older rows of privet and yew, the clusters of beautiful shrubs and beds of geraniums, verbenas, and calceolarias were in all the bloom and splendour of summer.

And many a delightful drive they had in the park when Gwenny usually took the reins of the pony-phaeton, for there the grass was smooth as a billiard-table, having been carefully rolled and mowed in season, ever since clover-seeds had first been sown in it, in 1708, by Sir Cyril Wedderburn—the same Baronet who drank the health of James VIII., sword in hand, at Greenlaw Cross, when the Comte de Forbin's fleet, with the Scots and Irish Brigades on board, was off the Isle of May ; who nearly rabbled out the Union Parliament, and played many other political pranks in his time.

The month was still March ; but already the park—or "policy," as the Scots called it—was sheeted with pale yellow primroses, where, in the next month the Lent lilies would be in all their golden bloom.

But their drives were not confined to the park, for frequently they had the open carriage. Then Lady Wedderburn and Miss M'Caw were always present ; and, as the large and handsome vehicle bowled along the smooth roads, Gwenny would laugh, and like a happy child, clap her hands to the two white-and-black spotted Dalmatian dogs, which bounded along on each side, caracoling amid the dust, and seeming to exult in the dignity of being outriders to such an equipage, reminding her of the bare-footed *suwaries* she had often seen running beside the elephant of a native prince on the plain of the Choultry.

Poor Horace, however, saw the views and wishes of his aunt pretty plainly, for she was unskilful enough to show her hand to all but Gwenny.

He knew, and felt keenly conscious, of all he owed to the uncle upon whom he had been cast in boyhood, a penniless orphan : his education, his commission and yearly allowance ; and though loving Gwenny passionately, and with all his soul —for she seemed the realization of the wife he could love, the ideal of his dreamy hours—he shrank from any declaration that might, perhaps, mar the plans of those to whom he owed everything in the world, and also may, it might be, the fortune of his relation, his brother officer and friend, for he was ignorant of the recent ties already formed by Cyril.

It was hard for Horace to know and feel that the love he had longed for, the wife he had pictured in many a vision of fervid fancy, was now daily by his side, and yet that he dared not look upon her as more than a friend ; while, at the same time, it was impossible to resist the charm, the delight, the intoxication of her presence, and the craving to seek her society; to listen to her voice, to look into her softly-lidded eyes, that were by turns shy, passionate, and full of child-like surprise ; to touch her hand timidly, and think of all that *might* have been.

Ah, what did it all matter ! A little time, and it would be a thing of the past, this delightful companionship. Miles upon miles of land and sea must be between them, and the Russian hordes would be before him.

Yet often was the perilous secret, that he loved her, on the point of his lips, on certain occasions that suddenly seemed to invite it.

Attended by a groom they had ridden one day past the house, the park, and woods of Ernescleugh, to the verge of the cliff over which Cyril had been dragged by his horse. The tide was out, and the isolated rock from which he had been rescued by the crew of the fisher-smack was plainly visible, with the gulls wheeling in circles, and the white waves boiling round it.

Gwenny was shuddering as she looked alternately down at the rock and upward at the ruins of Fast Castle, perched on the giddy verge of a tremendous cliff, the fragment of a baronial tower " 'twixt cloud and ocean hung,' with the blue sky visible through its fissures and gaping windows. Laying his right hand on her reins, as if to steady her horse, which the booming of the waves below and the screaming of the sea-birds above had startled, he sought in reality but to touch the pretty bridle-hand that was cased in its tight black leather riding gauntlet, as he said—

"I think you admire this sample of our grim Scottish scenery, Miss Wedderburn?"

"Before I answer you," said she, looking with a bright smile under her veil, which the wind was blowing out like a pennant, "you must tell me why you persist in calling me Miss Wedder-burn? Did I not say once before that you were to call me Gwenny? *Miss* sounds so stiff! All the family at Willowdean, and even cold and hard Lady Ernescleugh, call me Gwenny."

" And by that name I always think of you—in my heart."

" Then call me Gwenny, I insist, as I once did before."

" I do not like to do so, when, when——"

" Is not the name pretty ? It was my mamma's."

"Apart from itself, association will ever render it adorable to me."

"Well ?"

"Somehow I don't like to do so when Lady Wedderburn is present; something tells me that she would not be pleased," replied Horace, blushing in spite of himself, and then the girl blushed too, for she began to see something of his meaning and the inferences to be drawn from what he said. "But," he added, retaining her reins and hand in his for a little way, "let us leave this giddy verge ; it is dangerous with a shying horse."

The groom drew near to make the same remark, and so the occasion was lost.

At another time the news came that the Queen, in conjunction with the Emperor of the French, had at last declared war against Russia !

Gwenny's dark eyes were upon Horace as he read the *Times* aloud in the conservatory, with a flush on his cheek and a strange emotion in his heart.

"All leaves will be cancelled now !" said he.

"And you, cousin Horace, you will be quite anxious to find yourself in Turkey ?"

"I *was* anxious," said he, in a low voice.

"And what has made you change your mind ; surely not dread of danger ?"

Her question was a home thrust ; but he only answered curtly, while his heart beat quicker and his cheek grew pale—

"I am a soldier, Gwenny."

"Then what has caused the change ?"

"Dare I tell you ?" he asked in a low and tremulous voice, as he took her hand ; "but no, I dare not," he added.

Nor could he have done so then, for Lady Wedderburn was not far from them, feeding a screaming paroquet, whose neck Horace could have wrung with stern joy. Still he was venturing to say something more in an incoherent and desponding way, when Gwenny came close to him, with her soft, serene, and loving eyes smiling into his, and placing her rapid little hand on his mouth, she said—

"Now, Horace, if you love me, silence ; for sadness worries me, and I won't be worried or sad till you are gone ; and then Heaven knows I shall be sad enough."

She joined her aunt, and again the secret remained untold.

"If I love her !" thought Horace, with a choking sensation in his throat ; but Gwenny had begun to suspect or feel all that he had left untold, through "that silent method of communion which no crowd can prevent persons who know each other well from interchanging."

To all the beauty we have described, a beauty that was dark

and pale, yet sparkling, Gwendoleyne added a manner that came with her Welsh blood ; it was full of those nameless and indescribable charms which the French, ever so happy in apt phraseology, term *folâtre et caressante*, winning and playful ; but there is no perfection out of novels and romances, so Gwenny, with all her loveliness, was *not* perfect. She had a fiery little temper at times, which, like her dark eyes and their long lashes, she inherited with her Welsh blood ; but she was all perfection to young Horace Ramornie, and in the core of his heart he idolized her !

CHAPTER XXIV.

PARTED IN SORROW.

IN the dining-room at Lonewoodlee Mary was seated in the deep recess of a window. She was sewing, and singing merrily the while. She felt happy, light in heart, and high in spirit, unusually so for her ; but ever and anon she paused in her work and even in her song to contemplate her new ring and recall the exact words of Cyril when he placed it on her finger, the expression of his eyes, and the tone of his voice.

The window was open, for the time was noontide, the day was warm and sunny, and the spring freshness in the atmosphere was delightful. The bleating of the sheep that browsed close by the Tower, the voices of the birds that twittered in the old trees and shrubbery, with the hum of insect life, all came pleasantly to the girl's ear, so, as we have said, at times her song died away, and her needle paused as she sank into happy thought, and abandoning herself to her day dreams, repeated, " Wife of my heart ; ah, he called me so ; the wife of *his* heart !"

So pre-occupied was Mary that she did not hear the hoofs of a horse approach the Tower, nor the ringing of the door-bell announce a visitor, till Alison Home, her face a little flushed with surprise and importance, placed in her hand the card of

CYRIL WEDDERBURN,

Royal Fusileers.

" Where is he—this gentleman?" asked Mary, starting from her seat.

" In his saddle at the door ; but he asks if he can see you, Miss Lennox."

" Show him in at once, Alison."

When their past mode of meeting and corresponding are considered, it may easily be supposed that a visit from Cyril, openly, formally, and at such an early hour as noon, filled Mary with anxiety, excitement, and alarm ! To visit thus had long ceased to be his use and wont, after the quarrels ensued with his family ; so what could it portend ? With true feminine instinct she glanced at a mirror—one of those quaint, old-fashioned, carved plate glasses with bevelled borders, set in an ebony frame—gave a final smooth to her rich brown hair, and was not ill-pleased to find, that though she was scarcely dressed in a style to receive visitors, she wore a morning robe of spotted muslin that was very becoming, and from the frilled sleeves and neck of which her taper arms and slender throat came forth to the best advantage.

Save his ring, ornament she had none.

Cyril was ushered in with hat and whip in hand, and the moment their eyes met, her heart became filled with dismay. He did not approach her or take her hand, even the faint sickly smile that conventionalism or good-breeding had spread over his face passed away, and he stood looking at her irresolutely, and keeping the dining-table between them.

Grieved and exasperated as he was by the ugly story he had heard so recently, Cyril glanced sadly from Mary to the old faded portraits that hung on the walls—older they were than some of the ancestry at Willowdean—and much of sorrow and pity began to mingle with his indignation. And there, too, were the arms and monogram of Oliver Lennox, who had been a good man and true to his Queen in the stormy times of the Reformation, carved above the antique fireplace, which looked so quaint with its heavy Scoto-Italian mouldings of stone ; but in the old-fashioned basket grate there burned a cheerful fire, composed less of coal than of cuttings from the thicket without, roots, fircones, and peat.

" Oh, Cyril," exclaimed Mary, piteously, " what has happened —what *is* amiss ? You have such a pale and tell-tale face ! You neither take my hand nor seat yourself."

" Nor shall I do either until you have heard me—if I even do so then, Mary," said he slowly, as if to gain time or arrange his perplexed thoughts, and doubtful in what terms to break the purpose of his unhappy visit, she looked so charming in that plain undress, so gentle-eyed and dove-like. " Things were said of you last night by Everard Home, my mother. and Lady Ernesclough, that have rent my heart asunder. Long, long will their words haunt me. Oh, Mary, I shall not readily forget that dinner at Ernesclough !"

Mary now knew all ; the Master *had* recognized her on that fatal night, when, in her innocence and helplessness, she fell into the species of snare contrived for her by Chesters and his roguish groom. Dropping her needlework, she grasped the back of a chair for support, and asked, with something of *hauteur*, nevertheless—

"And what did you say, Cyril, when those people dared to say hard things of *me ?*"

"Say, girl ! what could I say ? I sat and smiled, I suppose. I was in good society, where people must hide every emotion, and had to smile like the Spartan boy I spoke of ; and to smile thus is too often the hardest portion of the weary battle of life."

"To the point, Cyril—oh, of what do they accuse me ?"

"On the night of the snow-storm, you visited the house of Chesterhaugh ; you were there for hours, and Everard Home saw you leaving the gate, at midnight, in Chesters' waggonette, and seated by his side. Home's groom saw this too ! Was such a visit, in such a time of supposed grief, and to such a man, becoming in the girl whom I loved, and who I thought loved me ? Even though I was believed to be dead, was it becoming in your father's daughter ? He is, I know, a ruined man ; but ruin or improvidence cannot blot out the past, or alter the fact that he is a gentleman descended from as good blood as any in Scotland—not that most folks set much store on that nowa-days, but I do. Oh, that I had indeed been drowned—that I had perished on that night of terror, rather than have lived to hear this said of Mary Lennox, that she is no longer worthy of me !"

"Cruel, Cyril ! Oh, how cruel is all this of you !" said Mary, wringing her hands.

"Oh, Mary, Mary ! God alone knows how I have loved you, and how I love you still ; but even were that story not true, that such should be said of you—my future wife—tears up my heart by the roots."

"But it *is* true," said Mary.

"What was your reason for such a visit and at such a time ?"

"Oh, Cyril, the best," said Mary, with a bursting heart, while she stretched her trembling hand towards him, for his some-what imperious manner chilled and scared her.

"Why were my informants of a circumstance so strange and improper first the Master of Ernescleugh, and then Chesters himself ? What was *your* motive for concealment ?"

"A good one. I felt assured that you might disapprove of it, and I was powerless ; I had no control over my stay there. I was in Chesterhaugh certainly, but I did not go to visit Captain Chesters. I was lured in ; the snow fell : I could not get away ; and—and—and, oh, how can you speak to me thus, and think such things of me !"

Cyril bit his nether lip passionately, for the jesting words, the sneer of Chesters, that "she was consoled in the end," seemed burnt into his heart.

"I care not now for your motive, or even to inquire into it. Mary Lennox, we cannot undo the past; what I have to think of is the future."

"Oh, Cyril, bear with me, and hear a very simple explanation connected with yourself."

But he would listen to nothing, and exclaimed, in a hollow tone—

"Oh, has God no pity for love lost, for trust misplaced, and a heart wasted as mine has been on you !"

"I am innocent, Cyril, innocent of wrong, even of error," said Mary, with simple dignity ; and had he not been goaded by his own angry thoughts and the galling words of others, he might have read the assurance of what she said in the expression of her face, in her clear earnest eyes, her parted lips, and her very attitude, as she stood with outstretched hands. "I am guiltless of all blame, and a day must come when God will clear me."

"The day may come—but too late," said he, hoarsely and gloomily.

"Never too late if we are both on this side of the grave, Cyril ; yet, thank Heaven, this life does not last for ever."

"And your father's ?" said he, reproachfully.

"Oh, Cyril, your rebuke is just !" said Mary, in a flood of tears ; "but your anger is not so, and it makes me so miserable."

"You can have no explanation to give, and I seek nothing beyond the admission of the fact," said Cyril, with a cold severity that afterwards surprised himself ; "and now I quit you. Thank fate, we are on the eve of a war. A few days—ay, perhaps but a few hours—and I shall leave you and all the folly of regret and love behind me, to enter on a stirring and a glorious career. Adieu ! Never more shall we be as we have been ; never more shall we meet where we have met so often ! All is at an end between us, Mary ; and from this hour our paths in life must lie for ever apart !"

The door closed ; she heard the clatter of his horse's hoofs die away in the distance, and then she knew that Cyril was gone—gone, without even asking, or learning the *cause* of her visit to Chesterhaugh.

She felt that he had treated her both harshly and unjustly, and the sense of that bore her up for a time ; but a time only.

As one in a dream, she still clutched the back of the chair to prevent herself from falling. The bleating of the sheep in the meadow, the voices of the birds in the trees and among the ivy that rustled on the old Tower wall, and the hum of the insects, were all in her ears as before. Her eyes wandered over the pastoral Lammermuir hills with something of a hunted and despairing expression in them ; of wild anxiety, as though peace and rest lay somewhere far beyond, and the whole interview seemed like a dream—an unreality.

Nothing was distinct ; she felt as if struggling with a nightmare.

After a time, and as the day wore on, she began to perceive the realities of her position, and to feel the imperative necessity for a complete explanation with Cyril; but she was overwhelmed by the false position in which she was placed, by shame, anger, and unmerited mortification, that such a story should have gone abroad in the fashion it had done, and she knew how it would be viewed by the severe and censorious.

She knew that "woman is woman's worst foe ;" and to be pointed at by stern spinsters, with rigid religious and moral opinions—spinsters who never missed sermon or communion, or omitted their names in such lists as *printed* the names of the charitable, and who had in their hearts only a pretended horror for the mammon of unrighteousness—would be terrible and humiliating in the extreme.

From the dinner-table at Ernescleugh, she knew, or feared, the story in many exaggerated forms would spread like wildfire among the professing Christians and stern Church—we beg their pardon—*Kirk*-goers, and nasal-singing Pharisees of Willowdean ; and that many hands and eyes would be uplifted in dismay at the "shortcomings of the daughter of Lonewoodlee."

She knew, also, how utterly merciless such local gossips were ; but to be an object of speculation to the self-righteous on one hand, and to be pitied and misjudged by those who had loved her on the other, was a fear that proved bitter as the waters of Marah—yea, more bitter than death could be—to the sensitive Mary Lennox. She felt humbled, and seemed to have made acquaintance with degradation, she knew not why.

Oh, how in her heart she hated that man Chesters, who had caused all this misery !

But Cyril would come again to Lonewoodlee, to console and to comfort her.

" After all the vows we have exchanged—after all our hours of happiness together—Cyril, Cyril ! how could you leave me thus cruelly and coldly?" she would exclaim, almost aloud, while wringing her poor hands in a paroxysm of grief.

Sometimes, when an emotion of anger at his determined injustice and assumption of her guilt got the better of her sorrow, she drew the betrothal ring *almost* off her finger, and as often kissed and slid it back again, loth, by removing it entirely to break the spiritual link or tie between herself and Cyril Wedderburn.

"He will come to me again," she often whispered in her heart, fondly. "Oh, yes ; he must come to me once more."

But days went by, and Mary watched and wept, for the days became weeks and months ; yet Cyril Wedderburn came no more to Lonewoodlee.

CHAPTER XXV.

THE TELEGRAM.

So infirm was he of purpose, notwithstanding his severity with Mary, that he had barely quitted her presence and ridden off, ere he began to relent towards her ; and then the mocking story of Everard Home, and the cruel and stinging passage of Chesters' letter, came back to memory, tearing the wound afresh to exasperate him : and now events succeeded each other with considerable rapidity.

The whole of the afternoon subsequent to his interview with Mary, Cyril secluded himself in his own room ; there he wrote three letters to her, full of sorrow for what he termed her error, with the earnest advice and hope that, if ever she required a friend—oh, how cold seemed the word !—she should remember him ; but each production in turn dissatisfied him. He knew not how the tenor of them might sound when read, so each in succession was concluded only to be torn up and committed to the flames ; and in this state of indecision he remained until the first gong for dinner resounded in the lofty vestibule below.

Under his very window, as he wrote, he could hear his father's groom openly relating to one of the gardeners Mr. Bill Trayner's very coarse and freely garnished account of the visit paid by "old Lennox's daughter to the Captain on the night of the storm."

It was evident to all how moody Cyril had become ; and on this day he felt relieved rather than bored, as he usually was, by the presence of the Reverend Mr. M'Guffog, a prosy old man ; the nervous, but good-natured Dr. Squills, and the Baron Bailie, whom Sir John had brought home with him, as he wished their conjunct advice about some local matter.

Cyril knew that the eyes of his mother, Horace, and Robert, were on him ; and although the two last-named suspected that he had some little interest at Lonewoodlee, the former knew to a certainty the cause of that gloom and depression which, to do him justice, he endeavoured to conceal. He strove to interest himself in the minister's chief topics, an augmentation of his stipend and repairs of the manse ; with the Doctor on the important subjects of compulsory vaccination, and his quarrels with the parochial board; and even with the Baron Bailie, who was a grocer in the Vennel of Willowdean, on the probable war-prices of butter and cheese; but he was glad, when he had done his duty thus, to turn to Gwenny, and rest his head thoughtfully on his hand, through the fingers of which his hair stole in dark and glossy brown locks, close, thick, and crisp ; and Lady Wedderburn, as she saw their faces bent near each other, looked at them admiringly, and thought how handsome they were, and how admirably suited to each other.

But the world is full of cross-purposes, and while Cyril poured some good-natured nothings into Gwenny's ear, her eyes, from time to time, sought those of Horace Ramornie.

An unusually important ring at the hall-door bell reached the ears even of those at the dinner table, and made all exchange glances, just as Lady Wedderburn and Gwenny rose to retire ; but the entrance of Gervase Asloane, with a suspicious looking yellow document on a silver salver, made them pause.

"A telegram for Mr. Cyril—for the Captain I mean," said the old man, in a subdued voice, and, as Cyril tore it open, his mother grew pale as a lily.

"From whom is it, dearest ?" she asked, drawing near.

"The Colonel."

A low exclamation escaped her.

"He telegraphs, 'We are to embark for the East on the 5th proximo, so you have not a moment to lose in rejoining. Provide yourself with a good six-chambered revolver. All ours have done so. Tell Ramornie that he is detailed for the Depôt, so his leave remains intact.'"

A bright flush spread over Cyril's face as he read. There in action, far away from Willowdean and Lonewoodlee, and from all his present bitter associations and mortifications, was a relief opened suddenly up ; yet his eyes turned to the sad, the earnest and anxious look of his poor mother, who, instead of retiring to the drawing-room, reseated herself at the table for a little time, with her eyes full of tears.

Heartfelt and well-bred hopes were expressed by the Minister, the Doctor, and the Baron Bailie, that he and all his comrades might have a pleasant and prosperous voyage to the land of the Turk and the Heathen, " whither," added the Minister, " no Christian soldiery had gone since the Twelfth Crusade, so ours was an epoch in the world's history ;" but there might be no actual war after all, for was not this an age of subtle diplomacy and peace-making at any price ; and to these last expressions of hope, his mother clung desperately, with a sob in her throat and a prayer in her heart; but Sir John, who was a bitter enemy of Lord Aberdeen's Government, and was suspicious of his Russian sympathies, pretty broadly "d—d the notion of peace at any price, and hoped the day would never come when Britannia, if smitten on one cheek, would quietly turn the other !"

"You'll not be long behind me, Horace, I fear," said Cyril, gaily, as he took off his wine; "the service companies are barely the full strength, and we shall soon have gaps to fill. Gervase," he added, turning to the old butler, who lingered nervously behind his chair. with an expression in his face that indicated a desire to "whimper," and to pat Cyril on the head or back, as he had often done in boyhood, "you'll have all my traps packed and brought down-stairs. Have the carriage brought round in time for the night train for England."

Before this, Cyril had been, perhaps, the most silent member of the company ; now it was he who talked most and was the gayest ; but his mother was voiceless ; and even Gwenny felt crushed (and would have been more so had Horace been going), for all knew they were looking on a face they might never see again, and listening to a voice that never more might fall upon their ear.

The fatal telegram !

It lay on the polished table, like an executioner's warrant, to Lady Wedderburn's eyes—the ukase that was to tear her son from her—and she forgot all about her matrimonial schemes and fears of Horace ; she only looked at her handsome and curly-headed Cyril, and thought of all that was before him ; that terrible perspective ; the long voyage in a comfortless hired transport, by the stormy Bay of Biscay, the Mediterranean and the Levant, the Bosphorus and the Black Sea ; of the varied climates ; and more than all—oh, more than all !—the chances of an unequal and disastrous war against the hordes of Russia. Then her maternal heart died within her ; she could only lay her face on his breast and weep.

Many a wife and mother over all the British Isles felt the same emotion at that fatal time, when, after forty years of peace, and Waterloo had become as a tale that is told, the clouds of war began to gather in the North and East ; and long, long in London, the mighty heart of the Empire, was remembered that early morning when the drum beat that summoned the Guards, the flower of our army, to the field ; on that same morning when sixty thousand citizens of Edinburgh accompanied the departing steps of the King's Own to the ship that bore them away, for all the land was full of sympathy.

Now Cyril hated "a scene."

"What's the row, mamma ?" asked he, indignantly. "How often have you seen me leave home to join the Fusileers, and always come back jollier than ever ?"

"But you never left Willowdean at such a time of war and peril as this—going from me perhaps never to return, my boy !"

and becoming less excited, she left the room, leaning on Gwenny's arm, and urging Cyril soon to join her.

All her future plans and minor considerations, even the dread of Mary Lennox, were merged now in one thought ; and when she regarded his fine face and stalwart figure, her memory went back over the sunny days of his boyhood, and to the tenderer time beyond, when, "like the callow cygnet in its nest," he clung to her bosom, when merry bonfires were blazing redly on the Twinlaw and Earlston Hill, on Beimerside, and over all the Lammermuirs, from the beautiful vale of the Gala to the terrible rocks of St. Abb, for the birth of an heir to the beloved house of Willowdean.

And now, now, what might it all come to—the care, affection, education, and pride of past years ?

A bullet shot from the musket of an unlettered Russian slave, and a tomb without a coffin or a stone !

So might the life of one so loved—the life she had hoped was to stretch so far beyond that of his parents as God should will—pass away. Cyril, whom she had prayed and trusted might live to see his children's children, long after she had been laid in the family vault at Willowdean church. And as she skilfully tormented herself by dark anticipations like these, she turned to Gwenny (who, sooth to say, was somewhat scared by the suddenness of the summons, and her excessive and unwonted burst of grief), and said—

" Oh, Gwenny, why did I ever permit him to be a soldier— why ? But regrets are useless now; yet I am very ill used, I think. Horace has neither father nor mother to regret him, and yet he remains with the Depôt, as that provoking Colonel says, while Cyril goes abroad with the regiment !"

She glanced at the magnificent French clock, a miracle of sculpture and gilding, that stood on a white marble console table.

In two hours she knew he must be gone.

" Two hours only, Gwenny !" she said.

The gentlemen soon joined them, and then she was compelled to preserve an appearance of calmness. Cyril did not immediately come in with them, and her heart misgave her that perhaps he had started to Lonewoodlee, but he had only visited his own room for a moment to give it a farewell glance, and issue to Gervase some final instructions. His mother now, however, grudged every moment he was absent from her side. Sir John drew near and took her hands caressingly in his own, for their sympathies of course were one, though her emotions were the keener of the two.

The long-looked-for and dreaded day, yea, the very hour, had come when there was to be a final parting ; when Cyril's place

and chair would be vacant once more, and Willowdean a broken
home ! His sword case and portmanteau were already strapped
in the entrance-hall ; and now the little family circle that had
lived together in such close and pleasant companionship was to
be severed.

The grief of Miss M'Caw was so noisy and uncontrollable
that she had to retire to her own room ; and Lady Wedderburn
looked almost hostilely, certainly with envy, at her unconscious
nephew, who "was detailed for the Depôt," and whose home
leave extended for nearly a month beyond that of Cyril, as the
spring drills had not yet commenced.

"I would to Heaven that Horace's leave had been up too,"
said Lady Wedderburn through her tears, in a whisper to Sir
John.

"Why, surely there is time enough for him to go, poor boy !"

"Because we should then have had but one leave-taking, and
—and this rioting and romping about with Gwenny is scarcely
proper."

"Oh, the old idea ! A month will see it all over ; a memory
of the past, and Horace will have other and sterner work on
hand than flying over the Merse with a pretty young girl."

"Yes ; but the memory thereof may last with the lives
of both."

"Scarcely. Where are now all the girls I flirted with when I
was the age of Horace ? Gwenny is only eighteen, at a time
when love is often a mere illusion, Kate, that passes away or
fixes on some other object, often with perilous rapidity ; so
Cyril may have the best chance after all when in a few months
he comes back to us," said Sir John, with an external air of
confidence and cheerfulness he was far from feeling, as he rose
and crossed the room to bid farewell to their three guests,
who, finding themselves rather *de trop*, after formally partaking
of coffee, were bowed out.

Poor Cyril's heart had been sorely divided and torn since the
arrival of the telegram. From that moment till the time of his
final departure by train, four hours, he knew, would intervene ;
his horse would in a few minutes have taken him to Mary's
presence, and so vacillating and unstable are the resolutions of a
jealous lover, that there were times when he felt strongly impelled to visit her once again !

Had he done so, how much suffering might in the future have
been spared to both ; but the golden moments passed and never
returned again.

"To what end or purpose should I go ?" he asked of himself,
almost fiercely. "Weakness, folly, disgrace ! No—no ! Once
in the train for London, and then all is over !"

Yet his soul was full of compassion and dread for what might yet be the fate, the future, of this delicate girl, whom he had loved so truly and tenderly.

Cyril was sincerely attached to all the household at Willow-dean, to his parents and family, and to none more than his mother, who had ever been, to his eyes, the *belle ideal* of all a lady and a mother ought to be ; yet he was glad, as he had to go, that the telegram and the rail would whisk him off, as he said, "double quick," for the solemnity of leave-taking bored and worried him ; so he shared not his mother's envy of poor Horace's more protracted visit.

He was now anxious only to have it all over and be gone !

After the dark turn his love affair had taken, he felt inclined to thank God for the relief he should find amid the turmoil of war and foreign service with the Fusileers ; he felt a gloomy joy, or grim satisfaction, in the idea that Mary might weep if she saw his name in the Gazette among the killed ; but instantly thrust aside the morbid thought, as he reflected compassionately on his tender mother, and loving father, and all the friends by whom his loss would be lamented ; and life certainly was more valuable than the tears of a false woman !

Already the carriage was at the door ; his luggage, sword, and rugs were placed in it ; he heard the horses' hoofs rasping impatiently among the gravel, as if they resented being har-nessed out at such an hour, and the spotted dogs were gambolling about them. Then Cyril's lips quivered, as he drew on his kid gloves with singular but nervous accuracy. His father, brother, and cousin proposed to accompany him to the station ; but he was affectionately peremptory, and would have no second leave-taking.

As his mother cut a parting lock from his thick brown hair, she fairly broke down again, and sobbing, fell upon his neck. By this Sir John, who had his emotions more under control, was greatly moved ; for to see Cyril joining his regiment *now* was so different from what his departure had been on any previous occasion, save on his first appointment, when he was under orders for India.

" Mother darling," whispered Cyril, " when going now, I have but one favour to ask of you ; be kind to that poor girl at Lonewoodlee, should aught happen. I have loved her well ; and for my sake——"

" I shall, Cyril—if I can."

Some hurried salutes, tears, and shaking of hands, a mur-mured adieu from the assembled servants, and all was over like a dream. He was lying back in the recess of the well-cushioned carriage, and heard the budding branches of the old avenue—budding now as they had done for two hundred springs and more—sweeping its roof as he was driven away.

The old minister, Dr. Squills, with many more, were already

at the railway station to see him finally off, with a farewell cheer ; and as the departing train plunged with a mad shriek into the dark tunnel and vanished, the former lamented aloud that "once again the Merse had lost the best angler that ever dropped a line in the siller Tweed ; the primest curler that ever shot a stone at the rinks ; the boldest rider, the best sportsman, and the lightest dancer in a' the country side ; but God's blessing and a' our gude wishes follow him "

Until far on in the coming grey dawn, even till the sun rose on land and sea, his mother lay a-bed, sleepless, with watch in hand, reckoning with anxious heart the hours and pauses in his southern journey. Now she knew he must be at Berwick; now York ; now at Peterborough, and so on, until in fancy she saw the train rushing into the roar and bustle of King's Cross Station.

How long a period might elapse, and how much would he have to undergo, before he traversed that route homeward to her again ?

After a little time poor Mary Lennox heard, and a dreadful shock it gave her, of his abrupt departure on the very night of the sorrowful day when last they met ; and she knew that he had gone without a farewell word or letter of explanation, and that he still thought hardly and strongly, even bitterly, of her, and the girl's heart waxed sore with its great grief.

They could meet no more at the stile by the triple thorn, or under the old pine-trees : and for her own peace she meant in future to shun those places.

Did she repine, even enviously, a little, when Dr. Squills told her incidentally, that Cyril had telegraphed home (and not to her) "of his safe arrival at headquarters ?" We fear she did.

Cyril's new line of conduct seemed so harsh! Had he wished to quarrel with her, and begun to love his cousin ? It almost seemed so. Well, she had still her poor old father, who clung to her and her only, even as a helpless and querulous child might have done ; but how long should he be spared to her ?

God alone knew.

CHAPTER XXVI.

MARY'S NEW TERROR.

SOME weeks elapsed after this, and yet Mary heard nothing of Cyril ; even the lingering hope that he would write to her died away ; she knew not where his regiment was stationed ; where it was to sail from, when, and for where ; and still full of deep and tender interest as her heart was for him, this ignorance of all concerning him was most tantalizing, till one evening she was startled by a sudden visit from Captain Chesters, who had been for some time absent in London ; and with all her horror of him, she hoped to glean in the course of conversation some tidings of the absent and the loved.

The month was April now, but the day had been rainy and gloomy, and Lonewoodlee, with its weather-beaten walls, its masses of dark green ivy and group of stern old pines, had worn its most grim aspect.

The live-long day the rain had been sowing moor and lea, gorging the watercourses and runnels, while masses of cold white vapour were rolling slowly upward from all the lower portions of the pastoral landscape. The desolate face of Nature around the Tower increased the desolation of Mary's heart, for she was at all times an impressionable creature, and the whole of that dreary day she had sat by her father's bed-side sewing, or reading to him, and thinking of Cyril Wedderburn ; where was he—on the land or on the sea—and did he ever think of her now !

On this day it had seemed to Mary that when her father spoke, a strange brightness and smoothing out of wrinkles spread over his withered face ; his brow became stern at times, his eyes sparkled with a new light, and she saw something of what his features must have been in the days of his youth, and in the time of her dead mother's bridal—in the happier years that had gone for ever.

Then as she watched and saw how the brow seemed to become broad and open, the cheek to flush, and a younger appearance to steal over all his face, she trembled in her heart lest the last great crisis and the Shadowy Hand were approaching, for most of the day he had raved of his dead son, and the now almost forgotten Indian war in which he fell. " It is always dreadful even to the accustomed watchers of the sick, when *the mind wanders*," writes the charming authoress of " Lost and Won ;" when the soul goes on some wild journey of his own, away from direct human associations, fighting with imaginary dangers, yearning for impossible delights, living among distorted shadows and amazing pictures that have their origin in some magic-lantern reflection of past and present life." So it was with poor Oliver Lennox. Sometimes he mistook Mary for her mother, who was in the grave ; then came scenes in the hunting-field, for he had been a keen and fearless sportsman, mingled oddly with terror and hatred of duns, and the fancied presence of his dead son Harry, to whom he had been tenderly attached. To these occasional aberrations of intellect, Mary never became used, and they always filled her with the keenest anguish and dismay.

And so for a long and weary day Mary had been enduring all this, till she thought her own brain would turn, when Alison Home announced that Captain Chesters was in the dining-room, where she found him booted and spurred, and warming himself before the large fire of coal, roots, and peat, and perfectly dry, apparently, his overalls and ample Inverness cape, which he had left in the hall, having protected him completely from the rain.

The same old portraits that had looked down on Cyril Wedderburn—portraits of the Lennoxes of past times, "seeming ghostly, desolate, and dread," were looking down on him, but they suggested no other idea to his mind than that they were "uncommonly seedy, and were in appearance only fit for Wardour Street."

Her father was slowly, but surely, passing away, and Mary, in the utter loneliness of her heart—she had so few visitors and fewer friends—now felt compelled (despising herself the while therefore) to receive politely this unwelcome visitor, for, save her father, she knew no human being to care for, or who seemed to care for her ; thus a kind of sullen desperation had been stealing over her since Cyril's sudden departure.

Aware that it was Chesters who had injured her with her betrothed, Mary regarded him with a secret fear, equalled only by her loathing, and summoned as she had been from the bedside of her ruined and impoverished parent, whom she knew to be in this man's power, made these emotions all the stronger.

To the *roué* Chesters there was something altogether delightful in the freshness and presence of this young girl, so plainly and modestly attired, and with her rich hair so beautifully dressed, as she came near him, and brought an odour of the dried lavender (from plants in the old garden), amid which all her handkerchiefs, collars, and cuffs were folded ; and in her bosom, fastened by her solitary brooch, were some of the first violets of the season, which Alison had gathered for her, singularly enough, near the stile at the old triple thorn.

Mary had not been without many a mortification since Cyril's departure, and since *the story* had gone abroad. Lady Wedderburn, Lady Ernescleugh, and others—even the unpretending Mrs. M'Guffog, the minister's wife—had eyed her coldly and curiously from under their parasols ; and some even had ventured to survey her more boldly than had been their wont—or she nervously fancied they did so—and all this she owed to the scheme and tongue of Ralph Rooke Chesters !

And now with the first glance, Mary discerned, to her alarm, that her visitor was, as the saying is, "flushed with wine," or too probably something more potent, as his face was almost purple in some places, his green eyes were bloodshot, and his utterance was somewhat uncertain. He held out his hand, without drawing his thick riding glove off, and regarded her with one of his cool, leering, and insolent smiles.

" Bravo, Miss Lennox ! How goes it with you ?" he asked. " Dull enough, I suppose, in this atrocious weather ?"

" Pray be seated," said Mary, retreating back a pace, after barely touching his hand.

" Thanks," he replied, continuing to eye her smilingly, and to twirl and untwirl the lash of his short riding whip.

Ignorant of all that passed at Willowdean between Lady Wedderburn and Cyril, or knowing only that the latter was gone, the advent of Gwenny gave Chesters some courage to renew his attempts to gain a place in Mary's heart, or at least to bend her to his purpose ; and when tired of her—for tire he knew he should—why, then in Cyril's absence, he might have a chance of winning the heiress, if he met her in London ; for Chesters was a man of the most unbounded assurance.

" So Wedderburn is off to join his regiment at last—ha ! ha ! —after engaging himself to his pretty cousin ?" said he, bluntly.

" You are surely misinformed," said Mary, faintly.

" I am *not*. He told me all about it in London."

This, of course, was utterly false ; but Mary could not know that it was so, and he was resolved on making her miserable by inspiring her with jealousy and mistrust.

" And where is his regiment lying at present ?" she asked.

" 'Tisn't lying anywhere just now," he replied, in a mocking tone, which, like his smile, was replete with insolence.

" I do not understand you, sir," said Mary.

" You're dying to know all about it, though. Well, after our mutual friend Wedderburn had been going it, as usual, among the girls at Chatham and Rochester—oh, I know the style perfectly—the Fusileers sailed from Southampton on the fifth of this month."

" For where ?' asked Mary, in a low, breathless voice.

" Oh, Malta, Turkey, or somewhere thereabout. What can it matter to you now ? Come, Miss Lennox—or may I not call you Mary ?

" ' See the mountains kiss high Heaven,
And the waves clasp one another.' "

And he proceeded to quote again his favourite and almost only piece of poetry, drawing nearer her as he did so ; but Mary arose, with lips compressed and eyes flashing, and so Chesters, whose ideas of love-making had not been acquired in the society of ladies generally, became correspondingly irritated.

" Well, if you won't be jolly, but are determined to be

10

unpleasant," said he, with an insolent laugh, "suppose we talk about business?"

"I am more and more at a loss to understand you, sir."

"You can understand *this*, I presume, Miss Lennox, that I took up the old gentleman's bill—not for his own sake, but yours?"

"Though you have been so often his guest in better days? Yet, from whatever motive you freed my poor papa from the terror of it, you performed an act of great kindness and charity, for which I shall ever thank you and remember you in my prayers."

"Bah!" said he, with gloomy scorn, "who prays nowadays? You treat me more like a dog than a gentleman, Miss Lennox; but," he added, as the fumes of what he had taken were beginning to mount upward, "do you know that for all the grand airs you give yourself, I could have your father arrested and marched off to Greenlaw Gaol; and if you continue as obdurate as you are now, what the devil is to hinder me from doing so?"

Terror of the man, and of his new and unwonted bearing, got the better of Mary's anger, and compelled her to dissemble. But she said—

"You talk daringly, sir; for what reason could you, or any such as you, have Oliver Lennox of Lonewoodlee arrested?"

"Debt. Have you already forgotten the bill I took up for him?"

"Never shall I forget your kindness. But has not the bill expired? I think the phrase is."

"No; it can never expire. I had it protested and renewed; so it grows daily in value—interest upon interest. The world is divided into two classes—at least, I have found it so—fools and scoundrels, or dupes and despots. Now, by Jove! I prefer being the last named; anything is better than being a fool or a dupe."

Mary was speechless. The bill! that fatal bill! She remembered how she had bathed her father's trembling hand in Rimmel and iced water, before he had achieved the signing and indorsation of it, with a signature so all unlike what his own was wont to be, that the bank people had eyed it dubiously for a time.

"How did your father ever expect to meet this bill, unless some good-natured fellow like myself had come forward? He is a veritable old goose, who seems to have thought his pasture land of Lonewoodlee a perfect California, a Golconda, or El Dorado, that no end of money could be got out of."

"And what have you thought of Chesterhaugh?" retorted Mary.

"Pretty much the same, by Jove! But though Chesterhaugh

is entailed, I have contrived to make all the timber march, and something more."

Amid all the difficulties, monetary and otherwise, that Mary had undergone, no man had ever before dared to address her in the tone and manner now adopted by this bold reprobate. A clamorous anxiety, a strong sense of weary confusion, a terrible, yet dull oppression of the heart and aching of the head, a sensation as if she was all pulse, pervaded her. She made a struggle to appear calm, and only after a time became conscious that Chesters was speaking again, but with thicker utterances than ever.

"Give me one kiss, Mary dear, and a promise of a little hope that you will love me in the time to come, and I shall be patient, though I want money horribly. Once I had only to draw upon my banker, now I have to draw upon my wits—a devil of a difference, you'll admit. So just one kiss, my sweet——"

"Stand back, sir, I command you!" exclaimed Mary, raising her hand to the bell.

"Why, hang it! you don't mean to mourn for ever about that selfish muff, Wedderburn, who has discarded you—cast you off for a richer engagement?"

"He could not well have made a poorer one," sighed Mary.

"Had he been a man of honour, he would never have concealed from his family the fact that he loved you."

This was perhaps the most stinging remark Chesters had made. and having some truth in it, Mary felt it more keenly ; so if fear made her tolerate the presence of Chesters, wounded pride now caused her to loathe him more and more. Remembering all the trickery of which Cyril—her absent Cyril—had suspected him, hinting even at intended murder, perhaps ; his sharping at cards, and the apparent snare into which he had lured herself, indignation for a moment got the better of her fear and policy, and with invincible hauteur in her face and manner, she said—

"I have to request, sir, that you never again mention the name of Captain Wedderburn to me. Indeed, I am astonished that you dare to speak of him to any one."

"Why? by Jove!"

"When you know that his horse was drugged on that terrible night."

"By whom?" he asked, with a frown.

"Your worthy groom, or yourself."

"Dare you say so to me—a gentleman?" he asked, making a stride towards her, and laying a hand heavily on her arm.

"I do. A gentleman? Take your hand away, Captain Chesters, or, though a girl, I shall——"

"Do what?"

"Summon aid, and have you expelled," replied Mary, feeling again all her own helplessness.

Her words and bearing had, however, the effect of completely sobering her tormentor, who took up his hat, and, while a cruel white glitter came into his green eyes, said, with a mocking bow, "As you please, Mary Lennox; as you please. But I warn you, that if you are not more complaisant when next we meet, my protested bill shall go into the hands of Grubb and Wylie, my solicitors. If you have no mercy on me, why the deuce should I have any on your father? And so I wish you good evening."

Mary made no reply to the unmanly threat of this would-be lover; but turned her back upon him and rang the bell, that Alison might usher him out. And as the sound of his horse's hoofs died away in the rain that lashed the windows, she felt as if her heart was dying within her, for never before had she undergone an interview so singular and insulting; and she felt, moreover, an intuitive foreboding that she had not seen the last of Rooke Chesters. "Sufficient unto the day is the evil thereof," saith the old Scriptural proverb. But she could not help dreading evil and gloom, misery and desperation, beyond the present; and that Chesters might, in his baffled rage at herself, be infamous enough to attempt to arrest her father, place him in prison, and so kill him outright, came on her soul like a new and hitherto unforeseen terror.

But strange events were to happen ere Mary and her tormentor met again. And after a few weeks she learned incidentally, from Dr. Squills, that Chesters had left the neighbourhood once more, and betaken himself to London. All that remained of Chesterhaugh, being entailed, had been put under trust for the behoof of his long-patient creditors; the house and grounds were advertised to be let by Messrs. Grubb and Wylie; so Mary and the district were alike freed from the annoyance of his presence for a time.

But she found her home gradually growing more and more intolerable to her. Cyril's sudden and unwonted visit just before his departure, and her subsequent anxiety for letters which never came, all betokened some mystery. Her rather stormy interview with Chesters, overheard, doubtless, by vulgar ears that were at the keyhole, and the total cessation of his visits afterwards; together with the great local esclandre of the snowy night at Chesterhaugh, had been made subjects for discussion at the village tap, the blacksmith's forge, and even beside her own kitchen-hearth.

Mary could gather much of this from the manner of Alison Home and her other domestic; and they had seen much that Mary wist not of, for, like all their class, they could read the faces of their superiors as one may read a book ; and in hers they saw only trouble and sorrow, distraction and care.

She felt that Cyril had deserted her, and she would say in her heart—

"His love for me was but one thought, one fancy, it may be, among many ; while mine, alas ! it was the die on which I staked my all—the chain whereon all the links of my life were strung."

CHAPTER XXVII.

IN BARRACKS AGAIN.

"As I informed you by telegraph, Wedderburn, we embark on the 5th—so you have a fortnight to get your outfit for the East, to see all your old flames in Rochester and Brompton, to prac-tise the use of the revolver at the Spur Battery, and every other little art of war or peace that may be turned to useful account in the land for which we are bound."

It was Sir Edward Elton, the Lieutenant-Colonel of the Fusileers, who spoke laughingly to Cyril, when the latter in uniform, with sword and sash on, reported himself in due form at Chatham Barracks, as having joined from leave, three days after his departure from Willowdean.

In the prime of life and manhood, Sir Edward looked every inch a soldier. Fully six feet in height, his strong and lithe figure had endured, without being impaired, the snows of Canada and the fierce hot sun of India : but his coal-black hair was becoming grizzled now. His dark hazel eyes were keen, but calm and resolute in expression, as those of one born to command ; and his voice was full, deep, and rolling, though apt to become husky after he had " handled " the regiment throughout a long field-day on the Lines or elsewhere. He was the beau ideal of what a British officer and a thorough English gentle-man ought to be ; and had seen some sharp service in the East Indies, when with Pollock's Brigade in Afghanistan. He was thrice wounded on the banks of the Sutledge, and was nearly finished off by a thrust from a Sikh lance at the battle of Aliwal.

" You'll find all our fellows pretty much the same as you left them," he resumed ; " Probyn as keen at billiards as ever ; Bingham always in a scrape with some enterprising maid, wife, or widow ; Pat Beamish always late for parade, breakfasting on seltzer and curaçoa, with a wet towel round his head, and the major giving, as usual, his song of ' The girl I left behind me,' to the last few who linger at the mess-table."

" He may sing that song with full effect, ere long," replied

Cyril, laughing at the Colonel's enumeration of a few regimental peculiarities.

"We shall have work enough and to spare in getting all ready by the 5th of the month; the baggage must be reduced to the smallest possible compass, and all we don't require, must be left, like the poor women and children, with the depôt. I am glad to say that the regiment is in the highest order and discipline, and able, thank God! to face more than its own strength of any troops in the world."

Elton's eye kindled as he spoke, for he was intensely proud of his regiment, the noblest qualities of which he had carefully fostered and developed; and perhaps no finer body than these Royal Fusileers existed in the service of the Queen, being all picked men, and in their ranks the three countries of the Empire were pretty equally represented; if there was any preponderance it was in favour of England, and among them were more "Good-conduct-ring men," than almost any other corps could produce.

"I shall see you this evening at mess, I presume. This is our last night there; to-morrow it is to be broken up. There is no parade this afternoon, save for the juniors and recruits; so I would advise you to fill up a spare hour in going over the company's accounts and so forth."

And, as the Colonel concluded, he once more turned to the "Register of Services," one of the thirteen great books which are kept in every regiment of Infantry.

Cyril shook his hand, quitted the orderly room, and once more found himself in the sunlighted barrack square, where squads of recruits are for ever marching to and fro, with or without rifles, practising the balance-step, or swinging the clubs or the dumb-bells, and mechanically he took his way to his old rooms, on the tree-shaded and somewhat gloomy old brick terrace which overlooks the parade-ground.

Though his quarters as a captain—one small apartment and a still smaller bed closet, their walls covered with mean and dingy paper of the cheapest material—were quite familiar to him, their poverty of aspect, the small and coarsely-glazed window that faced the blank brick wall enclosing St. Mary's Hospital, the lowness of the ceiling, the ugly wooden beam which crossed it and was covered with ten thousand indentations made with a poker (the usual mode then of summoning one's servant from his den above) together with the meagre and rickety furniture obtained on hire from some exorbitant Jew, all impressed him unfavourably, fresh as he was from the luxury and splendour of his own home at Willowdean.

He tossed his sword and crimson sash on the table with a sigh, and opened his blue surtout with its gold shoulderscales—the most handsome undress ever worn by the Line—as if he was choking from want of air.

Was it not a dream that since he had last stood there, matters were so changed between him and Mary Lennox ; that he had indeed lost her, and should never hear again the voice that found so soft an echo in his heart ?

He had received no explanation from her of that obnoxious episode, the visit to Chesterhaugh ; he had asked none, nor, perhaps, would he have listened to any in the mood of mind he was then. Yet he was not without a lingering hope that she *might* write to him in some fashion ; and so the craving to hear from her, or of her, combated fiercely with the sterner resolve to pluck from his heart the memory of her image, and all that she had been. It was so difficult—so bitter a conviction to entertain, that all was indeed over between him and Mary Lennox ! But he had never told her where his regiment lay, a singular omission, and in her sequestered home among the Lammermuirs, she knew none who could inform her, even if her little pride of heart would have permitted her to write. She, like him, longed and looked for letters ; but did so in vain. None were exchanged, so disappointment and mistrust grew fast between these two, who had hitherto loved so tenderly.

While in this mood of mind, Cyril Wedderburn had no desire for the tame monotony of overhauling his pay-sergeant's books, and seeing that Private Jones had been duly credited or debited the sum of ninepence ; that Private Brown's stoppage repaid the expense of the shako and ball-tuft he had lost in a row on St. Patrick's day ; that Private Smith's clearances had been paid to his wife when her last baby was born, and *not* to the clamorous canteen-keeper ; and that all the messing, clothing, and accoutrements of ninety odd non-commissioned officers and men, were right and regular.

But as idleness was impossible, he took his new-bought revolver-pistols, and went forth to the Spur Battery to practise in the dry ditch, at sundry imaginary Russians. Even of that he wearied, for in the ditch were already some thirty or forty noisy, happy, and heedless subalterns—boys fresh from Sandhurst or Eton, and chiefly ensigns of the Provisional Battalion, all cracking away to each other's peril with their revolvers, and emulous in their pistol practice ; and so, while numbers of his brother officers, with whom he was an especial favourite, were searching for him at his quarters, the mess-room, and all about the barracks, he was leaning over the lofty summit of the glacis, gazing dreamily at the old familiar scene, which spread far down below him like a map.

He saw the fertile plains of Kent, steeped in the light of the noon-day sun, stretching far away till lost in hazy distance ; the village of Rainham, and all the windmills that studded the green slopes ; the sleepy Medway with all its man-o'-war hulks

and freight of lesser craft, winding between its banks ; bustling
Chatham, its streets full of red-coats ; the great square stone
block of Rochester Castle, and the tower of the Cathedral,
both rising from amid a sea of sunny vapour, half in light and
half in sombre shadow ; and immediately beneath the lofty
bastion was the gloomier feature of the scene—the Military
Cemetery, where lie the bones of a vast army—of the thousands
who have escaped the battle and the pest, in every clime where
our drums have beaten, and who have come home invalided at
last, worn out by wounds and with constitutions broken, only
to die in Fort Pitt, and fated neither to see home or kind, or
to enjoy the hard-won pittance named in mockery a pension,
but to find an obscure grave under the brow of the great Spur
Battery.

Cyril looked long and thoughtfully over this scene so familiar
to his eyes, while those sounds so incessant in the adjacent
streets of barrack, the drum, the bugle, and often the shrill
Scottish pipe, were perpetually ringing in air, announcing
orders, parades, or dinners, and so forth ; and he marvelled in
his heart how he and all those in whom he had an interest, and
for whom he had a love, might be situated, ere that day twelve-
months came round ; for now war had been declared, and the
sword was drawn ; already the combined fleets of France and
Britain lay before the Russian harbour of Odessa, and none
knew what an hour might bring forth.

CHATTER XXVIII.

THE LAST NIGHT AT MESS.

" WELCOME back, Wedderburn ! Eastward Ho ! is now the
cri de guerre !" exclaimed the cheerful voice of Probyn—always
known as Jack Probyn—when Cyril entered the mess-room of
the Fusileers, just as the last notes of the fife and drum, playing
the " Roast Beef of Old England," died away on the Terrace
without, and most of his brother officers accorded him a hearty
reception as he passed along to his place. It was flattering to
find that he was so much a favourite, and on his mind there
flashed the thought, could Mary but have seen it !

It was the last day of the Regimental Mess—for the morrow
was to see it broken up, and those who had met together at the
same board so long and so happily, dining as best they might in
their own quarters or at hotels. Thus it was not without something of melancholy interest, for the casualties of war had to be
encountered before once again those silver trophies glittered on
the table ; and of all the happy, heedless, and handsome young

fellows who sat there now, who might be present at the next festal meeting? How many might be under a foreign sod, or mutilated and pining forgotten, upon half-pay.

God alone could tell. Soldiers are not much given to reflection luckily, and probably few thought on the subject.

The mess-room was far from being an elegant one, for in Chatham Barracks even moderate comfort cannot be found; then how much less, elegance! It was long, narrow, and somewhat low in the ceiling. Dingy red curtains draped the windows, and a few oil portraits decorated the walls. These were the property of the regiment, being likenesses of some of its colonels who had either been favourites with the Fusileers of past times, or were eminent in military history, such as George Lord Dartmouth, who demolished Tangiers, and whose breast-plate and black wig belonged to the days of the Revolution; the Great Earl of Orkney, who commanded the corps at Stein-kirk and the Siege of Athlone, and whose squinting Countess was the mistress of him of "the pious, glorious, and immortal memory." And there was fiery little Lord Tyrawley, in whose days, when the regiment was hunting Rob Roy in the High-lands, it was named the South British Fusileers to distinguish it from the 21st, who still retain their remarkably ugly cognomen of North British Fusileers.

The furniture was very plain; at one end stood a table covered by a red cloth, whereon lay the current literature of the mess, to wit: Army Lists, Racing Calendars, Peerages, the " Queen's Regulations," " Field Exercise for the Infantry," and various newspapers, the corners of which had been appropriated for lighting cigars when matches ran short; but what the room itself lacked in elegance, was amply made up for by the splen-dour of the long table, on each side of which sat some thirty officers all in full uniform, richly laced, with crimson sashes and glittering epaulettes, for in those days the free and easy mode of dining in shell-jackets and open vests, had not as yet crept into the service.

They were all men of a good style and more than creditable appearance; there was not a sub in the regiment, and very few of the captains, but could ride, row, shoot or fence, handle a cricket-bat, a billiard-cue, or single-stick with any man; and, as the old commandant said, at the farewell inspection, "They were a splendid set of officers, and such as England only could produce."

The mess-plate, the long accumulation of years, was indeed magnificent; and on the tall centre-piece, the chased epergnes, the massive goblets and salvers, large as shields, were graven the trophies and mottoes of the Fusileers—the Rose of England, the Garter and the Crown, with all their battles from the capture of Martinique to the field of Toulouse. Nor were softer luxuries omitted ; on this, the last day, the mess-man had done his best, and thus roses, carnations, and geraniums from neighbouring conservatories were not wanting to enhance the decorations of the table ; and the ice to cool the champagne was cut in square blocks of crystalline brightness, hollowed out to receive the bottles, when placed in the costlier coolers of gold and silver, carved and embossed.

The colonel, Sir Edward Elton, was in the chair ; Pomfret, the junior Lieutenant present—the corps had then *no* Ensigns —was Vice-President. The former wore his Cross of the Bath, and save a few who had Indian medals, he was the only man decorated there ; for the veterans of Walcheren and Egypt, the Peninsula and Waterloo, had long since become as traditions in the ranks.

Ten liveried servants, whose close shorn hair and stiffness of bearing showed them to be soldiers, were in attendance, and amid the buzz of conversation, half-drowned by the crash of the band playing certain airs from *Lucrezia* and *Fidelio* on the Terrace outside, Cyril heard dreamily the voices with which he had been so long familiar ; of his kindest friend, Major Single-ton, an old soldier who had suffered many disappointments in his time (as what old soldier has not?) and who, having little save his pay, would have retired but that war had broken out ; of Jack Probyn, arguing with the Doctor about a billiard match ; Pat Beamish, with his rich Irish brogue, quizzing Bingham, Captain of the first company, about some girl with whom he had been flirting furiously about three o'clock that morning ; and all the frivolous chatter and banter inseparable from the conversation of thoughtless young men who meet thrice daily at least—once at dinner and twice on parade.

But now after Cyril had related the story of his adventure with the horse, very briefly, for a rumour of it had reached the regiment, the usual light topics became diversified by others of a graver nature ; the crowded state of the garrison ; the pre-parations for war by land and sea ; the chances of promotion and staff appointments ; which regiment had sailed already, and what other corps were going ; was Odessa to be the base of operations, or some port in the Black Sea? Bets were taken in favour of Odessa, and lost in the end. The merits of the general officers, the probable formation of the brigades and divisions, and the supposed plans of the campaign, were all discussed pell-mell with the beauty of certain dancers and opera singers, the points of dogs and horses, quarrels and griev-ances, and the girls at the Rochester Balls, where the same set of pretty faces appeared weekly, and as Beamish said, "regu-larly tore one's epaulettes to rags by the vigour with which they held on while waltzing."

"I'll trouble you for a slice of that turkey, Wedderburn," said Probyn.

"With pleasure, old fellow," replied Cyril, starting from his waking dream ; "a little of the stuffing ?"

"Thanks—did you see this morning's Gazette ?"

"No—anything important ?"

"Only the names of a few fellows who are appointed to serve on the staff of the proposed Turkish Contingent."

"Any one we know ?" asked Major Singleton.

"Bedad," struck in Beamish, with a flash in his dark blue Irish eyes, "there's a fellow going out with the rank of major that is as big a blackguard as ever was drummed out of the Belem Rangers."

"Rather strong language, Beamish !" said Sir Edward Elton, with a smile, but a tone of reproof.

"Not a bit too strong for the occasion, Colonel," urged Beamish.

"Is it Ralph Rooke Chesters you mean ?" asked Probyn.

"The same," resumed Beamish, while Cyril felt his heart throb painfully ; "he was once in a Lancer corps, but proved a mighty deal too sharp for the mess at cards, and so had to sell out to avoid a court-martial ; and now here is the fellow going to the East with the rank of major, bad luck to him !"

"That comes of having swell friends at head-quarters," said Probyn.

"But it is only local rank," added some one despairingly.

"True for you," grumbled Pat, dragging at his big black whiskers; "but it *is* rank there anyhow, and it is small pleasure I'd have in taking orders from Rooke Chesters on an outlying picket, or in front of the enemy——Champagne, waiter ! By-the-by, Wedderburn, you'll have to call out Pomfret."

"Why, what has poor Pomfret been doing ?" asked Cyril, looking at the smiling and rosy cheeked subaltern, who was fresh from Sandhurst.

"Doing ? By Jove, he's been going ahead at an awful pace at the bandstand and the Rochester Balls with an old flame of yours, Miss——"

"Exactly—I know," said Cyril, nervously interrupting the name.

"The Canterbury girl who worked you an elegant cigar case."

"Pomfret is welcome," said Cyril, wearily, for the name of Chesters had put a finishing stroke upon his secret annoyance. In spite of the light-heartedness of those about him and the all-inspiring subject of the coming war, Cyril felt low in spirits, dissatisfied and unhappy, and the more champagne he imbibed, the more dull he seemed to become.

His old friend Singleton observed this ; but instead of rallying him as he might have done, he said in a low voice—

"You seemed livelier before you left us on leave, Wedderburn—pardon me, but what is wrong with you ?"

"Can't say, Major—but I do feel out of sorts."

"Out of spirits, rather——no little bit of white muslin in the
matter, is there ? Hah ! I am right—that glitter and half
closing of the eye—and the sudden pink in the cheek, tell me
all about it. Well—if you have no engagement to-night, come
to my quarters after the mess breaks up, and we shall have a
little friendly chat over a quiet glass of grog and a devilled
bone. Are you game for that ?"

"Thanks—I am at your service, Singleton."

"Never think of annoyances, or run after them," said Beamish. "Cyril, like creditors, duns, and the devil, by the Powers,
they'll find you out soon enough !"

"Going to the ball to-night, Beamish ?" lisped Meredyth
Pomfret, the junior lieutenant, save Ramornie.

"Where is the ball, my little man ?"

"At the Dockyard Superintendent's. The whole of the staff,
a swell set, will be there—some pretty girls, too, Beamish."

"And could I venture among that lot in white muslin and
tulle—I, an unprotected man ?" replied Beamish, who was a
black whiskered and square shouldered Irishman, with a deep
Kerry brogue ; "and on the eve of marching for foreign service
too, would it be fair to break any more of the darlings' hearts ?
No—no ; that cruelty I leave to such fellows as you, Pomfret
and Wedderburn."

"Foreign service—and so it has come to that again !" said a
married officer who was the Colonel's guest, and there was a
tinge of thoughtful regret in his tone.

"Well, Joyce, bedad it's a power sight better than being
camped at the Curragh of Kildare, or protecting Peelers and
process-servers in Tipperary, or hunting for whiskey stills (God
bless them !) in the Bog of Allen, when the mist lies thick on
the Slievebloom Mountains."

On this day Cyril had some food afforded him for speculating
or reflecting, if not on human affairs in general, on the muta-
bility of human love in particular. When returning from the
Spur Battery in the afternoon, he had passed a handsome
carriage bowling on the way past St. Mary's guard-house, towards the green Lines and the beautiful village of Gillingham.
A pretty brunette in a white crape bonnet peeped forth for an
instant. Cyril would remember—oh, how well !—the time
when the sight of that equipage, its horses, harness, and livery,
had made his heart leap, and now he barely accorded to its
occupant a salute with his forage-cap. Yet he could recall

vows that seemed now to have been traced in water or written on sand, and the flood of joy her smile once poured through his heart had subsided for ever! How the thought of her had been the first in the morning and the last in the night! How many an hour had he rambled and ridden, danced and lingered with her; and how often had he met her amid the woods of Cobham, the green leafy lanes of Gillingham and Rainham! How he had showered gloves, bouquets, music, and gifts more precious still upon her; loving her and clinging to her, though he knew that before this Hamilton of the Scots Royals, Musgrave of the Marines, and Sutton of the Artillery, had flirted with her, and carried on the same agreeable but perilous game! Yet he hoped that she loved really at last, and loved *him* better than any one; but the quizzing of the mess had saved him. She was beautiful, yet she had been talked of then in his hearing as "a knowing hand—an old stager—up to trap," and so on; and the warning drum, when it beat for the march after the *route* came, dissolved the spell, so others had succeeded him, and now it was on "Pomfret of ours." His idol had taken to bird-liming the unfledged ensigns and second-lieutenants; and she, so loved and petted by him once, was less even than a friend now—a mere bowing acquaintance. How strange to think it was so, after all that had been!

How often is much of this great game of life played out *unseen*, amid a crowded drawing-room, at the jovial dinner-table, at the social fireside, by hearts that seem to break, "yet breakingly live on," while sentiment wars and struggles in vain, for in the end time soothes all things!

How much, how dear, how close to his soul was that woman once! Alas, how little now—less, we have said, than a bowing acquaintance!

Would his love for Mary Lennox share a similar fate? Perhaps so—time alone could show.

As this was the last night of the mess, until long after the drums had beaten tattoo in the great echoing square; long after the subalterns of the day had collected the final reports of the present, the absent, and the tipsy; the last bugle had warned "lights and fires out," and silence and darkness gathered over the roofs where so many thousand soldiers were sleeping, that so long were to be in the tented field, the officers of the Fusileers and a few of their guests lingered at table as if loth to separate; but ultimately, leaving a few who were bent on "making a night of it," or a morning rather, Cyril and Beamish adjourned to the quarters of Major Singleton, to have a little quiet supper, the "devilled bone," &c., which had already preceded them from the mess-house.

CHAPTER XXIX.

CONFIDENCES.

"BOTHER this garrison order about 'lights and fires out' by tattoo ! here's my fellow actually extinguished the stair-lamp," said the Major, as they stumbled up the old wooden staircase which led to his quarters. "Where are you, Beamish?"

"Behind you, in the dark, Major—in the dark, bedad, like a Protestant Bishop, as we say in Kerry."

Singleton soon found the keys of his rooms at the back of the staircase window-shutter, the place where such are frequently deposited in Chatham and other barracks, and they soon found themselves in his quarters, where, by the application of the poker to the dormant beam above, he summoned his servant down.

"Now then, Bob, look alive, and let us have supper double quick !"

Bob Dacres had relinquished his white livery coat and aiguillette on leaving the mess ; but he still retained his yellow plush inexpressibles, white stockings, and buckled shoes. They consorted oddly with an old regimental coat, having white worsted wings—a garment which he had donned for kitchen-work.

The fire was stirred up in the small, meagre grate furnished by her Majesty's Ordnance Department ; four candles were lighted, two on the table where the supper was laid, and two more stuck in quart bottles on the mantelpiece, gave the Major's sitting-room a cheerful aspect, though it was minus carpet or curtains, and its furniture was of the plainest description, being the mere barrack allowance ; to wit, a couple of Windsor chairs of hard wood, a table of the same material, a set of fire-irons, a cast-metal coal-box, with three field-pieces engraven thereon between the letters V.R. and B.O. ; a pair of bellows, and a black iron candlestick. These elegant pieces of furniture, together with a few iron-bound baggage trunks that had been all round the world, completed the comforts and appurtenances of the Major's room, unless we add a couple of regulation swords and undress and dress belts with a double-barrelled gun and brace of horse-pistols that hung in a corner, and a wooden box of cigars that stood on the mantelshelf, "pro bono publico," as he said, for Conyers Singleton was a plain soldier of the old school, contenting himself with little, and always resolved to make the most and best of everything. He rarely or never wore "mufti," and when he did it was quite out of the mode.

He had a grave, almost sad face at times, with a remarkably soft expression of eye ; and it was currently supposed in the regiment that a shadow or a sorrow must have rested on some portion of his earlier life ; at least, all knew that prior to his joining the Fusileers he had been long a prisoner of war in India, and had thereby lost his chances of promotion. "There is no example of human beauty more perfectly picturesque than a very handsome man of middle age—not even the same man when in his youth," according to one of our fair novelists : and these words fully applied to the Major, who, though past the prime of life, was still a man of fine and commanding appearance. His features were noble, and slightly aquiline, and his thick, wavy hair, once a rich dark brown, was fast becoming grey and grizzled now ; but his hazel eyes were as clear and bright as when a boy ensign he carried the colours of his regiment fearlessly up the corpse-strewn glacis of Ghuznee, though *seven* reliefs had been shot under them in succession.

He had seen much service in other corps, but was an especial favourite with the Fusileers.

The supper, which consisted of something better than the promised " devilled bone," was soon discussed ; the Major's servant was dismissed to his roost upstairs, and amid a cloud of soothing Cavendish, the trio proceeded to make themselves completely comfortable.

"This is jolly !" exclaimed Beamish, as he tossed aside his sash, and threw open his full-dress uniform.

"I have wine, if you fellows prefer it," said Singleton ; "but here are brandy and some real Irish whiskey ; and neither will taste the worse for being in black bottles."

" The whiskey, by all means, with water *pur et simple*," said Beamish, "and no adulteration of lemon or sugar—orthodox grog, that is the mark, Major, for there's never a headache in a hogshead of it. Ah," continued Pat, while mixing his tumbler and eyeing the contents affectionately, "there is nothing on earth so true as a good glass of grog—nothing so fickle as a pretty woman !"

"Heresy !" said the Major, while Beamish heaved a mock sigh, and Cyril remained silent.

"I saw Miss—Miss What's-her-name !—you know it well enough, Wedderburn—passing in her carriage by St. Mary's Guard to the Lines to-day," resumed Beamish.

"And young Pomfret, no doubt, with her?" added Singleton. "A little fool that boy is !"

" She still looks young and beautiful, that brunette, though I have known her when younger and more beautiful ; but that was before we went to Burmah ; and, by Jove, 'tisn't yesterday I saw the big pagoda of Moulmein."

" It seems ages ago, and she's on the cards still !"

Cyril's heart beat quicker, and he coloured while he spoke, yet he scarcely knew with what emotion, as he had long ceased to care for the fair one in question.

" Don't affect to be soured with the sex, Pat," said Singleton. " Fill your glass again—it's down to zero."

" Soured ! not I; for I am naturally kind and attentive to everything with a petticoat on."

" Even a Scotch Highlander, eh ?"

" But we had one omission to-night at mess, Singleton."

" What was it ?"

" Your invariable song, ' The girl I left behind me.' It generally comes off about one in the morning."

" But we left at twelve sharp, and I am keeping it for the marching-out day," replied the Major ; and with a twinkle in his eyes, which were fixed on Cyril, Beamish began to sing in a mock sentimental manner—

> " My love is fair as Shannon's side,
> And purer than its water ;
> But she refused to be my bride,
> Though many a year I sought her.
> Yet since to France I marched away,
> Her letters oft remind me,
> That I promised never to betray
> The girl I left behind me."

" Well, Beamish," said Singleton, catching something of the other's spirit of raillery, " I hadn't the heart to sing when I saw Wedderburn looking so melancholy."

" What is amiss, Cyril ? Have you made a bad book on the Epsom, or the Whittlebury Stakes for three-years-olds ? Or is it some red-headed Scotch lass that you have left behind you?"

Cyril's eyes dilated and flashed ; and he coloured with vexation, but attempted to laugh while rising the glass to his lips.

" You seem awfully cut up about something, and it must be a girl, Wedderburn," said the Major. " I can see that with half an eye."

Cyril's colour deepened ; he was in no humour either for scrutiny or banter. But Beamish said laughingly—

" Don't grieve so about it, or her, or whatever it is. Little more than a week must find us on the sea, and if a girl has jilted you, forget all about it, or score it down to the bad drop that is in her, as we say in Ireland."

He winced decidedly under this unwitting home-thrust, but drained a huge rummer of brandy-and-water at a gulp, and then with a sudden burst of that communicativeness which seizes most men at times, and of which they generally repent when calm reflection comes in the morning, he exclaimed—

" I have been deceived, Singleton—deceived where I trusted; I own it, and am sick and sore at heart just now !"

" Hear that now. Bedad! I would have sworn it!" said Beamish, in whose eyes there shone a light that was all merriment, without an atom of the commiseration for which Cyril was inclined to look.

" I have been deluded, I say, Singleton, by a girl I loved well and dearly," he resumed, with growing bitterness ; " and in my heart I am constantly vowing—yes, swearing that I shall forget her ; but with every futile vow her gentle face, her soft voice, and all her image—the remembered charm of her presence— come back to me clearer and more vividly than ever ! Oh, what magic, what idiosyncrasy of the human heart is this !"

" By Jove ! it's like a bit of Moore's melodies !" said Beamish, while Cyril coloured deeper, with a sudden sense of his rashness in making such an admission.

" You are just what I was at your age, when a subaltern, though, luckier than I, you are now a captain," said Singleton. " I was hot-headed, generous, impulsive, and warm-hearted. Ah, what a devil of a treadmill is this work-a-day world, that it grinds both heart and soul out of us till nearly all trust in man, and too often in woman too, passes away with every scrape of our razor ! How many fellows have I seen come into the service since I was first gazetted—cultivate their whiskers, and the d—d Jews !—get into debt or matrimony, sell out or go to the devil, while I have still held on, and am only a major yet, when so many of my brother-subalterns are in command of regiments, or the enjoyment of snug staff appointments !"

" But you had a singular run of ill-luck," urged Cyril—"your captivity."

" True ; few, however, but myself, know exactly all that captivity cost me ; and now, if you have patience to listen to an old soldier's story, I don't care if I should spend a few minutes in telling you the incidents that cast a shadow on my life for many a year—a shadow that may never pass away or melt into sunshine."

The Major paused, and after a time said—

" It is a strange, but pretty true axiom, that ' a man is only as old as he feels ; a woman as old as she looks ;' thus I am not so old as to be past loving, or at least remembering what it was to love and be loved in return. So listen to my story."

And filling his glass and his meerschaum almost at the same time, Conyers Singleton related the following little narrative of his early life.

CHAPTER XXX.

"THE GIRL I LEFT BEHIND ME."

"THERE was a time when hope and enthusiasm were the mainsprings of life and action with me. Alas! their places are supplied alone by memory now. No battle in the field has ever been fought without some blunder ; then how much more likely is the battle of life to be full of error and mischance !

" In the year after the storming of Ghuznee, in Afghanistan (when both of you who now listen to me must have been boys at school), I found myself at home in Cheshire on sick-leave. I had been wounded by an Afghan lance, and was in comparatively feeble health ; so as our way to and from India then was always round the Cape, my leave was for two years from the date of leaving head-quarters, and I was bent on enjoying it all the more that I had come home on promotion ; for my corps, the **th, had been sorely cut up during Keane's operations amid the snowy mountains and deep and perilous defiles of Afghanistan. We lost by war and disease nearly all our captains, so we, the subalterns, benefited thereby.

" My aunt, Lady Singleton (dowager to Sir Guy Singleton, a general of the old fighting days of Wellington), received me with open arms, for I was almost the only relation she possessed, and at her old place, Stoketon Moat, near Warrington, but on the Cheshire side of the Mersey, I had always found a warm welcome when I came there for school holidays in the years of my orphanage (my parents having died young), then how much more welcome was I from far away India, and the perils of the Afghan war !

" Stoketon Moat—so called, for once in Saxon times a timber house had stood there surrounded by a moat, of which not a trace can now be found, though it was said to be deep enough when Hugh d'Avranches, after Hastings, slew the whole Saxon inmates of the place, sparing not even the dogs by the hearth —was a beautiful old mansion of the later Tudor days, with heavily mullioned windows that were half-shrouded in ivy, jasmine, and clematis, through the leafy masses of which the sun at times could scarcely penetrate the little leaded hexagonal panes, the upper rows whereof were emblazoned with the armorial bearings of the Singletons for many a generation, back even to Geoffrey Singleton, one of the two knights who represented Cheshire in Parliament in the reign of Henry VIII., who curtailed so greatly the absurd privileges of the county-palatine of Chester.

" The old house stood on an eminence overlooking the sweep made by the Mersey towards Runcorn : it was surrounded by fine old oaks, massive cedars, and dark yews, and the vista through these, as seen from its front, was terminated by the green hill that is crowned by the old ruined castle of Halton.

"Aunt Singleton was of a cheerful disposition, thus Stoketon Moat was seldom without visitors ; and on this occasion she had residing with her three handsome and lovely girls, the youngest seventeen, the oldest barely twenty, whose presence spread a new and bright charm to me about the quaint old house.

"Isabel, Lyla, and Katie Vane, were unusually attractive girls ; their beauty was great and of the most refined and delicate cast ; but the eldest proved the most charming to me. She was twenty now, and I had not seen her for four years before, when an incipient boyish and girlish flirtation had sprung up between us—a flirtation that with our somewhat maturer years was to take a more solid and lasting form amid the seclusion of Stoketon Moat, and the opportunities afforded by its woods and fields, green lanes, and leafy privacy.

"I was an object of interest now, to be flattered, coddled, and petted—pale, and with my recent wound yet green, and yet with all the glories of Keane's campaign to talk about !

"Thus my rival, her admirer Riversdale, had no chance when compared with me, though he was a very pleasant and good-looking young fellow. A doctor of the Royal Staff corps, Robert Riversdale was home on leave of absence like myself, but from America. It seemed to me that Isabel's blue eyes were always seeking mine, and that every glance we exchanged was half-complimentary and wholly caressing. They were glances of mute and secret intelligence, that we alone felt and understood.

"Riversdale's family lived in the neighbourhood of Stoketon Moat ; they were wealthy, thus he was everyway an eligible suitor, and had been a kind of privileged dangler after the Vanes for a short time prior to my arrival. He had driven and ridden with them to see all the sights in the county ; but his attentions were in no way decided, nor was his preference marked, until my decided admiration for Isabelle seemed as a spur alike to his jealousy and love.

"However, her residence in my aunt's house, our daily, almost hourly intercourse—the vast charm of propinquity, and the chances afforded by it—gave me every advantage over Riversdale; and after the snuff-coloured Bengalee girls, and the dreamy, tawny, and affected Eurasians or Indo-Britons, with whom we were compelled at times to associate when up country, the pure and soft English beauty of Isabel Vane, together with her sweetness of disposition, and a certain piquant playfulness of manner, were so pleasing, that, within a week after my return to the

Moat, I was fondly in love with her—madly, I may say, as 1 never did things by halves in those days.

"I was scarcely aware of the strength or depth of the passion that was growing up in my heart, until one day, when my aunt said—

"'Why is it, Conyers, that your talk to me is for ever of Bella Vane? You are never weary of extolling her accomplishments——'

"'But she has so many, aunt!'

"'Her graceful style of conversation, her elegance of figure, her beauty, and so forth ; do you love her, Conyers?'

"'Yes, dear Aunt Singleton,' said I, blushing like the boy 1 had been, rather than the man I was.

"'Then tell her so, Conyers, and God bless you ; for Bella, 1 know, will make a kind and loving wife to the man who is happy enough to win her.'

"My heart leaped within me, and my blood seem to course with renewed force through every vein, as Lady Singleton spoke thus, for already ideas of marrying, of being the actual proprietor, possessor, and protector of a girl so charming, came with her words.

"Well, encouraged thus, my declaration—fully expected, no doubt, by foregone conclusions—and her acceptance came about successfully in the usual fashion, or what I suppose to be such for I never loved before, and have never loved since.

"In a leafy lane, where the purple plum, the golden apple, and the damson trees entwined their branches overhead, excluding the sun from the thick rank grass below, and where the wild honeysuckle and flowers by the wayside, filled the air with fragrance, as we rode slowly together, side by side, on a summer afternoon, it all came to pass somehow.

"We were long of turning our horses' heads homeward, and the house-bell had summoned us thrice to dinner, ere I lifted her from her saddle with a caressing tenderness and an emotion of delight such as had never before thrilled through me, for we were engaged now ; she was my own Isabel, and to be the wife of my heart, before we sailed together for India.

"We were rallied by the laughing Lyla and the golden-haired Katie, about our delay and return at so late an hour ; and we must have had self-conscious or tell-tale faces, for the girls were not long in discovering our great secret ; and even Riversdale, who unluckily dined with us that day, detected quickly enough on Isabel's *engaged* finger, a ring which he knew well to be mine, for it was conspicuous enough to him, as he stood by her side to turn the music leaves, as she seated herself at the piano in the drawing-room, where usually music became the order of the evening.

"I, too, was near, and could detect the flush that mounted to his temples when his eyes fell on the ring, and how the words of compliment or flattery he was about to whisper in her half-averted ear, died away unuttered on his lips.

"He was too well-bred to question her, or make the least remark upon the subject ; but pleading an after-dinner engagement, took his leave soon after ; and I was weak enough to feel some triumph at being master of the position, and that the girl he admired so much and loved in secret, was mine—and mine for ever.

"For ever ? Alas, could I then have foreseen the future ?

"Three months afterwards the bells rang a merry wedding chime in the old church of Warrington, when Isabel and I knelt · at the altar and were declared 'man and wife' by the white haired rector ; and seldom, perhaps, has the sun shone through the quaint stained glass of those ancient windows on a lovelier bride than mine, or on two sweeter girls than Lyla and Katie, in their clouds of snowy tulle, as they knelt, sobbing, of course, behind her.

"A brother officer was to have been groomsman, but an accident detained him, and by an odd chance or fatality, his post was occupied by Robert Riversdale, who acquitted himself to the satisfaction of all—the six bridesmaids in particular, for very striking the fellow looked in his rich staff uniform ; though I fancied that his voice faltered when he congratulated me, and he turned deadly pale, as he kissed the cheek of Isabel ; but I could forgive him these little weaknesses *then ;* and as if to show that he had no secret repining at my success, he presented her with a magnificent suite of jewels, diamonds and opals set in gold and blue enamel—a suite an empress might have worn ; and that evening saw us off to seclude ourselves in Wales, until the honeymoon waned.

"As our carriage drove away from the Moat, and I drew down the blinds and embraced her, caressing her head on my shoulder, 'Oh Isabel !' I exclaimed ; 'my own Isabel—at last we are married and one !'

"'Married for life !' she murmured, with her face nestling in my neck.

"'Married for love,' I added.

"'Yes, but for life, dearest Conyers—for life, too—and the life beyond, if such can be !' she added with an energy that haunted me even as her words did, when our dark and sorrowful future came.

"I shall never forget the delight of those remembered days —for they are but a memory now—the blissful days I spent with Isabel, amid the green vales, the frowning cliffs and soaring peaks of the old principality ; in lonely places where the

wild goat, his long beard waving in the wind, leaped from crag
to crag, rousing the golden eagle in his giddy eyrie ; or by
secluded pools and mountain tarns, where the brown otter
would rise suddenly to the surface, and, with a spotted trout
between his teeth, vanish as quickly to his hole among the rank
green sedges. 'The world forgetting, by the world forgot,' at
least for a period, we spent it in a calm of joy and tenderness,
till Lady Singleton began to weary for us, and urged our return
to Stoketon. as I could spend but six months more in England,
and would have to report myself at the Depôt Battalion in
Chatham, whither Isabel was of course to accompany me.

"How well I can yet recal our long Welsh ramble, the flat
vale of the Teifi and the old church of St. David's ; the gloomy
pass of Llanberris ; Craig Ceffyl, where the Welsh made their
last brave stand against the 'Ruthless King ;' the lovely vale
of Llangollen with all its luxuriant greenness and fertility—for
we were never weary of wandering, and were full of love and
enthusiasm for each other and for everything.

"I had no alloy to my happiness, not even when I found, as
by chance I sometimes did, among Isabel's favourite books, a
withered flower between the leaves, that had *not* been given by
me, or 'To Isabel, from her friend R. R.,' pencilled on the fly-
leaf, for Riversdale's hopes were gone for ever now. But if I
progress thus, I fear you may find my story as weary as an old
novel written in letters, than which, perhaps, I know of nothing
more flat and prosy.

"After we had been some months at Stoketon, a child came
to add to our happiness.

"When you see me seated here, a plain and rough old soldier,
in his bare or half-furnished barrack-room—if not happy, at
least content, like poor La Vallière in her convent—content to
do without the luxuries and the tendernesses of life, you may
think there is little of the poetry of it in me ; but there was
much of it *then*, ere sorrow, care, and unmerited misfortune
came upon me.

"A new joy seemed to spread a holy light over all our little
circle when the baby came. I shall never forget the tender
emotions that made my heart swell tremulously and filled my
eyes with a moisture akin to tears. I felt grateful to God and
happy with everybody, with the old village doctor, the wrinkled
and tyrannical nurse, who assumed the command of the entire
household ; with my benignant Aunt Singleton : the radiant
girls Lyla and Katie (exalted now to the sudden dignity of full-
blown aunts), and more than all with my poor, pale darling
Isabel, for to my enthusiastic mind, something of sanctity
seemed to mingle with the love I bore her.

"I felt what the childless can never feel ; now more than

ever joined. as a certain writer has it, to the great community
of man. Here was a little unit, that in the time to come should
be a man, to live long after us, I hoped and prayed in my heart
of hearts, honourably and well, beyond the years, when the sod
had grown green above Isabel and me.

" So the baby grew the wonder of all our little community at
Stoketon Moat ; Aunt Singleton bestowed upon it a sponsorial
silver mug, the handsomest that could be procured, and the
white haired and red faced Rector gave it a name and made a
little Christian of it, under the double cognomen of Guy Conyers ; the latter for me, and the former for the old General who
had led his brigade so gallantly at Vittoria and Toulouse ; and
so, happily passed the days till the time came when I found
that I must appear in Chatham garrison, and our home was to
be, thenceforward, a broken one !

" If our baby was a hale and sturdy little fellow who throve
amazingly, it was otherwise with his mamma, for Isabel made
a slow recovery, and was so weak and ailing, when the terrible
time for my departure came, that by a consultation of physi-
cians, it was impressed upon me, that she must imperatively
remain at home, nor attempt to follow me to India, for perhaps
six—certainly for four—months yet to come.

" This was a sad dictum to me, who knew that the transport
which was to take me to the shores of Hindostan—the *Rangoon*
Indiaman—was already lying opposite Tilbury Fort, taking in
water and stores.

" I shall pass over our parting. It was sad, indeed ; and
long and frequently did I press both the pale mother and the
golden-haired child to my breast ere I tore myself away, with a
whirling brain and a bursting heart.

" ' To your care I confide them, dear Aunt Singleton,' said I,
as she embraced me at the door. ' I am going now, and perhaps may not be here again before my hair is grey and wrinkles
have taken the place of dimples.'

" The overland route had not then been developed, and going
to India was, to many, the affair of a lifetime. I had tried to
speak in jest, but, alas ! I knew not how prophetically.

" I travelled night and day until I reported myself to the
Commandant, old Sir William W., and assumed the command
of the men of my own regiment, that were to embark next day.

" In the hurry of our departure, I had no time left me for a
moment's reflection, luckily : and grey daybreak on the following morning saw us leave Chatham for Gravesend, five hundred
strong, all drafts for various corps in India. And as we marched
in the still and dewy dawn, to the air of ' The Girl I Left Behind Me,' every tap of the drums and every note of the sweet,
low fifes, went keenly to my heart : for I thought of her I had

left behind in Cheshire, my girl-wife, my Isabel, with our baby
at her breast !

"The cheers of the heedless and unthinking boys—for the
detachments were composed of little else—who were off to see
the world, each with sixty rounds of ammunition at his back,
and ready to face anything—Old Scratch himself if he came
against them—failed to rouse either my natural spirit or my
military enthusiasm ; though I could remember the time, when
the loud crash of the regimental band, the bright gleam of the
bayonets, and the waving of the colours above nine hundred
bearskin caps, with the measured tread of many feet, had
kindled both when *last* I had marched to India, through the
deep resounding arch of the old Picquet House, and under the
guns of the great Spur Battery.

"Seven miles of dusty road brought us to Gravesend, where
the *Rangoon* lay, a stately ship of eighteen hundred tons, hove
short on her cable, with blue-peter flying at the foremast-head.
All was confusion on board, for she was a great East Indiaman
of the old school, built alike for war and traffic, carrying twenty
eighteen-pounders, and eight thirty-twos on her main and lower
decks. Everybody was bustling about, and the ship was a
veritable Babel. Cuddy stores, with fresh and salt provisions,
were being hoisted in from lighters on one side ; rusty shot and
shell, as ballast, from a Woolwich tender, on the other. Casks
and cases encumbered all the decks ; paint, tar, beer, tobacco,
gin, and bilge-water, loaded the atmosphere above and below ;
a drizzling rain was falling, and a thick white mist enveloped
all the low flat shore ; the brick bastions, the curtain and fosse
of Tilbury, which is a fort as Dutch in aspect as in character,
since its chief strength lies, not in defending itself by fire, but
in being able to lay the surrounding district under *water*.

"More than a hundred women, sailors' wives and sweethearts,
were sent noisily ashore. Our men were 'told off' to their
berths speedily, and amid the noise and bustle, the voice of
Isabel, her face and the baby's came ever and anon as in a
dream before me ; and with something of a sickened heart, I
entered the great cabin.

"'Bravo, Singleton! How goes it, old fellow?' cried a
familiar voice, and from amid a crowd of officers who were
lounging and lunching about the table, some sitting, some
standing, and all laughing and chatting gaily, Doctor Riversdale in his blue undress uniform, with sword and black belt on,
came forward to greet me. 'So *you* are going out in the
Rangoon, eh !'

"'Yes, with two hundred men from the depôt. Are you?'

"'Bound for Bombay I am, to be stationed there on the staff.
But—but I don't see Mrs. Singleton with you.'

"I then explained, and my voice faltered as I spoke of her, that her health did not, as yet, permit her to accompany me to India. I know not now the words of Riversdale's reply ; but the spirit of it impressed me with the idea that her absence proved rather a relief to him. To avoid talking of Isabel, even to my late rival, was impossible. He seemed to like the theme, and perhaps felt a grim satisfaction in the idea that she and I were to be separated for a time.

"The voyage passed over pleasantly enough. At St. Helena, at the Cape, and with several homeward-bound ships, we left letters for those we had left behind us—those we loved, and hoped, if spared by war and disease, to meet again. And the month of December saw us with our various regiments in the army of Sir Hugh Gough, advancing from Agra against the Mahrattas engaged in that war, which was incident to the quarrel about the occupation of Cutch, all of which, however, has nothing to do with my story, save that I was a unit in the army destined to annex the principality of Scinde to the British Crown.

"On the 29th of December we crossed the Chumbal (a river which flows through Central India, from the Vendhya mountains to the Jumna) without loss or much trouble, and had just halted and piled arms to have a little tiffin, when the mails from Europe overtook us, and I got a letter from Isabel, the first I had received since leaving her and home, an event that seemed now to have happened ages ago.

"She was getting slowly better, and hoped to rejoin me soon—at least, to be in Bombay, awaiting the conclusion of the war in Scinde. My eyes suffused painfully, and my heart beat wildly, as I read on ; for though petty and trivial to others, situated as I was then, all that followed was dear indeed to me, for it was about our little Guy Conyers. He was growing *such* a baby, *such* a love as never was seen or heard of since babies were first invented ! His nose was fast resembling mine (I remember-bered it a most unpromising button), and he had such a pretty pouting mouth, just like Katie's ; his eyes were already noticing, and often smiled from his berceaunette at things other people couldn't see ; but they were *such* eyes ! How he crowed and laughed, and bit the nurse's finger with his toothless gums ; and would persist in kicking off the woollen bootikins Aunt Katie had knitted for him, and his little pink feet seemed more com-fortable without them !

"How I devoured all this. I who once upon a time thought all babies most stupidly alike, deuced bores and nuisances, to be avoided and shunned in all trains and steamers. And so while I read on, the picture of Isabel, with her downcast eyes and long lashes, turned to this particular and most wonderful baby, crowing on her knee, or nestling in her tender bosom, came vividly and fondly before my mental eye, till I was roused from my dream of home by the bugles sounding 'fall in,' and the voice of Sir Hugh's senior aide-de-camp saying to the Colonel as he rode past,—

" 'The enemy are in front.   Please get the battalion formed. Her Majesty's 39th will commence the attack—the 56th Native Infantry to support : stand to your arms !'

"I placed the letter in my breast pocket, drew my sword, and, with a sigh, joined my company.

"I need not detail at any length the battle of Maharajpore, though it proved a fatal field to me.

"The British were fourteen thousand strong, with forty guns; but the Mahrattas, a fierce and warlike race, trained to arms from their earliest years, mustered twenty-one thousand, horse and foot, with one hundred pieces of cannon.

"Under a terrible fire, which, in the end, killed and wounded seven hundred and ninety of our officers and men, we rushed upon them ; the old 39th, or Dorsetshire—*Primus in Indus*, as their colours have it—in the van, and the 56th Bengal Infantry supporting them well and gallantly, soon drove the foe from their guns, bayoneting the gholandazees on every hand.

"Rallying in the village, the Mahrattas again showed front, and fought with blind fury.   There the Gwalior troops, after discharging their long matchlocks right into our faces, flung them down, and, like the Scots Highlanders of old, charged us sword in hand, with target up and head stooped behind it. With frantic desperation they fell, like a herd of wild tigers, upon our regiment ; and the whole of my company got mingled with them in a confused *mêlée*, opposing their bayonets or clubbed muskets to the keen trenchant blades of the Indians, who were ultimately routed, with the loss of four thousand men, and all their beautiful cannon save *one*, which they carried off the field, and to which I was fastened by a rope, a mutilated and manacled prisoner of war !

"The catastrophe happened thus :—

"Amid the terrible *mêlée* in front of the village, and just when Major Stopford and Captain Codrington, of the 40th Regiment, fell before the very muzzles of the Mahratta cannon, the aspect of the enemy was wild and imposing, and I shall never forget it.   Their shrill, mad yells mingled with the cheers of the British, and added to the general roar of the conflict ; while their flowing garments and turbans of every brilliant colour, scarlet, yellow, crimson, blue, and white, studded with precious stones and embroidered with gold, made their excited masses seem gorgeous as a vast field of flowers.   Large round shields covered with brass bosses protected their breasts, and over these we saw their swarthy faces, their shining eyes, and crooked sabres, that flashed and glittered in the sunshine. Personally, they were all powerful men, and their strength and activity were only equalled by their recklessness of life and ferocity of purpose.

"'Save me! save me, Singleton, for the love of God!' cried a voice; and dismounted with his horse shot under him, his bare head (for he had lost his cap), exposed to twenty uplifted sabres, I saw Doctor Riversdale lying among their feet; and I did save him, by a superhuman effort, at the head of twenty determined men. But as we fell back, keeping our bayonets at the charge, a volley of grape and canister shot, from their last and only gun, swept away the twenty brave fellows who adhered to me. I fell among the enemy alone, was cut down by a tulwar, and dragged to the rear of the village.

"I fainted from loss of blood, and on recovering, found myself many miles away from the corpse-strewn village of Maharajpore, and in the hands of a Mahratta chief and a few of his men, now outlaws and fugitives among the mountains; for their army had broken and fled, totally defeated and irretrievably scattered."

CHAPTER XXXI.

THE MAJOR'S STORY CONCLUDED.

" My limbs were stiff and sore, for I was still bound to the cannon, which was a nine-pounder fieldpiece.

" The chief, Ali Khan, whose whim it was to keep me prisoner instead of cutting me to pieces, was an outlaw now; several regiments of Gough's army, both infantry and cavalry, were sent into the country of the Mahrattas at the expense of the Gwalior Government, to inforce peace and order; so he, with his followers, were compelled to lurk among the mountains in the north-west of Scinde.

" There were times when I repined bitterly, and thought that but for Riversdale's presence in front of the village, when he ought to have been in the rear of the attacking column looking after the wounded, I should not have made that desperate onslaught to rescue him, and so been *taken* myself!

" Alas! you see that my story, unlike most others, begins with a happy marriage instead of *ending* with it, as most novels do, and all comedies at the fall of the curtain.

" Like most, if not nearly all the Mahratta troops, the followers of Ali Khan were cavalry, hardy and ferocious fellows. Their only arms were swords, spears, and matchlocks, like those used in the wars of Cromwell; their only equipage, blankets

and horse-cloths. With these slight incumbrances they easily
rode fifty miles a day, feeding their horses on whatever they
would eat ; whether it was the ripe corn growing in the fields
or the dry thatched roofs of a village, was all the same to the
Mahrattas of Ali Khan, who was a stern and unyielding warrior,
vain of real or supposed descent from Sevajee, the founder of
the old Mahratta empire.

" *En route* he carried off several children, and I now learned
for the first time that his people were fond of possessing slaves,
and hence their capture of me.

" Over miles upon miles of a flat country covered with wild
bushes, and many more of desert sand, they fled from Maharajpore, till we entered upon a district studded by almost
impervious thickets and tamarisk shrubs which also entwine
their branches ; and beyond this desolate region we reached
the mountains that look down on Western Scinde, where they
halted, encamped, and lurked for several weeks to rest and heal
their wounds, subsisting the while by forays and the plunder
they carried off in their march.   Sometimes Ali Khan made
the neighbourhood too hot to hold him ; and then, by a swift
movement, he would favour other regions, perhaps in Beloochistan, with a short residence ; but he generally preferred to
hover in the hills to the north of Tattah, which are barren and
totally uninhabited, so that we were often compelled to plunder
for food, almost to the gates of Brahminabad, its ancient
capital.

" Chained to that accursed gun, my sole sleeping-place being
between its wheels at night, exposed to the dews with only a
horse-rug to cover me (while the Mahrattas lived in tents),
exposed to the risk of being helplessly strangled by Thugs,
devoured by tigers or jackals, or being bitten by serpents such
as the terrible Braminee cobra, stung by insects all day, and
having the disgusting green bugs among my matted locks and
beard by night—chained to the gun, I say, like Ixion on his
wheel in the Infernal Regions, I thought—oh, how deeply and
desperately—of her I loved, of my home, of free and pleasant
England, far, far away ; of Stoketon Moat and Cheshire with
all its shady woods, its lakes and meres ; its parks of emerald
green, its shady lanes and hedgerows ; of the broad Mersey
winding to the sea ; of budding spring and glorious summer,
brown autumn, with its golden harvest fields and crisp foliage,
and jolly winter, with its snow on hill and wold, its green bays
and scarlet berries in church-porch and in hall.

" Changes like these I had none !

" It was a period of horror, weariness, and despair—a despair
that was black and hopeless, and daily, with a sickened heart,
I surveyed the arid plains on one hand and the barren moun-

tains of Tattah on the other, hoping against hope for some
rescue or relief, and in this slavery more than a year passed
away, without an event save an occasional buffalo hunt, when
hides were wanted for shields or harness, (as the Mahrattas
cared not for the beef), or an occasional *kutha*, a popular
amusement of the tribe, when recitations and songs are given
by professional musicians or story-tellers; and frequently I
heard them sing of the battle of Maharajpore, and how the
great Sahib-log, Ellenborough Bahadour, had been amid the
thickest of the conflict, mounted on a snow-white elephant, in
the howdah of which I had certainly seen his lordship freely
exposing himself to the risk of shot and shell.

" My sabre wound had been allowed to heal as Nature chose,
and after hemorrhage ceased it closed rapidly ; but unluckily
for myself, by the skilful and tender manner in which I bound
up a bayonet-stab received by Ali Khan, the Mahrattas conceived that I was a doctor, and hence kept me closely secured
to the gun, to frustrate any attempt to escape.

" Isabel's letter was found upon my person, and conceived to
be some great medical secret ; the ink lines were carefully
washed off the paper, and the dilution swallowed on speculation
by Ali Khan and his favourite wife ; but I had many cures to
perform, many cuts and stabs and bullet-holes to probe and
patch and bind, with the terror of death hanging over me if I
failed, or a patient fevered or died ; but luckily for me the
Mahrattas were all Hindus, extremely temperate in what they
ate or drank, so I was pretty successful in my practice, and
earned the goodwill of all, particularly that of the women of
the tribe, who were as hardy and as muscular as the men, and
regularly shared every labour with them save that of fighting;
but it was long before I succeeded in convincing them that I
was *not* a doctor, and by that time I was so weary of existence,
as to care little whether they shot me, to save further feeding
or trouble.

" Released but at rare intervals, and even then always closely
watched, I had been *five* years chained to the gun, when it was
abandoned in a deep *nullah* as a useless incumbrance. I was
then worn to bone and brawn ; but I had lost all heart and hope.
Heaven knows how I had been fed, for I had been treated often
like a dog—a creature of the lowest caste.

" Offers of ransom I had often made in vain ; and chance of
rescue I had none. Neither had I any prospect of escape. I
was without horse, or arms, or money, or even a knowledge of
where I was, so devious had been our wanderings ; and at times
I could not say with certainty whether we were on the confines
of Beloochistan, or among the mountains of Kelat.

" The Hindu religion admits of no proselytes, so I was never

troubled with any attempts to convert me ; the institutes of
Menou, compiled 1200 B.C., had quite settled all that, so that
I was safer than in the hands of Mohammedans, who might
have compelled me to choose between the turban and the
bowstring.

"And so a sixth year passed away !

"Was my Isabel living or dead? Had she perished of a
broken heart ? I tried to remember of a widow that had done
so, but failed. Was our little child living now ? If so he should
be verging on seven years old. Seven years old—oh, my God !
I would press my hands over my eyes and strive to portray
him, for I knew that the child must grow, and change with his
growth ; but I could only picture him as I had seen him last,
nestling in his mother's bosom.

"Then I would think with a shudder, Alas ! how long may
he have been in his little grave ?

"Ever present were such thoughts as these ; of Isabel and
the baby in 'the woollen bootikins' which had been worked for
it, as her last and only letter told, by Katie—little Katie, whom
I remembered with her masses of golden hair; the rippling
locks of which would neither keep in knot or net, but hung
like an aureole, a shining glory round her smiling face.

"Kate would be four-and-twenty now, and most likely herself
a mother.

"I knew that I must long, long since have been gazetted out
of the service ; numbered with the lost, the missing, or the
dead ; that another must have filled my rank and place in
the regiment, where by that time my very name must be
forgotten !

"And so I grieved at the thought of these things, till my
heart grew sick with sorrow and grieving. Oh, how true it is,
that 'the heart knoweth its own bitterness, and a stranger
intermeddleth not with its joys.'

"Times there were when I longed for death, for, as Dryden
says in his 'Don Sebastian,' I felt keenly but bitterly that
'Death is to man in misery, a sleep;' but in that sleep, I should
have no dreams of Isabel or home.

"One day—I shall never, never forget it—these, and such
sad and bitter thoughts as these, were maddening me while I
was grooming the horses of Ali Khan, beautiful animals of
the Candahar and Thibet breeds, and when my task was over
I sat down beside a tamarisk tree, and actually gave way to
tears. We were then encamped, as I knew, not far from the
Indus, in a place where a grove of peepul trees grew round a
little lake beside a Hindu temple of white marble, the bronze
idols in which the Mahratta women were wont to fan for hours,
after smearing them with ointments, butter, and ghee.

" 'The Sahib-log (white gentleman) is always sad!' said a voice close by me ; and on looking up 1 saw Ali Khan, with his shield of buffalo hide slung on his back, and leaning on his Kelat spear, while his dark gleaming eyes observed me with something of wonder and much of contempt.

" 'I have thoughts, O Khan, that make me sad,' said I, rising and crossing my hands upon my breast.

" 'Are you not kindly used among us ?' he asked.

" 'I have certainly eaten your salt and bread ; but both have been watered by the tears of misery.'

" 'Why ?'

" 'I have a wife and child——'

" 'I have several wives and children too ; yet were I a captive, would they cost me a tear ? No. I am a man ! Go —our lives are in the hands of Bramah—our doom in the hands of Kali—even yours, a creature without caste or future.'

" And turning away with stolidity and scorn, he mounted the horse I had just saddled for him, and with his long tasselled spear in his hand, rode off on a scouting expedition—for the appearance of some Bombay cavalry in our vicinity had rendered him somewhat uneasy.

" He had scarcely left me, when I heard some shrill cries from the women of his followers who were dipping and bleaching their linen dresses in the little lake beside the peepul grove. A child had fallen into it from a rock where he had been gathering flowers ; it was the deepest part of the lake, and the little creature rose twice and sunk again before I stirred myself.

" 'What is it to me ?' thought I bitterly ; 'would that every Mahratta in the land were in the same perilous predicament.'

" A third time the boy rose and wildly threw up his little brown hands and arms, while his half-shriek came over the water as he vanished again. At that moment a thought of my own child flashed upon my mind, and plunging in, I dived successfully, saved and brought the little Mahratta cub to dry land ; but barely in time, for some hours elapsed before I succeeded in perfectly restoring him to life and consciousness, and ere I became aware that it was Sevajee, the favourite child of Ali Khan, I had rescued from a watery grave !

" With all his assumed stolidity and apparent sternness of heart, the Mahratta chief was melted towards me now, and in a burst of gratitude he gave me my liberty !

" 'Go,' said he ; 'here are a swift horse, good arms, my own, and a bag of rupees. You are free to join your people. Thirty miles from this, near a temple of Seva, on the left bank of the Indus, you will find them. Go—and Brahma, Kali and Vishnu be your guides, and may their arms overshadow you, even as those of the blessed banian tree overshadow the earth !'

"This was the best and holiest wish a Hindu could give me, as they pay divine honours to this enormous tree.

"You may imagine that I was not long in availing myself of the permission so suddenly given.

"Like one in a dream, one who had suddenly shaken off a long nightmare that has been protracted to the verge of madness, I rode all that afternoon at a breathless pace, not without fears that Ali Khan might change his mind, or my horse, arms, and rupees should excite the cupidity of some of his people who might follow me ; and ere nightfall I found myself in a little flying camp formed by a battalion of the Queen's troops (the 'old Springers'), and a squadron of the 1st Bombay Lancers, whose French grey uniforms, faced with white, I hailed with a shout of joy as I rode towards their videttes.

"On that day I had been exactly six years and four months a prisoner !

"On hearing my story, the officers treated me with every kindness and commiseration, and while the Lancers departed on a vain search for Ali Khan and his people, no time was lost in having me transmitted to Bombay.

"I had been returned among *the killed* at the battle of Maharajpore, and so circumstantial were the details of my having been cut down and dreadfully mangled by the Mahratta swordsmen, that I had some trouble in proving my own identity.

"The years of my captivity had seen many changes, and thus I, who had gone out by the *Rangoon*, Indiaman, round the Cape, and up the Arabian Sea, came home by the overland route, which was just being got into working order, but we crossed the desert with a caravan. So eager was I, that the six weeks of the homeward journey, with its ever-changing scenes, seemed interminable ; and telegraph, or Indian cable, there were none. I reached London well nigh destitute ; but burning with impatience for news of Isabel and home, having counted more than ever the hours since I was a free man.

"I attended the Commander-in-Chief's *levée* at the Horse Guards, where my weird and wild, or hunted aspect, excited considerable speculation among the fashionably-dressed loungers in the ante-room. He promised to look after me promptly ; but 'the Liberals were in office,' as he told me, with a peculiar and inexplicable smile ; so my back pay was refused on the plea that 'the country had lost my services for six years and four months ;' my progressive rank also was declined, so that I, who had been well up among the subalterns of my own corps at the battle of Maharajpore, was now, when gazetted anew, placed at the foot of twenty-four lieutenants of the Royal Fusileers.

" My wife ! They could tell me nothing about her. 'Why ?' I asked passionately.

" 'Because my rank and services did not entitle her to a pension ;' so I turned on my heel with mutiny in my heart, and on my lips a bitter malison on 'the Liberals' who were in office.

" On my aunt, Lady Singleton, depended all my hopes now ; so I set out for Stoketon by the first train from London.

" Already in the whirl of events my past period of love, and my marriage with Isabel Vane, had begun to seem but a tiny patch in the chequered web of my existence ; but it was a spot so bright and fair, so pure and happy, that I clung to the memory of it, as being well worth ten times all my other years together.

" My heart and soul yearned for her, and as the train bounded along the London and North-Western line my mind went back to the day when we set out from Stoketon on our joyous wedding trip to Wales, and the affectionate energy with which she insisted we were married 'for love and for life !' Would that gush of affection fill our hearts again ? or was it one of those joys which have no renewal in this world of change ?

" As I approached Stoketon Moat, and saw the dear old house with its clustered chimneys, its quaint oriels and deeply-mullioned windows shining in the sun, and half-hidden by dark green ivy, flowering clematis, and fragrant jasmine, I lifted my hat, and inspired by the memory of all the terrors and hardships I had undergone, exclaimed in a low voice—

" 'My God—I thank Thee for this day !'

" Is it blasphemy—oh, I hope not—to say that I had little perhaps to be thankful for in having escaped the perils of Maharajpore, and survived my sufferings among the mountains of Tattah and Beloochistan ?

" The house was occupied by strangers, who viewed me with coldness and mistrusted my appearance of agitation.

" ' Lady Singleton had died three years ago—Mr. Vane's people they knew nothing about—had never even heard of them,' I was informed by a sleek and well fed butler who was about to close the door in my face—the door of the house that was once my home.

" ' Are any of Dr. Riversdale's family in the neighbourhood ?' I inquired anxiously.

" Yes ; the doctor has resided at his father's house since the old gentleman died about a year ago.'

" 'Thanks,' said I, and turned wearily away, and conscious that I was a source of vulgar speculation to the menials of the

strange family now occupying what, as I have said, was once
my home, I passed down the old and well-known avenue to
issue out upon the highway that led to Warrington.

"Riversdale, I learned from the lodge-keeper, had retired
upon half-pay, and had now an extensive practice in the neighbourhood. From him, then, I should perhaps learn all, and a
few minutes' brisk walking brought me to his villa, a handsome
new house, embosomed among some fine old trees.

"'Doctor Riversdale is always visiting his patients at this
hour,' the servant informed me ; 'but Mrs. Riversdale is at
home,' she added, ushering me into a drawing-room, the splendour of which seemed wondrous to me after my sojourn among
the sordid tents of Ali Khan.

"'I have no card,' said I, having omitted to provide myself
with such a luxury, or forgotten all about such things, 'and the
lady cannot know me : but say an old brother officer of the
doctor is anxious to see her.'

"'Why did I become a soldier?' thought I, while surveying
the comforts of Riversdale's home, and seeing his children. I
had no doubt they were his ; two boys and a girl, fair haired
little things, gambolling on the lawn in the sunshine ; and all
the inclination for what Jean Paul Richter calls 'cottage smoke
and sitting-still-comfort' came over me. Thus might mine
have been merry among the Stoketon woods ! Oh, the years I
have lost—years of love and joy with Isabel !

"Escaping from her brothers, the little girl toddled through
the drawing-room window, which opened in the French fashion
down to the floor ; and then impelled, I know not by what
secret impulse, I drew her towards me and kissed her so tenderly on the forehead, that she shrank back abashed and eyed
me dubiously, for I was tanned to almost negro blackness, had
a bushy beard, together with what must have seemed to her
the eyes of an ogre—the eyes of one who for fully seven years,
had been daily face to face with Death !

"Just as the poor child shrunk from me, the drawing-room
door opened, and there entered a lady who bowed with a well
bred smile of inquiry and paused, surveying me earnestly.

"Though more matronly in form, and a trifle rounder perhaps, her face was still that of Isabel, the girl I had left behind
me. Womanly and thoughtful, her eyes were as sparkling and
inquiring as of old, but animated by wonder now and inexpressible tenderness (for my aspect seemed so war-worn', till
suddenly tears and terror filled them as they gazed into mine.
The mouth, so exquisitely cut, was full and fine, till it quivered
and blanched, while the skin of her delicate face was smooth
as the lining of a white and pink shell.

"'Isabel!' I exclaimed, and opened my arms ; but shrinking

back, she uttered a wild cry of anguish and despair, and sank on a sofa, half fainting, and holding up her hands deprecatingly, between herself and me. 'Touch me not,' was what her mute gesture seemed to say.

"I then perceived that she had two plain hoops upon her wedding finger.

"*Two?*

"I dared not approach, but stood bewildered as if rooted to the carpet, for now I saw it all—I saw it *all*, and that a great and terrible grief was about to come upon me!

"She was the wife of Robert Riversdale!

"We stood apart, she shrinking and I doubting. Oh! was this the meeting—this the moment—for which I had longed and yearned, and thirsted, amid the protracted misery of the years that were past? Gasping, she gazed at me, while she did so, clutching wildly the cushions of the sofa; and there was an expression of unutterable bewilderment, of keen intensity, in her eyes.

"'Oh, merciful Heaven! Conyers Singleton, can this be you?' she exclaimed, in a low voice, like a wail.

"There was no embrace between us—no gladness, but only intolerable fear in both our hearts; we did not even shake hands, and she was my wife!

"'Oh, Isabel, and is it so? while I, after all those years that I have been a prisoner of war, a hunted fugitive, a wretched Christian slave, chained by the leg to a field-piece, among people whose faces and voices were to me but as those of wild animals—is it thus we meet and thus you greet me?' I said, mournfully. 'Isabel, what weariness of the world is in my heart—speak, or I shall fall at your feet!'

"Indeed, the room seemed to whirl round me, and I clung to the marble mantelpiece for support.

"'You seem to have come back as it were from the grave to reproach me; yet, oh, Conyers! I have nothing to reproach myself with,' she replied, speaking with great difficulty, while she placed a hand upon her heart as if to stay its wild beating, and a ghastly whiteness blanched all her beautiful face. 'The misery of this meeting is known only to—to God and me.'

"'And you have in my absence given to another your heart, your affection, which I deemed my own—*for life*, you once said?'

"'Reproach me not; all the world told me you were dead. I read the Gazette myself, and but too keenly remember, even at this hour, the agony of that in which I saw your name as among the killed. My hand, in time, was given to another.'

"'To Riversdale?'

"'To Riversdale; but my heart never—never. Oh, I shall go mad!' She began to speak wildly and incoherently, and

then added, 'In those dear past days I loved you and you only
—oh, yes, I loved you then so dearly, so truly, Conyers!'

"'And now, Isabel!'

"'I love you still, dearest Conyers, but that love will turn
my brain. My little child—*our* little child, Conyers,' she added,
with moving pathos in her voice and eyes, 'was dead ; Lyla and
Katie were about to be married. I had no one to love, and no
tie seemed to bind me to you, but sad, sad memory. Oh, what
shall I say? how explain myself? A mother—a wife, and yet
no wife! Riversdale loved me before I saw you, Conyers.'

"'Nay, not before your girlhood.'

"'Before your return from Ghuznee; but that pleads nothing,
I am aware, for I loved you then and you only.'

"'And since, Isabel—since?'

"'Alas! do not question me—and yet you must.'

"'Surely some little explanation is due to me!' said I, with
the forced calmness of settled despair. 'Oh, that I had never
returned from Ghuznee or learned to love you ; or would to
God that He had permitted me to perish at Maharajpore?'

"I was lonely and helpless, Conyers—oh, so lonely and helpless in my supposed widowhood,' said she, making a great effort
to speak, for voice and sense seemed alike to be failing her.
'I respected the long-tried affection of Riversdale, which had
survived even my marriage with you. He told me that he
owed his life on that fatal field to you. Oh, how I mourned
for you and how I loved your memory are known only to myself
and *One* with whom there can be no secrets, and who knows
all things! Could I help myself? and now—*now*—now,' she
exclaimed, while casting her eyes despairingly to Heaven,
and striking her hands together, 'am I to be torn from my children
—his children, *his and mine*—even from the little helpless baby
in its berceaunette!'

"'Not by *me*, Isabel,' said I, while on my aching heart those
piercing words fell like drops of molten lead ; 'not by me. I
shall go forth again to seek death more surely now, and cross
your path no more. One kiss—only one kiss—even *he* could
not refuse me that, and then never again shall we meet on this
side of the grave.'

"We both sobbed bitterly as I took one brief but passionate
embrace. I laid her gently on the sofa and rang the bell,
because she had fainted. Then I quitted the house of Riversdale
never to enter it again!

"To me it seemed that I must be in a dream from which I
should surely awaken. The sun was shining in all the glory of
a summer noontide on the green woodlands and greener
meadows, but I felt no warmth in its rays, and my teeth

chattered as I walked on, I knew not, cared not whither. So ended this terrible meeting—this interview of agony.

"I felt as one who was enveloped in the horror of a great and sudden darkness—one who had gone from the world itself, into the cold shadow of death.

"I have but little more to tell you now. Believing that I was dead, my aunt, Lady Singleton, on the death of my infant boy, bequeathed all she possessed to charitable institutions ; and I cared not to dispute her will, for a few months after saw me again in India, and face to face with the hard-fighting Sikhs at Chillianwallah. I strove hard to throw my life away ; but it seemed to be charmed now. I never received a scratch, nor has bullet or blade been near me since the day of Maharajpore.

"A few weeks after our victory over the Sikhs, I read the death of Isabel in the *Times*, and then I knew that my interview with her, and the intolerable mental agony consequent to the falsehood of her position, had destroyed her? My poor Isabel !

"We were then on the march for Goojerat, and none of my comrades knew why in that battle, and for many a day long after it, the hilt of my sword was covered with crape—the only mourning in which I dared indulge, for the miserable fate of the girl I had left behind me."

<hr />

CHAPTER XXXII.

THE ROUTE FOR VARNA.

UNQUESTIONABLY Cyril was unhappy in his mind about the new state of relations between himself and Mary Lennox. There were times when he thought that perhaps he had acted rashly in yielding so suddenly to the dictates of jealousy and the angry pride it engenders. He thought, too, over Singleton's remarkable story, and remembered how he had conceived the idea of a private marriage, and had even urged it upon Mary—a measure by which he must have left a young and almost unfriended bride behind him. Singleton's wife had wealth, position, and relations to rally round her, yet her fate had been a hapless one ; and Cyril, as he reflected on the contingencies of war, felt somewhat consoled, that he and Mary were still free.

"Let me think of her no more—no more !" he said, mentally. "Ah, how true it is that 'violets plucked, the sweetest showers will not make grow again.' And now my flower of love has been crushed in its bloom !"

Fortunately for him, in the short time that intervened now before the departure of the regiment, his days were too fully

occupied to leave him great room for reflection ; and the tours
of duty entailed upon an officer in such a place as Chatham, even
in time of peace, are incessant; thus, if they engaged, they at
the same time bored him by their continuous hard work and
monotonous routine.

When not on guard or piquet, and when captain of the day,
he had to make incessant inspections of the barrack-rooms, to
see that the iron beds were turned up in the morning, and the
ventilators open ; also before and after, and at every meal, to
ascertain that the messes were in order, wholesome, and
sufficient.   Then came visits to the patients in hospital, the
prisoners in the cells and guard-room, the children in school,
for the number of each and all were to be inserted in his daily
report.   Then there were courts-martial and of inquiry ; com-
mittees of all kinds, mess and band ; the expenses of the last
ball ; and baby-linen for soldiers' wives ; the foreign outfit for
his company to be provided ; the settlement of women who were
to sail, and those who were to be left behind (to starve,
perhaps)—a mournful fate determined by ballot ; then came
squabbles about barrack damages, broken glass, nail holes, and
candle blisters, over which barrack-sergeants groaned and
quarter-masters became furious, as they were generally found in
the "married corners" of the rooms, for in Cyril's corps the
angles of each apartment were still appropriated in the old
fashion, to the wedded couples, because experience had taught
Sir Edward Elton that the motherly and domestic care of the
women, when thrifty and respectable, added to the comfort of
his men.

Add to all these, the arrangement of little scrapes into which
Pomfret, Jack Probyn, and some of his younger comrades had
fallen by "flying kites to raise the wind," as they phrased it,
among the Jew usurers and money-lenders, the Shylocks of
Hammond Place—fifty per cent. wretches—whose eyes, unlike
those of poor Banquo, were full enough of "speculation."

He had to leave his card on several garrison belles, who had
bloomed, and blushed, and faded ; but by the triumph of art
over nature, had bloomed and blushed again through many
fruitless seasons, amid a vast number of military changes, which
saw the beardless ensigns they danced with at one period, come
back at another as bronzed captains or majors.   Invitations
were showered upon him ; there were even attempts made to
revive one or two dead flirtations—sickly attempts indeed,
for his love-wound was still green, and his heart was with the
solitary girl at Lonewoodlee.

Besides all these little occupations, there were revolver
practice in the dry ditch, pontooning at Rochester Bridge, where,
under the shadow of the old Norman Castle of the Bishop of

Bayeux, the Medway runs so fast, that it sometimes swept away a life or two ; and escalading with storming ladders about daybreak at the walls of the Spur Battery, a dangerous style of practice, too, when the bayonets of one's mimic forlorn hope are unpleasantly close behind. As a finale, he had to get his own Crimean outfit, for which Sir John enclosed him an ample cheque : to wit, gutta-percha jack boots, waterproof cloak and cape, camp bed, ground sheets, and blankets ; a canteen for two persons ; lantern, basin, and bucket ; bullock trunks and slings, and much more lumber, all of which he got for the small sum of eighty guineas, "dog sheep," from a Jew contractor ; so one way or another, it must be acknowledged that Captain Wedderburn's hands were pretty full, and that his sword could be seldom from his side.

Thus the days were got rapidly through ; but in the morning when he awoke, like a flood of gloom, his hopeless quarrel with Mary—his Mary, once so loved and petted—rushed upon him, and despite the bustle around, for many an hour his eyes and heart were far away at Willowdean and Lonewoodlee ; and a fair face he had last seen there—Mary, tearful, trembling, and pale in her muslin dress, with her delicate neck and adorable arms--haunted him.

Torn by conflicting emotions and unstable in purpose, he had come to the merciful resolution of writing to her, when a letter was placed in his hand by the drum-major, who acted as regimental postman.

It was from his mother, Lady Wedderburn ; and after a great deal of verbosity about Gwenny—to the effect of how much and how often she spoke of *him;* how *sad* she had looked since his departure ; a wish that Horace was safe with the Depôt (*why,* she did not add), which she hoped would be stationed in England and *not* in Scotland—she mentioned Mary Lennox, and as he read on, Cyril felt the blood rushing to his temples.

"As for that unfortunate girl at Lonewoodlee, the popular verdict, I regret to say, is still against her. Your father alone talks in an extenuating manner, but then we all know that he is so exceedingly simple ! I am so glad that you are beyond her dangerous influence now, dearest Cyril. Only think of what would have been your fate—your future, if you had been lured into an engagement with one whom society could not have received after what has occurred."

He crushed the cruel letter up, but after a time smoothed it out and read on.

" I hope my darling boy is now happy in his mind, and quite cured of his absurd *local* fancy ; for Mrs. M'Guffog, the minister's wife, told me that she has heard on all hands the rumour confirmed, that the visit to Chesterhaugh, of which we know, and which caused you such suffering and annoyance, was too probably not the only one."

Cyril placed his mother's letter in his desk, which he locked, and buckling on his sword with a vicious jerk, set forth to attend to his duties, so there was no letter written to poor Mary Lennox.

The mess, the great solace of barrack-life, was now broken up completely; the splendid epergnes, trophies, and plate, either packed or "handed over" to the Depôt; and Cyril hailed with satisfaction the dawn of the day that was to see the Royal Fusileers off to share in the coming perils and glories of the Eastern War; and every heart in their ranks beat high, save those, perhaps, who were leaving hearts that were swollen with sorrow behind.

The notes of the *réveille*, now low, now high and swelling, with the drowsy, softened roll of the drums, rang through the square and echoing streets of the great barrack just as the grey dawn stole in. It is an air sweet and mournful in its cadence, and is known in the service traditionally as the Scottish Réveille, with which the English was originally played alternately; and ere the last soft notes of it had died away, Cyril heard the pealing bugles of his own regiment sounding loudly and high the "turn out."

The brief, restless, and half-sleepless night passed away, and ere long, belted and accoutred, he yawned and shivered in the cool atmosphere of that spacious and roughly-gravelled barrack square, where, since the middle of the last century, so many hundred thousand men have been drilled and sent forth to all parts of the world; for Chatham is our great military school— "a mighty military hell," Beamish was wont to term it.

The pale morning star was melting into the amber sunrise, but the purple shadows yet lay deep along the wooded terrace and the lower barracks. The voices of the birds were heard as they carolled merrily in the old bushes and tiny gardens before the quarters of the commandant, the staff, and other officers, when the adjutant, about half an hour after daybreak, began to form the regiment, which was in heavy marching order, in open column of companies.

The colours, borne by Pomfret and another subaltern, were in their oilskin cases; the officers and men wore white canvas haversacks; but Bingham and a few of the former affected smart courier bags. The Fusileers were in complete order for service in the field; their blankets rolled on the top of their knapsacks; their great coats folded; their canteens and camp-kettles strapped on; thus their aspect was such as no soldiers had been in Chatham Barracks since Bonaparte landed from Elba.

A few of the Fusileers had been late of coming into barracks over-night ; others had undoubtedly got groggy at the rural tavern known as the Hook and Hatchet, or other places ; but not a man was absent on this auspicious morning, though some were noisy and jocular.

"Answer to your name, sir !" cried Beamish to one of his men as the roll was called.

"Faith, but it's blisterin' dry my tongue is this morning, Captain dear."

"Dry, after all you drank last night, Barney ?"

"Faith, if I had drunk more, may be I wouldn't have been so thirsty this blessed morning."

"Silence !" This was the sole rebuke for Barney's chatter, which on any other occasion would have secured him a sojourn in the guard-house.

Mounted on his fine black horse Vidette, Sir Edward Elton was in front of the line, conning over the *route*, an official document, which stated that it was "Her Majesty's will and pleasure," that he was to proceed to Chatham, with thirty-five officers, forty-seven sergeants and drummers, and eight hundred and twenty-eight rank and file of the Royal Fusileers, to South-ampton, "there to embark for the coast of Bulgaria, on board of such tonnage as may be provided," for so the formula ran.

The officers were around him in a group, and all were chatting gaily.

"So we are bound for Bulgaria ; but wherever that may be, the devil a bit of me knows," said Beamish, whose whiskers were so black that they seemed a mere continuation of his bearskin cap ; "and there is small honour in being a traveller now, when all the world is rushing about by steam and rail, and fellows go to pot tigers in Bengal and lions in Africa, when their fathers were content to look after snipe in an Irish bog, or grouse in the Highlands."

"Good morning, Wedderburn," said Sir Edward, as Cyril saluted him and presented his hand ; "whatever it may be at Southampton, here the wind is fair for running down the Channel. We don't go by steamer I find," he added, pointing to the great vane on the barrack-roof—an iron rifleman, the size of life, who has levelled his weapon in the wind's eye ever since the days of Waterloo.

"Well, Bingham," said one, "have you had a tender leave-taking before breakfast ?"

"Breakfast !" repeated the other, twirling the tassels of his sash ; "who could make one at this inhuman hour? I have had a dose of brandy-and-seltzer."

"A bad beginning," said Beamish. "I have breakfasted at the mess-house by candle-light (which made me think it sup-

per), on devilled kidneys, fried mackerel, and a jolly glass of
Sauterne, to make a man of me for the day."

"And what is that huge flask slung over your sword-belt, Pat?"

"What would it be, Wedderburn, my boy, but 'condensed
sunshine'—the best condensation I know of."

"Sunshine?"

"Well—poteen. Would you like a *doch an dorroch*, out of
it? *We* can understand that, though Bingham and these English fellows don't, or pretend they don't."

The light-hearted banter of the majority contrasted strongly
with the gravity, even unconcealed sadness, of one or two of
the married officers, particularly Joyce, who but a short time
before, hand in hand with his wife, had lingered beside the
bed where their two children lay fast asleep and nestling in
each other's arms. As he kissed them softly, the poor man's
tears had dropped upon their golden hair, and then he came
forth to take his place at the head of his company; but their
little cherub faces, though they haunted him for many a day
and night, amid the sufferings of our army at Varna, and the
perils of the Crimea, poor Joyce was fated never again to see.

And now, gnawing the brass chain of his cap, he stood on
parade, tearless, but with his eyes bent wistfully on the window
of the room where his children slept, and from whence their
mother was watching him. He kissed his hand to her and
even tried to smile, so true it is, that in the wealth of our
emotions, at times we can give nothing.

Many of the married soldiers were in the same predicament,
and the sobbing of the women became at times painfully audi-
ble, as they stole forward into the ranks, and held up their
children to be kissed by the father who was too probably leaving them for ever; for before Sebastopol whole companies
perished, and were renewed but to perish again. "Soldiers
have hearts like other men, and they share the lot of other men,"
says Florence Marryat. They love and leave and lose occasionally, and occasionally also they have a soft spot left wherein
to keep the memory of such things; for the military profession
and a careless roving life, do not necessarily render men dead
to human feeling.

How often do we hear the contemptuous or careless remark,
"*he* is only a private soldier;" but, thank God! our private
soldiers are generally made of better stuff than those who seek
to sneer at them, and no nobler or finer army ever left the
British Isles, than that which landed under Lord Raglan on the
shore of Bulgaria; and the letters that came from its humblest
members, the mere voices from the ranks, with which the newspapers of the day soon teemed, formed a splendid example of
epistolary literature, displaying inherent manliness strong

affection and fearlessness, resignation and hope ; high moral and religious principles, together with a singularly graphic power for describing all they saw and felt.

" Gentlemen and soldiers of the Royal Fusileers," cried Sir Edward Elton, when the officers had fallen in, and he wheeled the battalion into line ; " prior to this we have all been soldiers but in name. Now the day is coming—nay, it *has* come—when we shall be soldiers in stern earnest, with battles to fight and glory to gain. Though nine hundred strong, we are *one* in heart, my lads—one in heart, officers and men—and ready to face anything. We are of various ages—your captains and field-officers being senior in years to most of you. Half a century hence, how many of us shall be alive ? A whole century, and as surely as the sun now shines the grass will be growing over us all ; but the deeds we shall achieve must be borne on the pages of history and live for centuries after us. So comrades, while shoulder to shoulder, let us be all as brothers, and never forget that we must be ready to die with honour to the Queen we serve, and the country which gave us birth !"

To this short, but remarkable address, the regiment responded by loud cheering, and began its march at the word of command.

"Flam off !" cried the tall Drum-major, flourishing his splendid staff (which was surmounted by the Horse of Hanover in massive silver), and using the old fashioned command now almost forgotten in the service ; then crash went the music of the brass band to the air of " The Girl I left behind me," while the deep, hoarse, but hearty hurrah that Englishmen can give so well, burst from the throats of the thousands of their comrades of other corps that were soon to follow, and who had assembled to watch the departure of the Fusileers. Cheering and waving their caps, they followed into the streets of Chatham.

Other troops, Infantry, Artillery, and Marines, were on the march that morning, and other bands were heard to break the stillness of the ambient air, as their music floated over the level fields of Kent, scaring the lark and the blackbird in the budding woodlands.

Soldiers always muster and march merrily, so even the usually grave faces of Singleton and Joyce looked bright on this eventful morning. Patrick Beamish, who was a " devil-may-care" sort of officer, and had contrived to get several Irishmen into his own company, struck up the popular marching song, and nearly eight hundred men, while waving their bearskin caps or brandishing their muskets, made the clear blue welkin ring to the merry chorus ;

" Though I bask beneath another's smile,
  Her charms shall fail to bind me ;
  For my heart flies back to Erin's isle,
  And the girl I left behind me."

How many brave young hearts were bounding there with
wild and vague ambition, with the hope of that which they
could scarcely have explained! There was, of course, the
stirring novelty of departure for foreign service, to engage in a
great European War after forty years of peace, and a glow
swelled up in every breast as the cheers, the songs, and the
music loaded the morning air, reverberating with a thousand
echoes in the streets of the town through which they marched.
Even Conyers Singleton, we have said, seemed to feel this
proud emotion keenly—he who had marched many a time to
battle, and had heard given the orders of the pre-percussion
times—"Gentlemen, uncase the colours—examine your *flints
and priming ;*" and leaning with his hand on his horse's flank,
he looked back with bright and glistering eyes on the marching
column, the flushed faces, the black Fusileer caps, the sloped
arms and the fixed bayonets that flashed so keenly in the
sunshine.

Among the women who saw them march there was no enthusiasm, but there were commiseration and tears for all ; for
none, perhaps, more than the smooth-cheeked boy ensigns, like
Pomfret, in their first red-coats ; or the little drummers who
beat so lustily in front of the column, and the half of whose
whole height, seemed a tall bearskin cap.

By rail they were soon swept away to Southampton, and that
evening saw them all stowed on board the *Victoria* transport
ship, and "told off" to their berths ; the muskets racked ; the
belts and knapsacks hung on their cleats ; the messes formed,
the quarter-guard on duty, and silence and order prevailing
through all the crowded vessel, the result of discipline, strict
obedience, and military etiquette.

By sunset, the *Victoria* had been towed by a steamer below
Portsmouth, where through the evening haze, loomed the great
modern tower of the church which forms a landmark from the
sea, the forest of masts, and the long line of ultramural fortifi-
cation extending along the beach to Southsea Castle. Now,
her canvas was let fall and sheeted home ; the tow-line was
cast off, the last connecting link with dear Old England ; a
farewell cheer was exchanged ; the steamer dipped her ensign
thrice, and the great transport with its human freight stood
upon her own pathway, with the high lands of the Isle of
Wight upon her weather-bow gleaming white and pale in the
cold lustre of the clear star-light ; but the chalky Culver Cliffs,
the Cove of Ventnor with all its pretty villas, and the Black-
gang Chine, soon melted into the midnight sea as the transport
bore down the channel before a spanking breeze.

CHAPTER XXXIII.

THE OLD, OLD STORY.

LADY WEDDERBURN's fond desire that Gwenny should be married to Cyril was still uppermost in her mind, and ever present in her thought and day-dreams, though Cyril was far away and thinking now of other things—had, perhaps, almost forgotten his cousin's existence. Thus she viewed with extreme impatience the intimacy that was ripening fast between her wealthy niece and the penniless Horace Ramornie ; an intimacy which led her to fear that ere Cyril could return to Willowdean the love of the beautiful heiress, if he cared to win it, might be lost to him for ever.

In a farewell letter from Cyril, dated at Southampton, Lady Wedderburn had heard of the embarkation, and she already trembled at the idea of the many perils to come. The *Victoria* transport, with the Royal Fusileers, had sailed ; and the same newspaper which announced that circumstance contained an account of the destruction of the *Europe* troop-ship by fire, off Cape Finisterre, with a body of the 6th Dragoons on board, when the Colonel, so many of the men, and all the horses perished.

It has been already mentioned how love for Gwenny was dawning in the heart of Horace Ramornie ; how twice he had been upon the point of a declaration, but was restrained by an intuitive perception of his aunt's views. And though a secret passion was swelling up in his heart, fear of the family aims and wishes made him actually long for the expiry of his leave of absence, as a suitable excuse for quitting his uncle's house, where he had ever been welcome and always a favourite.

Gwenny was a sensitive creature ; one of those who shrink from the world's rougher touch. By nature she was all gentleness, sympathy, and enthusiasm. The blue waves rolling in light, and breaking in shining ripples on the sandy beach, or thundering in white foam on the bluff coast of the Merse, where the rocks are literally alive with wild seafowl ; the songs of the birds, so new a sound to her, as the birds of India are mostly voiceless ; the perfume of flowers, a novelty too, as the most gorgeous plants of the land she had left are scentless ; the balmy coolness of the spring days, the dark purple tint of the heather on the hills of Lammermuir ; the songs of the sturdy peasantry, so different in cadence from the monstrous polyglot rubbish of the dusky Hindoostanees—all served to fill her with joy and vague yearnings, in which Horace, her usual attendant or companion, was associated. For Robert Wedder-

burn, anticipating, perhaps, the day when he should have the
field to himself, was usually, to all appearance, immersed in his
studies.

Horace was master of all the legendary lore of the Merse.
Thus, when with Gwenny, he enlivened many a solitary ride
by the tales he told her—weird ones some of them—about the
witches of Auchincraw, who became cats or crows, as suited
their purpose ; the terrible goblin known as the Bogle of
Billymore, who devoured children like shrimps ; of St. Mary of
Coldingham, and the Skeleton Nun who was found built in the
convent wall, and the last words in whose ears had been the
awful three, *Vade in pacem*.   And often they rode to the deep
rocky ravine and the two abrupt hills, which form the famous
foreland named St. Abb's Head, from whence they could see
the coast of England, stretching in the distance far away.

There an undulation in the velvet turf, and a few gray stones
lying one upon another, indicate where the convent church
stood in an age that is now remote indeed ; a low fence of sods,
a few tufts of hemlock and wild nettles tossing in the keen
sea-breeze show the old burial-ground, where the dust of the
Pict, the Scot, and the Briton, mingle on the bleak verge of the
giddy cliff, three hundred feet below which the ocean roars
and boils, hurling the huge waves that have come unbroken
from the Naze of Norway and the mouth of the Skager Rack.

There he would tell her how the church that had passed
away, had been founded in gratitude to God, by the Saxon
Princess Ebba (daughter of a Northumbrian prince), when
escaping shipwreck there.   And how, when the Danish rovers
came, in the days of the Flame-bearer, the pious nuns, to save
themselves from capture, cut off their own lips and noses ;
which made her think of some of the barbarous tales she had
heard in India.

And often Horace paused in stories such as these, bewildered
by the love that filled his heart and loaded his tongue, while he
gazed into the soft, inquiring, or wondering eyes of Gwenny,
or admired the graceful mode in which she sat her horse.

Horace knew well that it is not every woman who looks well
on horseback ; but a slender girl like Gwenny, whose spirits
were light as ether, whose dark eyes were always sparkling,
and whose complexion, if not brilliant, was clear, pale, and
pure, looked a very Aurora in a plumed hat and riding-habit.

Those who love truly and tenderly, seem to have had no
past, for love seems always a part of the present ; thus Horace
felt as if he had known Gwenny all his life, or rather to have
begun a new existence by knowing her.

One day as they rode home together slowly, after having
lingered at Wolf's Crag, and talked of Lucy Ashton and Edgar

of Ravenswood, as if they had been real characters, rather than the shadows of a romance—

"Thank God!" exclaimed Horace, suddenly, after a pause, "that this is my last week at Willowdean!"

"Why that exclamation?" she asked, with surprise.

"Because, Gwenny, I shall soon see the last day here of a love that is without—hope."

She made no further inquiry, but cast down her long lashes, for right well did Gwenny know that her young companion loved her. By one electric glance which once had passed between them, like a flash of light, she had learned it instinctively.

"Oh, Horace," said she, tremulously, though she seemed to have more courage in the matter than he. "How lonely will all these places seem to me when you are gone!"

"And how will it be with me, Gwenny, when a memory shall be all I have of you?"

The girl cast her dark eyes down again, and blushed and smiled.

"There is a poet, who says," continued Horace—

"'How many meet who never yet have met,
To part too soon, but never to forget!'

So it is with you and me, Gwenny—with me, at least. Times there are when I almost wish we had never met; for never, never can I forget you, or the hours of delight we have spent together. Oh, Gwenny Wedderburn," he added, while checking her horse's bridle, and taking her hand in his own, "I love you—love you dearly; but—but, you are rich, and I so poor—and then our aunt——" He paused, and then resumed, while the girl trembled in her saddle, and was covered with confusion. "Gwenny, dare I hope that the distinction I trust to attain on service—such, at least, as may fall to the lot of a mere subaltern—may be a pledge to me—of—of—that if I live to return, I may claim your love as my reward—my recompense?"

"You have my love already, dear Horace—all that my heart can bestow," was the almost breathless response of Gwenny.

Their horses were side by side; so passing an arm around her, he drew her close to his breast, and kissed her brow and cheek. There was something wonderfully soft and loving, tender and respectful—mutely eloquent, in fact—in the manner in which Horace gathered the girl in his embrace, when words failed him, and Gwenny seemed to feel it as such. "No two declarations of love are alike, any more than two leaves on the same tree," says a writer who has had some experience in such pleasant matters. But it was thus that the great secret, which had trembled so long on the lips and in the heart of Horace Ramornie, was shared now by her whom it most concerned.

Long did they linger on their homeward ride, these two young lovers, reiterating the old, old story that has been said or sung by others so often, and will be so, till the end of time—how much they loved, and how unutterably dear they were to each other *now!*

"But what will Aunt Wedderburn say when she hears of our engagement?" said Gwenny, after a long pause, as they entered the shady avenue which led to the house of Willowdean.

"She will learn to hate me, I fear. And yet I am her sister's only son," said Horace, sadly.

"Hate you—why?"

"As yet we shall say nothing about it, Gwenny, love," replied Horace. "Ah, it is a pity you are so rich," he added. "People could not then talk as many do ; our Aunt Wedderburn would not then deem me a fortune-hunter, and I could marry you at once, and take you away with me."

"To live on your lieutenant's pay, with a share of a barrack-room, a bungalow, or a tent! Oh, cousin Horace—Horace, darling, it is very romantic, but not to be thought of," said Gwenny, laughing.

"I have thought of it often in my day-dreams."

"Yes ; but even the proverbial love in a cottage were better," she continued, looking down with a beautiful smile, and toying with her horse's mane.

"Aunt Wedderburn wishes you to marry Cyril."

"But Cyril never asked me, nor seemed to care for me, but as one to talk to and laugh with," said Gwenny, looking surprised.

"I feel that such is her wish, however ; even Robert has hinted as much."

"But let us speak of ourselves," she exclaimed, as her eyes suddenly filled with tears ; "oh, how long may this horrible war last?"

"It is scarcely begun, so far as we are concerned, but when once shots are exchanged, Heaven alone can tell the issue. However, I may not be away from you for more than a year—perhaps," he added, with a quivering lip, for he strove to speak hopefully, though his heart misgave him.

"A year? Good Heavens! a whole year!" exclaimed Gwenny, ponderingly.

"Yes, Gwenny : what is a year, at most?"

"It will be an eternity for us to look forward to, though it is so little to look *back* upon."

"True, my own Gwenny ; and when I think of looking forward to a whole year,—twelve months, fifty-two weeks, three hundred and sixty-five days, with all their weary hours of separation——"

" And a year of such peril to you, it may be—of anxiety and terror and sorrow to me !"

" Oh, my darling—my beautiful darling, it is horrible to be separated so soon when we have just learned to love each other, and to find existence so dear and that love is so sweet !" said Horace, with a burst of tenderness, as he assisted her to alight, and would certainly have kissed her, but for the appearance of that solemn personage Asloane, the butler, between the pillars of the peristyle.

The future life of Horace Ramornie—the life of ambition and of military glory he had hoped to live—seemed to have passed from his mind and desires. He could imagine no scene and form no scheme for the long years to come, in which Gwenny was not concerned, and in which she did not bear a part. His ambition had evaporated, and with it, for the time, his military ardour, vanity of uniform, and the " pomp and circumstance of war" seemed to have faded sorely. The joys of the mess ; the glitter of the military ballroom ; the splendour of the parade ; the perils of the field and the chance of being even a unit in the great game about to be played by Europe in the East, were all as nothing now, when contrasted with the charm of Gwenny's presence, her voice and her society.

Ideas of the life of splendour and display he might spend with a beautiful girl possessed of such wealth as Gwendoleyne Wedderburn, never occurred even once to single-hearted Horace. He was too young, too impassioned, too genuine in heart and impulse to be mercenary, or to love the orphan-heiress for anything save herself alone.

He felt that he could almost without a pang relinquish his old world of hope, for she had become a new world to him.

But his sword was his sole inheritance, and now duty and honour alike combined to separate them ; yet as the few remaining days of his leave of absence flew past, the happy consciousness of mutual love grew stronger between him and Gwenny ; though the hour of his imperative departure was viewed with an apprehension that was mixed with sadness— an intense sadness, that was all the more keen that they were compelled to conceal it from the searching eyes of Lady Wedderburn.

" If poor Horace has nothing but his pay as a lieutenant, and I love him so, why should we not be married ?" thought Gwenny ; " surely I have wealth enough for two—even for a dozen. Horace is a dependant, I have heard Aunt say ; but what of that ? Who that love as we do, care for riches !"

And as she thought thus, a grand scorn for wealth curled the beautiful lip of the little proprietrix of three hundred thousand pounds in gold mohurs and rupees.

" It would be hard indeed to marry only to please Aunt Wedderburn, when I should much rather do so to please myself and dear Horace."

But that was not the time for marrying or giving in marriage. They had to content themselves by a solemn ratification of their engagement—an exchange of rings, of locks of hair and photographs—a long, long stolen embrace amid the flowers of the conservatory, and then the hour came when they were to part, to all appearance as merely affectionate friends; when they had that task to perform which is so difficult to those who are unused to the world, and are young and love tenderly—to veil their secret emotions, to smile when they would weep; when each had to conceal their great grief at parting with the other, while their passion was so new and keen in their sensitive and impulsive hearts.

But the fatal hour came, and as the carriage rolled away through the avenue with Horace just as it had done with Cyril, Gwenny felt with a sobbing emotion in her throat, and a suffocating sensation at her heart, as if the sun of her existence had set at Willowdean, and she never knew till then how much she loved him.

To her, his departure seemed the breaking of a spell—the mockery of a dreamy fancy, till ultimately his vacant place at table and in the house generally, served to bring the truth home to her, that he was gone, gone perhaps for ever—Horace so loving in manner, so gentle in voice and eye—and then the tide of sorrow welled up in the girl's heart, all the more that she had none with whom to share her secret.

The memories and visions of love remained with her; but they were visions and memories only.

Meanwhile, Horace felt sensibly that, save with Gwenny, there had been far less fuss and *empressement* about his departure, than that of Cyril Wedderburn ; and poor little Miss Flora M'Caw was the only one who gave free vent to her tears, which were always ready for service on a suitable occasion.

CHAPTER XXXIV.

DARK DAYS.

"WELL, thank Heaven, they are separated at last !" was Lady Wedderburn's mental congratulation, as she saw, but not without emotions of pity and suspicion mingled, the pale girl—her soul wrung with uncontrollable anguish—retire to her own room after the departure of Horace ; but she knew not how inex-

pressibly dear they had become to each other, by that very
separation.

In oppressive dulness the weeks succeeded each other now,
for as the family were in mourning still for Uncle Wedderburn,
the visitors were fewer than usual at Willowdean ; and it was
not until the fourth or fifth day, and when a letter arrived,
dated at Chatham Barracks from Horace and addressed to his
aunt, that Gwenny realized to the full the fact of his absence.

" Horace gone," thought she ; " Horace (like Scot's ' Quentin
Blanc') so gentle-voiced and gentle-eyed, who looked like one
whom all the world had frowned on, oh ! what a dreary void,
what a blank her life would be now ! There were no more
drives, or walks, or rides together; no more reading together,
and no more sweet companionship."

But Horace, she knew, would be sad, even as she was herself ;
and who could comfort him ? and who fill her place ?

And the confidence and innocent truth of her own heart told
her—*none !*

How happily the past three months had fled ! Oh ! how she
missed him, and wept and sorrowed in secret for his absence from
a house where no one seemed particularly to care for him ;. for
Robert Wedderburn was cold and selfish, hence perhaps his
legal predilections ; Sir John was incessantly occupied by all
the cares that take up the time of a sporting country gentleman ;
by politics, county meetings, and the internal affairs of the little
burgh of Willowdean, where he was viewed as a species of
potentate, even by the ministers of the three Presbyterian de-
nominations who had churches there and Christian hearers who
hated each other most cordially. As for Lady Wedderburn,
she had special views and wishes, that made her approve of
Horace being away, though he was soon to be face to face with
death and suffering.

The piano Gwenny would touch no more, for the music so
powerfully reminded her of his presence and voice, as to give
her absolute pain. Her worsted work, her embroidery, her
flowers and the birds she had brought from India, had all become
distasteful to her ; and so were her books, though these were
full of passages he had marked, poor boy—for he was not much
more than a boy after all ; and fast fell her tears as she re-read
them.

" Alone—alone ! oh, I am now so much alone !" she would
say.

Her engagement-ring, which, curiously enough, escaped Lady
Wedderburn's attention among the others that glittered on
Gwenny's white fingers, and which had cost poor Horace a
couple of months' pay, she was never weary of looking at, during
the first few weeks of their separation ; even as another sad girl

was looking at her plainer— but equally, or perhaps more beloved hoop, which from its form was emblematic of something more than a mere betrothal ring.

In her separation Gwenny had no wound to her self-love, such as that which tortured the heart of Mary Lennox ; the consciousness that one of whose whole soul and thoughts she had been empress, to whom her least word was law, her smiles and glances happiness, had cast off his allegiance, was neglecting and ignoring her, and seeking to forget her as one who would disgrace him.

The joy and excitement of Gwendoleyne when letters came from Horace, and her normal condition of sadness, were alike ignored by Lady Wedderburn, though the latter was viewed with some concern by good-natured, but unthinking Sir John.

" Well, Gwenny, my summer blossom, why so sad ? Thinking of your Indian home and poor papa—eh ?" he would ask at times, and suppose that such were her thoughts as he received no direct reply ; and then his handsome sunburned hand would caress her dark hair, which was always dressed to perfection by the skilful fingers of her ayah Zillah, the Madrassee ; but she wore fewer ornaments now, for there was no one at Willowdean whose eye she cared to please.

And so the summer months stole on.

Horace was as yet at crowded and bustling Chatham, where the drills and duties were hard and incessant ; and unremitting too were the departure of troops for the East, amid the cheers of the people, the crash of music, and the clangour of bells ; and he knew that the time for him to go must arrive soon, for the grim fever king was thinning fast the ranks of his regiment at Varna. But never before had Horace seemed in such an affectionate mood to his aunt, and never had he written to her so many letters, so that at times she had, most unwillingly, to depute " the task " of answering them to Gwenny, the first sight of whose handwriting made Horace start as if electrified when he received a letter in Chatham barrackyard.

" Dear Aunt Wedderburn has desired me to write in her place ; she has one of her nervous headaches to-day, and neither Dr. Squills, nor Miss M'Caw, with Rimmel, can make anything of her."

He could read no further, for now the bugle sounded ; but Gwenny's presence seemed beside him—Gwenny in her innocent love and artless girlhood—and he became so bewildered, that as the exasperated adjutant said, " he made a mull of the whole day's drill by his blunders, by twice marching a camp colour through the centre of his company, and repeatedly throwing the whole line out !"

Attended by an old groom, Gwenny often rode to the places she and Horace had visited, and his stories of the quaint old

world that was past, came back to her memory with many a
sweet and pleasant association ; but how dull, how lonely and
valueless seemed all those places now, for he whose presence
had shed a charm over them, was no longer by her side.

The evening sun setting in gold and amber clouds beyond
the purple ridges of the Lammermuirs ; the beautiful flowers
in the garden, even those he and she had planted (the seedlings
" from dear papa's house in the Choultry"), expanding under
the summer warmth ; the rippling grass, the growing corn on
the upland slopes, the green waves breaking in surf on the
rocky shore, were all alike gloomy and discordant, for Horace
was not there, and never more might be, the most terrible
reflection of all ! Had she but known the solitary Mary Lennox, what delightful companions they would have been, with
their community of thought and wishes ; for though their
positions in fortune were widely different, their hopes were one.

Arrangements had been made to join Lady Ernescleugh in
London during the season ; but now Lady Wedderburn, on
hearing, from Cyril's letters and the public prints, of the disease
and horrors by which, through the utter inertia of the Ministry,
our splendid army was literally withering away at Varna,
shrunk from the idea of leaving Willowdean for a house in
town and entering into gaiety, so the family remained at home.

Though it has been truly written that "three months of a
London season teach us more than six months in the country,"
Lady Wedderburn had no desire that her niece's mind should
become so much enlightened : so even the mixed and melan-
cholly gaieties of Edinburgh were eschewed, and young gentlemen visitors by no means encouraged. So the girl would sigh
with utter weariness when visitors came who talked only of
crops and cattle, or the county pack ; or when the Reverend
Mr. M'Guffog paid a solemn and fussy visit, for then the conversation ran entirely on matters clerical. And thus Gwenny
learned for the first time that there was a Scottish Established
Church, a Dissenting Episcopal Church with bishops, a Free
Kirk which had none, and other roads to heaven without number; and she heard of petty squabbles about religious forms,
if the utter absence of any could be so called. The pharisees
seemed the most powerful sect of all; and she would listen in
vacant wonder to the discussion of affairs that seemed as
incomprehensible as the difference between Parsees and Hin-
doos, Brahmins, Bheels and Khonds ; but much less picturesque.

Summer we have said had come; the scarlet poppies and
blue cornflowers studding the golden fields of the Home Farm,
pleased the eyes of Gwenny more than those of Sir John, who
viewed them as weeds, and a bore ; and Lady Wedderburn
sighed when she thought of all that might happen, and all

her eldest son must face before that corn was reaped and
ground, for it was evident that our army would soon take the
field, and be where hard knocks were going, as the Ministry,
with a stupidity, if not worse, that has few parallels in history,
was only waiting for *winter* to commence the Russian campaign.

Once, peace and war had only been empty words to many a
heart and household; but they had a terrible significance now.

The Turks had compelled the Russians to raise the siege of
Silistria, and driven them across the Danube; our ships of war
had destroyed the batteries of Sulina, a Bessarabian village at
the mouth of that river; the battle of Bayazid was fought in
Armenia; Bomarsund, in the Baltic, had been bombarded by
land and sea, and utterly destroyed by old Sir Charles Napier;
and now many new and barbarous names of places almost
never heard of before became at every table and fireside at
home in Great Britain familiar in the mouths of all "as household words;" and even Lady Ernescleugh wrote Lady Wedderburn, to announce that, with some friends, she was actually
thinking of going to Constantinople in Everard's yacht.

"My friend Lord Cardigan's yacht has already sailed; would
you care to join us?" she added; and then followed a catalogue
of many events of the London season : the debts and difficulties
of some, the flirtations, matches, and jiltings of others—threatened duels, for that fashion of adjusting disputes had barely
gone out.

"What if Cyril saw Gwenny now, or after the lapse of some
months?" thought Lady Wedderburn. "Yes we shall go; and
perhaps I may get leave for him to come back with me on
'urgent private affairs,' as so many contrive to do now. Yes—
yes, I must bring my dear boy away from that odious place
before the fighting begins with us."

But Sir John was opposed to the scheme as eccentric, and so
far as regarded Cyril, incompatible with honour. The yacht
required complete refitting, and the plans of Lady Ernescleugh
were delayed for a time.

Though an active and obstinate opponent of Lord Aberdeen's
government, and one who mistrusted him personally and as a
minister, Sir John gave a large dinner party to a few neighbours
and local notabilities, on news coming of the surrender of Bomarsund to Napier and General Baraguay d'Hilliers, when two
thousand two hundred Russians were taken prisoners; and to
his guests he bitterly reviled the Ministry for their delays and
utter mismanagement of the war, and the mode by which,
through their previous reductions and retrenchments, they had
crippled our power by land and sea, so that our very arsenals
could scarcely furnish shot for the first siege trains, while the
entrenching tools issued to the troops had been condemned as

worthless by the Duke of Wellington in Spain forty-three years before; and in conclusion, he quoted that fine sentence of Sir William Napier, whose words are terrible in their significance and truth. "In the beginning of each war, England has to seek in blood the knowledge necessary to insure success, and, like the fiend's progress towards Eden, her conquering course is through chaos, followed by Death !"*

"Sae that evil-minded ne'er-do-weel, Chesters o' Chesterhaugh, has gone to help the Turks in person," said the Baron-Bailie of Willowdean, who officiated as croupier ; "think ye it is true news, Sir John ?"

"Yes ; he has been gazetted to a majority in the Turkish contingent," replied Sir John, laughing.

"A major o' Bashi Bozooks, whatever they be !" said the Reverend Mr. M'Guffog, lifting up his dreary eyes ; "the Lord be good to us !"

"It's just what we micht hae expected o' siccan a loon, sirs," resumed the irate bailie, who, being a grocer and general dealer, ranked heavily as a creditor against Chesters ; "he's mair a Turk than a Christian by nature, and will find himsel' quite at hame amang their harem-scarems, I warrant."

The mention of Chesters' name by a direct association of ideas caused a reference to be made to the decayed Laird of Lonewoodlee, and the esclandre concerning his pretty daughter.

Sir John, his son, and several gentlemen who were present, were disposed to express their disbelief of the matter, or their hopes at least, that the Master of Ernescleugh had been mistaken on the night in question ; but the Baron-Bailie, who was a strict Sabbatarian, and vehement expounder in public on religion and morality, and who naturally took the worst views of human nature, maintained that "the young leddy had doubtless gude reasons o' her ain for her mysterious visits to such a man ; and evil or no evil, there was aye some water found where the stirkie droons," a Scottish proverb which is supposed to infer a vast deal more than one may dare to say ; and as she listened, again in her heart did Lady Wedderburn congratulate herself on the escape of her eldest son "from the snares of that designing girl."

Singularly enough, the next day was to behold somewhat of a change in her views regarding Mary Lennox.

Just as she and Gwenny were setting forth in the basket-phaeton which was drawn by a pretty pair of Orkney ponies, for a drive as far as the town of Greenlaw, a man whose face seemed not unfamiliar, approached, and respectfully lifting his bonnet, craved a few words "with her Ladyship."

" History of the Peninsular War."

"I think I know your face," said she, pausing, whip in hand, and bowing pleasantly to encourage him.

"I am Tony Heron, my lady, a gate-keeper at Chesterhaugh."

"Well, Tony, what can I do for you?"

"Much, madam, if you are but willing, and a' in the Merse ken how kind you are to the poor. I have a wife and five wee bairns that can neither work nor want. They are a' thrown on my hands, which are empty, for the Mansion House is you know shut up ; Chesters has gone to the wars ; the servants are all dismissed, and I have got notice to quit too, from Grub and Wylie, the writers."

"Poor man !" said Gwenny, beginning to open her purse ; but Lady Wedderburn checked her, for the man, who saw she had mistaken his intended appeal, blushed scarlet and drew back.

"You want employment, I presume?"

"Just so, my lady ; and if you or Sir John could find me something to do about Willowdean, to put a little bread into the bairns' mouths, I'd be beholden to you for life. I have been twenty years in service, and have a good character."

"But from a bad master."

"I was servant to the good laird his father, before him."

"I fear you may find it a poor recommendation to Sir John having been at Chesterhaugh."

"So I hear on all hands now," said the other, with a sigh of bitterness ; "but no man can say a word derogatory to the character of Tony Heron."

"Well, I shall speak to Sir John and the ground bailie, and do what I can for you, Tony, were it but for the children's sake."

The man's eyes kindled with gratitude ; but he was not profuse in thanks ; for Scotchmen, reserved at all times, seldom are so. Suddenly, checking her ponies again, Lady Wedderburn asked—

"Were you the gate-keeper who was cognisant of the visits Miss Lennox paid your bachelor master?"

"Miss Lennox never visited my master," replied the man with a glance of genuine surprise.

"But you must have heard it said that she did?" continued Lady Wedderburn, looking astonished in turn.

"I have heard, my lady, what a' the country-side has been ringing wi'; but Miss Lennox was never, to my knowledge, at Chesterhaugh save once, and then she came to visit *me*."

"You—about what—or for what reason?"

"She came in the evening, about the sunset time, to make some inquiry anent the terrible night when Mr. Cyril—that is, Captain Wedderburn—went amissing ; to ask me the hour he left—if his horse was restive, and so forth?"

"What interest could *she* possibly have in the matter?" asked

Lady Wedderburn, rather haughtily, and with a heightened colour.

"Interest, my lady ! Through a' the Lammermuirs, secret as they thought it, it was well kent that they loved each other well and truly, till some quarrel came between them. Just as she was asking me all about the captain, poor thing, her heart seeming to be in her mouth the while, the master lured her inside the gate, and then the storm of hail and snow came suddenly on. She wished to take shelter in my lodge ; but the master would not hear of it, and half led, half pulled her into the house, where he kept her till midnight, as his hellicate groom, Billy Trayner, told us, by pretending that the springs of his waggonette were broken ; and that is the whole story, my lady ; and if I have told you a word that is untrue, may my puir bairns lack the bread I'm seeking to win them !"

"Why did you not state this before ?" asked Lady Wedderburn, angrily.

"To whom, my lady ? Besides, it was not my place or interest to speak against my master."

"True," she replied, and a keen emotion of remorse inspired her, as she now saw that the poor girl in her love for Cyril—artful though it might be—and her burning anxiety to learn tidings of him, after that terrible night and time of suspense and dread, had permitted herself to be lured into the false position we have so fully described elsewhere, and which was so destructive to her peace of mind and place in society.

"Call again to-morrow, Tony, and I shall see what can be done for you. Meanwhile," she added, turning to Gwenny, "we must call openly on Miss Lennox, and see if we cannot in some measure repair the serious injury that has been done her."

" I don't think she will see you, my lady," said Tony Heron.

" Not see me—why ?" she asked haughtily.

"Because as I passed the tower gate this morning, I heard the women lamenting, for the Laird of Lonewoodlee had died in the night ; and he is the last of the auld Lennox line, my lady," added the man, with an emotion of respect.

Lady Wedderburn, to do her justice, was inexpressibly shocked and grieved when she heard of this, notwithstanding all the old quarrels and coolnesses in the past time. She relinquished her idea of driving, and sent Gervase Asloane with cards of condolence ; and she even in the first emotion of generosity wrote to Cyril on the subject ; but he never got her letter (as she was pleased to think, on after-thoughts), for the mail steamer by which it went was cast away in the Gulf of Salonica.

And, though she knew it not, times there were when Cyril's thoughts flashed home, quicker than the electric wire could

have brought them : when he sat in his tent at Varna, gazing
listlessly out upon the flat shore, the vast blue semicircular bay,
and the hideous, gloomy, and dilapidated Bulgarian town, while
his heart grew filled with irritating doubts and vague regrets,
and with the mournful image of his lost Mary. Was she indeed
false, as had been represented, and with Rooke Chesters of all
men ? Had she forgotten him ? Had separation and time
effaced his memory from her heart ? Was he now as one she
had never known and never cared for ?

"Well, well," he would think, "a few more weeks must see
me at Eupatoria, and a Russian bullet may solve all my doubts
and difficulties."

But we are somewhat anticipating the regular progress of our
story.

CHAPTER XXXV.

THE SHADOWY HAND AT LONEWOODLEE.

DURING all this time that the summer had been verging towards
autumn, and the corn yellowing on lea and upland, Mary Lennox
had been unremitting as usual, in the lonely task of tending her
father's sick-bed.

She had only heard incidentally of Cyril's departure for the
seat of war—that he had gone without a word of kindness or
farewell to her who loved him as her own soul and more ; and
for a time, that soul had seemed to die within her.

Her betrothal ring was a fond link—a species of sentimental
fetter—from which she had no wish to free herself, otherwise
she might have drawn it from her finger and cast it in the fire !

The first time that Cyril had called her Mary—her Christian
name—still dwelt in her memory with exquisite tenderness,
from the very novelty of the circumstance. The *last* time he
had called her Mary, dwelt in her memory too ; but with anguish,
for then it had been uttered in a tone of wrath, of sorrow and
upbraiding.

Music was the great solace of old Oliver Lennox's lonely
days. He loved to hear the rich and glorious voice of his
daughter, and thus, for many an hour she played and sung to
him, while her heart was full, nigh unto bursting, with thoughts
that would not be repressed.

Like an angel of mercy had poor Mary hovered about that
sick-bed, where her only tie to earth was about to be severed ;
for at last there came a day, she was never to forget, when the
doctor assured her that all his skill could "protract life no
longer, and that ere nightfal, too probably, all would be over ;"

and Mary heard him without tears, for now they would not flow ; but the old anxious and clamorous sensation about her heart, became replaced by a gnawing concentrated agony too keen for description ; and as she listened to the fatal words of Doctor Squills, felt the kind pressure of his hand and heard his steps die away as he left the house, she gazed in a kind of stupor across the landscape, where the setting sun shone so warmly, and, it seemed, so mockingly, in his summer splendour, on the green pasture lands, and on the trees where the birds were singing so merrily, while through the open windows the hum of the mountain bee, and sweet perfume of the honey-suckle came together.

" Must it be—must it be—at last—at *last !*" she murmured through her clenched teeth ; and creeping once more to his side, she kissed her father's brow and caressed his silvery locks, that were now as thin and fine as floss silk ; and as she did so, there flashed on her memory the old tradition that "a grey head was ne'er kamit " (*i.e.*, combed) by a Lennox of Lonewoodlee, for in domestic brawls or foreign wars, they all perished early ; but the manners were changed for the better now.

For a time he seemed unconscious of her presence, and spoke only of her dead brother.

" Oh, my Harry," he murmured, "your mother was in her grave, and never knew how gallantly you led your squadron on that terrible day against the Sikhs."

" Mamma is in Heaven, and oh, papa, may know it all !" whispered Mary.

Then suddenly a light seemed to penetrate the darkness of his mind ; he recognised her, and drew her close to his breast in a tremulous embrace.

" Mary, my own little Mary," said he in low and laboured accents, "the bitterness of death is not in dying, but in leaving you without a home — without a friend — for all passes away with me."

" God will guard and guide me, papa !"

" Our past, with all its traditions and history, has been an honourable past ; yet we Lennoxes have been going down in the world—*down* so surely as I shall go to my grave—my poor child !"

After a long pause he spoke again ; but more feebly.

" Play me something, Mary, while I can yet listen ; for the music soothes me into dreams and fills me with prayerful thoughts ; play to me once again, Mary," he added with a smile that made her heart sicken, for it was the last flash up of the dying light, ere that light went out for ever !

Mary seated herself at the piano in the adjoining room, and while tears streamed over her face, and her tremulous hands

could barely touch the keys in accompaniment, she slowly sung
two verses of a hymn :—

> " Gentle Jesus, look with pity
> From Thy great white throne above ;
> All the night my heart is wakeful
> In Thy sacrament of love.
> Shades of evening fast are falling,
> Day is fading into gloom ;
> So when shades of death fall round us,
> Lead thine exiled children home."

For a time the old man had beat feebly with his fingers on
the coverlet ; then all motion ceased, and when Mary stole in,
a cry escaped her, and she sank on her knees, burying her face
in the bedclothes.

The day had indeed faded into gloom ; the old man had
passed away to the foot of the Great White Throne ; and, a
terrible reality, the unseen, yet shadowy hand was resting on
Lonewoodlee.

    *   *   *   *   *   *   *

There were now silence and utter desolation in that sequestered tower among the moorlands. The blinds were drawn
down ; old and dingy blinds they were, making the deeply set
windows look more gloomy in the walls which were of such
strength and thickness.

Alison Home, after the first noisy explosion of her grief, when
she uttered spasmodic sobs, and rocked herself to and fro before
the kitchen fire, moved about stealthily and softly in list shoes,
as if fearing still to disturb the old Laird, who died where so
many of his forefathers had lain, and where many of their
brides had slept.

The stillness, the solemn hush of death were over all, and
nowhere more than in the desolate heart of Mary. Everything
connected with such an event in Scotland is so grim, so stern,
so funereal, and utterly without aught to alleviate the mind of
the survivor, that it becomes harrowing in the extreme. There
are no prayers for the dead ; no pretty offices, such as the decoration of the body with flowers : no service of any kind is
performed beside it, so that the living may linger near in a
labour of love to the last. A white sheet is simply spread over
to hide *it*, and then the body is left to stiffen into ghastly
rigidity of outline.

And this death had not come unaccompanied by omens ; the
watch-dog had moaned painfully all the preceding night ; and
Alison Home, and the other domestic, had of course heard the
dead-bells tinkling in their ears, according to the peasant superstition in the old ballad :—

" Yestreen I heard the death-bell sound,
When a' were fast asleep ;
And aye it rung, and aye it sung,
Till a' my flesh did creep."

Though in days and months past, Mary had otten, in anticipating
the present terrible contingency, thought of her own future, she
forgot all about it now. She had even ceased to think of Cyril
Wedderburn till his mother's card came, and a bitter smile
crossed the girl's pale face as she placed it on the table, where
lay an open letter from Messrs. Grub and Wylie, the solicitors,
" threatening legal proceedings anent the bill handed to us by
our client Captain Chesters of Chesterhaugh."

It might safely lie on the table unheeded *now !*

Mary Lennox was indeed alone ! Sorrow-stricken as she was,
there was not on all the earth a being who could share her terrible
emotion of grief. She had no friend nigh to soothe her awful
loneliness by a single word that was not so conventional as to
be repellant. She had no home, no house, no shelter now from
the too probable want that must soon overtake her !

Dark and cheerless indeed was the prospect of the bereaved
girl ; there was affliction and agony for the present, with vague
terror of the future. No hand was near to caress, and no voice
to soothe her, as she lay weeping on her bed, sleepless and without rest, though prostrate from over-wrought emotion. There was
something terrible in the desolation of that young heart, thrust
back upon itself, even in its craving for sympathy. She had
not even that relief afforded to sorrow by having around her
friends to whom she might speak of the dead, and hear his real
or imagined virtues extolled, remembered, and descanted on.

The two old female servants sat cowering by the kitchen fire,
talking in low whispers of the Shadowy Hand on the wall, and
wondering if it was visible now ; but then there was no moon.
According to an old custom, or superstition, they had covered
up with white every piece of furniture the chamber of death
contained, and then the door thereof was carefully closed, for
in rural districts the people fear the dead may speak if it is left
ajar, though the whistle of the locomotive is fast banishing all
such foolish fancies.

The minister of Willowdean, a cold and somewhat pompous
personage, came on the morrow, and his extempore prayer—
one stereotyped in his mind, having been delivered on a thousand similar occasions— though hard and unsympathetic, and
most jarringly intoned, soothed her a little, because his meaning was good, and he wished to be kind apparently. The
Reverend Gideon M'Guffog was a burly, hard-featured and
sandy-whiskered Galwegian, who seemed more like something
betwen a bluff grazier and a sleek attorney, than a clergyman.

At the close of his prayer, which he delivered with his eyes shut, he glanced with surprise at the open piano, on which the music Mary had last used was yet remaining neglected or forgotten.

"Music," said he, in a tone of reprehensive inquiry, while glancing at Mary, under, over, and finally through his spectacles.

"It is the hymn I sang to my darling papa last night ; he loved it so, next to *Adeste fideles*, indeed ; and it was while I was singing it, he passed away from me," said Mary in a choking voice.

The measure of the Reverend Gideon's reprehension became full when he read over the hymn in question.

"It is ritualistic, even popish in spirit, Miss Lennox, and I deplore that the last sounds heard on earth by the ears of your esteemed father, were such as these. But oh, let not me bruise the bruised! My poor young lady, this sort of thing comes of your being so sadly left to yourself."

He retired, promising to call again. But nothing that he could say had the effect of crushing Mary's spirit lower, though she felt that in life or in death she had nothing to reproach herself with as a daughter.

As he was in haste to address a meeting of the Sabbatarians and self-righteous folks of Willowdean, who were getting up a petition to the Home Office to prevent the working men of Edinburgh from entering the Botanical Gardens of that city "on the Lord's Day," and indulging in the desecration of it by enjoying flowers and sunshine, he hurried away ; but permitted his wife, who had latterly ignored Mary's existence (at least since the Chesterhaugh story), to remain with her, till the funeral matters were arranged. This was but an act of Christian charity ; and when it became known in the neighbourhood, that the impoverished Laird of Lonewoodlee was dead, many shook their heads regretfully, when remembering, like honest Sir John Wedderburn, his stately manners, his steady seat in the hunting field, his convivial qualities, his dignified, old-fashioned courtesy, his queer feudal notions ; and all agreed that a link with the past was broken. A few others speculated on what would become of his beautiful orphan daughter.

The funeral day came at last, the great and final wrench to poor Mary, who was secluded in her own room, as men alone are present when "the Prayer" is given in Scotland ; but she heard that Sir John Wedderburn and his youngest son were present in deep mourning, and she sobbed more heavily at the intelligence.

Cyril's father ! Cyril's brother !

"Dead!—dead!" she would whisper in her heart. "How shall I struggle through the world alone? Who will love me

So Oliver Lennox was buried in the Lennox aisle of Willow-dean Kirk, where are lying the tombs of his race for three hund-red years, back even to Oliver who built the Tower, as the legend above its door records. And with a face of due solemnity, specially got up for the occasion, his solicitor from Edinburgh acted as chief mourner; for neither kith nor kin had Oliver left to stand by his grave on that solemn day when the turf fell like a green curtain over the last scene of his history.

"Better in his narrow home than in the Tolbooth of Willow-dean or Greenlaw; for it was coming to *that*, sir!" whispered his solicitor in the ear of Sir John Wedderburn, to whom, as a Baronet and man of property, he had stuck like a barnacle dur-ing the whole of the melancholy ceremony.

CHAPTER XXXVI.

A SURPRISE.

WHEN Oliver Lennox passed away, he left Mary little that she could call her own, save her paraphernalia and a few jewels that had been her mother's. Lonewoodlee had been sold piecemeal in times long past, and the little that remained was mortgaged to the turret-vanes. The spot of ground around it was mortgaged too, even to the last tree that grew thereon. There was the old furniture of the days of the Regency, now scarcely worth removal; there were some grim old portraits, by Ramsay and Aikman, and even two by Sir Peter Lely, which would sell readily to those who were "getting up" galleries of an-cestors elsewhere. There were some old arms, even bits of armour that had seen service in the Border Wars; steel caps and jacks, and Jedwood axes; old cabinets, and eggshell china in the chintz-covered drawing-room; old books, old rods and guns, and whips; and many a household god, to which Mary's heart clung yearningly now that she knew she must leave them all behind her; for whichever way her eyes turned they fell on some object through which, by the mere association of ideas, she was tortured. But she strove to cast such thoughts aside, as she reflected on the littleness of life and the worthlessness of it—a bitter conclusion when formed by the heart of one so young, and when that heart should feel all the best impulses of hope in a joyous future, and in a long life of lasting happiness.

Had her father been more provident in his hot fox-hunting youth; had her brother, the lancer, contracted fewer debts of honour, her fate might, she knew, have been different now. But her father was dead, and Harry was dead—buried in his Indian grave, far, far away; so she crushed the thoughts that would upbraid them. Yet when taken in conjunction with her

broken engagement, and the whole details of her luckless love
affair with Cyril Wedderburn, her heart

"Ached with thoughts of *all* that might have been,"

had her fortune and circumstances in life been more prosperous
and suitable to her birth.

When the gloomy excitement of the funeral was past, and
she came steadily to see the necessity for facing the future, she
felt at times an irritation—an almost angry and defiant emotion
at Destiny; while sharing with Alison Home the hope that
"when things are at the worst, they are sure to mend—at least
they couldna' weel be waur." But she knew that with her they
must mend elsewhere than in her old ancestral home. And
knowing that the Chesters' story had caused her to be coldly
and malevolently regarded in the neighbourhood, now she felt
only the most intense longing to quit it, and for ever.

In the years of the future, if God spared her, when her name
had been forgotten here, she might, if she choose, return again
to see her father's grave, and perhaps to erect a little monument
over it. And so, thinking over these possibilities, pondering
alone—for the minister's wife had that day gone back to the
Manse—Mary, seated in her modest black dress, gave herself
up to thoughts that became most difficult to unravel. She
leaned her head upon her right hand, and sat in the deep recess
of one of the dining-room windows. She heard only the beating
of her heart, save when the intense solitude that reigned around
the old house was broken by the cawing of the black rooks in
the ancient thicket—the *lone wood*—from which the Tower took
its name, or the bleating of a sheep on the hillside close by.

A day was coming, she knew, when her eyes must rest on
other lands and prospects than the old familiar view she saw
from her window now; and never did the fields, laden with
golden grain, or the green pasture meadows and the purple
heather of the hills now bathed in the amber hues of sunset,
look more lovely than in this her time of sorrow.

With all her anxiety to begone now, she dreaded the change.
She was so young, and so totally ignorant of the world and all
its crooked ways; the uprootal from old associations amid which
she had lived from infancy; the risk of venturing among the
cold, hard, suspicious, and perhaps unpitying strangers—more
than all, of precipitating herself into a human wilderness so
vast, and to her unknown, as that of London, appalled her—for
to London she was bent on going! She felt herself little able
to work, but alike ashamed and unable to beg! These, and
such as these, were crushing thoughts to a tender girl in the
sensitive time of youth, when all around her should be happiness and sunshine.

Her former friends and school companions now in London were, many of them, girls of good and high position. But in her change of circumstances she shrunk from intruding on any of them as a supplicant ; and resolved that among strangers only should she look for work and bread.

So immersed was Mary in her own sad thoughts that she heard neither the sound of horses' hoofs, the rolling of wheels, nor the barking of the Dalmatian dogs ; nor was she roused from her reverie till the startled Alison Home placed before her an old and well-worn silver salver, whereon lay two black-edged cards. Almost immediately after there was a rustling of silk and crape, as Lady Wedderburn and Gwendolcyne entered ; and, being both in deep mourning, their appearance was most consonant to the occasion. Lady Wedderburn at once introduced herself, adding, " Miss Lennox—my niece, Miss Wedderburn."

A flush crossed Mary's pale face, and her quickened heart beat painfully as she rose to receive visitors who were entirely unexpected. But still, in the native pride of her heart, she strove to restrain her tears.

" Lady Wedderburn," said she, " it is most—most kind of you to come to me——"

" Surely not at a time like this, my dear child," replied Lady Wedderburn, seating herself on the deep old horse-hair sofa, and thinking how beautiful and how perfectly ladylike the pale girl looked in her black dress—an orphan in mourning for her father.

" Yes, at a time like this—the darkest of a blighted, a stricken life !" continued Mary, deeply moved by the soft and kind manner of her visitors.

" My son Cyril asked me to—to— ;" poor Lady Wedderburn paused, conscious that she was beginning to blunder already.

" Cyril—Captain Wedderburn—did he——"

" Yes. He asked me to be kind to you if aught happened. You understand, Miss Lennox ?"

Mary *did* understand, and she began to weep hysterically, while her visitors, unused to grief of this kind, glanced at each other uneasily.

The elder had ignored, slighted, even " cut " her. But could Mary forget that she was the mother of Cyril, who once loved her, and whose ring was yet on her engagement finger—Cyril, whom she still loved so well ! Her heart was crushed by her own great grief : she felt weak and tender, and had the desperate longing in her utter and intense loneliness for some one to love her, for something to cling to. And she had now all the passionate desire to throw herself into the arms of Lady Wedderburn, as she might have done into those of a parent, and then

14

weep freely and fully, pouring out her sorrow ; but a remnant of family pride — the genuine old Scottish instinct, of not "letting oneself down," sustained Mary's spirit, and withheld the generous emotion which the other was too motherly and too kindhearted to have misunderstood.

She had admitted Cyril's interest in Mary's welfare, and she resolved to ignore that she knew or suspected more ; but somehow the conversation always turned to Cyril.

"I have now learned,—I think it right to tell you, my dear Miss Lennox—the true story of that visit you paid to the house —the gate, I mean—of Captain Chesters. I learned it quite incidentally," she added, perceiving that a momentary flash of anger lit up Mary's eyes ; "but I do think, as a friend, that it was most unfortunate for yourself that you concealed it so."

"I concealed it, knowing the character of Captain Chesters, and in dread of the very event that took place."

"And this event?" asked the other, looking a little perplexed.

"Was your son's just indignation at that which I had no control over ; indeed I had not," replied Mary, referring thus to her engagement in the most straightforward manner, and not ill-pleased that the attractive eyes of the beautiful cousin were occupied by an album in the recess of a window.

"Control?" stammered Lady Wedderburn, not knowing well what to say.

"Before that, he loved me very truly, madam."

"For long?"

"Almost ever since he brought my dear papa my brother's sword and rings from India."

"And you loved him?"

"Yes," replied Mary, in a low voice like a sigh.

"It is great duplicity on Cyril's part, when he knew our families were on bad terms ; and *latterly*," she added, with a glance at the unconscious Gwenny, "an unfortunate folly on yours, under all the circumstances."

"You refer, madam, I presume, to the engagement with his cousin of which Captain Chesters told me?"

Lady Wedderburn was silent ; and thus, unwittingly perhaps, permitted Mary to adopt a painful error.

"Well, well," she sighed, looking sadly down the while ; "I can have no more bereavements now. My papa's death leaves me alone in the world."

"Alone?"

"Yes ; God and myself only know how fearfully alone !"

"This is most sad," replied Lady Wedderburn, kindly, as she took Mary's hands in hers, and gazed tenderly into the sweet young face. "Can I not assist you, Miss Lennox ? In anything you may command me," she added, for secretly her heart went forth to the girl who had loved her absent son, and had the courage to honestly avow that love; so with charming inconsistency, forgetting all about her past accusation of art, of cunning, and decoying on Mary's part, with much of pity and sudden affection, she surveyed her; for Mary was so wasted and worn by past watching, nursing, and sorrow, that she was more like a spirit, having dark brown hair and large violet eyes, with bluish unhealthy circles under them, than a living being. "You do not seem strong, Miss Lennox," said she.

"Nor am I; my health may never recover the shocks I have sustained of late, with dear papa's long illness, and the hard task—a labour of love—watching him by night and day; so Dr. Squills tells me, that unless I am very careful, my grave is not far distant, and at best, assuredly not far off."

"Poor child! And what do you mean to do? Pardon me, but you cannot live here alone."

"Here!" repeated Mary, and as she glanced at the old faded dining-hall, the bitter smile stole over her lip again; "no, not here—not here. I mean to get some teaching if I can."

"And if not?"

"Then I can but—die!"

"Do not speak thus, I implore you!"

"My voice is thought to be a good one, and has been well cultivated, for papa was vain of it; but I fear I have lost a note or two since—since——"

"Since when?"

"Last March."

("That was when Cyril left this," thought Lady Wedderburn.) "And you mean to go to London, I have heard; is that true?"

"Yes; in a few days."

"Have you friends there?"

"Not one."

"This is a terrible—a bleak prospect!"

"Bleak indeed; fatherless, motherless, and in time, it may be, penniless! But not hopeless, while God spares and helps me. Assuredly, Lady Wedderburn, this world is not the place where our fondest hopes are realized, or where our brightest dreams are always embodied. It is a place, rather, where we should bear and forbear one with another, striving to be happy if we can; and if we cannot be happy, to be at least resigned and content."

"My poor child, by living so much alone, you have learned to talk and think painfully beyond your years," replied the other, who could not help contrasting the probable fate, fortune, and future of Mary and Gwenny, both alike so young and beautiful.

Somehow her visit proved a very protracted one. She found

the charms of Mary's mind and manner were such, that even her loveliness seemed to be but a secondary excellence. She pressed her to visit Willowdean—to come away with her now in the carriage ; to spend even a single day there ; but Mary remembered her father's luckless and expensive quarrels and disputes with Sir John ; she thought, too, of the bitter slights and mortifications that had been put upon herself ; and now that all was over between her and Cyril, and that another possessed the love that had once been her own, she steadily declined, so her visitors ceased to press ; and all this seemed very strange to the blushing and simpering Mrs. M'Guffog, who had just returned, happy that she was in time to have an opportunity of even shaking hands " wi' her leddyship."

She prevailed upon Mary, however, to accept of a letter of introduction to a lady friend in London, who had two little daughters, and who, she was assured, would befriend her ; and for this, Mary felt herself compelled to express gratitude ; and there the interview, which afforded sincere pleasure to Mary, ended, and the splendid carriage, with its liveried servants and brace of spotted dogs, rolled away from the door of the desolate and dilapidated house.

When Gwenny, after kissing Mary and weeping with her at parting, in the mode adopted by most young ladies, who so readily share each other's joys and griefs—expatiated on the romantic solitude of the old tower, and the quaintness—so she was good-natured enough to term it—of its furniture and so forth, Lady Wedderburn reminded her that the Lennoxes were but as mushrooms when compared to the old Welsh line of Ap-Rhys of Llanchillwydd ; but so she might, with a safer conscience, have added were the Wedderburns of Willowdean ; for so, even in this advanced age of the world, will some people talk, and set a mighty store upon their real or fancied little bit of heraldry, as if there had been more Adams than one in Eden.

CHAPTER XXXVII.

MARY BEGINS HER PILGRIMAGE.

WITH that promptitude which women can so often exert when in grief or adversity, Mary made all her preparations for leaving Lonewoodlee. It was already in the hands of creditors or their agents, and every day she remained she felt as if they were conferring an obligation upon her, and that idea was intolerable ! A few relics of her father she secured for herself. The embroidered slippers he had last worn—her own working ; his spectacles, an old riding-whip, and other mementos, were put away as sacred treasures, over which she often wrung her poor little hands, and as the emotions of the child welled up in her heart, would weep—oh, so bitterly !

Mary had sometimes—especially latterly—repined at the dulness of her impoverished home ; but now, with an emotion of repentance, she shed salt and silent tears, at the misery of leaving its shelter for a future which she could not foresee, and some dark forebodings of which had already begun to steal upon her.

The last day there was a dull and melancholy one indeed. A dense mist had set in from the German Sea, and was rolling in masses along all the glens and ravines of the Lammermuirs ; the wind seemed to sigh with a deep "sough" in the old pine wood, and the old house-dog, as if sensible of some impending change or calamity, uttered ever and anon a low and dismal howl.

Mary was taking away with her only a trunk, for everything that had belonged to the family in past times, and all their most treasured household *lares*, were to be left behind for the hammer of the inexorable auctioneer. Jealously tender of her dead father's honour, Mary had changed into money everything in the shape of jewellery that the solicitors would permit her so to turn (for even the stony hearts of Grub and Wylie were moved); she had thus paid to the last penny all he owed in the neighbourhood ; and leaving herself but a very little stock in gold—enough, perhaps, to maintain her for a few weeks, till she discovered some one to appreciate her musical talents and those little domestic accomplishments by which she hoped to feed herself in the great metropolis of the world.

So the fatal or eventful evening came at last, and Mary, with her little trunk, was driven over to the railway station by Doctor Squills, who, as he had always admired her greatly in secret, was somewhat moved on this occasion. As he turned the gig down the roadway from the hills, Mary begged of him to pause for a moment, while she gave a last long, wistful glance at Lonewoodlee, which—save that no smoke ascended from its chimneys now, and that all the windows were closed—looked just as it must have done for three centuries, a grey and stony mass, with its four turrets standing sharply up against the evening sky.

The little garden, once so trim and neat, was a mere wilderness now, where the jasmine grew in wild masses round the old lichen-spotted dial-stone ; and the ancient pines of the thicket which her usually improvident father had spared for beauty's sake, and where she had been wont to meet Cyril, were marked by the axe for cutting down and "sale by public roup at the Market Cross of Willowdean," as a large placard informed the passer.

There had been a time when she had pictured herself leaving Lonewoodlee—if she ever left it—as the bride of Cyril Wedderburn, happy, joyous, and filled with the natural anticipations of a long and brilliant future.—Now! tears choked her under her veil, as she felt keenly all the bitterness of the present, when contrasted with the vanished hopes of the past. It was all over —all—all; and certainly on this side of the grave they would never meet again.

"Drive on, Doctor, please; I fear we shall be late for the train—I am sure I hear the whistle already!" said she, making a prodigious effort to be calm.

In her motherly heart, Lady Wedderburn viewed with much of pity and more of terror, the fact of a solitary and beautiful girl, one so gently bred and nurtured and so totally ignorant of the world, setting forth on a pilgrimage so hazardous; while Sir John, with his usual open-handed liberality, thought of enclosing a cheque to her for a handsome sum, pretending it was some debt he owed her father; but his wife assured him that the spirit of Mary Lennox was such, that she would too probably return it as an insult; so the good man sighed as he relinquished the idea, adding—"Ah, poor thing—she was so fond of our Cyril, you say;" and he sighed again over his wine that evening, and said, "Kate, Kate, I cannot now, without regret and emotion, regard this utter destruction of an old Border family, with all its local and historical associations. Poor obstinate, passionate Oliver Lennox! I would, for the girl's sake, he had guided his patrimony as he might have done."

Lady Wedderburn agreed with him; but Robert thought "the sooner such geese as old Lennox were plucked and in the market, the better."

"There speaks the lawyer," retorted his father; "but poor Lennox knew one art only—that of squandering."

Meanwhile, Mary was standing as one in a dream on the platform of the little station at Willowdean, where the Reverend Gideon M'Guffog and a few others waited, either to see her off, or more likely to see the train come in, that event being then somewhat of a novelty in the secluded locality. He omitted to warn her, an inexperienced girl, of the perils that might so easily beset her path in a city so vast as London; but he did not fail to warn her to beware of "prelacy, popery, ritualism, and other errors and snares of the Evil One, abounding in the land to which she was going."

Sobbing bitterly as she bade her adieu, old Alison Home forced upon her acceptance a pair of worsted boots of her own knitting, "to keep her feetie warm in the train," as she said, though the season was the end of summer; and a tall footman in plush brought her from Willowdean a beautiful bouquet and a pretty basket of fruit, with "the compliments and best wishes of Miss Wedderburn."

Her rival—her supplanter! yet she received the graceful gifts quietly, and returned a polite message of thanks.

To keep up appearances, she had taken a first-class ticket to Berwick, resolving to exchange there where she was unknown to a third-class for London, consoling herself by the reflection, that as an unprotected girl, she should doubtless be safer among the many, though more humble, who might be in the latter, than with one or two in the former class of carriage. And as the train glided away, Mary gave a last and piercing glance at the familiar scenery around her, at the village spire, whose shadow at sunset fell upon the grave of her parents, and then she sank back into a recess of the carriage, to weep and commune alone, with all her thoughts turned inwards.

Every tie between her and her home was broken now ; and she had but one all-pervading idea, that on the day of her visit, Cyril's mother, by her *silence*, had tacitly admitted the fact of his engagement to his cousin Gwendoleyne.

" How soon, oh, how readily he forgot me !" she exclaimed, for she was alone.

Mary felt truly grateful to Lady Wedderburn for her letter of introduction, which was addressed to a Lady Wetherall in Piccadilly, and on the latter all her hopes were based. She wondered whether Piccadilly was a street or square—a park or suburb, and what manner of person Lady Wetherall might be— whether old or young, grave or gay. Would she be kind to her? oh, if so, how very soon she should learn to love her and her two little daughters. If the girls were her daughters, then *she* could not be very old—middle-aged, pleasant and motherly, perhaps ; for now when alone, and entirely among strangers, Mary began to feel a little timid ; she had heard and read so much of the unmerited humiliations of governess life.

She had changed carriages at Berwick ; the waters of the bordering Tweed had vanished, and she strove, but in vain, to court sleep in the comfortless third-class vehicle, while the swift night train sped on in darkness along the bleak Northumbrian coast line, by Morpeth, and by Newcastle, the lights of which she saw with astonishment from the famous High-level Bridge ; and as the train "slowed," then with growing fear and wonder did she look down on the quaint old bridge of the Tyne, on the pigmy figures in the gas-lit streets, and on the masts and yards of the shipping, more than one hundred and twenty feet below her !

So the monotonous night wore away, and weary, pale and nervous, with her black mourning dress powdered white with dust, she saw the train enter London, and run on for miles upon miles between dense streets, which being all of brick, seemed strange and even foreign to her eyes, till she began to imagine it would never stop at all,—till about ten in the forenoon, when she found herself standing lost, bewildered, and literally stunned, amid the bustle and roar of the Great Northern Railway! But last night—only last night, she had been amid the sequestered solitude of the healthy Lammermuirs, where, save the bleating of a sheep or the whistle of a curlew, no sound broke the oppressive silence!

CHAPTER XXXVIII.

IN LONDON.

THE space, the crowd and the bustle in and around the terminus of the Great Northern Railway, scared poor Mary, and literally took her breath away. Wearily, and with a haggard and almost despairing eye, the girl threw up her black veil and looked about her. The train had disgorged its hundreds on the spacious platform; all seemed to have some decided object or path to pursue—some home or hotel to go to; nearly all seemed to have friends to greet them, were able to select their own luggage, and depart on their way in confidence and security.

" Now then, young lady—move on, please," said a policeman, and she moved on accordingly, but mechanically and forgetting all about the little trunk which contained all her worldly goods, till she suddenly saw it on a barrow, with many others, when she claimed it, and was instantly surrounded by clamorous porters, and even cabmen seeking her as a fare, and using strange slang terms of which she was totally ignorant.

" Where was she to be driven to?" some one asked her.

She could not say, but stood helpless and burst into tears. At that moment the guard of the train by which she had travelled—a ruddy complexioned, brown-whiskered, and jolly looking man—remembered that she was the young lady to whom the showily-liveried footman had brought the bouquet and fruit at Willowdean. He came forward and, touching his cap, politely said—" Can I do anything for you, ma'am—'seem a stranger in London—'been here before?"

" Never."

" Where do your friends live?"

" I have none in London."

" Then where would you like a cab to take you?" he continued.

" That I cannot tell you—I am so utterly a stranger."

The guard began to look puzzled, and a policeman who was standing by, and had hitherto been gazing stolidly over his glazed leather stock, now seemed to take an interest in the conversation and to look suspicious, while one or two men of shabby appearance whispered together and drew near, till his eye fell on them, and then they slunk away.

" Do you know Lady Wetherall's house in Piccadilly ?" asked Mary, timidly.

" I knows Piccadilly pretty well, ma'am—but can't say as I knows Lady Wetherall. Are you going there ?"

" To-morrow—meantime I must rest for to-day and to-night ; I am quite exhausted."

After a pause, the guard said, " I daresay my missus wouldn't object to taking you in for a night till you could look about you, and do it cheap too. She prefers Scotch folks—queer, but every one to their taste. If you choose to cab it, I'll go along with you myself."

" Is she your wife of whom you talk, my good man ?" asked Mary, feeling the necessity of rousing herself to action, for the eyes of many loiterers were now upon her.

" Wife—no, my landlady—poor woman she has seen better days, has Mrs. Long Primer."

" Of course—who ever knowed a landlady that hadn't ?" said the policeman, laughing.

" She's a respectable woman—a printer's widow, ma'am ; and though her name be Long, she's little enough."

" Well, Tom," resumed the policeman, "I think you'd better take the young woman away with you ; she may get into trouble else, being, I see, quite a stranger—a jolly green one too, sure as my name is Finnis."

This style of dialogue was Mary's first taste of a new kind of humiliation. The distribution of two or three three-penny pieces procured the cab, on the box of which her trunk was hoisted ; she stepped in, and the guard, Tom Gubbs, in his railway livery, followed her. As they drove through the streets the double lines of vehicles of all kinds, laden carts, drays and waggons, the multitude of sounds that mingled and united into a species of dull roar ; the vast and ceaseless human tide that surged along the pavements, at first appalled Mary, and then seemed to lull her senses into a kind of stupor, from which the voice of her new companion roused her at times, as he kindly named the thoroughfares through which they were passing, or drew her attention to some great church or other public edifice.

At last, after traversing what seemed to be an enormous wilderness of streets, the cab turned to the left from the crowded Strand, down a quiet and narrow alley, where all was still and nearly noiseless, and at the foot of which a glimpse could be had of the Thames, with its shipping, and the crowded steamers

gliding past.   And now the vehicle stopped at the green-painted
door of a large house, where people lodged on the various
floors, according to what they could afford to pay.   Then the
guard, Mr. Tom Gubbs, after a chaffing wrangle with the cabby,
who insisted that his fare should be five, instead of two
shillings, informed her that this was "Norfolk Street, Strand."
To Mary's ear this conveyed no particular idea, but to her eye the
houses looked gloomy, dingy, and strange, and she could not
determine whether they had been built yesterday, or two hundred years ago ; though with their quaintly corniced doors, old
fashioned brass knockers, and general aspect, they looked like
mansions at which Johnson and Garrick might have visited,
near which Savage might have wandered in his hunger and
misery, and where crown bowls of punch had been drunk over
the defeat of "The Rebels" at Culloden, and the fall of Que-
bec,—for the quarter seemed decidedly London of the Hano-
verian times.

Mary's *introducteur*, whose apartment was at the top of the
house, vouched to the landlady for the respectability of her
"new wisitor," who he said "had come from Scotland by the
night train, and was going to Lady Wetherall's in Piccadilly—
to service of some kind, as he thought—to-morrow ; but that
she wished a few hours' rest, being well nigh wore out."

Indeed Mary looked as if about to sink, and when Mrs. Long
Primer, a plump and motherly looking little woman in a huge
white cap, asked her " on which floor she wished an apartment,"
she replied that it was a matter of total indifference to her ; so
the landlady solved the difficulty by conducting her at once to
a little room, one window of which faced the gloomy street ;
but the other afforded a narrow glimpse of the shining river
with all its bustle.

A little breakfast was prepared for her, and now Mary with
a swelling and thankful heart, shook hands with Gubbs the
guard (who, on the morrow, she knew, would be speeding past
the Lammermuirs, with the down train), and the worthy fellow
blushed scarlet, for it had not been often his lot to have in his
a hand so white and beautiful as that of Mary Lennox.

A reference to the London Directory assured Mrs. Primer
that there was a Lady Wetherall in Piccadilly.   The weight
and appearance of Mary's trunk, as it stood in the passage,
suggested respectability, and it was filled with genuine wearing
apparel.   Her courier bag too, with all its little appurtenances,
seemed faultless.   Mrs. Long Primer studied all these things
acutely, for she had been deluded, "taken in," more than once
during her career as a landlady ; but in the course of conversation with Mary, she soon learned her circumstances, her object
in coming to London, and all her wishes ; and the good woman

felt her mother's heart stirred within her, as she surveyed the sad, weary eyes, the pale little face and the black dress of a creature so young and attractive east on the world alone ; and more sadly perhaps would she have surveyed her, had she known how very few pounds the poor girl had in her pocket.

Unslept though she had been all the previous night, Mary felt unnaturally wakeful all day. The street was still and quiet, though close to the roar of the mighty Strand. No sound came to her ears there, save an occasional street cry, the paddling of a steamer shooting past with its human freight, or the bell of St. Clement's church, as the clock struck the slowly passing hours. She prayed in her heart and felt hopeful, for she had made her first essay in life and met with kindness.

She studied the advertisements in the *Times*, and the number of situations vacant filled her with wonder. Could people ever be found to supply them all ! On the other hand, the number of applicants, their talents, qualifications, and recommendations rather scared her, and made her happy to rest all her hopes on Lady Wetherall. Yet she could not resist turning again and again, nervously, to the monstrous list in the *Times*. There were, " Wanted, a young lady for a millinery department— salary for the first year £50." " Wanted, a young *person* of strictly Christian principles, as governess to five little girls ; solid English education, French, Italian, music, drawing, and the use of the globes necessary, salary £10 per annum ; and the share of a comfortable home." " Widow, wanted as housekeeper to a single gentleman, not over forty " (which was to be "not over forty," the advertisement did not say). " Wanted a cook" —the cooks seemed decidedly to have the best of it, so far as salaries went ; but Mary's heart sank as she read on, and then she cast the paper aside.

Quitting the rickety little calico-covered sofa, she frequently rose to look from the window into the street without. The architecture, material, and construction of the houses seemed novel to her eye, while the window panes being almost flush with the external walls, suggested alarming ideas of insecurity. The voices of the passers, and the names on the signboards, like the sound of the church bells, all spoke to her of being in a strange place, and of being utterly among strangers.

Slowly passed the day, and after she had been some hours alone, she began to feel forlorn and nervous. Oh, the gloom of that London lodging-house—she should never, never forget it ! Her liberty, her being so unheeded and uncared for, almost terrified her. There were none to greet her, and none whom she could greet. She felt as if her existence was already being ignored. To add to the gloom of her thoughts, she had read in that day's *Times* of two cases of death from starvation—death

amid the wealth and luxury of London. And in one instance
the victim had been a governess, a lady of many accomplishments, but out of employment. Starvation ! the idea filled her
with horror ; but, with God's help, such could never be her fate,
for was there not Lady Wetherall, whom Lady Wedderburn felt
assured would refuse *her* nothing ?

The very opening and shutting of the house door, and the
rat-tat of its knocker, suggested the idea of temporary lodgings,
and not of home. *Home!* alas, she had none now, though even
the dog's kennel or the half-ruined stable at Lonewoodlee, would
have seemed as such to her then. Never more — never more,
should she feel the sublime sense of security afforded by home
and a father's roof !

She felt somewhat relieved, however, when gossipy little Mrs.
Primer came to ask her to "join her at tea, with a chop, quite
cheery in her own back parlour." The kind woman had hot
muffins, shrimps and watercresses—even a little flask of Old
Tom—provided as a relish ; and she was very anxious to hear
all about Scotland (the late Mr. Long Primer's mother having
been a native of that country), her ideas of which were decidedly
cloudy, and somewhat pre-railway, being chiefly deduced from
a cheap edition of Miss Porter's "Scottish Chiefs," and "Rob
Roy," as she had seen it performed at the Lyceum or Surrey
Theatre.

"And if Miss Lennox would like to go to the play to-night,
or any night," she added, "they could get a pit order from the
first floor front, Miss Madelena de Montmorencie, who was
leading lady at one establishment, or her third floor back, Mr.
Algernon Sidney Spangles, who was the light comedy gent at
another ; or to see funny little Mr. Robson in 'Jones the
Avenger,' when one didn't know whether to laugh or cry, and
so did both at once ; or to see Mr. Harley, as—begging your
pardon, Miss — was Bottom at the Princess's." But Mary nervously declined all these kind offers of patronage, urging that
she was in deep mourning, and had been face to face with sorrow
too recently.

Even amid her intended civility and benevolence, Mrs. Primer
came out at times with little remarks that jarred on Mary's,
perhaps, overwrought sensibility.

"I think, my dear," said she, as she slowly stirred her tea
and balanced the spoon from time to time on the edge of her
cup, "you said it was a situation as governess you were a-looking
after ?"

"Yes."

"Oh, I quite forgot to ask—have you got a character ?"

"A what— Mrs. Primer ?" asked Mary, with genuine surprise,
while the other began to fidget and cool her tea in the saucer.

" Testimonial of any kind from your last place ?"

" No, I have never been in a situation, and consequently never thought such things were necessary."

" No character—no testimonials—not even a line from the rector or parish clergyman ?"

" I have nothing of the kind."

" Oh lor, oh lor, you are simple as a new-born babby ! Why, child, you'll not get a place even as a lady's maid, without some such papers."

" I have a letter of introduction, such as one lady may give to another," replied Mary, coldly and proudly, yet feeling crushed in heart and broken in spirit, for that such things should be said to her, plainly showed already how poor and dependent her position in life was becoming.

And Mary—she who, in her pride of heart, had shrunk from kissing Lady Wedderburn, while under the roof of her dead father's house—now in the utter loneliness of that heart, kissed with real affection the cheek of the plain little Englishwoman, as she left her for the night ; for she felt gratefully conscious that Mrs. Long Primer had been kind and good to her.

But the word "character" continued to rankle in her memory; and at times, especially in the darkness and silence of her bedroom that night, ere she slept, there crept into her soul an intense longing to be laid at rest by her father's side, where she might never—too probably should never—lie, in the Lennox aisle at Willowdean.

CHAPTER XXXIX.

LOST.

REFRESHED by a deep and dreamless sleep, after her hands had been folded in prayer for assistance and guidance, Mary rose, inspired by a hope that ere the new day was past, she should have come to the end of her chief doubt and difficulty ; but she had to count several weary hours until the time would be suitable for her to call on a person of Lady Wetherall's position.

The smart and bustling little Mrs. Long Primer suggested that Mary should take an omnibus so far as this or that point, changing here and changing there, as a matter of economy. However, Mary became so bewildered by the strange names and infinite number of changes to be made, that she preferred going by cab ; but before setting out she met with a terrible shock. Mrs. Primer suggested some little change in her travelling costume, which Mary had forgotten all about ; but she had the required alteration in her trunk.

"And that, I forgot to say, has gone before you to Lady
Wetherall's, my dear," said Mrs. Primer, rubbing her hands
over each other and smiling with pleasure.

"Before me—how?"

"Her ladyship's own man came for it this morning early,
and left her compliments, with the message that you were to
follow as soon as you chose."

"It is impossible—it is incredible!"

"Lor, Miss. How?"

"Lady Wetherall knows nothing about me, and nothing of
my being in London. She never even heard a word of me!"
said Mary, becoming very excited as she hurried to the passage
and saw that her property was indeed gone.

"What can it mean?" asked Mrs. Primer, growing pale.

"The man must have been a robber."

"A robbery in my 'ouse, Miss Lennox—take care what you
say, ma'am!" exclaimed Mrs. Primer, growing red, while all
the quilling of her cap quivered with her anger.

"By Jingo, it looks very like it, missus," said Tom Gubbs,
the guard, who had overheard these remarks, as he was about
to depart for the midday train; "it's a regular do, Mrs. Primer,
and has been done by one of the fellows as was a loafing and
listening about the platform at the Terminus yesterday—perhaps it's the cabby himself, for all we know or may ever know,
that's away with the young lady's box, and she'll never see it
again on this side o' time."

Mary was dreadfully harassed by this loss. The trunk—apart
from a few little family relics—contained all she possessed in
the world, and what she was totally without the means of replacing. She seemed so crushed that Mrs. Primer, in pity, felt
the necessity of saying something.

"Her ladyship *may* have sent for it, after all. Might not
your friend in Scotland have written to say that you were about
to visit her?"

"Yes. But how were either of them to know that I was here?"

"It is impossible to say. The telegraph tells things wonderful now-a-days."

"And then she would have sent her carriage for me," said
Mary, wearily and dreamily.

"If she has one."

"She must; for I have heard that she is very wealthy."

Tom Gubbs was off by this time to give information to the
police, while Mary, unable longer to delay, procured a cab and
set out for Piccadilly; but not before her kind landlady—whose
prevailing idea was that people should eat under all circumstances, whether joy or grief—had forced her to partake of a
little luncheon, and followed her to the door with the warmest

Mrs. Primer's little ones were all dead, and the good-hearted woman having known much of sorrow in her time, felt a genuine interest in Mary and sympathy for her. She seemed so gentle, so thankful for any kindness, so unsuspecting and truthful; and yet withal, as a stranger utterly ignorant of London and its ways, most helpless. She awaited her return with considerable impatience, and calculating that she might be away at the furthest about three hours, put off the usual time of tea (her most important meal, if it could be called such), that they might have it cosily together, with a pleasant chat about Lady Wetherall's house and establishment; what manner of woman her ladyship was; how she dressed; what her two little girls were like, and so forth.

She wondered if Mary would come to see her after she was fairly established in one of those great mansions in Piccadilly. Mrs. Primer hoped she might, for the young lady didn't look in the least proud; but the idea of herself returning the visit, and being admitted by a huge footman, all calves and whiskers, never entered the timid little woman's head.

The summer afternoon wore drowsily on, and the shadows began to deepen and then to darken in the gloomy brick streets and alleys off the Strand. The clock of St. Clement's struck six, and Mary had now been absent four hours. Mrs. Primer could wait no longer. She took her tea alone, but left the pot to simmer on the hob, beside some hot muffins, for she was certain the poor young lady would return harassed and weary.

Another hour passed without her appearing. Still Mrs. Primer did not feel alarmed; she knew that great folks dined very late, almost in the middle of the night, she had even heard; and what could be more likely than Lady Wetherall keeping her visitor to dinner. So she looked forward with real pleasure to a description of the marvels thereof. Eight, and then nine, were duly chimed in succession from the church tower, and still Mary was absent; and when ten o'clock and darkness came together, Mrs. Long Primer began to feel a real anxiety mingled with alarm. She knew the snares and pitfalls that beset the steps of the unwary in London, and more particularly would one so beautiful as Mary Lennox be subjected to peril; for she was an orphan, and utterly friendless and unknown. Mrs. Primer knew from an article she had lately read in the *Times*, that many more than a thousand beings disappeared in the streets yearly, being literally lost beyond all human ken; and dreadful stories of abductions and robberies, of concealed traps that opened over the river in the floors of nefarious dens and mysterious houses, recurred to her memory, for the slow rolling current of the mighty Thames hides many a terrible crime.

A sudden terror seized her: that the man who had stolen

the trunk that morning might have got some deeper plot in
hand ; that Mary might not have been taken to Piccadilly at all ;
that some wicked woman might personate Lady Wetherall, and
lure her away to where she might never be heard of again.

Midnight came, and still the girl was absent ; and then the
good woman's anxiety of heart amounted almost to an agony,
but she knew not what to do, or where, or to whom to go.
Despite her fears of rheumatism and toothache, with a shawl
over her head, she remained long at an open window, watching
and listening.   Twice or thrice a cab dashed along down
Howard Street, and then her heart leapt with hope : but, as it
turned into the Strand, the hope, like the sound of its wheels,
died away.

The noises without became less and less.   The gaslights in the
adjacent houses had all been turned off ; silence and deeper
darkness seemed to be settling all around her.   Miss de Montmorencie and the light comedy man, who were always late, had
both returned long ago, and it became evident that the lost lady
would not return until the morrow—if she ever returned at all !

Then another vague terror, that she might be held somehow
responsible, personally, for this disappearance, occurred to Mrs.
Long Primer, and added greatly to her perturbation of spirit.

At last she closed the window with a sigh, and was about to
retire to bed, when suddenly, about two in the morning, a hansom cab dashed up to the door, and there was such a vehement
use made of the brass knocker that the whole house resounded
like a drum.

Mrs. Primer sprang again to the window, and a cry of alarm
escaped her on beholding a night policeman, flashing his bull's-
eye on her brass plate, while alighting from the vehicle.   And
then the conviction came over her that some terrible catastrophe
must have occurred to Mary Lennox !   She must have been
robbed, maltreated, or ridden over at least !

CHAPTER XL.

PICCADILLY.

WITH her heart full of sore anxiety concerning her loss, out of
the quietude of gloomy and shabby Norfolk Street, Mary had
been rapidly taken by the cab into the roar, the rush, the racket,
and the breathless heat of London, in one of its hottest months,
when every breath of air seems to have passed away, and the
sunshades of the shop windows cast strong dark shadows on the
heated pavement.   Guiding his lean horse with marvellous
skill, the cabman tore along between the endless tides of busses,

crowded inside and out; drays and hansoms, splendid equipages, and costermongers' carts, and Mary felt again as if in a
dream ; for ages instead of hours seemed to have elapsed since
she had left her sequestered home—the gloomy tower, the
solemn thicket, the pastoral hills, and the months of close
attendance on a sick bed, in a half-darkened and silent room.
All, all seemed to have happened long, long ago ; and all to be far,
far away. So far that it seemed incredible to realize the fact,
that little more than ten hours by rail, would set her among the
lonely Lammermuir hills again.

Along all the line that Mary was driven, none of the sordid
squalor peculiar to some of the humbler parts of London was
visible. All savoured of wealth, to be won or wasted, of
splendour, and of luxury. There were stately buildings of vast
magnitude ; beautiful equipages, with shining liveries bearing
past beauty and fashion : there were enormous plate-glass
windows, glittering with jewellery and gold and silver vessels ;
rich dresses and fabrics, and good things of all kinds, from every
portion of the habitable globe, and from the very waters that wash
its furthest shores ; everything that fancy can create or appetite
suggest was there, for London is the true metropolis of the world.

As Mary looked on all this, hope began to spring up in her
heart. Once established as an inmate of Lady Wetherall's
house, she would earnestly and honestly do her duty to her
pupils there ; and perhaps elsewhere, in time to come, might, as
a teacher, make her voice, so vaunted at home, the means of
further acquisition. She would toil for money—not that she
cared for lucre in itself—but as a means to an end. That she
might relieve the wants of the indigent, and do good unto
others, to people who might be as poor and forlorn as she
herself was then forlorn and poor. She would seek the abodes
of poverty and affliction, and God would reward her for all this
by the blessings that would be poured upon her by grateful
hearts. Among other fond projects for the future, was the
erection of a monument to her parents at home ; and as she
thought of it, there stole over the soft face of the pretty day-
dreamer, weaving her plans even as Alnaschar wove his of
fancied greatness, over the basket of crystal—a divine smile as
she sketched the design in her mind's eye, and traced the
inscription to their beloved memory.

The girl was young, yet it was strange that no thought of a
lover or of marriage ever entered her scheme of the days to
come, till the appearance of a splendid battalion of the Foot
Guards marching past the National Gallery with all their
bayonets glittering in the evening sun, and the crash of their
brass bands waking the echoes of peristyle and dome, recalled
Cyril to her memory with a keen pang ; and she reflected that

15

it was better to have loved and lost than never to have loved at all, for their passion had been a sweet one while it lasted.

"God pity the desolate loving heart, the only star of whose hope is gone out in utter darkness ;" and so thought Mary, as she clasped her hands in bitterness.

From the Strand, where she had close glimpses of the mighty river, with its dark forests of masts and rigging, past the great façade of Somerset House, up the Haymarket, and across Great Jermyn Street, she had been driven into Piccadilly, and along that splendid thoroughfare, to Mary it seemed that they must have proceeded many miles, when the cabman suddenly drew up at the number she had given him, and, having successfully extracted from her double his legal fare, he whipped up his horse the moment she alighted, and disappeared, leaving her on the pavement, looking wistfully at the house ; for among all the stately, gay, and brilliantly decorated mansions in Piccadilly, Lady Wetherall's alone seemed gloomy and deserted, and Mary's heart now began to palpitate, for it was the first time she had ever found herself about to face a total stranger in the attitude of a dependant or a suppliant.

The blinds were all down ; the steps and entrance, which stood between four white pillars, seemed dusty, unswept, and neglected, and hence a foreboding chill, with a hope that Lady Wedderburn had mistaken the number, came over Mary's mind. She rang the bell, and had to do so thrice ere the door was opened by a sharp-featured little woman, who was dressed in rusty black with a widow's cap of portentous size, and who eyed Mary somewhat suspiciously and superciliously.

"Is this Lady Wetherall's—or have I made a mistake?" asked the visitor, timidly.

"Yes ; it is Lady Wetherall's 'ouse ; but what do *you* want, Miss?"

"I have a letter for her——"

"Then you must post it, for her ladyship ain't at 'ome," replied the little woman, in a sharp falsetto voice.

"Not at home?"

"No ; nor in England either."

"Where is she?"

"With the family in Paris."

"But when does she return?" asked Mary, clinging still to chances.

"Can't say, Miss ; but when the London season will be over, she will be sure to go down to the country. Can I do anything for you, Miss?" asked the housekeeper, civilly enough, but gradually closing the door nevertheless.

"Nothing, thanks," said Mary, in a gasping voice as she turned away, and the woman watched her with some interest.

for her steps seemed to totter when she reached the pavement. She felt the absolute necessity of getting out of the stunning and breathless bustle then, to consider the future. Immediately opposite Lady Wetherall's house a gate of the Park stood invitingly open, and the shadow of its trees looked tempting. She soon found a seat, and there, for more than an hour, Mary sat lost in thought and bewilderment—in fear and dejection, totally oblivious of the number of men who passed and repassed; of one or two who seated themselves near and sought to attract her attention ; of the equipages and equestrians pouring past, and more than all of the policeman, who, perhaps luckily for herself, "had his eye on her," for to him there seemed something mysterious about her, and she evidently "didn't seem an every-day young woman ;" for it is one of the peculiarities of London that no person can be too respectable in aspect, too attractive in face or manner, too richly or plainly dressed, to be above suspicion ; and she frequently clasped her hands as she said in her heart—

"God help me ! What *am* I to do now ; in London, unknown, without employment, and robbed of all but a few pounds ?"

Lady Ernescleugh was in town ; she knew that her address was at a place called—she thought—Cavendish Square ; but Mary Lennox felt that she would rather die by the curbstone than appeal for aid or patronage to her, at whose table the odious story of Chesterhaugh had first been mentioned, to render her the victim of local impertinence, malevolence, and envy.

The sun had set ; the shadows in the Park were deepening, and the appearance of a few lamps twinkling at intervals, brought to Mary's mind the necessity for seeking the only roof of which she had any knowledge, kind Mrs. Primer's in Norfolk Street, from whence she resolved to write without delay to Lady Wedderburn for advice, and to obtain, perhaps, a letter to some other wealthy friend in London. Already humbled and crushed by loneliness, by grief and misfortune, all foolish pride on the score of the Willowdean family had completely left her heart. Her cab fare had been so excessive or extortionate that she resolved to make her way back on foot, trusting to the directions of strangers. Giving a small coin to a little fellow who had been going round and round her in wheel-fashion on his hands and feet with wonderful rapidity, she inquired of him "the way to Norfolk Street in the Strand."

Whether inspired by mischief, or in mere ignorance, Mary could never afterwards determine, but this imp of the pavement —one of those intensely sharp and funny little vagabonds who are so peculiarly of London growth, a denizen of the streets and gutters, where like wandering curs they hunt for chance morsels—sent her in exactly the opposite direction by pointing towards Hyde Park Corner, and telling her that when there she was to turn to the right and go straight on ; the consequence was, that when darkness set in, and in her serious alarm she inquired of some one to "direct her to Mrs. Long Primer's, Norfolk Street, Strand," she was greeted with a rough laugh, and the inquiry if "she thought the Strand was to be found about Paddington," for near that quarter of London she found herself, or supposed she found herself, misled, weary, and sinking with fatigue.

Never before had she been in the streets of a vast city by night, and the new scenes and sounds, the brilliant gin palaces, the music from occasional casinos and dancing-rooms, the strange words that were said to her, the vivid light at times, the strong dark shadows at others, all conduced to confuse and terrify her.   Once or twice she received proper directions and wandered on in the desperate hope of recognising some landmark of her morning drive, such as St. Paul's dome, the Nelson pillar, or the National Gallery, but sought in vain.   The loss of her handkerchief, which had deen filched from her—deliberately twitched out of her hand, indeed—suggested that she should take care of her little purse, which she secured in her bosom. She feared to offer money for a guide lest she should fall into some perilous snare ; more than one man had already addressed her in bantering terms of endearment, which only terrified, but failed to excite anger in her heart ; and, to avoid one of these who had begun persistently to follow her, in a pitiable state of irresolution she unfortunately turned down a quiet street, where she suddenly became involved in a miserable catastrophe.

CHAPTER XLI.

THE LONELY STREET.

AFRAID lest this strange follower should accost her rudely or even molest her, Mary took advantage of the shadow in a portion of the street, to spring into the recess of a doorway, where with palpitating heart she laid a hand upon the bell, determined to seek succour at all hazards if he came near.   The man evidently missed her, and while he was gazing about him irresolutely, three fellows of a suspicious aspect, who appeared as suddenly as if they had been shot up through the pavement, flung themselves simultaneously upon him !   There was a brief—very brief—struggle ; a choking sound as of strangulation, a half-stifled cry in which a shriek from Mary mingled, and then the ruffians, one of whom she perceived to be tall and thin, sallow-visaged, with a hooked nose and long moustache, vanished, leaving their victim on the pavement, partially garrotted and *minus* watch, purse, and hat.

It was a common case of cruel assault and robbery by street thieves.

Breathlessly Mary approached the stranger, who lay still and motionless. She had no fear of death—the dead had lain in her arms too recently—"a heavier weight than lead ;" and as she looked down on the unfortunate man, she could perceive by the light of a gas-lamp close by that his hair was white and glistening. She thought of her father's silvery hair, and forgetting how this man had so recently scared and annoyed her, while stooping down and calling for help, she endeavoured to loosen his cravat that he might respire more freely.

While she was thus acting the part of a little Samaritan, several passers-by gathered around her, and four officers of police came up with a man handcuffed and in their custody ; the tall sallow man with the hooked nose.

" I am so glad you have captured this wicked wretch !" said Mary, tremulous with excitement. " Oh, I saw it all happen— a horrible act of cruelty !"

" Ah ! this is fortunate ; then you fully recognise this person as one of the culprits ?" said one who seemed by the difference of his dress to be an Inspector of police.

" Yes ; perfectly."

The prisoner uttered a terrible oath mingled with a threat.

" That is well, ma'am. This fellow, Ben Ginger, *alias* 'the Captain,' is an old offender ; but we'll have him finally locked up for this. Your evidence will be necessary, however. What is your name, Miss?" he added doubtfully, while peering into her face, as ladies are not wont to be abroad in the streets of London at that hour afoot, and especially alone.

Mary began to sob, and said—" My name is Lennox. I shall be so glad if you will direct me ; I have lost myself since this afternoon in the streets, and cannot make my way——"

" Where to—home ?"

" Home !" she repeated in a strange voice, for she felt that she had no home ; and none but the homeless can tell how that little word thrills through the heart. Even he who composed " Sweet Home," the sweetest of our ballads, is said to have died without one, a mendicant in the streets of that great metropolis whose magnitude so terrified our little wanderer.

" You seem respectable ; in mourning, too," resumed the Inspector, surveying her with the aid of a bull's-eye held up by one of his men.

" Mourning is a common dodge among this ere lot," said one of the latter, "and respectable gals don't ramble about the

streets at this hour, so we'll just take her along with us, and
lock her up till morning."

"Unless you can show us your house, and give a proper
address, I fear there's nothing else for it," said the Inspector.

"So look lively, little one, and keep up your pecker," said
the captured thief, with a fierce grimace; "you're one of ourselves, you know, and as you've taken such a precious interest
in me and my doings, you're welcome to a share of my bunk in
the lock-up. Any objection, Inspector Tappleton!"

"Silence, fellow!" said the Inspector; "we are wasting time.
Disperse this gathering crowd; help this poor man to rise, take
him to the nearest surgeon's, and get his name and address.
But you must come with us to the station-house, girl, if you are
as you say, and as I suspect, a mere wanderer in the streets."

Mary started back with great horror, and, clasping her hands,
exclaimed incoherently—"Oh, sir, do not take me there—what
have I done? Oh, my papa, you are in your grave, and Harry,
my brother, lies in his at Chillianwallah, but where will mine be?"

"The dissecting-table first, I hope," said the garrotter, with
a bitter grin, while mutterings of commiseration, doubt, and
ridicule, were heard among the listeners.

"At Chillianwallah?" said a constable, coming forward, and
Mary's quick eye saw the Indian ribbon on his breast. "What
was his regiment?"

"The **th Lancers."

"And did you say your name was Lennox?" said the official
with increased interest.

"Yes."

"Lor, Miss, I know'd your brother well; I was in his troop,
and, more than that, Miss, I was his own servant through all
the campaign in Central India; and a kind master he was to
me. A Captain Wedderburn of the Fusileers, and I, rolled him
in a horserug and buried him with our own hands, the same
day he was killed in the charge."

"My good man, I thank you," said Mary, almost choked in
tears. "He was my only brother. Are you the John Finnis of
whom he used to write?"

"Yes, Miss; the very same."

"I have no time to listen to all this," said the Inspector, impatiently.

"Beg pardon, for one moment," urged the constable. "Did
you come from Scotland t'other day by the morning train?"

"Yes; to King's Cross."

"Then I'm sure you are the young lady I told Tom Gubbs,
the guard, to take care of."

"I am; and he took me to Mrs. Primer's, near the Strand."

"Oh, sir," said Finnis the constable, turning to the Inspector, "this young lady's respectability is unquestionable. I shall find her in the morning when wanted; but, in the meantime, how is she to get home?"

"Call a cab, and take her with you," replied the Inspector, while making by gaslight a brief memorandum of Mary's full name and present address (not an aristocratic one) in his notebook; and saying that she would certainly be required in the morning, or next day at latest, he proceeded to take care of the garrotted man.

"Come along with me, Miss Lennox, please," said Finnis the ex-Lancer, conducting her into the next street. "Cab!"

"Here you are; fus cab! But what lark is this? A gal and a blue-bottle," exclaimed a strange and tattered-looking being, who seemed to spring out of the gutter, and placed his hand on the door of a hansom.

"Get in, Miss, please. Norfolk Street, Strand."

"Bah! only a couple o' bobs' worth," said the driver, surlily, as he whipped up his lean Rosinante, and away they went.

Mary felt her heart full of gratitude, and so pleased at her escape, that she would have driven in the hansom with Finnis through the streets at noonday perhaps, without thinking of the incongruity of the situation; but, after a time, it *did* occur to her.

"Oh, Heaven!" she thought, "has it come to this with me, that I am grateful for the countenance and the protection of people so humble as these? and when my money is gone, what shall then be my fate?"

Her new ally treated her with the utmost deference, and expatiated at great length on the kindness, the bravery, and high spirit of his late captain, her brother; and he was still full of this subject when the hansom drew up at the door of Mrs. Long Primer's house, to the infinite relief in one way, and terror in another, of that little woman, who had a wholesome dread of "the Perliece," as she named them.

A few words rapidly explained all; but Mary had no sooner reached her room than she fainted, and for a few minutes was quite insensible. She was comparatively safe now; but that episode in the street by night was only the beginning of Mary's most serious sorrows, and with morning came the terror and repugnance of having to appear as a witness against the captured culprit. In her dreams the live-long night had the past and the future haunted her, and if for a few minutes she dropped off to sleep, she awoke with a convulsive start. She saw the struggle, the robbery, the hook-nosed ruffian, and cries for aid rang in her ear, or left her lips mechanically.

Her trunk, with her little all, had never been heard of, so she was compelled to abandon all hope so far as concerned it. The next day passed, and she heard nothing of the affair of the robbery in which she was the chief, or only witness, so she spent a little time in writing to Lady Wedderburn; it was so pleasant now amid the black desperation of her situation to write to the mother of Cyril, and to cast herself upon her for protection, telling of her sad disappointment concerning Lady Wetherall, and asking if she would kindly give her another letter of introduction to any friend in London; and with a sigh of longing, and a prayer of hope, she had the letter posted in the nearest post-office, and her soul went with it back to the Lammermuirs! There came a kind and motherly answer in due course; but poor Mary Lennox was not at Norfolk Street to receive it. Dark horror had closed over her by that time!

CHAPTER XLII

ALDERMAN FIGSLEY.

THE clamorous fear and sense of extreme mortification at having to figure in a petty local court in some obscure part of London, as a witness in such a cause—her very name to go forth in print too, as connected with it — haunted Mary keenly, till a climax was put to her endurance on the morning of the second day, when Finnis arrived with the announcement that her presence was required before Alderman Figsley at the office in W—— Street, when the prisoner, familiarly known as "Ben Ginger," would be brought up for a preliminary examination and committal.

A close cab was summoned, and they set out together, Mrs. Primer assuring her that she must keep up her courage, as this petty annoyance would soon be over.

When they arrived, Mary was politely enough handed to a seat within the bar, near a table covered with books and printed papers; and there she sat with a palpitating heart while the Alderman, a fussy, portly, and wealthy city man, with a bald head, a rubicund visage, and several double chins, disposed rapidly of numerous cases and accusations by fines, committals, or remittance to a higher court. The heinous crimes of poverty and sleeping in the open air, were always visited severely; and a little orphan urchin, whose nightly couch was the iron roller of the neighbouring park, was locked up without mercy.

The court in W—— Street was a dingy looking apartment, the windows of which were placed high in the damp and discoloured walls. It was a metropolitan court, and consequently presided over by an alderman; all other magistrates are stipendiary— carefully selected barristers—else Mary's case might have been managed differently had she been before one of them.

A gentleman of fashionable appearance, calling himself Mr. Jones Robinson, was brought up for extinguishing and smashing a street lamp in the exuberance of his spirits ; and Mary drew her black veil closer on recognising Everard Home, the Master of Ernescleugh, who after tapping playfully, and perhaps contemptuously, with his cane, on the iron spikes of the dock before him, paid his fine, and departed with the air of one who deemed the affair a joke.

" Call the next case—what is it ?" said the magistrate, impatiently, for as none of those before him possessed any particular interest he was getting a little weary, and proceeded to polish his bald head with a silk handkerchief in irritation till it shone.

" William Trayner—livery servant, your worship, accused of assault in a Betting House," was the reply ; "his master, an officer about to embark for the seat of war, will be ready to pay any fine you may impose."

And to her astonishment, Mary beheld the impudent looking groom of Ralph Chesters—the same long-bodied, short-legged, and gimlet-eyed individual who had aided and abetted him in the scheme against herself—step into the dock with a remarkably airy and confident aspect, while at the same moment Chesters entered the court, attired in a fashionable morning costume, and certainly looking more bloated and dissipated than ever.

Mary was too thoroughly Scottish by blood and education to be without a tinge of superstition in her character ; and to her it seemed ominous of misfortune—a conjunction of three evil stars,—a strange coincidence,—that those three men who had brought her so much mischief at home, should be there, in that London Court, at this unhappy juncture.

Chesters' quick eye immediately fell upon Mary seated near the Alderman, a remarkable piece of courtesy which roused his curiosity ; but as yet, her veil totally prevented recognition. The assault in the Betting House was fully proved against Mr. Bill Trayner, who was wont to make up a book on coming events as well as his master, who immediately paid the fine. Trayner touched his fore-lock to the Magistrate, and vanished at once ; but Chesters, inspired by curiosity—and, perhaps, a deeper interest—lingered a little in a corner, to the infinite chagrin of Mary, leisurely sucking the white ivory handle of his riding whip the while.

" There is but one more case, your worship," said Inspector Tappleton ; "the assault upon and robbery of Mr. Fenchurch, solicitor, by garrotters, of whom we have, unfortunately, but one in custody as yet."

As he spoke, a pale, cadaverous, and savage looking fellow in very worn habiliments appeared in the dock between two officers, and glanced at the magistrate and all about him with defiance and malevolence. He had been brought from the House of Detention, and was heavily ironed, as the authorities seemed to fear that he was quite capable, unless under powerful restraint, of destroying himself or some one else, as he frequently threatened to do. He boldly and furiously denied all knowledge of the circumstance of which he was accused, averring that he was in another place at the time.

"We have a competent witness, your worship," said Inspector Tappleton of the 1st Division.

"Stand forward, Mary Lennox, and draw off your glove," said a voice, authoritatively.

Chesters gave an undisguised and almost convulsive start on hearing the name; and still more was he astonished when Mary came forward.

"Lift your veil, please," said the Alderman, with a very curt nod.

Her face was pale as that of death, and her eyes were full of alarm, shame, and a restlessness of expression; the very sweetness of her mouth had departed, and a hard line replaced the curve of her once beautiful upper lip.

"Are you married or single? speak quickly," said he, pausing, pen in hand, after the usual preliminaries.

"Single, sir," she answered faintly.

"No objection to be the other, I suppose," said he, hazarding the attempt at a jest.

"Yes, I guess as she's a rum un' your worship," said a constable, encouraged by this; "for she vears a kind o' vedding ring on the wrong finger."

"Silence!" said the Inspector, severely.

The portly Alderman now turned to Mary, and politely enough required her to relate all she had seen, and to confirm her full recognition of the prisoner. Her evidence was deemed quite conclusive to warrant the committal of the culprit for trial before a higher court, and he was accordingly removed, partly by force, muttering vengeance against Mary if she ever crossed his path again, as being herself an accomplice.

"Don't be afraid, Miss," whispered Finnis, on seeing how terrified she was; "'taint likely as the streets of London will be troubled by him again."

"Search her pockets!" bellowed Ben Ginger, as he was dragged away. A constable approached her; Mary shrunk back, but instinctively put her hands into the outer pockets of her jacket, and drew forth from one, in utter confusion and bewilderment, a leather portemonnaie, which was found empty of money, but contained the cards of Mr. Fenchurch, to whom it undoubtedly belonged,

"This looks ill, young woman—deuced ill for you," said the Alderman, frowning.

"It may all be a plant, your worship—they've perhaps put it in the young lady's pocket," said Inspector Tappleton.

"Still, why did she not find it there before, and produce it?" was the suspicious question of the magistrate.

Mary's tongue clove to the roof of her mouth; she vainly strove to say that she had never, until then, thought of looking in her pockets, or on going home that night; she was crushed, terrified, bewildered, and unable to speak, till she faintly implored a glass of water.

After some inquiries concerning Mary, as to where she lived, what friends she possessed and so forth, the magistrate said, coldly—"I find that your account of yourself is so unsatisfactory, that I must require you to give your personal recognisance that you will appear at the due time to give further evidence against this man."

Mary stared in utter bewilderment; she failed indeed to understand what he meant, but feeling only that money was somehow required of her, she put her hand to her purse, and then nervously withdrew it. With some irritation of manner, for though obese, he was not blessed with overmuch patience or temper, the Alderman repeated the information that she must give the necessary security for her appearance whenever required.

"Sir, I have not above six pounds in the world—it is impossible; if that sum will do, take it, and keep it; but permit me to go, I entreat of you. I am so sick of this place!" she said imploringly.

"Mr. Fenchurch is very ill, you say, Tappleton?"

"Dangerously, sir—we have here a doctor's certificate," replied the Inspector.

"Then, if anything serious befell him, the prisoner will be liable for manslaughter—or worse—a double reason for procuring security to insure the ends of justice."

Turning to Mary, he said, "The discovery of this purse upon you is awkward; can no one be found who will be bail for you?"

"None, sir—oh, whom could I ask?"

"That is your affair; not mine."

All this time she had studiously kept her back to Chesters, but the sense of his odious presence, if it oppressed her in one way, gave her a species of false courage in another.

"You positively cannot find bail?"

"Oh, no, sir—no."

"Then I have but one alternative," said Mr. Alderman Figsley, dipping his gold pen in the ink bottle; "sorry for it, but I must at least commit you to prison till this fellow's trial comes off."

"'To prison—to prison !" repeated Mary in a voice of anguish
that is indescribable, while she clasped her hands and gazed
into the round stolid face and shining gold spectacles of the
city Solon with intense fear and entreaty mingled, while on her
quivering lips a prayer seemed to hover.

"If I may venture to speak a word, your worship," began
Finnis the ex-Lancer, with irrepressible anxiety ; "I served
under this young lady's brother in the war in Central India,
and elsewhere under Brigadier— "

"What the deuce has Central India to do with the case !"
exclaimed the Alderman, testily, as he looked at his massive
repeater, and remembered that he had an appointment in the
city ; "the girl has no business to be prowling about the streets
alone at the hour mentioned ; I don't like that affair of the
purse, and I must insure her presence ; she will be safer a
prisoner than at large.   You are a soft-hearted fellow, Finnis,
and this is not the first time you have been the dupe of a pretty
face and an artful manner.   You hear me, sir !"

Whatever was the instance to which the Alderman referred,
in which Finnis had been guilty of softness of heart, the rebuke
had the effect of completely silencing him, and the good-
natured fellow slunk back abashed.

"You have positively no friends in London to whom you can
apply ?" said Figsley, pausing as he looked doubtfully at the
girl's horror-struck face.

In her despair Mary thought of poor Mrs. Primer.   But could
she, a total stranger, expect a widow struggling for subsistence
by letting a humble lodging-house, to be her surety for some
amount—she knew not what ?   Then she actually thought
again of the haughty Lady Ernescleugh ; but, as before, shrunk
from an appeal to her.

"No—no," muttered Mary ; "better let the daughter of Oliver
Lennox die unknown in the very gutter, than appeal to any—
to any, but God !"

"I have a letter," faltered Mary ; "a letter from a lady of
rank in Scotland to a friend in London, but found, sir, that
she had gone to Paris, and—and——"

"Where is this letter ?   I cannot open it, of course ; but the
address may be some clue or guarantee."

Mary searched her pockets in vain ; her letter was gone !   In
fact, she had pulled it forth with her handkerchief, and it was
now safely deposited under the left foot of Chesters, who had
cleverly twitched it towards him with the lash of his riding
whip unseen.

"Oh fatality !   The letter is lost—I have it not, sir !"

"This is all, I fear, some specious pretence ; we are too much
used to such trickery in London.   If you were at all so respect-

able as you pretend, and as your appearance certainly warrants, you would find no difficulty in getting some humane person to be security for you. Every one has some friend——"

"Save the poor; and God knows how poor am I !" she added, with touching pathos.

"I have no time for all this sentimentalism ; you must go to prison," replied the magistrate, as he proceeded deliberately to fill up the warrant for her committal.

"Oh, Chesters—Captain Chesters," exclaimed Mary, suddenly turning in her dire extremity and fear, and stretching her hands towards him ; "will you not speak for me ?"

"Whew—what is this?" asked the Alderman, frowning at her over his spectacles, and thoroughly filled with suspicion now. He had been actually beginning to conceive the idea of making some other arrangement concerning her. But now he rapidly dismissed the thought from his mind, and felt irritated that he had permitted her to impose upon him for a single moment.

"I thought, girl, that you had no friends in London ; yet you suddenly recognise one here—here in this very court, and in the master of that disreputable groom, who I have just permitted to go under a fine for a very unprovoked assault. There must be some collusion here ! Captain Chesters, your town address is the Army and Navy Club, I believe?"

"Major Chesters, Mr. Figsley ; I am Major Chesters, of the Turkish Contingent."

"Do you know this young person ?"

"I know her intimately."

"Can you speak for her in any satisfactory way ?"

"On one condition, and I must name it to herself."

He drew near her, and in French whispered something rapidly to Mary, who surveyed him with a sublime expression of scorn and loathing.

"What is all this?" said Alderman Figsley, becoming now seriously angry. It is doubtful whether a knowledge of French was among the number of his accomplishments, but he frowned portentously, and muttered something about "contempt of court."

"Oh, sir," exclaimed Mary, "this gentleman—if I may venture to call him so now—knew my father, knew my family, knew me almost as a child, and he might have the common humanity to speak one gentle word for me here."

"I only know, Miss Lennox, that in your own locality at home, you were spoken of lightly enough, latterly," he replied with a malevolent glance.

"Oh, papa ! my poor papa !—thank Heaven you know nothing of all this ! What have I ever done to you, sir, that you should

treat me thus, in a strange place, too, when you might, and
ought, as a Christian to befriend me ?"

"Bah! your name and mine have been mixed up enough,
and oddly enough already, Mary ; so it is no use attempting to
play genteel comedy or act injured innocence here."

The subtle villany of this speech, in such a time and place,
made all present exchange smiles of intelligence, and caused
the magistrate to be less inclined to pity Mary. He was far
from being a hard-hearted man in the main, and thought there
might—nay must—be more in all this scene than met the eye
or ear. So he signed the fatal warrant, and leisurely placed
the blotting paper over it. Then he handed it to an officer,
saying—

"It is for Tothill-fields Prison ; but, in case of mistake, let
her have a separate sleeping cell," retired at once to an inner
room, as if to cut short a matter that had already occupied too
much of his valuable time.

"Tothill-fields," repeated Chesters to himself ; "good, I'll
have you yet, my proud little minx ! Bravo ! here's Ralph Rooke
Chesters against the field ! Unless in despite of the fate that
is hurrying her downward, she take some silly qualm of conscience, as it is called, bar accident the race is mine ! How
lucky that Trayner fell into that scrape and brought me here.
I should have known nothing otherwise of her being in London.
Ta, ta," said he aloud, with all the coolness of practised effrontery,
"I am going to soldier again, but in Turkey, my girl, for I am
sorry to say that my creditors are much more attached to me
and my fortunes than you are, my pretty Mary ; so it is better
to have a shy at the Russians abroad, than become a billiard-
marker, or a gentleman rider at home. Any messages for our
mutual friend the Fusileer ? Shall be happy to take them, I'm
sure."

And kissing the tips of his kid gloves, with an ironical bow
and a leering smile, for both of which he deserved to have been
blown from the mouth of a gun, the heartless *vaurien*, gamester,
and spendthrift mounted his horse and rode off to the Lady's
Mile, and "to do a bit of park," followed by his groom in
accurate livery, while Mary Lennox of Lonewoodlee, in a state
more dead than alive, and looking as if transformed to marble,
was taken away to the prison in which she was to be detained,
in a common dark and grated police van !

CHAPTER XLIII.

MEPHISTOPHELES AGAIN.

A PRISONER, and without a crime ! Mary Lennox felt that fate was indeed dealing hardly with her. When the first wild paroxysms of grief and mortification were passed, she learned to understand that she should be released and free the moment the robber's trial was over ; but whither was she to turn then ? Could she seek for any employment, however humble, and say that her last abode had been a public prison ? Her purse would be restored to her she had been told ; but how long might its contents avail her, especially when all the wardrobe she possessed was the fast fading suit of black she now wore.

All these reflections, and others, coursed through her mind, causing such pangs of pain in her heart, that each was like a probe of hot steel.

There was a valuable diamond in Cyril's ring, but the idea of parting with it never occurred to her, or that it possessed other value than accrued to it in her own estimation, from being his gift to her in a time of vanished happiness.

Three weeks after the scene we have narrated saw Mary still in a cell of the prison, gazing in listless abstraction, and with eyes that were becoming dull and stony in aspect, from a grated window at the high brick boundary-wall of the place, a barrier to liberty and the external world, defended by two rows of crooked spikes. The chaplain had been kind, and gave her a few dreary books and pious publications ; while the matron, whose occupation rendered her naturally suspicious, and who could not be convinced that Mary was not an evil girl in some way, otherwise she should certainly have friends of some kind, supplied her with work, and urged her to "do a little white seam," that she might have more money by her when set at liberty.

But she had ever one thought which rankled bitterly in her heart, that she was a prisoner, though guiltless of a crime ! Should she ever smile—ever sing again—she who had so often sung with an aching heart ? Deadened by the massive walls, the roar of mighty London came to her ears like a drowsy hum, and dreamily she listened to it.

Within every shadow there is a deeper shade. To Mary it seemed strange that she should have been able to undergo so many shocks to her nervous system, so many humiliations to her proper pride, so many bitter mortifications, so many sorrows and affronts, and not have died ! Yet she was still living, with all the impulses of life strong within her, save its best and brightest one—hope, for that was fading now.

Her lover !   He was a feature of the past ; yet she could not
look on his betrothal ring without a strange thrill running
through her bosom, while fond memory flew back to many an
hour of quiet joy beside the lonely stile and by the old pine
wood.   Anon she dismissed these regrets as unworthy of her ;
but she longed and yearned amid the solitude of her cell for
one caress, one kind word from the poor old man who had so
loved and petted her !

"Never more—never more !" she would moan and mutter.
Could she but join him !   The attempt would be a crime against
her Maker—-yea, even the thought thereof, was a sin ; but the
dark idea would come to her again and again.

Memories grew strong and keen out of the monotony of her
existence.   And the most vivid were of her father, so fond and
doting, so passionate and querulous, and yet, withal, ever so
gentle and affectionate to her.   So, then, would come before her
with morbid and painful distinctness the scene of his death-
bed, his passing away, and the wistful look which, when once
seen, is never forgotten—the glance we must all give one day,
when the world is receding from us, and its smallness appears
more small than ever.   His was a smile of unutterable fondness
and sadness, and there came the great change that chilled her
heart then, and chilled it now—the pallor of death—the forerunner of eternity and peace.

On whose face would her last smile rest?   And who would
close her eyes when the hour came?

Times there were when a terror filled her soul lest she might
come forth only to fall lower than poverty could make her ; for
she remembered painfully one or two poor girls whom she had
seen brought up before Alderman Figsley.   But—no, no, she
could only die, and be at rest for ever !

She knew that while she was gazing at the smoke-blackened
brick wall or into the paved yard, where not a blade of grass
was visible, the leaves would be thick and green in the rustling
woods of the Merse ; the blossoms of the white and pink
hawthorn and of the golden laburnum must have passed away ;
but the honey bees would be humming drowsily in the sunshine among the flowers she had planted, and over the beautiful
heath-clad hills that looked down on what was once her home.
There still, in the breezy and sunny morning, the mavis and
merle were singing, and the voice of the cushat-dove would
sound in the old coppice, the *lone wood ;* but never more for her !

A pile of odious work for the matron was lying untouched
before her, when she was roused from these dull thoughts by a
warder announcing that "a gentleman, with an order from
Alderman Figsley, had come to visit her."

She started from her seat with heightening colour ; a fore-

boding of the heart told her who this visitor would too probably be—and Chesters, bowing and smiling, was ushered in.
He presented his hand ; but Mary drew back, and covered her
eyes with her hand and arm, as if to shut out the sight of him.
"That man—that man again ! You here, sir ?"

"As you see, Miss Lennox ; or will you permit me, as an old
friend, to call you Mary ?"

"Friend !" she exclaimed, with loathing in her half averted
face.

He was now attired in a blue undress uniform, elaborately
frogged and braided about the breast. He wore a gilded waistbelt, and a sabre with a white ivory hilt, and carried in one
hand a scarlet fez with a long blue silk tassel ; for he was in
the undress of an officer of the Turkish Contingent. His appearance was always that of a gentleman, but there was in his
eyes the jaded and dissipated expression habitual to them :
and there were certain hard lines about the mouth, at least the
angles thereof, that indicated him to be a roué or worse, and a
gambler who played at high stakes with honour, fortune, and
destiny.

"So, you foolish little girl, it has come to this," said he,
surveying the bare walls of the whitewashed cell. "Why would
you not permit me to become your security—to speak for you,
I mean ?"

"Rather would I have died than have accepted from your
hands the smallest favour on any terms, and least of all on such
as you dared to offer me—the daughter of a gentleman, every
way your superior ! And how basely done—in French, too,
lest the magistrate should overhear or understand you. Begone,
sir ! What seek you here ?" she demanded, while surveying
him with intense disgust, and drawing herself up the while
with the air of a little tragedy queen, her eyes sparkling with
resentment, and her hands clenched with energy. "Why in-
trude upon me, unasked, unwanted, and so abhorred as you are ?"

"This is a cell in a prison," said he mockingly.

"True. But here my privacy is as sacred as if I occupied
the saloon of a palace ! And I am here—here—a prisoner,
without crime !" And her voice died away as she spoke.

After a pause she asked,—

"Is it manly of you to come here and mock me in my misery ?"

"I did not come to mock you, Mary."

"Leave me, sir. Whatever be my fate, I am stainless and
guiltless."

"Notwithstanding all that, your character will be utterly
gone, and a taint shall be upon you that will cause all to shrink
from befriending you. If you seek for work, or aid of any
kind, however menial, however humble, can you refer people

16

only to the chaplain or the turnkey of a prison ?   I should think
not !   Oh, Mary Lennox, you will starve, or do worse, in the
streets of this vast modern Babylon !"

Mary trembled in her soul, for he was speaking her own
terrible thoughts ; but he was minute in his wish to torture her,
and pitiless in his desire to bend her to his wishes.

"There are, of course, houses of refuge for casuals, and the
hospitals for those who are ailing ; and when the unknown or
the unclaimed die there, where do their remains go ?   To the
surgical theatre, where your beauty, which is undeniable, and
where the very perfections of your person, may be made a
source of speculation, perhaps of banter, for a rabble of young
sprigs of anatomy ; and thence to a grave, God knows where or
how !   Avoid the contingencies of a fate so terrible ; I entreat
you, dearest Mary, to listen to me, and—and——"

"Go with you ?"

"Yes."   And he drew nearer, as he spoke, earnestly.

"Never," said she, through her clenched teeth, while shrinking back.   "Better death—any death, however black and
desperate !   Oh, how have I the patience to degrade myself by
talking with you on such a subject ?   But I am becoming
familiar with humiliation now and misery too !"

"I can prove a strong friend, Mary."

"Hitherto you have been a dangerous enemy—a veritable
fiend."

"As you please, as you please.   In this epoch of ours, much
as we boast of enlightenment and advancement, passion is as
strong, hate as bitter, and Destiny quite as inexorable and
pitiless, as ever they were in the dark and middle ages."

Mary cowered and shivered as she spoke ; and in the depth of
her misery—a misery rendered all the more keen by the girl's
extreme sensibility, he surveyed her with exactly such a
glance or smile, as one might fancy in the face of Mephis-
topheles, while watching Goethe's heroine, poor Margaret, when
she lay prostrate on the straw in prison, with a piece of
brown bread and a pitcher of cold water beside her.

Mary's unconcealed repugnance and aversion for him, kindled
at last the rage of this would-be lover ; and, in revenge, he
adopted an undisguised insolence of tone.

"So you hate me ?"

"Say rather that I—despise you !"

"So you won't come with me to the East on any terms ?   By
Jove, I could give you such a pretty gilded kiosk on the shore of
the Bosphorus, where you might see all the gardens of Pera on
one side ; Scutari, with its mosques on the other, and all that
sort of thing.   I daresay that, as senior officer, I could get you
out with me in the transport somehow ; and we should do the

Mediterranean and the Levant at her Majesty's expense, and without requiring even a 'John Murray.' Say you'll come, and I shall get you out of this den in a twinkling. I shall soon make it all square with yonder Alderman, who made such a fuss about you. I am in funds, my girl, I can tell you : cleared two thousand odd, by a few strokes at billiards last night, after getting the I O U's of two noble lords—swell friends—by whose aid my leave at home has been somewhat protracted, as I threatened monetary pressure. Say you'll come. I have plenty of gold to pave the way, and won't we be jolly while it lasts ? 'See ; the mountains kiss high heaven'—you know the rest. Ah, you will find it better fun steaming past the isles of the Levant, than moping here or mooning at Lonewoodlee !"

Even his brusque insolence failed to rouse anger in her heart. "Lonewoodlee—oh, Lonewoodlee !" she repeated, pressing her slender white fingers interlaced upon her sunken eyes and speaking in a soft and agitated voice ; "my father's home ! It is gone, and I have but the memory of it now, and of all I have lost, to remind me of the words of David," and lifting up her hands and eyes with much of sublime resignation in the expression of her pallid face, she said, "Dominus dedit, Dominus abstulit, sed nomen Domini benedictum !"

After a pause,

" Are you mad that you begin jabbering Latin in a place like this ?" he asked, with an air of astonishment that was really genuine.

" I am not mad, sir, though I might well be ; and now I have but once more to entreat—nay to command you, as you are a man, to leave me to my fate and trouble me no more."

" I shall do so—and be assured it will be a sad and degrading one."

" As God pleases."

She turned her back upon him, and with a glance in which rage and baffled desire triumphed over pity, he retired and left her in an almost fainting condition.

CHAPTER XLIV.
THE TROOPSHIP.

" THE detachment of the Royal Fusileers, under Lieutenant Horace Ramornie, proceeding to join the service companies at the seat of war, will embark on board the *Blenheim* transport at Gravesend, with others, under the command of Major R. R. Chesters of the Turkish Contingent."

Such was the garrison order, which Horace, to his infinite

16—2

chagrin, perused in a little vellum bound book, handed to him
by a corporal, one evening, as he was proceeding to the mess of
the provisional battalion. He had no desire whatever to find
himself under the special command of such a man as Chesters;
but there was nothing for it save obedience; and the various
anecdotes elicited at table, or recalled to the memory of officers
present, confirmed his dislike to the prospect before him, for
the mere mention of Chesters' name seemed sufficient. He
seemed to be as well known in the service as the goat of the
Welsh Fusileers, though not so harmlessly. One remembered
"how completely he had done Black of ours in that affair of the
spavined mare;" another "how he had been jockeyed by him in
a race at the Curragh;" "how he had so rooked Blake of the
Rifles at Malta, that the poor fellow had to sell;" how he had
abandoned one girl, run off with another and so forth; with
many other things that would never figure on his tombstone,
or opposite his name in Hart's Army List.

Three days after Horace read the order, and after the interview recorded in the preceding chapter, saw H.M. transport
Blenheim, with fully three hundred officers and men for various
corps in Turkey, under weigh and steaming down the river,
greeted by many a cheer from the crews of passing ships.

Horace remembered all that had passed at home between his
cousin Cyril Wedderburn and Chesters; and though he had
secretly a peculiar detestation for the latter, it would have been
alike unwise and unsafe to exhibit it, now that they were to sit
at the same table, to meet daily on the same parade, to encounter each other incessantly on the deck or in the saloon
during a voyage of so many thousand miles; and more than all
now when Chesters bore the local rank of major, and was
distinctly his *superior* officer.

All irritation would have to be repressed and all disagreeables
avoided, for Horace could not but remember that his commission
was his sole inheritance, and that Chesters would care little
"to smash him" if he got an opportunity. So he resolved
to shun him as much as possible by seeking the society of other
officers, of whom there were some thirty captains and subalterns
on board.

Though Chesters hated responsibility of any kind and would
very willingly have been second in command to any one on
whom the trouble of authority and risk of direction might have
devolved, he was not the less disposed to be overbearing in
manner, and to attempt to "talk down," all about him, especially at and after the mess, which took place at an earlier hour
on board than is usual ashore.

He soon became heated with wine and rather quarrelsome, dis-
puting with Ned Elton, a brother officer of Horace, about the odds

on the last Epsom; how *he* should have apportioned the weights, and how shrewdly he had guessed at the winning horse, yet, as if the devil was in it, didn't make a successful book after all, having been "sold," though he knew it not, by his own particular confidant, Trayner, who generally knew the contents of Chesters' betting book as well as his own.

"I'm safe on the Oaks, however," he added with an oath— "backed the winner at long odds there."

"A bad style of fellow this," whispered Elton to Ramornie ; "we'll have many a case of row and arrest before we see the coast of Bulgaria, unless we combine and put him 'in Coventry.'"

Chesters had on board his faithful rascal Mr. Bill Trayner ; but that amiable individual was at present enjoying his own society in the seclusion of the cable-tier, where, though a civilian, he was in irons for behaving insolently to a young officer of the Rifles, whom he taunted as "a carpet-bag 'cruity," a slang barrack-room phrase for a recruit who joins with a quantity of useless luggage ; and on appealing to his master, the latter only laughed at him, and said—

"The bilboes and bread and water will do you good, Trayner, —you have been getting too fleshy of late."

And Trayner swore secretly that he would be revenged on Chesters for this at a future time. When idling over their wine and fruit, and while the transport was steaming slowly past the flat but fertile shore of Kent, and the salt marshes of Essex, Chesters with his habitual insolence of spirit and disposition to be obnoxious began to annoy the inoffensive and gentle Horace Ramornie.

"Heard of our friends at Willowdean lately, eh, Ramornie ?" he asked ; "we are neighbours you are aware."

"No," replied the other curtly (though he had just received a letter from his aunt before embarking), and he turned away.

"Wedderburn is at Varna, isn't he ?"

"Yes."

"With yours ?"

"Ours."

"You are fond of monosyllables, I think?" said Chesters, with a white gleam in his pale eyes.

Horace gave a haughty smile, and was turning to Elton, the Colonel's nephew, when Chesters resumed his scheme for "trotting him out," as he would have phrased it, and when he spoke the buzz and laughter around the table subsided, for all feared that a scene of some kind would ensue ere long, and felt exceedingly uncomfortable.

"When I was last at the Horse Guards, Ramornie, I heard some talk of a waggon train being formed ; and as we have no Belem Rangers, your cousin will be looking for his spurs in that force. He is a pleasant fellow, but a muff, and was an awful griff when he first came out to India."

Horace grew crimson with anger at the triple insolence of this speech ; for to any military man the inference to be drawn from the first part of it, was most offensive.

"Major Chesters," said Horace, rising, while a chill seemed to fall on all at the table ; " dare you impugn the honour of my cousin Captain Wedderburn of the Royal Fusileers ?"

"No—far from it," replied Chesters, coolly, "whatever I may think," he added insolently, but aside. "Come, come Ramornie, take your wine, though it is a little corked, and let us be jolly. You could little imagine where I recently saw his last flame— that girl Lennox."

"Indeed—where ?"

"Sent to prison from a London police court, where I had gone to bail out Trayner, who got into a row somewhere ; to prison in London, by Jove ! though I don't know exactly for what, unless it was involvement in some robbery affair."

"Miss Lennox ?" exclaimed Ramornie, with genuine surprise and concern.

"Yes—Miss Lennox as you call her ; hope she enjoys the silent and separate system peculiar to the London model prison, and so conducive to reflection and all that sort of thing."

Horace was inexpressibly shocked, but hoping that Chesters was telling what was untrue, he disdained to make further in- quiries, and once more turned to his friend Elton, seeking to divert the conversation from himself ; but Chesters was not to be baffled and began again, while leisurely dropping the ice into his champagne glass.

"And now Ramornie, to change the subject, how is the fair heiress—well and jolly I hope ? You fellows—I mean you and the Wedderburns—will surely not let her slip through your hands. She is worth entering stakes for—a handsome girl, so well weighted, with a pot of money and no end of fun in her. A noble bird to bag, before the fields are in stubble."

"Silence, if you please, Major Chesters," said Horace, whose face from crimson had now become pale with passion, while his voice grew concentrated and low. " I have to request that the name of the lady in question be not uttered here, by your lips at least."

"That is very quarrelsome wine, surely—try the pale sherry; I have mentioned no name as yet," said Chesters, laughing.

"Then take heed how you do," added Horace, with his dark eyes flashing fire. How he cursed in his heart—even he, the quiet and gentle Horace—the rules of discipline, the amenities of society and civilized life, which prevented him from flying at this man's throat and dashing him under his feet. As for "calling him out," the idea certainly did occur, only to be dismissed, for duelling had gone out of fashion, and he had not the greatest of Job's virtues—patience.

His soul was full of love and tenderness for Gwendoleyne—worshipping her as a pure and beautiful spirit, with all a young man's generous enthusiasm and joy; and thus it revolted him to hear her spoken of jestingly by any man, least of all by one such as Ralph Rooke Chesters!

"I am going on deck, Ramornie," said Elton, "try these cigars with me;" and taking the arm of Horace, he succeeded in drawing him from the cabin to the poop, whither the majority of the party followed, leaving Chesters with one or two more at their wine.

"Ramornie," said young Elton, drawing his friend apart, "I warn you to beware of that fellow of the Turkish Contingent. From the first moment he saw you on parade in the Barrack-yard, he evinced a determination to annoy and fix a quarrel on you. You remember how closely he inspected our fellows in particular, and found so many sham faults, actually bringing four of our best privates to the front, to have them put through their facings as if tipsy, and then made them ground arms as a final snare, that they might topple over. It was an insult to us all. So be wary. I can see that he is an utter scoundrel, and as Oldham says, 'he could outrogue a lawyer,'—aye, even a Scotch one, or a Jew; but at the same time he is your senior officer, and in all rows a junior invariably is sent to the wall. Besides, old fellow, I think we have had quite enough of that ship champagne."

"You are right, Elton," said Horace; "he is beneath my attention. But my head still aches with the memory of that champagne breakfast we had at Brompton with the Rifles, before we marched out."

"Clicquot and fun; eh, Horace?"

"They are all very well," added a blasé-looking officer with sleepy eyes and long fair moustaches; "but when to these you add hazard and écarté, as we had them, the breakfast becomes something to remember."

"And repent of; eh, Ponsonby?"

"Yes, decidedly—doocidly so, as I know to my cost."

"Was Chesters there?" asked Elton.

"Of course; d—n him!" was the rejoinder of Ponsonby, who was a 23rd man.

"Well," said Ramornie, thoughtfully, "the Essex shore looks flat and low now; we shall soon be in blue water, and see the last of Old England."

"Not the last, I hope," said Ponsonby, smiling.

"For some among us, certainly, if knocks are going."

"Anyway, thank God, we are off in earnest," said Elton; "I was so sick of Chatham, with its boredom of drills and sham duties : besides, it will be so jolly to knock about the world a little."

"Yes ; and better still to knock about the Russians a great deal, eh ? ha, ha !" lisped a languid Hussar officer, as he twirled his bandolined moustache and laughed at his own mild joke.

The transport was now clearing the Thames, and rounding the floating light on the sandbank that runs eastward from the Isle of Grain. The waters of the Medway opened wide upon her starboard beam, and as the setting sun shone through the golden haze, the buildings of the dockyard, the tall masts of the war-vessels in the great basin at Sheerness, and the outline of the guardship, came all darkly and minutely forward to the eye. A red flash and white puff of smoke from the black hull of the guardship caused all the loungers on the poop of the Blenheim to turn towards her.

"The evening gun," suggested one.

"Impossible," said another : "the sun is still high above the Essex marshes."

"What's the row yonder?" asked the Hussar, languidly; "the guardship has hoisted a signal at her main ?"

The evening was beautiful ; the poop was crowded with officers in their shell jackets, or undress uniform, and the air was redolent of cigars of all kinds ; their men grouped amid-ships were looking at the fast-receding shore ; others at the cat-heads, were gazing wistfully seaward, and some at the passing craft, bearing up Thames from every quarter of the globe, and all were merry, heedless, and thoughtless of the future that was before them.

"What the deuce is up?" was now the general exclamation, as the steamer slackened her speed, and drew in shore nearer to the point of Sheerness.

"What is the signal?" asked Ponsonby.

"Red, blue, and yellow—nautical, perhaps ; enigmatical, certainly," said the Hussar.

"Some fellow on board has got his swell friends in town to telegraph for him at the last moment, to come back with the pilot-boat, perhaps," suggested Ponsonby.

"Urgent private affairs—that his book on Coutts' is all square ; that his uncle is dead, the will is all right, and that he'd better return to mamma."

"Hush, gentlemen," said a grave old Captain of the Rifles, who perhaps was thinking of his wife and little ones. "We shall soon learn what is wrong."

"There is nothing wrong, sirs," said the Captain, testily, from the bridge ; "but the guard-ship has signalled that we are to lie to for a boat from the shore ; and here it comes, hand over hand," he added, as a man-o'-war gig, with its oars feathered in beautiful and steady regularity, came sheering out from the basin direct for the transport, which lay heaving and plunging slowly on the heavy ground swell.

Meanwhile that distinguished officer Chesters had been left in the cabin alone to " soak over his wine," as he phrased it, for he was constitutionally and systematically a deep drinker. Amid all the quiet insolence and tipsy banter in which he had indulged, no sentiment of regret or pity for the poor girl whose interests he might have served, but to whom he had wrought so much mischief, and whose terrible sorrow he had witnessed, occurred to the callous and hollow-hearted Chesters. But he had peculiar and regretful thoughts of her, nevertheless.

" Had I possessed but more tact and time, to have waited a little till her confinement had broken her spirit and dulled her perceptions ; had I pressed her more tenderly perhaps, during that last interview ; or had I spoken favourably of her to that old pump of an Alderman, she might have been mine—mine, by this time ! Now, descending fast from scale to scale in misery and degradation, her noble qualities, for she has them, wasted ; her pure sentiments dulled, her affections blasted, her perils equalled only by her beauty, she may become the prey— the facile prey of *others !*"

And he gnawed his yellow moustache and bit his thin cruel lip at the galling idea. Had he only traduced and repudiated her, to the end that she might become the prize—the prey of some person unknown ? Jealousy became a keen pang, but the waters were rolling between them now, and every revolution of the inexorable screw—and now it suddenly occurred to him that the motion thereof had ceased, and he was just about to come on deck and have another bout of banter with Ramornie, when Lieutenant Elton, who acted as adjutant of the various detachments, placed in his hand a long official letter, which he tore open in haste and surprise.

It was from the Quartermaster-General, informing Major Chesters, that Lieutenant-Colonel Louis De la Fosse of the 34th Regiment, Infantry of the French Line, having come to London on a special mission from Marshal St. Arnaud, would have a free passage on board H.M.S. *Blenheim* to Varna ; and it was trusted that as a stranger and officer of the allied army, all courtesy and attention should be shown to him during the voyage.

" The devil ! De la Fosse !" muttered Chesters, changing colour. " Where is this fellow, Elton ? this Frenchman ?"

" He is here," replied Elton, as a very handsome man about forty years of age, with regular features, curly hair, a long dark moustache and closely-shaven chin, in the blue uniform and gold epaulettes of the French Line, with a few orders glittering at his scarlet lapelles, his little kepi in one hand and his sabre in the other, entered the cabin and bowed low to Chesters, who returned the courtesy, but with a coldness and restraint that were as marked as the surprise and hauteur that immediately spread over the face of the other, when his open and pleasant smile passed away, and he recognised the man he looked on.

CHAPTER XLV.

THE VOYAGE.

" COLONEL DE LA FOSSE, I bid you welcome to her Majesty's ship *Blenheim*," said Chesters, presenting his hand, which, however, the Frenchman did not take, but contented himself with another bow and a very perceptible elevation of his black eyebrows. " I have also to congratulate you on promotion since—"

" Since when, monsieur ?"

" We last met."

" Ah !" said the other a little contemptuously, " I thank you. I have just been in time to reach your vessel ; the telegram left London this forenoon, about the same time I quitted it by rail ; and here I am."

" So we are to have the pleasure of voyaging together so far as Varna."

" So far—yes," replied the Frenchman, shrugging his shoulders, and causing the bullion of his epaulettes to glitter, whilst his face said so plainly that he saw little pleasure in the companionship that Elton laughed behind his forage cap.

" Will you eat anything? the messman will bring you partridge pie and *pâtés de foie gras.*"

" No, thank you."

" The wine is here," said Chesters ; "shall I assist you ?"

" Thanks ; I shall help myself. What is this ? St. Julien !— très bon !" and the Colonel took a bumper of wine, without according a smile or a glance to Chesters, who felt far from comfortable as several officers had left the deck, all anxious to converse with the stranger, and be attentive to him. But after seeing to his berth on board, and having his baggage arranged by a Fusileer, who was to act as his servant during the voyage, he lit a cigar and went on deck without bestowing the faintest bow on Chesters, who bit his lip, and muttered something under his breath.

The *Blenheim* was under full steam now ; the wind was fair for her down channel ; her top-sails and topgallant-sails were sheeted home ; the Isle of Sheppey was sinking fast upon her starboard quarter, and the bugles having ere this sounded the tattoo, save by the watch under a subaltern officer the main deck was deserted. The French colonel was of course the centre of attraction, and a group gathered round him. The stiffness and restraint, even hauteur of manner he exhibited in the cabin, passed away completely now, and he chatted gaily and freely on the chances of the war, and spoke with a Frenchman's hereditary hate of Russia and the Russians, for the Gaul has never for-given Moscow. He expatiated on the sufferings undergone by the armies at Varna, and denounced as criminal the conduct of our Ministry in waiting only for winter to begin the campaign. He spoke lightly of his own past military experience, but would seem to have seen some sharp service in Algeria in the regiment of General Bazaine ; he had been side by side with Canrobert in the breach of Constantine, and had served as a volunteer with the 3rd Chasseurs à Pied, in the terrible conflict at the Pass of Djerma, where the Arabs were totally routed and their prin-cipal sheiks captured.

" Monsieur le Major, who commands you," said he during a pause, " has *he* seen much of the world ?"

" I should say a deuced deal too much—for my taste at least," replied Ponsonby, caressing his whiskers.

" Ah—but in the way of military service, I mean ?"

" A little in India," said Horace Ramornie. " I don't think you seem to like him much."

" Sacre Dieu ! no. I should think not," replied de la Fosse, tipping the ashes off his cigar.

" To me it is like a dream that I have heard of you and him having met in Scotland."

" In Scotland," repeated the Frenchman, who spoke English very fairly ; " you are but a youth—from whom did you hear of that ?"

" From my uncle, Sir John Wedderburn, of Willowdean."

" What do I hear—you a relation of Sir Wedderburn, who was so very kind to me ?"

" I am his nephew."

" Mon Dieu !" The Frenchman shook the hand of Horace with great cordiality, and drew him a little way aside.

" And Madame Wedderburn—how is she ?"

" Well—I thank you."

" I was a captain then, at the time you refer to—home after the expedition to Morocco—travelling in Scotland, of which the Walter Scottish novels had made me enthusiastic. (Horace smiled at the compound word.) I met this Monsieur Chesters, who pressed me to have a little shooting in Berwickshire. I went there—no shooting at all ; it was all one humbugs ! play,

play, play : écarté, hazard, vingt-un, and so on, till I was left
without a centime, and but for your kind uncle, to whom my
case became known, I should never have reached France again,
never have seen my regiment, never have been now, as I am,
Colonel of the 34th Infanterie de Ligne ; for even my watch
and rings I had staked at his table and lost, among them a
valuable onyx, that belonged to one of my ancestors, and which
I see he has the bad taste now to wear ; consequently, I have
no particular favour for M. Chesters. And now that we have
met again, I would call him out," he added through his clenched
teeth, while a fierce gleam came into his black eyes ; "yes! and
force him to fight me on the first land we see ; but then, mal-
peste ! I know that Marshal St. Arnaud would resent on me
severely a quarrel with any British officer at the present juncture;
so I most dissemble, if I can, till I find him among that rabble
the Turkish Contingent, when I may shoot him, begar ! with a
safe conscience, under pretended belief that he was a Turk !"

The first few days of the voyage passed pleasantly enough ;
the weather was fine, and when the few duties incident to a
troop-ship, such as the parade of the men in their canvas frocks
and of the quarter-guard for bayonet duty, on the poop, fore-
castle, and scuttle-butt, were over, idling, smoking, single-stick,
revolver practice at the passing birds, or at a bottle slung from
a yardarm, and too often gambling, became the mode of passing
the time.

Gaming is strictly prohibited in transports as in camp or
quarters ; but the evil example of Chesters speedily infected the
younger officers, who, as they all belonged to different corps,
and would be separated on landing, had little interest in each
other personally ; so if the tedious monotony of the voyage
was partially dispelled by the excitement of gaming, they cared
nothing for the monetary risk they ran, and kept up a cross-fire
of I O U's, that would rather have astonished their parents and
guardians ; and were all the more free with these from the
knowledge that ere long they must be before the enemy, and a
bullet might pay off the heaviest score. Thus every evening,
after the mess-table was cleared, cards and dice made their
appearance regularly, and large sums were staked and lost or
won, to the manifest deterioration of discipline and good-feeling;
and all this was caused solely by Chesters, whose special office
and duty it was to have repressed the practice at once, instead
of becoming a leader in it : but this cosmopolitan Scot was
"a gambler for gain : that foul amalgam of the miser and
the knave." This state of matters continued to increase until
the evening after the transport entered the Mediterranean, when
a very unpleasant fracas took place. The weekly parade of all
the troops on board in full dress and in heavy marching order

had just occurred, and the soldiers had been dismissed to rack
their arms and resume their free and easy canvas frocks, when
the Bay of Gibraltar, glittering under a clear and brilliant sunshine, opened on the port bow of the *Blenheim*, as she steamed
onward between lovely Andalusia on one side, and the black
mountains of arid Tetuan on the other, gliding past the shores
of Europe and Africa into one of the greatest water-highways
of the world. In outline a couchant lion, starting there to the
height of fifteen hundred feet from the pale blue ocean, that
seemed to ripple in gold and silver against its base, the Rock of
immortal memories, terminated in the ruin known as O'Hara's
Tower, on which the British flag was flying in the distance
diminished to a speck. The *Blenheim* did not run close in, but
steamed steadily onward into the Mediterranean, and as the
vast citadel began to lessen on her quarter it seemed to all as
if they had seen but a glimpse, and a passing vision it certainly
was—of gardens of brilliant green; terraced houses of dazzling
whiteness, with sunshaded windows; batteries bristling with
uncounted guns, and dotted by redcoats whose bayonets glittered like stars; cliffs honeycombed into galleries and perforated
by round holes, through which grim cannon peered, and, below
all, the bay full of shipping, where the variegated flags of all
the nations of the maritime world were fluttering in the breeze
of a pleasant August afternoon.

There were special orders that unless stores were required she
was not to touch at Gibraltar, so, to the disappointment of many,
the *Blenheim* held on her course. Horace experienced this in
particular; but several officers on board had been quartered
there before, and cared less about it.

"Were you ever stationed in old Gib?" asked Elton of
Ponsonby.

"No; never. And shouldn't care much to be cooped up
between the bay and the Spanish lines."

"Old Gib is not without his amusements, and I have twice
had a run with the Calpe hounds," said Chesters, who was well
up in all kinds of field sports. "The meet always takes place
at San Roque, six miles from the Rock on the Andalusian side."

"You can scarcely have it six miles from the Rock on the
other side," said Colonel De la Fosse, twirling his moustaches.

Chesters frowned, but resumed: "People don't usually
course in the sea, Colonel. The last time I rode yonder, after
we had a dose of milk-punch at the nearest posada, the
fox broke cover at the end of the Malaga Garden, and away we
went powdering along at a rasping pace. We had a devil of a
run over the most awful ground in the world—the Stony Road
they name it there, and by Jove, it *is* stony with a vengeance,
being a slope at the angle of forty-five degrees, covered with

thousands of cart loads of rocks, boulders and loose *débris* that have fallen from the mountain above; but across it we went with a whoop and a cheer, some eighty riders or more, all in red, for no true born Briton can either hunt or fight comfortably in any other colour; and if any of the 12th fellows were there, you might be sure to hear them shouting ' *Montis Insignia Calpe!*' because that motto is on their colours with the castle and key. I can almost make out the coursing ground from here with my glass, though the old Rock is sinking fast astern. I had I remember a strange bet there, with Bob Riversdale, a staff surgeon——''

"And you won it?" asked De la Fosse drily.

"Yes."

"Aha, begar, I thought so—I'm sorry for Monsieur Bob," said the Frenchman, whose manner made the speaker colour with anger, while Horace turned away wearily, for he was heartily tired of Chesters' everlasting topics, horses and gambling dice and cards; so he followed the Frenchman, who proceeded to the taffrail; there a few officers were leaning over it, smoking and keeping their eyes fixed on the fast receding pillars of Hercules, which were defined in dark outline against the sky, and melting into the evening sea, which was all aflame with the amber and crimson tints of the setting sun.

A young officer in a shell jacket with bright yellow facings, politely touched his cap, and made way for the French Colonel.

"Thanks, Monsieur,—do not allow me to disturb you," said the latter; "ah—pardon," he added, as he took a button of the other's uniform between his fingers; "you belong to the 34th of the Line—my own Number!"

"Yes, Monsieur le Colonel," said the young Ensign, proudly; "ours is the Cumberland Regiment, and was raised in 1702."

"'Albuhera,' 'Arroya del Molinos,'" continued the Colonel, reading the motto on the button. "I could tell you a good story about your Regiment and mine, when my father, the Marquis De la Fosse, commanded the latter in that very battle of Arroya del Molinos in Spanish Estremadura, in the brave old war of the Peninsula, that we are forgetting all about now.

"In that little village, which is situated in a plain that was then quite covered with wild laurels and mignonette, and at the base of a ridge of rocks that start abruptly up in the form of a crescent, the whole Regiments comprising the division of Marshal Gerard, when getting under arms amid the rain and mist of a dark morning, were suddenly surrounded and attacked by the troops of Sir Rowland Hill, who had made a forced march for that purpose from Alcuesca. To be brief, they were nearly all taken to a man by your people, and my father fell from his horse severely wounded. The French had to form two squares and began to retreat, when suddenly there was a shout of—

" 'Voilà, les baionettes Ecossais !' and one square was entirely cut off by a Regiment of Highlanders, who dashed at it out of the mist. The other, which was chiefly composed of the 34th of the Line, under the Chef de Bataillon, my father—now sorely wounded and afoot—was surrounded by the British 34th, and he told me that in the grey light of the breaking day each Regiment simultaneously recognised the other's *number* on their shakos, and the French officers as they tendered their swords to those of your corps, exclaimed—

" 'Voilà, messieurs—nous sommes des frères, nous sommes du trente-quatrième régiment tous deux ! Les Anglais se battent toujours avec loyauté, et traitent bien leurs prisonniers !'

" The sword of my father was returned to him by the commander of your regiment, who politely said something about 'les malheurs de la Guerre,' and the fighting ended."

" It is quite true, Monsieur le Colonel," replied Hunton, the young officer, smiling ; " for at the Head quarters of our regiment, we still possess the brass drums, and the drum-major's staff of the French 34th, and if I ever have, as I hope, the pleasure of presenting you to our mess, you shall see them under more pleasant auspices than the Marquis your father last saw them.* But now that we are allies, are not such memories better forgotten ?"

And now we have to record the less agreeable portion of our story, already referred to.

CHAPTER XLVI.

UN BON COUP D'ÉPÉE.

As the troops on board were divided into three watches, there were always about a hundred men on deck at a time exclusive of the seamen. On this evening, Horace was subaltern of the watch, and as such, was solitary on the poop, while his men, muffled in their grey great coats, trod to and fro on the main deck, or lounged between the guns on each side, for the transport was partially armed.

As the evening deepened into night, the stars came brilliantly out in the blue sky of the Mediterranean ; the atmosphere was calm and serene ; the wind light, but fair, and the great troop-ship, with its living freight, glided silently and swiftly on the watery path, with its three great lanterns, green to starboard,

* This military coincidence is an historical fact.

crimson to port, and white at the foretop, emitting weird and strange gleams at times on the bellying sails, the lofty spars, and the passing waves. The time and place were very conducive to thought and reflection, and undisturbed by the laughter, exclamations and other sounds that issued occasionally from the great cabin, where wine or brandy and water, dice and cards were the order of the evening, Horace Ramornie gave himself up to the solitude of the sea, and with a fragrant havannah in his mouth, leaned over the taffrail, watching the white and phosphorescent sparkle of the vessel's wake, as the water boiled and bubbled in two eddies under each counter, to meet in one around the propelling screw.

Horace had certain unpleasant forebodings that Chesters would yet work him some mischief, in the spirit of his feud with Cyril Wedderburn, and the fear of this grew strong within him, together with a loathing of the man ; for his commission and his honour were the young man's sole inheritance now, and he knew that despite the sword and epaulettes which gave Chesters the rank of field-officer in the Turkish Contingent, he was a reckless desperado ; so this dread conflicted with the solemn thoughts that occurred to him, as they do to most think- ing men, while at sea in the silent night, when the clear stars are reflected in the passing waves, and strange phosphorescent lights seem to glide mysteriously under the bosom of the vast and shadowy deep.

And soft and tender memories came of his Gwendoleyne— memories blended with "the perfect love that casteth out fear." She loved him well, he knew, though their mutual aunt knew it not, for both were aware of her *wish ;* and Horace blushed to himself as he thought of a sentence in a novel which Lady Wedderburn had once read to him rather pointedly, and which was to the effect, "that disproportion of fortune was an insur- mountable barrier to married happiness ; that the sense of perfect equality in condition was the first requisite of that self- esteem which must be the basis of an affection untrammelled from all unworthy considerations."

If he fell in the coming strife how long would Gwenny sorrow for him ? Long, he was assured : but sorrow cannot endure for ever. Time consoled all, and soothed all, even as it avenged all things ; and others would come who would teach her to forget him, and perhaps—to love them. Aye, there was the rub, the gall and the bitterness ; and his whole soul revolted at the idea that when he was lying forgotten in his foreign grave, amid the festering heap in some battle-trench, another might gather in his arms that Gwenny whose beauty was so sweet and tender, and whose heart as yet, was wholly his own !

Yet he would not have her to pine as one who had no hope

on earth. That would indeed be too selfish ; so with a sigh, he strove to thrust these thoughts away.

While thinking thus, eight-bells struck, and Hunton, of the 34th, whose duty it was to relieve him and take the middle-watch, which extends from midnight to eight in the morning, came promptly on deck to his post, while the old watch went below, and a hundred fresh soldiers in their great-coats and forage caps came thronging up the hatchway.

"You'll scarcely find the cabin so pleasant as the poop," said Hunton significantly, " for Chesters and Co. are at it again."

" I mean only to have a glass of sherry and a devilled biscuit from the messman, and then turn in," replied Ramornie, to whom the long and handsome saloon presented a very exciting scene as he entered it.

By the rules of Her Majesty's Service all lights in the fore part of a troop-ship are extinguished at eight o'clock P.M., save such as there are sentinels posted over ; even the lights of the officers aft are put out by ten. The captain of this transport, an old master of the Royal Navy, had retired to his own cabin, leaving particular orders that "the lights were to be doused before the first hour of the middle watch was past ;" but by permission of Major Chesters, "the officer commanding," they were kept burning as long as there was a card to be turned, or a dice-box rattled.

Overcome by wine and excitement, some of the juniors had dozed off to sleep on the sofas and cushioned lockers. Two were singing, and others were arguing noisily as to the place where the troops would probably make their landing against the Rus-sians—if they ever landed at all. Some were offering and book-ing ridiculous bets, for the evil example of Chesters was painfully prominent now. The wine decanters had passed freely and frequently round, and as a result, the clamour of voices rose at times to a most unseemly and discordant din ; but fortunately, laughter and fun were predominant, for most of those present were heedless subalterns, lads fresh from Eton, Sandhurst, or Harrow.

Chesters was seated at a table playing vingt-un with young Elton, whom he had lured or taunted into gambling with him, and whose face, alternately flushed or pale as he won—which was seldom—or lost, which was frequently, presented a strange contrast to that of his bloated adversary, or to the placid aspect of Colonel De la Fosse, who, while catching the turns of the game with an eye expressive of disdain, leant quietly against the foot of the mizen mast, with a half-lit cigar between his fingers, and muttered to Horace as he passed some-thing about " le régiment de la Calotte " (i.e., madmen).

Horace had been at sea in troop-ships ere now. In one he

17

had gone round the Cape to India; but never before had he beheld a scene like this at such an hour in any vessel in her Majesty's Service; it was so entirely subversive of discipline and good feeling.

"Here comes Ramornie from the deck, looking as usual, cool as a cucumber, rather reprehensively perhaps, too," said Chesters, mockingly; "will you join us, and have a little mild play, 'to improve the shining hour'?"

"I would rather be excused, Major. I never gamble," replied Horace.

"Ah, you have no small vices. You, then, Ponsonby?"

"Play with *you*?" replied Ponsonby, who had imbibed sufficient wine to make him exceedingly rash, "not if I know it!"

"Why so?" asked Chesters with knitted brows.

"Can't afford it; that is why," replied the Welsh Fusileer, coolly.

"You have grown cautious?"

"No. But you are always so deuced lucky with the honours, and when the ship rolls, do exactly what you please with the kings and aces."

"A home-thrust, egad!" said Elton bitterly, for he had been losing fast.

"I'll have a turn with you, Major," said a little tipsy ensign, stepping up from a sofa.

"I don't bet with boys under age."

"But you play with them, and to some purpose," retorted the lad angrily.

Chesters darted a furious glance at the speaker (who returned it by an unabashed stare), and then he proceeded to sort and shuffle the pack of cards anew, prior to determining the deal.

"Mon ami," whispered Louis De la Fosse to Elton at this juncture; "beware of him whom you play with. I know him of old; he is one of the luckiest fellows in the world."

"How?"

"He is ever a winner, always cool, always quiet and observant, and seems to possess the eyes of Argus instead of two."

"What is all that whispering about?" asked Chesters, with suspicion.

"You, Monsieur," replied the Colonel, so quietly that the blotches on the Major's face deepened in colour.

"A knave! the deal is mine," said he. "My transactions with *you*, Colonel De la Fosse, if it is these you refer to, were a trifle compared to my single affair with Prince Galitzin, the Russian Attaché at Paris."

"They were serious enough for me, any way, Monsieur."

"I won eight thousand pounds odd, at a sitting: we played

vingt-un, this very game. But then he owned more roubles and Russian peasants than he could well reckon."

Elton was still losing fast, and the exasperation of his temper, the pallor of his face, his straining eyes and general disorder of aspect, became painfully apparent, while the bead drops of perspiration glittered on his temples.

" You had better abandon vingt-un," said Horace. " The run of luck is against you, my dear fellow ; or won't you turn in, the hour is waxing late."

" Early, rather," replied Elton to this advice, which was rashly given, so far as the giver was concerned, for Chesters immediately said in a threatening tone—

" What the devil do you mean, sir, by interfering with us ? By what right do you permit yourself to do so ?"

" The right accorded by friendship and kindness."

" Attend to your own affairs, sir. You've not had much experience of life, my young friend ; but like mild, trashy Cape Madeira, you'll improve by a sea voyage, I hope."

Horace kept his temper by an effort, or felt himself compelled to do so, and turned away towards the rudder-case, recalling the fears he had fancied, and the wise resolutions he had formed on deck to avoid this dangerous man ; but a loud laugh elicited by some remark of the latter, from the tipsy ensign—a remark in which he heard his own name mentioned, drew him again to the table near the mizen mast.

" And you came home with her over land ?" he heard Chesters say.

" Yes, by Jove I did," replied the boy.

" She is a girl with a thundering lot of money in Indian stock, bonds, a palace in the Choultry, and the deuce knows all what more. I suppose Ramornie can tell us all about it."

" Of whom are you talking, sir ?" asked Horace.

" Wedderburn's cousin— the Madras girl."

" That subject again, Major Chesters?" said Horace, absolutely trembling with passion, for there was a deliberate and languid insolence in the other's tone that maddened him.

" You should not find it an unpleasant one," said Chesters, still mockingly. " A girl worth her weight in gold ; in fact, her weight in mohurs and rupees."

" A la belle millionaire !" said De la Fosse, smiling, as if to preserve good humour. " If beauty be the test, parbleu ! every girl I saw in England is worth her weight in guineas."

" They say she is to marry Wedderburn of the Royal Fusileers," continued Chesters, resolutely bent on insulting Ramornie. " Ha, ha ! but many a fellow will be run to earth ere we return again, and why not Wedderburn among the rest ? He may go to

Old Scratch with the *down* train, for a hotter place than Varna, and have no return ticket."

"Sir, I appeal to all those present, if this is not a most brutal jest?" exclaimed Horace, now as white with passion as Elton was with his losses.

"This to me, sir?" exclaimed Chesters, starting up. "I am a gentleman——"

"By the courtesy of the turf."

"I am a Major of the Turkish Contingent!"

"Much that is to boast of," replied Horace, whose voice was tremulous with rage and scorn.

"Look you, young fellow," said Chesters, in a bullying tone, "hitherto, so far as you have been concerned, I have been holding my stride——"

"Sir, *I* am a gentleman ; neither a jockey, nor a groom, consequently your phraseology——"

"Is obscure, you would say?"

"Yes."

"Then, by Jove, I'll make it plain enough to you. I am your superior officer, and as such I order you under arrest ; aye, close arrest in your cabin. Mr. Elton, as acting adjutant, receive Mr. Ramornie's sword. At Malta or Varna he shall figure before a general court martial."

Ramornie, little foreseeing the use to which it would soon be put, handed his sword and belt without a word to Elton, and bestowing on Chesters a glance of supreme disdain, retired to his cabin, but in such a mood of mind as the reader may conceive.

This untoward affair caused a chill, a gloom to fall on all present, and they formed little groups to whisper over the probable result of it.

"And now to finish our game, Elton," said Chesters, coolly reseating himself. "We have but a few minutes only, ere the lights must positively be put out. Where were we?"

"I scarcely remember," sighed Elton, who had already lost stake after stake, and given I O U's to a considerable amount, for to him, as a younger son, the losses he had sustained were ruinous, and he despaired of retrieving his fortune.

Colonel De la Fosse, who had beheld the scene between Chesters and Ramornie with silent indignation, now proceeded closely to watch the conclusion of the game between the former and Elton ; and while humming a French air, he had taken up Ramornie's sword, drawn it from the scabbard, and with apparent curiosity was examining the edge, and more particularly the *point* of it.

As dealer, Chesters turned up a *vingt-un* with wonderful celerity and success on every occasion. And at last poor Elton, pale as death, with bloodshot eyes, trembling hands, and clammy brow, placed his last stake, a very heavy one, upon his *last* chance! But Chesters might still have a fatal *twenty-one*, and thus rook him completely!

The hand, on a finger of which the latter still wore the large onyx ring he had the bad taste to win in former days from De la Fosse, was spread out on the table somwhat ostentatiously; and on this hand, or on the ring, the keen dark eyes of the Frenchman were fixed as if by some strange fascination. On the stone was engraved a gauntlet on a sword's point. All who were sober stood hushed in silence round them, their eyes fixed alternately on Elton's excited face and the fatal cards which roused such evil passions, when suddenly an exclamation escaped the watchful Frenchman.

"*Imposteur! Mon Dieu—un 'imposteur—*ah, pitiful *carabinade!*" and he dashed the sharp point of Ramornie's sword between the second and third fingers of Chesters' outspread hand, which he instantly and instinctively withdrew; and then was seen by all an ACE, which he had concealed beneath it, for purposes of his own—the ace being always reckoned as one or eleven according to the exigencies of the holder's play—pinned to the table by the steel weapon!

* * * * * * *

CHAPTER XLVII.

UNDER ARREST.

MEANWHILE Horace Ramornie was in his little cabin (nearly one half of which was filled by a 24-pounder), ignorant of the strange event that had transpired in the saloon; and anticipating only the evils, the affront, and shame of a court-martial, before which he knew not in what artful fashion the charge of Chesters might be framed against him; and in which, perhaps, spitefully, and for the mere purpose of annoyance, the name of Gwendolcyne Wedderburn might appear as the cause of quarrel, and this itself might ruin him with her for ever.

Knowing but too well that for the maintenance of discipline, the authorities at the Horse Guards generally supported—even to injustice, seniors against juniors—he passed the hours that remained of the morning in a most unhappy mood, fearing that ruin stared him in the face, and resolving—for he was full of desperate and bitter thoughts—that if he were cashiered, he would join some regiment as a volunteer, if permitted, and still serve, to perish, if he won not honour, in the war!

What would Sir Edward Elton and the regiment—those Royal Fusileers, of whom he was so proud to be one, and

among whom he was so well thought of—say, when they heard
of his being placed under arrest, close arrest too, a double
degradation, when on his way out to the seat of war, for an
unmeaning gambling row (such it *might* be called) with his
senior officer?

Gwenny and the Wedderburns too! His heart grew sick
when he thought of her and of them; the disappointment his
good uncle must feel; the indignation of Lady Wedderburn
and Cyril; and the cold, legal, and reprehensive comments of
Robert. So his ideas became a mere tumult, a chaos of rage;
for the catastrophe his fears foreshadowed had come to pass
sooner than he expected.

Separated from Ramornie only by a bulkhead or two, Chesters was in his more spacious cabin, in a frame of mind that
was still more unenviable; for he had yet the hollow and conventional feeling of honour, or knew the necessity of affecting
to have it, for outward purposes. As to what people at home
might say he cared little, for there he was forgotten by all, save
his creditors; but here, in the Allied Army, he would have to
face exposure, disgrace, and, too probably, a court-martial, if
not summary dismissal from the Turkish Contingent; for even
the singularly recruited ranks of the Bashi Bazooks might
decline to receive him.

Deep were the blasphemies against Fate, and bitter the curses
against Louis De la Fosse that fell from his lips! He drank
brandy and seltzer water as if he had a consuming fire within
him; his features, all save the grog-blotches, were pale and
livid; his hands trembled and moved by convulsive twitches
—all the more so when a message came from the Frenchman,
through young Elton.

"Tell him, Monsieur le Lieutenant," said the former to the
latter, cuttingly, "that I can neither be bullied nor jockeyed
like some of his boy ensigns; and that I will fight with sword
or pistol, or both, on the first land we sight, even were it no
larger than this table."

"Something must be done," replied the rather bewildered
Elton; "but I fear arrest also, if I become the bearer of a
challenge. Duelling is fairly put down in our service."

"But not in ours. People cant and talk of steam and telegraphy, of progress and civilization, but the science of human
destruction keeps pace with them, for human nature never
changes. We shall never be without crime and passion. And
tell this man—if he is not what I should blush to call any man
who wears an epaulette?—I shall fight him, if he will come, a
duel à mort, though I fear that my old comrade, St. Arnaud,
would resent such a *fracas*. And yet he does not always keep
his own temper under control. *Mon Dieu!* I was close by his

side on that terrible morning in the Tuileries, when General Cormeneuse accused him of extracting a valuable document from the portfolio of Napoleon; and before one of us could speak, the sword of St. Arnaud was plunged to the hilt in his heart."

Chesters strove again and again to write an insulting acceptance of the challenge from the Frenchman, but his fingers failed to guide the pen. And when he remembered that, too probably, not an officer on board the troopship would become his messenger or second, he dashed his desk against the cannon in his cabin, with blind and impotent wrath.

A jockey, a gambler, a *roué*, he had never before been so openly and publicly stripped of the character of " gentleman ;" and now he knew and felt himself to be exposed, lost, disgraced, perhaps beyond redemption, and all through the means of that quiet, stern, and observant Frenchman, whom he resolved that he would yet shoot like a dog, if he had the opportunity. How he loathed and literally cursed him ! Well, if he escaped dismissal, which he could scarcely hope, he should in future scrupulously avoid his own countrymen, and fraternize with the Orientals—perhaps turn Turk altogether, like the Croat, Omar Pasha ; for this gambling scrape would not, he conceived, injure him much in the estimation of Osmanli officers, whom he knew to be but an indifferent set of fellows, often originally the *acancoglans*, or men who do the meaner offices of the Seraglio, or attendants of the pashas, such as *tirnaktzys* (nail cutters), carpet-spreaders, *chiboukgis* or pipe-bearers, and so forth. But being literally covered with merited shame, he became seriously ill, and his uninterrupted libations of brandy increased his ailment, so that a few hours saw him in a raging fever and placed on the sick-list.

The next officer in command, a Captain of the Rifle Brigade, ignoring alike his past authority and the whole affair, released Horace from arrest, and restored to him his sword. The incident, however ugly, had a salutary influence among the youngsters. Dread of a court of inquiry still existed ; so the gambling in the cabin ceased, and a vast number of bets were cancelled, and I O U's that had been interchanged were, by mutual consent, destroyed, torn to pieces, and sent whirling over to leeward.

To do him justice, amid all the contempt he had for his character, the soldierly Louis De la Fosse felt some pity on learning that Chesters was so crushed in spirit.

" My own life has not been always *couleur de rose*," said he to Ramornie, as they promenaded on deck one evening, while the little green coloured isle of Pantellaria, with Il Bosco, its volcanic cone, were faintly visible on their weather beam ; "it has been cloudy enough at times—such as that when this same

Chesters reduced me to the verge of starvation and despair;
and when for months I was a prisoner among the Arabs in the
mountains of Auress, which look down on the sandy waste of
Sahara, and when every morning I had the pleasant anticipation of dislocation of the neck, by having my head
twisted one way and my body another, like a pigeon in a poul-
terer's shop. *Ma foi! un bon coup d'épée* I have struck many
a time, but for you young fellows, the best I ever struck was
that with your sword blade through yonder trickster's hidden
card !"

Save through the surgeon on board, nothing was known of
Chesters, who only began to recover his senses one evening
when he could see through the open port-hole near his bed the
waves careering past before the pleasant breeze that fanned his
throbbing brow, and land visible a few miles off; but he gazed
at it dreamily, for what shore it proved he knew little, and
cared less.

The ocean was all of a very light blue; but the bases of the
mountains were of a dark indigo tint, while their peaks were
tipped with crimson and purple, as they started in outline
against a sky of gold and amber, that gradually turned to fiery
red as the sun went down behind the land. Then blending
tints of opal and crimson began to steal across the sea; while
darkness deepened on the shore of Sicily, for such it was, and
the cape—some call it the isle—which terminated near Passaro.
The chargers were whinnying on board as they gladly snuffed
the land—the Pachynum Promontorium of the classic ages;
but it might have been the coast of Bulgaria or of Baffin's Bay
for all that Chesters cared, as he closed his blood-shot eyes, and
dozed wearily off in slumber.

When next morning he awoke a little calmer, and looked
forth once more, he knew instantly where he was. Around the
open port-hole swarmed a flotilla of little boats, full of tawny,
black-haired and keen-eyed men and lads, almost in a state of
nudity, looking like great monkeys as they clamoured for
money to be thrown over, that they might dive for it. He
recognised the streets of stairs ascending to the Strada Reale;
the solid batteries rising tier above tier, and bristling with a
thousand cannon over the freestone rocks, on which the glittering sea was dashing; the Cathedral of St. John, where the
keys of the Holy Cities hang; the Castle of St. Elmo; the
harbour full of shipping, chiefly war vessels and transports,
crowded with troops, the boats in hundreds shooting to and fro,
full of seamen and marines, food and warlike stores, coals,
powder, shot, and cannon. He heard the occasional drum and
bugle-call in the garrison, and the tolling of those solemn bells
that whilom had rung for mass and prayer in Rhodes; and as

Chesters turned wearily in his bed, he knew that the *Blenheim* swung at her moorings in the harbour of Valetta.

A great French line-of-battle ship, the *Ville de Paris*, crowded with Zouaves, lay near her. They were swarming about her decks, and even out upon her booms, laughing, singing, and chattering like marmosets, in their short blue jackets and baggy red breeches, and ever and anon their long brass trumpets rang shrilly out upon the ambient air.

For all these he had no eyes : he was feverish, and though, in a moral sense, not naturally courageous, at that moment he actually longed for death. He could remember his father, a gallant and irreproachable veteran officer, whose ideas of honour were based on the old military school, when men entered the service, not as a lounge, but for the duration of their lives, and when the standard maxims were, never to give, but never to *take* an insult, and to be ever prompt with your pistol ! He could recall this fine old officer, scarred with many an honourable wound, his breast decorated with the medals he had won in Egypt, at Corunna, and Waterloo, commanding his regiment in yonder citadel of Valetta ; and he felt that if the dead are conscious, his father would be regarding him with sorrow, if not with shame !

And shame and rage Chesters felt keenly, but no dread of the future and no regret for a misspent past ; no thought of reformation for the time to come, and short enough that might be. He was devoid of all religion, yet, strange to say, not entirely destitute of a species of superstition ; and in times of danger, was wont to recall with confidence the prediction of a gipsy woman at Yetholm, who, when he crossed her hand with silver, had predicted, "That he should neither be drowned, nor die a violent death—yet that he should not die in a bed, as his father had done."

So he began to gather a little hope. He might survive the present disgrace, and be a Bimbashi or Colonel yet—ay, a Pasha with two tails, or a Brigadier ; and thus, while trembling in his heart lest the late affair should recall fully to memory the half-forgotten play-transaction, in which his name was once involved before, compelling him to quit the Queen's service, he schemed, in fancy, out the future.

The saloon of the great ship was empty, voiceless, and he knew that every officer who was not on duty would be on shore, to see the wonders of Malta, to smoke cigars at the Auberge de Provence, have tiffin with sliced melons and Maltese oranges at Spark's in the Strada San Paoli, and a donkey ride as far as Monte Benjemma, or the wood of Boschetto, where the knights of St. John kept their game of old, for he had done all that himself in happier and more innocent days.

Suspense and hope, the heaven and the hell of the systematic
gambler, he had endured and triumphed over; but to be pointed
at by the finger of scorn, for what he had been discovered to
be—he, who had alternately bullied or chaffed and rooked the
boy-subs of his detachment—all proved too much, however, for
the brain. The cognac was again appealed to in absence of the
assistant-surgeon, and again a raging fever seized him.

He became oblivious of everything and everybody now, save
his close attendant, Bill Trayner, whom he never failed to recognise, and to anathematize most freely—a circumstance which
excited only a smile from that well-trained jockey, who was
already looking to the reversion of his effects, and taking the
opportunity of dividing the contents of a well-filled purse, with
great fairness, between himself and his master, with whom he
was left in charge, for when the _Blenheim_ got up her steam for
the Archipelago, Chesters was in the Military Hospital at Malta,
where we shall gladly leave him to recover at leisure from the
results of his own folly and debauchery.

It was generally supposed that he would die, or resign and
slip quietly home ; so, as if by common consent, the officers on
board the troop-ship resolved to commit his story to oblivion.

CHAPTER XLVIII.

THE BRIDGE OF SIGHS.

ONE more brief glance at home, ere we find ourselves face to
face with the disgusts of Varna, and the hostile columns of
Russia.

Many, many weeks had passed away; and during these Mary
Lennox knew nothing of what was passing in the outer world.
She knew that busy world was there, beyond her prison—"the
huge lock which shut her out from it," for during the monotonous hours of the day, and the drearier watches of the night
between her intervals of sleep, she heard the hum of the vast
multitudes around her—a hum that, though less at midnight
than at noon, seemed never to become, even for an instant, still.

She was weary—weary indeed of life ; but felt too strong to
hope that death was near her. In the morning she longed for
night; and when night came she thanked God that another day
of her dull pilgrimage had passed into eternity ; and then she
prayed for the oblivion of that sleep "which covereth a man
all over like a mantle :" but sleep was not always forgetfulness,
for sad dreams of the past and vague terrors for the future
haunted her, till, one memorable evening, the chaplain and an
official of the prison appeared with the startling tidings that
she "was _free !_"

" Free, sir! How?" she asked, doubtfully.

" By the death in prison of the man against whom you were bound to appear. It is fortunate for you," added the chaplain, " as he confessed your perfect innocence."

" Poor wretch! I hope he made his peace with Heaven?"

" Can't say as he did, Miss. You see he died in a hurry," replied the warder.

And so it proved to be the case, that the miserable desperado, Ben Ginger, otherwise known to the public as "the Captain," was soon after found dead in his cell; whether of atrophy of the heart or by some secret agency of his own, the learned coroner and the intelligent jury, who viewed or sat over his remains, failed to elicit; but Mary was free.

" You may leave this, Miss Lennox, as soon as you choose," said the chaplain, with a smile of encouragement; "for you the gates of the prison are open at last, and the days of your bondage are over, I am happy to say."

Intolerable as the prison had been to her, she was not without fear of issuing forth once more into the vast human wilderness around it; yet she knew that the essay must be made, come what might of it, and like one in a dream, she put on her hat and shawl. Her garments were sorely worn now, and from black had turned to a kind of rusty-brown tint. Her purse was restored to her, and walking mechanically, she found herself at the strong iron-barred gates. The chaplain still accompanied her; but with that mistaken acuteness peculiar to some people, both he and the matron had their doubts about Mary; and the diamond ring on her " engaged finger " completed the measure of these.

" Where are you going to-night?" he asked, drily.

" As God may direct me. Would that it were to my father's grave at home," said she, as with trembling hands she tied her worn veil under her chin.

Those little hands were gloveless now, so their extreme whiteness and delicacy caught the observant chaplain's eye.

" Home; it is ever home you pine for," said he, kindly, but reprovingly; "why are you for ever looking back?"

" Because, sir, I dare not look *forward*," replied Mary, with a morose gloom of manner all unusual to her.

" Are you then as one who has no hope?" he asked, with folded hands.

" Yes, sir; one who has no hope here, at least," and her smooth white eyelids and long dark lashes drooped as she spoke.

A trite text or two suited to the occasion—a word of conventional advice were given, the wicket clanged behind her, and they had parted; he to repair to his snug little room, with its comforts and well-filled bookshelves, and Mary to wander through the streets, aimlessly, and in a tumult of terrible thoughts. It was the month of September now, and darkness soon set in amid the dense and smoky thoroughfares of London.

The girl was in utter desperation and bewilderment, and walked on through the ceaseless throng and past the brilliantly-lighted shops, with the old stunned sensation that the whirl of omnibuses and other vehicles will always impart to those who are, as she was, country bred ; it came over her, all the more, perhaps, because latterly she had been secluded so long in utter solitude. Within her heart there was a sense of desolation that was fast becoming unendurable !

She had vague ideas of once more seeking the abode and advice of kind little Mrs. Long Primer, as the only being she knew in London ; and with this view inquired her way towards the Strand ; but was fast becoming weary, footsore, and in her agitation, oppressed with an intense thirst, which she knew not where to allay.

Alone, she feared to trust herself by night in a cab, and whither, or in what direction, those strings of gay, swift, and crowded omnibuses went she knew not. The Bank, Pimlico, Piccadilly or Paddington, Cornhill or Islington, conveyed no meaning to her; and so she wandered on, enduring a horrible sensation of com-bined loneliness, emptiness, and gloom, finding herself at times in densely crowded thoroughfares, and at others in stately streets and squares, where the lights and music that came through the tall and draperied windows, the glimpses of rich dresses, of liveries in marble and pillared vestibules ; and where the carriages that rolled up to the doors with flashing lamps and glittering harness, bespoke wealth and luxury, gaiety and splendour.

Lady Wetherall might be in town now ; but dared she present herself at that great mansion in Piccadilly in such faded attire, and without her letter too ? The thing was not to be thought of !

And it had come to this at last !

"Homeless, near a thousand homes she stood."

Mary Lennox, so delicate and tender—so loving and true—so formed and calculated for home and home affections ! What a fate to be houseless and shivering in the busy streets of London, where the vast human tide went surging by, ceaselessly —ceaselessly, as it has done for centuries past, and shall do for centuries yet to come ; its very magnitude appalling her ; though she knew that under happier auspices, and with some protection, she would get used to it in time ; but at present she felt only a desperate longing for rest, for the face of a friend—a yearning for the safe solitude of that home she never more should see ; and she recalled now with vivid distinctness all the terrible things said to her by Chesters, so cruelly and so artfully, of what her fate in life, and even after death, might be, if she died there friendless and unknown.

It was night in London now, but the pulses of the mighty city were throbbing still. In some streets the roll of carriages and the echo of hurrying feet had passed away ; but in the main arteries of the modern Babylon the full flood of life was flowing strongly as ever. Night or day seemed to make little difference in them.

Thus as Mary wandered aimlessly on, the strange combinations of extreme light and dense darkness, with the peculiar aspect that buildings and certain objects assume by night, all served to bewilder her more, and she remembered with growing terror the episodes of the last and only night she had ever been thus adrift in the streets at such an hour before.

To add to her extreme misery, rain began to fall, and came down with a heavy, steady, and apparently ceaseless determination. She was without cloak or umbrella, and was often compelled to take shelter in doorways and chilly passages, from which she was driven by men accosting her in terms of mock gallantry, or by policemen flashing their lanterns suspiciously into her eyes ; for she had a most rustic fear of those to whom she ought to have appealed for advice and protection. But all the little courage she ever possessed was gone now, and the poor girl, bred and reared as she had been, was as a child lost or astray in the streets of London.

The rain was still falling fast, and gusts of wind began to sweep the drenched thoroughfares and to ripple up the puddles and gorged gutters that reflected the gaslights. The atmosphere became murky as the smoke and soot of the countless chimneys were forced downwards by its density. Mary's clothing was wet and sodden now ; but in the terror and disorder of her mind, she was scarcely sensible of discomfort, for a man of suspicious aspect had been pertinaciously following her, and to escape him she ran onward till suddenly she found herself in an open space upon a great bridge, the double lamps of which were reflected in the wide river below.

It was the Thames, with all its bordering streets of stores and wharves, and its gathered fleets moored side by side, packed and densely, and yet so orderly.

Thousands of lights were gleaming across the murky bosom of the river, and through the open balustrade Mary looked at its current wistfully, thinking, as so many have thought, while lingering on that bridge of sighs, that there was peace—there an escape from all misery and sorrow.

She looked round her with a haggard eye ; in one place rose a square dark mass from out of the general obscurity ; in another a vast dark shadowy dome, that seemed to shimmer amid the dusky haze. One was the Tower, the other St. Paul's; and once more, sighing heavily, she bent her gaze on the turbid water. It flowed steadily, swiftly, and darkly onward—that mighty river—onward to the distant sea—but far down below her. Strange white things seemed to shine there in a lambent or phosphorescent light amid its rippling current. These objects made her shudder for a time and recoil. Then she looked at them steadily—it might be sternly. They were, she knew, only pieces of rag or rope, old hats, sailcloth, straw, or dead animals — and—"to be found drowned," amid all these!

"Oh, no—oh, no! God forgive me and guide me!" cried the girl, wildly. "Let me not think of *that.*"

She cast her eyes upwards as she prayed; but no star caught her imploring eyes, and the fast falling rain plashed heavily on her pallid face and sodden tresses.

She remembered her father as he lay dead in the old wainscoted room at Lonewoodlee, calm, peaceful, and triumphant over the world and all its ills. But his was a death so different from what such as *this* would be.

"Now then, young 'ooman, wot air you hup to?" said a voice, sharply, in her ear, startling her like a galvanic shock; and a well-whiskered guardian of the night, in his felt helmet and dripping oilskin cape, confronted her.

"I am doing nothing, sir," she faltered, and shrunk from him.

"Nothink! Then you'd better come along with me. Prison, I think, is the place for such as you."

"Prison!"

She uttered a wild despairing cry, and throwing herself over the balustrade, sank beneath the still, black current of the stream below!

The startled constable looked over, and as he sprang his rattle, saw something like a little hat and veil floating downward on the surface, but nothing more.

All seemed over!

CHAPTER XLIX.

THE VALE OF ALADYN.

By the time that Horace Ramornie with his detachment of the Fusileers reached Varna, and after a six hours' march, joined the headquarters of his regiment, which was then encamped in the green and beautiful Vale of Aladyn, the magnificent army which had left the shores of Britain so full of hope, so high in ardour and spirit, by the gross mismanagement, the vacillation, or something worse, on the part of the Home Government, had lain inactive and been literally decimated by disease, during the breathless months of a hot Bulgarian summer, and deliberately kept waiting for the approach of the Russian winter with its icy terrors, of which the French army at least might certainly have had a traditional memory and wholesome fear.

Cholera had cut our men off by thousands, and their graves lay thickly all over the slopes in the Vale of Aladyn, where the Russians had buried more than seven thousand of its victims a short time before ; hence it was not inaptly termed by the Bulgarian peasantry the Valley of the Plague.

The 7th, the Welsh Fusileers, the Connaught Rangers, and all the other Infantry had suffered severely, the Highlanders perhaps excepted ; the peculiarity of the Celtic costume, by the warmth it affords round the loins, having proved an admirable protection, which saved many a life in their ranks. Two of our cavalry regiments were reduced to skeletons, and about two hundred and fifty sabres formed the average muster of the other corps. So severe was the pest that many men died and were buried within five hours of their being attacked ; and now stern doubt and louring discontent become visible in the faces of the survivors. "Though no act unbecoming British soldiers was committed—though no breach of discipline could be charged, it was impossible to refrain from discontent. Murmurs, not loud but deep, made themselves heard. No man there but burned to meet the enemy. The entire army was prepared cheerfully to face death in the service of the country to which it had sworn allegiance ; but to remain in inactivity, exposed to pestilence, which struck down its victims as surely and nearly as speedily as the rifle-bullet, beneath a burning sun, with no power of resistance and no possibility of evasion, was a fate which might quell the stoutest courage, and raise discontent in the most loyal bosom."

The French army had come to Varna by marching over the great mountain barrier of Turkey, the Balkan ; our fleet the while had been seeking in vain to lure that of Russia from under the gun batteries of Sebastapol. The Turkish army had been carrying all before it on the left bank of the Danube ; and at Citate and Oltenitza had actually routed and covered the Russian armies with disgrace : but the last days of August still saw our army lingering hopelessly in Bulgaria, while the Russian forces whom they were ultimately to oppose were gathering fast in the land of the Tartars.

Horace shared the cool bell-tent of Cyril in the camp, and on the forenoon of his arrival, while lying on the pleasant sward which formed its floor, enjoying cigars and bitter beer, with belts off and coats open, and when looking forth on the scenery, who could imagine that death was hovering so near, and that more than ten thousand graves lay around them in that smiling valley! On one side of the camp lay a beautiful lake, and on the other the ground rose high and was covered with varied foliage, over which the storks were always flying in long lines. And there too were eagles, vultures, and kites, soaring in mid-air, on the outlook for dead horses, or, it might be, a camp follower who had perished in a lonely place, and lay blackening in the desolate glare of the sun, covered with flies, with dim glazed orbs and open jaws.

Near Cyril's tent were the ruins of a kiosk or country-house which the Russians had destroyed ; but its arabesque white marble fountain still remained in the centre of a beautiful garden, where the great Persian rose-trees yet loaded the air with fragrance ; where the foliage of the greengage, the apricot, the apple, and the purple plum, waved pleasantly in the soft wind ; and the beautiful orioles, all yellow and green, the gaudy woodpecker, the blackbird, and the thrush, darted after the flies at times in veritable coveys, and sung sweetly in the shadow.

A group of soldiers in fatigue dress, filling their camp-kettles, canteens, and horse-buckets, or washing their linen, might always be seen about this fountain. These visitors had long since "looted" the garden of its golden-coloured melons and great scarlet pumpkins ; the Egyptian palm, the Indian fig-tree, the gorgeous aloe, and the solemn towering cypress, still grew side by side, though the billhook of the forager had abstracted many a branch to feed the camp-fires, and had the French been near, not a twig had been left.

Now the allied forces, some eighty thousand strong, were under canvas over the whole vast plain which extends from Aladyn to Varna. Horace found Cyril looking pale and changed, for he had undergone a touch of the pest, and he was bearded to an extent that would have astonished the folks at home, whom he had never informed of his illness, as Dr. Rivers-dale of the staff had "pulled him through it."

" If we don't take the field soon," said he, " the Russians will find but few to fight with. The army, though recruited fast, is rotting away, Horace, literally, and just as our army rotted at Walcheren in 1809, when thirty-five thousand entries were made in the fever hospitals ; so you see that in forty-seven years Britain has learned nothing in the art of war ! But how fresh you fellows look just from home, in your new uniforms and bright epaulettes, as if you had just stepped from band-boxes. By Jove ! you do form a contrast to those who have been under canvas here so long."

Cyril had, of course, overwhelmed Horace with questions about all who were at home ; and the latter had related, in confidence, the affair with Chesters in the transport. It, however, excited no surprise, as Cyril knew the worthy's character well ; but the mention he had made of Mary Lennox's name stung, grieved, and bewildered him. In prison! The story seemed mere malevolence, and altogether incredible ! How could it come to pass ?

While they were speaking the same Drum-Major who had been wont to act as regimental postman at Chatham—ay, even in Candahar and many other places—appeared at the tent-door, coolly as usual, with letters for both, the mails having come on in the *Blenheim* from Malta. Each tore his missive open in haste, and became absorbed in its contents ; for a letter there was as a voice from home, and the hearts of both were instantly far away from the tented vale of Aladyn, among the green braes of the Merse and Lauderdale. Cyril's was from his mother, to whom he was tenderly attached. That to Horace was from Gwenny.

"For a reason, of which I may tell you at a future time," Lady Wedderburn mentioned among other matters, "we have employed Chesters' old gatekeeper, Tony Heron, in the stable-yard, where, by-the-by, the long projected new wing and clock-tower are progressing. Robert is busy with his studies, and will come out for the English Temple. Your father thinks that as he is not brilliant he might shine amid the aspiring mediocrity of the Scottish bar (where there is such utter poverty of position and of talent) ; but in London, we fear, that he will never be *heard of at all !* The Reverend Gideon M'Guffog, not content with 'the flesh pots ' he enjoys, is raising an action, chiefly against us, for an augmentation of his stipend, through Grubb and Wylie, the writers (or wretches rather), who, like too many Scotch legal desperadoes, are ready to do anything for cash or a case. As your regiment does not wear the kilt, Dr. Squills urges that you should wear a belt as a safe precaution against that cholera which seems so terrible at Varna ; and Gervase Asloane says he has in the cellar some fine old Glenlivat, which would be a better protection still, had we but the means of sending it to you."

Other things followed, of as little importance as these, but there came one remark which found an echo in Cyril's heart.

"That foolish old man at Lonewoodlee is no more, as Horace, perhaps, by this time may have told you, and his proud, but penniless, daughter has left this part of the country for ever."

Mary's face, her sad, earnest eyes, her last words, and her helplessness, all came painfully before him. Dead—old Oliver Lennox dead ! Cyril in imagination saw all the grim details of the last scene, with poor Mary alone—so terribly alone—in

18

that old rambling and gloomy Tower.   Had his mother been—
as he implored her to be—kind to that orphan girl whom he
had loved even as his own soul ? The coldness of her letter gave
him slender hope of that. Who, then, had befriended, who aided
her ?   Chesters ?   He writhed at this thought, and though he
had never ceased to love her, but false as he deemed her, had
sworn never to see her more, the interest he felt in Mary's fate
would never die.

The cousins tacitly, and with one accord, exchanged letters,
and Cyril, from the tenor of Gwenny's, guessed at once how
matters stood now, and said—"Bravo, Master Horace ! So you
have not been idle in my absence ? But I congratulate you, old
fellow, for Gwenny, wealth apart, is a girl among ten thousand !"

Horace blushed with pleasure, and replied, with a laugh—
"For Heaven's sake, Cyril, don't tell Lady Wedderburn that
we have committed the enormity of falling in love. You know
what her *wish* is, so far as you are concerned ?"

But Cyril did not answer, for another pang was inflicted on
him by a passage in Gwenny's letter to Horace, and it almost
seemed to corroborate the remark of Chesters in the troop-ship.

"There has been some talk among us from time to time of a
trip eastward in the Ernescleugh yacht, so don't be surprised if
we should see the Russians before you do. I should like to get
a Turkish husband for Zillah, my ayah (the men here won't
look at her), and I don't think that Miss Flora M'Caw, at her
mature years, would have much objection to a Muscovite, even
if his name were like three sneezes with *off* or *iski* at the end
of them. The orphan girl, Miss Lennox—perhaps you may
remember, dearest Horace, it was she of whom such unpleasant
things were said by the Ernescleughs—was visited by Aunt
Wedderburn and me after her father's death, and before she
went to London. Aunt gave her a most kind letter to the
Wetheralls in Piccadilly, and another was sent to her address
somewhere near the Strand ; but it was returned by the post-
office people, with the information that she could not be found
in London—had disappeared, in fact."

Disappeared, and in London !

Cyril grew ghastly pale as he read those words, which seemed
to burn themselves into his heart, and in a gust of jealous bitterness, he connected this disappearance still with Chesters. He
started up, shouted for his servant, and ordering horses, added,
suddenly and impatiently—"You have reported yourself to Sir
Edward, the Colonel ?"

"Of course, Cyril."

"Well, come, Horace, there is no parade this evening; all
hands are turned to pound green coffee. Let us ride into Varna
and have some tiffin, such as it is, at the Military Café. Any-

thing to kill time and thought. till we can kill the Russians! Ned Elton, Probyn, and ever so many more of our fellows will be there by this time, for it is the only place in this dreary hole where any fun is going."

Horace agreed, and a few minutes after saw them mounted and off.

CHAPTER L.

VARNA.

"AND so you and Gwenny are engaged? By Jove! Don't wonder at it! She is a most attractive girl; and there are worse-looking fellows in the service than you, Horace. But I've not been lucky myself lately in this game of love-making. And you should hear old Conyers Singleton of ours tell the story of the girl he left behind him. It is quite a warning," said Cyril, as they trotted towards the line of advanced sentinels posted round the British camp.

"Going to Varna?" asked Captain Joyce, of the Fusileers, whose guard tent was in that quarter.

"Yes. What is the parole?"

"'Bomarsund.' Countersign, 'Baltic.'"

"Thanks. That Zouave heard you?"

"Perhaps; but it can't matter much. He is a Captain, I presume?"

Had Horace not been full of Gwenny's letter, and had he not found ample occupation in repeating to himself certain pleasant passages thereof, he must have been aware that there was a forced or spasmodic gaiety in the manner of Cyril Wedderburn that was not real, for he tugged at his moustache nervously, and viciously switched at the flies which buzzed about his horse's ears.

Troops of every kind; Lancers, with gay bannerets; Hussars, with their glittering dolmans; Carbineers, with brass helmets and slung carbines; Artillery, in dark blue; and Infantry, in red, covered all the plain. Our Household Brigade of Guards, in their bright scarlet coats, with large white epaulettes and bearskins; the Highlanders, who were in the same division, in their varied tartans, with their sturdy bare legs and tall-plumed bonnets, exciting the wonder of the starved-looking little Arabs of the Egyptian Contingent. There, too, were the Rifles, in their sombre green uniform, which looks almost black at a distance.

All the bustle of preparing food went forward at hundreds of impromptu fires, by soldiers in their shirt-sleeves; and the sound of chopping wood was heard on every hand, while the sun of the afternoon blazed hot in their fires from the unclouded Bulgarian sky. Fatigue parties went to and fro, laden with bundles of sticks for the cooks, or corn or swathes of grass for the horses; and songs and merriment came at times from the tents where the soldiers lay smoking on the sward. But the camp had its darker pictures.

Here and there a ghastly and attenuated sick man might be seen carried on a stretcher to the hospital tents ; and, ere long, the same stretcher would be borne in another direction, with some victim of the Fever King, to be cast into the graves which honeycombed the low range of hills that overlook the Vale of Aladyn, or it might be to yonder "City of the Dead," in the plain, where the solemn rows of giant cypresses stand like guardians round the tombs of "the Faithful."

Beyond the British lay the French camp, with all its gaily-clad, untidy, but somewhat purpose-looking little soldiery. The Infantry of the Line, in long blue tunics, with scarlet epaulettes, and brass eagles on their tiny shakos ; the splendid Cavalry and Artillery of the Imperial Guard ; the Chasseurs à Pied ; the Tirailleurs Algériens, dressed like Arabs, but in light blue ; and the active Zouaves, in their (to us) well-known uniform, which excited great surprise and speculation among the stolid Turks and the Bulgarians who swarmed about the camps in great numbers, clad in jackets of undyed wool, wide white trousers, girt with sashes of silk, caps of brown sheep-skin, and sandals of hide ; and who failed to comprehend how Christians should be going to battle wearing the turban of Mohammed ; for the poor Bulgarians loathe the Turks, whose slaves they are ; and as such, dare not carry a knife, while all the former, down to the lowest *hamal* (or porter) go armed to the teeth, with pistols, sabre, and yataghan.

Amid all its splendour and order of military array, this camp, like our own, had also its dark features ; the sick and dead were hourly borne through it ; and there too were the intoxicated, courting disease and death, as they lay by the way-sides, in ditches or kennels, stupefied with raki or peach-brandy, their faces blistering in the sunshine, and covered by clouds of odious flies. Others, despite all warnings, might be seen gorging themselves with scarlet pumpkins, cucumbers, gages and plums which the acquisitive Greeks offered for sale ; and the Turks of Omar Pasha were nearly as reckless, for they were always eating of the perilous green fruit, when not engaged in smoking, praying, or covertly reviling "the Christian dogs," who had to fight their battles.

As Wedderburn and Horace were passing a mass of Araba carts, all drawn up wheel to wheel, there darted from under them a long snake of dark green colour mottled with white, and having bright protuberant eyes that flashed like carbuncles. As the reptile came forward, writhing, wriggling, and almost

dancing on its tail. Cyril's horse reared back upon its haunches ;
but a Turkish *Yebosha*, or captain of cavalry, who was riding
by, drew a long brass pistol from his belt, and with singular
adroitness shot it dead ; and with a pleasant smile and a low
salaam rode on. Once or twice the reptile quivered all its
length in the dust, and then lay still.

"Ma foi, mes camarades, but that was well done !" said a
voice, and they found themselves joined by the same Captain
of Zouaves whom they had seen near Joyce's guard-tent. He
was now mounted on a stout little Tartar horse and seemed to
have made a *détour* round the French lines, instead of coming
through them. The cousins scarcely noted the circumstance
then, but subsequent events made them remember it. "Going
into Varna, Messieurs ?" he asked, reining in beside them.

"Yes," replied Cyril.

"A horrid place—dull as a vast catacomb ; even the French
can scarcely make it lively. Any word yet of when the troops
are like to take the field, or for what point ?"

"I have heard nothing yet, Monsieur," said Cyril, with some
reserve, as the manner of the questioner seemed abrupt and
authoritative.

"Your cavalry force is dwindling fast," resumed the Zouave.
"Why, diable ! all your regiments put together would barely
make *one* efficient Russian corps of four squadrons," he added,
with a mocking laugh.

"I don't understand this Captain of Zouaves," said Cyril, in
a low voice : "he spends his whole time in our camp, and seems
to have fallen in love with perfidious Albion. What can his
object be ?"

"Are you sure that he *is* a Captain of Zouaves ?" said Horace.

"I have no reason to doubt it—but hush ; he may understand English."

It might have been some peculiarity of his dress which made
Horace think what he said, for the Zouave had features that
were more finely cut than usually appertain to Frenchmen. His
eyes were black, glittering, and closely set together ; his nose
was somewhat hooked and a fierce moustache stuck sharply out
on each side of it ; but his hair, which was dark as a raven's
wing, was shorn close to the scalp.

"Sang, Dieu !" he exclaimed, as if he had penetrated their
thoughts and doubts, "but I am tired of this work. Ugh !
when we pound the green beans here, between two friable
stones, which add dust in plenty to the condiment, I think of
the fragrant coffee I used to get at home, and the little pats of
sweet butter on a honey-cake, or on a cool green ivy-leaf—the
breakfast of my schoolboy days, at home in pleasant Gascony.
I have been a soldier for twenty years ; but I have never forgotten those days."

"He is a Gascon—ah, that accounts for his peculiar accent," said Horace.

"I am not much of a gourmand," resumed the Captain of Zouaves. "In Africa, I have often dined on a slice from an old trooper—a horse I mean ; but still I have a predilection for *fricassées*, and *fricandeaux et galettes*, which mean *collops Ecossais*, or thin cakes (though the Scotch stole all their cooking from us, in the days of the old alliance), and I doat on broiled chicken and cream-tarts, such as I used to get from my old mother in Gascony, before I betook me to the rough-and-ready trade of soldiering."

"And now, Horace," said Cyril, whom the Frenchman's empty chatter bored, "behold our thriving city of Varna !"

It was a dreary looking place, and rose from a bank of white sand that stretched far along the flat Bulgarian shore.

Imagine a low and half-ruined wall, a mile in length, broken and battered as the shot of the Scoto-Russian Alexis Greig had left it in 1828, but all loopholed and painted pure white. Before it lies a ditch, over which a number of 68-pounder guns are pointed. Above it rise the round leaden domes of four mosques, with their tall, white, slender minarets, encircled by wooden galleries ; the solitary campanile of the Greek church, and round these a little sea of dingy red-tiled roofs, and one may picture that Varna on which so many of our soldiers looked their last, and before which Ladislaus of Lithuania and Poland perished in a futile attempt to drive the stupid and brutal Osmanlees out of Christendom.

Prior to the arrival of our troops, its filthy streets had been deserted and silent as the grave. Save when a wild dog—the unclean and forbidden animal of the Prophet—panting with out-lolled tongue on a heap of decayed melons or festering offal, uttered a melancholy howl ; when a stork, with flapping wings, came swooping down on the eaves of a dilapidated house, and loosened a tile or two, to fall with a crash ; or when a bare-legged *saka* (a water carrier), with his brown feet in low slippers, and his greasy buckets slung from a shoulder-strap, shambled along the narrow and tortuous, yet sunbaked, thoroughfares, no sound was ever heard there.

But now French and British soldiers filled every street and alley with noise and bustle ; the bazaars were crowded by Zouaves chattering like magpies : by Rifles and Guardsmen ; by grave and observant Scottish Highlanders in search of food, *soochook* sausages, and kabobs, or little articles of finery for wives and sweethearts far away at home ; by quarter-masters and sutlers, seeking corn and flour, beef and mutton, Greek wine and peach-brandy ; in short, everything eatable and drinkable. Drums were beaten, bugles sounded incessantly, and incessant too was the marching to and fro of guards, escorts, pickets, and fatigue parties in their canvas frocks. Tumbrils, limbers, cannon and tents, encumbered the five arched gates ; war-ships, transports, and pestilent looking little gunboats, crowded all its once empty harbour. The black kites and mangy pariah dogs were alike scared from its streets and market place. The lazy and blasé Turkish householder secluded himself in his *divan hanee*, or zenanah if he had one ; and hourly held up his hands, or stuck his fingers in his ears, at every fresh wonder, for to him it seemed that the end of the world was nigh, for the sons of Anak, the children of Perdition and the Devil himself, had all possessed the city together !

French names were actually painted up at the street corners, and to crown all, an old deserted caravansera had been taken possession of, *sans permission*, by a speculative Parisian *restaurateur*, who papered, painted, and furbished it up gaily, and hung out an immense sign-board, on which an artistic Corporal of Zouaves had painted the French eagle, with the words, "*Le Restaurant de l'Armée d'Orient, pour Messieurs les Officiers et Sous-Officiers ;*" and under this sign-board Wedderburn and Horace Ramornie dismounted, gave their nags, with a few piastres, to two half-naked *hamals* to lead about, and then entered the café.

CHAPTER LI.
LE RESTAURANT DE L'ARMÉE D'ORIENT.

" We are going to have cigars and a bottle of Greek wine," said Cyril to the Zouave Captain, who seemed at first doubtful about entering, and then acceded with a bow. Cyril thought that perhaps he was a man of high French family and did not care much to mix with the *sous-officiers*, many of whom were then mingling with their superiors, playing chess or dominoes, laughing, smoking, chatting gaily, or perusing the *Charivari ;* even *Punch* and the *Illustrated News*, which were not wanting for the amusement of the British officers, many of whom were in the large and strange looking coffee room, which had been the place where the horses and camels had been stabled when the house was a khan of high repute. On many parts of the walls were coloured prints of Parisian girls, opera and ballet dancers, pirouetting in the shortest of drapery, and round them the Turks were wont to gather in amazement, and to mutter that such beauties were worthy of the Padisha himself.

Everything that he saw filled Horace, like every new comer,

with wonder, or excited his interest ; strange dresses, manners, voices and faces ; but Cyril had already become intimate with all these as if he had known them from boyhood.

He who arrives in any place which is to be his quarters for a time, feels as if the strange streets, the public edifices, the churches, and the sound of their bells, would never become familiar ; yet Horace was so much of a soldier that he had not been three days in and about Varna before the aspect of the itinerant Dervises, who received his piastres or paras with a malediction ; the shrill invitation of the Muezzin from the minaret ; the Turk kneeling at prayer on a bit of tattered carpet in the open street, counting his *colomboio*, and scowling with horror at the passing Highlander ; the French *vivandière* riding at the head of a battalion of Chasseurs à Cheval, and waggishly kissing her hand to some fat old Pasha ; the women stealing along like sheeted spectres in their white yashmacs and yellow boots ; the jolly gangs of British tars, trundling up their Lancaster guns from the beach like toys, became all familiar, for the sense of novelty was gone.   They had scarcely entered before several of their brother-officers came forward from amid the various tables and groups to accost them, for the cousins were decidedly popular among the Fusileers.   There were Bingham, Jack Probyn, old Conyers Singleton the Major, and Pat Beamish, with his black whiskers more bushy than ever.

"Welcome to Varna, Horace, though bad luck to it for a hole, anyhow !" said Beamish ; "for if we don't get out of it sharp, between raki and unripe fruit, we'll leave half our men behind us."

"Orders and advice go for nothing, so far as these are concerned," added the Major.

"Bedad, the arms of Briareus and the eyes of Argus won't keep these Greek devils with their fruit out of the camp ; and there's Bingham of ours narrowly escaped a slash from a yataghan for peeping through the holes of a woman's yashmac in a sherbet shop yesterday, and giving her a chuck under the chin."

"Is that Home of the Guards with a cocked hat?" asked Horace, as he saw the Master of Ernescleugh seated jauntily on a table, laughing with some French and Turkish officers.

"Yes ; he's on the staff."

"An aide-de-camp?"

"Yes, and enjoys the fullest confidence of the General," said Beamish ; "but here, unfortunately, he cannot have that which is so indispensable to the position of an aide-de-camp—the confidence of the General's wife and daughters."

Colonel De la Fosse, who was seated at a table with a few officers of the French 34th, now rose and lifted his cap to Horace, who said, "Allow me, Colonel, to introduce my brother officer, Captain Wedderburn. It was De la Fosse," he added to Cyril, "who in some measure revenged you on Chesters ; but, by the way, in the troop-ship we agreed not to refer to that subject."

"Ah, now, comrade, it was to your kind father I believe that I owe the favour of being what I now am," said the Colonel, as he warmly shook Cyril's hand ; "for his opportune assistance saved me, when yonder brigand put me in a sore strait indeed !"

Wine and cigars were speedily brought, and the new arrivals proceeded through their medium to enjoy the buzz and heedless merriment around them. The restaurant was soon densely crowded, and the mixture of languages, French, English, Turkish, Greek, and often a polyglot of them all, and bad Bulgarian, were heard on all sides. The only silent person was the observant captain of Zouaves who accompanied Cyril and Horace, and who, oddly enough, seemed far from being at ease.

"Drink with us, Monsieur," said Colonel De la Fosse. "You are very silent for a Zouave ; your fellows have the reputation of being more noisy than even the Tourlourous," he added, laughing, as he used the sobriquet for the French Linesmen.

"I am thinking of Paris," replied the Captain. "But we must rough it as best we may, for potages and jellies, ragoûts, and pâtés are all unknown here."

"But you can have kidneys fried in champagne," said Beamish; "or claret mulled with a dash of clove or a slice of pineapple, and sure these are luxuries enough for any man on service."

"Yes ; but here one longs for the cafés chantants, the theatres, the casinos, and the girls of Paris, with their sparkling black eyes and white shoulders."

"*Ah, ces épaules blanches ?*" said a sous-lieutenant, throwing up his eyes. "True ; for the women here look hideous in their shapeless mufflings."

"Your regiment, mon Capitaine, is the——" De la Fosse paused and twirled his moustache.

"The 1st Zouaves, mon Colonel," replied the other, curtly. "Ah, encamped at present a mile or two beyond the Devna Lake."

"Exactly, Monsieur," replied the Zouave Captain, who seemed to dislike the expression of scrutiny he read in the keen eyes of the Colonel, who wore the square peak of his scarlet kepi close to his nose.

"It was your regiment that led the van at the pass of Djerma ?"

"Yes, Monsieur," replied the Zouave, while the Colonel tugged at his moustache more than ever.

"I too am sick of Varna," said a gay-looking Chasseur à Cheval, "and long, if not for active service, for the pleasures

of Paris ; a ramble in the Place de la Concorde, or the Gardens
of the Tuileries, or to take my ease in the Hôtel de Lausanne,
instead of the devilish old tumble-down Restaurant de l'Armée
d'Orient."

"Yes ; and perhaps to run after the nurse and grisettes,"
said the Zouave Captain.

"Tra la la la, l'amour est là !" sang the Chasseur. "Well,
perhaps, yes."

"But," said Cyril, "there are no grisettes such as we find in
the romances of Paul de Koch and his predecessor, the author
of the 'Conquests of Mademoiselle Zina' (over which the
Emperor slept on the retreat from Leipzig)—the grisette is
now a *petite dame.*"

"Any way you take it," replied the Zouave, with a growing
irritation of manner. "We have but a dreary time of it here,
nursing the sick and burying the dead ; no fighting, no glory ;
patience—always patience. *Mal peste!* what we have endured
since our troops came down the passes of the Balkan !"

"Your reward is at hand, Monsieur," said De la Fosse. "In
four days we leave this to attack the enemy !"

A burst of applause followed this announcement, and hearty
English cheers, mingled with shrill yells of " *Vive la France!*"
" *Vive l'Empereur!*" the old cry that rang over Waterloo, and
many a field of the past !

"In what direction is the attack ?" asked the Zouave, eagerly.

"I am not yet at liberty to say."

"But your authority is undoubted, Monsieur ?"

"I had it from Marshal St. Arnaud himself."

"I am glad to hear of it," added the Zouave. "Gunpowder
is the incense amid which the souls of the brave go straight to
God."

"Somehow, that bit of bombast is the only thing this fellow
has said like a true Frenchman," whispered Cyril to Horace.

"In four days," exclaimed the young chasseur. " *Ouf, ma
foi !* we'll eat the Muscovites up—train oil, tallow, and all the
rest of it !"

" And now, Messieurs, adieu," said the Zouave, as he drained
his wineglass, put his sword under his arm, and with a low
bow quitted the café. The keen glance of De la Fosse followed
him, and then fell on Cyril Wedderburn. Each read doubt in
the other's eye.

"Is that Captain of Zouaves much about the camp ?" he
asked.

"Daily ; but he keeps more among the British than the
Turks."

"I am sorry to hear this."

"Why, Monsieur ?" asked Cyril.

"Because it adds to my suspicions," said De la Fosse, lowering his voice. "He showed a purse with more gold in it than usually falls to the lot of a captain of Zouaves ; and he spoke of the First leading the van at Djerma, when it was *I* who led the van there, at the head of the 3rd Zouaves, and 3rd Chassenrs à Pied."

"Do you mean to say that you think——"

"I know not what to think ; but fear to be rash. To detain him might excite a bad feeling between the Zouaves and ours, if he be innocent ; but anyway, I shall ride to Devna to-morrow and see his regiment on parade."

"You had not many scruples about unmasking our Major of the Turkish Contingent," said Horace, laughing.

"Ah! but then I knew him of old," replied the Colonel ; "and I detected his false play while watching, with regret, a signet ring he wore ; an onyx graven with my crest, a gauntlet on the point of a sword, with the motto, *Droit en avant*—a ring that had been long in my family, and which we valued highly, because there is a terrible story attached to it. He won it from me, however, at play, when I madly staked and was stripped of everything."

"And what is this story, if I may inquire?" asked Wedderburn.

"It belongs to the old days when duelling was alike a passion and a vice with the French, who carried it almost to a pitch of insanity ; and if it while a little of this time, which we find so irksome in Varna, I care not if I relate to you the affair, as illustrative of the days of our grandfathers—in France at least."

"*Bon ! très bon !* Agreed ! Very good ! Fire away ! Colonel," said several voices in French and English ; and after more wine and cigars had been brought, the Colonel related the following story.

· ˙ ˙˙ ˙˙˙ ˙˙˙ ˙˙˙

CHAPTER LII.

THE DUEL A MORT.

"Louis XV. of France died in 1765. It was in the year preceding that event that my grand-uncle, Louis De la Fosse, whose ring that man Chesters now wears, fought the famous duel I am about to relate to you ; but prior to doing this, I must go a little way back into the history of himself, and that of the time, now some ninety years ago.

"My family is of Languedoc, and for several generations we have resided near Montpellier ; thus it chanced that when my great-uncle Louis was a student attending the Royal College there, he became acquainted with a youth named Renée de

Taillevant De l'Isle, from Provence, and a friendship sprung
up between them. The circumstance of Louis' only sister
Henriette, a beautiful blonde, being not indisposed to view the
handsome Renée—for Renée was so—with favour, conduced
greatly to cement this regard ; and at the house of Louis most
of the spare time of Renée was spent, when studies were over.

" Both lads were destined for the army ; every gentleman of
good family in France took a turn of military service then, in
some fashion, with the Mousquetaires, the Line, or as a volunteer ; and knowing that the time would come when they should
be inexorably separated, their friendship, the spontaneous
growth of two generous and affectionate hearts, of similarity of
taste and thought, was all the stronger.

" They had gone through the same classes at college ; they
practised together the use of the sword, and soon taught each
other to excel all their companions in every trick of the science
of self-defence. They hunted together in the mountains, boated
together on the Rhone, and, accompanied by Henriette, had
many a wild gallop among the beautiful groves of olive and
mulberry trees, which grow there in much luxuriance, for
Languedoc is one of France's most favoured regions ; and on
these occasions the fair Henriette, with her golden hair dressed
à la Marquise, looked like a beauty by Watteau, in her riding-
habit of *gris-de-lin*, then the fashionable colour. I have seen
her portrait, taken then, and she must have been lovely, though
she did wear the stand-up collar—the *collet-monté*—of the time
of Louis XIV. to please her mamma, who was somewhat old-
fashioned in her tastes, and was full of recollections of the
brilliant entertainments she had seen at Marli.

" And Renée de l'Isle idolized her ; but though wealthy and
noble—for in those days people made a great fuss about their
heraldry ; to marry was to get a coat of arms, quartered, im-
paled, or so forth ; now we are thankful if we marry a good
monogram. So the world wags—*très bon !* Well, though
wealthy and noble, he was too young to think of marriage, and
so was Henriette. A little time, and they should be happy, for
they were betrothed solemnly in the church of Saint Pierre ;
but that little time was to be spent by Renée in the army ; and
one morning which brought him but a dubious throb of excitement and which filled Henriette's heart with anguish, he found
himself appointed a sub-lieutenant in the Regiment of Mazarin
(the 54th of the old French Line, under the monarchy), as a
letter from the Minister of War, Lieutenant-General the Duc
de Choiseul, informed him. So now Damon and Pythias were
to be separated. The days of their joy were to terminate.

" The lovers were impulsive and young ; so their hearts were
wrung with sorrow at parting. Henriette gave Renée a white

scarf embroidered by her own hands with blue *nonpareille*, a narrow ribbon then much used by ladies in decorating silk or velvet, and weeping as if her heart would break, she placed it round him, and then sank into the arms of her mother.

" 'Oh, Henriette, cease to weep thus. Your life was never made for sorrow,' murmured Renée, as he hung over her pale face. 'It should be all love, kisses, and sunshine ; and such shall it be, my beloved, when in two years I return.'

" *Ah, mon Dieu !* two years !' she exclaimed, and would not be comforted ; for two years seemed a long, long time indeed to look forward to.

" While Renée for a time could feel no military ardour, even while contemplating himself by the aid of his mother's great crystal-framed mirror in the white uniform, the scarlet vest, and gold-bound hat of the Regiment of Mazarin, he strove to comfort himself by remembering that in the scene before him the term of probation would soon glide away.

" But he could think only of Henriette, her tears and her fair beauty, her love and her promises of fidelity, and while posting away to the frontier of Germany, he longed to be again as he had been, a happy boy in the woods of Languedoc, conning over with Henriette the charming story, 'La Belle au Bois dormant,' and others, before they learned to relish the writings of Scuderi, Mademoiselle de la Fayette, and the Countess d'Aunenil. So they parted, but looked forward to the coming time when they could marry, and be happy for all the days of their lives, as the old stories have it.

" The following month the tears of Henriette flowed afresh, for her only brother, Louis De La Fosse, was appointed to the Regiment of Languedoc, which was the 53rd of the old Line, prior to the Revolution of 1792 ; but though the numbers of their respective corps were so *near*, the friends were placed far apart ; for while Renée was doing duty on the banks of the Rhine, Louis was sent to broil in Martinique for two years.

" In all that time he never heard of Renée, and but seldom of his own family. In those days there were no steamers, no telegraphic wires or deep sea cables ; and the letters of those who were separated became indeed as the visits of angels, few and far between.

" However, the famous treaty of Paris, by which France lost Canada and Louisiana, enabled her to bring home great numbers of her troops from far and foreign shores ; thus the year 1764 saw the Regiment of Languedoc quartered in its native province ; and as it marched into Montpellier to take quarters in the strong citadel which Louis XIV. had built, how great was the joy of Louis De la Fosse to find the Regiment of Mazarin drawn up to receive and salute it with all the honours of war, bayonets fixed and colours flying; for by a singular coincidence, the 54th had come in but a few days before from the Rhine.

"Mademoiselle De la Fosse had been taken to Paris by her parents, as her health had been delicate; but the two young lieutenants speedily met and renewed their friendship amid the same scenes where it had first grown and been cemented, and for some days they were incessantly together before they remembered that they now unfortunately belonged to two regiments which had long been rivals in camp, field, and garrison; and following up some absurd feud, old, perhaps, as the latter days of the Cardinal, from whom the 54th was named, had fostered an unremitting hatred, which was apt to break out between the officers and men of each on the most trivial occasions. Such feuds were but too common then in the French service, and officers of hostile corps would fight, whenever they met, upon the least imaginary affront, even a glance, though when out of uniform they were the best friends in the world.

"The 53rd had been raised in Languedoc in 1672, and the Comte de Douglas was its Colonel at the time of our story. The 54th had been raised the year after, and was commanded by the Marshal Duc de Mazarin.*

"The friends knew of this spirit of folly, but it was nothing to them; they would soon be brothers, they loved each other dearly, and would never do otherwise. One evening they had dined together at the *Fleur d'Amour*, a cabaret in the Place du Peyron, a promenade outside the city, and as they sat at the open windows, which from the lofty terrace enabled them to survey all the old familiar views, their hearts swelled with happiness, and they grasped each other's hands.

"'*Peste!*' exclaimed Renée, 'but this is pleasanter work than lying on out picket before Frankfort!'

"'True, Renée, *mon ami*,' responded Louis. 'When looking down as we do on dear old Montpellier, with all its quaint, old-fashioned streets, and the groves and vineyards of our beautiful Languedoc, spreading yonder far away even to the Pyrenees, the blue Mediterranean in the distance, dotted with white sails, it seems as if it were but yesterday that we trudged together to college, with Livy, Horace, Juvenal, and Euclid in our satchels, and yet thousands of miles of ocean have rolled between us since then, and I have been among the Caribbean Isles, have seen the green savannahs of Martinique, and the lightning of a tropical tempest play round the summit of Mont Pelee!'

"'*Morbleu!* but yesterday indeed, and yet an age since we saw Henriette—*our* Henriette, Louis!'

"'Let us be happy in the hope of seeing her soon; and

* " Liste Historique des Troupes de France."

meantime, let us have a little turn at piquet, for here comes
Gustave Lapierre of ours, a horrid quarrelsome fellow, with
whom we had better have nothing to do.'

" So they seated themselves at piquet just as Lapierre, a tall,
thin, and swaggering looking officer, with his triangular cocked
hat very much over one eye, his left hand planted on the hilt
of his sword, the fingers of his right twirling his moustache,
entered the room, bowed to De la Fosse, gave a supercilious
glance at the face of Renée and the uniform of the 54th, and
with a loud and imperious voice, ordered wine and the ' Gazette
Française.'

" Renée felt his face flush, but he affected to attend to his
game, and he and his friend played for small sums, as neither
of them ever gambled ; but Renée being annoyed by the presence and general bearing of Lapierre, played ill, and the run
of the cards went in favour of Louis, who won every game.

" ' Pardonnez moi, Louis,' said Renée, laughing ; ' but how
is it possible that you always win so ?'

" ' In what way ?'

" ' Contriving *always* to have such excellent hands.'

" ' No contrivance at all, my dear Renée ; 'tis chance ; but
keep your temper.'

" ' Could I lose it with you, Louis, when your voice and eyes
so remind me of Henriette ?'

" ' Well, cease to think so much of her, and the next game
perhaps may be in your favour,' said Louis, laughing.

" ' Hélas non !' sighed Renée, and again Louis laughed, for he
won, and then they separated with an arrangement to meet on
the morrow. De l'Isle repaired to his quarters in the citadel,
while De la Fosse took his horse and rode off to his father's
chateau, which stands on the road to Nismes, and is still a
fine old place, though it was sorely battered and burned by the
Huguenots in 1622.

" Lapierre had been an attentive listener to all that had
passed ; the imprudent jest of Renée at losing so often, the
jocular hint at unfair pl. y, and Louis's laughing advice that he
should ' keep his temper.' Repairing straight to the citadel, he
gathered a few of the quarrelsome spirits of the 53rd about
him, and to them he retailed the story, but in such a manner
that the whole affair took the tone of an affront passed upon
the corps, through the regimental antagonism of the 54th, and
he was deputed to represent to De la Fosse that he must
' demand immediate satisfaction alike for the sake of his own
honour and that of the Regiment of Languedoc.'

" Louis was inexpressibly shocked when he heard how the
matter was likely to turn, and felt inclined to pass his sword
through the body of the meddlesome regimental bully who so

smilingly confronted him ; but that would not have mended
the affair, though it might have benefited society, as Lapierre
was a professional duellist, and had killed and wounded many
men, by a peculiar feint followed by a thrust, of which he alone
was master.

" 'Come, come, comrade, you must have him out and kill him,
or we shall be obliged to call out every officer of his corps in
succession, and give them their *sauce Robert* to perfection.'

" Louis knew that this was meant by Lapierre as a sneer at
the family of Renée, who was descended from Taillevant, Master
of the Kitchen to Charles VII. of France, for whom he invented
no less than seventeen different sauces ; so the remark, which
might have made him laugh at another time, inflamed him with
passion at the speaker.

" 'Beware, Gustave Lapierre,' said he, 'for if I am taunted
to fight my dearest friend—which cannot be thought of—I shall
fight with *you* next.'

" 'Perhaps that cannot be thought of *either*,' sneered the
other, with a contemptuous glance of his grey-green eyes, which
were totally destitute of lashes ; 'but as you please ; I shall
lay before the corps your doubts and scruples in this matter,
and we shall solve them for you, *après la mode Française.*'

" 'Dare you, Monsieur, impugn my courage ?'

" 'It seems I must; but the omission of that in your com-
position is a little oversight on the part of Providence for which
you are in no way to blame,' sneered the other.

" 'Sangdieu, but I will kill you, Lapierre !"

" 'You may try ; but you must first kill this Renée Taillevant
De l'Isle.'

" Knowing but too well where all this tended, and aware of
the fashion of the time, Louis at once sought out his friend, in
a state of mind most difficult to describe.

" Duelling, I have said, was then alike a passion and a vice
in French society ; so it was carried to a pitch of ferocious
madness in the army. Louis XV., and the two Louises his
predecessors, had issued many an edict in vain against it, but
the rage for fighting, wounding, and killing by the sword continued, though not quite so bad as in the time of Henry IV.,
during whose reign, as Lomenie records, no less than four
thousand French gentlemen perished in single combat ; and by
the civil law of France, as it existed in 1764, the period referred
to, 'the body of a person slain in a duel was ordained to be
dragged through the streets on a sledge, and refused Christian
burial ;' but there were ways and means for evading this ordi-
nance, as we shall see in the end.

" With sorrow and horror in their hearts, and with tears in
their eyes, they found themselves compelled to take their swords

and repair to a solitary part of the old rampart that girds Montpellier, and there, in presence of Gustave Lapierre and several officers of both regiments, they threw off their white uniforms, and engaged in their shirt sleeves, each as he did so seeking only to be wounded, rather than to wound, and to avoid meeting the glance of the other.

" 'Guard, Louis—oh, mon Dieu—guard!' exclaimed De l'Isle.

" 'Guard you, Renée; cover yourself well,' replied De la Fosse.

" 'Enough of compliments—enough of griefs,' said Lapierre, scornfully; 'fall on, like French *gentlemen!*'

" 'Would it were with thee!' exclaimed both together.

" 'I am at your service, Messieurs, this affair once over.'

" In the peculiar manner they fought, they each received a sufficient number of flesh wounds with the sword's point to have satisfied even the artificial scruples of the spectators, and actually to disable themselves from continuing the conflict longer, for that day at least. So they separated and retired each to his quarters.

" The moment that Renée had his wounds dressed he presented himself before the senior officers of his regiment; but they one and all turned their backs upon him, with the taunt that he 'had been *forced* to fight.'

" 'In the name of God and St. Denis, what more must we do?' asked Renée, in utter bewilderment.

" 'Fight till one is killed on the spot, or be for ever disgraced among us as a couple of poltroons!'

" 'He and you, and all of you who would say so are liars and pitiful *capitaines!*' cried Renée, transported with rage; but their insulting laughter rang in his ears as he quitted the citadel, and again sought the presence of his friend.

" In the distraction of their minds, they resolved that they should meet again on the morrow, rush simultaneously upon each other's swords and die together!

" Early next morning, Louis De la Fosse was seated in the library of the château, writing a farewell letter to his parents and to Henriette, when the latter suddenly appeared by his side. Accompanied by her old nurse, she had preceded their father and mother, who had loitered in Montpellier; but she had heard that with which the whole city was ringing, that her affianced husband had insulted her brother; that they had fought and were to fight again.

" Fear was in her face, but in her eyes were mingling a gleam of anger with the light of love, for she idolized her brother Her eyes were beautifully set, with a half droop in the lids that gave them great sweetness and softness, though her short upper lip and chiselled nostrils—it is a great word "chiselled," and I

don't know how we should ever get on without it—told of spirit
and will and high breeding too.

" 'Oh, Louis! after our separation, what a meeting is this for
us all !' she exclaimed piteously.

" 'Then you have heard all, my sister ?'

" 'Yes; that you have quarrelled, have fought, and hate each
other so that though covered with bloody bandages, you are to
fight again. Oh, Louis, my brother ! tell me in pity can such
things be ?'

" 'You have but come in time, sister, to see me before I die;
for Renée and I have sworn, hand in hand, not to survive each
other.'

" 'Oh, this is a madness !'

" 'It is the crime of others, Henriette.'

" Then he told her how they were situated ; how the supposed
quarrel and the duel had been forced upon them by the insane
suggestion of a barbarous code of honour ; and a great horror
came over the heart of the girl, for she knew that the matter was
irremediable, and she clung to his breast and wept in a paroxysm
of grief and despair ; till at last the fatal hour approached when
he had to tear himself away, and leave her.

" 'Farewell, Henriette, my sister, my sweet pet-bird ! It is
dreadful indeed to die so soon, and by dear Renée's hand too ;
but you shall see us again, and pray over us, when all is ended.'

" Alas ! though she could not foresee it, even that melancholy
office was denied her.

" To be brief, they met again upon the ramparts, when all
the officers of both regiments were present, those of each corps
eyeing the others with hostility, malevolence and exultation.
The morning was cold and grey, not a bit of blue was visible in
the sky ; the sun, as he rose from the waters of the Mediterranean, was shrouded in dun and sombre coloured haze, and
the wind came in fitful gusts and sighed mournfully through
the embrasures of the old rampart. The two friends were
deadly pale, their eyes were bloodshot, their handsome and
usually cheerful faces wore an expression of intense sadness,
for each felt himself forced into the commission of a dreadful
crime, against which all his nature revolted. They moved with
difficulty too, for their limbs were stiffened by the wounds of
yesterday.

" The words to 'guard' and 'engage' were given by Lapierre,
and with half-closed eyes they rushed upon each other's swords,
and both fell at the same instance, each pierced by a dreadful
wound.

" A cry of mingled agony and anguish escaped Renée ; but
from the quivering lips of Louis De la Fosse there came not a
sound. He was pierced through the heart !

" While writhing himself forward to embrace his dead friend, Renée, whose wound was perilously near the left lung, was lifted up and borne away by some officers of the 54th to the house of a surgeon, where he was kept in concealment for three months, till his wound was cured so far that he could fly and escape the civil authorities. But to prevent the latter from putting in execution the final disgrace of the law upon the dead body of Louis De la Fosse, the officers of the 53rd threw it into a hole which they had ready dug for the purpose ; and round that hideous grave they stood in a ring, with their swords drawn, till the remains were almost utterly consumed by quick-lime, so that the sentence I have quoted elsewhere could not by any possibility be put in force upon them ; but prior to their destruction thus, Lapierre drew from his victim's finger the onyx ring to which I have referred. My father wore it for his lifetime and then transmitted it to me.

"Renée De l'Isle fled from Montpellier in the night, and perished of want in Spain ; and so ended this most barbarous tragedy !"

  ❉   ❁   ❋   ❈   ❋   ✳   ✳

"And Mademoiselle De la Fosse : what became of her ?" asked Cyril, whom the little love bit of the story interested.

"More like a heroine of romance than of real life, she never married ; but on proving her eight quarters of nobility became a *Chanoïnesse* in the chapter of Ste. Marie, and lived to be a very old, and, notwithstanding her brilliant beauty in youth, a very ugly woman. Often have I sat upon her knee in my infancy, for I was a great pet of hers, and she loved me most perhaps for bearing the name of Louis. She died so lately as 1818, when Louis XVIII. was king of France."

By the time the story of Colonel De la Fosse was ended, the shrill trumpets of the Zouaves and the brass drums of the French Infantry had been giving warning that the time was at hand when, without reference to rank, all should be in camp or quarters ; so the *Restaurant de l'Armée d'Orient* began to empty fast, as each visitor departed to the *place d'armes* or head-quarters of his regiment. As that of De la Fosse (the 34th) lay encamped on the side of Varna nearest to the British lines, Cyril, Horace, and he, rode off together leisurely, just as the soft and very brief twilight began to close over the flat shore, the most unpicturesque city, with its four flat leaden domes, and the sea of white tents that spread over the plain to the westward of it.

"By Jove !" exclaimed Horace, "there is our Captain of Zouaves again !"

"Where ?" asked De la Fosse, sharply, as he reined up his horse.

"Coming from among the tents of Omar Pasha's people."

"And he is *not* riding towards the lake of Devna, where the 1st Zouaves are under canvas, but quite in an opposite direction."

"At a devil of a pace too," added Cyril.

"Let us follow him. There is something in all this I don't like," said the French colonel.

Skirting the camp, and riding under the concealment of a long grove of olives, they followed him at a short distance, as they thought unseen ; but on clearing the group of trees they could perceive that he had urged his little Tartar horse almost to racing speed, and was riding fast towards the sea.

As the brief twilight passed away, and darkness closed over the flat landscape, they lost all trace, but still rode on in the hope of overtaking, or perhaps meeting him when returning ; and after continuing this vague pursuit for some miles, they found themselves on a lonely part of the sea coast some seven or eight miles from Varna, and near the port of Baldjik, where no sound broke the silence but the dash of the waves as they rolled on the shingle.

"Well, Messieurs," said Colonel De la Fosse, "we have had a bootless gallop."

"But see—there is some signal !" exclaimed Cyril.

About a mile from them, in the very direction they had come from, a small blue light was suddenly burned for a second or two, but close to the shore ; another light upon the water responded, and then came the half-muffled sound of oars in the rowlocks distinctly over the surface of the sea. Then all became still but the dull clang of their horses' hoofs, as the trio galloped along the sands to where the mysterious lights had shone.

Alone on the shore, with ears drooping, stood the little Tartar horse, minus saddle, bridle, and holsters ; a scarlet Zouave turban and blue Zouave jacket lay near ; and about two miles at sea, but visible nevertheless, was a large lugger or small schooner—which you will—with all her canvas spread, standing away to the north-east out of the Gulf of Baba, as if heading for that portion of the Black Sea which runs towards the Isthmus of Perecop, in the rear of Sebastopol, before which the British fleet lay.

"Death and the devil !" exclaimed the French colonel, "we have had a spy among us ; but the fellow, however daring, overacted his part of Frenchman. Ah, *morbleu !* there will be no need for me to visit the camp of the 1st to-morrow ; our friend, 'the Zouave captain,' is in yonder craft, with all the information he has been able to glean up in and about Varna, and a few hours hence will lay it all before Prince Mentschicoff."

They were intensely annoyed to find that he had escaped

them ; but regrets were useless now. Wedderburn and Ra-mornie returned to their camp in the Vale of Aladyn, bidding farewell to De la Fosse *en route ;* but the information he had given in the restaurant proved to be quite correct ; for the 5th of September saw the long lines of tents struck on the plain— the charnel-house—of Varna, the great armament embarked for the Crimea, and the smoke of the steamers alone visible from the ramparts when the sun set on the shores of the Black Sea.

CHAPTER LIII.

THE ALMA.

WE have small space for much detail of the Crimean War, and so shall confine ourselves chiefly to the personal adventures of our *dramatis personæ* there. But it seems strange to think how after the lapse of a very few years the terrors, the tears, the sufferings, and the glory incident to that campaign, are already half forgotten, and the whole seems but as a tale that is told ! Yet great were the endurance, steady the discipline, and noble the heroism of those who followed Raglan, our one-armed veteran, to the field : and there were men of all ages in his army, from those white-haired warriors who like himself had seen the night of horrors at Badajoz, and the corpse-strewn plains of Vittoria and Waterloo, down to the fair-cheeked boy-ensigns fresh from school ; for when the death-lists of the Crimea appeared, many a name therein was recalled with pride and sorrow in the class-rooms and playgrounds of Eton, Har-row, and Rugby.

Yes, it is indeed all as a tale that is told—the night of our landing at Eupatoria, when without tents or baggage sixty thousand men remained on the bare ground, under torrents of rain, thus adding fearfully to the scourge of cholera next day ; the march towards the enemy under a blazing sun ; the mad-dening thirst, that thousands broke their ranks and rushed to quench in the Bulganac ; the skirmish there with our advanced guard ; the heights of Alma bristling with cannon and bayo-nets ; the death ride of " the Six Hundred " at Balaclava, when

* The episode of a Russian spy at Varna was not without a parallel during the siege. "A captain of Zouaves was observed in the French trenches for the last four or five days. As he was always bothering the men working at their guns, the officer commanding the battery called out, ' Who is that captain of Zouaves that is interfering with my men, and not attending to his duty.' The fellow appeared confused, and the men began 'to smell a rat.' He jumped over the works, and though fired upon, got safely into Sebastopol."

cannon blazed in front, on flank, and in *rear* of them ; that
dull November morning, when amid the grey mists the rumble
of the Russian artillery was heard while Mentschicoff poured
his hordes into the valley of Inkerman, and the butchery
of our wounded there and in the quarries. Then came the
half-frozen trenches and rifle pits, while the iron voice on the
grassy slopes of the Mamelon, the lines of the Redan, and the
mighty batteries of Sebastopol, was never still ; and though
last, not least, the ghastly horrors of the great hospital at Scutari !

On the morning of the 20th September, the allied army was
face to face with the Russians, led by Prince Alexander Mentschicoff, and then entrenched on the heights above the Alma, a
stream which rises among the western slopes of Crim-Tartary,
and falls into the sea twelve miles from Sebastopol.

Cyril Wedderburn had been on active service before in India,
but this was to be Horace's first battle ; and such was also the
case with most of the young subalterns in the army.

High on the southern bank of the Alma riscs a ridge of
picturesque rocks, which terminate in a cliff which overhangs
the Euxine ; in the ravines of these rocks grew groves of turpentine and other trees, many of which had been felled to form
abattis to encumber the advance of our troops. The Russian
lines were formed along that ridge, two miles in length, and by
the aid of field glasses their flat caps, their spiked helmets,
glittering bayonets, and grey-coated masses, could be seen as
the allied columns came on. Every available point was mounted
with cannon, trenches were dug, redoubts and breastworks
thrown up, and on the Kourganè Hill, six hundred feet above
the Alma, to protect his right, Mentschicoff had constructed an
enormous triangular battery, mounted with heavy cannon and
24-pounder howitzers. There too was the great Kazan column
with the holy image of St. Sergius, and also, oddly enough, a
train of carriages full of ladies from Sebastopol and Bagtche
Serai, "the Seraglio of Gardens," waiting to see the defeat of
the "Island curs," as they termed the British, whom, strangely
enough, they believed to be chiefly seamen.

The morning of the Alma was a lovely one. From the Black
Sea, where our steamers—their smoke ascending high into the
clear air—were creeping in shore to shell the Russian left there
came a soft breeze that played along the slopes, and whirled in
wreaths the smoke from the blazing Tartar village of Burlink.
The leaves rustled pleasantly in the beautiful groves of olive and
turpentine trees, and a peculiar fragrance that filled the air
came from the leaves of a little aromatic herb (which grew there
wild) when bruised by the feet of the marching column, or the
wheels of the field artillery. Many places were covered with

orange-coloured crocuses, growing thick as buttercups, in the fields at home.

"It was now that after forty years of peace the great nations of Europe were once more meeting for battle !"

The enemy was at last in front—those dark grey masses, so often spoken of, written of, and thought of—the hordes of half-savage Russia, and as the Fusileers (under Sir Edward Elton, who was mounted on his black barb Vidette, and looked every inch an English soldier) with the rest of their division halted, the altered demeanour of the officers and men became apparent to themselves. All foolish banter and idle conversation had ceased. There was indeed a cessation of sound—a kind of hush—over all the army, save when the neigh of a horse, or the clatter of a field-gun, woke the echoes of the rocks in front.

No man, unless a fool, goes into action, especially for the first time, in the same mood of mind with which he enters a ball-room, or joins a dinner party. Decent gravity pervaded the entire ranks, and many a heart was doubtless filled with prayer and thoughts of home and loved ones far away. Now and then a brotherly emotion of anxiety for Cyril occurred to Horace Ramornie, and to Cyril for him. Which might survive the day to speak of the other? If both fell, would they be buried together?

"Bother such thoughts!" muttered Horace, as he ventured to light a cigar in rear of his company.

They and others waxed a little more kind in their bearing to those about them; and one or two who had small coolnesses, shook hands or bowed and smiled in passing. Some, like Joyce the married captain, leant thoughtfully on their swords ; and he, poor fellow, was thinking, no doubt, of the two little faces he had last seen, side by side and asleep in the dingy room at Chatham barracks on the morning of the march.

Sir Edward sat motionless on his horse, till an aide-de-camp, passing at a quick trot—he was Nolan—the gallant and heroic Nolan— said—

"The General wishes the men to get loose their cartridges. This, Sir Edward, will be a field day for most of us to remember."

Elton repeated the order ; and under their bearskin caps a grim kind of smile lit up the faces of the Fusileers, as they opened their pouches and loosened the ammunition from its packing paper.

In losing Mary Lennox, life had—for a time at least—lost much of its charm for Cyril Wedderburn ; and somehow on this morning he felt as if danger and death had been for him divested of half their terrors ; and he had the longing desire to do that which rarely falls to the lot of those of subaltern rank,

something great and brilliant ; something that would make his
family and friends—aye, even the lost Mary—proud of him ;
yet with all this wild enthusiasm he seemed perfectly cool and
unmoved.

But alas for poor Cyril ! as we shall see in the sequel, he
longed and hoped in vain for such distinction as he honestly
coveted ! And he looked wistfully at the armed and hostile
heights with the thought that it would be hard to die there
without leaving his mark upon the world—some footprint " on
the sands of Time."

"Breathless and exhausting work this is, gentlemen," said
Sir Edward Elton, taking off his bearskin to cool his forehead,
for the heat was intense, and the troops had been some hours
under it.

"It suggests vague desires of iced champagne," said Jack
Probyn.

"Egad, it's mighty glad I'd be of a glass of pale ale, and a
pipeful of birdseye or cavendish," added Beamish ; "but here
comes a Frenchman who has been on some final mission I hope
to Lord Raglan."

"Colonel De la Fosse, by Jove!" exclaimed Horace, as that
officer trotted past the British lines. " Good morning, Colonel—
are we likely to come to blows soon ?"

"Soon enough, it may be, for the Russians yonder, Monsieur,"
replied De la Fosse, pausing. " The moment I rejoin Bosquet
the attack will commence. I have been pretty close to those
Russian fellows already. They look resolute and determined ;
but what of that ? We shall teach them that to win glory or die
in the field, is all a soldier need care for."

"Well," said old Major Singleton, " I should prefer half-pay
with a snug pension myself."

"Every man to his taste, mon camarade," replied the Frenchman gaily, as he laughed and galloped off to the right, of which
the French had contrived to possess themselves, and an awkward
post of honour they might have found it, close by the sheer
cliffs which overhung the Euxine, had they been defeated, or
had the British left been turned.

After two protracted halts, during one of which the French
division of Bosquet coolly cooked their coffee and made a comfortable breakfast ; and after two consultations between Lord
Raglan and Marshal St. Arnaud (who had taken the field in
almost a dying condition), and after the troops had been irritated
by seeing parties of Cossacks scouring the ground in front,
while the flash of steel could be seen amid the olive groves and
breastworks above the Alma, and at times a Russian standard
brandished as if in defiance of the lines that were approaching,
now wheeling, now deploying, extending and taking ground to

the right or left—a roar of musketry far away on the right flank announced that the fiery French had begun the attack, and were pouring forward in impetuous masses under a terrible shower of missiles of every kind. These masses were chiefly the fierce and active little Zouaves, flushed with their victories in Africa, and they were seen to swarm up the heights at the point of the bayonet, in their blue jackets and baggy red breeches, till they formed in two lines, and with a truly French yell, rushed on to close with the enemy !

On went our columns to close with them too, opening fire at half-past one. By that time, the cannon shots fell thick and fast among our ranks. Bursting at times in mid air, the shrill whistling shells fell in iron showers among them ; others ripped up the earth, scattering stones and splinters on every side. Now a bullet swept past unseen with a deep humming sound ; the next might tear a man in two, or hurl him away, doubled up like a muslin scarf ; another would bury itself deep in the ranks, making a lane of blood and death, of shrieks and agony.

" The slow ping, ping, *ping* of those Minié rifles—don't at all like it," said Probyn.

" Daresay not," replied Meredyth Pomfret, whose face was flushed with boyish ardour and pride in carrying the Queen's colours. " But why particularly so ?"

" It is such deliberate potting, always suggesting that every bullet takes a human life."

" Well, it is just what a soldier's work is," replied the boy, bravely. " By jingo ; let us only get close to them !"

The burning village with its flaming stack-yards formed the centre of the British position.

To the right of it the 41st Welsh and the 49th regiments forded the Alma under a heavy fire from the Minié rifles of the Russians who there lay snugly *perdue* in rear of some vineyard walls, over which the purple grapes were hanging in ripe and heavy clusters ! while on the left of Burliuk the whole Light Division under old Sir George Brown (who had first smelt powder at the capture of Copenhagen in 1807) dashed across the stream and proceeded to storm the heights, which were so steep in some places, that in several instances the enemy's bullets traversed the spinal column, as they were shot sheer down upon the assailants.

Cyril's regiment was in the same division with the 33rd, the Welsh Fusileers, the 19th, 77th, and 88th, all which pressed on with such fury that they speedily routed the Russian riflemen out of the vineyards, carrying the walls at the point of the bayonet, and pushing on beyond these, a few only pausing at times to snatch a handful of those grapes which proved so de-

licious to men furiously excited, and sorely athirst, after their
long march in a hot and breathless morning.

Waving their caps and swords in front, their officers led them
on, amid tumultuous cheers.

"Forward, the Fusileers !"

"Forward, Twenty-third !"

"On, on—Nineteenth and Seventy-seventh !"

"Forward, forward ! aim under the cross-belts."

Such were the cries from officers and men on all hands, as
·the scarlet tide pressed upward ; but they were mingled with
many a shriek and groan, for the Russian shot fell thick as hail,
and every moment the dead and wounded were dropping in the
ranks. But now began that famous up-hill charge, by which
the field was won ; the dark Rifles meanwhile taking the hills
in flank, as coolly as if at drill on Chatham Lines.

The supports were the Duke of Cambridge's Division of
Guards and Highlanders.

Cyril could see before him but a cloud of smoke, amid which,
at times half seen, half lost, were the figures of Sir George
Brown, on a grey charger, and Sir Edward Elton, on his black
one. A shower of lead, heavier than usual,.tore through the
ranks of the division. Colonel Chesters, of the Twenty-third,
and eight of his officers, fell almost at the same moment, and
their brave Welshmen were nearly decimated. Sir George
Brown fell amid a cloud of dust, and, for a moment, it was supposed that he was killed.

The Royal Fusileers then wavered for a moment, but re-
formed, shoulder to shoulder, as Sir George sprang to his feet
and again led on the whole. The first of Sir Edward's officers
who fell was Captain Joyce ; a bullet shattered his head and
his body rolled down hill. The three next were Bingham,
Jack Probyn, and young Pomfret. The first was literally cut
in two by a round shot ; the second was pierced in the heart by
a ball, and bounded into the air ere he fell dead. The third
had the standard-pole splintered in his hand by a ball, which penetrated his breast, and he was left behind to die in great agony.
Ned Elton snatched the colours from his relaxed hand ; but in
a minute after he too fell, a leg being smashed by a Minié bullet.
Relief after relief were shot under that fatal colour ; but still
the human tide went rolling upward and onward, cheering
wildly as their growing enthusiasm became mingled with a thirst
for vengeance, and a longing to grapple with the foe !

A roar as of thunder, was in the air, and a hell of fire seemed
in front of them.

Meanwhile, wounded officers and men, in hundreds, were
being borne to the rear by bandsmen, on stretchers, or crawling
to the river side to quench their thirst—in many instances the

thirst of the dying. Though nine hundred of all ranks fell on the slope of the great redoubt, amid the vineyards and the perilous abattis of trees; and though the colours of the Twenty-third Welsh Fusileers were actually planted on it, and the Russians expelled by the bayonet, the victory was not yet decided.

From a higher range of the hills, there rushed upon our now breathless, blown, and shattered troops, a heavy double column of Russian Infantry—the regiments of Ouglitz and Vladimir; one wearing flat caps, the other with spike-helmets. A great, grey, solid mass, they came on with equal ardour and fury, strong in the belief of the conquest which the Bishop of Moscow had predicted would accompany the image they bore—that of St. Sergius—a hideous idol of carved and painted wood.

It was then that the British ranks began to waver, and even to fall back a little way, leaving in and near the redoubt several wounded, who were mercilessly bayonetted, or brained by the clubbed muskets of the Russians, who, in some instances, hewed off fingers in their eagerness to possess the rings of those they murdered.

By this time, no less than nineteen serjeants of the Thirty-third had perished, chiefly in defence of the regimental colours; and most fatal would the temporary repulse have been, but for the re-advance of that corps, with the Fusileers and the Guards and Highlanders of the Duke's division, when the conflict was renewed in all its fury.

The appearance of the Highlanders, in their strange costume, as their brigade advanced in successive *échelon* of regiments, with their tartans and black plumes waving in the wind, seemed to impart some superstitious terror to the Russians, who almost immediately began to waver.

A close and deadly volley was poured upon them. No sound in particular followed, save the yells of the wounded, while the Highlanders "cast about" to reload; but after their next volley, a strange rattling was heard, as the bullets fell fast among the tin canteens and kettles which the enemy carried outside their knapsacks, for they were all *right-about-face* now. Then a cry—a literal wail of despair—came from them, as they broke their ranks and fled, throwing away muskets, packs, caps, and everything that might impede their speed.

Holy Russia was no longer invincible! "The Angel of Light had departed from her, and the Demon of Death had come!" Three generals, seven hundred prisoners, and about seven hundred and fifty of their wounded, remained in our hands, according to Mr. Kinglake, though other authorities have given them as many, many more.

The Heights of the Alma were won; but three thousand three hundred of the Allies lay killed and wounded on their green slopes, which were dotted for miles by spots in scarlet, blue, or grey—each *spot* a human corpse, or a man in mortal agony from bayonet or gun-shot wounds !

Among the latter was Cyril Wedderburn !

At the very moment when his splendid, but sorely cut-up regiment, led by Sir Edward Elton, was rushing with the bayonet in pursuit of the foe beyond the Kourganè Hill, he was lying near the river, covered with blood and dust, and presenting a piteous spectacle. On two crossed muskets he had been borne there, to have his maddening thirst quenched and his wounds attended to.

When the troops were recoiling, after the capture of the great redoubt, he had found himself close to Horace Ramornie, who was endeavouring to assist a Russian officer of rank, as the number of his medals and stars evinced, and who was lying, half smothered, under his dying horse, in the chest of which a cannon-shot was imbedded.

They succeeded in dragging him out, and raised him to his feet ; but the barbarian—in whom, with the speed of thought, Cyril recognised the spy of Varna, the pretended Captain of Zouaves—drew a revolver from his belt, and, inspired by all the terror of capture, and the hatred of race and religion—for by these emotions his face, a handsome one, was quite distorted—he fired at both his protectors, and retired among his advancing men, escaping several shots that were sent after him by the exasperated Fusileers.

Horace escaped uninjured, but poor Cyril had his left arm wounded by one ball, while another penetrated his left breast. He sank into the arms of his kinsman, who uttered a cry of mingled rage and commiseration, and had him borne to the rear by two of the band ; but he could do no more, having to lead his company, of which he was now the only surviving officer.

By this time, the Turks and French were in full pursuit of the enemy, whose last efforts were a few faint struggles, and a disorderly and scattered fire. Hereditary hatred and religious rancour alike inspired the Turks, whose shrill cries of " Allah, Allah Hu !" came at times, upon the wind ; for they still boast themselves to be the *Assakiri Mansurei Mohamediyes*—the " Victorious troops of Mohamed," and until the day of Balaclava they had always fought with honour.

CHAPTER LIV.

THE 21ST OF SEPTEMBER.

It was not until the next day that Horace could discover—and only after a long, painful, and exciting search—where his cousin Cyril was lying, and had lain all night, in extreme suffering and misery.

The night after the storming of the Russian intrenched camp, Horace slept soundly—the deep sleep of that utter exhaustion consequent to intense bodily toil, the heat of the march before the engagement, and over exhaustion of the mind. He did awake once or twice, to see around him, as in a confused dream, the darkness of the chilly night, and, that something of the picturesque might not be wanting, groups of soldiers, lying or sitting, and smoking or chatting round fires of turpentine, olive and willow trees, of Russian muskets and gun carriages, that flamed high above their heads, and caused the piles of muskets to glitter in light. These were the men who, but a few hours before, had been amid all that wild carnage, and were now quietly toasting little scraps of food in the blaze by which they warmed themselves, and which lit up their bronzed faces with a ruddy glow, and displayed their varied and, in many instances, torn and blood-stained uniforms.

Some were moaning over a wounded arm, or a bloody and recently bandaged stump, which they rested on a bed of branches, and thousands were lying about, in every attitude expressive of exhaustion.

So most of the army passed the night after we won the Alma ; though some who were less worn out than others spent it in seeking over the field for those whom few or none could help them to find.

By the first ray of dawn, and while the red sun was rising above those hills that, on one side, look down on Simpheropol, and on the other overhang the windings of the fatal Alma, Horace, with a few of the Fusileers, had left the bivouac, and, without seeking food or refreshment, engaged in the melancholy and heart-rending task of searching over the field for his cousin, Cyril Wedderburn.

The two bandsmen by whom he had been borne away had been killed subsequently, and no one could say where they had laid him down, to bleed to death of his wounds, too probably.

Horace thought sadly of the many fine fellows gone for ever —those whose faces he should never look upon again ; Jack Probyn, with whom he had played so many keen games at billiards ; Bingham, whose handsome figure and winning manner made him a favourite with all women ; Joyce, poor old Singleton (the man with the secret sorrow), and merry little Meredyth Pomfret, who was such a first-rate "bat," and so many of the brave rank and file too. He was full of depressing and harrowing thoughts.

Unstripped by "death-hunters," or a plundering peasantry (as those were who fell in the wars of Wellington, and left bare

and ghastly under the eye of heaven), the soldiers here were all
lying, whether dead or wounded, fully clothed and accoutred,
just as the shot had struck them down in their ranks.

Many of the killed lay on their back, with their arms uplifted, as if still levelling their muskets, in all the cataleptic
stiffness which so often results from gunshot wounds. "The
upstretched arms of dead men were ghastly in the eyes of some;
others thought they could envy the soldier released at last from
his toil, and encountering no moment of interval between hard
fighting and death." And over this scene rose the cloudless
sun of a lovely September morning, glowing on the tender
green of the willow and olive groves tossing their leaves in the
warm, soft breeze, and suggestive of delicious tranquillity rather
than the carnage of war.

The unfortunate braves of the Welsh Fusileers lay over each
other literally in piles, amid dark pools of blood, in which the
flies were battening; and wherever the cannon shot had bowled
in their deadly career, lay bodies without legs, or heads, or
arms, crushed, rent, and torn in some instances out of all
semblance of humanity; and there were grey haired officers
who had fought in other lands, in India, Persia, and Afghanistan, lying side by side with our poor boy-subalterns, slain in
all the splendour of their *first* red coat—fresh from school and
from their parents' arms.

Many a familiar face of his own corps was seen by Horace as
he passed along, but they were pallid and still; no glance of
recognition came back from the fixed and glazed eyes; no
smile was on the open marble mouth. Among others, he
saw young Meredyth Pomfret, lying dead with his hands as if
yet clutching the colour-staff, the belt of which was still over
his shoulder. He turned away with a sinking heart, and he
knew that Cyril could not be there.

All who could speak were inquiring for water, or to learn
when they would be taken to the rear and have their sufferings
alleviated. Others begged only for a match or a pipeful of
tobacco.

In their long grey coats, in many instances cuffed and
collared with scarlet, the grim Russians lay thick, like swathes
in a harvest field, along the Kourganè Hill, and all about the
great redoubt. Many had fallen in the act of reloading, and
lay with a steel ramrod in their hand, or a half-bitten cartridge
between their teeth. A ghastly grin or defiant smile was
visible in some of their dead faces; and in many instances there
were men of the 23rd and other corps of the Light Division,
who appeared to have perished in the act of supplication or
entreaty.

These were the wounded whom the merciless Russians butchered, when the division wavered on the crest of the hill.

Hairy knapsacks, glazed helmets, and the coarse, clumsy firelocks of the Russian infantry lay scattered there in thousands, just as they had been cast away; and clouds of ammunition paper were whirling over the sward.

Many acts of perfidy, similar to that by which Cyril fell, had been perpetrated by the enemy. In some instances our soldiers were shot down by the wounded whom they were supplying with water from their canteens. In this manner, Captain Eddington of the 95th perished under the eyes of his brother, who fell in the attempt to avenge him; and enraged by such treacheries, our soldiers clubbed their muskets and dashed out the brains of the perpetrators, as creatures totally unworthy of mercy or life.

Horace felt his heart growing more and more sick as he looked around him, and heard the incessant and afflicting exclamations of suffering, the result of wounds of every kind, and in all parts of the tender human form; stabs by bayonets, cuts by swords, musket shots, and the more dreadful casualties inflicted by cannon balls, grape, canister, and splintered shells; and if his tongue clove to the roof of his mouth with the intensity of his thirst, he thought, "What must these poor creatures be enduring!" But ere long the regimental and naval surgeons, with fatigue parties and seamen from the fleet, began to be busy among them.

Wandering down from the heights by the extreme British right, he came among the wounded of the French left flank, and there the Zouaves were lying thick as leaves in autumn. Two, who had each a limb bandaged tight by a bloody handkerchief, were seated with their backs against a large stone, smoking cigarettes, while a pretty vivandière, in a smart blue jacket and scarlet skirt, with the number of some regiment embroidered on her cap and shoulder-straps, was tripping about giving mouthfulls of brandy from her little barrel.

"Is she not charming—Pauline of ours!" exclaimed one of the smokers, admiringly.

"Mais certainement oui, charmante!" responded the other, and with great politeness they both saluted Horace as he passed them, though unable to rise; "and like ourselves she has breakfasted à la carte on grapes and cold water, most likely."

"Your regiment must have suffered severely," said he, "if we are to judge by the numbers lying here."

"Oui, Monsieur, we have lost twice as many as we did at Constantine. Diable! la fortune de la guerre est bien capricieuse!"

"True, Adrien," said the other, laughing; "but we gave those

Muscovites a sharp taste of our little Charlemagnes—our cabbage-cutters ;" for so the French soldiers name their sword-bayonets.

A man on the ground with his head propped upon some loose stones, attracted the eye of Horace at a little distance, for he was an officer and in the scarlet uniform of the Royal Fusileers, and proved to be Major Singleton !

He hastened to him, and found that he was just expiring of wounds, with a staff-surgeon, a somewhat elderly officer, had just been examining with great tenderness and care. The latter held up his hand warningly to Horace, as if to say, "Do not speak—it is useless." He had been pierced by two balls, each of which had inflicted a mortal wound. His filmy eye dilated as Horace bent over him ; then his jaw fell, the breath passed away, and the brave soldier who, yesterday had been face to face with the Russians, was now face to face with—his Maker.

"We can but leave him till the burial party comes," said Dr. Riversdale, with great emotion ; for, by a singular fatality, it was in his hands, almost in his arms, that the first husband of Isabel Vane—poor Conyers Singleton, died ! "Another officer of your corps," he added, "is lying near the river severely wounded—a Captain Wedderburn."

"In which direction ?" asked Horace, starting.

"Where those turpentine bushes are. I have just dressed his wounds."

"Oh, how shall I thank you ! It is he I have been in search of. Are the wounds dangerous ?"

"One may prove so. A ball has entered the left breast, and injuring the lung, has passed out under the shoulder-blade. I am not without hopes of him, however."

Horace hurried in the direction indicated, and there amid the turpentine bushes, the branches of which were quite alive with brown larks and golden linnets, unscared by the din of yesterday, in full melody, lay him he sought !

Cyril was lying on his back and breathing heavily ; his handsome face was pale as marble, and with his thick curly brown hair and well-curved moustache, Horace thought he looked like a manly and beautiful statue. His eyes were closed, but a quiver of agony at times passed over his features. His epaulettes had been torn off, probably by some passing Tartar of Burliuk. His uniform was open and sorely soiled, for bloody bandages traversed his breast. His whole aspect was intensely pitiable and forlorn. Alas for Cyril ! once so particular in his toilet, in the quality of his perfumes, the exquisite fit of his gloves and boots, and the general perfection of his apparel. His sword was still lying near his hand, and on hearing a step, he instinctively clutched it nervously, thus causing the blood to well forth anew from the wound in his breast.

Poor Horace was deeply moved.

"Oh, Cyril," thought he, "if that poor mother who dotes on you were to see you thus, sodden and damp with dew, splashed with blood and pierced with wounds ! Cyril !"

He opened his eyes, and a faint smile of recognition passed over his face as he took the hand of his cousin, who knelt by his side.

"Thank Heaven you have escaped, Horace," said he.

"Yes, Cyril, my dear fellow. Would to God that you had been so fortunate. I had my left epaulette shot away by one bullet, my cap knocked off by another, and my sword hand grazed by the splinter of a shell, but I am untouched. If that Russian scoundrel—the spy——"

"He may have got his deserts by this time and be lower than he has brought me. You will write to my father,—say, to break all this gently to my mother ; but then she will unfortunately see the Gazette first !" said Cyril, and now his voice failed him.

After a time he asked—

"Who of ours have fallen, and who escaped ?"

"I know not who have escaped, but I know that Bingham, Jack Probyn, Joyce, and Pomfret are all gone. Ned Elton had a leg smashed under the colours, and poor Conyers Singleton is lying dead among some stones yonder."

"Poor Joyce—his wife and children—he loved them so !"

"The colonel had his black horse shot under him, and then led the regiment on foot."

"I feel utterly sick of life, Horace. I hope I shall die— and I must, if this agony endures," said Cyril in a low voice through his clenched teeth.

"Do not speak or think thus. You shall soon be comfortably cared for. The wounded are ordered to be sent on board the fleet, and I shall see you off among the first."

Yesterday Cyril really had a mad desire to court danger—to tempt death, but not to be stricken down thus—almost assassinated, when assisting in an act of mercy ! Yet why should he have wished for death ? he began to think now. Did not his tender mother, his affectionate and manly father, love him, and Bob too, after his somewhat cold and legal fashion ? All his brother officers were his friends. The passing emotion was morbid and ungrateful ; yet, as he lay there, he sighed in his soul for one glance from Mary's eye—one touch of Mary's hand again !

Just as Horace was about to leave him in quest of assistance, a little midshipman with four seamen bearing stretchers passed

near, and he hailed them.   Into one of these he was carefully,
even tenderly, lifted, and conveyed towards the shore, while
Horace, with a prayer of hope that he might recover soon—for
he and Cyril were especial friends—turned away to attend to
his duties with the now shattered regiment—and these duties
were the reverse of cheerful.

Many vessels sailed with their melancholy freights for
Scutari; but on the voyage of three hundred and thirty miles
which lie between that place and the mouth of the Alma, many
a body was committed, coffinless, to the waves of the Euxine;
for many brave fellows were uselessly shipped who were mortally
wounded, and through routine, circumlocution, and infamous
parsimony, "there were not medical necessaries on board for
five out of fifty sufferers."*

"Ten men per company to bury the dead!" was the order
issued to each regiment on the morning of the 21st September.

During the two days subsequent to the battle, Horace was so
busy with one of the working parties who were ordered to
separate the dead from the wounded; to bury the former and
get the latter out of the field; collecting the abandoned Russian
arms and destroying them by fire, or otherwise, that he could
barely snatch a few minutes to dispatch a letter to Gwenny—
think what his aunt might of it, he could not resist the tempta-
tion of writing to *her*—with a brief detail of all that had
transpired.

And from this pleasant office which brought her bright face
and sweet presence and all the distinct *individuality* of the girl
so vividly before him, it was hard to turn to the grim task of
having those ghastly trenches dug, tenanted, and filled up.

Though reflective, he was not much of a sentimentalist; yet
as he stood by one of those hecatombs and heard the solemn
words of the surpliced regimental chaplain, reading the English
burial service—now that the fury of the battle had passed away,
his soul was stirred.   "The bitter pains of eternal death;"
"The certain hope of a resurrection to eternal life;" "For a
thousand years are in Thy sight as yesterday, seeing that is
passed as a watch of the night.   As soon as thou scatterest
them, they are even as a sleep, and fade away suddenly like
the grass."

An old sergeant of the Welsh Fusileers, whose son lay in
that grave, all belted and accoutred as when in life, made the
responses tremulously, and Horace felt moved by an emotion of
great pity.

To what end, or for what useful purpose had all this carnage
been?   Why had all those strong and, many of them, handsome
young men been cut off thus in the flower of their manhood?

* Letter of a medical officer.

For a time he thought war horrible—an utter desecration of God's fair earth; but anon the trench was filled, the drums beat for dinner, and the living soon forgot those dead with whom they might be sleeping on the morrow.

"My poor fellows! there lie one hundred and sixty of them!" said Sir Edward Elton, as he stood at the head of the long trench, with his sword arm slung in his crimson sash; "by this time they have learned the grand secret that lies between Time and Eternity. Well—well! God rest them! General and drum-boy, king and clown, we must all lie alike in our graves; there is no distinction there!"

CHAPTER LV.

WOUNDED AND MISSING.

THE summer was past, and the mellow tints of its successor were beginning to steal over the woods at Willowdean. September had come, the month of in-gathering, and brown autumn, the evening of the year, was creeping on.

There is usually then a great variety of tints in the Scottish woods; all gradations of green, from the tender paleness of the willow to the bronze-like branches of the sombre pine, mingling with every shade of fading foliage, from bright yellow to russet, brown, and red.

Autumn was beautiful as ever in the fertile Merse; the cattle lowed as usual on the pastoral hills of the Lammermuirs, over which the sun cast the flying shadows of the white clouds that came from the German Sea.

In the household at Willowdean, as elsewhere over all the British Isles, the public prints were eagerly scanned for their contents at that time; and the slow progress of our army in the East was watched with the keenest interest, for there were few in the land who had not either a relative or a friend who faced the pestilence at Varna, and the perils of war that followed it.

And every letter that came from the camp added to the craving for another; but during this anxious and eventful autumn, Willowdean House did not seem to wear its usual aspect. Lady Wedderburn had not her general circle of guests, and no friends were invited to pass the shooting season with Sir John. Robert was not much of a sportsman, so the gun-room was unentered, the preserves remained undisturbed, and the speckled grouse and the golden pheasants kept holiday together, the latter venturing even to feed among the barnyard fowls at the home farm.

Robert Wedderburn was far from being insensible to the beauty of Gwenny, and still more to the pleasing fact that she was an heiress ; and, regardless alike of his brother and cousin, he had striven to effect a footing in her good graces from the time Horace departed ; but strove in vain : for Gwenny's impulsive and susceptible heart was far away with our army of the East. His futile attentions, however, had been apparent enough to Lady Wedderburn, and had secretly pleased her.

"If Gwenny should happen not to care for Cyril," thought she, "let Robert have her by all means. Her fortune would quite enable him to cut the Temple and the dry study of the law."

Alone, the girl thought ever of the absent Horace Ramornie ; and all the scenes they had been wont to visit, even the objects of nature, seemed to the fanciful Gwenny full of his memory by association of ideas. The gurgle of the clear trouting stream that came from the hills and flowed under the old bridge in the *Dean*, or Den, which being fringed by overarching willows, gave a name to the place ; the voices of the birds, the thrush, the, blackbird and woodlark, among the shrubberies of the garden and the stately trees of the lawn, where they always sang most joyously after a shower had gemmed every leaf and flower ; the sweet perfume of the clover fields, where many a day they had ridden together and rushed their horses at the fences and turf-dykes, all somehow reminded Gwenny of Horace, the first and only love of her passionate girlhood, now far away facing peril and hardship, it might be to return no more !

That a change had come over her, even when visitors were present, was perceptible alike to Sir John and to Lady Wedderburn. The latter flattered herself that she was at last thinking of Cyril—that she had begun to see his merits, and to remember how attractive he was in person and manner ; but the former more shrewdly suspected the real state of matters, for Gwenny could not control her change of colour when the name of Horace was mentioned incidentally, though she betrayed no emotion whatever when that of his cousin occurred.

She never opened the piano now. To sing when Horace was no longer there to listen or to accompany her ; to laugh and talk or seem to enjoy the society of others when he was absent —oh, what might he not be enduring !—proved a bitter ordeal to her ; and to her kind uncle's observant eye it was evident that the girl was love-sick, but time he knew would cure all that.

We have shown by her treatment of the hapless Mary Lennox that Lady Wedderburn was neither an unjust nor unkind woman. The presence of her son in the field, and the obvious risks he ran there, led her, unlike Lady Ernescleugh, who was immersed in the gaieties of London, to turn her attention to works of charity and benevolence, even more than was her wont; to schemes for the amelioration of the poor ; to schools, emigration, little allotments of land on the estate—for her husband denied her nothing ; to teaching, visiting the peasantry and so forth, a system which soon caused her and Gwenny to be idolized at Willowdean, for she felt when doing all this good as if she gave hostages to Heaven for her son's safety.

Like every one else who had friends in the army of Lord Raglan, the Wedderburns were kept on the rack of keen expectancy during all that memorable week which ended the month of September. Even in mighty London every kind of business gave place or became secondary to this anxiety and anticipation. All knew that the allies had landed at Eupatoria, and all calculated to a nicety the day on which a battle must be fought—a battle in which the dearest and best-beloved of many might fall.

But it was not until the morning of the tenth day, *after* we won the Alma, that faint rumours through mercantile sources were heard in London, and with that evening came the telegram which announced the total defeat of the Russians, and that again, as in the glorious wars of old, our arms had been victorious !

By the following day (Sunday) it was known in Scotland, and in remote places where no electric wire could flash the intelligence ; for a whisper seemed to pass over all the land—a whisper which at first was full of exaggerations and mistakes, but it found an echo in every heart, from the apple bowers of Devonshire to the storm-beat isles of Orkney—a whisper of the great battle that had been fought in the strange land so far away. More keen and agonizing now became the expectancy. Lady Wedderburn thought of her son ; Gwenny of her lover Horace, —wounded or dying ; yes, it might be dead and buried afar off in that hitherto almost unknown land, so far as we were concerned, and the names of the places in which sounded so strange to the ears of those at home. That already all might be over for ever, was the haunting thought that wrung the aching heart of each.

Three days more passed ere Lord Raglan's telegraphed account of the battle in the *London Gazette* reached the secluded little town in the Merse ; and with a hand trembling Sir John unfolded the morning paper which Gervase Asloane had taken from the despatch box, while Lady Wedderburn and Gwenny quitted their places at the breakfast table, and drew near him with their faces pale and their eyes so full of eagerness and fear that an expression of expostulation escaped the calmer Robert ; and even the white-haired butler, and the stolid and bewhiskered footmen in plush, paused to listen for intelligence,

Skipping all the details, Sir John glanced nervously and hurriedly through the paper, seeking first the casualty lists of the battle ; and after running his eye down the regimental numbers, he suddenly exclaimed—

"Kate—Kate ! oh, my God, our poor boy !" and crushing up the paper, buried his face in his hands.

While both Lady Wedderburn and Gwenny burst into tears, fearing the worst, and a cry of terror escaped little Miss M'Caw, Robert quietly spread out the paper and saw the fatal line which had so moved his father. It came after the list of killed :

"Royal Fusileers ; Captain Cyril Wedderburn severely wounded. Since MISSING !"

CHAPTER LVI.
THE WINTER OF THE YEAR.

WHEN a little more composed they began to consider this catastrophe in its various lights. That he was wounded severely they could not doubt, but that he should be *missing* was a most perplexing and harrowing thought.* He might be a prisoner in the hands of the Russians ; or he might too probably have crept away, as many did, to bleed to death and die unseen—a terrible thought ! and thus his fate might never be known.

His pale mother had but one distinct idea—Cyril was wounded and missing too ; wounded and suffering she knew not, and might never know, in what fashion or degree ; and her motherly hands were not there to nurse and tend him. Her pet boy— the apple of her eye—Cyril, always so tender and loving to her !

All her worst, her darkest, and most terrible anticipations seemed to be fulfilled now—so suddenly too, in the first battle. Oh, that she could fly to him ! Oh, that she had acceded to the Ernescleugh scheme of the yacht voyage ! Horace had escaped ; but why was Cyril missing ? Horace could, should, and *must* know all about it. And, as she wrung her hands she thought, amid all the luxury and splendour of her home, how futile it was to reckon on earthly joys, they were at best so fleeting !

Then as she looked over the lists and saw how many other mothers must be suffering even as she then suffered, she prayed for strength and calmness to bear her cross ; and prayed too as only a mother can do, who yearningly supplicates for her son's safety and cure.

* From the time of the first landing in the Crimea till the capture of Sebastopol, September 8, 1855, no less than 13 of our officers, 23 sergeants, and 468 rank and file were reported missing and never traced.

A few more anxious days and the same despatch-box which has already figured in our story contained tidings from the seat of war—the letter from Horace to Gwendoleyne Wedderburn. It simply announced that we had won a great victory; and then detailed the mode in which Cyril had been wounded.

This added anger, even an emotion of rage, to the grief of his mother on learning that he had fallen when performing an act of mercy and compassion. How bitterly in her heart she thought of that treacherous Russian! If her son should indeed die of the wounds his hand inflicted, the malediction of a sorrowing mother would follow his assassin to the grave! Never, never would she forget or forgive

"The deep damnation of his taking off."

For Gwenny's behoof Horace could not resist saying a little about himself:

"I had a narrow escape from a shot, nearly the last fired by the Russian artillery. I was in the act of closing up the ranks of my slender company (Probyn by this time was killed), when a *round black spot* caught my eye. I knew what it was by instinct, Gwenny; for I had heard it said by old soldiers, that you can never *see* a cannon ball unless you are in its line. I threw myself flat on the turf with a breathless exclamation, and at that instant it cut in two one of my men, and his covering file also. I felt the wind of the shot as it passed over me!

"We are eager to attack Sebastopol before the fortifications are increased, as they are sure to be if any more delay ensues; and when they echo to the drums of the British Grenadiers, the latter will prove better arbiters than those absurd Quaker fellows who lately tried the peace-at-any-price dodge with old Nick, the Emperor. We go in for any amount of shot and shell, risk and danger here; we endure much more than I can describe; but I care little how the time passes as it is not spent with *you* at home. My very soul seems to go with this to you—*all*," he felt himself compelled to add, "and my tears are falling on the paper, Gwenny. I know not what I write, or what I have written; I have no time to read it over, for already the bugles are sounding for the advanced guard to fall in, as we move at once when the last of the dead are buried."

And Gwenny's voice broke as she read that letter which poor Horace had penned on a drum-head, amid the harrowing carnage of the the field—amid that terrible grey "acre of Russian wounded," groaning for water, tobacco, and sour-krout, while his thoughts travelled forward to the time when the white hands of her he loved would open and read it, and when her dark eyes might look so earnestly and sweetly over the lines his hand had written, perhaps drop a tear on them in secret and unseen.

"It is always of himself, and not of my Cyril he writes," said Lady Wedderburn, almost with anger; "but continue."

"Already Gwenny," she read, "our once gay uniforms are in rags, the lace black, the epaulettes vanished. Our once splendid bands have been turned into the ranks, or are decimated by cholera and the bullet. We have no mess, and all the brilliance of military life in time of peace has gone. We are wretched and filthy, tattered, unkempt and unshaven as gipsies, or the homeless poor of London."

"He calls you simply 'Gwenny,'" said Lady Wedderburn, looking over her gold eyeglasses; "it is scarcely courteous, as I have often said you are *not* cousins."

Gwenny blushed in silence, but the blush was seen and noted too by Robert.

"He does not seem to have fallen in again with that odious fellow Chesters," said Sir John.

"Horace is frightfully vague about Cyril after the battle," resumed Lady Wedderburn, who could not but resent something in the tone of the letter; "he says that he saw him borne *towards* the boats, but why did he not see him carried on board of the ship personally? Oh, my boy—my poor boy may have died, or been taken prisoner on the way!"

"Scarcely prisoner, in rear of our lines," said Robert, sententiously.

"And if dead, dear Kate," added Sir John, in a low and husky voice, "he must have been found, and not returned as missing. I cannot understand it."

And so for a time sorrow and perplexity reigned at Willowdean, while all there waited each successive mail in hope and fear; and while letters and cards of condolence poured in from all the county, together with an address from the inhabitants of the little Burgh of Barony, signed by the Bailie thereof, and an exhortation from the Reverend Gideon M'Guffog, stuffed with the usual stereotyped crumbs of comfort.

Though she sorrowed for Cyril, and deplored the mystery that seemed to envelope his fate, Gwenny nightly, and on her knees, thanked God for the safety of Horace; but then natural anxiety suggested the fear of what might not have happened since that 22nd of September, when he wrote his hasty letter on the Russian drum, and the bugles were sounding for the advance to the front!

On discovering the mistake in the Gazette, Horace lost no time in telegraphing direct to Willowdean, stating that Cyril was *not* missing, but was in the hospital at Scutari, and was believed to be doing well. Then he further wrote to mention that the announcement which gave such pain to the family, was caused by his inability to report to the adjutant who made up the lists, that he had seen his cousin carried out of the field by seamen, as he was busy for two entire days with a working party interring the dead ; and now the army was before Sebastopol, in the harbour of which, to bar all entrance, the Russians had sunk their splendid fleet, adding the crews, in battalions, to the strength of the garrison.

Some endearing terms to Gwenny were perceptible enough in this letter ; but his aunt felt that she could forgive the writer out of the great relief he gave her heart.

Cyril was safe, and, as she hoped, recovering !

The newspapers teemed with harrowing details of the war ; the bombardment of Sebastopol began ; the terrible slaughter of our Light Brigade at Balaclava made all Britain thrill with sorrow and enthusiasm ; the two battles in the valley of Inkerman followed ; the carnage of the last saw Horace a captain ; but still he escaped without a wound ; and then began the protracted sufferings in the trenches and rifle-pits—the horrors of the close siege during a Crimean winter.

The letters of Horace were always cheerful ; but he had now learned the policy of writing them to Lady Wedderburn alone.

The winter of the year came on with great severity at home —with greater still by the shores of the Black Sea. Flights of wild Norwegian pigeons were seen on the hills of Fife and Lothian, and such are always a sign of heavy and protracted snows in the north of Europe.

It was Christmas-day at Willowdean, as it was all over God's fair world. A few friends, the minister and his wife, the Baron-Bailie, and so forth, were there ; but when Lady Wedderburn saw the luxuries around her, the blazing fire, the glittering crystal, the fine linen, rich china service and massive plate, the chandelier decorated with shining holly and scarlet berries, the various courses at the table, the fish, and beef or mutton ; the fowls, puffs, custards, and creams ; the rich wines placed before Sir John, after being solemnly and carefully decanted from cobwebby old bottles in secret binns known to Asloane only, she sighed and thought with sorrow of her poor Cyril, lying in his hospital bed, a wretched pallet, fed on meagre broth or *bouillon ;* and she thought too of those who were shivering amid the mud of the frozen trenches, or dying of cold and starvation within sound of the bells of Sebastopol, or crawling back to their huts half dead with exhaustion, bearded, tattered, and squalid ; and where their only luxury might be a little half-ground and half-green coffee, boiled on a wretched fire, made of damp wood from the nearest thicket, or the wrecks made by the great hurricane in the Euxine.

Gwenny's astonishment when she found one winter morning her window panes all frosted over in the fashion of thistle leaves, was great indeed, and she wondered if the cold was as great in the Crimea as at Willowdean. And in common with all the ladies in the land, she and Miss M'Caw knitted all manner of worsted things—a labour of love for our poor soldiers.

Crisp lay the snow over all the level park, over all the hills, and nowhere so crisp as in the broad gravelled walks of the garden. Long icicles hung from every eave and cornice ; the Leader and even portions of the Tweed were frozen hard, and the linns where erst the torrent roared between rock and scaur, were congealed and white as the beard of Father Christmas.

It was a season when the flakes lingered long on the Lammermuirs. The white snowdrops did not appear till April ; and the purple lilacs and gold laburnums, the pink and white hawthorns, did not bloom till after midsummer in the woods of Willowdean ; but ere that time came great events had taken place there, as well as elsewhere.

After the first month of spring, mail succeeded mail as usual from the East ; but to the terror and grief of Gwenny, the letters of Horace ceased altogether, and a great horror filled the heart of the girl, lest something fatal had occurred !

On the other hand, to give joy to the soul of Lady Wedderburn, there came to her a letter from Cyril himself ! He stated that at Scutari all had nearly been over with him ; but he had found one of the dearest and most loving little nurses in the world ; and that through God's grace and her care he was now almost well—quite convalescent, able to ride about the streets, to have a sail on the Bosphorus, and bully the extortionate Caïquejees. Then suddenly in one letter he seemed to write in an agitated and disturbed state of mind, saying that a great grief had come upon him, and that he would not—yea, might never—return home on leave as his mother wished and urged ; but he was to rejoin his regiment, and be "in at the death of Sebastopol."

The silence of Horace, and the mysterious grief to which Cyril so abruptly alluded, occasioned endless surmise and much perplexity at Willowdean ; but now spring had come, and with it came a letter from Lady Ernescleugh, then in England. After the usual details of the gaieties of some friend's country-house where she had spent much of the winter, she wrote thus :

"The commander of my son's yacht writes to me stating that she is quite ready for sea, and I mean to sail with her for the East next month, Lord Cardigan's yacht and others are now in the harbour of Balaclava. *Will you accompany me ?* Many officers' wives are content to endure the discomforts of a residence at Constantinople, for the purpose of being nearer the scene of those terrible events which are daily occurring ; and there, or even at Malta, letters and news will reach one much sooner than when in England. I am sick of London, and Ernescleugh is odious to me without Everard. The doctors have prescribed a change of scene, and I do so long to see my dear boy. or be near him. As yet, thank God ! he has only been slightly wounded at Inkerman ; but matters will go hard with me if I do not bring him home in the yacht, and his father also, from Corfu."

This letter, together with her desire to unravel the mystery of Cyril's conduct, which she attributed to a love freak for some Turkish damsel (an odious creature, who wore trousers, sat cross-legged, smoked a chibouk, and eat pilau with her fingers), together with the strange silence of Horace, decided Lady Wedderburn on travelling with her friend.

So slowly had passed the days at Willowdean, that Gwenny hailed with rapture the prospect of a change, and the antici- pated voyage. To see those places towards which the thoughts and hearts of all were turned ! Perhaps--oh ! what joy—to see Horace himself ! The girl became wild with delight. Stamboul, Varna, the Crimea, and the Black Sea should no longer be as mere names to her when she had seen and could remember them distinctly, as she did " dear Madras and papa's lovely house in the Choultry."

And so it was arranged that Miss M'Caw was to govern at Willowdean in their absence, and that Robert Wedderburn should escort them to London, whither Sir John—who was in Parliament representing some snug little English borough in the Conservative interest—had preceded them.

" My foolish Kate," he wrote to Lady Wedderburn, " in this proposed Crimean escapade of yours, you will be compelled to behold many a scene of horror you do not reckon upon !"

CHAPTER LVII.

SCUTARI.

In the reference to Cyril's letters, we have somewhat anticipated a portion of his story.

The steam frigate on board of which he had been conveyed, ran straight for Scutari with her freight of sufferers, whose number lessened every hour. as the mortally wounded, or those who were totally exhausted by loss of blood, expired, and were shot over to leeward, tied up in a blanket, or, more simply still, in their grey great-coats. Cyril endured great agony from his principal wound, together with an extreme difficulty of respi- ration, and even when awake he lay as one in a kind of dream, in the cabin generously resigned to his use by an officer of the ship. At times he seemed still to hear the din of battle in his ears; the sharp roar of the musketry, the booming of the artillery, the crash of exploding shells and rockets, the demon-like yells of the Russians, and the tumultuous cheering of our own troops as they closed in upon them, and the cries of the wounded, as they rolled in their agony, and tore up the grass with their fingers. But this was only the result of an over-heated fancy, for the only sound he heard was the rush of the shining waves as they passed the open gun-port while the frigate sped on her way.

On the third day after the battle he was very languid and weak, yet his listless eyes could see, through the gun-port, that land was in sight. Beautiful green hills were there, tall minarets of snowy whiteness, great round leaden domes; and recognising Scutari as they neared it, he closed his eyes wearily.

After a time he was sensible of being lifted on a stretcher tenderly and kindly, by the hands of sailors, and found himself in the open air and on a quay, with many more of the wounded, surrounded by a staring crowd of picturesque-looking Greeks, in scarlet fezzes, blue breeches, and laced jackets; stolid look-ing Turks, with great turbans; swarthy Arabs, Negro slaves, and filthy Jews, with their sly, gleaming eyes and long gaber-dines; all of whom the Marine escort put back with their bayonets, and without much ceremony. Through this motley mob he was conveyed, past the magnificent pile of buildings which an Italian architect constructed as a barrack for the Turkish troops (but which was then full of our own conva-lescents), to the hospital, which was filling fast with wounded, as ship after ship arrived from the shore of the Alma with her human cargo, in the shape of mangled, emaciated, moaning, and quivering unfortunates, in uniforms that became rags, sod-den and saturated with mud and gore; and they were laid side by side in the wards, pell mell, many of them on the bare floor, where, through want of sufficient attendance, the atmosphere soon became tainted with the horrid odour of undried blood; causing the shocked onlooker to long for the day—if it will ever come—when the shedding of it should cease, and "when war shall be no more."

The name and rank of each man, together with the number of his regiment, were asked, as the patients were borne in. Some could reply to all that was required of them; but many a poor fellow was past utterance, and could only gaze with listless and lack-lustre eyes at the questioner, who would enter him in the hospital books as "a private of the Seventh Foot," "cor-poral, Twenty-third Fusileers," or the "Guards," or "Cameron Highlanders," and so forth.

Thus they were carried in, in too many instances to die un-

named and unknown, by their fate recalling the touching lines
that appeared in a periodical :—

> " Into a ward of unwhitewashed walls,
>   Where the dead and the dying lay—
> Wounded by bayonets, shells, and balls—
>   Somebody's Darling was borne one day.
>
> " Somebody's Darling ! so young and so brave,
>   Wearing still on his pale, sweet face,
> So soon to be hid by the dust of the grave,
>   The lingering light of his boyhood's grace.
>
> " Somebody wept when he marched away,
>   Looking so handsome, brave and grand ;
> Somebody's kiss on his forehead lay ;
>   Somebody clung to his parting hand."

Cyril's room was in a lofty portion of the hospital, and, from a
window which was near his bed, he could see the blue Bosphorus sweeping by the base of the dark-green mountains of
Scutari, and all the far-famed Golden Horn—seeming such indeed, for the waters round it were tinted with all the splendour
of the Eastern sun. And, while thinking sadly of the slaughter
that had fallen upon his regiment, and of the faces he never
more should see, his eyes gazed with a species of vacant wonder
on Constantinople, which seemed like a cluster of fairy cities
beside the strait, each a very wilderness of shining domes,
painted cupolas, gilded and red-tiled kiosks, tall minarets, and
marble fountains, the snow-white palace of the Sultan towering over all ; the background, dark cypresses and hills, and, in
the middle distance, a forest of masts, each bearing a flag, for
the waters of the Bosphorus were full of merchant ships, war-
steamers, swift caiques that cleft them as if instinct with life,
and shoals of glittering dolphins surging past from wave to wave.
    For a time he was tormented by the groans and cries of an un-
fortunate young Chasseur d'Afrique, who, by some mistake, had
been brought away with our wounded, and who shared his
room. The left shoulder of this unhappy creature had been
shattered by a large grapeshot, and the wound was perfectly in-
curable ; but life was wonderfully tenacious within him. On
the second day his ravings ceased, and turned to prayer :—
    " *Sainte Vièrge, priez pour moi—pour moi !*" he would say
imploringly, and then murmur softly, with quivering lips and
tearful eyes, " *Ma Mère—O, ma Mère !*" in that touching and
childlike spirit of devotion which the French soldier has peculiarly for his mother.
    On waking one morning, Cyril found that he was alone ; for
the poor Chasseur had been taken to his last home, near those
solemn cypresses which cast their shadows on that city of tombs,

outside the walls of Scutari—the seven miles of cemetery where the followers of the Prophet lie.

For many days Cyril Wedderburn hovered between life and death, while patients poured into the hospital so fast, that the surgeons and nurses had more work on their hands than they could attend to. There was a perpetual and offensive odour of poultices, *bouillon*, preserved meats and jellies about the place, as they were carried to and fro ; while the rending of the shirts and sheets of the dead into bandages for the living, together with the manufacture of cushions and pillows for limbs that had undergone amputation, went briskly forward in the passages and yard without.

A night of restlessness and weariness—with its occasional waking fits, during which, to the eye of the sick or ailing, a kind of phantasmagoria peoples the darkness, strange faces come of it, and fancy fills the air with odd sounds—was passing slowly away. Dawn stole into Cyril's room. The Bosphorus and all the domes and windows of Constantinople were beginning to glitter in light, as the sun rose above the hills of Scutari ; and like many others in that abode of suffering, Cyril woke with a sigh, to think that another weary day of pain and inertia was before him. So faint and weak had he become, that there were times when he wished to die, and would mutter, as he lay with closed eyes—" If I have not done much good in the world, I have not done much harm, and now I could pass peacefully away."

He was too dimsighted by the loss of blood to be able to read, even had he been supplied with books, and thus his days were days of utter weariness.

On this morning his throat was parched, and he called feebly to the soldier who usually attended him for water ; but the soldier—one of the Black Watch, whose left hand had been shattered by a canister-shot—did not reply, so Cyril sighed and wearily closed his eyes again.

Something like a tear fell on his face, and starting, he looked up, but only to shrink back with emotions of alarm and fear, so he covered his pale face with his thin hands.

" Cyril," said a voice, and a sob mingled with his name. Then he trembled, for it sounded like a voice that once had power to thrill his heart to its inmost core.

Was it all a dream, or was he going mad? Had the excitement of the battle, or the crash of the bullet as it traversed his body, given his brain a shock so rude, that sense and imagination wandered now?

No ! she on whose shoulder his aching head reclined, whose hand caressed his now tangled hair, whose tear had fallen on his cheek, and whose loving, yet deep and thoughtful eyes seemed to speak of a strange future, and of a sorrowful, it might be awful, past, was—Mary Lennox.

Cyril had been dreaming of his mother, and it had seemed as if her voice—the one he loved most and best in boyhood—was murmuring in his ear, calling him back to life ; and now it was the voice of Mary, and her soft earnest face, with a mingled expression of tenderness and agony, was turned towards his own.

She was very pale, rather emaciated, and dressed in a plain black costume, somewhat like that of a Sister of Charity, but without a hood.

" You here, Mary—here in Scutari—in this frightful hospital, and attending me ? Oh, explain this riddle, or I shall go mad —speak to me—place your hands in mine !" said he, huskily, in a low and imploring voice, as if he feared she would melt into thin air. But she answered, calmly—

" I arrived here, Cyril, three days ago from London, with Miss Nightingale and the staff of ladies who have come to nurse the wounded. Oh, Cyril Wedderburn, what was my emotion—my horror—when I learned that you were here !"

" Mary, it is frightful this, such work—such scenes—you will perish. Scenes of utter horror and affright ! What madness brought you here ?"

" It was no madness, but the prompting of my own heart, Cyril—a light that came to me from Heaven above, and the hope that I might be nearer—*you*, and now, now, oh my God !" she suddenly exclaimed, while placing her interlaced fingers on her forehead, and looking wildly upward ; "after all the sufferings, the terrors, and sorrow I have undergone; after all the most unmerited shame that was put upon me ; after enduring all the emotions of love, desertion, and despair, have I met you, but to see you thus—dying perhaps ?"

That Mary should have accompanied Miss Florence Nightingale —a young lady of good family, whose benevolent occupations fully qualified her for that remarkable and romantic undertaking, which made her and her trained nurses the idols of our soldiers, whose sick-beds they soothed, and whose pains and anxieties they did so much to console—fully explained to Cyril the reason of her sudden and most unexpected appearance in the Hospital of Scutari ; but we leave their subsequent conversation to explain how she escaped the death to which, when last we saw her, she was hastening.

Miss Nightingale and her ladies were as ministering angels in the terrible wards of that hospital ; and to the death-drowsy ear of many a wounded and sinking soldier there, how sweetly came the prayers and words of comfort they uttered in his *native* tongue.

CHAPTER LVIII.

HOW IT CAME TO PASS.

" Oh, Cyril," said Mary, in a low and earnest voice, and in her forcible way, after the first emotions excited by their sudden meeting had subsided a little, " I have undergone much that might have made my poor father's bones turn in their grave, by reason of my exceeding misery ! Though young in years, I am old in suffering: for in my brief time I *have* endured much."

" My poor Mary !" exclaimed Cyril, gazing with love and admiration on her pale beauty, which in its calm patrician style, consorted ill, or oddly at least, with her plain black stuff dress ; " tell me all that has happened since last we met."

" Since last we parted so unhappily, you should say, Cyril."

" My darling, tell me all !"

Then she briefly narrated her story up to that time when in despair, and in an evil moment overcome by shame and terror, she threw herself into the river, and a cry of horror escaped the listener as he struck his hands together ; but she had been providentially rescued by a waterman, and conveyed to a London hospital in a raging fever.

Cyril, who had listened to her in sorrow and commiseration, closed his eyes for a moment, and said in a hissing voice, through his clenched teeth—

" Oh, Chesters, there is a terrible account to be closed one day between you and me, and close it *shall*, if lead and powder avail men yet in their wrath and vengeance ! The rascally affair of the drugged horse — my beautiful bay hunter ; the foul cheating at play ; the attempt to disgrace you, my sweet Mary, at home and elsewhere ; poor Horace too in the transport —all, all make up a heavy score indeed, to be cleared between Ralph Rooke Chesters and Cyril Wedderburn."

" I was at first ungrateful enough not to thank Heaven for sparing my life," said Mary, " when I slowly recovered and the fever passed away. I was very, very weak, Cyril, and the professional politeness or conventional kindness of the hospital doctors and the hired nurses proved cold, hard, and unsoothing. I longed for the clasp of a friendly hand ; for the glance of an affectionate eye ; for a shoulder whereon I could lay my poor head and be at rest. Cyril, alas ! you were far away—you were no longer mine—and I felt myself lonely—oh, so lonely in the world ! I have endured and felt the bitterness of death when I sinfully sought it ; but not more bitter than what I endured on losing you."

" Do not heap ashes on my head, I implore you, Mary."

" In that hospital I recovered, yet only wished to die, for it seemed better, holier, purer, and every way safer to die then and be at peace, than to live and struggle on, friendless and hopeless ; and yet Chesters had artfully said such terrible things of the dead who die in such places, unknown and unclaimed, that my heart shrunk within me. But one day there came a lady, with a comely face and pleasing manner—a lady who seemed to take a great interest in me, who talked to me kindly and consolingly, whom I kissed, and who actually permitted me to press my thin, wan cheek to hers—yes, even to nestle on her breast, while I told her all my hapless story. Then she took a deeper interest in me—a lonely girl without father or mother—and spoke much of the good works one may do in this world.

" Prior to her coming, I had sometimes in my heart rebelliously questioned the justice of God in creating creatures such as I, only for trial and sorrow ; but she taught me that these thoughts were evil, and that I had no right to consider His reasons or purpose for chastening me. Then she spoke of her own mission, and said—" 'Come and be one of us in the East, where we are going to nurse our poor soldiers. Our hands are weak, but our hearts are strong and true.'

" I immediately agreed to be one of these good Samaritans, and then I thought myself at peace with God, the world, and—myself.

" ' I have been so long the nurse of my poor papa,' said I, 'that I shall be useful, I trust. I owe God some atonement too, for what I attempted—to rush unbidden into His presence !'

" The desire to devote myself to the cause of suffering humanity became an enthusiasm within me. Existence and its personal interests seemed to have lost all value to poor Mary Lennox. I had learned to feel that out of all grief we may attain to a nobler state of life than that of the world, and as I cherished these emotions, I felt myself growing better, holier, almost sublime, in my longing to do good. I have read that ' it is well for us to remember that we are only travellers and wayfarers on this earth ;' but sometimes it seems a little hard to think how few traces of our footsteps we leave behind us when the journey is finished."

" And these emotions and purposes brought you to this horrible Seutari ? To nurse all kinds of fellows, with all manner of wounds and dreadful diseases incident to camp and field ?"

A little colour came into her face as she replied—

" Yes, Cyril ; and perhaps a lingering desire, or hope, to be nearer you ; for though you had cast me off so cruelly, I felt that you were still—the husband of my heart. I did not desire to meet you because—because—but God has willed it otherwise. It is enough ! I resolved by doing good to consecrate to Heaven the life I had so wildly, in my despair, attempted to take away."

"My poor Mary! my poor Mary! my own love!" moaned Cyril.

Her voice was grave and sweet; even so was her soft, pale face, as she replied, meekly—

"You have no longer the right to love me, Cyril Wedderburn."

"Mary?"

"Your wealthy cousin——"

"She is engaged to Horace Ramornie!"

"And you never loved her?"

"Never! I have had many a flirtation, Mary, but never loved woman save you!"

"Chesters told me——"

"Chesters again! Curses dog his steps!"

Mary said nothing more, lest she might agitate him, and while her heart began to beat happily, and even some colour mantled in her cheek, she could not but recall that painful interview, when Lady Wedderburn, by her silence, seemed tacitly to admit of his engagement with that terrible and dreaded cousin!

"Oh, my Mary, my own!" said he, while caressing her hand, "such joy it is to hear your voice again—to feel your hand in mine. But your engagement-ring——?"

"Is gone, Cyril. It was taken from me after I was picked up senseless in the water, as I have told you."

"I will soon replace it, darling, by one that shall never be taken off your finger in life or death! I begin almost to believe in magnetic influences—in Mesmerism, and the Odic force."

"Why?"

"For never did the touch of a human hand thrill through me as yours does, dearest Mary. Now, why is this?"

"Because I love you!" she answered, with a beautiful smile.

If it be true that "to people who are in love each casual meeting is a new miracle," in which they fancifully see the finger of fate, or destiny, or the hand of Heaven itself, how bewildering to Cyril Wedderburn was this sudden re-union with Mary Lennox!

"The past is gone for ever," said he, after a happy pause; "let us forget it; but the present is ours yet, Mary, darling—my wee heather lintie," he added, sliding into the idiom of his schoolboy days; "my cushat doo, that has come all the way from the purple Lammermuirs to be my nurse and guide."

"Now you must not speak more, dearest Cyril. Already you have said too much," said Mary, drawing back from his extended arms.

Cyril was becoming flushed and excited, and it was fortunate that the arrival of the staff-surgeon, Dr. Riversdale, caused Mary to withdraw to another ward.

From that day Cyril's progress towards convalescence was marvellous ; and to get chicken broth, arrowroot, calf's-foot jelly, and an occasional glass of wine from Mary's pretty hand, was marvellous too ! Clever, versatile, full of expedients, she made an excellent nurse, and was adored by the soldiers, though they soon discovered that her chief favourites were the wounded of the Royal Fusileers.

Their separation, quarrel, and sorrow ; time, and their singular isolation in that remarkable place, made his love keener, stronger, and more tender than ever. Glory had suddenly become a myth and a sham ! He had fully earned his war medal, if the army was to have such a decoration ; he had acquitted himself as a soldier at the passage of the Alma, as he had already done in India. He had a fair claim for sick leave, prior to selling out, without the hollow pretence of "urgent private affairs ;" and leave he should have, and bring home a bride with him to Willowdean !

And in sketching out this joyous programme, he quite forgot any scheme for the exposure or punishment of Chesters.

Cyril saw it all—that happy future. All doubts cleared away, and Mary's wrongs atoned for, by the devotion of a life to her !

As he grew towards convalescence, however, he saw less and less of Mary. The rules laid down for her guidance as a volunteer nurse, the amenities of society, and proper policy alike required that she should only visit him at stated times, especially after he became well enough to ride about Scutari, to visit Chalcedon (and linger in the beautiful garden and plantain grove of Haider Pacha), remembering he had read in his schoolboy days, that Pliny had called it "the City of the Blind :" or to ride up the eastern shore of the Bosphorus as far as Asia, and once by the daily steamer to the Islands of the Princes, to see the tomb of Irene, and other places set forth in his "John Murray."

He was intensely anxious to get well, that he might put his plans in operation and remove Mary from the perilous and, as he thought them, degrading tasks to which she had devoted herself ; and, as a preliminary, he resolved to place her at Misseri's Frankish Hotel in Pera, where several officers' wives with whom he was intimate resided.

But man proposes, and God disposes !

CHAPTER LIX.

THE NIGHT MARCH TO TCHORGOUN.

"THE Royal Fusileers will parade in light marching order, and in their great coats, at twelve o'clock to-night, and march to

the rear of the Defence Works, to join the brigade of Sir Colin
Campbell, in his *reconnaisance* of the enemy's lines.   Officers
commanding companies to see that the men's ammunition is
completed to sixty rounds."

Such was the Brigade Order read by Horace on the evening
of the 20th February ; and he muttered, " Great coats, by Jove!
I should think so ;" for the atmosphere was bitterly cold, and
the unexpected parade was annoying, as he had provided a
little supper in his hut ; and being popular in the division, to
say nothing of the regiment, his guests would be sure to come,
each bringing his own knife, fork, and spoon ; and to some
such social gatherings they had sometimes to add their own
" grog and prog ;" for before Sebastopol an entertainment was
somewhat of a scramble, so far as viands and table appurtenances were concerned—a wretched picnic, with a perpetual shot-
and-shell accompaniment.

Horace, with the assistance of the Fusileer, his servant, had
contrived to make his hut pretty comfortable, and felt extremely
loth to quit it on the night in question.

He had constructed an arm-chair out of an empty flour-cask,
by sawing off the half of one side to the middle thereof, and
therein he took his repose, and enjoyed a " quiet weed " after
the fatigue of the trenches, or having a few hours' shooting
behind a sand-bag in the rifle-pits, while Beamish and others
who might drop in had to perch themselves on his " overland " or
bullock trunks.   But to turn out for a night march in the then
state of the thermometer, when he expected guests, and was
getting his bedfellow heated, was a decided bore—the aforesaid
" fellow " being a sixteen-pound shot which he was wont to
warm in the fire by which his supper was cooked, and placed
thereafter at the foot of his camp bed.

Rearward of his hut the wind was howling up from the
valley of Inkerman, where the graves of those slain in the two
battles lay under the winter snow ; it came into the hut by
many a crevice and cranny, together with a cloud of white
drift whenever the door was opened, so that his candle end,
which was stuck in a horn lantern, was often on the point of
extinction.

The swords of Probyn, Bingham, and two other poor fellows
who had fallen, were hanging on the wall until Horace could
get them transmitted home to sorrowing parents or friends.   A
few Russian muskets and leather helmets gleaned up from the
adjacent field (to be sent as trophies to Willowdean), with a
bucket, some black bottles, full or empty, tins of preserved
meat, a few cooking utensils, with a truckle camp bed, formed
the entire furniture of Horace's abode, which measured some
ten or twelve feet each way, and might have passed for the

wigwam of Robinson Crusoe ; but to see stray numbers of *Punch*, the *Illustrated News*, and monthly " Army List " would be an anachronism there.

The first who arrived was Everard Home, the Master of Ernescleugh, from the Guards' camp ; then came Beamish, young Hunton of the 34th, Ned Elton, limping after his wound received at the Alma, and two Cavalry men ; but save their swords and belts, little trace of regimentals (that good old word which is now going out of fashion) could be found upon them. All wore fur-trimmed over-coats of different kinds, caps with ear-covers, and huge warm gloves and mufflers, comfortable knitted things, the offerings of fair friends and tender-hearted Englishwomen, far away at home ; and all were thickly coated with snow.

" Welcome, Ponsonby, though the last," cried Horace to one of the Dragoons ; " but you can't close the door too quickly."

" True for you," added Beamish ; " that intrusive beast Boreas blows the snow in everywhere."

" I wonder what Beau Brummel would have thought of such ' damp strangers' as you ?" said Horace, laughing, as they shook the snow from their caps and outer garments.

Alas ! now for those who had been particular in their toilettes, who were careful in parting their hair, in the choice of colours for their cravats, and were puppyish in the tint and fitting of their gloves and curve of whisker ! In aspect all had become ragged and wolf-eyed, like desperadoes, and were no way ashamed of seeming so, for each made the other's costume a source of jest, and the cleverness with which he patched his own a boast.

Men who had been of the " best style" in London, and should be so again if spared ; the Brahmins of Society, the Flower of the Lady's Mile, the pinks of the Household Brigade, now frequently appeared in clouted boots and strange garments of their own stitching. Their dainty straw-coloured or lavender kids had given place to worsted muffatees and mits, cut out of old forage caps, and the waxen heath blossom at their button-hole, like the delicate exotics that accompanied it, were all things of the past.

Handsome fellows who had made many a white bosom flutter and many a beautiful eye grow brighter in Belgravia, and who had hitherto given much of their spare time to the cultivation of their whiskers, and staring through a plate glass of a club-room window, were now reduced to grease their own boots, thankful if they had the grease to do so, and glad to boil their own coffee, thankful if they had the coffee and the fire to boil it ; while Sybarites, who whilom had lisped slightingly of pale sherry, because it was " corked," condemned mess-room port,

and talked largely of vintage wines, had now to content them
with a mouthful of burning raki out of a wooden canteen, or of
Jamaica rum, the gift of a casual man-o'-war's-man.

And such were the condition and aspect of those who assembled in the hut of Horace Ramornie on this night of the 20th
of February ; but all were lively, laughing, full of pluck, and
only sorry that *their* regiments were not detailed to join in the
reconnaissance.

" A devil of a night to go though !" said Elton. " Are we to
be joined by the French ?"

" Yes ; Bosquet and Villenois come with four thousand men,"
replied Home, the Guardsman.

" And Colin Campbell's force——"

" With your corps, will muster about eighteen hundred
bayonets."

" There are some dragoons of the Turkish Contingent going
under that fellow Chester," said Hunton.

" A scoundrel who is knave enough to cheat the 'cutest fellow
in the Scottish Law List—and that is a strong one," added
Horace, aside to him.

His servant had by some means provided an ample supper
of ham and eggs, the savoury odour of which filled the hut ; to
this was added a little pie of larks, which the Zouaves were in
the habit of shooting and offering for sale.   When these viands
were discussed, cigars with brandy-and-water became the order
of the night.

" By Jove ! your cookery does you credit, Ramornie,"
exclaimed Home, who was seated on an inverted basket, with
his plate on his knees. " My fellow is clever in his way too.
He made a mess for me yesterday out of a slice from a goat
' found dead,' that Lucullus might have smacked his lips on
tasting."

" Had Lucullus been ass enough to come here," grumbled a
cavalry officer, " and not *do* ' Banting.'"

" It was quite an Apician meal."

" A truce to your classics, Home," said Horace, " or I shall
fancy myself at Sandhurst again ; and, in truth, I'd rather be
before Sebastopol."

" You here in the Crimea, Home ?" said a dragoon, suddenly
recognising the half-disguised Guardsman.

" By Jove ! I wish I was anywhere else," replied Home ;
" we last met at Maidstone, I think ?"

" Are you detailed for the trenches to-night ?"

" Yes ; at twelve o'clock we go to the front."

" I have not seen you, Ponsonby," said Horace, " since the
Balaclava day. By the way, how did you feel in the Cavalry
charge ?"

" Feel !" exclaimed the dragoon officer, as he tipped the ashes off his cigar, and his eyes sparkled ; " I felt as if impelled on, and on, and onward by some new and terrible impulse that amounted to mad exultation—the impulse to ride over, bear down, cut, thrust, and hew, to annihilate man, horse, and every-thing ! Our Colonel led us nobly till we were in the heart of that Russian horde, and then he fell, crying—

" ' Cut your way back, my lads ; go through them again like bricks ; they are only Cossacks, mounted on wretched screws !'

" But three of these Cossacks pinned the fallen man to the earth with their lances, for thus he was found by some of Scarlett's Brigade, when the heavies went in for work."

" Any more news of that spy, who has figured so often among us as a Captain of Zouaves ?" asked Beamish.

" No ; there is a sharp look out kept for him, but he seems to be a very ubiquitous personage."

" It's in luck I am," said Beamish, " having a supper like this, after actually eating a dinner to-day."

" I dined on nothing particular," said Ponsonby.

" But I had a veritable dinner, bedad ! and it is not every man who can make that boast before Seblastherpoll, as my servant Barney calls it. By the merest good luck I found a Turk lying dead, and in his havresack a chicken and a bottle of sherry—the forbidden of the Prophet. I have left only the bones of the one and the cork of the other, and did so with regret."

" Had you thoughts of swallowing them too ?" lisped Pon-sonby, who, though tattered and unshaven, still retained some-thing of his " man-about-town" air.

" What was going on at the left attack last night, Hunton ? There was an awful shindy made with those two Lancaster guns in your quarter."

" Can't say, Horace ; I was fast asleep—worn out. Never heard it, in fact. Besides, we are so used to the incessant pounding with those heavy cannon."

" Any word of Wedderburn from Scutari ?" asked Beamish.

" Getting rapidly well, and going home on sick leave."

" The wounding of him by that Russian was a rascally affair !"

" There goes the warning bugle for our fellows !" said Horace, as the notes of the signal rose and fell on the fitful wind, and he proceeded to invest himself in a thick overcoat. " I must leave you here to finish the night as you like—only please don't burn the hut down. House property is valuable here ; and there is one more bottle of brandy in the corner."

" I'll finish what I have here," said Beamish, with a sigh of regret, as he drained a bottle beside him ; " for who among us can be sure of coming back again ? The drink is uncommonly good. Who's your confiding merchant, Horace ?"

"A Sutler at Balaclava—oddivee : he writes it in his accounts. There's the bugle again, the men are falling in."

None would remain behind ; all were intent on watching, if possible, the *reconnaissance,* and so all rose to quit the hut together.

"By Jove ! Horace, in such an atmosphere as this——"

"What—of frost, Beamish ?"

"No, tobacco : it *is* mighty difficult to find the door of your —bungalow."

"If he doesn't think himself in India again, and the thermometer twenty degrees below the freezing point. Hope you feel warm, Pat ! What an imagination you have !"

"But an utterance getting thick and feathery," replied Beamish, who had imbibed more than sufficient of the cognac.

"What *are* you about ?" asked Horace, laughing heartily.

"I am searching the wall in vain——"

"For what ?"

"That orifice popularly known as a door."

"Here it is, and, by jingo, a soberer with it !" cried Horace as he opened it, and the keen fierce blast of hail and snow came in together. Giving his arm to Beamish, whose steps were unsteady, Horace set out for the muster place.

"Good-bye, Beamish," cried Ponsonby. "Look me up to-morrow, if you escape to-night."

"All right ; I'll put Balaclava on my visiting list. Steady, eyes front," hiccuped Beamish, as he floundered on through the blinding drift, clinging tenaciously to Ramornie's arm. "Well, if we don't leave footprints in the sands of time before Sebastopol, we'll leave some in the snow ; but, d—n it, don't it look very like madness in a parcel of fellows in red coats going out in the snow to pot a set of other fellows in grey or green coats, when all might be comfortably in bed beside their wives, if they had them."

Horace thought of his cosy sixteen-pound shot, and laughed— some thoughts of Gwenny came into his mind too, as they stumbled on. Gwenny would doubtless be fast asleep then, with her soft cheek on her laced pillow in her pretty room at Willowdean, and dreaming, perhaps, of him, with one of the last batch from "Mudie" lying at hand.

"Are those two stars West Inkerman Lights ?"

"There is but *one* light, Pat ; and no wonder that we see it so well beyond the river : it is four hundred and two feet high."

"There go the ' whistling dicks !' "

Some cannonading was going on at the right of the French batteries, which were shelling—even in such frightful weather —the earthen works that lay between the South Fort and the Quarantine Bastion ; thus, the bombs which in daylight were discernible like black globes soaring through the air, now seemed like meteors of brilliant fire, as each described an are to the spot where it was expected to spread destruction and death.

They could hear the church bells of Sebastopol, tolling midnight, as they trod on.

The Fusileers were soon under arms, the battalion "told off," and the march began through the darkness and drift along the left bank of the Tchernaya and beside the aqueduct which had been destroyed by the Allies. The night was intensely gloomy and the snow fell heavily, impeding the progress of the regiment, which, however, successfully joined the force of Sir Colin Campbell on the high open ground which lies two miles and a half westward of Tchorgoun, and then there occurred that which, for a time, appeared to be an indecisive halt.

"One might live to the age of those old fellows who figure in the Pentateuch, and not endure what we do here before Sebastopol!" said Ned Elton, who felt his wounded limb aching in the cold.

"What the deuce is wrong? Why are we halted here?" asked his father, Sir Edward, impatiently, of an aide-de-camp who trotted slowly past in the dark, looking like a white phantom in his coating of snow.

"There's some infernal mistake," was the reply. "The French have not come up, and the Russians are in great force—five thousand men at least—in Kamara, under General Prince Galitzin."

"The French seldom fail us."

"A messenger from General Canrobert to Sir Colin Campbell has stated, that in consequence of the extreme severity of the weather to-night, the regiments he had under arms to take part in the *reconnaissance* have been ordered back to their tents; but the messenger lost his way in the snow. He was too late to inform the fiery old Highlander, who was already on the march, and here we are!"

"And here a few of us are likely to remain, if the halt lasts long," added Sir Edward, for the cold was intense, and many cases of frost-bitten noses and fingers were occurring in the ranks.

Notwithstanding the state of the weather, old Sir Colin was all on fire to have a brush with the enemy under Galitzin; and it happened, as he thought, fortunately, that General Villenois, having learned that his leader's change of plans had been communicated too late, got his Zouaves under arms, and amid the dark and the snowy tempest, had moved down from the heights to join in the expedition.

A cheer from the Rifle Brigade and Royal Fusileers greeted the two dark columns of the French when they were discerned

moving through the gloom ; and after a brief consultation
between the Generals, the command " Forward" was given, and
the advance began towards Tchorgoun and Kamara at four in
the morning, with the Rifles and Highland Light Infantry
extended in skirmishing order.

A few cavalry of the Turkish Contingent, under Major Chesters, who had now recovered and joined the army, hovered on
the right flank.   The river Tchernaya lay on the left.

The orders of Sir Colin were, that not a shot was to be fired,
even if they came upon the enemy, as he hoped a body of them
might be surprised and quietly attacked by the bayonet ; but
the snow-flakes fell so thickly, that the extended files had
difficulty in keeping each other in view, and the fingers of the
men were so benumbed that very few could fix their bayonets !

In profound silence—for the tread of the marching columns
was completely muffled, even as their appearance was hidden
by the snow—they proceeded thus, till suddenly there was a
half-stifled shout !

Three Russian advanced sentinels had been taken by the
skirmishers of the 71st Highlanders, who literally stumbled
against them in the obscurity.

"Flash, flash ! bang, ping ! There go the carbines !" cried
Beamish, as the Cossack Videttes of the picquet at Kamara
began firing at random in the dark ; and then followed the
hoarse din of the Russian drums, as their Infantry began to get
under arms in the town.

The order was then given to retire, for the *reconnaissance* was
a failure, and Sir Colin—by the absence of Bosquet's troops—
had no supports to fall back upon in case of being vigorously
attacked ; besides, the snow was falling more heavily than ever.
" One company could not see its neighbour ; each regiment was
hidden from the other, and the regiments were becoming, mo-
mentarily, less able to advance." Then the cases of frost-bite
were increasing fast, especially among the Highlanders, who had
been ordered to take off their warm fur caps and resume their
plumed Scottish bonnets.

A few random volleys were exchanged, and then the retro-
grade movement began with speed. Horace was earnestly
wishing himself back in his hut, and surmising that his sleeping
partner, the sixteen-pound shot, would be cold enough by that
time.

"We can't be back to camp sooner than mid-day now," said
Beamish. "We have a horrid road to march by—the road that
leads to glory and Sebastopol. Bad cess to both of them !
Have you a drop of anything in your canteen, Horace ?"

Ere Ramornie could reply, the power of speech seemed to
pass from him. He received a dreadful blow in the back, and

fell on his face among the snow. The entire regiment seemed to vanish from his sight, and he found himself left alone; for a half-spent shot had struck him in the back, and in the darkness, drift, and confusion, his fall was unseen, as he had been in rear of his company, which was covering the rear of the battalion.

An emotion of despair at the prospect of being left there to perish, made him stagger wildly up ; but all trace of Campbell's force, and of the Zouaves of Villenois had disappeared. Nothing was visible around him but whiteness—a sheet of snow beneath his feet, and white flakes falling blindingly aslant on the biting wind that came in fierce gusts from the Black Sea.

To advance was as perilous as to retreat ; for he might be staggering towards the enemy, and to remain still was impossible. But his difficulties were soon solved, as he stumbled against a party of Russian soldiers, who were already in possession of a prisoner, a mounted officer.

To these he was fain to surrender himself, and escape being butchered, as he had not power remaining to use his revolver ; and he found himself marched off towards Tchorgoun, a prisoner of war, in company with the other who had fallen into their hands in the confusion : and that other proved to be— Major Chesters, of the Turkish Contingent !

CHAPTER LX.

A PRISONER OF WAR.

OUT of the whole army, Chesters was the last man whom Horace Ramornie would have chosen for a partner in misfortune, or in anything ; and he marched along by his side, preserving a grave and contemptuous silence. Twice or thrice Chesters, who seemed in no way crestfallen, attempted to open a kind of "chaffing" conversation, by offering bets about their destination, the probable term of their captivity, and so forth. But Horace made not the slightest response. And now, as day dawned and the storm abated, about eight miles distant he could see Sebastopol, with all its tremendous batteries, its green domed churches, and lofty houses, the walls of which were white as the snow that covered all the landscape.

He could see the steamers about Balaclava, and the camps of the Allies ; and of these he seemed to take a farewell glance, as he and his escort descended into the valley through which the Black River runs.

An irrepressible emotion of sadness crept over him. When should he see his comrades or be free again ? What account of

his fate would be conveyed to Willowdean? Letters had informed him of the grief and consternation there, consequent
to the report of Cyril's being "missing" after the Alma; but
how would *his* disappearance be accounted for? and what an
amount of sorrow it would cause to Gwenny! Ideas of escape
occurred to him ; but he had been deprived of his sword and
revolver, and the six Ruskies who formed the escort, were
fellows not likely to stand on trifles with those who were in
their hands. They had rifled his pockets, deprived him of
watch and rings, and stripped the lace from the collar and cuffs
of the faded uniform he wore below his pea-jacket; and
Chesters was treated in the same scurvy fashion.

They were all men whose raw-boned figures indicated clumsy
strength. Their features were hard, angular, and ugly. Their
long great-coats were of mud-colour, with flat metal buttons
and scarlet shoulder-straps, and their canvas havresacks contained their coarse tobacco and materials for manufacturing
sour-krout, while their canteens smelt strongly of raki—the
three prime luxuries of their stupid and perilous lives.

One of them, who seemed rather a good-natured man, offered
Horace a mouthful from his canteen, and then a piece of black
bread, but it looked too like a portion of peat from a bog, and
he declined both.

But to be a prisoner almost at the commencement of a war
was a galling and oppressive thought to the young man! How
long might he remain so, and what might his treatment be?
The greatest empires in the world were involved in this mortal
contest, and his captivity might last for years—for the natural
term of his life perhaps ; for at that time strange and dark
rumours were afloat in the Allied camps of the French having
found in some Tartar castles prisoners who had been gleaned
up on the retreat from Moscow, and kept chained as slaves
since then. Whether such was the case or not, it is impossible
to say now ; but the idea of such a doom being his, froze the
blood in the veins of Ramornie ; and he thought with agony
of Gwendoleyne Wedderburn becoming—perhaps when he and
his fate were alike forgotten—the bride of another.

A body of Russian cavalry from Kamara was now upon the
march rearward, under General Prince Galitzin, as Horace
ascertained from a passing officer who spoke French, and
behind this force he and his companion in misfortune were
marched under a new escort of dirty and unwashed Cossacks,
who to make sure of them and save themselves trouble, mounted
the captives on two spare Tartar ponies, and tied their hands
to the shaggy manes thereof.

These Cossacks were all beetle-browed, ill-favoured looking
fellows, with high cheek-bones, piggish-like eyes, and wore fur

caps, in colour and quality closely resembling their own beards. Their uniforms were coarse and quaint, but their arms were bright and good, and each rode with his knees up to his saddle-bow, and so surrounded by forage, bags of Ghiska wheat, and other plunder taken from the poor Tartar peasantry, that little more than the head and crupper of their little horses could be seen. They were doubtless brave and resolute men, for the copper medals stitched on their coarse green uniforms showed that they were Don Cossacks, and had faced alike the rifles of Schamyl's Circassian cavaliers, and the keen sabres of the Khirghee outlaws.

This Cossack force continued riding eastward, and ere long they were at the base of the Tchatr-Dagh, or "mountain of the tents"—a flat hill not unlike the famous Table Mountain, but all of red marble, towering above groves of large trees that were leafless then, and clumps of dark green cypresses, where many a huge eagle, and whole clouds of other wild birds, hovered in mid-air. Here they shot and roasted a few bustards, which were plucked, cooked, and eaten, without being per-mitted to cool—there was no time for that—and Horace and the obnoxious Chesters came in for a share of the birds ; though sooth to say the drumsticks were tough enough to have been used on a drum. With these they had some *yourgourt*, or sour milk and Tartar cakes, taken sans cérémonie by the Cossacks from the house of a neighbouring farmer.

The snow had disappeared now in the changeable climate of the Crimea, having melted so fast that scarcely a trace of it remained even on the bare scalp of the Tchatr-Dagh, or the grotesque-looking Dimirdji Mountain, which towered on the opposite side where the halt had been made, and which was soon to be the scene of a very dark incident.

" Alexis, Ivan," said a smart looking aide-de-camp, in the rich uniform of the Princess Maria Paulovna's Hussars—for that lady was sister to the Empress, and was proprietrix of a regiment of cavalry — " bring those two prisoners before the General, Prince Galitzin."

Then the two weary wretches who escorted Horace and Ches-ters, and who had just lit their short pipes to enjoy a brief whiff, started simultaneously from that dirty piece of felt on which they were squatted, and which economically serves the Cossack warrior in the triple capacity of bed, tent, and cloak.

We should have mentioned in its place, that it was Chesters who commanded the force of Turks that so disgracefully abandoned the 93rd Highlanders at Balaclava, but not through any fault of his own, as he killed several of the fugitives with his sabre in vain attemps to stay the rest. Left behind sick at Malta by the transport, he and his affair on board that ship had

been forgotten amid the bustle of embarking for the Crimea,
and the subsequent passage of the Alma ; so that he had been
permitted to join his corps of that peculiar force, the Turkish
Contingent, where his story was unknown, or if known, would
not be understood, and now he thought that all his gambling
scrapes and sharp play had been forgotten, so he was little
prepared for what was before him. And now we have to apo-
logize to the reader for an introduction to a very unpleasant
personage indeed ; but such introductions are misfortunes which
the historian and novelist cannot avoid.

Apart from where more than a thousand Russian heavy
cavalry had hobbled their horses, and were cooking, smoking,
eating sour krout and drinking bitter quass or fiery raki, some
lounging at length on the still damp grass, with their belts and
leather helmets off, for the air was steamy and moist, as the sun
had so rapidly melted and exhaled the snow of the preceding
night in mist, Prince Galitzin and a few noisy Russian officers
were partaking of a hurried repast near the wall of a Tartar
vineyard— an erection which, from its massive thickness, age, and
height, must have been a remnant of one of the many fortresses
erected in the Crimea during the fifth century against the Goths
and Huns.

Near it rose several of those green tumuli which are so
common over all the Peninsula, and mark the graves of those
who had fallen in the ages of classical antiquity—old even as
the days of Mithridates.

The Prince occupied a stool beside a kind of table, both of
which had been brought from the house of the Tartar farmer,
and his brother officers stood or lay on the grass around him,
laughing and smoking. Under a loose grey great-coat, which
was open, he wore a rich uniform of grass-coloured green, richly
laced with gold. His epaulettes were massive, and several
medals and orders of the empire were sparkling on his breast.
He seemed rather an undersized man, with a handsome face,
having dark and sparkling eyes, set indeed unpleasantly near
each other ; his nose was hooked, with a somwhat delicate
nostril, indicating Tartar blood, and his jet black moustachios
were well and fiercely curled up.

He did not rise as the two prisoners approached him, each
with proper politeness yielding a salute, in reply to which he
simply lifted his cocked hat a few inches ; but ere he replaced it,
his face and his shorn black hair recalled at once to the memory
of Horace a former acquaintance—the person who had figured
as Captain of Zouaves among the British at Varna and elsewhere ; and the fallen officer who so infamously pistolled poor
Cyril Wedderburn after performing an act of mercy at the battle
of the Alma, where he dragged him from under his dying horse.

In short, the notorious Russian Spy, and Ivan Tegoborski, General Prince Galitzin, were one and the same man !

As there are upwards of three hundred Princes of that distinguished name in Russia, we shall have no fear of "being called out" for mentioning *one* of them here ; but he in question was the poorest among them, having now only his military pay.

The first emotion of Horace was astonishment, and then genuine contempt, that any officer should so far have degraded himself and his epaulettes ; next he thought of the kind, gentle, and manly Cyril Wedderburn, and his heart grew hot with indignation. He involuntarily turned to Chesters, but in the face of that person read considerable alarm and disquietude ; for *he* too had recognised a former acquaintance, who, like De la Fosse, had a gambling grudge to remember.

" So, Messieurs," said the Russian, coolly and with a strange smile, " we three recognise each other, it seems ?"

" I am sorry to say that we do," replied Horace Ramornie, haughtily, in French, which he did not speak nearly so well as the Prince ; but, as a traveller remarks, " the Russians have this advantage over other nations—namely, that they are endowed with the gift of tongues, having an extraordinary facility for acquiring and speaking with a pure accent any foreign language ;" yet one who can speak Russian or Chinese may easily achieve anything vocable. " Monsieur le Prince, how about the coffee, the broiled chickens, and cream tarts you were wont to get from your dear mother, in Gascony ? Was it honourable to act as you did at Varna, and elsewhere ?" asked the young officer, boldly.

There was a triumphant and malicious but cruel glitter in the eyes of Galitzin, as he replied, coolly—"All plans are fair in war and love, my friend. Thanks to me, Alexander Mentschicoff knew to a nicety every bayonet and sabre you had yonder in Bulgaria ; yes, and every cannon too. So now we shall drop *that* subject. You are sorry to recognise me ? By the bones of all the Moschti of Russia, and by every shrine in Holy Mother Moscow, *one* here shall be still more sorry at this meeting !" and his eyes flashed like a sword-blade as they turned to Chesters. He then added, to Horace, " What is your name ?"

" Horace Ramornie, Captain in her Britannic Majesty's Royal Fusileers."

Galitzin made a note of the name — " Oraz Ramhornoff, Capitan" — in a fashion that would have puzzled Horace's friends had they seen it on his calling cards.

" Your companion's name I know but too well, as Captain Chesters."

" He is Major Chesters, here at least."

" That will matter little by-and-by," was the ominous response.

" What was the object of the sudden night march from Balaclava towards Tchorgoun?"

" To attack you."

" Bah ! I thought so ; you didn't succced though."

" The snow——"

" Ah, Nicholas, our glorious Emperor, was right. Holy Russia has two generals who never fail her — January and February ! What was the strength of your force? There were Turkish dogs among it, I know—the Asiatics."

" For that very reason I cannot tell. Moreover, I must decline to say more."

" I might compel you," retorted the other.

" Am I to have my parole of honour?"

" That we shall consider elsewhere. Meantime a glass of wine with you."

" Thanks, Monsieur le Prince," and Horace, however repugnant the pretended cordiality, felt himself constrained to clink his glass against that of the Prince and drink with him. After which, the latter said—

" And now, Monsieur Chesters, for *you*."

" Shall my parole be granted?"

" No !" was the abrupt response.

" What am I to understand by that reply and your peculiar smile, Prince Galitzin?" asked Chesters, uneasily, for his captor was known to be at heart a savage, "but a savage of health and vigour, smoothed and shapened in accordance with the prejudices of civilized life."

" Oui ; you smiled when I lost roubles to you by the thousand. I then learned to beware of the smile of such polished villains ; but it is my turn to be merry now."

" Why, Monsieur le Prince ?"

" Because you are the loser."

" In what way, beyond being a prisoner of war, I have yet to learn," replied Chesters, with ill-assumed hauteur.

" The odd trick is against you, Monsieur."

" I am indifferent about the stakes."

" That we shall see, très bon ! Come here, you fellows !" he cried to some soldiers who were loitering near, observantly. " Throw off your accoutrements, and dig me a hole here some six feet long !"

" A hole?" exclaimed Chesters, enquiringly.

" *A grave !*" replied the hollow-hearted Russian, smiling with his false smile and black glittering eyes.

" Have you no sense of honour?" asked Chesters, growing very, very pale.

" Some of its kind. Quick ! deeper and deeper yet ! Throw out the earth, you accursed Asiatics !" he added, kicking one of the soldiers with his jackboot, and bestowing upon him the most opprobrious epithet in Russia, the name of the race which closed his order. " Ah, Monsieur Chesters, you thought that some fine day, sooner or later, you would repent of your mis-deeds ; and now you have not time, ah ! ah !"

" Then, have you no compassion ?" urged Horace.

" Bah ! I parted company with that long ago," laughed the other.

" Do you actually mean to assassinate him ?"

" No !"

" What then ?" asked Chesters.

" To punish you."

" Give me pistols, and I shall fight you at twelve paces—ten, if you prefer it !" said Chesters, who gazed at him with a haggard eye.

" I don't fight with cheats or tricksters, and men who use loaded dice, and know the backs of cards quite as well as their fronts, if not better. Tie his hands behind his back, and tie his feet too !"

By this time the sharply ringing brass trumpets had sounded ; the cavalry had all mounted, and formed in quarter-distance column of troops, prior to the resumption of their march ; and it was evident that whatever was about to be *done* would soon be over now.

Chesters was all that was vile and bad, yet he was the son of a gentleman—the scion of a family long honoured in his native Merse. The Crimean air had bronzed his cheek ; time, and still more, dissipation, had whitened his hair. He had done deadly wrongs to the kinsman of Horace, yet the latter looked on the impending scene with horror, and prayed Galitzin, but in vain, to be merciful.

Horace remembered that there was a local story of the prophecy of a half-crazed female gipsy of Yetholm (at whom Chesters, in his mischievous boyhood, had thrown stones), to the effect that he " would never die of a sudden death, nor yet die in his bed ;" and now it flashed upon the mind of Horace ; but to judge by the piteous expression of his face, Chesters put no faith in the prediction, if at that moment he remembered it at all.

A couple of dragoons had unslung their carbines and were in the act of loading, ramming their cartridges home, and return-ing their steel rods, with a *sang froid* that was more French than Muscovite, when Chesters, who was powerful and athletic, proud and fiery, struggled fiercely with those who sought so ignominiously to bind him. Big bead-like drops of perspiration oozed over the unfortunate man's forehead, his face was deadly pale, his lips a ghastly blue, and his usually light-coloured eyes glared with all the anticipation and the terror of a sudden, merciless, and violent death, which he knew to be inevitable, yet he could not resist the natural desire to shun it as long as possible, for at that moment life seemed dear—oh, so dear! Yet in his blind despair, he sought aid neither from Heaven nor earth.

Horace called hoarsely, piteously, and then threateningly to Prince Galitzin, who only waved his hand in contemptuous silence, and then the two Cossacks once more seized him, one administering a prod from his lance to quicken his movements, and they again mounted on the Tartar pony, re-tying his hands to the mane thereof. They then forced him away, but, on looking back, he saw a strangely horrible scene.

In his mad terror of death, or in his utter despair, Chesters, with his clenched teeth, had seized fast the coat sleeve—perhaps the arm—of one of those who were binding him. Another dragoon on seeing this clubbed a carbine and dealt him a blow on the head, a blow which, though it inflicted no wound but only a flesh bruise, completely stunned him, and he fell senseless.

"In with him as he is and cover him up," said Galitzin, remorselessly. "Keep your ammunition for others! Quick—obey me, or it shall be the worse for yourselves!"

The two dragoons who had paused with loaded carbine in hand, now relinquished them, for they knew that Galitzin was not a man to brook delay, or have his temper trifled with; and taking a couple of Tartar shovels, they proceeded to assist in filling up the grave upon the yet living and breathing man, whom the cold earth so speedily revived that a sense of his situation dawned upon him!

A half-stifled cry of despair, that made the blood of Horace congeal, came out of that hole; another and another followed, each, however, more faint than the last, as the load of earth grew heavy upon him. Then came a sound like a convulsive groan or snort; anon it was completely filled, and they batted the heaped up mound with the flat of the shovel. Four feet below that heap writhed the yet living man, bound hand and foot; and while the *Pulkovnick*, or Colonel of the Russian Dragoons, gave his hoarse words of command to "break into sections" and "march," while the kettle-drums rolled and the trumpets pealed forth a lively and martial air, Horace, as he looked back, thought he could see the mound of earth heaving, as the strong man struggled in his death agony amid the depth of his living grave!

So thus, in some fashion, the prophecy of the revengeful Yetholm gipsy came true after all; and the onyx ring of Louis De la Fosse, with its heraldic gauntlet on a sword's point, and the motto *Droit en avant*, became the prize of an ignorant Cossack, who tore it with his teeth from the finger of the half-

This was all base revenge on the part of Galitzin, as he was a man stained with a thousand crimes and immoralities. So there Ralph Chesters found his grave by the ruin of an old wall of the Gothic days, and amid a lonely clump of caper-trees and juniper-bushes in Crim Tartary!

CHAPTER LXI.

THE PAROLE OF HONOUR.

THE Russian troops in the Crimea were always being changed, with what object it is impossible to say; but those who were once engaged with the Allies seldom saw them again. Thus the Heavy Dragoon force of Prince Galitzin wheeled off towards Simpheropol, *en route* for the Isthmus of Perecop, while he, accompanied by his aide-de-camp and a few Cossacks, proceeded direct to Yaila, carrying with him one of the few trophies lately secured by the Russians—Horace Ramornie.

The repugnance the latter had of his captor was intense, yet he was compelled by policy to dissemble to an extent that made him almost despise himself; for he had to smile and bow his thanks whenever that personage proffered—as he not unfrequently did—his cigar-case, with a bland yet cunning glitter in his eyes. With all his bad points of character—and Horace knew not the half of them—he sorrowed for the sudden and terrible fate of the hapless Chesters, and justly deemed his death, and more than all, the mode of it, an outrage on humanity, on the laws of war and of nations; for whatever their private quarrel may have been, Galitzin should have respected the rights of a prisoner.

But the butchery of our wounded in the Valley of Inkerman, the massacre of a boat's crew under a flag of truce at Hango, and the cannonading of our ships that were perishing amid the terrible storm that swept the shore of the Euxine, go far to prove that the Russians are not particular in their mode of dealing with an enemy, or remarkable for their nice notions of chivalry.

So the close of the second day, after some forty miles march, saw Horace Ramornie a prisoner in the Castle of Yaila. Along the route he had noted every path and defile, every Tartar village, every wall and tree, that might guide him if he succeeded in escaping. That project, if put in execution, had with it many perils; for he might be shot, or shut up among the rank and file and sent inland he knew not where! He writhed under the restraint of the present, and anticipated the future with doubt and dread.

22—2

However, once within the gates of Yaila, his parole of honour was accepted by Galitzin, as commandant of the place, to the effect that he should not go more than *one* mile beyond its walls, reporting himself every night at gunfire to the *parooschick* (a lieutenant) of the main-guard ; that he would be made a close prisoner if he failed in these conditions, and eventually shot if he attempted to escape.

Horace was fain to accept of these hard terms, stipulating on the other hand, that his life should be safe, and that he might write to his friends at the camp by a Tartar messenger.

This was peremptorily refused by Galitzin, lest he should in some hidden terms describe the locality of Yaila and strength of the garrison ; for distrust of everything and everybody was a second nature with this impoverished Prince.   Moreover he had been more than once a spy himself ; so hence came much of the mystery that involved the disappearance of Horace Ramornie.

When he found himself isolated thus in that sequestered fort, amid the mountains of Crim Tartary, at times a stunned sensation came over him.   He felt like one who wanders in the unknown places of dreamland, or under a species of nightmare ! Was he the same Horace Ramornie who had lately so many friends, a position and rank as Captain in the Line—who had been riding between a file of filthy snubnosed Cossack Lancers, in coarse uniforms and mangy-looking fur shoubahs, with his hands tied to the shaggy mane of a stolen Tartar pony ; and was he actually to pine there, under the shadows of the Tchatr-Dagh and Dimirdji Mountains, for some unnamed period of time? If this was reality, was Gwenny a myth ?

The longing to escape was intense ; but then he had given his parole ; and to ask it back, would be to announce the intention of flight, and cause him to be made a close prisoner, who would be well watched in one of those cells or dungeons of the place, the bare thought of which made him shudder. He could but hope that some body of the Allies might by chance assault Yaila, and effect his rescue ; if the Ruskies did not bayonet him, to prevent him from falling safe into friendly hands ; and *that* he knew they were quite capable of doing.

Rising from the slope of the hill, on rocks of red and white marble, the Castle of Yaila consisted of four towers of very picturesque aspect, connected by an embattled curtain, or wall, before which lay a deep ditch of recent construction ; and, in its time it had witnessed many changes, and had many masters.

The basement was originally part of a citadel erected by the Emperor Justinian against the barbarians.   The family of a Khan of the house of Zingis, leader of the Golden Horde, who came from the deserts of Tartary to conquer Russia, had occupied it for several generations.   It had been demolished by

the Genoese, when the Superb City was mistress of Lesbos,
Cyprus, and "Scio's rocky isle ;" and it had been restored, to
undergo a cannonading by Mohammed the Second, when he
swept her industrious colonies from the shores of the Black Sea.
Now, each of those sorely-patched round towers, was surmounted by a Russian cupola, the copper of which was of a
brilliant green colour. Two were shaped and striped like
water-melons, and two like pine-apples, being cut into knobby
points to make the resemblance more complete. Each terminated
in a great cross, and over all, on the mast of a ship brought
from the Euxine, waved the white standard of the Empire,
charged with the blue saltire of its patron, the Fisherman of
Bethsaida.

The garrison (Horace, intent on rescue if he could not escape,
took note of everything) consisted of two four-company battalions of Finland Infantry, under the *Pulkovnick*, or senior
Colonel, Alexis Tegoborski, a kinsman of the Prince—a grim
old soldier, who had lost the half of his left hand by a Turkish
sabre, at the siege of Varna. and wore a gold medal for the war
in Transylvania. As each Russian company is supposed to be
two hundred strong, this garrison should have consisted of at
least sixteen hundred bayonets ; but as Galitzin was one of those
good old-fashioned Muscovite officers who peculated whenever
he could do so, he had barely two-thirds of that number in his
ranks ; but when the (obliging) General of the District inspected
them, the rest were borrowed from the next officer of the same
school at Simpheropol, Kertch, or elsewhere ; and the General,
pocketing a share of the pay, said nothing about it.

In general vulgarity of appearance, as well as in coarseness
of face, it was difficult to distinguish the officers from the men
on parade. All wore the same long grey coat, that hid everything, to their gaiters ; but under this each had a dark green
coatee, faced with red and trimmed with yellow, like their flat,
round forage-caps.

Heavy cannon, all painted green, with white crosses on the
breech, commanded the approaches to the place on every side,
and Horace saw with a sigh, that even if some General of the
Allies suggested a sudden expedition of the troops to Yaila, as
Campbell did to Tchorgoun, that the Castle would not be taken
without a terrible loss of life ; yet, he was fond of imagining
the joy with which he would see the Red-coats, or the active
Zouaves, in their baggy madder breeches, crossing the ditch
under grape and musketry, and swarming up the rocky glacis
at the bayonet's point. And then his heart would leap within
him, only to sink lower in hope than ever. For when was it
to be ?

Though a Russian Prince, and, consequently, we may suppose,

a gentleman, Galitzin had but vague ideas of the position held
in English society by an officer of any rank : and though the
superannuated nurse of the Emperor, and even his coachman,
have the nominal rank of Colonel—for everything is judged by
the standard of the sword and epaulette in Russia—he was
disposed to treat the "Hospodeen Ramhornoff," as he called
him, rather coldly, and all the more so when reverses came thick
and fast upon the garrison of Sebastopol.

So February passed into April, and wistfully and yearningly
did the prisoner gaze upon the blue waters of the Euxine (piquancy being given to that glimpse by the sails and smoke of
our war-steamers, cruising between the Straits of Yeni Kale
and Sebastopol), "the highroad to Old England," which lay
about two miles from his place of detention. And his soul sickened of the same eternal view. Yet that view was not without
its charms.

There were the stupendous peaks of the Dimirdji and Tchatr
Dagh ; the picturesque little Tartar villages with white walls
and green roofs ; a peep of the wooded valley of the Salghir—
the silver rivulets stealing between the slopes of emerald green
towards it and the sea. Groups of passing natives ; the Asiatic
women, with loose trousers and flowing headdresses—the Russian, with high-waisted petticoats ; the turbaned and slippered
Turk, with a bundle of weapons in his sash ; a mounted Tartar,
in a red striped jacket with blue trousers and scarlet sash ; a
Russian Mujik, in jackboots and sheepskin jacket ; and troops
of all arms, perpetually pouring forward to or from Sebastopol ;
and high over head the black eagles soaring in the blue sky.
But Horace sighed for his little tent in the British camp ; for
his perilous tour of duty in the trenches ; for creeping towards
the rifle-pits in rear of a sap-roller ; and to hear once more the
ding-dong of the great guns, night and day, in and around the
beleaguered city !

The greatest terror of Horace was a snowy or, as the season
opened, a wet day, for then he was of a necessity confined within
the walls. Minus umbrella and wrappers, he could not even
enjoy his paroled mile, but was compelled to keep within a
dingy whitewashed room, heated by a *peitchka* or wall stove,
with a tattered copy of the *Times* or *Galignani* three months
old, which somehow found their way there, and from which the
censor of the press had carefully obliterated everything of the
slightest interest ; otherwise he would encounter General Prince
Galitzin, who was most exacting of salutes, at every other turn
of the old tumbledown Tartar stronghold, every stone of which
he loathed.

The weeks were marked only by a bearded Greek priest, who
performed service on Sunday in the armoury, clad in white,

with gorgeous vestments of cloth of gold, bordered by the richest lace. Sometimes he had the honour of dining with the Prince, and the pleasure of having his usual meal of beef, black bread, and beer, especially after wrecks in the Black Sea, varied by a repast à la Russe, where everything was excellent, from the preliminary kimmel and caviare, to the coffee that closed it. There would be turbot from the Euxine, wild boar from Khutor Mackenzie, potatoes garnished with parsley and butter, salted beef and green borsch, plenty of fruit from Achmetchet and crimskoï or Crimean wine. and that of the Don which so often passes for champagne in Russia. Galitzin, to Horace, seemed then a kind of Belshazzar in a green coat and epaulettes, but discontented, and sighing for the beauties of St. Petersburg and the bells of Paris and Baden-Baden. He never asked Horace to play, however, as he knew the industrious Cossacks had stripped him of everything, even to half the buttons on his uniform.

On these occasions, when under the influence of the wine, Galitzin would relax a little of his stiffness, and Horace would strive to forget that he was the guest of a spy and assassin—yea, a double one (for by this time Cyril might be dead at Scutari); and once he begged "that his parole might be extended to two miles;" as he had an intense longing to stand by the shore of the free rolling sea—but dared not hint that.

Galitzin bent his keen dark Tartar eyes inquiringly upon him, and said significantly :—" Are you ill-treated here ?"

" Monsieur le Prince, do not misunderstand me ; I simply wish to wander out to see——"

" What, Monsieur le Capitain, if the Tchatr Dagh, the Trapezus of the Greeks and the Palata Gora of the Russians, together with the mountains of the Yaila, are where they were yesterday ?"

" Well, life has come down pretty much to that sort of thing with me. To find that any of them had vanished like the Palace of Aladdin, would cause a new sensation—a surprise at least."

" An alerte from Balaclava would be more acceptable ?"

" Decidedly, Monsieur le Prince," said Horace, smiling.

" You are weary of your imprisonment and of our Tauric scenery."

" How much I weary, heaven alone knows !"

" Well, empty that bottle of Donskoi ; your exchange or release is only a matter of time."

And Horace thought sadly in his heart—" Patience, patience yet awhile. What is there on the land or sea that is not a matter of time ?"

How regretfully, yet proudly, he thought of his regiment, the Royal Fusileers—of that splendid group of English officers, who gathered round the farewell mess-table at Chatham—the table

that is at once the model of aristocracy, democracy, and dinner
society—men so high-hearted, noble, and generous, of all those
who drew their swords that morning beside the Alma ; of Jack
Probyn, of old Conyers Singleton whose blighted life was closed
by a Russian bullet ; of Pomfret, Bingham, and Joyce, and all
who had fallen ; of Sir Edward, Ned Elton, Pat Beamish, and
others, who, he hoped, were surviving still. His heart turned
to them with affectionate longing. He felt himself so much
alone among all those hostile foreigners, with whom he had no
community of feeling ; alone with his sorrows, doubts, and
harrowing fears of liberty, promotion, and more than all perhaps—a love lost !

The yearning for letters that could never come, and for news
of those at home, became keen and poignant. How drearily
the round of each day passed ! The utter sameness of place
and view and occupation, or rather lack of the latter ; so that
each night he thanked heaven that another day of his life had
gone, and he was twenty-four hours nearer the end of his captivity.

But the *end*—when might it be ?

Surmises of how the war was going on were incessantly in
his mind, with thoughts of Gwenny, of Lady Wedderburn, and
of their health, or where they might be, whether at Willowdean
or in London, where Gwenny would certainly be the object of
so much attention ! Poor girl ! he flattered himself that her
sorrow for him would be great indeed—all the greater that she
had still perhaps to keep the secret of their engagement in the
recesses of her own heart.

And so while he pined thus within the narrow limits defined
by his *parole d'honneur*, the soft Crimean spring stole on towards summer, and the soldiers of the garrison were changed
many times. Then came the hum of the mountain bee as it
floated over the little caper bushes or the purple heather of
Yaila ; the plash of the brown scaly fish in the stream that
bubbled towards the Salghir or the sea, and these were the only
sounds that broke the stillness of the lonely hours Horace spent
on slopes outside the fortress (for he loathed the in), while the
fertile soil around began to teem with mint and thyme, wild
parsley and aromatic herbs ; the great dahlias, sweet-briar, and
whitethorn flourished amid the marble rocks and the crumbling
walls of the days of Justinian and the Genoese, and every breeze
of summer as it swept past was laden with delicious perfumes.

Meanwhile, the Czar Nicholas had died ; the great sortie of
the 4th of April had been repulsed ; the rifle-pits had been captured ; the terrible conflict took place in the cemetery ; Sebastopol still held out desperately, but the Russians were hemmed
on all hands within it.

Galitzin was a great tyrant. Seldom did a day pass without finding an officer under arrest for some petty fault ; or a soldier mulcted of his miserable pay for the Prince's behoof, flogged, tied neck and heels to a musket, or sent to shot drill ; and these punishments generally took place in the evening, after Galitzin had imbibed his full share of crimskoi ; and after witnessing them, and saying prayers before a gaudy print of his patron, St. Ivan Veliki, he generally retired to smoke a cigar in the apartments of his kinsman, the Pulkovnick Alexis Tegoborski, with whose florid and fair-haired wife, Norina Paulovna, he seemed on remarkably intimate terms.

So thus the spring wore into summer, and Horace Ramornie was still a lonely prisoner, pining in the Castle of Yaila ; but new, strange, and terrible interests were to grow up around him ere he saw the last of its four green-domed towers and heavy gun batteries.

CHAPTER LXII.

THE YACHT.

ON the evening of one of those same summer days which Horace was spending so sadly among the green slopes outside the fortress of Yaila, a beautiful English yacht was seen stand-ing before a fair wind between the European and the Asiatic shores, between the fortress of Karibdsche on its barren rocks, and the lighthouse of Anatali Kawak.

At this place, the narrowest part of the Bosphorus—the waters of "the Sacred Opening"—the waves seemed to be sleeping in golden light. A strong flush of splendour from the sun, then sinking towards the Thracian chain of Hæmus, fell in all its glory on " Olympus high and hoar," and all the undulations of the Bithynian range ; the purity of the atmosphere, bringing clearly to the eye the shining windows of many a gaily-painted and gilded kiosk, the marble peristyle and leaden dome of many a little mosque ; the pretty villages, the gigantic cypresses, and the beautiful groves of fig trees ; the water being so trans-parently pure and clear, that nearly all these objects were reflected downward in its glassy depths, exactly as if in a mirror.

The yacht was a smart little schooner of some two hundred tons, straight and low in the water, and coppered to the bends with metal bright as burnished brass. She carried a vast spread of fore-and-aft canvas, which was white as snow ; the masts raked well aft ; the deck was flush, the only encumbrance being six small brass carronades, for ornament rather than use, though a garland of shot for them was round the coamings of the hatchways.

The elaborately carved figure-head was the effigy of a hand-some woman, with flowing tresses, bearing a gilded wand, which was always unshipped when the yacht went to sea; and now the empty hand was pointed as if directingly towards the Black Sea. The yards were light, and the spars tapered away aloft like fishing-rods; the union-jack and ensign of the Royal Yacht Club were duly displayed, one at the gaff-peak and the other at the mainmast-head in answer to the crescent and star on the ramparts of Caribdsche.

The tiny companionway, all walnut wood and brass, was like a toy staircase, and the cabin was furnished like a lady's boudoir, save that it was hung with coloured prints of operatic favourites and dancing-girls, in the shortest of skirts, photographs of "some fellows of ours" in the Household Brigade, French crayon heads and studies, some of them slightly objectionable in character—for this was the yacht of the Master of Ernescleugh, and that handsome girl with the fine features so delicately pale and minute, with dark eyes and hair, to whose fashionable costume a piquancy was given by the dark-green Sardinian Bersagliere plume which she wore in her little velvet hat, and who was gazing through her lorgnette alternately at the European and the Asian shore, is Gwendoleyne Wedderburn.

Lady Ernescleugh and Lady Wedderburn were below. They had been more than once to the East before, and the Bosphorus was nothing new to them. A heavy gale had been encountered the preceding night in the sea of Marmora, and they were now lying on the luxurious velvet cabin sofas, each fanning herself, bathing her face with Rimmel, in which a handkerchief was dipped, and both eager for the time, when after traversing some three hundred and odd miles of the Black Sea, they should be able to embrace their sons. The yacht did not anchor at Constantinople, as Lady Wedderburn had been given to understand that Cyril had left Scutari for head-quarters.

"Oh, the foolish fellow!" she exclaimed, "to risk himself again, when he might have come home with honour!"

She was anxious that Cyril should see Gwenny as soon as possible; not that the trenches before Sebastopol were quite the place for marrying or giving in marriage, or a Crimean hut the place wherein to spend a honeymoon; but she had begun to have certain jealous fears of secret views entertained by her friend, the fair Ernescleugh, for *her* son, whose extravagance was boundless, and for whom the wealthy Indian heiress would prove a very seasonable match. Once, when she exclaimed in admiration—

"Oh, it is quite a fairy ship this!"

"Were my son to hear you, he would doubtless make you a

present of it," replied Lady Ernescleugh, kissing her cheek. "Would you like to be mistress of it, child?"

"Gwenny!" exclaimed Lady Wedderburn, not knowing very well what to say.

"I am so enchanted with everything, and yonder beautiful shore!"

"If the Sultan heard you, Miss, he'd likely wish to make you mistress of *that* too!" said Bob Newnham, the commander of the yacht, with an air of gallantry.

Many a day at Cowes and Ryde had the Master of Ernes-leugh figured on the deck of this yacht with other guardsmen, wearing sou'westers and the roughest of Petersham dreadnoughts, with glazed boots and scarlet neckties, and with shirt collars of marvellous size and pattern, all over ships and anchors, all thinking they "were doing the thing uncommonly well;" and now he was toiling in rags in the trenches, or the occupant of a hut inferior to his dog-kennel at home, while more than one of his brother yachtsmen—poor fellows!—were lying quietly in their graves on Cathcart's Hill, or in the valley of Inkerman.

And now as the yacht bore on, careening gracefully over, when the wind drew more abeam, a breeze which, however gentle, sufficed to make the sea chafe in surf about the Cyanean rocks, Gwenny filled up her time by chatting gaily with Newnham, who, though a soured and somewhat homespun character, could not but be charmed by her beauty and vivacity.

To Gwenny, secluded so long as she had been at Willowdean, this voyage to the East had been a source of uninterrupted joy. Gibraltar with all its batteries, Malta with its churches and streets of stairs, and but lately the Cyclades—Sirpho with its steep mountains, Thermia with its caverns, barren Joura (the Botany Bay of Ancient Rome), Andros with its mountains covered with arbutus, and all the other "Islands of the Blest;" and then came the Dardanelles and Constantinople, her crowning wonder, for she saw only its beauties and knew nothing of its streets of mud.

A joyous and light-hearted girl of eighteen to be transported into a world of such novel sights and sounds, new scenes and tastes, new pleasures and daily excitements—more than all, to be going to behold with her own bright eyes that great belea-guered city, of which all the world was talking, thinking, or writing, where daily and nightly her mysterious—was it pos-sible?—naughty Horace, who had ceased to write to her for so long, was facing danger—all proved a source of thrilling excite-ment.

Bob Newnham, the commander of the yacht, was as enchanted by her questions as she was bewildered by the utter incompre-hensibility of many of his answers, for nautical terms were as

Hebrew to her. He was somewhat tall for a sailor, with a fair
but saddened face, in the lines of which disappointment was
too evidently written. He was nearer fifty than forty years of
age, quite bald, only a lieutenant R.N. yet, and never hoped to
be more, even in this time of war. Poor Bob Newnham! He
had neither patronage nor interest; ambition was dead within
him now, and he was content to be a kind of "upper servant,"
as he sometimes said in the bitterness of his honest heart; for
he thought the skipper of a lord's yacht was only a degree better than his butler or gamekeeper ashore, and not half so comfortable a berth as either had; and he had more than once lost
his situation for threatening to "colt," or ropesend, for their
aggressive insolence, some of the young sprigs and *parvenus* in
whose service he had been since he was last paid off in Hamoaze,
after long service in the horrid African squadron, where he had
learned too well to know the truth of the sad rhyme,—

> " The Bight of Benin,
>   The Bight of Benin;
>   But *one* comes out,
>   When *three* go in."

Newnham was by birth a gentleman; but he had gone early to
sea in the rough old sailing-ship times, when steamers were
stigmatised as "smoke-jacks;" when the midshipman's berth of
Marryat's days was not much improved since those of Tobias
Smollett; and he had been more used to tar and slush, than
white kids and perfume, or even a white tablecloth, "though,"
as he often said, "he was obliged to affect all these sort of
things now."

Lady Ernescleugh thought his solecisms dreadful, deeming
him a creature only to be tolerated because "that absurd boy
Everard rather likes him, for they played chess, cards, smoked
and made much noisy fun together, when the former chose to
be nautical, and have a few miles' voyage in the yacht with a
few friends from London;" and the maintenance of the said
craft, with her crew of some twenty-two hands, all told, cost a
pretty sum annually, when added to the little brigade expenses
of the Honourable Everard.

"And those little cannon, they are so beautiful and clean!"
continued Gwenny, who was still enchanted with everything.

"We generally give 'em a polish on Sundays, Miss, when the
men are idle," replied Newnham, who stood near her with a
telescope under one arm and his hands thrust into the pockets
of his reefing jacket,—a semi-uniform, as it had gilt buttons
and gold lace.

"I think I could fire one myself! Would you permit me?"

"With pleasure."

"But I mean if the Russians attacked us."

Newnham laughed, and while looking down on the bright face and its wonderful long eyelashes, replied, "Thank God that, for your sake, there is no fear of the Russians attacking us, Miss. All their craft are choke full of stones, and lying low enough at the bottom of Sebastopol harbour. We are as safe here as if we were off Blackwall !"

"You would like to fight them though, I suppose ?"

A gleam passed over his clear blue eyes, and the colour deepened in his cheek, as he replied, "You talk of practical fighting—I can't get the chance,—but that would be nothing to me. I am one of those luckless dogs, Miss Wedderburn, who in the mighty battle of life have had to fight before the mast, thankful that I could keep my place there, and maintain myself and my poor mother—for she is living yet. But to fight a Russian gunboat, however small," he added, laughing, "and with these toy carronades, would be exactly like scuttling a ship to get rid of the rats—we should lose her anyway."

"And our liberty ?"

"Yes, if we did not lose our lives."

"Oh, that would be dreadful !"

"Though there is no fear of that sort of thing ; there are some frightful squalls at times in these waters, and my advice to Lady Ernescleugh should be, that as soon as she has landed at Balaclava harbour all the good things we have for her son, the preserved meats, cases of wine and stout, (Rimmel's perfumes)" he added, parenthetically, and with a peculiar smile ; "and after she has seen him—that is, if he ain't already under the turf, we should haul up for Constantinople, and wait awhile there, to see what turns up in the Crimea. The infernal work can't last much longer there. We are to have a rough night, I fear."

"Worse than the storm of last night ?"

"Storm—bless me, Miss Wedderburn, it was only a capful of wind. We had the mainsail and fore and aft foresail close reefed, to be sure, and the sea made some breaches over the deck, washing a few buckets to leeward, but that was all ; she went through it like a duck. Unfortunately we were too near the Isle of Prote, and when it blows I like a good offing and plenty of sea room. We are not in the Mediterranean now, and I believe (even when there) with the old Admiral Doria, that 'its three best harbours are June, July, and Carthagena.' It is freshening already, by jingo !" he added suddenly, as the lofty schooner careened over more heavily to leeward ; "and I didn't like the look of the sun, as he went down behind the hills, looking yellow and pale at last."

"It *is* coming much stronger, sir," said the mate, in a low voice, and after a consultation, and much anxious gazing at one particular quarter of the sky, where to Gwenny's amazement nothing was to be seen ; but where, with the true instincts of seamen, they seemed to discern much to excite solicitude.

"House those carronades alongside (we only showed our little teeth as we passed Constantinople, Miss Wedderburn); lower away and lash the gun ports fast, for I see that it will be a night of close-reefed canvas again," said Newnham. And ere long the wind increased so much that sea after sea pooped the yacht, and her commander donned his oilskins, while she rolled fearfully on the long and heavy swell which is so peculiar to that ocean. Gwenny was compelled to go below, and Newnham handed her down just as the light of Faranaki-in-Asia began to glitter like a star across the darkening water, and Mount Hæmus on the opposite shore was sinking faint and blue, while the schooner bore on her course, northeastward, into the lonely Euxine, for not a sail or trace of smoke was visible as gloom and obscurity descended on the sea.

CHAPTER LXIII.

FATE.

CYRIL was still full of his project—his most earnest desire to remove Mary Lennox from the perilous atmosphere of the Hospital at Scutari, and place her in the care of an officer's wife, whom he knew, and who resided in Misseri's Frankish establishment, the Hotel l'Angleterre ; if not there, in the *pension* of Madame Giuseppino Vitale, so famous for the views from her windows, though that there *was* an awkwardness in a young unmarried officer procuring quarters for a young unmarried lady, he could not but admit ; however, ere he had quite decided what to do, there occurred an event which he had dreaded, yet could not bring his mind to anticipate.

He had recovered with marvellous rapidity, having suffered more from loss of blood than from actual severity of the wounds inflicted by Galitzin, though that near the lung had been certainly dangerous ; but what astonished and distressed him for a day or two was that Mary, who had long since ceased to attend or visit him, had entirely disappeared, and his servant, the soldier of the Black Watch, could tell him nothing about her. He could no longer meet with her light figure in its sombre dress, flitting about the passages that led to the wards, crossing the square from the laboratory or soup kitchen, and he began to fear that she had left the place for some reason or purpose known to herself alone.

Could she be ill? Alas! that was likely enough. He remembered that since he had first seen her in Scutari, she had been daily growing thinner, even as he waxed in strength and flesh. Her figure, once so fair and round, had seemed to be fading away ; her cheeks had become hollow, and her white temples too. Her hands had become painfully attenuated and almost transparent, all bespeaking what some one terms "the lingering decay of the delicate physique."

Cyril Wedderburn was sorely distressed by the recollection and conviction of all this ; and, blaming himself for remissness in not having her removed sooner, after three days had elapsed without seeing or hearing of her, he went forth to make inquiries.

"Depend upon it," thought he, "inspired by an emotion of false delicacy, or something of that kind, she has given me the slip and bolted for England perhaps, by the steamer from Galata."

Alas ! he little knew that poor Mary had not a sixpence in the world she could call her own.

"I was anxious, of course, to get her out of this horrid place ; but I hope she has not anticipated the move by any rash plan of her own," thought he ; "but anything is better than being here," he added, for with something akin to terror, he had seen her hovering in the cholera wards, where the patients were in all stages of collapse, with cold extremities, rigid muscles, and faces white or blue ; and yet among them she had gone cheerfully, gliding about, with her doses of opium, brandy, soda and calomel ; and old Doctor Riversdale, who was now there on duty, affirmed that she was worth any dozen nurses put together.

"It is all very fine, but by Jove, a fellow don't like the girl who is to be his wife doing all that sort of thing among the rank and file," said Cyril to her one day when he expressed his genuine astonishment and grief to find her thus occupied. "It may be enthusiastic, self-sacrificing, and so forth, but it is not the work for an English lady. In the French Sisters of Charity it seems somehow altogether different, but in our Protestant folks I can't understand it."

"Oh, Cyril," she had replied, gently, "we must bear patiently —I at least have learned *that* now—and with proper fortitude and resignation, the ills and the work Fate has marked out for us."

But Mary's frame was ill-suited for such tasks and for such an atmosphere ; and now Cyril learned, with horror and dismay, from a passing staff-surgeon, that "the poor girl was down with cholera, and was in that wing where the women's ward lay ; have a cigar, old fellow," he added, proffering his case, "and don't go near that place if you can avoid it." The

medical officer said all this quite in an offhand way, little
dreaming that he was planting a sword in the heart of his
hearer, who hurried away, stunned and overwhelmed, to the
place he indicated.

It was a great rambling Turkish house, which had once been
the residence of some wealthy merchant of Stamboul. Some
Turks were on duty that day about the Hospital, and a stolid-
looking Mahommedan soldier, in his scarlet fez, blue jacket and
red knickerbockers, stood sentinel under a sunshade, leaning
on his musket and smoking a cherrystick chibouque. He
started and saluted Cyril, and something expressive of astonishment that a man not a *hakim* should come to visit women,
escaped him ; but Cyril pushed him aside and strode in ; for
all our notions are reversed in that peculiar land where the
ladies wear trousers and the gentlemen often petticoats ; where
the ladies ogle through the eyelet-holes of their yashmacs, and
the gentlemen look demure and abashed ; where the men wear
all the gay colours and women the sombre.

An English soldier's widow who had acted as nurse there
since her husband died of his wounds, soon led Cyril to the
room where Mary lay—a small apartment that opened off the
stately Divan Hanée, having walls painted white and the roof
a flaming red, lighted by pointed windows of stained glass ; and
in this kiosk (a term signifying a room, or a house indifferently)
she was stretched on the floor, the occupant of an hospital
straw-pallet and covered by a coarse brown military rug, on
which were stamped in tar, the broad arrow and the inevitable
letters B.O.

The only furniture in this comfortless room was a *tandour*,
the Turkish substitute for a fire-place, being like the *brasero* of
the Spaniards, a wooden frame holding a copper vessel full of
charcoal, covered•by a wadded cloth. She was dashing her
head against the wall and the pillow alternately as she rolled
about in pain or delirium ; her beautiful silky hair hung all
dishevelled over her snowy shoulders, which were quite exposed.
Her lips were parched and black, while her face was deadly
pale and her eyes unnaturally bright and dilated. Her voice
was changed, yet the sound of it thrilled through Cyril to his
heart's core. She was raving, and she knew him not.

" God help us—God help us !" moaned Cyril, as he knelt by
her side in a passion of tears, and sought caressingly to smooth
her tangled tresses and reclose her night-dress which she had
rent at the neck.

" Poor young lady," said the soldier's widow, commiseratingly,
" she's done a power o' good among our poor fellows ! Is she
your sister, Captain Wedderburn ?"

" No."

And in his agony and answer, the woman seemed instinctively to know all; for after a pause she said—"Doctor Riversdale says, sir, it's more fever than cholera, and so there might be hopes if—"

"If what? Oh, speak out."

"If her system wasn't so low—but she can't stand the shock. I saw two children of mine die at Varna—die when the blue cholera mist rose like a tide about the tent-pegs, and I saw my poor Tom die here, after his leg were ampertated, and—and," she continued, bursting into tears, "I knows a look when I sees it in the eye now, and I see it here—so she can't last long, poor thing!"

"How long has she been thus?" asked Cyril, in a choking voice.

"Some hours, sir."

"And before that?"

"She was as calm as a lamb, sir, wishing for a clergyman, and expressing fears that a Captain Wedderburn—you, I suppose, sir—might visit her, and catch the infection."

And this was his Mary—his plighted wife—she whose nature was so full of those charms which are more attractive than the most brilliant or classic beauty—such winning and pretty ways! Oh how, as he knelt by that wretched bedside, and sought to capture and keep the quick small hand that eluded or repelled him, while her eyes sparkled dangerously—through the mists of the past and horror of the present, memory went back to many a happy, happy day, and to episodes all gone for ever now!

She was raving by turns of her father, of her dead brother Harry, of Cyril himself—and his reproachful heart seemed to bleed as he heard her—of little Mrs. Primer, of the Alderman in London, of the prison, and of a host of persons and places whose names bewildered him; then starting into a sitting position she pressed her hands on her temples, threw back her hair, and with eyeballs starting from their sockets, uttered a piercing shriek, as she sprang into an imaginary river, and then lay back calm and still, with her arms by her side as the fancied waters closed over her head.

"Please Captain Wedderburn, do leave us for a little, and when she is a little more composed and sensible, I'll fetch you;" and the female nurse half led him out into the Divan Hanée, which is the central hall of every great Turkish house, and off which all the other rooms open. She closed the door—dropped the curtain we should rather say—and Cyril wearily, and as one in a nightmare, seated himself on the divan, or luxurious sofa, which is placed all round this apartment, and there he remained for a time, like a man in a dream—but a dream which, with all its bitterness, did not pass away.

CHAPTER LXIV.

THE CITY OF THE SILENT.

WAS it the vision of a distempered brain, he asked of himself, this strange and fantastic Turkish hall (through which the sunlight fell in golden flakes from a double row of upper and lower windows of square form), with all its green and gold arabesques and pious sentences from the koran traced round on scrolls beneath the cornices ; was it not like some scene he had witnessed in a theatre, that line of twisted columns and horse-shoe arches dividing the room, beyond which he saw a marble fountain playing, and places like pigeon-holes holding vases and beautiful jars, once filled with cool water, sherbet or flowers? And could it be possible that Mary Lennox—she whom he used to meet in the old pine thicket, whose cheek had so often reposed on his shoulder by the lonely stile in the glen, was lying there on a wretched straw pallet, amid such strange and foreign surroundings, and at the point of—death? So he sat in a kind of stupor, gazing at a group of the Turkish guard seated drowsily under a sunshade, smoking and listening to the lascivious story of a dervish, whom they would reward with a para or two.

Anon the nurse came, and told him in a whisper that "she was asleep ;" and he blessed God for it, in the fervent hope that it might be the forerunner of returning health and strength, and that the crisis might be past. So he went forth to soothe his nerves by a stroll and a cigar, and in about two hours returned to find that Mary had been awake, and that a chaplain of the Duke of Cambridge's division (whom the splinter of a shell had wounded) was with her ; that she was quite calm, and preparing and wishing to die.

"But not to leave me !" he exclaimed with sorrowful reproach, and he issued forth again, repassing the Osmanli sentinel, who thought he must be mad to grieve about a woman —"Mashallah ! a sick one too !"

In the yard he met Doctor Riversdale, and questioned him ; but the old staff surgeon shook his head sorrowfully, and his reply recalled to Cyril the convictions of the nurse.

"There are two expressions in the human face, which when we once see them, Wedderburn, we never forget—the first quick glance of love, and the last long look of death ! I have been in love in my day, like most men ; and as a soldier have seen many die on the field and in hospital ; and I have seen death in that girl's face, but blended with love too !"

"How, Riversdale ?"

"When her lips uttered *your* name."

After a time, when he re-entered the Divan Hanée, the curtain veiling the door was lifted by the nurse, who beckoned him eagerly, and as he drew near, the woman, with good taste, withdrew, while Cyril, in a fresh burst of anguish, threw himself on his knees by Mary's side, striving, but in vain, to control his grief. She stretched out her thin hands towards him, and gave him a soft sad smile.

Oh, that glance! that too often furtive glance which all lovers know, and which is too subtle for description, has much of power; but it was *not* the glance that was now in the weird and pursuing eyes of Mary,—it was the earnest glance seen only in the eyes of the dying, but blended with much of sweetness. So Riversdale was right.

"I am dying, Cyril," said she, in a low voice; "I feel it in my heart."

"You—you, my Mary; oh, it cannot be!" he whispered with quivering lips and in a passion of tears.

"Yes, Cyril, my love, I can't last long now."

"Oh! would that my wound had been mortal, and that I had died before you, darling; we should then have been re-united, never more to part. But God knows what is best for us."

"And blessed be His holy name, Cyril! Kiss me, darling, while—while I can see you, and can feel my hand in yours. The sun has set very suddenly, surely—on the forehead, darling —on the forehead, not the lip—not the lip!"

"Why, my Mary?"

"There may be death in such a kiss."

"Then welcome be the death!"

"Oh, Cyril!—husband of my heart!" she murmured.

"My plighted wife—my Mary!"

"I am going to my poor papa," she said with childlike simplicity. "He clung, Cyril, to the fragment of his patrimony even as a gallant captain clings to the wreck of his ship, and— and—"

"Yes, Mary; though rash, a true gentleman to the last."

"And he loved me so—my poor papa!"

Then her mind began to wander a little again. Far away from Scutari, from where the hastily buried dead lay on the plain without the walls,—from the wards of the horrid hospital her thoughts went as in a dream,—for so her mutterings showed while her poor head rested on Cyril's neck,—back to Lonewoodlee, to the old grey tower, with its turrets and cape-house of the stormy Border times; to the mossy stile and the thorn trees; to the old Scottish firs, with their red stems, gnarled branches and bronze-like foliage cutting the clear blue sky; to the mountain burn that brawled amid grey rocks and stones, purple heather and golden broom; from the green slopes of the

Lammermuirs, to the lonely pastoral hills, where the black-faced wedders browsed and bleated ; to places where the scarlet rowan grew, and where the pink and white hawthorn loaded the evening air with fragrance ; and in the girl's heart there waxed strong the desire to die—not among her kindred, for kindred had she *none*, but that she might die in her native land, and be laid among the graves where her forefathers lay, in the Lennox-aisle of the old kirk at Willowdean. But fate had willed it otherwise.

For an hour she lay with her head pillowed on Cyril's heart, and barely conscious of his presence. She was hovering on that Borderland which lies between Time and Eternity—that mysterious frontier from whence the world, and all its interests, must look very small indeed ; smaller still its wrongs and its sorrows ; dim its doubts, its loves, and allurements. After a time a shiver, that passed over all the delicate form ; a sigh that escaped her ; and the fallen jaw, revealing all the pearl-like teeth, announced that all was over !

The light was fading as the sun shed its last red rays on the Bosphorus, but Cyril lingered long with the dead in his arms ; and tenderly, and while his tears fell on them, he kissed her white eyelids after he had closed them for ever, smoothing the long dark lashes on the marble cheeks ; and the widowed nurse, who was hovering without, could not restrain her tears when on peeping in she saw the handsome young officer on his knees, in his blood-stained and tattered uniform, engaged in prayer by the humble pallet whereon the dead girl lay, looking in death purer and lovelier than ever.

   *   *   *   *   *   *

By the hospital regulations all fever patients were buried immediately, to avoid the spread of infection, and so that night saw the last scene of this tragedy.

Four soldiers—wounded Fusileers of Cyril's company, men selected by himself—bore her on their shoulders in a hastily-made coffin to the cemetery without the walls, where lie so many of our dead, the gallant, and in too many instances, perhaps, forgotten victims of the war and pest. The only pall that covered her was a ship's union-jack ; it had already served for many in Scutari, and would serve for many more ; and Cyril, as he stood at the head of her grave, could see the full round silver moon as it rose up in beauty from the sea of Marmora, throwing far across the plain the shadows of the spectre-like cypresses that overlook the vast Turkish "City of the Silent," the seven miles of tombs ; and after the chaplain had concluded the affecting burial service of the Church of England, not a sound was heard but the splash of oars in the Bosphorus, throwing showers of seeming diamonds upwards, as some light caïque that shot to and fro ; or the prolonged howling of some houseless dog, the ever accursed of the prophet, prowling along the streets of Scutari.

It was the night of the 20th February ; so the same moon that through a tempest of snow looked down on the capture of Horace Ramornie near the Tchernaya, saw his cousin acting in a very different scene in the great cemetery opposite Seraglio Point. For a time he sat on a tombstone close by, the picture of thought and grief, his hands clasped over the hilt of his sword, which was placed between his knees, and his chin resting on his hands, his eyes bent on vacancy. In the last hour or two he seemed to have become older, thinner, greyer, and more stern.

The chaplain kindly gave him his arm, and his four comrades urged him, in their own plain fashion, to be comforted, though they could not comprehend the cause of his grief ; but then he was a favourite officer, and as they put on their caps and saluted him, ere withdrawing to their quarters in the convalescent portion of the hospital, they all in unison sympathized with Captain Wedderburn.

And there she lay alone in her grave upon the Asian shore, under the shadow of those giant cypresses, poor Mary Lennox, the last of that ilk of the Lonewoodlee. After all her miseries, it was a strange and wayward fate !

How bitterly and unavailingly now he repented of his past harshness, suspicions, and injustice to her who was gone — bitterly too, for the time lost by their needless separation ; for the false position in which she had so long been placed with his family through mistaken ideas of policy ; and he felt in his heart, that surely we suffer our punishments on this earth, and not hereafter.

He had but one embodied thought ever present now—that he had found her in this strange land among Miss Nightingale's good Samaritans ; that he had seen the face, again heard the voice of Mary, and held her hand in his ; and that never, never more would that beloved face turn to his, and never more her voice fall on his ear ! And she had been true to him, and had loved him to the last ! He remembered her warning words of fear and love when he kissed her, and he was not without hope that he might yet die and be laid by her side, for Mary seemed so lonely in her grave ; but Cyril Wedderburn was not one of those men who die easily.

Many a solitary hour he lingered by Mary's grave, as if he felt the influence of her presence about him still, and many a fresh chaplet of white roses he hung there ; for he could not altogether leave the place where she lay alone—so utterly alone ; and times there were when he thought he might have her remains transmitted home and laid beside those of her father at Willowdean. There seemed a soothing yet sorrowful companionship in sitting there and repeating her name to himself, and looking at the turf which covered the grave, and at the little marble cross which marked where she who on her death-bed had called him "the husband of her heart," was lying at peace with God and man.

Poor Cyril! His life was purposeless now, and more than the half of it seemed to have passed away. His thick brown hair came out in handfuls, and he could detect—yet heeded it not now—a grey hair or two in his beard and moustache. All zest for existence, for exertion, for anything, had gone with Mary Lennox; but, nevertheless, idleness soon became intolerable. He speedily reported himself fit for active service, and Riversdale struck him off the sick list. So the tenth of March saw him on board of a steam transport, filled with enthusiastic and cheering convalescents who had partly recovered from their wounds, all anxious to have "another shy at the Ruskies"—all longing to be once more before Sebastopol, where the ceaseless cannon boomed and the bullets went *ping-ping* from the rifle-pits, where the dead lay half buried on the hill slopes, and where in rags and misery the trench guards toiled,—God alone knows for what now : but when steaming up the Bosphorus, the eyes of Cyril were turned to the point of Scutari and to the diminishing outline of the cypresses that overlook "the City of the Silent," for his heart was lying there. Had Lady Wedderburn known of the catastrophe that imparted such a tone of distraction to the letters of her favourite son, she might have thought, with mingled remorse and satisfaction, that her *wish* would probably be gratified after all.

CHAPTER LXV.

DREAMS REALIZED.

IN Yaila the days and even the nights were passed by Horace Ramornie in a species of mental torture. The longing for freedom took the form of dreams when darkness fell, and visions haunted him like those of one who suffered from fever. He beheld Gwenny at times encompassed by absurd and fantastic perils, from which he sought in vain to save her. Once she appeared clinging to a fragment of loose rock above a raging sea—the cliffs of the Ernesclough, or Fast Castle, perhaps—and ere he could aid her—for his limbs felt as if powerless, weak, or fettered—the frail thing to which she seemed to cling gave way, and Gwenny disappeared beneath the waves, eliciting a cry from Horace, which brought the Russsian guard in wonder to his room.

On other occasions, he wandered in pursuit of her through endless and mysterious galleries, arched passages, and long, long chambers, where, though he could hear her voice, he lost all trace of her in the end, and sought in vain with terror and bewilderment of heart.

But then he had other and more pleasant dreams. He was free! He was again with his company of the Fusileers, in the trenches, among wooden gabions and fascines of straw or sand bags, and the booming of the cannon in Sebastopol came to his ear. He saw the white walls and the green spires of the city rising in the sunshine above the curling smoke of the gun batteries. Then would come the music of the band on the march; again he saw the heights above the Alma glittering with Russian bayonets, and he heard the pleasant voice of Cyril Wedderburn; there was a sound of pistol shots, and then came the pale face and glittering cold eyes of Prince Galitzin; or it might be that he had memories of the mess-room of the corps—the billiard table at Chatham or Canterbury, and he was at pool or pyramid with Bingham and Probyn; and often it was of Willowdean and the days when he came there an orphan from his dead mother's side, and then he saw the stately house with its white peristyle and all its windows glittering in the sun, old Gervase Asloane in his ample waistcoat and black suit hovering about; his aunt, Lady Wedderburn, bowling through the ample lawn in her smart pony phaeton, or Sir John in tweed suit and leather gaiters going with his gun to the preserves, or rambling about, weeder in hand, and Horace could hear his pleasant voice and see again his bright and benign smile; but only to waken and find himself—a prisoner still in Yaila! It was after visions such as these, that by the mere force of contrast, his captivity felt intolerable, and equally so, when, after being lost in thought—indulging in some bright daydream, perhaps—he would be roused by the hoarse Russian drums, beaten for parade or some tour of duty, and, starting, would bethink him how, or why he was here in Yaila.

Though the idea of violating his parole of honour, attempting to escape or to quit his prison without being properly exchanged, never occurred to Horace, the manner of Galitzin offensively showed that *he* was suspicious of something of the kind being attempted. Horace was conscious of being watched; that eyes were upon him; and that whenever he went abroad for a solitary ramble, somehow, as if by a singular coincidence, the two Cossacks, Alexis and Ivan—he never knew, nor cared to know their surnames—were always hovering near. But to have spoken of this would have been unwise, and would have excited suspicion

To a Russian of Tartar descent, subtlety and craft were
familiar, even as caprice and tyranny, from the days of his
wooden cradle, when he had been taught to thump or kick the
image of his patron, Saint Ivan Veliki, and even to thrust it in
the fire if he suffered pain from overeating himself with
pastillia or other sweetmeats ; if he lost his top or marbles, or
got cuffed for his impudent petulance by any of his companions.
He suspected that few things in this world were ever done for
the motives really assigned to them, and he believed that under
all that went on, something *else* was going on unseen.   So there
was a terrible distrust of everyone and everything pervading
his whole existence.   He was Muscovite to the heart's core !

One morning Horace was sensible of an unusual commotion
in Yaila, after Galitzin's *aide-de-camp*, the Lieutenant of the
Princess Maria Paulovna's Hussars, who had been sent to the
seashore on some special duty, returned with important tidings
for the Prince.   The preceding night had been one of dreadful
tempest.   The rain had fallen in torrents ; and, amid the wild
bellowing of the wind, the thunder had been heard, as it rattled
in appalling peals over the red marble cliffs of the Tchatr Dagh,
and the four copper-covered domes of Yaila.

The drums were beaten, and a certain portion of the garrison
got under arms after breakfast.   Horace felt a thrill of hope in
his heart !   Was there about to be an attack—a chance of
escape after all, and after those weary, weary months of spring
and summer he had endured there?   Day was just breaking,
and, in anticipation of some event, which, if it did not set him
free, would at least vary the stupid monotony of his existence,
Horace came forth, just as Prince Galitzin, after buckling on
his sword, was mounting his horse.

The usual strange and malicious glitter came into his eyes, as
he seemed to read the hope of Horace in his eager and excited
face ; and the latter's emotion seemed to strengthen when he
saw the troops bring forth two eighteen-pound guns, and, with
their muskets slung, tally on to the drag-ropes, as the field-
pieces were without horses.

"By Jove, it did rain and blow last night, Monseigneur le
Prince," said Horace, loth to ask any questions, while wishing
to invite information.   "I have not passed so many sleepless
hours since I was in the trenches before Sebastopol, and heard
the Lancaster guns pounding away on the right attack."

"And you are longing to be there, again—eh ?"

"I cannot deny that I am, indeed."

"You must be patient, Monsieur le Capitaine."

Horace sighed bitterly, and then ventured to say. "But
what is the matter ?   Have you had an *alerte*, or are you going
to be attacked ?"

"Nay. 'Tis we who are about to attack!"

"What, or who?"

"I know not whether I should reply, but it is no matter. Well, an English ship—a yacht, apparently—is reported to be ashore on the rocks, a few miles northward from Alushta; and we are just going to knock her to pieces with those two eighteen-pounders, if the waves do not anticipate us ; for Kaminski, my aide-de-camp, reports that there is a heavy sea on, and that she can't last long now."

"A wreck—an unarmed yacht. To fire on a wreck—is this fair?"

"*Morbleu!* Did I not once before say that all things are fair in war and love? and we are at war just now, I believe. Come on, Tegoborski, we have no time to lose!"

"I dreamed of rats last night, and I thought something would be sure to happen after that, and the wind being so high," grumbled the superstitious old Pulkovnick, as he mounted his horse, while Madame, his wife—in a very becoming *deshabille*, appeared at an open window, where she kissed her large white hand repeatedly to the Prince, who waved his smiling adieux in return.

The hoarse and guttural commands were given, and, at a double-quick, the Infantry—about four hundred in number—left Yaila, dragging the guns and limbers, and having with them several kabitkas, or covered Tartar carts, for plunder, or whatever came ashore.

Some hours elapsed, and Horace felt his heart swelling with indignation. He pictured, in fancy, the shattered ship, the helpless drowning seamen, and the Russian guns firing round-shot — perhaps grape and canister — upon them from the heights ; just as they did during the dreadful hurricane in the preceding November, when so many of our ships perished along the iron-bound coast of the Black Sea. Much bitterness was now being imparted to the war on both sides ; but chiefly owing to the barbarity of the Russians. Doubtless, there were a few instances of humanity that are worth remembering. Many Russian prisoners who were *paroled* at Lewes, expressed in print, on their return home, their gratitude for the kindness and hospitality they had experienced at English hands ; and several of our officers who were prisoners of war in Russia, related the kind treatment they received while there. So, perhaps, Ivan Prince Galitzin was a somewhat exceptional personage.

About noon his cruel expedition returned, and Horace, who had secluded himself in his room, full of disgust and anger, heard the noisy applause with which the soldiers in Yaila received those who came back, though their exploit was far removed from being a noble or gallant one. The kabitkas were filled with pieces of shattered wreck, sheets of copper, sail-cloth, rigging, several cases of wine, London porter, and casks of beef, which had come ashore ; and now hearing by chance that prisoners had been taken, Horace again came forth to see them, and seek for some intelligence of the outer world, from which he was so completely debarred by the measures and ex-treme reserve of Galitzin. To be sure he might always have gained some news of the war from Madame Tegoborski, who was not indisposed to view him with favour, as a handsome young man; but he had a wholesome dread of exciting the jealousy of the Prince in that quarter.

"How many prisoners have you got, Monsieur le Colonel ?" he asked of Tegoborski, who was proceeding leisurely, limping, for he was lame, towards his quarters, anticipating a cup of hot tea after his morning's work.

"One," was the brief reply ; "at least only one of any con-sequence."

"And the rest ?"

"Are in the sea."

"Drowned ?"

"Or shot, as the case may have been."

In the yard of the fortress, Horace perceived one whom he took to be an Englishman, handcuffed ; he had on only a tattered white shirt and pair of blue cloth trousers ; he was tall and athletic in figure, fair complexion, bald and bare-headed, for in lieu of a cap he had a bloodstained handkerchief round his head, showing that he had been wounded ; and he was seated moodily, and as if lost in thought, on the trail of one of the fatal eighteen pounder field-pieces.

He looked up listlessly as Horace approached, and said—" A prisoner, like myself, I see."

"Not precisely, as I have not the misfortune to be fettered ; but I have been here for four months—ever since Sir Colin Campbell's night march to Tchorgoun. And you ?"

"My ship went ashore in the middle watch last night, on a reef that is not laid down in any of our charts."

"Where ?"

"Within a quarter of a mile from the cliffs that rise near Alushta, a Tartar village on the coast. We had undergone a rough night and were blown far out of course beyond the head-land of Alupka, where Prince Woronzoff's castle stands ; our rudderbands had given way, and we couldn't help ourselves. Finding that the craft wouldn't last long, I lowered the boat and got the ladies ashore, and at the hazard of my own life returned on board ; but I was scarcely on the deck, when, bang, bang, bang from the cliffs came a fire of round shot from these rascally guns ; so they and the sea, which was a heavy one, soon made an end of the schooner and of my men, for every poor fellow perished, those who threw themselves into the sea to escape the cannonade being killed by the lances of the Cossack beggars, as they struggled half fainting ashore."

" Most rascally—most base !" exclaimed Horace.

" Luckily I had my naval uniform below, and put it on. As I swam ashore the sight of my epaulettes saved me from being butchered like the rest ; but they were torn from my shoulders, and I was handcuffed as you see. I am a lieutenant in Her Britannic Majesty's service ! As a signal of distress I had the union-jack reversed at the gaff-peak ; but I was glad when the spar was knocked away and it fell into the sea. It went to my heart to see the old bunting under fire and never a shot in return. I thought of Nelson, and the signal that flew along the line at Trafalgar ; of old Charlie Napier's in the Baltic, ' Sharpen your cutlasses, lads !' I thought too of many an old shipmate who is lying in the Bight of Benin with a cold shot at his heels, and strong in my breast grew the genuine old English contempt of all these foreign beggars ! But now that I look at you again, I think I have had the pleasure of meeting you before. Are you not Captain Ramornie of the Royal Fusileers—the nephew of Sir John Wedderburn of Willowdean ?"

" The same ; and you ?"

" Lieutenant Robert Newnham, R.N."

" And your ship ?" asked Horace, faintly.

" Was the Master of Ernescleugh's yacht. I have seen you aboard of her at Cowes more than once."

" And the ladies you spoke of ?"

" Were Lady Wedderburn and Lady Ernescleugh ; they *would* come out here after their sons in the Crimea. Lord Cardigan's yacht had come, and the Countess of Errol had accompanied her husband who is in the Rifle Brigade, so the two mammas were determined to come too, and bring no end of comforts and condiments for their ' dear boys' in the trenches; but by jingo! they'll rather repent of the expedition now, though they were sent with their maids under escort in a kabitka towards Bala-clava ; for the worst of the story is yet to come."

" What could well be worse than that which you have told me?" exclaimed Horace.

" Another prisoner was brought on with me here, and my heart bleeds for the poor young lady in the hands of those d—d Russians. She is too young for sorrow, and was so kind and affable to all the poor fellows before the mast, they idolized her."

" Of whom are you talking?" asked Horace, whose heart began to tremble with apprehension and conjecture.

" Who should I mean but Miss Gwendolyne Wedderburn ?"

" She here ?"

" Aye, here in this fortress of Yaila—a prisoner like ourselves
—but not half so safe in some respects."

" My God !" exclaimed Horace, and he shivered from head
to foot ; "how came it to pass, Newnham, that she was not also
sent to Balaclava ?"

" In this fashion, for I was standing by, and to my sorrow
and disgust heard every word.

" ' I am rich, Monseigneur le Prince,' said Lady Wedderburn,
in the greatest agitation, to the Russian commander, whom I
understood to be a Prince Galitzin — but that's a name like
Smith in England, they are thick as Mother Cary's chickens in
Russia ; 'and so is my friend ; we can afford to pay a ransom,
if it will be taken.'

" ' And your niece or daughter, which is the young lady ?' he
asked.

" ' My niece—Mademoiselle Gwendoleyne Wedderburn.'

" ' Wedderburn, Wedderburn,' repeated the Russian, 'she is
wealthy too ; an Indian heiress, I understood.'

" ' Yes, Monseigneur ; but how knew you that ?'

" ' A Monsieur Chesters told me all about it at Balaclava ;
and of her being the intended of your son ; who was wounded
or killed at the Alma, I believe.'

" ' Only wounded, thank Heaven ! but do you know Monsieur
le Capitaine Chesters ?'

" ' I *did* know him ; but, Madame, he is dead and buried now,'
replied the other, with a grin.

" ' And now about a ransom ?' said Lady Wedderburn, full
of anxiety.

" ' Well, Madame, no ransom can be taken for the young
Hospoza ; we are Russian troops, not Circassians, Bedouin rob-
bers, or brigands.'

" ' But her liberty ?' urged Lady Wedderburn, to whom Miss
Gwenny clung in terror and despair.

" ' Her liberty shall be well cared for. I shall keep her for
myself ; heiresses are scarce in the Crimea,' was the bantering
reply.

" ' Surely you will permit me to accompany her ?' urged poor
Lady Wedderburn, piteously.

" ' What the deuce should we do with old women in Yaila ? It
would only be people to feed unprofitably, and in this nothing-
for-nothing world, my dear Madame——'

" ' Oh, dearest aunt, are we to be separated ?' exclaimed Miss
Gwenny, in dreadful agitation.

" ' Instantly, by St. Ivan Veliki !'

" The wretches tore them asunder, though the aunt and niece
clung to each other with the death-like clutch of the drowning,

and their cries wrung my heart. The two elder ladies were sent in a Tartar waggon towards Balaclava, in charge of the aide-de-camp Kaminski and four Cossacks, one of whom carried a white handkerchief as a flag of truce on the point of his lance, while we were brought on here. But Heaven help the poor girl, Captain Ramornie. Galitzin sees that she is young and beautiful, and he knows that she is wealthy, for I heard him remark, laughingly, to Kaminski, his aide, 'This war can't last for ever; another winter will see those allies frozen or fought out; then I shall go to England with my wife, turn her rupees into roubles, and spend them in Holy Russia.' Holy Russia be d—d, say I."

Horace listened to all this with the air of one quite stunned by a calamity; and he was again about to address Newnham, when the voice of Galitzin was heard.

"No talking—no communications between you two. Separate them," he added to the *parvoschick* of the main guard; "and as the sailor has declined to give his parole, keep him a close prisoner."

So poor Newnham was led away.

"I was only hearing some details of the—well, I suppose we must call it the shipwreck," said Horace, making a prodigious effort to appear calm and to conceal the agony of his spirit; for the idea of Gwenny being a prisoner in Yaila seemed too fantastic, too unexpected, and too horrible for conviction.

"Ah! we let him put the women ashore; for whatever you may think, we are not quite devoid of gallantry, we Russians; and then we knocked the schooner to pieces," said Galitzin, laughing; "but the chief prize we brought on here."

"I do not understand you," faltered Horace.

"Then understand this. I have caught the rich cousin—the brunette—the little Anglo-Indian millionaire, whose intended I pistolled at the Alma——"

"Cyril Wedderburn?"

"Well, yes, if that *was* his name; I suppose we may speak of him in the past tense now."

"From whom had *you* all this private information?"

"From Monsieur Chesters, *le scelerat!*"

"When?"

"When I met him in the camp of the Turkish Contingent."

"Explain, Monseigneur le Prince?"

"A few days before your silly night march to Tchorgoun, and when I was figuring, as the play-bills say, 'positively for the last time,' as a Captain of Zouaves," replied the unabashed Russian.

"Will not the offer of a bribe set her free?"

"Not twenty bribes!"

"Why, Monseigneur le Prince?"

"You shall hear in good time."

"And where is she now?" asked Horace, with an affectation of carelessness that certainly cost him an effort.

"In the apartments and under the matronage of Madame Tegoborski. She was dreadfully offended when I attempted to give her a little salute *à la Russe.* St. Ivan Veliki—bah! a time shall come when she will think little of my wiry moustache—though it *is* like a hog's-bristle—being rasped on her damask cheek!"

"By Jove! this *is* a pleasant situation," thought Horace, as he wiped his brow, and longed to plant his foot upon the neck of Major-General Prince Galitzin, who added with pleasing condescension—

"I shall introduce you to her at old Tegoborski's to-night; but perhaps you don't care about it."

"Thanks, Monseigneur le Prince, I shall come with pleasure," said Horace; and he retired to his room with a heart that was full, nigh to bursting, with sorrow, terror of the present, and apprehension of the future.

That night Newnham was dispatched on foot, escorted by two Cossack Lancers, towards Yekaterinoslav, and a deadly fear came over Horace that unless he dissembled, and he and Gwenny played "their cards" remarkably well, some such distant transmission might await himself, if Galitzin discovered the deep and tender interest they had in each other. And how to conceal it? for the first meeting might, most perilously, reveal all.

"Gwenny here—my Gwenny here in Yaila?" he repeated to himself again and again.

He felt himself trembling from head to foot; a pallor came over him repeatedly, as the blood rushed back upon his heart. Though loving her with all the devotion of which his life and heart were capable, he had no desire, even while longing passionately to see her, to have her with him there, and his voice shook while, clasping his hands, he said fervently—"God protect her —my darling Gwenny. Oh! I fear she will need all His protection here in Yaila!"

CHAPTER LXVI.

TEA WITH MADAME TEGOBORSKI.

HORACE naturally wondered how it came to pass that Chesters should have spoken of the Wedderburn family or of their private interests to an utter stranger—a foreigner—a mere chance visitor, such as this pretended Captain of Zouaves in the redoubts before Balaclava; for the visit of Galitzin had been paid to them prior to the assault made by the Russians on the day of the battle there; but it only proved that the enmity of Chesters to Cyril was an ever-rankling subject, and the matter might have come about *apropos* of the misfortune which befel the latter at the Alma. And then the luckless Major of the Turkish Contingent had failed as yet to recognise in the turbaned Zouave his quondam gambling acquaintance ; but the latter knew *him* only too well, and treasured up his secret vengeance. However the matter came to pass, Horace was certain of one thing, that the information of the needy Russian Prince as to Gwenny's fortune was unpleasantly accurate.

His next idea was, as to how he and she were to meet, and how to greet each other—betrothed lovers, who had been so long and so perilously parted—in the presence of Galitzin, after the openly-expressed views of that personage concerning her—views so suddenly and distinctly stated. For Horace knew that the Prince had nothing in the world but his sword, his epaulettes, and a truly Muscovite spirit for the most daring peculation ; and he knew also how resolute, how cunning, and how savage he could be when roused. And now, by the contingencies of war, this man was to become the arbiter of their destinies !

Longing, with all a young lover's ardour, to fold Gwenny in his arms, and to cover her sweet face and hands with kisses, he would, nevertheless, be compelled to appear before her as a stranger, and, as such, to be introduced by the Russian ogre, who had them both in his power. It seemed intolerable and absurd, and times there were when Horace was on the point of saying boldly that the lady was his betrothed, his intended, and almost a kinswoman ; but then prudence suggested that such a confidence might be unwise, and might, moreover, cause Galitzin to dispatch him, under escort, to Yekaterinoslav, if he did not *dispatch* him out of the world altogether. For Horace could not forget the fate of Ralph Chesters, and knew the refined cruelty of which the Prince was capable.

Gwenny, ere evening came, had got over much of her terror of the shipwreck ; but her mind was still brooding with horror over the memory of the cannonade, the mangled and drowning seamen, and the strange manner in which she had been so rudely separated from her aunt and Lady Ernescleugh, and brought she knew not whither. But the Prince had pacified her for a time, by the assurance that when he could get a carriage worthy of conveying her, she should be also sent to Balaclava. She was full of these things, and in no mood to construe, or attempt to understand Madame Tegoborski, who, as she could not speak English, addressed her in Russian, mingled with a few words of German, seeking to interest her in a certain handsome young " Capitaine Ramhornoff," whom she was so soon to see, and whom Gwenny supposed to be some odious Russian, who ate tallow candles and took his morning libation of train oil.

Horace felt the absolute necessity of losing no time in letting
her know the line of conduct they must adopt towards each
other, lest she should become inspired by doubt or apprehension
of his seeming coldness. On the flyleaf of a Russian book he
pencilled a few words in the smallest possible space, simply
informing her that under the eyes which were on them there,
they must seem to be only *friends*, not what they really were ;
and that, on the first opportunity, he should explain all ; and
he had barely achieved this tiny billet, when Galitzin appeared
to inquire " If he was ready to accompany him and his aide-de-
camp, the Lieutenant Kaminski ?"

The Prince was in full uniform, with a pair of splendid
epaulettes set very high upon his shoulders in the Russian
fashion. He was evidently bent on making an impression, for
he wore a gold embroidered waistbelt, and in addition to the
order of St. Anne, had that of St. Andrew, an order founded
by Peter the Great in 1699, and only bestowed on officers of
high military degree. It was a blue enamelled saltire with the
Muscovite eagle, and four initials, signifying *Sanctus Andreas,
Patronus Russiæ.* Horace had only the poor remains of his
red coat, on which none of the lace and few of the buttons
remained ; but he knew that to Gwenny's eye "the old red rag
that tells of England's glory" would be dearer and more significant than the most splendid costume in the world. However,
he felt that he cut but a sorry figure in comparison with Galitzin. He was greatly agitated on entering the whitewashed
vaulted chamber, which, in one of the old towers, passed as the
drawing-room of Madame Tegoborski ; but though the latter
was there, and received Horace with a bland smile, and the
Prince with a particularly bright one, Gwenny had not yet left
her room, so the visitor glanced uneasily about him, after
shaking the hand of the grim Pulkovnick, or *Chef de
Bataillon.*

Most of the furniture in the apartment seemed strange to the
eye, and extremely nautical in fashion ; for save a piano, taken
sans cérémonie from the house of an Armenian merchant at
Alushta, most of it was the spoil of that hurricane in the Black
Sea which strewed the shore with wrecks in the preceding
November. Wafered on the wall were two Russian caricatures,
which at that time were thought prime jokes. One represented
John Bull in his well-known top boots, occupying an island so
small that he had not room to turn in it, and which was divided
into three parts, entitled " Leinster, Oxford, Cambridge." The
other was a grotesque figure of Sir Charles Napier, presenting
a fish from the Baltic Sea to the British Parliament, as the spoil
of Cronstadt and Bomarsund. An *eikon* or Byzantine Madonna
stood in a corner, with metal halo like a gilt horseshoe around

the head ; but now there was a muslin veil drawn discreetly over it, lest it should see old Tegoborski become tipsy, or the Prince saluting Madame, which, we must admit, he was wont to do somewhat oftener than friendship warranted, or platonic affection required.

Madame Norina Paulovna Tegoborski, a stout and very fair woman, with a dazzling neck and bosom, was beautifully dressed in honour of the evening, and wore Schologoleff earrings, each like four tiny cannon-balls, a fashion adopted in honour of an imaginary artillery officer, who with only *four* guns, was alleged by the Russians to have sorely mauled and repulsed the allied fleets at Odessa ! On her large, fair arms were glittering bracelets ; but on this occasion she was fated to display her charms in vain. The room door opened, there was the rustling of a dress, and Horace felt a mist before his eyes and a wild throbbing in his heart, as Gwenny, looking pale and startled, yet somewhat defiant in bearing, entered. The Prince hurried to kiss her hand, and next Madame Tegoborski hastened to present to her the Aide-de-camp Kaminski, and "le Capitaine Ramhornoff."

"Horace !" exclaimed the poor girl in utter bewilderment, "you *here ?*"

"And you, Gwenny?" He clasped her hands, and—had death menaced them both, to resist the impulse was impossible —for a moment their flushed faces were pressed together, but the hands remained closely locked, while her agitation found relief in a flood of tears.

"The Prince has told me all," said Horace, "and more than I could wish to have heard."

"I certainly expected to see you in the Crimea—and dear Cyril too," said Gwenny, sobbing.

"Alas ! I know nothing of him ; I have been here for more than four months."

"We heard that he had left Scutari and joined the Fusileers again."

"Recovered ?"

"Yes."

"Thank Heaven—poor Cyril."

"What is all this?—you are old friends, I find !" said the Prince, as Horace drew back (after contriving to slip his billet into the hand of Gwenny and to whisper, "Read at leisure"). "But, I suppose," he added, laughing, and pointing to one of the caricatures, "all the people in your little island know one another, it is so small."

For a traveller writes : "The notion that the great want of England is want of land, is a very popular one in Russia, where land is so plentiful in proportion to the population that no proprietor thinks of reckoning his fortune by his acres, but by the number of peasants he can put to cultivate them."

And now Horace and Gwenny sat on opposite sides of the room, their eyes and hearts full of each other ; but all external emotion was repressed by the consciousness of publicity—the odious presence of strangers.

"And you were taken prisoner, my poor Horace?" said Gwenny, in a tender tone.

"Yes. In the dark amid the snow I fell into the hands of the enemy, in the night expedition to Tchorgoun."

"And hence the mystery of your disappearance and the total cessation of all letters. You know, of course, the catastrophe of last night and this morning?"

"I have heard all from poor Newnham and the Prince," replied Horace, in a sad voice.

Gwenny looked at him earnestly. She could see that captivity, irritation, and the suspicions of Galitzin had done no good to Horace. His eyes, she thought, had lost much of their open, candid, and kind expression ; they seemed sunken, furtive, and at times defiant and stern. He looked more manly, however, for campaigning and trench work had developed and hardened his frame ; but he was bearded to the eyes, and tattered as a digger at Ballarat.

The figure of Gwenny, he thought, had attained more of the roundness of womanhood ; her face was pale and pure as ever, her smile as winning, and her bearing as full of grace.

"Horace—Horace !" she exclaimed, with a touch of her old waggery, "such a coat you have—why, it is in absolute rags !"

"Yes, Gwenny ; my kit is not at its best—or my wardrobe, I should have to say, were Aunt Wedderburn here ; but the Cossacks took a fancy for the lace and most of the buttons ; they appreciate finery, those fellows. But your own attire is rather odd. That dress never came from Swan and Edgar's !"

"It is a yellow silk of Madame Tegoborski's—as you see, a world too wide for me."

Galitzin, who was equally master of English as of French, laughed at these remarks. But now the *samovar*, or brass urn, made its appearance, hissing and hot, and the important business of the evening, tea drinking, commenced.

The four Russians all turned to the *eikon* and crossed themselves, while a servant poured out the tea, and another—a pretty Karaïte Jewess, whose white *fereedjè* gave additional lustre to her beautiful eyes—handed it round, with cakes and preserved fruit. It was served in crystal tumblers* for the four gentlemen, but in china cups for the two ladies ; and the im-

---

* The use of the tumbler is being gradually banished.—" The Russians at Home."

bibing of this fluid is such a passion with the Russians, that in the *Traktirs*, or tea-houses of Moscow and St. Petersburg, visitors have been known to take from twelve to twenty cups at a sitting. Gwenny made more than one wry face over her cup, for in lieu of cream, a slice of lemon was floating in it. Old Pulkovnick Tegoborski added to his tumbler a good jorum of rum, and after having it filled five or six times, hobbled into a corner, where he proceeded to intrench himself behind the columns of the *Moskauer Zeitung*, and was soon enveloped in a cloud from his meerschaum. The Prince sat by the side of Gwenny and sought to draw all her attention to himself, while Madame Tegoborski looked at them vindictively over her tea equipage.

We have mentioned that the Pulkovnick was lame, and we may add that he became so in a very remarkable manner. He was the aide-de-camp whose foot—as M. de Custine relates—the Emperor Nicholas pinned to the floor with the point of his sword, to convince a distinguished foreigner how perfect was the submission of his officers ! A serf by birth, he had attained to the fifth *tchin*, or grade of nobility, with his colonel's commission, through the *oukase* issued by Nicholas in 1842, when serfs were first permitted to make civil contracts and to hold property.

CHAPTER LXVII.
GALITZIN AS A LOVER.

GALITZIN was well educated and knew all the little that existed then of Russian literature ; thus he made many an excuse of translating to Gwenny the tender passages which he had marked off in the poems of the Countess Rostopchin (which being secret literature, circulate in *MS.* only) or the verses of Puschkin, who has sung so sweetly of the Fountain of Tears in the palace of the Crimean Khans, or in the story of Voinaroffski, the lover of Aurora of Konigsmark ; but she listened vacantly or with ill-disguised impatience, and would irritate him by ever and anon addressing Ramornie.

" And so, dear Horace, you are a captain now ?" said she, in the middle of one of Voinaroffski's most passionate appeals.

" Yes, Gwenny ; but I got my promotion through the death of the very man who would have been the first to congratulate me on it—yes ; to have ordered a fresh cooper of port at the mess to wet the new commission—poor Jack Probyn ! But it was no fault of mine ; it was the fortune of war ; yet I would rather have remained a lieutenant still, and had jolly Jack to make fun with."

" We shall have peace soon, Mademoiselle," said the Prince, adding the same in Russian to Madame Tegoborski ; and Horace shivered, for he knew what idea was associated in the mind of Galitzin with peace.

" But peace always ends in war," said Madame Tegoborski, " just as war must end in peace. What you say reminds me of a passage in Kriloff, the Fabulist, about the friendship of two dogs."

"And what says your Kriloff?" asked Galitzin, knitting his brow.

" It is a fable only."

" Well, go on with your fable."

" Two dogs in a court-yard become affectionate friends ; how they fawn and love each other, and will never fight again. It is charming ; but suddenly a bone is thrown from a window, and they straightway proceed to tear each other to pieces."

" Yes ; and Kriloff has another fable of a sleeping peasant. who is about to be stung by a serpent ; but a friendly fly bites him on the nose and awakes him. The shepherd kills the serpent, but he also destroys the fly. A warning to the meddlesome, or the jealous, not to be too officious in *opening the eyes* of any one," added Galitzin with considerable significance of meaning, after which Madame coloured, lapsed again into silence and took up a cigarette, but she had to twist it up for herself that evening.

Monseigneur le Prince was otherwise occupied, he forgot all about the little duty which had been a pleasure yesterday ; and now desiring Kaminski to open the piano, he begged Gwenny to favour them with a little music.

With a horrid memory of the events of the morning hovering in her mind Gwenny was about to decline, when a glance from Horace decided her, and she seated herself at the instrument—a very indifferent one, and not at all improved in its recent transmission from Alushta, by Cossacks, on the limber of a brass field-piece. All the music placed before her was Russian, but Gwenny's fingers and ears were clever, and after a few efforts she was able to read off and play in very tolerable style—" *The Red Sarafan*," (so called from the old Muscovite dress worn by ladies at evening parties), Vielgorski's *Buicala*, and even the " Nightingale," a traditional song and air of the Russian gipsies, to the great enchantment of Galitzin, who was flattering himself what a creditable little wife she would be ; and even of old Tegoborski, whose grizzled and closely shorn caput and grim visage (seamed by the edge of more than one Osmanli sabre), appeared approvingly above the columns of the *Zeitung*, as he waved his meerschaum and beat time with his lame foot ; but more than all were they pleased when her rapid little fingers dashed over in quick succession all the melodies of the inevitable and inimitable *Trovatore*.

And Horace listened like one in a dream. Was it reality, or was it a madness that had come upon him, that he seemed to be sitting in Crimean Yaila, and under the shadow of Tchatr Dagh, listening to Gwenny Wedderburn playing the self-same airs which she had played to him in the early days of their loverhood, and on many a delicious and half-dreamy evening in the beautiful drawing-room at Willowdean.

"I have been tired of my own company," said he in a low voice, as he bent over her, "and have longed—with all the longing of a desperate and a loving heart—to be beside you again, but *not* here. Oh, no, not here; in my wildest imaginings, no such idea or wish could have occurred to me, and yet it has come to pass. Oh! what madness tempted Lady Wedderburn and Lady Ernescleugh to venture here?"

"To see their sons. Besides, Lord Cardigan's yacht, and ever so many more, have come out. And you mentioned having seen the Countess of Errol with her husband in the camp of the Rifles."

"True; but what of that? This barbarous land is no place for delicate English ladies; and I would to heaven that I saw you safe on the watery high road for home."

Much more they rashly succeeded in whispering to each other, for Galitzin was at that moment in conference with Kaminski. How tender and delicious to themselves—but themselves only—are the little nothings that make up the conversation of lovers!

Was it Ennemoser's theory of polarity, or what? But it seemed that in the same mysterious fashion as that on which the learned doctor expatiates, through spirituality, or may it be the force of a strong love, a kind of magnetic current had passed between these two at times, for on comparison they found that they had simultaneously thought of, or dreamt each of the other, and imagined the same things at the same identical moment. It might be all nonsense, or a mistake; but anyway it was a delicious theme to talk about, till the eyes of Galitzin were upon them, and he had begun to feel first piqued, and then jealous of Horace as an *Anglais;* but luckily, he was equally so of the aide-de-camp Kaminski, who having discovered a pair of glazed boots and some kid gloves in a chest that came ashore from the shattered yacht—some of poor Newnham's holiday finery, perhaps—had appeared in them as for special service this evening. Giving the obsequious Kaminski a hint to draw off Horace and engage him in conversation, Galitzin bent over Gwenny's chair.

"Ah, Mademoiselle, your singing enchants me; that *Miserere* was indeed divine!" he whispered, in what he deemed his most seductive tone, as he proceeded to turn over the leaves really

like a well-bred man of the world rather than the savage
he was in heart. "But," he added, as the cruel glitter came
into his dark eyes, "excuse me—I have begun to dislike your
friend."

"Who ?" asked Gwenny, impetuously.

"He in the tattered red coat."

"What—poor Horace ?" she exclaimed, and then blushed
with confusion and irritation.

"Oracc—what you mean the Hospodeen Ramhornoff ?"

"He is indeed an old *friend*," replied Gwenny, in alarm, for
ere this she had read the pencilled note, and could think of no
safer term for him.

"Bah ! I hate such old, or rather such young friends." Then
after a pause, he added with a loftiness that made her smile,
"I am the Prince Galitzin, Major-General under the Emperor,
Knight of the Imperial Orders, and Colonel of the Tambrov
Regiment of Infantry."

She only gave an acquiescent bow ; had he been that worthy
grocer and self-righteous elder of the kirk who officiated as
Baron-Bailie of Willowdean, she could not have seemed less
awed. Now Galitzin knew enough of the world, of Europe, of
that isle of it named Britain, and of the "snobbery" thereof, to
believe that she would be greatly impressed by his announcement, as well as by his stars, medals, and enormous epaulettes ;
but she had come from a land where Rajahs, Maharajahs,
Begums, Nanas, and Princes were thick as leaves in Vallom-
brosa, and where she had seen them trotting about on white
elephants with all their half-naked *suwarri* yelling at their
heels, so she "saw nothing in it."

But as the evening wore on, an eventful one in the life of
her and Horace, Madame Tegoborski strove, but in vain, to
open a flirtation first with him and then, as he was too *c tete*,
with the staff-officer, Kaminski, and to turn the tables on the
heedless Prince. The latter was, however, too fully occupied
with Gwenny to perceive this, or to care one jot about it ; and
certainly, the grim old Pulkovnick, Alexis Tegoborski, appeared
to care quite as little ; he seemed entirely occupied with the
pot-hooks and endless lines of consonants which seemed to
make up the letter-press of the *Moskauer Zeitung ;* and for
the remainder of the evening, Horace discreetly kept apart
from Gwenny.

With the views of Galitzin so openly stated and now attempted
to be put in force, they felt that to observe a distant reserve to
each other was absolutely necessary ; for if the gallant commander of the Tambrov Infantry had suspected that his
prisoner was a secret—and still more, an accepted—lover, he
would have no more compunction for telling off a file of Cos-

sacks to take him into the nearest wood, and there despatch him with their carbines, than for taking an extra glass of kinmel, or spoonful of caviare before saying his prayers at dinner time. However, after that evening Horace was invited no more to tea-drinkings or other entertainments at the apartments of Madame Tegoborski ; not that the latter was to blame there, for the wishes of the Prince came to her through her husband, and they were law, for the Russian wife must not forget the symbolical whip which her husband receives from her father on the bridal day.

Long, long were the watches of the night in which he thought, and thought, and considered of what was to be done, till it seemed as if his brain would turn. Then came sleep, full of nervous starts and dreams, and then came the morning. It was a horror to wake with the first thought that rushed upon him, like a black and overwhelming flood, the knowledge that by an extraordinary turn in the wheel of fortune—a cast of evil destiny—Gwendoleyne Wedderburn was in Yaila, at the mercy of that lawless Russian officer, and in the care, custody and apartments, of one whom he had too much reason to deem alike unscrupulous and jealously hateful of her—Madame Tegoborski. Of what vengeance might not such a woman be capable ! And if Gwenny, a helpless being, a stranger and prisoner of war, escaped the bold designs of the Prince, might she not, by poison perhaps, fall a victim to the vengeance of the forgotten mistress ! *Galignani* and the *Times* record such vengeances every day. So what might not occur in the sequestered fort of Yaila?

CHAPTER LXVIII.

THE PROGRESS HE MADE.

LITTLE knowing the peculiarity of the perils that surrounded her, Gwenny felt tolerably secure in Yaila, chiefly because Horace Ramornie was there, and only once or twice did she reflect on how strange and horrible her isolation and detention would have been had he *not* been there by being a prisoner elsewhere, or with the army before Sebastopol. But Gwenny did not like gloomy thoughts, so she speedily thrust these aside. When safe at home and free it would be something great to talk about, to remember, and to think of—it would be like a leaf from a romance, the fact that they should have *both*, he and she, been together prisoners of war in a Russian fortress. And then the revelation of their engagement (that terrible secret) must eventually come about pleasantly, even to Aunt Wedderburn ; as for good, easy Sir John, Gwenny stood in no awe of him.

She complained to Madame Tegoborski that she saw but little of Captain Ramornie, for repeatedly when he had called at the quarters of the Pulkovnick, the Karaïte maiden in the white fereedji, made incomprehensible excuses for not admitting him. Horace knew well why this came about; but Madame, who only half understood the queries of her guest, could only shrug her shoulders and make grimaces in reply. Galitzin, however, stated to her, that it was deemed improper to permit frequent conferences between those who were prisoners in a fortress, on the principle of military expedience. This explanation, though utter nonsense, partially satisfied the girl for a time, and she could only sigh and watch incessantly at the window in the hope of seeing Horace pass through the yard before the barracks.

So never dreaming that danger menaced her, she sometimes took merry bursts of laughter at the abrupt and inflated love-making of Galitzin which he sometimes conducted in French as well as English ; but her untimely merriment caused his dark eyes to gleam and his brow to become purple with passion, while bitter and evil thoughts of violence flashed upon his lawless mind. But Gwenny, though she knew it not, had one great safety in the fact that the love of Galitzin was almost destitute of all passion ; and provided that he obtained her hand and fortune by an undoubtedly legal marriage, which not even the law of England could break, he cared for little else. Yet it *was* pleasing to him, the conviction that the girl so completely in his power and at the mercy of his passions, was one possessed of beauty, accomplishments, and vivacity.

And poor Horace as he walked about in the gravelled yard or square, under the irritating observation of a long grey-coated Russian sentinel, chafed when he heard Gwenny's voice through the open window as she sang and played in the drawing-room of Madame Tegoborski, for the delectation of Galitzin ; and also on other occasions, when he saw the latter mounted to accompany her and her " matron" for a drive in the Tartar pony-carriage of the latter to the village of Alushta, Babugan Yaila, or to Bagtche Serai, from the high road to which the valley of Inkerman, with its perforated cliffs and ruined fortress was visible, with an old Genoese bridge in the foreground ; and in the distance, by the aid of a telescope, they could from thence see the green domes of Sebastopol and the white tents of the right flank of the British camp, at which Gwenny would cast many a wistful glance. Ramornie always viewed their departure on these expeditions with something of terror, lest they might not *return*, for he knew not what nefarious plans might be forming in the inscrutable mind of Galitzin, and his best hope lay in the chance of their falling in with and being carried off by some foraging or scouting party of the allied cavalry.

But on one evening after their return from a drive, and when Madame Tegoborski had gone on some mission to a Russian church among the mountains close by, Galitzin found himself alone with Gwenny and hastened to improve the opportunity ; for the old Pulkovnick, shrewdly conceiving himself to be in the way, had taken his forage cap and meerchaum and limped forth to enjoy the latter on the gun-battery which faced the road to the Tchatr Dagh.

"What say you, Mademoiselle," he whispered with a soft smile during a pause in her playing ; "how should you like to become a Princess ?"

"I know not—I never thought of such a thing."

"The dignity would well become your beauty, and you could then be the mistress of peasants who should be to you as slaves—people whose teeth you might even draw, if you could find among them one white enough to replace a lost one of your own."

"A most shocking idea ! I never saw a princess ; but in India I have seen a Begum riding on a snow-white elephant, in a golden howdah, hung with scarlet silk."

"I could not exactly give you all that," said the Prince (and indeed he might have added, "nor anything else ;") "but I can assure you that there is no nobler title in Russia than that of Galitzin."

"Oh, I perceive ; you are pleading for yourself !" said Gwenny, laughing, amid her well-acted surprise.

"Do you not understand the spirit of all I have said to you ?" he asked, gravely.

"I think so."

"How then, this laughter ?" he asked.

"We are here in a horrid old prison, apparently, as in a dull house in the country," said Gwenny, still endeavouring to parry his addresses. "You have paid me certain well-bred attentions, such as every pretty girl expects. You praise my singing, which I know to be tolerable—my playing, too, which I know to be good ; and you seem to like my society, which I am vain enough to conceive must be much more pleasant than that of old Tegoborski, or of Madame his wife, but all this must end."

"How so, and when ?"

"I shall soon be released ; I am a non-combatant," said she, smiling ; "to detain me is simply absurd, and I have powerful friends who will not forget me."

"St. Ivan Veliki ! we shall see what we *shall* see !" said he, through his set teeth.

And Gwenny laughed again with her head waggishly on one side, as she ran her fingers over the ivory keys of the piano.

She knew not what Horace did ; that she was in the hands

of a dissipated and *blasé* wretch, a world-weary reprobate, who had long since done with all human emotions, save avarice, and perhaps a little of lust. He was artful, however, and thought to enlist her vanity in his favour.

"Your life must be dull here?" he resumed.

"Very," said she, sighing.

"I could soon remove you to the wonders of St. Petersburg."

"Thank you—but dull as it is, I should prefer remaining here."

"Why?" asked he, with surprise.

"I am nearer the British before Sebastopol."

"I don't think that will matter much to you now," said he, with a wicked glitter in his eyes ; but the expression was unseen by Gwenny, for during this conversation she never turned her face towards him.

"As the wife of a Galitzin you will be equal in rank with the Dolgourukis, the Volhonskis, and the noblest in Russia—even with those who boast of their descent from Rurik of Kiev."

All this did not convey much to Gwenny's ear.

"I am utterly sick of this place and of old Tegoborski ; a married officer is never a good boon companion or a jolly comrade. He becomes a man with selfish interests. Ah, if his wife were only like you !"

Gwenny did not understand this wish ; but it conveyed a volume. He then proceeded to expatiate on the gaieties to which he pretended he could introduce her, and on the post he could get her in the household of the Empress ; on the charms of the opera house at St. Petersburg, where she might hear the national hymn and grand military chorus composed by Lvcoff, who in the latter had always at his disposal forty-eight pieces of artillery, which are discharged by him with the aid of a galvanic wire ; he next dwelt on the splendour of the palace of the Czars, with its Granovataya Palata, or reception-room ; of the hall of St. George with its alabaster walls ; of that of St. Andrew, which seems to have been carved out of rose-coloured marble ; of the brilliant entertainments, the promenades *à la Polonaise*, the balls and banquets to which he should introduce her ; but Gwenny only smiled wearily, and relinquishing the piano, proceeded to fan herself.

"Think too, Mademoiselle, of the grand field days in the presence of the august Emperor, when you shall see a glittering array of perhaps three hundred thousand men, of all the races composing mighty Russia, the infantry of Muscovy and Poland, the horsemen of the Don and the Dnieper, and from the steppes of Circassia, defiling past the grand stand, where you sit among the ladies of the Imperial Court. Oh, what is all the army of your little island, when compared to a show like that ! Then there are masked balls at the Kremlin in Moscow ; ah, you must see that Kremlin," he added, with something of true enthusiasm, " at the hour of vespers, when, as Mouravieff says, 'to the call of the golden-headed giant, Ivan Veliki, suddenly respond from all sides those bells, the voices of his numberless children, and the sound reverberates through the startled air—the many, silver-voiced sound, formed not out of the tolling alone, but out of thoughts, feelings and words which fall not to the earth.' "

And thus translating rapidly from memory, Galitzin spoke all this as if he actually felt it ; but Gwenny only muttered " barbarians," under her breath, however, and fanned herself more vigorusly than ever ; while Galitzin—who in reality was tabooed by his sovereign, and had not the power to have intro-duced her anywhere, though he sketched so freely castles in the air out of her own fortune—as he looked down on the dazzling whiteness of her slender throat, and the little delicate ears, at each of which a simple jet-drop dangled, thought to himself, " how could I ever, for an instant, have admired the amplitude of Norina Paulovna, with her Schologoleff cannon-balls, and large fat fingers covered with rings ?"

" I shall even try to get you an elephant to ride upon," he resumed. " I suppose you rode one in India ?"

Amid her vexations, and they were not small, Gwenny could not help laughing at this offer ; and Galitzin, finding her still in the mood to ridicule him, twisted up his moustachios angrily and left her with a haughty bow. Her child-like entreaties that she might be permitted to write to her aunt, only excited the genuine merriment of the Prince ; but Horace was not without hope that the wretched exploit of pounding the stranded yacht with cannon shot, and the sudden appearance of the two ladies at Balaclava, might have the effect of getting an expedition dispatched, for the purpose of capturing and destroying the somewhat paltry fortress of Yaila.

From thenceforward, all the conversations of Galitzin with Gwenny tended towards St. Petersburg and Moscow the holy. The officers and troops in the Crimea were daily being changed, and he would get his command transferred from thence to one or other of those cities ; and she devoutly hoped he might be successful.

He saw that the hackneyed, " the venerable protestations which lovers from time immemorial have uttered," were useless with her ; yet he felt himself compelled to recur to them. Once, when he held her hand almost forcibly and kissed it, she said to him with quiet energy, " I entreat you to respect me, and be kind to me here, in my unfortunate position, as if I were your younger sister, or your daughter."

"My sister, perhaps," replied Galitzin, making a grimace, as the alternative suggested an unpleasant disparity of years; "I have seen much of life in all its phases; I have felt much, suffered much, and enjoyed much; but never knew till now that a passing glance, a smile, could be so priceless to me—never till I met you. Ah, there are higher prizes in this world than courtly rank or military glory; and how often need I reiterate that I love you! You must marry me, Mademoiselle."

"Remember that there are others whose permission is requisite."

"Others?—whom? where?" asked Galitzin, with genuine surprise.

"At home in Britain."

"Ah, the little cock-boat of an island, where people jostle each other at every step; bah! you may never see it, till we visit it together after this foolish war against Russia is over, and peace proclaimed."

All this was becoming unpleasantly plain, she was to be coerced, perhaps; so she said haughtily "I am weary of all this—obey me, Monseigneur le Prince, if you please, and leave me."

"I am more used to command than to obey," he replied, while seating himself with perfect deliberation.

"Yes, your serfs, and soldiers, who are little better; but you have no right to command me."

"That we shall see," said he, laughing, for her grand airs amused rather than piqued him.

"Come," said she, giving him her hand, which he kissed tenderly; "do not let us quarrel; I fully believe that at heart you are a gallant soldier, and—"

"One you could love?" he added, with his moustachios close to her ear.

"Nay," she replied shrinking, "my husband—pardon me—must be younger, and have fewer lines—"

"These are Circassian sabre cuts! You will not have me then?"

"On a fortnight's acquaintance? it is impossible."

"Am I to suppose then," he asked, in a low and concentrated tone, "that you love another?"

"Perhaps," said she, with a provoking smile.

"You dare to say this to me?"

"Who are you that dare to question me?"

"*Who* am I?" he exclaimed, in a loud and imperious voice, while he started to his feet, and Gwenny became dismayed. "Mademoiselle, is this a vaudeville we are acting?"

"Prince," said she, "the conversation is again becoming unpleasant. In accepting the offer with which you honour me, I should be guilty of dishonesty to you, to myself, and the world at large."

"I don't understand all this. Please to explain?"

"To accept you, I ought to love you."

"Well, I suppose so—if not now, at least by and by," said he, leisurely and playing with the tassels of his sash.

"But what if I love another?"

"Again that hint! Who *is* this other?"

"I have not said that I do; I merely said *if.*"

"Well?"

"Then I could not marry you, and what is more, I *won't,*" she added, suddenly losing all patience, and beating the floor with her foot, while her eyes sparkled with resentment. "Set me free from this horrid place; send me to Balaclava to my aunt and friends—send Horace too."

"Oh, the devil! Ramhornoff, eh? Perhaps you prefer the society of this dilettanti young countryman of yours to mine?"

"I have not said so," replied Gwenny, feeling herself on dangerous ground.

"Ah! we shall know each other better by and by."

"With you, Prince, this alleged love is caprice; to me it may be fate—destruction!"

"I know that I am your senior in years—not much though; but when better acquainted you shall find no disparity in our tastes, or temper; and if you entrust me with your future happiness, you shall never have cause to repent of becoming the Princess Galitzin."

"Never but *once,*" thought Gwenny.

Again the high-spirited little beauty was exasperated by his confident mode of annoying her; and when Galitzin saw the bright flash of the usually soft dark eye, the quivering of the cherry-like nether lip of her exquisitely cut mouth, and the curve of the proud nostril, he knew that he had nothing to hope from her concession or complaisance. He could win her, but by force or fraud only; and by one or other he was resolved she should be won. She was his prisoner, and he would take time to consider the matter well.

"You are very haughty and coy, Mademoiselle," said he, giving her one of his darkest glances, while he took his flat green foraging cap and jerked his sabre under his arm; "but if I find that your friend—your cousin, or whatever he is—this Captain Ramhornoff, stands in my way, or will not use his persuasive powers for me, I may dispose of him as I did that fellow Chesters, who robbed me in Paris!"

And with these threatening words, which he closed by some tremendous Russian oath, he left her. She remembered Rebecca and the Templar in the castle of Torquilstone, and ever so many more heroines and melodramatic situations with which the contents of the box that came quarterly from Mudie's to Willowdean had stored her mind ; but she gathered no comfort therefrom, or from the conviction that there are " greater novels in real life than in stories."

They were all perilous scrapes—unpleasant, desperate, and so forth, and in this age of gas, steam, and electricity, absurd and unsuited to the case : yet a spice of her Indian breeding came at times to her mind, and she felt, that if sorely pushed and she had a weapon, Major-General the Prince Galitzin, Colonel of the Tambrov Infantry, &c., might stand a very fair chance of having a hole punched in his skin.

CHAPTER LXIX.

HORACE'S PLEASANT TASK.

SOON after the last interview we have narrated, Galitzin went in search of Horace Ramornie. He had not to seek for him long, as the nearest sentinel pointed to where he lay on the grassy slope of the glacis outside the fortress, listlessly, to all appearance, though sunk in sad and exciting thoughts. However, he started up and, as policy required, saluted courteously the person who now approached him, but whom he loathed with an intensity that words cannot pourtray.

" Still contemplating the road towards Sebastopol, and the sea ?" said Galitzin, with a smiling countenance, and in French. " Ma foi ! you'll not require to make a sketch of it, as it must be graven pretty well in your mind by this time. Will you have a cigar ?" he added, proffering a handsome silver case, which had been found in the pocket of one of our Guards' officers on the field of Inkerman.

Cigars were luxuries of which Horace had long been deprived, and as declining might have savoured of insult or open dislike, he accepted one and lit it at that of the Prince, the two looking into each other's eyes pretty much as we have all seen John Mildmay and Captain Hawkesly do in the latter's " Office in the City."

" So you are anxious to be free, eh ?" said the Prince.

" Why taunt me by a question so tantalizing ?"

" I do not taunt you ; far from it. Well, I don't care if I afford you an opportunity for being so."

" How ?" asked Horace, whose heart, while longing for liberty, revolted at the idea of having it without that of Gwenny Wedderburn also being secured. " I have given my parole, and your Government——"

" Know nothing about you as yet. I have troubled Mentschicoff with no reports for some time back. I can make you a close prisoner and yet afford you a chance of escaping. A horse —yes ; even a Tartar pony, would soon take you to Balaclava."

"But what means this sudden change in your views, and where are your fears that I might detail the strength, the defences, and so forth, of Yaila ? What am I expected to do in return for this favour ?" asked Horace, suspiciously.

"You are right to ask, for, as I always say, it is a nothing for nothing world ours. Well, you may do much for me."

"Explain, Monseigneur le Prince—pray ?"

There was a pause ; the usual detestable glitter came into the cold and half-closed eyes of Galitzin, and Horace rightly surmised, that if he were once out of Yaila with the aforesaid Tartar horse, he should find—whatever favour he granted or service he performed—the road beset a few versts from the place, and that then he would be shot down without mercy or despatched as a close prisoner to Yekaterinoslav ; for he knew that his present companion was capable of any act of treachery, however dark, or base, or cruel.

"As your friend Chesters would have said——"

"Excuse me ; he was no friend of mine," said Horace.

"Your brother officer then ?"

"Nor that either," replied Ramornie, haughtily. "The unfortunate fellow had only local rank in the Turkish Contingent, and had to quit Her Britannic Majesty's service for malpractice with cards."

"Well, your fair friend Mademoiselle Wedderburn and I have had one or two long conversations together, and as Chesters would have said, in his sporting *parlance*, she is a stake I mean to enter for. You understand me ?"

"You mean to make her a proposal of marriage ?" said Horace, with a smile that in spite of himself was somewhat ghastly.

"Precisely ; and I wish you to use your influence—that is, if you possess any, with her, for me. Tell her that if she will marry me without any fuss or absurd resistance, I shall open up to her a life of wealth and brilliance at St. Petersburg or Moscow— she can have her choice—at Baden-Baden, and elsewhere, such as she cannot conceive and could not have in England—that land of fog, of exclusiveness, and insular prejudices, where everything foreign is deemed ridiculous and judged by the standard of Pall-Mall or the Old Bailey—your *Times* and your *Punch*. I know all about it ; I have been in London, and was there too long for my own profit."

He certainly had not been there for the profit of others, as "this interesting foreigner" had been required more than once at Bow Street, and was not forthcoming.

"Have you not already proposed?" asked Horace, quietly tipping the ashes off his cigar.

"Yes; but she can't make up her mind. It will after all be, at best, a poor style of ingrafting, as the gardeners say; yet the blood of the Tegoborskis may be perpetuated through my pretty one for all that."

Ramornie made a violent effort to control his rising rage, an exhibition of which would have been useless, and only serving to spoil all, so he said, simply—"You are unfortunately older than the lady, Monseigneur le Prince."

"Yes—perhaps—somewhat."

"Old enough indeed to be——"

"Don't say, her father—that would sound unpleasant. I know that with a disparity of some twenty years between us, I shall have all the ordinary commonplaces of well-bred life said of me on *that* score, and perhaps to me, for the girl seems wonderfully cool and self-possessed. She will talk to you, no doubt, of the brevity of our acquaintance, our partial ignorance of each other's tastes and dispositions—perhaps also ask whether I have not already a Princess elsewhere," he continued, with his ugly smile. "Seek to explain all this away, and to assure her that, save with me, she has no hope of ever returning to England. But though there be a difference in our years, as I am a Russian Prince, it is not necessary that I should sue for this girl in a tone of humility."

"I do not quite comprehend all this," said Horace, bewildered by stifled rage.

"Well, I mean that my renewed offer is not to be blended with an apology—by you at least."

"Have you no humane or religious scruples in this matter?" asked the other, scarcely knowing what to say.

"Oh, as to religion," replied Galitzin, laughing heartily, "you don't think surely that I am particular to a shade about the tenets of the *raskolniki*," for so dissenters from the Russian Greek Church are named.

"But she, I hope, has some scruples."

"She has told you so?—perhaps you are more in her confidence than I am?" said Galitzin, with flashing eyes, for his suspicions were ever prompt to kindle.

"If I am *less*, why seek my aid or influence? Besides, you forget, Prince Galitzin, that we are almost cousins;" and as Horace spoke, he remembered again how Lady Wedderburn used to resent the term or idea; but there it proved most useful, for his hearer felt and knew from a Russian point of view that ties of blood barred both love and marriage within the fourth degree; and so his suspicion lulled again, and he said—

"Monsieur le Capitaine, let us seek to understand each other."

"You are sure you love her?" asked Horace in desperation, to gain time and to think.

"I always dreaded a regular love fit as I dread the evil-eye of the devil ; but how could any man escape with her, she is so perilously handsome? She has a lovely hand, and an irreproachable foot and ankle. What a ravishing peep I had of them yesterday as she stepped out of the pony-phaeton. Say to her, that I implore her to come to terms for her own sake, as she is perhaps far from safe where she is."

"Terms—safe," stammered Horace.

"I have put her in Norina's charge—under Madame Tegoborski's care, I should say. Now, Madame has been absurd enough to conceive a mad fancy for me. Of course, I am a Prince and Major-General, while Tegoborski is only a Pulkovnick, and has been a serf (though a relation of mine), who joined the army with one half his head shaved, for so we always mark our recruits to prevent them from running away. But she threatens me——"

"Who—Madame?"

"Yes," said Galitzin, lowering his voice, and glancing furtively about, as if he feared being overheard, "she threatens me, and might, for all I know, poison the poor girl ; women are terribly vindictive, and that would never do, with such a fine fortune as she has. Will you expatiate on all these dangers as an old friend? and if your advice weighs well with her, you shall have a horse for Balaclava to-morrow."

"But if it does not weigh with her? For I may fail as an adviser, if you as a lover have failed already."

"Then I shall try other means, I shall take her away with me alone to Bagtche Serai or elsewhere for a few days, and that will compromise her honour in her own eyes and those of the world, if the world cares about the matter. She will then see the absolute necessity of a marriage with me. Beautiful as she is, I may frankly tell you that it is not her person I value so much as her purse. I have rank, but I must have roubles as well. I want money, and this war will soon be over now ; yet in my time I have drunk and gambled away serfs enough to be the population of a moderate city."

"But even this last scheme may fail ; and what will you do then?"

"Resort to *force!*" hissed the other through his teeth ; and thinking that to say more might lessen the strength of his instructions, which did not seem very clear to Horace Ramornie, he lifted his forage cap, bowed, and withdrew, leaving his listener rooted to the spot in a storm of indignation, rage, and natural fear, though not for himself.

"Scoundrel !—open and confessed as such !" muttered Horace,

as he watched the figure of Galitzin disappear through the arched gate of the fort ; "you little know your man, or the task you have set him ! Anyway, I will have an interview with my beloved Gwenny, and may concert something with her. But what can that something be ? Have I not thought of all, in vain, before ? Oh, God aid us !" he added, looking upward with clasped hands.

It was dreadful to contemplate the idea, or rather the fact of his idolized and highly-bred Gwenny being in the hands of a man who could conceive such schemes, and canvass them openly ! In the course of a few minutes, what had he not hinted, suggested, or threatened ; and now there was a new terror, in the jealousy of Madame Tegoborski ! He threw himself on the cool grass, to think ; but how often had he thought in vain before ! And there he lay scheming—considering this doubt and that probability, this plot and that plan, till his brain grew giddy with intense perplexity. The Russians he knew to be corrupt and ready to take bribes ; but he was not the master of a copper kopec. And in yonder Tartar village there was no one whom he could intrust with a message to Balaclava, or whose aid he could seek. He looked wistfully at its flat-roofed cottages, almost buried among the green leaves and golden apples of luxuriant fruit-trees. He turned to the fertile valley that led towards the Black Sea, which blended with the sky in sunny haze, and then to the dark pine forest, that clothed the southern slope of the Tchatr Dagh, the marble cliffs of which seemed to vibrate in the rays of light. But no shelter for her could be found there. Did his parole bind him still, at a conjuncture so terrible ? He feared that it did. He felt powerless, and weaker by having Gwenny's fate linked there with his own ; and he envied now the stupid and monotonous existence he had enjoyed before her peril, and anxiety for her safety came to torture and agitate his mind. Great was the horror of sitting there helplessly unarmed, penniless, and powerless ; and not knowing what an hour—yea, a minute, might bring forth ! Anyway he would see Gwenny at once ; and, with a prayer for inspiration and guidance in his heart and on his lips, he passed the *tête du pont* and entered the fortress.

CHAPTER LXX.

GWENNY'S PLAN.

IF, even to save Gwenny Wedderburn, he broke his parole of honour and escaped, he knew that he should inevitably forfeit, at home, his position as an officer and gentleman for ever. If he withdrew it, that would be simply a warning to Galitzin that he meant flight, if he could achieve it; and to preclude that, he should be made a close prisoner, helpless to assist her, and probably sent away to the rear, like poor Newnham, who, exasperated by the brutality of his capture, had declined to give his parole at all in any way. It was, every way, a horrible dilemma! Could he by any means communicate with the officer commanding the nearest allied forces or outpost? He had by this time, however, ascertained that the Russian troops in Tchorgoun—that place which had proved so fatal to his destiny —the nearest point to Yaila, were very insignificant in number, though their position was strong, and connected with that held by their army along the whole line of heights between the Tchernaya and the Belbck. He inquired for the Hospoza (i.e., Madame) Tegoborski, of the pretty Karaïte Jewess, who had, doubtless, received her full instructions beforehand, as she at once ushered him into the bare and chilly chamber which we have already described as the "drawing-room" of the Pulkovnick's lady, to which some additional ornaments had been added, in the shape of gildings washed up by the sea from the Ernes-cleugh yacht; and there Gwenny was seated alone, busy with some needlework, which she tossed aside, and hastened to receive him with a bright and tender smile. They were alone, and were instantly hand in hand! Ramornie could perceive with concern, that since he had last seen her, there was a change in her face, the result, doubtless, of the "worry" occasioned her by the absurd and obtrusive attentions of Galitzin and her separation from himself, when they had so much to say, so much to ask and to tell each other. She had become thinner; her large, dark, and finely-lidded eyes — usually so full of brilliant expression and emotional changes—looked dull and weary, till they caught some vivacity from his.

"Oh, Horace darling, how have you been enabled to visit me? I feared they were about to keep us for ever apart, those horrid people! Do they fear our conspiring, or what? Four whole days, Horace, and I have not even seen you!" she exclaimed.

"I have come at the suit of a lover of yours," said Ramornie, with a smile on his lip, but a stern expression in his eyes.

"Who? that odious Galitzin?" asked Gwenny, laughing.

"The same, darling. But this is no laughing matter for us —for you especially. I dare not tell you all that man has ventured to hint, and commissioned me to say."

"Well, I don't want to hear it. Pet Horace, sit beside me here, and talk to me; we shall speak of each other and not of him—the Russian toad!" and drawing closer to her lover, she nestled her sweet face in his neck; and yielding to the charm

of the situation, they forgot all about Galitzin, and sat dreaming
in silence, or talking of Willowdean and the Lammermuirs, of
St. Abb's Head, and the wild sea shore, of scenes and places far
away, of past times, their earlier emotions as they stole into
their hearts, and of much more on which their *listener*—for they
had one—could not enter.

"And Galitzin has been making you proposals?" said Horace,
suddenly coming back to their present predicament.

"Yes, frequently; ridiculous, is it not?"

"And how do you receive them?"

"I laugh; but there are times when I become angry. He is
an absurd old creature; I loathe the sight of him, with his
strange cruel smile, and sincerely hope that he won't come here to
pester me with any more of his solemn, hard and deliberate love
making, that has not one atom of softness or tenderness in it."

"Could I get pistols and an opportunity, I should blow the
brains out of this middle-aged Russian cupid!" said Ramornie,
in a low voice of concentrated passion.

"Oh fie, Horace; he cannot mean anything serious," said
Gwenny, her eyes dilating with surprise at his quiet vehemence.

"Ah, my love, you know not the man or all he is capable of;
unfortunately, I do. My letters informed you how infamously
poor Cyril suffered at the hands of a Russian officer whom he
was succouring, when we stormed the heights of the Alma."

"Yes."

"Well, that Russian officer, so wantonly ready with his pistol;
the notorious spy so often found in our camp at Varna, and
even in the trenches at Sebastopol—he who could so well act
the part of a Frenchman, is Ivan Tegoborski, the Prince Galitzin;
but—but—did you not hear a noise?"

"Oh what is all this you tell me? A noise! no, I heard only
the beating of my heart, dear, dear Horace."

"Poor little heart! It may have much to make it palpitate yet. If I had only some money for bribery. Oh, if
Heaven would only give me the means——."

"Money, Horace, is the root of all evil, says the proverb;
and but for the reputation of wealth, I should not be troubled
by this Galitzin."

"True; but money is also the root of all good; for none can
be done without it."

"How well he speaks English."

"Ah, and French too—the *mouchard!*"

To a certain extent he explained to her, the views, the wishes,
but not the ulterior threats of Galitzin in case of her non-
compliance; his tender love and her natural delicacy, made
him shrink nervously from a hint so odious; but she fully
understood and recognised all the danger of the position

occupied by Horace and herself, though she could not quite understand the difficulties. On Horace Ramornie rested all her hopes for weeks past; they must meet some time alone, she had thought, when they should have a careful conference and sudden flight together; though the chief obstacle seemed the want of money, a vehicle and horses. But when he set the latter wants before her, with the moral and military obligations enforced by his parole, the penalties of breaking it, the Cossacks' eyes that seemed constantly to watch him, and the chance of his transmission to Yekaterinoslav, her heart, so full of hope and fond anticipations, seemed to die within her. And little thinking that they were watched by jealous eyes, they would frequently clasp each other's hands by the instinct of sudden affection, and sit thus for precious minutes in silence, gazing into each other's eyes that were full of tenderness and light. When they did speak, it was fortunately in a tone that was low, and heard by themselves only.

"Good Heavens, darling!" said Gwenny, suddenly, "it cannot be that in this time of civilization and progress, as the newspapers call it, we have got into a scrape of the Middle Ages—an adventure worthy of some old castle on the Rhine!"

"I am afraid it looks deuced like it, Gwenny," replied Ramornie: "but oh, if the Allies would only take an airing this way, and knock the whole place to pieces! One Lancaster gun should do it in two hours! but they devote all their energies to Sebastopol, and never think of the petty outposts."

"And oh, Horace, if this man should take me away from you?" suggested Gwenny, in a really piteous tone.

"I would kill him in front of his men!" was the husky reply.

"And be bayonetted or shot instantly?"

"I ran those risks daily with the Fusileers, for no reason that I could see, Gwenny; but Heaven alone knows what you and I shall do!"

"And I had formed such a nice plan for our escape!" said she, mournfully.

"You, my pet, love?"

"Yes," she sobbed.

"And your plan, darling, what was it?"

"Simply this—it involved a little horse stealing, however."

"Go on, Gwenny, go on."

"You know that Madame Tegoborski often drives me out, without any attendants, in her little phaeton, which is drawn by two Tartar ponies; and I thought that if you could contrive to meet us, unexpectedly as it were, a mile or so from this place you might simply assume her seat and whip, and we should drive off together! She would soon give an alarm, of course——"

"Nay, I should tie the old hag hand and foot to a tree——"

"But oh, Horace, wolves might come!"

"Let them," said Ramornie, savagely. "Yours *is* an admirable plan, and I am astonished that it never occurred to me
before ; but it is woman's wit, and you have such a clever little
head, darling. Then," he added, with a sigh, "there is my—
parole !"

"Oh that weary parole !" exclaimed the girl, and her head
and spirit drooped again ; "it destroys our only plan, our sole
remaining hope ! This very evening we are to drive so far as
the pine wood, on the road between those two great mountains
with the fantastic names."

"The Tchatr Dagh and the Demirdji."

"Yes ; you know it, then !"

"I have seen the wood from the gate ; it lies some versts
beyond the distance I am permitted to go from the glacis of
Yaila."

"Can you *not* break this promise ?" she whispered, imploringly, with her hands on his shoulders and her bright eyes
looking imploringly into his.

"No, it is impossible ; an officer's word once given thus is
irrevocable !"

"Then I am in despair ! Oh, Horace, Horace, what is to
become of us ? What is to become of me ?" exclaimed the girl,
in a passion of grief, as she flung herself upon his breast and
clung to him, so full of her own and their mutual sorrow that
she was quite unconscious of the door having opened and shut,
and that Galitzin stood behind her with lowering, inquiring,
and malevolent eye.

"You here, Monseigneur le Prince ?" exclaimed Ramornie
indignantly, and not without alarm, as he tenderly deposited
the half-fainting girl upon a sofa.

"Oui, ma foi !" replied the pale, unhealthy-looking Russian,
with his detestable grin ; "and what then ? I was simply
adopting the privilege of Le Diable Boiteux, and peeping in
here."

"And, doubtless, you have overheard all ?"

"I am sorry to say that I have not."

"How so ?" asked Ramornie, greatly relieved.

"You spoke rather too low for that ; but I can guess its
interesting nature, as I have *overseen* all."

"Silence, for Heaven's sake, Prince Galitzin ; do you not see
that this young lady is almost fainting, and cannot even speak ?"

"Ah, indeed !" replied Galitzin, scornfully. "'Silence adorns
the sex,' says Sophocles ; perhaps silence, seclusion, and sal-
volatile, together with a glass of kimmel will be advantageous
here. Have the goodness to see to this, Madame," he added, as
the wife of Tegoborski entered, and with an exhibition of considerable agitation, the exact source of which it might be

difficult to discover, seated herself by the side of Gwenny, while Galitzin, saying to Horace, "Follow me, Monsieur le Capitaine," led him into an adjoining room.

"Now, Monsieur, I must speak plainly," said Galitzin ; "we understand each other perfectly, I believe. How often have I made love, as people say, St. Ivan Veliki alone knows ; but this time I am in earnest—I have an additional incentive, and shall not be crossed by you. A turn of the wheel of fortune has thrown a golden opportunity in my way, and I shall not be such a fool, such an utter Asiatic, as to neglect it !"

Galitzin paused and breathed hard ; for opposition to his wishes had begun to pique and inflame him ; while, on the other hand, young Ramornie, proud and fiery by nature, inspired by all the genuine emotions of a gentleman and a free-born Briton, felt as if on the verge of madness, and yet had to be most guarded in all he said and did.

"Beware, Prince Galitzin," said he, as the drowning will cling to straws ; "in proposing to marry this orphan girl, you, a foreigner, a stranger, one of a different religion——"

"Bah ! you said all this before. What care I, though she were a Hindoo ?"

"You promise yourself a month's amusement during the *ennui* of Yaila, forgetting that to her it may be the destruction of a life."

"You mistake me, my would-be Mentor. I promise myself the enjoyment of a fine fortune when the cannon of Cronstadt and the Kremlin announce peace to Europe. But by Heaven I don't understand you, or this tone of insolent advice that you have ventured to adopt !"

"She has trustees—if you understand what I say—and you may not be able to get at her fortune without *their* consent, even if you married her to-morrow," said Ramornie, quietly.

Galitzin seemed to be transported with rage by this new suggestion, for he felt the too probable truth of it.

"Vassili blajennoi !" he exclaimed ; "this to me? Say as much more, and I will not give a copper kopec for your life !"

A bitter smile escaped Ramornie on hearing the pious invocation of a saint blended with a threat of violence against himself. For this man had no religion or real veneration for holy things ; yet in his superstition or adherence to outward forms and to traditions of the Russian Greek Church, he would as soon have thought of pistolling himself as of sitting down to his dinner of green borsch and stuffed carrots without first bowing to the *cilion ;* or of killing and eating one of the countless pigeons, which at Yaila, as in every other Russian edifice, are to be seen clustering in clouds over the roofs, belfries, and cupolas, and sitting in long rows like cornices along the eaves ;

for it is pre-eminently the holy bird of the Muscovites. On fast days he would not even look on butter or cream ; but in place thereof, used plenty of oil for his *ouka*, or fish-soup of sterlet or salmon cutlets, pleasantly boiled in vinegar and flour *à la Russe*.

"Do you actually threaten me, a prisoner, an unarmed man ?" asked Ramornie, after a pause.

"I do ; so beware, Monsieur le Capitaine, of what you are about. It is not known, I am almost sure, to the Allies that you are in our hands, as you stumbled among us amid the snow on that dark night march to Tchorgoun ; and as yet I have never sent in your name to Prince Mentschicoff. Hence I might, without the slightest risk of being questioned, make as short work with you as I did with that fellow Chesters when on the march to this place. If inclined to be more merciful I could send you inland with a note—a mere note of a few words would do—which would ensure your safe transmission to Tobolsk or Irkutsk. The mines there, if not favourable for the lungs, are admirable for the development of the muscles, and you have been getting fleshy in idleness, though having a thirty-two pound shot at one's heels is apt to cure one of all taste for dancing. Now we understand each other, I think ?"

"And this is said to me within fifty miles of the British camp before Sebastopol ?" said Horace, with crimsoned brow and sparkling eyes.

"Well, perhaps a few versts more or less."

"Such threats are alike ungenerous and outrageous !"

"I could hang you by the wrists from a tree with a cannon ball for one toe to rest on ; and how should you like forty-eight hours of that without food or water ?"

Even that threat was more than sufficient for Horace Ramornie.

"Enough," thought he ; "I shall be at the pine wood this evening, and trust to Heaven and my own wit for the rest !"

"Take care how you trifle with me," said Galitzin, almost as if he understood or read what was passing in the mind of Ramornie. "You will wish yourself among the graves of Inkerman, rather than here, if you bring my jealous vengeance on you."

Horace could scarcely understand to what all these threats tended, but drawing himself up and eyeing the Russian sternly he said, proudly and haughtily—"I demand, Prince Galitzin, that you shall remember that I am a British officer on parole of honour, and in no way subject to you."

"A British officer—bah ! I do not forget it. In three days we shall have a convoy proceeding to Yekaterinoslav. Prepare, Monsieur, to accompany it with your hands tied again to the mane of a Tartar pony if you are not marched there on foot !"

And, as Galitzin said this, he bowed and left the room. "This again more than ever renders my parole null and void," said Horace, in a low and concentrated voice, in which passion and satisfaction were curiously mingled ; "three days ! now for Gwenny's plan of escape, and this very night too ! Blessed be Heaven, that Muscovite rascal did not overhear her !"

CHAPTER LXXI.

A NEW FRIEND.

THERE was something of fierce elation in the mind of Horace Ramornie when he found himself alone ! On giving his parole of honour that he should not go beyond a mile from the glacis of Yaila, it had been, of course, distinctly understood that his life must be respected, and his personal liberty too. Now the former had been threatened and the latter also ! The compact had thus been vitiated by the Russian Major-General, so Ramornie was free—free to escape when or how he could. He knew the contingencies ; that he was certain of a degrading captivity if three days hence found him in Yaila, and certain of death if he fled from it and was *retaken*. Anyway, to free Gwendoleyne Wedderburn was worth risking all for, and that evening he resolved the attempt should be made, minus though he was of arms, money, or a guide. He would simply adopt the plan she had conceived ; he should meet her and Madame Tegoborski at the pine wood ; assume that lady's place in her vehicle and drive off, testing the speed and muscle of the Tartar ponies to the utmost, and the whole matter seemed very easy, provided no interruption occurred by the way. The plan was only a little horse-stealing from the enemy, and under the high pressure of the circumstances quite justifiable.

About an hour before the projected design, he left Yaila by the barrier-gate, as if for one of his usual solitary strolls, but not without an increased beating of the heart, as he fancied that every stolid-looking Russian sentinel in his flat cap and hideous long clay-coloured coat, eyed him more keenly than was their wont ; but this was the mere result of feverish anxiety ; and he proceeded slowly along the ancient road that led towards the Black Sea, whose waters he could see in the distance, rippling in golden light at the end of a valley. He frequently paused and seated himself on the grass, again to walk slowly on, thanking his stars that the two Cossacks, Alexis and Ivan—their surnames he never knew—who had been wont to hover, singly or together, so mysteriously on his steps, or within his range of vision, were now absent, having been sent with poor Bob Newnham to Yekaterinoslav.

Sometimes he clasped his hands and looked upward. Was it possible that this night might see him a free man ; free, with Gwenny by his side, and within a few miles of the British outposts ? There are few places where one has been resident even for months only that they do not quit with regret; but Ramornie simply loathed Yaila in all its features ; the green painted cannon, each with a red cross on its breech, the brick-faced curtains and embrasures, constructed by Baron Todleben, who had also patched up the old towers of the days of Justinian and of the Genoese ; the angular visages and tattered uniforms of the garrison ; the green slopes around and the flat outline of that "table mountain," the Tchatr Dagh towering over all !

Heaven be thanked, he was about to see the last of them—and with Gwenny, too ! He had read of, and fancied many a melodramatic incident ; but scarcely conceived that in sober, civilized life such things could come to pass as had happened to him ; yet our Afghan war, a few years before, and the subsequent Indian Mutiny, were alike full of terrible situations, painful and harrowing escapes and perils, undergone by lovers and friends, by husbands, wives and their children ! But who can foresee the sudden and startling contingencies that are consequent to a state of warfare, especially in wild and lawless lands ?

And now, beyond all their present peril, as he threw himself on the green sward to think and ponder, Horace Ramornie looked forward fondly to spending his future life—a happy home life—with Gwenny, as to a promised land, where they should talk over the *present* with wonder, and even with pleasure ! He was now on the skirts of the pine wood, and being quite concealed by some little caper bushes, could watch the road that led to the quaint old fort on the green hill slope. The crimson light of the setting sun was glowing redly on the gnarled stems and twisted branches of the old forest. All were shining as if with flame, and the birds were singing their last notes loudly amid the wiry foliage. The dry cones were dropping, and the field mice were scampering homeward to their holes under the long rank grass.

Beyond the green Babugan mountains, he could see that the road wound through a shady dell, where the tall white poplar, the dwarf almond and the pretty linden tree grew together in luxuriance ; and by that valley he knew they should have to pass in their flight, after he had possessed himself of Madam's equipage. But how was he to dispose of *her*, and prevent her giving an alarm that in ten or twenty minutes would ensure pursuit ! His eyes seldom turned from the gate of Yaila, as every instant he expected to see the shaggy ponies appear ; and how, if Galitzin took it into his head to accompany them, as he frequently did ? He always rode with a pair of revolver pistols in his holsters. As this idea occurred to him, Ramornie looked round for a suitable stone—but hark ! There was a sound of hoofs and accoutrements in the valley, and very soon a detachment of Russian cavalry, some fifty files or so, came along at an easy trot, evidently from Tchorgoun.

They were all Don Cossacks, with grey fur caps and huge red moustaches, the twisted points of which were quite visible from behind ; their blue tunics worn halfway to the knee were girt by scarlet sashes, and their wide loose trowsers were thrust into their coarse jack-boots ; and so defiling past, and chanting a rude hoarse ditty, they passed through the archway and entered Yaila, greatly to the mortification of Horace ; for thus Galitzin had at hand swift, ready and instant means of an effectual pursuit and recapture in every direction ! Another hour, to the anxious lurker a seeming eternity, passed away, and the sun, which had been above the marble summit of the Tchatr Dagh when he first came forth, had sunk behind it now, and his ruddy golden rays spread skyward among the light floating clouds, like the spokes of a fiery wheel, while the singular outlines of the Dimirdji and Babugan mountains rose in purple and black against the red evening clouds. The odour of the wild thyme came pleasantly on the passing wind. The monotonous plash of the water sounded ceaselessly from an ancient stone fountain near—a relic of the Genoese ; but though athirst with feverish anxiety Ramornie never drew near it. Close by too were purple grapes, ripe figs, soft peaches and blooming nectarines all growing wild ; but he heeded nothing. He ever turned his eyes to Yaila ; but the archway appeared only as a black spot in the walls, from whence nothing seemed to issue.

A knowledge that the place where he lay was beyond his paroled distance, added to his anxiety, so his suspense, dread, and doubt, amounted ere long to actual pangs of bodily pain. Was she ill ?

"Oh what *can* have happened—why do not they come ?" he continued to exclaim from time to time, long after there could be any chance of the Hospoza Tegoborski taking her evening drive.

Suddenly the boom of a cannon gave him a species of electric shock. A thin white puff was curling upwards from the northern bastion of the fort, and he saw the Russian Cross streaming out upon the wind, which brought the sound of drums towards him. Had the garrison received information of an attack ? What had happened ? He had not a moment to lose now, for even if he saw the columns in red pouring through yonder valley, he must return and report himself to the officer of the main guard—more than all he must return to where *she*

was, and on entering, he found the whole garrison under arms,
in two quarter-distance columns, with bayonets fixed, and a
fresh supply of ammunition being rapidly distributed from
casks which were strewed in front of each regiment.

His heart beat high and happily. An attack, he thought,
must be expected ; and those Don Cossacks were the fore-
warners of it !

" Do you expect an attack, Monsieur le Colonel ?" he inquired
in French, of old Tegoborski, as that personage limped past.
" I presume those Cossacks brought the intelligence ? "

" They have brought none, Monsieur," said Galitzin, ere the
Pulkovnick could reply, " They are simply the convoy I spoke
of, *en route* to Yekaterinoslav, whether you shall go with them
in two days now," he added, with his old smile. He had a
peculiarly malevolent pleasure in hurting the feelings of others
—of the young especially ; for as his own youth was long past,
he hated that joyous period of life in any one else.

There was no attack, and the night passed away in peace ;
but the whole of this sudden alarm and preparation, which
thus baffled the plans and hopes of the prisoner, were the mere
result of Russian superstition.

The *bell* of the chapel had fallen from its rusty hook, decayed
by time and exposure. This was deemed by the garrison in
general, and by Galitzin in particular, as significant of some
dire and impending calamity, because the Muscovites deem all
bells as something sacred, and when in the preceding February,
a great bell fell in the tower of St. Ivan Veliki at Moscow,
crashing through four floors in succession and killing all the
inmates, it was regarded as the omen of some much greater
calamity to Russia ; thus, on the day after, news reached the
Holy City of the death of the Emperor Nicholas !

Ramornie cursed, in his heart, the wretched superstition by
which his only plan had been marred. But one evening now remained to the fugitives, and if it proved one of rain ; if Madame
Tegoborski had the vapours, or was indisposed to drive, the
noon of the third day would see him once more under escort,
and accompanying those red-whiskered Don Cossacks, towards
the Isthmus of Perecop.

Though Ramornie knew it not, and feared the worst from the
plump fair Muscovite with the sleepy eyes, large hands, and
snowy arms, she was neither an enemy to him or Gwenny.

With all a woman's quickness, she had seen and discovered
their secret—that they were lovers. From a quiet point,
through an eyelet-hole, she had overlooked their recent interview which Galitzin had so unceremoniously interrupted, and
she became earnestly desirous of succouring them for their
sakes, and somewhat for her own, that she might remove from

Yaila and the Prince's vicinity, a rival so wealthy, beautiful, and young, though she had a wholesome terror of him on one hand, and a little, perhaps, of her spouse, the Pulkovniek, on the other.

Lack of language—for she knew only her native Russ and a few stray words of German—rendered the difficulty of arrangements and explanations very great ; but, most luckily for the conspiring trio, it chanced that at this very time there had arrived with the detachment of Don Cossacks, an officer of rank, deputed by the Princes Mentschicoff and Gortchakoff to inspect the garrison with its stores and report thereon, as both Kertch and Yenekale had been captured by the Allies, and several discrepancies had been detected in the nominal returns of Prince Galitzin ; in short, the "men of straw" in his muster-rolls had been suspected, and the pressure of affairs in Sebastopol rendered further trifling impossible. So His Excellency had his hands full.

One interview with Gwenny and Ramornie sufficed to complete their new plan. Madame's arrangements were simply and speedily made for their flight, and, in a burst of gratitude, he threw his arms around her ample waist and kissed her on both cheeks—a process to which, as he was a more than usually good-looking young fellow, she submitted with the best grace in the world.

Taking advantage of the confusion—almost consternation—and occupation of Galitzin and the Pulkovniek, Madame arranged that she should ride her saddle horse, a fine and active Tartar one, next evening to the pine wood, accompanied by Gwenny on foot. There Ramornie was to precede them, and lie *perdue* as before. She would mount the lady, and he must lead her bridle ; their way should lie through the Baider Pass, some fifty miles to Balaclava. They must travel in the night, conceal themselves by day, and trust for the rest to God, she added, bowing to the *eikon* in the corner.

She did more : knowing the great risk run by Ramornie if he travelled in a red coat (or the remains of that which once had been a *red* coat) she supplied him with a Russian caftan of canvas, girt in the approved fashion with a rope. Still he was without arms, and he donned this ungraceful attire, never reflecting the while, that if he appeared thus within range of a sentinel of the Allies, he might be shot ere he could answer a single inquiry.

All succeeded beyond even their fondest anticipations : and when, next evening, the shadow of the Tchatr Dagh fell on the pine wood and the valley of the wild almond and linden trees, Madame Tegoborski was lingering on the Yaila road, looking back, and kissing her hand to the retiring figures of Ramornie and Gwenny, whose newly acquired horse he led by the bridle, as they descended into a steep dark glen that they believed was ultimately to lead them to the Pass of Baider.

CHAPTER LXXII.

THE LOST PATH.

"FIFTY miles, and for you afoot! Oh, Horace, Horace, I can never be so selfish as to ride!" said Gwenny, in sorrow and commiseration.

"It is only two very long days' marches, Gwenny," he replied, cheerfully, for his heart was beating happily, and he paused a moment to look back, to caress, and kiss the gloveless hand that held the reins. "The last portion we may take leisurely," he added, "for then we shall be near old Colin Campbell's headquarters. What a trump Madame Tegoborski has proved after all! and yesterday I actually thought of tying her neck and heels with a vine trailer. Thank Heaven, the darkness comes on fast!"

But unfortunately, with the darkness there set in a dense white mist from the Euxine. It came rolling in masses along the grassy valleys and up the rocky mountain slopes, and ere long amid it and the obscurity of the night, all trace of the narrow roadway became as completely lost as if it lay under the snow drifts of that night of the fatal march to Tchorgoun! Muffled in a warm cloak of the Hospoza's. Gwenny did not feel cold ; but her heart, like that of her companion, became filled with natural anxiety. They had completely lost the path now, and the horse, though led carefully by the bridle, stumbled and lost its footing every moment amid loose stones, caper-bushes, and stunted turpentine trees, on what seemed to be the slope of a mountain side. At last Horace paused in utter irre-solution, and the bead drops rolled from his temples. For aught he knew to the contrary, he and his companion might be pro-ceeding straight to, and not from, Yaila, and daybreak might find them in sight of it! Lost together on a dark mountain side in Crim Tartary, how strange it seemed to Horace, the knowledge that the girl whose soft and plaintive accents came to his ear from time to time, was the same bright and light-hearted Gwenny from whom he had parted in the drawing-room at Willowdean when he left home to rejoin the Fusileers, and dared only press her hand—she whom he had clasped to his breast so tenderly before. Yet so it was, and truth is stranger than fiction !

The livelong night they wandered slowly and irresolutely

there, and Gwenny was sinking with fatigue, while Horace, preternaturally wakeful and nervous, listened for every passing sound ; but none came on the soft breeze that sighed through the waste so lightly as scarcely to roll the mist before it. No Russian drum or bugle, no sound of alarm-bell, and no Cossack halloo were then "piercing the night's dull ear." All was still, and when grey dawn began to break and the mists to exhale upward, the wanderers found themselves yet somewhere about the base of the Tchatr Dagh, and near a Tartar farm or large cottage. Horace swept the landscape with a keen and haggard eye ; no vestige of Yaila, with its four green domes, and no sign of scouting horseman could be seen. All the land seemed woody and fertile, but desolate of people. That was well and his mind was relieved ; but his delicate companion required instant rest and succour, so he approached the dwelling of the Tartar with mingled hope and anxiety.

Early abroad, the Tartar farmer met them at his door, and surveyed them with doubt and distrust. He was a keen-eyed and sharp-featured man, of middle age ; his shaggy black brows seeming to mingle with the fur of his sable cap. His features were not of the flat Mongolian type, but were pleasing, regular, and fair. He saw that the lady was weary, and required alike food and rest ; and when she had dismounted, he led them into a room, softly carpeted and cushioned, with a fireplace in it—a mark of civilization—and a little table, some twelve inches high, in the centre, whereon he placed milk, curds, and cake ; but Ramornie made Gwenny imbibe some Crimskoi wine from a crystal cup ; and being without money, she pressed upon the Tartar's acceptance one of the rings she wore, and he took it, glancing with undisguised covetousness at those which still remained upon her slender fingers.

To his alarm, Horace discovered that they were not far from the hated Yaila. In fact, amid the mist, they had been describing a kind of circle in their peregrinations overnight, at the base of the Tchatr Dagh, and even the southern end of the pine wood was still visible ! Gwenny seemed already so worn and weary, after all she had undergone of late, that Ramornie had great fear of her ability to keep in her saddle till she could reach Balaclava ; and he conceived the idea of getting succour from thence half-way. In a strange Polyglot kind of language, partly Turkish, English, and Italian, cked out by signs, he contrived to make the Tartar understand that he wished a message taken to Balaclava, and his host averring that he had a swift horse, offered to bear it, if paid therefor ; so all Gwenny's rings were to be his on the answer coming back, and she freely proffered them.

"May Allah increase the glory and the substance of my

lord !" whined the Tartar ; "and mayest thou never know hunger," he added to Gwenny, giving her the kindest wish of his
people. "Drink," he continued, giving her more of the effer-
vescing and refreshing Crimskoi ; "it is pure as the holy well
of Mecca :" but she closed her eyes wearily, as if to sleep. and
Ramornie surveyed her with apprehension and solicitude, as
she lay back on the cushioned divan, listless and pale.

Oh, if she should become seriously ill on his hands in that
wild and out-of-the-way place—so near Yaila, too ! He asked
for writing materials. None were to be had ; but a quill
plucked from a hen's wing, a little gunpowder mixed with
water, and a fly-leaf, torn from an old Koran, thus making the
message more sacred, supplied the three requisites : and Ramornie wrote a note to be delivered to the officer commanding
the nearest out-post, imploring that succour should be sent
along the road that led by the seashore from Balaclava towards
Alushta ; and adding, that if an attack on Yaila were projected,
there were only in the place two Russian battalions, of four
companies each, and twenty pieces of cannon, the heaviest
being 32-pounders. He added his name, rank, and regiment ;
and requested the Tartar to depart at once, showing him all
the rings that glittered on the white hands of the now sleeping
girl, as the reward of his speed and fidelity.

"May Allah increase the glory——" began the Tartar again.

"There, now," interrupted Horace, "that will do. Be off ;
spare not spur nor whip, and the reader of my message may
also reward you for our sake."

"Speech is silver ; silence is gold," replied the Tartar, sententiously, and a few minutes after saw him mounted and away
at a gallop southward, by the road towards the headquarters of
Sir Colin Campbell ; and again hope began to dawn in the
breast of Ramornie.

In front of the flat-roofed farmhouse there rose a steep ridge
of rocks. Up these he clambered to watch the progress of his
messenger ; and how great was his disgust, his disappointment,
and anger, when he saw the fellow, after conceiving himself
quite out of sight, ride directly north, and disappear past the
edge of the old pine wood, along the road direct for Yaila. He
had gone to betray them to Galitzin—to that Galitzin, whose
scouting Cossacks might even now be within a few versts of
them !

Inspired anew by anxiety and alarm, he hastened to rouse
poor weary Gwendoleyne, and replacing her in the saddle, after
appropriating a sabre that hung on the wall, they set forth in
search of another place of rest or refuge. A narrow, winding,
and sombre path, overhung by oaks and beeches, soon hid the
house of the traitor from the fugitives. The morning was clear

now, and the sun shone cheerily along the mighty green slopes and impending cliffs of the Tchatr Dagh. After a time the trees were left behind, and rocks alone bordered the way. Ramornie looked for a place of shelter, and if possible, of repose, for his delicate companion, for Gwenny was sinking fast. At length, his keen and haggard eyes detected a dark fissure in the red marble cliffs. He hobbled the horse in a little thicket of turpentine trees, and half leading, half carrying his tender charge, he conveyed her into what ultimately proved to be a cave, strewed apparently with dry chips and white branches of trees ; but these, in fact, were human bones—the relics of a Tartar slaughter—for they were in the famous grotto of Foul Konba.

He placed her on a ledge of rock, and wrapping her cloak about her, kissed her on both eyelids, and bade her sleep if she could, while he would wait and watch. Looking forth from the mouth of this uncouth hiding-place, he could discern about six miles distant the four white towers of Yaila shining in the sun ; but no figures were stirring in the open ground between. Again he turned to watch his sleeping charge, and then what were his horror and dismay to see the figure of an armed Cossack, who had evidently issued from the inner part of their retreat, bending over her with curiosity, pistol in hand.

CHAPTER LXXIII.

PERA.

Robbed and stripped by plunderers, in short by the Cossacks of the escort, of their money, jewels, and even their outer garments, Lady Wedderburn and Lady Ernescleugh reached Balaclava, the neat white houses of which were now almost hidden by more recent erections of huts, stores, and so forth, even as its slender population of Arnaouts had become lost amid the overwhelming numbers of its new occupants, the Highland Brigade, Rifles, and other British soldiers of all arms and uniforms : and in the distance their anxious eyes could see the three-tiered batteries, the green domed churches, and the lofty houses of that Sebastopol, whose name was then in the mouths of half the world.

They reached the headquarters of Sir Colin Campbell in such a plight, and in such a state of excitement, that the testy but warm-hearted old Scottish General, after telling them that it was alike impossible for them to go to the front, or to remain in Balaclava, as deaths were occurring every hour by cholera, and that the Sardinians at Tchorgoun had lost a thousand men in three weeks by disease, transmitted them without much ceremony on board a steamer, then just starting for Scutari; and before the poor ladies quite knew where they were, they found her steaming out of the harbour of Balaclava, amid all the *débris* of wreck and drift-wood, and the festering and floating carcases of cavalry horses which encumbered it. There, at Scutari, they had been told by some one, they knew not who—a staff officer apparently, in tattered uniform, with a haversack under his arm, and wearing a prodigious beard—they "should get intelligence of their sons."

The boat left the vessel's side and he was gone.

"Has Cyril been wounded again?" thought Lady Wedderburn; but ere long, on board the steamer, she learned all!

Poor Cyril had fallen at the head of his company, on the 8th of the preceding June, in the memorable attack, when the great Mamelon, the Quarries, and the White Works were stormed and taken by the Allies. On that occasion, among a host of others, the Master of Ernescleugh had been wounded and sent to Scutari, so it was to him that Sir Colin Campbell's aide-de-camp had referred.

Who can open the Book of Destiny, or see the slender thread, the link or chain of events, that leads to fortune or to fame—to misery or calamity? Happy it is for us that we can never see the future! Cyril had fallen by a ball through the chest, at the base of the Piquet House Hill, and there he lay, while the tide of his comrades swept on—lay dying and alone, under the sultry sun, while the dull mist of intense heat mingled with the smoke of the conflict, and settled down in the breathless valley, where there was no air to rend it aside; and as his blood and his life ebbed together, there seemed to come to his drowsy ear the voice of Mary Lennox, singing, and he thought himself again listening to her in the garden at Lonewoodlee. It was the voice of a French sister of charity, at a little distance. She was chanting the *De Profundis* amid some dying Zouaves, and when her song ceased the soul of Cyril Wedderburn had passed away.

Upon the table in his hut the poor fellow had left a will, hurriedly written. Therein, after piously giving his soul to God, and his body to be buried by the finders, if he fell, he bequeathed certain sums to wounded soldiers of the Fusileers and to the widows and orphans of others who had fallen in the war. His love he left to his parents, brother, and all friends, adding that he would die at peace and with goodwill to all men. And so he was found lying on his face stone dead when the burial parties came. Nightfall saw the handsome and gallant soldier shovelled away, with hundreds of others, into the trench-grave —"the vast lumber-house of death"—and the secrets of Mary's love, and of all her sorrows, were buried with him.

Cyril dead! Oh, could it be, thought Lady Wedderburn, that all the objects and wishes of her life had changed within so short a space of time?

"Oh! my Cyril, my son, my pride! and has it ended here, and ended thus?" she wailed out on the breast of Lady Ernescleugh, when she read the last letter sealed for her, and left in his hut. "Oh, where now are all my fond aspirations! oh, my hope! my joy! they have ended now in death! Oh, Cyril! why did I ever bear or nurse you? Yet, I am enduring only what many a poor mother has endured since this fatal war began."

And she wept long the tears of unavailing sorrow, while her maternal heart went sadly home, and back to the sweet days of his tender and loving childhood, when he, who had fallen a handsome and stately soldier, had clung to her skirts, clambered at her knees, and nestled in her bosom, a beautiful, a happy and smiling child with dark eyes and golden hair; and so the loss of her son, combined with keen and sharp anxiety for Gwendoleyne, brought on a species of low and nervous fever, under which she lingered on for many weary weeks in Misseri's Frankish Hotel at Pera. She was not confined to bed, but lay propped on a sofa at the open window, from whence she could see the vast and glittering panorama of Stamboul and all the Golden Horn, with the three-deckers of Abdul Medjid lying at anchor, with the star and crescent flying; but nothing could rouse her. She thought ever of the dead Cyril, the lost Gwenny, and her now futile *wish*.

"Oh, wherefore should we heap up riches," she would say, "when, as the Scripture tells us, we know not who shall gather them! Oh, Juliana dear," she added to Lady Ernescleugh, whose son was now convalescent, and was able to lounge about Pera with glazed boots and carefully parted hair, "I did not think it possible that I could have heard of my Cyril's death, though daily I knew he risked life, and yet live on as I am living. But I don't think I shall survive it long. See, my poor hair has become quite grey, and is coming out fast."

"Use cantharides, dear," lisped Lady Ernescleugh, as she lounged on a satin divan and fanned herself with a bunch of feathers in a pearl handle; "it is an excellent specific," she added, as she saw that her friend's "division" *was* becoming wider than its wont.

So the quiet, unsentimental and unenthusiastic Robert Wedderburn, who had in his time "spoiled more foolscap than cartridge paper," plodding over his books in the Temple, became the heir of Willowdean and the old baronetcy, the stately mansion, and the Burgh of Barony, with all their political interests, while a grass-covered mound at the base of the Piquet House Hill, was all that remained to his elder brother.

CHAPTER LXXIV.

THE CAVE OF FOUL KOUBA.

"A Cossack, a dog of a Cossack, by Heaven!" exclaimed Horace Ramornie, in a low voice of intense emotion, as he unsheathed the sabre with which he had provided himself at the house of the Tartar, and saw his apparent foe, a wild-looking fellow, with matted hair and cap to match, and clad in a rough shoubah, come hastily towards him.

"English, now thank God!" exclaimed the seeming Cossack, in whom Horace instantly recognised Newnham, the commander of the yacht. "May I never!" he added, turning to the sleeping girl, of whose face only the handsome mouth and set of small white teeth were visible. "By Jove! if this isn't Miss Wedderburn, and you—you in the caftan like a Ruski?"

"Captain Ramornie, of the Royal Fusileers."

"And don't you recognise me—Bob Newnham?"

"Of course I do," was the response; and they shook hands heartily, each being intensely relieved by discovering *who* the other was; and the sound of their voices awoke the sleeper. Alarm was her first emotion, and then her natural sense of fun caused her to laugh at the odd figure cut by her old friend Newnham; for they had been great friends on board the yacht, the poor and soured Lieutenant R.N., having sunned himself for a time in the charm of her society, though he knew that the pleasure would end some day, but not so disastrously as it had come to pass.

"By Jove, Ramornie, I feel almost comfortable now and quite happy, for the idea that Miss Wedderburn was in the hands of those beastly Ruskies was maddening to me," said Newnham, when he had heard their story. "I wish I had a pipeful of tobacco or a cigar, however I have often made both one and t'other do duty in place of fire or a tot of hot grog on a cold night-watch."

"But how did you escape and obtain these arms?"

"And this elegant costume? Well, if you guessed till your hair was grey and as long as the Atlantic cable, you never would hit on the right thing. It happened in this way. The two fellows who escorted me proceeded for, I don't know how many miles, towards Perecop, passing between Karasu Bazar and the Putrid Sea, till one fine day, about a week ago, they made a halt on the banks of the Karasu, in a fertile and beautiful valley, covered with yellow and green tobacco fields; and though we had gone so far, still the flat scalp of this mountain, the Tchatr Dagh, was visible at the southern horizon. That I might share their black bread and quass they took the devilish handcuffs off me, but each had by him a sabre and loaded pistols, as a hint of what I might expect if I attempted anything unpleasant.

" The scenery was lovely, the air delightful, and the halt most welcome ; for I was weary and thirsty; but the *dolce far niente* character of our little picnic underwent a rapid change. It chanced that the Cossack named Ivan had planted his butt-end fairly upon a hollow place, containing a large wasps' nest. On finding himself stung by one, he furiously discharged a pistol into the hole, and in a moment the air was black with them. They came not alone from that hole, but from a score of others. I sprang to my feet and bolted a little way, for in a trice the two Cossacks were covered with them, wasps and bees too, were on their faces, necks, ears, and hands. They buried their heads in the long grass; they roared, and raved, and rolled about in utter agony, so I resolved to lose no time in making the best of the opportunity. I seized the cap of one, the shoubah of another, then provided myself with the arms of Ivan and the horse of Alexis, and leaving them to their sorrows rode as if the devil was after me, by the very way we had come. In fact, I rode till my horse dropped under me, and I was compelled to leave it, poor animal, to the vultures. Then I lost my way, and for days have been wandering, feeding myself on whatever I could pick up, till chance last night brought me this way, and here I am."

Newnham related his adventures so briefly and jauntily that even Gwenny could not help smiling through her tears.

"Come, Miss Wedderburn," said he, "don't have a faint heart in harbour, after having shown a brave one at sea."

" But we're not in harbour yet, Captain Newnham."

" We soon shall be, and laugh over all these things. You have had a lucky escape from that rascally Russian, and in my heart I thank God for it," said he, kindly patting her fingers with his strong brown hand. " It is a queer bunk this," he added, surveying the cave, and looking at the sunny landscape that stretched far away below its mouth or arch of rock, which seemed to form a frame for it like that of a picture ; "but what are all these that strew the floor ?"

" Bones," said Horace, in a low voice.

" Bones !"

" Yes, human ones. Hush !"

In this cavern a party of Genoese had been smoked to death by the Tartars (just as the French used to make a razzia among the Arabs in Algeria), and their bones are still lying there. So at this hour the tourist in the Scottish Hebrides may see in the cavern at Eigg the bones of the Macleans, who were there smoked to death in a similar fashion by the Macdonalds. This

Crimean den is of vast extent ; for Monsieur Oudinet, a French-man, is said to have "penetrated half a day's journey into it, without reaching the end." Be that as it may, our fugitives contented themselves with lingering at the mouth thereof.

Though they had no food, the day passed rapidly ; they had all so much to say and to tell each other, and it was proposed that at nightfall Gwenny should mount again, and some pro-gress be made towards the valley of Baidar. Balaclava could only be some thirty-seven miles distant. So, when evening came and the shadows of the Tchatr Dagh fell far across the sun-lit valley, and melted away in general darkness, Newnham crept forth to scout and listen ; for mist was stealing in from the sea again.

Secure for the time, as they deemed themselves in that uncouth place of shelter and secrecy, Gwendoleyne laid her throbbing temples on the breast of Ramornie, nestling herself there, as if sure of peace and security, while he pressed his lips to her brow from time to time ; and so they remained silent, hand in hand, heart speaking to heart only, till a sound aroused them.

"It was Newnham creeping in to announce that "some infernal Ruskies were in motion in the valley below, as he could hear by their horses' hoofs ;" doubtless a scouting party brought by the treacherous Tartar.

A low cry of alarm escaped Gwenny,

"Now do take heart, Miss Wedderburn," urged Newnham ; "remember that, as some writer has it, 'no pleasure is lasting that is not dashed with a sense of danger.'"

At that moment the Tartar horse hobbled in the thicket below neighed ; after a few seconds there was a response from another amid the mist below. Then came the sound of voices, and of feet, as if many men were scrambling up to the mouth of the cavern, and Horace felt his heart beating painfully and wildly, as he clutched his sabre, resolved to die hard. To do that was easy, but what of Gwenny then ?

Through the gloom and obscurity of the misty night they could see the figures of the dismounted Cossacks making their way up the slope ; but just as the foremost had come within twenty yards of the hiding-place there was the report of mus-ketry on the road below, and by the flashes it became evident that an exchange of shots was taking place between the Rus-sians and some hostile force.

The leading Cossack paused, and next moment a huge stone, hurled from the hand of Ramornie, dashed him into the mist below. His comrades lingered doubtfully in the ascent, as if they knew not whether to fall back or advance, for the firing continued to increase in the dark below, and by the distance between the flashes it seemed to have been opened by troops extended in skirmishing order, feeling their way as they slowly advanced.

Suddenly a loud and authoritative voice rang out, and once more the ascent to the cave of Foul Kouba was resumed, while a large and brilliant fireball, thrown almost into its mouth, revealed all within. Steadily it burned in the still atmosphere of the breathless night, casting a green and ghastly glare on the red marble walls and arched roof of the vast natural grotto, lighting up many a point and feature hitherto unseen in its gloomy recesses, on the wild weeds that grew in luxuriance about its entrance, on the whitened bones that strewed its floor, on the shrinking figure of the pale and terrified girl, and on her two guardians crouching, each with sabre and pistol in hand, behind a mass of rock, intent only on defending her to the last gasp and dying as hard as possible.

Steadily, we say, burned the weird and ghastly light, and the first face it fell upon was that of Galitzin. He had lost his cap in the ascent, and was clad in his light green uniform lapelled with white. He was armed with a sabre and revolver pistol.

He fired the latter thrice at Ramornie, but the balls only starred the rocks behind him, and the echoes found a hundred reverberations in the black profundity beyond. The sneering courtesy, the sleek aspect, the cold and glittering smile of Galitzin, all were gone now, and the eyes, the bearing, and the expression of the human tiger had replaced them. The man looked all instinct with ferocity and recklessness. He was haggard, ghastly, and savage, as he cast one furious and inquiring glance to where the rifles were flashing through the gloom below, and then sprang into the mouth of the rocky den with uplifted sword, to be instantly cut down by Horace; for the sharp and trenchant Damascus blade, of which he had so opportunely possessed himself, clove the truculent Muscovite to the left eye, and he fell prone at his feet without a groan !

Another who followed him was shot by Newnham, who speedily despatched two more with his sword ; and now, scared by the fall of their leader and by the increasing fire of musketry in the mist below, all who were ascending fled down the slope and disappeared, leaving the fugitives free ; but one, ere he went, discharged his carbine back at random, and by this Parthian shot Ramornie had his right arm broken above the elbow.

" Vive la France !" cried a voice out of the obscurity. " Mes Zouaves, suivez-moi !"

Then, after a time, came the sound of the Scottish bagpipes, and of the shrill Zouave trumpets, sounding the advance.

" By Jove ! an attacking force at last, and not a moment too soon !" exclaimed Bob Newnham.

The tread of feet, passing double-quick along the valley below, re-echoed for a time, and occasional shots were heard and flashes seen, dying away in distance and obscurity. Newnham, to prevent Gwenny being shocked, trundled the fallen Russians down the slope ; and the remainder of the night was passed in hope mingled with suspense and anxiety.

When day dawned, the white flag had disappeared from Yaila, and two of darker tints were floating over its leaden domes, doubtless the union and the tricolour ; and two columns of infantry, one in red and one in blue, were encamped on the plain within a mile of Yaila.

Still the fugitives did not venture forth, though Ramornie was enduring the greatest pain in his wounded arm, and Gwenny was overwhelmed with grief about him, as she sat by his side watching his pale face, while he clenched his teeth to conceal his agony. About noon two mounted officers in French uniform came galloping back to the lurking-place to discover who had been firing from thence over-night ; and one of these proved to be Colonel De La Fosse, who informed them that Sir Colin Campbell, on ascertaining the exact whereabouts of Yaila, had dispatched a regiment of his Highland Brigade with a few guns towards it, in conjunction with the 34th Infanterie de la Ligne and a battalion of Zouaves sent by General Bosquet. To this combined force the Pulkovnick Tegoborski had surrendered without firing a shot, and all his garrison were prisoners of war.

"Sacre tonnerre !" added the Frenchman, "and yonder fellow lying dead on the slope is the spy,—after all—aha, *le scelerat !*"

"He is the Prince Galitzin," said Horace.

"Cut down by Captain Ramornie, and serve him right," added Newnham.

"And you, Mademoiselle, ma douce amie," said the Colonel, approaching Gwenny, cap in hand ; "this is no place for you, so we shall forward you to Balaclava in a Tartar kabitka ; and meantime I shall send the surgeon of the Scottish regiment to dress your wounded arm, Monsieur le Capitaine. Aha, mon brave ! we have just come in time ; but by the horns of the devil, I would rather have cut off my moustachios than have had that pitiful Russian mouchard to escape. And now, adieu ! for I must ride back to Yaila."

"We shall meet again, I hope, Monsieur le Colonel?" said Ramornie, cheerfully.

"Allons ! I hope so ; all the roads in the world lead to Rome —or to Heaven. Adieu, Mademoiselle !" he added, and lifting his kepi, bowed low and hurried to where his horse awaited him. But they were fated never to see the gallant Louis De la

Fosse again, as on the 8th of the following September, he fell at the head of the 34th Infanterie, at the storming of the Malakoff Tower.

~~~~~~~~~~~~~

CHAPTER LXXV.

CONCLUSION.

THEY joined Lady Wedderburn at Misseri's in Pera, and her reunion with Gwenny was the first gleam of joy that had visited the poor woman's heart since that morning on which the stranded yacht was so foully cannonaded by the Russians.

After his wound was dressed, Horace had paid a farewell visit to his comrades at the trenches, and brought away his cousin Cyril's baggage ; but the packing thereof—slight and slender though his fighting wardrobe was—proved a sorrowful task ; for few mementos bring the presence of the dead so powerfully before us as garments they have worn, or the objects of their solicitude. Among other things Horace found Maltese crosses, Gozza buttons from Valetta, roseleaf bracelets full of sweet perfume from Stamboul for his mother, Gwenny, and even little Miss M'Caw ; a Turkish pipe for Bob, swords from the Alma, bayonets from Inkerman, a fragment of an iron shell from the Valley of Death for Sir John—suitable present for everybody.

His tattered Fusileer uniform, his bruised epaulettes, his Indian medals and rusted sword were brought away by Horace. Then too his photos, little mementos of the happy home circle, each and all treasured as sacred *lares* by Cyril in that Crimean hut, and often looked at fondly and lingeringly in the long hours of the weary night, while the great guns were heard pounding away, and men were dying fast amid the frozen mud and gore of the fatal trenches.

A few letters there were, at which Horace glanced ; they were in a lady's hand, and tied up with a white riband. Ramornie dared not read more than a line, for the secrets of the dead are sacred ; but they were full of earnest, passionate, and girlish love, frank, tender, and adoring ; for they were the few—a dozen or so—that Cyril had received in happier days from Mary Lennox.

Now both hearts were still—still for ever ; and the spirit that had invoked spirit were perhaps together now, in the Shadowy Land that lies beyond human ken.

Horace placed the packet in the camp fire that burned outside the hut, and after watching the embers smoulder, resumed his sorrowful packing with one hand. These letters seemed now but as "the vague shadows of a vague existence."

"Life is made up of bitterness, Gwenny," said Lady Wedderburn, as she caressed the girl's head in her bosom, "and I have brought a few upon myself and you ; but ere long we shall be safe at home. Yet Cyril, my darling Cyril, can never be restored to me, and it seems so cruel and strange that I shall never see him more !" And as she spoke all her mother's heart —and God knoweth how great a heart that is—went forth for the dead son. "My poor Cyril !" she resumed, as she resigned her to Horace. "I cannot conceal from you, Gwenny, that I had other views and another wish concerning you ; but God hath willed it otherwise, and may you and Horace be happy !"

A few days after this saw them all "off for Old England, as fast as black diamonds and boiling water could turn the screw-propeller," to quote Bob Newnham, who was left behind in command of a large transport, a post procured for him by Lady Erneseleugh.

"Oh, I am so thankful !" exclaimed Gwenny, looking at the canvas as it was sheeted home to accelerate the vessel's speed.

"Thankful for what, darling ?" asked Horace ; "to be free ?"

"Not that alone, but to be once more upon the sea—the great ocean ; it is like the beginning of home."

"Home, Gwenny, darling ? we are not yet past Seraglio Point. Yet I understand your feeling."

"So do I, Miss Wedderburn," said Newnham, whose boat was alongside, and who was gazing on her admiringly. "You feel like myself ; that when on blue water you are on the high road to Old England. Ah, you should be a sailor's wife !"

"Ah ! but she is to be a soldier's," said Horace, "and the water is green here."

"And green water always shoals," replied Newnham ; and bidding them a laughing farewell he descended the side ladder and shoved off to his transport.

Though clouded by natural regret for Cyril, the heart of Gwenny was full of happiness, and her dark eyes shone with liquid light, while all her face seemed to beam with sweetness and bright intellect as she surveyed Horace Ramornie, her future husband, and admired his perfect features, his erect air, broad chest, and lithe figure so full of strength and symmetry, all save the poor wounded arm in its scarf of black silk.

She was with him she loved and who loved her. She forgot the past and all her tears, and absolutely blushed at her own joy as the great steamer sped on its homeward path, their eyes ever seeking each other, and never, never wearying of the search.

Her glossy black hair was simply braided and girt by tiny diamond stars upon a narrow velvet band round her head, displaying the pretty ears and fine contour of her neck and throat. Her dress was black silk, trimmed with narrow white lace, and she had silver bracelets, necklet, and cross, all enamelled with black, as mourning for her cousin.

" Ah," thought Horace, as he surveyed her, while she sat on the poop twirling her parasol under the awning, "who in the world, with any idea of joy or happiness, would be a bachelor ! " But neither could say all they felt then—

> " For words are weak and hard to seek,
> When wanted fifty-fold;
> And then if silence will not speak,
> Nor trembling lip, nor changing cheek,
> There's nothing to be told !"

If it is difficult to describe our own happiness it becomes next to impossible to pourtray that of others. So we shall not attempt to expatiate upon the emotions of Gwenny and Ramornie ; yet, like all happiness, it had its alloy, for they could not but revert to the memory of him who lay in his lone grave by the Picquet House Hill.

" I couldn't send in my papers, Gwenny, even as your rich husband, while the war lasted, but this broken arm luckily settles all for me," said Horace. " It is England and sick leave in the first place."

" With me for your nurse—and your dear little wife, Horace."

They looked back from the poop, for now they were in the Sea of Marmora. The tall cypresses of Scutari, the mosques, the domes and minarets, and all the flags of Stamboul, the city of the Sultan, had lessened in the distance, and were blending with the golden evening haze as they sped on the world of waters ; and when the night came down, and the stars came out in the deep calm blue of the sky, Gwenny still sat there, with her hands clasped in those of her future husband—the realization of a young girl's dream.

THE END.

BILLING, PRINTER, GUILDFORD.